IN THAT QUIET EARTH

IN THAT QUIET EARTH

Roy Hattersley

M

MACMILLAN LONDON

First published 1991 by
MACMILLAN LONDON LIMITED
Cavaye Place London SW10 9PG
and Basingstoke

Associated companies in Auckland, Delhi, Dublin, Gaborone,
Hamburg, Harare, Hong Kong, Johannesburg, Kuala Lumpur,
Lagos, Manzini, Melbourne, Mexico City, Nairobi, New York,
Singapore and Tokyo

ISBN 0-333-47033-8

A CIP catalogue record for this book is available from
the British Library

Typeset by Rowland Phototypesetting Limited
Bury St Edmunds, Suffolk

Printed in Great Britain by
Billing & Sons Limited, Worcester

CONTENTS

CHAPTER ONE

Alice Thomson Comes to Call

William Skinner was suited to his job neither by temperament nor by training. He was a gardener by instinct and the little education he had acquired owed more to afternoons enjoyed in his father's fields and orchards than to mornings endured in the church vestry at Whittlesey. But his employment was no more decided by his inclination than it was by his aptitude. He was the second son of a farmer – a farmer who was both magistrate and Poor Law Guardian. So, in 1875 when the workhouse of the Union of Wisbech Parishes needed a new superintendent, no one was surprised that William was offered the job and accepted it with gratitude if not enthusiasm. His elder brother laboured behind the plough like a hired man, waiting impatiently for his inheritance to be earned, but with no legacy in prospect William had to take whatever fate, and family connections, offered.

He was not the first Skinner to take charge of the workhouse, which had been built to shelter the paupers of North Cambridgeshire. His uncle, Young Skinner – so named to mark the extraordinary achievement of surviving until christening day, despite being the seventh child of elderly parents – had been master at Lynn Road for almost twenty years. During his boyhood visits, William came to loathe the institution. He hated the smell – a combination of wet wool, boiled cabbage, carbolic soap and urine. He was horrified by the inmates, who dragged their feet aimlessly across the yards and stared at the ground in self-denigration when a person in authority came near. Worst of all he was terrified by what he regarded as the moral of the workhouse. The wages of sin were only death, but the penalty for sloth and foolishness was a living hell. So, whilst he accepted the appointment without question, he looked forward to assuming his new responsibilities with fear and loathing.

The work was even more uncongenial than he had anticipated. Most of the two hundred inmates aroused in him a compassion so personal and intense that he felt permanently guilty about the poverty

1

and degradation that the Poor Law required him to impose upon them. A few paupers excited feelings of disgust mixed with shame that he could so despise one of God's creatures. His punishment for the sin of the Pharisee was hours of unhappiness heightened by the belief that a natural right to perpetual happiness had been stolen from him.

Only two small parts of his work – plants and children – provided him with pleasure and consolation. The young paupers, who were separated from their parents to protect them from contamination by wilful poverty, offered endless opportunities for little acts of kindness and consideration. The kitchen garden, behind the washhouse – where the able-bodied men grew cabbages and turnips – occupied more of his working time than the Poor Law Guardians, had they known of it, would have thought justified. His own little plot, in bloom from the daffodils of April until the gladioli of September, consumed more affection than a recently married man should have been able to spare.

William Skinner proposed to Elizabeth Saunders on the day of his appointment. He was no more suited to her than he was to the job of workhouse master, and she knew it, but she accepted his proposal at once. Although the workhouse was a rough trade and generally thought to be beneath the dignity of a master mariner's daughter, she was the youngest of five sisters whose father had been beached by drink. Life was stormy and William was a port. Elizabeth decided that she could make those changes in her husband's character which were essential to a peaceful married life and then bully him into getting himself a shop or business.

William had no doubts about why he wanted to marry Elizabeth. Although she was not a lady, she possessed a lady's airs, if not a lady's graces, and was therefore the nearest thing to that station in life that he had ever known. No one else he knew was so aloof in manner and austere in habit. Elizabeth, he decided, was unusual and, in consequence, a catch.

Though handsome, she was handsome in a forbidding way.

> 'She was just the sort of creature, boys,
> That nature did intend
> To walk right through the world, m'boys,
> Without a Grecian bend.'

William had sung the song to himself, with pride and pleasure, a hundred times during their brief courtship. Elizabeth always wore dresses of the same pattern – black bombazine with high, tight collars topped with lace. William thought with pride that inside them she

2

had no option but to live an upright life. William was an affectionate, indeed passionate, man, and he knew from the moment of their first meeting that Elizabeth did not share his disposition. Although he did not possess the arrogant nature which kept his wife's nose in the air, he felt an unjustified confidence in his power to make Elizabeth's passion come alive. Indeed, he looked forward to cultivating the stony ground of her emotions.

In appearance they were admirably suited. William was a good-looking man who took unreasonable pleasure in his looks. He was tall and because of his excessive concern with his appearance he was invariably neat in a way which was unusual for a man of his size. His beard was always carefully trimmed and his parting was the straightest in Wisbech. He wore clothes which were slightly above his station and washed his hands as often as if he were a gentleman. It was generally agreed that they were a well-matched couple.

After the wedding Elizabeth moved into the workhouse master's quarters with an equanimity which few young women could have emulated. The rooms put at the superintendent's disposal were huge, cold and forbidding. They were furnished in a style more appropriate to a prison governor's office than to the first home of a young bride, and despite their chilly grandeur and spacious proportions, they were as claustrophobic as the rest of the institution. Elizabeth could not cross the corridor from dining room to kitchen without the stench of the wards sticking in the back of her throat. When she drew her bedroom curtains in the morning, inmates – padding about in the yard outside – stared into her window. If she walked into Wisbech she ran the gauntlet of a dozen paupers on outdoor relief. Inside the workhouse she felt herself to be in receipt of the parish's charity, sharing indoor relief with the wretched men and women whose lives she helped to govern with great determination but considerable distaste.

From the first day of her marriage, she supervised the workhouse bakery, distributed patent medicine, admonished dirty-faced children, berated enuretic ancients and generally imposed discipline as rigid as her spine. She had a special talent for dealing with pregnant girls, who never left her presence without understanding that He would wreak a terrible vengeance upon them for the sin of reproducing His image in less than respectable circumstances. Sometimes she regretted that the Guardians no longer allowed the shaving of heads and the public identification of miscreants in special clothing. Elizabeth gave thanks that a just Providence had called upon her to impose the discipline that the weak-minded Poor Law no longer made mandatory in all its institutions.

One task, although pursued with equal dedication, proved to be

3

beyond her. Her husband, she decided, possessed a distressing inclination towards compassion and a tendency to see the best in people which was inappropriate to his profession and wholly unsuited to the vale of tears through which they passed together. No matter how hard she tried, she was never able entirely to extinguish the unfortunate characteristics.

Elizabeth Skinner came nearest to achieving her ambition during the months immediately after the birth of her first child. The pregnancy – discovered to her distress three months after the wedding – was a martyrdom for which her mother's rudimentary explanation of a wife's tribulations had not prepared her. There was periodic bleeding at the beginning and a constant headache at the end. The sickness, which her sister had told her would last for only a few weeks, persisted into the last week of her confinement. She felt as if every part of her body was as swollen as her belly.

As Elizabeth struggled to discharge her duties, William made genuine but ineffectual attempts to share her burden. She always dismissed them with the complaint that he would not do the job right or that she would have to do it again after he had finished his poor attempt at home-building or housekeeping. William looked forward to the birth with a mixture of terror and impatience. He had hoped to anticipate fatherhood with pride in his achievement, yet he prepared for it with nothing except guilt, anxiety and resentment that humans do not reproduce themselves with the easy facility of plants and flowers. He tried to remember that his suffering was nothing like the agony that his wife endured but his resentment increased with the suspicion that he was blamed for every stab of pain and spasm of nausea.

It was a long and painful birth – so long and so painful that, whenever during that terrible time Elizabeth thought of anything except her agony, she imagined that she was giving birth to a ten-pound boy. The baby was a six-pound girl who looked so like her mother that she was christened Elizabeth Anne. The choice of names was, in part, intended as a memorial, for nobody except the sick woman herself thought that Elizabeth Anne Skinner would live. Six weeks later, when the doctor changed the prognosis of certain death to the possibility of survival, the convalescent attributed her recovery to merciful Providence and her own indomitable will – adding that, in William, she had been blessed with an understanding husband and indefatigable nurse. She also announced that, since she was not going to die, it was no longer necessary for the baby to bear her name. Henceforth her daughter would simply be called Anne.

It was during the painful pregnancy that William decided that the disappointment he had felt during the early weeks of his marriage

4

was likely to persist throughout the long years which he and Elizabeth were to spend together. He was, he had no doubt, in love with his wife, for – being far more naïve than he realised – he confused love and admiration. She was not, however, in love with him, and William knew it. She exhibited none of the emotions William thought were essential ingredients of that condition. She was particularly deficient in admiration.

William consoled himself with the thought that perhaps she was incapable of loving anybody and he determined to make the best of what life and marriage had to offer. Making the best of things came naturally to William, which did not mean that he passively accepted whatever fate befell him. It is a gardener's duty to challenge the elements and improve upon what nature, left to itself, would provide. It was no use complaining when cuttings failed to take root. Next year they might grow – as long as the soil was better prepared and the weeds more ruthlessly removed. He was not always a happy man, but he was always hopeful that he would be next year.

He could remember the exact day when he concluded that, since marriage was less pleasant than he had once hoped, he would concentrate his energies on making other parts of his life as pleasant as possible.

It was during Elizabeth's long recovery from her daughter's birth. Dinner was prepared at noon in the workhouse kitchen and carried into the master's quarters on a tray, but the evening meal William made himself – much to his wife's disapproval. As always, he pushed open the bedroom door with his foot and made his triumphant entrance with his achievement held before him. The triumph did not last long. Although most of his attention was concentrated on balancing his precarious load, out of the corner of his eye he could see his wife moving in the bed so as to obtain a better view of the mark he had made on the paintwork with the toe of his boot. Even after the damage had been done, she could not help warning him against it.

'Careful.'

Irritation instantly replaced the pleasure he had felt at having shown his affection in the shape of two eggs and as many slices of toast.

'Careful about what?'

'You'll spill the milk. The jug's too full.'

As William approached the bed, his wife pushed herself up on one elbow to examine the state of the tray cloth. The milk spilt at that second. The damp patch was barely visible between the crockery but Elizabeth struggled to move plates and saucers so that she could fold back the embroidered linen and discover how much harm had been done to the inlaid wood beneath it. Little Anne, disturbed by the upheaval in the bed which she shared with her mother, began to whimper.

'I don't know why you don't let the inmates do these jobs.'

'I want to do it. I like looking after you.'

'But it only worries me.'

'What do you worry about?' William forced himself to smile in the hope that he could create the impression that the whole idea was a joke.

'I worry about you breaking things. I worry about you wasting food. I worry about the pots not being washed properly.'

'In a year I've broken one plate.' That, William believed, was all the carnage of which Elizabeth was aware. Remembering the real total of destruction, he began to feel nervous about the tea service on the tray. Holding it during the initial skirmishes with his wife had made his arms ache and fearful of incapacitating cramp, he laid down his load on the bed by his wife's side. She recoiled as if she anticipated carnal assault by the sugar bowl.

'Take it off, take it off straight away. It's wet underneath.'

William responded so quickly that the teapot rebelled. The lid throbbed under the knitted cosy and tea spewed out from its spout. Since it was situated at the edge of his tray, a brown stain began to spread across the sheet by Elizabeth's side. She spoke with calm contempt.

'Take it away and put it on the window sill. I'll have to get out of bed and clear all this up.'

'Why will you? It's just a spot of tea.' William was speaking from near the window. Even as he argued, he obeyed his wife's instructions.

'It'll soak into the mattress. Pick up Anne for a minute.'

William seized his daughter as if a moment's delay would ruin the whole bed. Anne's whimpering turned into a wail and the wail became a scream.

'You *still* don't know how to hold her. You *still* can't pick her up properly.' Elizabeth had swung her legs out of bed and, sitting on the edge of the mattress, she held out her arms to take her daughter.

'Go and get a cloth – a damp cloth from the kitchen. And bring a towel.'

As William hurried off, he decided that eggs were no more attractive to him than they were to Elizabeth. He would discharge the several duties imposed upon him and then take refuge in his garden with a slice of bread and a piece of cheese. He calculated that he would have a full two hours to himself before he had to prepare his wife and their daughter for sleep. He determined to enjoy every second.

Even when Elizabeth was not explicitly critical of William's conduct she was able to engender a constant atmosphere of disapproval in the parlour, disappointment in the living room and dislike in bed. A year after the baby was born, when the doctors pronounced Elizabeth fit and well, her distaste for close proximity to William turned into outright hostility. Although she returned to her duties in kitchen and bakehouse with apparently undiminished commitment, she spent her nights lying with knees and ankles clamped together as securely as the locks on the pantry and coalhouse doors. When her husband even brushed against her, she shuddered with an uncontrollable terror so out of keeping with her daytime composure that William was bewildered as well as wounded, frightened no less than humiliated.

Only once during the next year did they make love and, the moment it was over, William regretted that it had happened. It had provided no real pleasure for him and only grief for his wife. Indeed, it was so unsatisfactory an experience that it seemed hardly credible that three months later she announced – with undisguised resentment – that she was going to have another baby. The months of pregnancy were passed by Elizabeth in fear and by William in guilt. Elizabeth suppressed her terror, but William exhibited his conscience in a way which irritated, rather than comforted, his unhappy wife. Even when the baby was born – with an ease that convinced the mother she had given birth to a five-pound girl – there was no forgiveness, and, although the child was a nine-pound boy, the father felt none of the pride in achievement which he once would have expected. An insurmountable barrier had been built between husband and wife. At night, Elizabeth continued to curl herself up in bed in a way which reminded William of a hibernating hedgehog. He lay by her side at a safe distance from the bristles and felt sorry for himself.

A more enlightened man would have tried to talk about his wife's trauma and a less civilised husband would have forced himself upon her. At first William simply lay in uncomprehending pain, wondering when and how something would happen to release the frustration that burned inside him. Then he longed for the liberation which would allow him to talk to Elizabeth about a wife's proper feelings for her husband. He decided that, since the angel of love and passion was not going to appear to Elizabeth, he would nurture those parts of the marriage which both gave him pleasure and seemed likely to benefit from his careful cultivation. It was his nature to turn acorns into oak trees. He would look after Elizabeth, however great the difficulty. In the spirit not of a martyr but of a knight errant, he would bring up his son and daughter in an atmosphere of respect and affection. By effort of will he abandoned all thought of living a normal married life. But he did long for Elizabeth to know the pain that he was suffering. Even that consolation was, at first, denied him for his wife seemed incapable of comprehending what an extraordinary life they led. Then, during the fourth winter of their marriage when Anne was almost four and Ernest, her brother, nearly two, the sins of the flesh forced their way irresistibly into her life.

Alice Thomson was a pauper of unexceptional appearance and conduct. She was grubby, but no grubbier than anyone else in the women's ward. Her straggling hair fell over her brow in just the same way and in about the same quantity as it flopped over other brows during the scrubbing of floors and the black-leading of grates. If Elizabeth Skinner thought about Alice Thomson at all, she thought of her as a malingerer but that in no way distinguished her from the other workhouse inmates. Mendicants were malingerers by nature. It was that characteristic which made them mendicants.

When Alice Thomson asked Mrs Skinner for a private audience, her request was granted with the usual graceless reluctance. Meetings between the master's wife and the female paupers were organised according to rules laid down by Elizabeth herself. They took place at times when William could be relied on to be out of his office. Interruption, even by the master, would have been intolerable. Elizabeth stood, erect and imposing, against the light of the long windows which opened out on to the courtyard. Once she was in position, she signified her readiness in a voice which, although neither loud nor strident, easily carried to Gerrard Knock, the foreman who waited on the far side of the solid oak door.

Gerrard Knock was a tiny, wizened man who, though barely thirty, already looked lined with age. Like his master he had once hoped to earn his living at work he enjoyed. But whilst William Skinner still harboured a vague hope of one day spending his life amongst plants and flowers Gerrard Knock felt only despair about his future. He had tried to become a jockey and he had failed.

As soon as he heard Elizabeth Skinner's cry, the foreman pushed Alice Thomson into the room. Then, leaving the door just ajar in case the girl turned violent, he retreated out of earshot into the corridor. Elizabeth regretted that Knock could not be present during the interview as a symbol of her authority, but the more brutish girls sometimes spoke of subjects which it was not right to discuss in front of a man. Elizabeth stood in silence in anticipation of the required curtsy. Even when it had been made, she did not speak at once. She maintained the silence in order to destroy any confidence which might have survived the long wait in the hall and Gerrard Knock's instructions about proper behaviour.

Then the master's lady spoke. 'Well?'

The single syllable was intended to remove any thought of conversation. Conversation was neither appropriate nor necessary. Elizabeth Skinner could always predict what she was going to be asked. Alice Thomson was undoubtedly about to counterfeit illness and ask to be excused heavy work. All that was necessary was the quick, halting request and the swift categorical refusal.

Alice Thomson sniffed, snuffled and coughed. She said how difficult it was to say what must be said and she confessed to the hope that she would never be forced into telling such a story. After a full minute, when she had got no further than the insistence that she 'didn't want to cause no trouble', Elizabeth Skinner lost patience.

'Either say what you've come to say, or be off to your work.'

The stern injunction had an instant effect. With a sparse clarity which few of her casual acquaintances would have thought possible, Alice Thomson delivered her message.

'It's the master, mum. He's had his way with me twice. I wouldn't say nothing about it but I think there's a baby coming.'

Elizabeth's first thought was the importance of betraying no emotion. She was afraid that she had turned white. But she was sure that if she swallowed hard she could speak without her voice trembling.

'How dare you!' She hoped that her tone left no doubt that she knew the girl was lying.

Absolute belief in William's innocence increased her outrage. She was not so much horrified by the accusation that her husband had defied the commandments and broken the marriage vows as disgusted by the suggestion that he might have made bodily contact with the dirty and dishevelled pauper who stood, head bowed, before her. Alice Thomson, she decided, must be mad to imagine that anyone would believe such lies. She thought of William – his pink face glowing above his neat beard – and she did not so much shudder at the thought of his adultery as recoil at the idea of his defiling himself with such a person. She knew that her first feeling should have been horror at the thought of the act itself but she could only think of the absurdity of the suggestion that the act had ever taken place.

'Out. I'll not spend another moment listening to your wicked nonsense. Stand outside the door whilst I tell Mr Knock what's to be done with you.'

The girl did not move.

Elizabeth smoothed down a straying hair. She was determined not to lose either her temper or her dignity and she paused before she spoke again to make sure that she was in complete command of her emotions. She had kept her self-control so far and to lose her temper at Alice Thomson's disobedience might suggest that she had been wounded by the allegations. She had decided how to deal with the girl and vengeance would be swift and terrible. But her verdict would be delivered in her own time and with cold detachment.

'Will you come in for a minute, Mr Knock, please?' She spoke with unusual courtesy to demonstrate her complete composure.

Alice Thomson did not move. She shuffled her feet, twisted the hem of her apron between her fingers, stared at the floor, sniffed and bit her lip. But she did not move.

'Did you hear, Thomson?' The question was not a reproof, but a genuine enquiry. 'I told you to wait outside.'

To Elizabeth's astonishment, the pauper began to argue. 'I can't go on working in that laundry. I'm sick almost to dying every morning, mum. As God's my witness, if I go on folding them blankets and carrying them buckets of water the baby will die and I'll go with it.'

Elizabeth had tried not to be curious about the girl's motives, for curiosity would have been demeaning, but she could not suppress all interest in the causes of such lunatic behaviour. The outburst had answered her question. The girl – as bone-headed as she was wicked – believed that by inventing her calumny she would be able to blackmail her way into an easy life.

'Do you think that I'm as stupid as you are?' Being thought stupid was, to Elizabeth Skinner, the unforgivable insult, far more offensive than the allegation that her husband was unfaithful to her. She raised her voice and called to the foreman. 'Mr Knock. I want this woman to go into the casual ward until the master returns.'

The girl howled. 'Who's to look after m'mam? She can hardly get out of bed. And m'brother Billy can't help. You won't even let him in the ward to see her. Who's to feed her?'

'Your brother's lucky still to be in this workhouse. After the way he beat that old man, all he deserves is penal servitude. You should have thought about your mother before starting to spread your wicked lies.'

'I've told no one, mum. Only you. As God's my witness. And it's true, mum. I swear it. May I be struck dead on the spot if I tell a lie. Twice he did it. Twice.'

'Out. Out of this room and out of my sight.' For a moment the veneer of composure cracked. 'When the master gets back you'll be out of the workhouse as well.'

10

'It's true. You ask him. It's true.'

'Take her away, Mr Knock. I've got better things to do with my time.'

Gerrard Knock put his hand under Alice Thomson's elbow in the manner of a man who was encouraging her to walk with him in the garden. She screamed as if she had been viciously assaulted.

'Come on, Alice. No sense in being silly.' Knock put his arm around her shoulder.

Elizabeth began to wonder what she would do if the girl began to kick and shout, strike out or sweep the china ornaments from the sideboard.

Suddenly, Alice lost her nerve. It was panic which made her forget the required curtsy as she rushed from the room. Shame not anger caused her to push Knock out of the way as she ran down the corridor.

When the sound of Knock's hobnailed boots was almost too faint to hear, Elizabeth Skinner pushed the door shut and rattled the knob to make sure that it was securely latched. Then she leaned forward and rested her head on the cool wood. She had come very near to losing her self-control and that would have been unbearable. She was determined to regain her poise by the time her husband returned. It was not her practice to display emotion in his presence and she had no intention of allowing Alice Thomson to force her into an uncharacteristic exhibition of humanity. The first step back to composure having been taken, she began to feel the pins in her hair. If they had worked loose her appearance might not be as severe as she wished. It was three o'clock. William would be home in an hour. She knew exactly what she would do until he returned.

CHAPTER TWO

Make Believe

William Skinner always spent Saturday afternoon at Wisbech Market and invariably arrived home punctually at four o'clock. At that time, the last casuals of the day were admitted to indoor relief and the master thought it right that he should be there to see them into the bathhouse. At the same time Henry Stainton left the workhouse and returned to March. William never returned home until he was certain that his wife's brother-in-law was clear of the drive.

Despite the antipathy he felt towards Henry Stainton, William had appointed him teacher to the pauper children. He had been convinced by his wife that it was his duty to keep the job in the family. Stainton was schoolmaster in the parish of St John's and as his duties in March occupied him for all of the normal teaching hours he could only visit Wisbech in odd corners of his days. He taught reading and arithmetic on Tuesday and Thursday nights and arithmetic on Saturday after-noons. Six hours' schooling a week was, William knew, an inadequate preparation for the cruel world beyond the workhouse gates, but six hours was all that the Guardians would allow. The master waited impatiently for the day when his employers had the sense to send the children to the church school at St Peter and St Paul, so that they could receive a real elementary education and he would be spared the risk of meeting Henry Stainton.

The schoolmaster was scarcely more popular with his sister-in-law than he was with her husband. The feeling of family duty had prompted Elizabeth to press for his appointment and forced William into accepting his wife's suggestion. The same emotion required her to behave towards him with the respect due to a male relative. On Saturday afternoon she always visited his makeshift classroom to show an interest in his work, a feeling she demonstrated by sitting silent and menacing at the back of the classroom. As she knew well, Henry Stainton loathed her weekly visits, but her brother-in-law's happiness was less important than the proper observance of genteel propriety. In any event, her presence could not possibly have made Henry more

12

nervous than he already was. His nervousness made him pompous and it was his pomposity that made him unpopular.

On the afternoon of Alice Thomson's accusations, Elizabeth – determined not to disturb her normal routine – left for the classroom as usual at half-past three. To her astonishment, the children had already been dismissed and her sister Beatrice, who, to her knowledge, had never condescended to visit the workhouse before, stood with her husband in the doorway. They were in animated, but obviously guarded, conversation. When they saw Elizabeth, they looked at each other in guilty silence.

'What a pleasure. And a surprise.' Elizabeth congratulated herself on the neat blend of courtesy and aggression.

'To tell the truth, we've come to see you on a matter of some importance.'

'Well,' said Elizabeth to her brother-in-law, 'if it's a matter of some importance, we'd better discuss it in the house, particularly if we are all to tell the truth.'

The Staintons were offered but refused tea. Henry sat on the edge of his chair.

'If I may take the lead, I think it would be best if your sister began. I feel that I must be present. For I am the source of the original disturbing information and I must vouch for it as necessary. But it is clearly best if Mrs Stainton charts the course, so to speak.'

'No, my dear. You said . . . We agreed. You heard it. You must say.'

'Forgive us, my dear Elizabeth, for adding to your distress . . .' Henry wrung his hands.

'What distress?' Elizabeth offered a clear challenge.

Henry did not accept. 'We were deciding how best to proceed when you caught us unaware. Beatrice, please tell your sister what went on.'

'It would be far better for you just to tell Elizabeth what happened. I wasn't there. I only heard your account of it when you got back to the vicarage.'

Henry looked hurt. 'It was a perfectly honest and accurate account. Very clear, I would have thought. You ought not to speak as if you doubt my word.'

'Of course I don't doubt your word . . .'

Elizabeth filled the moment of resentful silence with what she hoped was a practical suggestion.

'Why don't *I* tell *you*? Some child in the class was heard to say either last Tuesday or last Thursday that a woman in the workhouse is going to have a baby and that my husband is the father. Ever since

13

then you have been trying to make up your minds whether to tell me, when to tell me and how to tell me. Unfortunately, you have not yet made up your minds *who* is to tell me.'

'I must say . . .' Henry sounded genuinely offended.

'If you must say, Henry, why don't you say? Especially since I know already.'

Beatrice gasped. 'How on earth do you know?'

Elizabeth Skinner just managed to keep her temper and preserve her dignity.

'I know because the girl came and told me.'

'My dear . . . !' Beatrice produced an impressive imitation of concern. 'And what did you tell her?'

'I told her not to invent wicked stories and sent her away. William will punish her when he gets back.'

Henry was outraged. 'If we'd known that before, we needn't have had all this trouble and embarrassment.'

He bustled out of the master's drawing room without another word. His wife followed him in silence. As soon as they were outside the door they began to hurry down the drive. Beatrice slowed the pace to ask him a question before she reached the gatehouse where, it being four o'clock, the horse and trap were waiting.

'Do you think she believes what she said about William being innocent?'

'I don't know. You can never tell with her. She's a strange one.'

'Do you believe it?'

'I don't know that either. He's a strange one too. But I have my suspicions. With all respect, I have my suspicions.'

'I'm sure he wouldn't do it. Not with a pauper.'

'I'll tell you this, my love, if you'll forgive the unavoidable coarseness of my story. I've had my doubts about him before. I've watched him at Guardians' meetings when they've been deciding on candidates for indoor relief. The Board sit round a big horseshoe table with the chairman, naturally enough, presiding. William sits next to him – on his right, as a matter of fact – and I sit at the side in case I'm required to advise on the children – their chances of gainful employment, and so forth. Sometimes I actually speak to the parents and—'

'Yes?' Beatrice hoped that her interruption would sound more like loyal impatience to hear more than irritation at the unnecessary detail.

'Well, the paupers are brought in and they stand between the wings of the table for the cross-examination.'

'Yes?' The tension was becoming too much for his wife to bear. She willed him to hurry towards the climax of his story.

'Well . . .' Henry was reluctant to reveal the full bestiality of William's behaviour. 'Sometimes when they stand there, he looks at the women as if they weren't paupers at all, just women.'

It was clear from Beatrice Stainton's expression that her husband had exposed a major flaw in William Skinner's character. She spoke with the relish of the righteous savouring the punishment of the ungodly.

'She'll have it out with him as soon as he gets home. Any minute now. Now we've left, he'll be back any minute.'

But, on the one Saturday that his wife actually needed him, William Skinner was late home from Wisbech Market for the only time in his life.

Market Day in Wisbech had been the highlight of William Skinner's week for as long as he could remember. From the age of seven, his father had brought him into town from Whittlesey each Saturday. At the end of his first visit, he had seen the masts of the grain ships above the houses which separated the market place from Neme Quay and, from that moment on, a full decade of Saturday mornings was spent in an agony of impatience, waiting for his father's permission to run to the docks and stare down the steep sides of the river walls at the crowded decks of the moored merchantmen. For ten years he fantasised about going to sea. Then the dream changed. At an age when other young men sauntered aimlessly along the High Street and through Castle Square, staring at girls whom they would never meet and glancing into shop windows at luxuries they would never buy, William Skinner developed a passion for plants, flowers, vegetables and fruit. He was infatuated with anything that grew 'and was bigger than grass, but smaller than trees'.

As a youth, he always spent the last hour of his Saturday in Wisbech wandering amongst the market stalls. At first, he was a joke with the farmers and market gardeners, who told each other that they would have earned twice as much for their day's work had they not been distracted by Jacob Skinner's boy and his questions about the sort of soil which produced the best potatoes and how they protected their seedlings against the frost. Gradually amusement was replaced with grudging admiration for William worked as hard on the books in the town museum as he laboured in his father's fields and in time his Saturday tour of the stalls took on a different character. Instead of asking questions, he answered them. When it became clear that he knew, at least in theory, more about horticulture than any of the working market gardeners, there was much speculation about whether he would, one day, put his knowledge to the practical test. When

Jacob Skinner died, the farm in its entirety would go to his elder son but there would be a few pounds in the will for William. The nursery-men and vegetable growers looked forward to the investment of that legacy in a smallholding – some hoping to see his enthusiasm rewarded and others anxious for proof that all the book learning in the world will never make up for practical experience.

Then William accepted the security of workhouse superintendent and when he visited their stalls – with the official purpose of compar-ing their prices with the cost of his home-grown produce – they greeted him with the modified deference due to his standing and status and the unqualified sympathy appropriate to a man who is not happy in his work.

The comparison of prices was one of the fictions which both cemented and lubricated his relationship with Elizabeth. Had he said openly that he visited the market for no better reason than to enjoy himself, his wife would have looked at him down her immaculately straight nose as a sign of the moral danger into which he was advanc-ing. Looks were her favourite method of complaint and comment, for they allowed her to criticise and condemn, resent or reject at will – and then deny that she had expressed any opinion if it suddenly became convenient for her to withdraw from the battle. The admission that he was going to Wisbech Market for pleasure (which was a sin) rather than for work (which was a sacrament) would have produced one of her most eloquently contemptuous glances. William would have asked his wife what message she meant to convey. She would have replied with the assertion that she did not know what he meant. The result would have been a disagreement too intangible to produce any emotion except frustration. So William pretended that he was working.

Even the deception that Saturday afternoons were spent comparing prices did not totally protect William from Elizabeth's disapproval. As he left, she always reminded him, 'Don't forget to call on Cousin Alfred.'

Alfred Ellison was a man of some substance. A bachelor of almost sixty, he was only distantly related to the Saunderses but, as the sailor's daughters were all the family that he possessed, he com-manded them to call him cousin and tried hard to treat them with the sentiments suitable to that relationship. Cousin Alfred was most anxious to be thought a man of affectionate and charitable disposition. The girls were not, however, easy to love and as, one by one, they married husbands to whom they were richly suited, Alfred Ellison almost despaired of finding a sympathetic recipient for his counterfeit concern and a gullible audience for the fantasies which made up most of his conversation. Then he met William Skinner, who seemed to

16

believe every word he said. The strange friendship excited the hope in Elizabeth that where his bogus affection led, his considerable fortune might follow.

His heart and his bank balance pulled Alfred Ellison in different directions. The fortune had been made from building houses of no great distinction but he dreamed of designing great churches, magnificent museums, monumental town halls and magistrates' courts which would proclaim justice from every slab of granite and block of Portland stone. When he and William sat down together in the Rose and Crown at three o'clock on a Saturday afternoon, the conversation was always between a workhouse superintendent who craved to become a gardener and a builder who longed to be an architect. Their mutual attraction stemmed from a common passion – the desperate need to hear the echo of their own regrets.

The meeting invariably began with Alfred denouncing the recent alterations to the front of the hotel which, in his aesthetic opinion, had ruined the façade. Then the two men took it in turns to express views on the separate subjects which interested them most. William would describe his latest discovery about the reproductive habits of the auricula and would provoke a response from Alfred concerning the gothic revival. Praise or condemnation of a new local building would be countered with a brief disquisition on the grafting of roses. Both men recognised the importance of sometimes dreaming out loud. Neither man shared the other's interests. There was never any practical discussion about the likelihood of dreams coming true and for years the Saturday afternoon conversations ended in make-believe.

William was, therefore, quite unnerved when, on the afternoon of the fateful events in the workhouse, Alfred told him, 'I've got something important to tell you about the business. Something I'd be grateful if you'd keep to yourself for the time being.' He was afraid that there would be talk of wills and inheritance. He did not want the hope of reward to spoil their relationship. 'I'm thinking about trying for a big new contract. I've got three months to work out the price and put it in.'

The news itself William found unremarkable. He assumed that the builder tendered for work during almost every week of the year and he was astonished that an account of the most recent venture was to be passed on to him. Normally his friend was as reluctant to talk about building as he himself was to discuss the Wisbech Workhouse. The real world which they inhabited for the rest of the week was not a suitable subject for Saturday afternoons. Yet Alfred began to elaborate on his announcement.

17

'It's in Lincoln and it's a bit unusual. I think that I could do it, but it'll be a handful. Nothing like any job I've done before.'

For the second time that afternoon, William misjudged his friend's motives. Alfred, he thought, was nervous about bidding for the job and talked about it to build his confidence. Putting all thought of sweet peas out of his mind, William offered a selection of comforting platitudes. 'Of course you can do it, with all your experience. You could build anything, anything reasonable.' He struggled to show real interest as well as real concern. 'What sort of building is it, anyway?'

'It's not a building at all. Though there's a lot of retaining walls. And there's a lot of flagstones. And there's terraces with balustrades. That sort of thing. There's one building, a keeper's lodge, that I'd design myself. And a glass pavilion. I think I'd sub-contract for that. It's more civil engineering than building. Apart from the big band-stand, that is. Really, that isn't much. It's mostly civil engineering.'

Although William knew that he ought to be infected by Alfred Ellison's enthusiasm, he felt betrayed. By talking about a park Alfred was trespassing on his dreams. He was not sure how he would react to real flower beds and herbaceous borders coming vicariously into his life with Alfred possessing the right to sow and plant them. He reminded himself that the whole idea was almost certainly fantasy. Even reassured he still exhibited his resentment. 'A park doesn't seem your line of business.'

'It's an arboretum. At Lincoln. There's an arboretum committee buying something called Brown's Close from the cathedral. As soon as it's bought they'll ask for tenders. It's nearly thirteen acres. It's a sloping site, but I can manage that.'

Trees came as a great relief. Alfred planting trees would not be so bad as Alfred growing flowers. William felt that he could afford to be generous, especially since he decided that the idea was not to be taken seriously.

'I'm sure you can do it.'

'Not without you, I can't. I'd only try for the job if you came with me.'

'How could I? I've got the workhouse and I've got Elizabeth and the children. It's a lovely thought and I bless you for it. But you'll have to do it without me.'

'I'm not ready to take no for an answer. You'll think about it. I'm in Peterborough next Saturday. Think about it for a fortnight.'

'It doesn't need thinking about. In a couple of years the job will be finished and I'll not have a penny coming in. It's not possible.'

'You'd stay with me. There'll be parks and botanical gardens to lay out all over the country, and greenhouses and conservatories and

18

tea rooms to build inside. We'll become landscapers to the gentry and gardeners to municipal councils. You'll be a real gardener, and I'll get as near as I'll ever be to a real architect – a landscape architect. You don't need qualifications. Paxton was just a gardener. I've made a bit. I won't let you starve if things start to slow.'

'No, Alfred. Anyway, you know it's only talk. It won't come to anything.'

'Elizabeth would like it. She doesn't like living in that workhouse.'

'She'd like it if I became Paxton or Capability Brown. She won't like it so much if I wear a leather apron and come home with mud on my boots.'

'Are you going to stay at the workhouse for ever?'

'Until we run out of paupers. So I've got some years left. Anyway,' William spoke slowly to demonstrate determination, 'it's quite impossible. I don't want to talk about it any more.'

They talked about it for the next hour – as if it were all a dream. They discussed the outline plan which had been drawn up for the Lincoln City surveyor by a London consultant and they talked about the details of his scheme – the Grand Entrance and the paved avenue which led to the heart of the arboretum, the lodge, the tea room, the terrace and the replica of the Crystal Palace which would be erected upon it. Alfred's excitement caught and held William. They talked about shrubs and plants – the rhododendrons in the spring, the roses, red, cream and white, throughout the summer, the hollyhocks which would be planted along Alfred Ellison's perfect stone walls and the lines of trees which would stand guard along every path and around every lake. They talked without thinking of time, until well after five o'clock. It was not until William broke the spell by repeating, 'It's quite impossible and we both know it,' that the enchantment was ended.

As always, Alfred, with no family of his own waiting at home, walked back with William to the workhouse. As usual when the strange silhouette came into view, he launched into an attack on the turrets and crenellations which could be seen against the evening sky and on the Guardians' pretentious claims for their building.

'It's a monstrosity. I'd be ashamed to have built it. Don't tell me it looks like a country house.'

'It certainly doesn't feel like one inside.'

'It looks like a barracks in the middle and stables at the sides. I'd be ashamed to put my name to it. It's enough to give you night-mares. Nobody believes it, but I could have done something twice as good.'

The complaint was the regular conclusion to the walk back to Lynn

19

Road. Rarely was a reply expected or given. On that special night William knew exactly what he must say.

'Well, now you've got the chance to show them what you can do. You can build an arboretum to rival the Hanging Gardens of Babylon.' He was no longer certain if the arboretum was part of the real world of Alfred's business or the other existence of his private life.

Alfred's response was disturbingly realistic. 'I can do the civil engineering, all right. I can shift the soil and put up the bits of building. But I can't manage trees. I need you for that.'

'I know nothing about trees. I can barely tell a sycamore from a chestnut. I know about flowers and vegetables. It's not the same, you know. Trees aren't big vegetables.'

Alfred, misjudging his man, tried to tempt William with exotica.

'Then there'll be all the foreign bushes. Japan, India, South America. Places like that. You could read all the books and find out about the different sorts. You could go to Kew Gardens and get cuttings and plant them in the right sort of soil. You could write out their Latin names and where they came from and we'd have them put into little cast-iron frames stuck into—'

'I could do none of those things. And, what is more, I don't want to. I want to grow the flowers and vegetables that I know. I want to be an English gardener, not an Indian or a Chinaman or anything foreign. Anyway, I can't be a gardener of any sort. I've got my family to look after. Alfred, I'm tired of this game.'

They stood uneasily together outside the workhouse lodge, reluctant to part in disagreement but certain that they could not agree. Then William noted that, although the arms of the windmill turned slowly in the evening breeze, there was no sound of corn being crushed between stone and stone. Milling was over for the day. It was after five o'clock. The day's casual inmates would already be in the bathhouse and the regulars would have started their supper. The monotony of his wife's uneventful afternoon would have been extended by an unnecessary hour. He said goodbye to Alfred and hurried apprehensively through the forbidding gates. As he passed the foreman's lodge, he noticed that Gerrard Knock pushed his wife inside the door and slammed it shut without paying the master his proper respects.

CHAPTER THREE

Hopes and Fears

Dusk had come early that evening, but Elizabeth Skinner still sat in the drawing-room window as if she hoped that the light would again illuminate her sewing. For over an hour, the needle had not moved in her hand.

'I'm sorry, love. We got talking.'

'Sorry for what?' She knew very well. Tea always came on Saturdays at half-past four. Normally Elizabeth was too proud to lie but on that day pride made conflicting demands.

'I had tea early. Then, I think I must have fallen asleep.' She glanced at the clock on the mantelshelf. 'I'd no idea of the time.'

'I was afraid that you would be worried.'

It was, William knew, a stupid thing to say – Elizabeth never worried – but it was the proper apology for a husband to make to a wife. He did not expect a proper wife's reply.

'Why should I be worried? You're often missing when there's trouble. I dealt with it.' She gave him her justified-resentment look.

'Dealt with what?'

'A girl came. A girl called Alice Thomson.' She paused. There was not the slightest sign that her husband had ever heard the name. 'She's pregnant.'

'Not another one. How do they do it? Do they climb over the wall into the men's yard? Or do they . . . ?' He decided that it would be indelicate to speculate about the possibility of copulation in the laundry or chapel, so he speculated about compulsion rather than location. 'They're driven to it by nature, I suppose. Original sin. It's a powerful force.'

William thought for a second of using the opportunity to introduce the subject of man's irresistible impulses. He then remembered his self-imposed vow of silence. Elizabeth seemed preoccupied with work-house management.

'Do you know her?'

21

William gave an answer which might have been absolute proof of his guilt or complete confirmation of his innocence.

'Of course I know her. She's a delicate little slip of a girl. Looks as if a strong wind could blow her over. She had rickets. She has the brute of a brother who you wanted to send to prison. Of course I know her. Why do you ask?'

'Because she said that you are the baby's father.'

When he was a little boy, William Skinner had always feared that he reacted to even the most unreasonable accusation by looking guilty. As he spoke, he could feel the credibility draining from his face. He tried to sound amused. 'You didn't believe her?' He waited for the blow to land. He was certain that, by his behaviour, he had convinced his wife that the accusation was true.

'Of course I didn't. How can you imagine that I might? But that didn't make me feel much better. A girl like that coming in here and telling me that my own husband . . .'

William was relieved but only partly so. If his wife did not believe that he was the father, she almost certainly thought that, by his liberal management of the workhouse, he had encouraged the girl's lunatic behaviour. He had no doubt that he had been right to sweep away the old regime of rigid regulation and savage punishment, but he knew that Elizabeth had never held with his radical notions of reform and rehabilitation and that she was silently blaming him for causing her pain. He did not expect the silence to last or to be ended with reassurance.

'I'm sorry. I really am.'

'Nobody's blaming you. I just want you to understand that it wasn't very pleasant.'

William could not think of anything sensible to say. He knew how his wife would have resented the indignity and he struggled to be appropriately sympathetic. But he wished that she was concerned with something more important than her immediate discomfiture. He was not sure what that higher emotion should be – outrage at the libel against him, pride in the certainty of his innocence, guilt at the thought that the shortcomings of their married life might cause such a transgression. He was certain that she should feel something more important than outrage at a moment's humiliation.

'Well, it's all over now. Best put it out of your mind.'

'I shan't ever forget it. Never. How could anyone forget a thing like that? Would you forget it, if it had happened to you?'

Elizabeth clearly expected some sort of reaction. William responded with the best practical suggestion that he could think of at short notice.

'I'll see her and make her tell me who the man is. If he's single, we'll see that he marries her.'

'She'll brazen it out. I know her sort. She'll swear to your face that you're the father. She'll describe the time and the place where it happened and she'll enjoy telling you about it. And, for good measure, she'll tell you how much you gave her afterwards, when she promised to keep quiet.'

'Did she say all that to you?'

'She did not. She wouldn't dare. But I could see her little mind working away. She'll invent every detail and enjoy spilling it all out. She'll invent more and more and say more and more.'

'I'll see her.' It was an inadequate response but, for the moment, it was the best that William could do. 'I'll go straight away.'

'She's in the casual ward.'

'What's she doing there?'

'I sent her. I won't have her in the women's ward spreading her lies. I have to see those women every day.'

'I suspect that she's spread a few lies already.'

'She has. Beatrice told me that Henry heard a lad shout something about it in the yard. That woman said she'd told nobody, but she's a liar. Talking to everybody makes it worse. That's why she's got to go.'

'My God. I hope Henry thrashed him.'

William was so outraged by the thought of the boy making dirty jokes at his expense that the full implications of his wife's explanation took some time to digest.

'When did Beatrice tell you all this?'

'This afternoon. She came round this afternoon, especially to tell me.'

'I'm sure she enjoyed it.'

'It's why this girl has got to be turned out, William. She really has. I mean it, William. She's got to go.'

'Go where?'

'Go anywhere, except here. Go out of this workhouse and out of my sight. We can't have her saying those things here.'

'Nobody will believe her.' William was no longer sure whether or not what he had said was true but he knew that there was no question of Alice Thomson being ejected from the workhouse. She was in receipt of indoor relief, duly approved by the Board of Poor Law Guardians. She could discharge herself at three hours' notice, or the Guardians, at a subsequent and properly convened meeting, could decide and determine that she and her mother had no further legitimate demands upon the parishes of North Cambridgeshire. But she

23

could not be turned on to the street for saying that she had been impregnated by the master, so William repeated his hope. 'Nobody will believe her.'

'You don't mean you'd let her stay? You don't mean that you'd allow her to go on saying those filthy things under this roof? I'd see her every day. You couldn't make me face such disgrace.'

'I tell you. Nobody will believe her.'

'They will if you don't turn her out.'

'You know I can't do it. I can't turn a girl out on to the streets, a girl of seventeen . . . or whatever she is . . . a girl who's pregnant by heaven knows how many months. She's nowhere to go. God knows, if she had she wouldn't be here. She'll walk for a day, sleep in a haystack and eat turnips until she dies under a hedge like a cat that's gone wild.'

'You've turned paupers out before. What's the difference?'

'I've turned out great healthy men. She's a woman. That's the difference. She's having a baby. That's the difference. The others were men I'd caught fighting or stealing. They'd been warned or threatened. I didn't even turn her brother out when he threatened violence to Knock. I could have handed them over to the magistrates and they would have been in Ely Gaol for a couple of months, breaking stones on bread and water. They chose to go instead of being dealt with by the police. They weren't seventeen-year-old girls who had rickets and probably have consumption.'

'How do you know that she probably has consumption?'

William could not remember how he knew, though to him the knowledge seemed a matter of little significance. He knew which of the old men were dying from cancer and he could recognise the children in his care who had come into the workhouse with ringworm. He had half an idea that the girl's mother was consumptive.

'Are you asking me if I really did it? Is that what this performance is leading to? Do you believe her? If you do, it's best to say so.'

'It's no good bullying me. You just ought to save some of your tender feelings for your wife and what she'll have to face because of you. I shan't be able to get away from it. I'll be living in humiliation all day and every day.'

'I can't turn her out. And I wouldn't if I could.'

'Then what are you going to do to stop people talking?'

'I'm going to do what's proper and right. On Monday, I shall tell the clerk to the Board that a woman is pregnant. That's the rule. At the same time I shall write to the chairman and tell him about . . . about what she said.'

William said 'do what's proper' as if the words were an incantation,

24

for he intended them to cast a spell over his wife. Propriety was the guiding principle of Elizabeth's existence. If she could be convinced that the course of conduct he proposed was the only choice consistent with conspicuous respectability, the argument would be over. The charm worked only part of its usual magic.

'And what about the girl?'

'There can't be any question of punishment. The days of bread and water are over, thank God.' William played his trump card. 'Think what a scandal there would be if something happened to her. Neither of us would enjoy it if I were accused of ill-treating one of the young women. You know what the papers are like these days. I wouldn't be the first workhouse master to be pilloried by a jumped-up journalist. Think of the scandal if we were up before the Guardians for brutality.'

William pulled an old copy of the *Wisbech Advertiser* from under one of the cushions on the sofa.

'I've been keeping it to prove what happens these days. Just in case the Guardians start on about discipline again.'

He read the date at the top of the page, 'Thursday, 9 June 1868,' and continued,

'"At Preston, last Tuesday night, an inquest was held on the body of Patrick Burke, son of Stephen Burke, executed in September 1866 for the murder of his wife. The deceased was an inmate of Walton-on-Dale workhouse near Preston. The day before Christmas Day the governor obtained from the surgeon a pot of blue ointment and rubbed half a tablespoonful on the head of each boy in the house in order to make them ready for inspection by visitors. The next day four of them were salivating and Burke died shortly afterwards. The blue ointment contained a large quantity of mercury. The jury returned a verdict of accidental death, but cautioned the governor as to his practices in future."

'These days you have to be very careful if you don't want to be accused of mistreating the paupers.'

'You've been accused of worse today. Rather a reputation for discipline than a reputation for being a fornicator.'

'But I'm not a fornicator, that's the important thing. I would be a brute if I turned her out. And we both know it.'

William walked towards his wife. When he was within arm's length of her chair, she stood up as if she were afraid of being touched. They were less than a foot apart, Elizabeth looking over her husband's shoulder into the dark room behind him and William staring at the

25

floor. Without a word, he turned on his heel and left the room. He was late starting his evening rounds. It was, he decided, important not to keep his wife waiting for supper as well as tea. He would not have time to visit the women's casual ward.

Gerrard Knock, ever faithful and always conscientious, had already carried out the inspection. He was surprised by how quiet the ward had been. Most of the older women were already asleep, for it was after six o'clock, the last meal of the day had been swallowed down and there was nothing left for them to do. A girl – the foreman guessed that she was no more than fourteen – sat in front of the fire suckling her baby. Coughing came from the corner in which old Mrs Thomson slowly capitulated to consumption. Knock silently closed the door behind him and limped slowly home to the lodge.

At every step of the way, he thought about horses – horses galloping in the half-light of early morning, horses steaming under their blankets in stable yards, horses restless as they were shod and groomed, and above all horses straining at reins held by jockeys in the brave colours of the great racing families. The foreman wore a smock which he thought of not as faded yellow, but as straw. Straw was the racing colour of the Devonshires.

The letter was still behind the clock on the mantelshelf, though it was not in quite the place where he had left it. His wife had read it whilst he had been out – read it, he guessed, for the tenth time that day. She was thinking about the decision they had to make. Gerrard Knock sat down to his supper determined that, by the end of the meal, they would have decided to leave Wisbech and its workhouse for ever.

'Have you thought any more?'

Rosie Knock shook her head so emphatically that every auburn curl danced and, catching the candlelight, sparkled for a moment before it fell back perfect and still.

'We've got to make up our minds this week. If we don't decide this week, it'll all be decided for us. It'll be gone.'

'I don't want to go, Gerry. I really don't.'

'Not even now?'

'What difference does all that make – another girl having a baby and lying about who the father is?'

'But what if she's not lying? It'll be hell open to Christians if Mr Skinner did do it. New master, for certain. Doubt if he'd be as easy as this one. This one's not usual.'

'He didn't do it.' Rosie's green eyes were steadfastly focused on the tablecloth. She sounded completely certain of the master's innocence.

'You can't be sure. If we're not careful, he'll be discharged and we'll be left here with some brute who treats us no better than he treats the paupers.'

Gerrard Knock had no doubt that Alice Thomson was lying, but her lies might be used to his advantage. The letter behind the clock contained the news that Mr Henry Sweet Hodding, squire of Harness Grove, Darfoulds in the County of Nottingham, was looking for a coachman and groom. Gerrard Knock, who could think of nothing except the chance to work with horses, was desperately searching for arguments in favour of leaving Wisbech.

'You don't know that you'd get it.'

'I want to try. Anyway, Billy Macdonald says I would.'

'What does Billy know? Billy always talks big.'

'He knows all right. This Mr Hodding asked him to look out for somebody when he was at Mr Robinson's stables.'

'Is Mr Hodding a racing man, then?'

'He's a hunting man with six horses to look after. He hunts with Mr Robinson – with the Rufford.'

'Can you manage the carriage?' Rosie was growing desperate and Gerrard was losing patience.

'A little two-hander! Lord save us and spare us! I could drive one of them when I was ten.'

'That was before your accident.'

The freckles, which began on Rosie's forehead and stretched down beyond her throat and neck, faded under a deep blush of shame. The accident should never be mentioned. It had happened almost ten years before and had ended all the great ambitions her husband had cherished since he was young. Gerrard Knock could not remember when – thanks to his stunted growth and the way he had with the ponies that his father bought and sold – people had first made jokes about him riding at Leopardstown or the Curragh. But he recalled the morning when the parish priest had told him that, in the wicked world beyond Dublin, there were great English races where horses owned by the licentious Prince of Wales competed against horses that belonged to members of the alien government which ruled Ireland. The morality tale had not had its intended effect. That night, little Gerrard Knock stole his father's takings from the Arklow horse fair and set out for Liverpool and the Sport of Protestant Kings.

He spent his first year in England mucking out stables in Doncaster. Then he moved to Newmarket, where he was allowed to work with brush and curry-comb. Just as he gave up hope of ever being allowed to sit astride a saddle, he was sent out fifth in the string on early-

27

morning gallops. He rode out twice. On the second morning, the horse he was exercising first reared and then fell. Gerrard Knock's leg was smashed as the kicking horse rolled across him. Worse still, the mare broke her back. The accident happened without cause or reason so he was held responsible and the word of his incompetence was passed to every stable in Newmarket.

'A stiff leg won't stop me driving a little two-hander.'

'I know your heart's set on it . . .' Rosie had meant to add that, despite her understanding of his passion, she hoped he would consider the possible consequences of such a leap in the dark. But it was too late. The wizened face lit up.

'I knew you'd understand, Rosie. I knew you would. And when you get there you'll love it.'

Gerrard Knock knew his wife to be one of nature's enthusiasts. It was that – as much as her auburn hair, green eyes and freckles – which had made so many men pursue her with unrequited, but unquenchable, passion. Her reluctance to move to a new job, a new cottage and a new world bewildered him. But he had no doubt that once they were installed in the grandeur of domestic service she would bubble and sparkle again.

'But you've done so well here, Gerry.'

He had arrived as a pauper and, after a year of hard work, had been offered the job of nightwatchman. He had made the rounds of doors and windows to such good effect that he had first been promoted to chargehand and then, when William Skinner arrived and the foreman had left muttering about soft ways only storing up trouble, Gerrard Knock had been offered his place.

'I've done well enough. But there's nowhere now for me to go. And if we get a brute we'll be done for.'

He might have added, 'and there are no horses'. But despite her Irish ancestry – the hereditary good fortune that had taken her to mass on the very Sunday when her husband went to give thanks for being made foreman – Rosie Knock did not understand about these things.

'So we're going to go, whatever I say.'

This, Gerrard decided, was the moment for courage – the time for a touch with the spurs and a single slash with the whip. He was within sight of the finishing post.

'Yes, we're going.'

He had often seen his wife weep little tears of joy but never before had he seen her sob in uncontrollable grief. For a moment, he could barely resist hobbling round the table, taking her head in his arms and telling her that he would be a workhouse foreman for ever. Then he hardened his heart and told himself that he must be strong and sensible for her sake as well as his own.

Rosie, he reminded himself, knew nothing of the world. She had come to England as a girl of fourteen hoping to work in service and had drudged for a year at the White Lion Hotel. Because she was round and tawny she had been a favourite with those guests who expected no more than a cheerful smile from a pretty girl – but because she kept herself to herself she never enjoyed the same popularity with the porter, the tapman, the valet and the waiters. In consequence she was required to work twice as hard as the more accommodating maids. She had first met Gerrard Knock when he was no more than nightwatchman at the workhouse and, like everybody else, had laughed at the funny little wizened man who drank a solemn pint of bitter beer each night. But Gerrard had discovered that they both hailed from Galway and befriended her with a persistence which she first suspected but gradually came to realise was prompted by the goodness of his heart. When he asked her to marry him she had no hesitation in accepting. She wanted to be comfortable and she believed that, by becoming Mrs Knock, she could have comfort and respectability for no greater price than the performance of a wife's proper duty. Since she was, by nature, a warm and loving woman who enjoyed work and longed for a family of her own to wash and cook for, she paid the price willingly. Gerrard loved Rosie with a purity which owed much to pride, surprise and gratitude. But he did not trust her judgement. He was unyielding in his determination to do what was right for them both by bettering himself.

'When will we go?'

'As soon as I know that the job's definitely mine. I'll write tomorrow.'

'And when will you tell Mr Skinner?'

'When the job's certain. I don't want him to know until it's definite. I'll tell him when I get an offer, when the letter comes.'

The letter from Squire Hodding arrived four days later. It did not offer Gerrard Knock the position, but asked him to travel to Worksop in order to be interviewed as to suitability. To the applicant's surprise, he was invited to wait upon the squire at a solicitor's office. Rosie expressed neither pleasure nor regret. Her only concern was her husband's obligation to make an honourable departure from the workhouse.

'You'll have to tell Mr Skinner.'

'I know I will, damn it. It's not the right time. Not till the job's definite. But I'll tell him soon enough.'

To Gerrard Knock's gratified astonishment, no enquiry was made about the reason for the trip to Worksop and no mention was made of the necessity of docking a day's wages in compensation for the time spent on the mysterious expedition.

The ancient river-port of Wisbech was in temporary decline. The years of growth and glory when half of the Fenland trade had passed through its docks were over and, since the railway companies had chosen to run their lines through other market towns, young men looking for new work moved to King's Lynn, March and Ely. Old Wisbech families talked increasingly of the past – of the year when the New Sutton Dock was sunk, the canal had made money and the Outfall had been dug to drain the increasingly prosperous farmland to the east. They talked with particular nostalgia about the brief moment in 1840 when Wisbech shipped more corn across its quays than was exported from any other port in the country. It was a subject which – to his increasing exasperation – dominated more and more of the conversation over Alfred Ellison's dinner table.

Alfred Ellison was a sociable man but his social instincts were precisely geared to his own pleasures. On Sunday evenings when he entertained his two closest friends at his strange new house at 23 North Brink, he expected to talk about subjects of his own choice. Despite his popular reputation as a man of gregarious instinct and generous disposition, under the castellated gables (which would not have looked out of place in Amsterdam) and behind the over-decorated window sills and door arches (which would have looked out of place anywhere) he expected proper repayment for his outlay on food and drink. He was happy to talk about business, particularly his own business, but he wanted to describe his prospects, not his past – for his history, though honourable, was a matter of hard fact. The future could be invented and invention was his greatest delight. When he found the conversation particularly oppressive, he always tried to shock his visitors into a change of subject. So when he grew bored with speculation about the imminent closure of the New Sutton Dock, he turned to Thomas Leverington, the chairman of the Poor Law Board of Guardians.

'I tried to abduct the master of your workhouse last Saturday.'

It was Thomas Leverington's response which stopped all other conversation. 'I wish you had. He's not making much of a fist at the workhouse.'

Alfred almost came to the defence of his friend. But he questioned rather than contradicted. 'You've never said anything like that before.'

'He's never written to me before, telling me as cool as you please that a young woman in the casual ward is in the family way and saying that he's the father of her child.'

'You don't mean that he admitted it?' Alfred Ellison was properly incredulous.

'Of course he didn't,' the chairman said.

Alfred Ellison feared that asking the question might have undermined his reputation for loyalty so he rallied to the support of his friend. 'He didn't admit it because he didn't do it. He couldn't do it. Anyone who has ever met him must know that.' He concluded his robust defence with a question that raised doubts about the confidence with which he argued his case. 'What did he say?'

'He said nothing on the subject of guilt or innocence. Took it for granted that I would not even suspect him of such a thing. Of course, he was right. The woman is clearly a liar and Skinner's no lecher. Even if he were, his wife would keep him on too tight a rein for him to cause much trouble. Elizabeth Skinner—'

Canon Winston Wheatley woke just in time to hear the lady's name mentioned. 'Splendid woman that. Worth twice her husband. I can't imagine why she married him.' He sank back in his chair.

'I don't understand your complaint. What has he done wrong?' Alfred Ellison hoped that his question was a compromise between enquiry and argument.

'It's the way he runs Lynn Road. No order. No work. No discipline. The teacher's been to complain about him – and he's related.'

'Teachers and masters argue in every workhouse in England. It's one of the reasons why we should send children out to school.'

'They argue', Leverington retorted, 'because the teachers want more time to teach and the masters want the children to work. At Lynn Road, it's the other way around. Skinner's always wanting more schooling. The teacher says that they hardly work at all.'

'I think that admirable,' said Canon Wheatley, who believed in patronage far more devoutly than he believed in the Trinity.

'It's not just that. He lets the children, boys and girls, play together on Sunday afternoon. If old men come back early from their walks he lets them straight back into the ward – whatever time of day it is. He makes money, I grant him that. He sells potatoes and cabbage—'

'Much to the annoyance of the market gardeners whose prices are undercut,' interrupted Alfred Ellison, who briefly forgot which side he was on.

'I don't mind that. Market gardeners complain about everything.' Leverington believed that only farmers had the right to resent bad weather, high wages and fierce competition. 'What I mind is that he spends all that he makes on extra food. Fresh milk. Meat or broth every day—'

Canon Wheatley woke again. He had heard the word meat. 'I read in *The Times* that in Lancashire they give the paupers meat every day.' His tone changed from horror to amused contempt. 'But they don't give them knives and forks to eat it with. Too expensive!' Chuckling, he fell back to sleep.

Alfred Ellison decided to polish his image as a radical and a reformer. 'Skinner's doing no more than is being done in dozens of other workhouses. It's the times, Thomas, it's the times. We're getting old and set in our ways. I'm not so sure that the old ways were best.'

'In the old days, there was respect. Respect for the Guardians and for the master. Can you imagine a pauper making such an accusation twenty years ago?'

'Unless he'd done it.' The canon was awake again.

'Twenty years ago,' said Alfred Ellison, 'paupers were being poisoned with bosh butter.'

'I spoke out against that. It was my first year as a Guardian but I spoke out as soon as I knew that they were being given horse fat and engine grease. It was William Skinner's father who defended the master then. And I know him, he'd do it again today given the chance. He saved the old master and, whether he knows it or not, he's saving the master now.'

'How do you make that out?' asked Alfred Ellison, who wanted to be William's saviour but did not want to take any risks by mounting the rescue. 'I can't see old Jacob being very happy about what's going on. Does he know about it?'

'He does not. That's what I mean. If Master William Skinner wasn't old Jacob's lad, he would have been out months ago. But, whilst his father is alive, he's safe enough.'

'So he's safe for years,' Canon Wheatley said. 'I drove through Whittlesey yesterday. They're late with the harvest. Jacob was riding about on that old horse of his like a Cossack general, shouting and cursing whenever a man stopped to whet his scythe.'

'The women should do that,' said the chairman of the Poor Law Board. 'That's women's work.' Thomas Leverington was a traditionalist.

Out at Whittlesey, work started before dawn. For five days, reaping had begun in half-light and gone on until nightfall with every capable man that Jacob Skinner could hire advancing in line abreast against the massed ranks of golden wheat. On cloudless nights they marched on after the sun had set with the moonlight casting long shadows on the stubble behind them. From start to finish, the scythe blades hissed through the air in what sounded like rhythm. When the sun was at its height, it flashed off the steel as if a hundred heliographs were sending irregular messages across the fields. Down south in Suffolk, scythes were being augmented by machines with flailing scarlet wheels that cut twenty-foot swathes through the standing corn, but at Whittlesey the scythe was still king. Jacob Skinner waited until the moment when his cornfield was just ready for cutting and then put his faith in men and muscle power.

Jacob was mean, but that was not what caused him to rely on the scythe. His instinct was for old things and old ways. He was not a romantic who followed tradition out of sentiment – often, he found it comfortable and economical not to change – but he was not moved by fad or fashion. When the customs of the country conflicted with his convenience, he spoke passionately of the need to move with the times.

In every other Fenland farm, the reapers were led by the man who, by general consent, had been the champion reaper of the previous year. That man wove poppies and dog daisies in his hat as a mark of his authority. He decided how long the line of scythes should be, at which side of each field the work should start, when heat and exhaustion justified a brief pause in the work or if the light was good enough for the men to work on safely.

Once upon a time at Whittlesey, a man with flowers in his hat had taken too many rests, started from the wrong side of too many fields and stopped work whilst the silhouettes of reapers were still visible above the standing wheat. Ever since then, the line of reapers had been led by a Skinner – first by Jacob himself and then, when he was half crippled by rheumatoid arthritis, by Joshua his elder son.

Joshua was not allowed to take any of the crucial decisions. With his straw hat garlanded to excess, he took his place on the right flank of the line that reaped at Whittlesey. Behind the line of reapers, the women collected the cut wheat, bound it into sheaves and left it to dry. The same sight could have been seen on any East Anglian farm in September but at Whittlesey an old man with stiff legs and crumpled hands shouted orders from the back of an ancient horse. He shouted more than orders. When the panting dogs saw a frightened rabbit and rushed – tongues hanging out – into the uncut wheat, he commanded them to keep clear of the scythe blades. And if a woman's scarf slipped from the crown of her head and the sun glistened in her hair, he instructed her to retie the knot before she collapsed with heatstroke. Jacob Skinner shouted to such good effect that his entire crop had been reaped and set up in stooks to dry in

33

five days. Not a dog had been ripped open by a scythe and not a single woman had collapsed in the sun.

The five days of reaping had been frantic. The five days which were to follow would be frenzied. Failure to reap when the wheat was ready would have risked damage to part of the crop. Failure to cart, stack and thatch before the next rain would result in the destruction of every mildewed sheaf so at dawn the hired men began to pitchfork the dry bundles on to the great carts and stack them higher than a barn. Pairs of Suffolk Punches – flowers in their harness to match the poppies and dog daisies in Joshua Skinner's hat – pulled the tottering loads back to the yard where the ricks were built.

At noon, the women – with no real work to do – brought bread and cheese out into the fields and sat in the shade of the hedges waiting for Jacob to give the word that the time had come to loosen the stoppers in the stone ginger-beer bottles. The midday break was the only rest allowed during the last days of the harvest. When it was over, even the miniature barrel made for Jacob Skinner by the coopers of Lynn to commemorate his twenty years as a magistrate was sent back to the farmhouse as a sign that he would suffer the deprivations of the hired men and work without rest or refreshment. In the afternoon, the morning's pace was doubled and the cutting was interrupted only if a load collapsed, a boy fell from the very top of a full cart or a pitchfork went through a man's foot. Everybody knew the rule. That is why every man in the Top Meadow stood still with astonishment at the sight of Joshua Skinner's ten-year-old daughter running through the field from which the sheaves had already been cleared. She was waving wildly, shouting and pointing behind her as if pursued by a dragon.

Before she reached Top Meadow, the dragon was breathing fire. Behind her a plume of smoke had begun to climb into the clear blue sky. Without a word Jacob Skinner pulled his horse round and kicked both his heels into its mangy flanks. The men dropped their pitchforks and ran with him.

Despite the kicking and cursing, the old nag could not match the speed of the running men. Within half a mile, Jacob Skinner, with one or two of the older farm labourers by his side, was in the rearguard. By the time he reached the farm, the fire-fighting was already under way, though it was too late to save much of the rick – the first stack to be built and therefore the nearest to the house.

It was a bad day for fighting fires. The summer had been dry and the duck pond was half empty. The men could fill their buckets only by wading knee deep into the soft ground which, when winter came, would once again be two feet under water. After every ten minutes, the pump in the yard ran dry and the handle hung limp until someone claimed to hear the spring gurgle again underground. Bolder spirits climbed up the side of the rick furthest from the fire, crawled across the top and – coughing and crying from the smoke – emptied their buckets on to the flames below.

Jacob Skinner, the moment he had time and breath to spare from directing operations, looked down at his son, who was leaning, panting, on the old horse's withers.

'When I find out who started this, I'll have the skin off his back.'

'These things just happen, Father. Fires start inside stacks.'

'Not when the crop was as dry as that. And not when the rick had only just been made. Somebody was smoking near that stack. Somebody knocked his pipe out and then went against that stack with a young woman.'

'Not at three o'clock in the afternoon, Father. Not within thirty feet of the house.' Joshua rarely contradicted his father but it was a moment of especial emotion and the usual disciplines had broken down.

'I'll find out who did it and I'll have every penny he owns. If he's a lad, I'll have it off his father.' Jacob pointed at a farm labourer who was blowing into a burned palm. 'Tell that lazy good-for-nothing that if he wastes any more time he won't be working for me tomorrow morning. At this rate, it won't be out before dark.'

It was not out until after dark, for the cloudless autumn had ended that day and there was neither a golden sunset nor a harvest moon. Jacob Skinner sat in the farm kitchen and calculated how much he would lose if it rained that night. Each calculation was worse than the one before. He was just beginning to contemplate bankruptcy when the stone came through the kitchen window.

At first none of the family understood what had happened. A pane of glass had smashed. Something had landed on the kitchen floor. The women screamed. Joshua Skinner jumped to his feet. Jacob eased himself painfully round and looked into the corner where he thought the object rested. But nobody quite realised that it had been a wilful assault. Even when they absorbed the facts of the outrage, nobody thought of running outside in the hope of catching the assailant. They had all been born and bred in the peaceful Fenlands and had no experience of violence or any idea how it should be dealt with. There was a pause before Jacob nodded in the direction of the stone missile. Joshua picked it up. To his surprise, it was wrapped in a sheet of paper which had been torn from a ledger and tied to it with coarse gardener's hemp. He handed the parcel, intact, to his father.

Jacob Skinner read only with difficulty. So, having untied the string, he handed the paper back to his son. Joshua was barely more literate.

It was more appropriate for him to suffer the indignity of spelling the letters out, one by one, than for his father to expose a more venerable ignorance. He spoke the words syllable by syllable, concentrating too hard on mastering each one to give any meaning to the whole message.

'"We shall never forgive your son for what he did. And we shall repay."'

'What have you been up to?' Jacob asked, even before the women had left the room.

'I've done nothing,' Joshua answered with resignation. 'I don't know who threw it. Some man I sacked in the spring? That horse-dealer in Wisbech who said we sold him a winded mare? The gypsies we turned out of Holm Wood? I doubt if they'll come back. I'll nail boards across the window tonight and we'll tell the police in the morning.'

'Somebody better keep guard on the ricks.'

Joshua, who made no claim to intellectual agility, had not connec-ted the two incidents.

'I'll go down to the cottages and get a couple of men straight away.' He reached down the shotgun from over the fireplace. 'I bet it was that Irishman I sacked. I sacked him for getting fighting drunk. Great Fenian brute. Just the sort of thing he'd do. I bet it was him.'

Had he gambled, Joshua Skinner would have lost his wages. In the early hours of that day, Alice Thomson's brother had discharged himself from the workhouse and, having stolen fourpence from the poor box in the doorway of the Octagon Church, had first drunk five pints of ale and then set out on a crusade of vengeance against the whole Skinner family.

CHAPTER FOUR

Gerrard Knock Improves His Prospects

Gerrard Knock arrived at the Worksop offices of Brodhurst and Hodding almost half an hour later than his appointed time. As he sat in the dark waiting room, he had little doubt that the job was lost. His crippled leg ached and his stomach churned with tension and disappointment. The stiff collar he had put on with such difficulty was limp from the sweat and rain which had added to his anxiety as he hobbled from the railway station to Cheapside. He was kept waiting for so long that he almost avoided the anticipated rejection by slipping silently away. Then a bearded, burly man banged the door open. He continued a sentence which he had apparently begun outside in the corridor. Gerrard assumed that he was an employee of the partnership.

'. . . And the train was late.'

'I've got an appointment to see Mr Hodding, sir.'

'Always is, I tell you. Are you interested in railways?'

'No, sir. Horses.'

'Well, if you work for me, you'll have to learn about trains. Timetables, anyway. A lot of my work's done for the Midland – the Midland and the Grand Central. Come through. I'll lead the way.'

Henry Hodding swept out of the room leaving the door swinging and Gerrard astonished by both the youth and the verve of his prospective employer. Briefly he cherished renewed hopes that the prospect might become a reality but they were again dashed when he was left standing on the threshold of the office whilst a window was opened, the roll-topped desk was closed and, more surprisingly, the swivel chair behind it was wound down to a height suitable to accommodate the limping visitor.

'What's wrong with your leg?'

Gerrard was convinced that having survived being late he was confounded by his disability. He replied bleakly, 'A horse fell on it.'

'How did that happen?'

'I was a stable lad at Newmarket, sir. Mr Horace Walker-Smith's stables.'

'Jumpin'?'

'No, sir. Early-morning gallop. The horse just fell, sir. I never knew why.'

'For heaven's sake, come in and sit down.' The chair was still difficult to ascend for it turned on its pivot when Gerrard attempted to obey Mr Hodding's instruction.

'Your answer does you credit.' Hope was renewed. The applicant waited for the cross-examination to begin. 'Let me tell you what I want. I live at Harness Grove at Darfoulds on Chesterfield Road. Part of it's Newcastle Avenue since I got it metalled and widened. I called it after the Duke. I'm the steward of Worksop Manor under his patent. Now, why do I need a coachman? I travel a lot. London most weeks. I've promoted four parliamentary bills and no doubt there'll be more. So it's Darfoulds to Nottingham most Mondays. I'm clerk to Ollerton Highways Board and the Newark Turnpike Trust. So that's more regular journeys . . .'

Mr Hodding paused. It was, Gerrard decided, impossible that he was exhausted by the recital of his commitments. Perhaps he was creating an opportunity for the would-be coachman to say something intelligent and knowledgeable.

'Am I to understand that you are an engineer, sir? I assumed from your letter that you were a solicitor.'

'Of course I'm a solicitor!' Gerrard's hope fell and then rose again. 'I act professionally for the railway companies and for the engineers. But they're only part of the practice. I'm clerk to the justices and I do private work – now that Mr Brodhurst has left.' Gerrard Knock believed that the interview was about to begin. He was wrong. 'But engineering's in my blood. At least, acting for them is. My grandfather worked for Brunel and Rennie – Thames tunnel and Waterloo Bridge. He wrote both bills. Makes the Worksop and Bingham line seem small beer. But I did the Worksop water. That's something to be proud of . . .'

Gerrard realised, at last, that the pauses were intended to allow him to provide a small peg on which Henry Hodding could hang more of the seamless and all-embracing garment which was his autobiography.

'Worksop water, sir?'

'I got the clean water. The Board opposed me, root and branch. But I raised the money and set up the undertaking. I had cause, you know. I had cause.'

Mistaking the signs, Gerrard almost repeated 'Had cause?', with what he believed to be the proper degree of interest. But, before he had fully pronounced the first syllable, Henry Hodding had answered the unasked question. 'Two of my sons died of scarlet fever. Two sons and a daughter. The doctors all said that bad water was the cause. Every one of them said the same thing. That's when I decided that this town would have a decent water supply. And now it has.'

A long silence followed. Gerrard had lost all confidence in his own ability to judge the response expected of him and Mr Hodding had suddenly turned his attention to a paper tied in pink tape which was lying on one of the side tables. After the agonising interlude the solicitor-of-all-trades spoke again. 'Is there anything else you'd like to ask me, Knock?'

'The duties, sir?'

'Well, there's the carriage and the hunters. I try to hunt on every Saturday in the season. Sometimes on Wednesday. But only twice or three times a month.'

It was Knock's chance to sound intelligent again.

'Is it the Rufford, sir? Do you hunt with the Rufford?'

'The Rufford *Hounds*, man. They like to be called the Rufford *Hounds*. I hunt with them and the South Notts. Though I miss too many South Notts meets to be regarded as a good member. Since I was promoted to captain in the Volunteers, I've not been able to hunt on the last Wednesday of the month. I parade at Welbeck Abbey in the evenings. You shall drive me there.'

'I shall, sir?'

'Of course you will. I enjoy driving myself. But, with the uniform and the accoutrements, it's best to sit inside the carriage. You've not asked me about money. Or about the cottage. I hope that you want this job. I've no time to waste just listening to your chatter. I'm a very busy man.'

'Oh, I want it, sir. I'm sorry if I've given any other impression. And I'm sorry if I've talked too much.'

'Well, let me do the talking now.' Henry Hodding set out – with great speed and in incredible detail – the annual salary, the Harness Grove establishment and the required duties. He then went on to describe the livery which he proposed to purchase, the horses he already owned and his plans for filling his idle hours with more energetic activity and gainful employment. The house he described last, for he was particularly proud of the offer he was about to make. 'There's a cottage, one of a pair. You shall have a tenancy agreement that gives you rights. I've seen too many servants turned out overnight.'

'Thank you, sir.'

39

'I've got two more questions for you.'

'Yes, sir.'

'You're not a Liberal, are you? It wouldn't do to employ a Liberal.'

Gerrard, who – thanks to the Reform Bill – would soon enjoy the privilege of voting for the first time in his life, answered with perfect honesty, 'No, sir. I am not.' He felt no obligation to add that his instincts were Fenian.

'Good, very good. But this one is even more important. Why are you leaving Wisbech? I don't like a man who doesn't know his own mind and tries to do different things because he's not sure what he wants. It's a good post you have there. Why are you leaving it? Not in any trouble, are you?'

'No, sir, I am not.' Gerrard knew that it would be sensible to say, 'But the workhouse master is,' and, having described Alice Thomson's accusations, proclaim his unwillingness to work for a known adulterer. All he offered was the truth, for he could not bring himself to betray William Skinner even though Worksop was a world away from Wisbech and the name would never be heard in Nottinghamshire again.

'I want to work with horses, sir. I always have. I get on with horses better than I get on with people. I was brought up with them.'

'Have you got a wife, Knock?'

'Yes, sir.'

'Is she keen on horses too?'

'Yes, sir.' It seemed a very little lie.

'Will she help in the stables when you're ill and so forth?'

'Willingly, sir.'

'Then there's only one more thing. I shall need a reference. I take it that your employer – the Guardians or the superintendent – will give you a character reference.'

'Oh, yes, sir. Mr Skinner the master certainly will. He promoted me to foreman.'

'Then you'd better start on the first of the month.' Henry Hodding took three half-crowns from his waistcoat pocket and handed them to his new coachman. 'That's for your expenses—'

'That's very generous, sir.'

'It's not all for you. I want you to take a package to the station and have it put on the Chesterfield train for collection. It should cost about eightpence.'

Henry Hodding was out of the office door before the last syllable was finished. Gerrard Knock, his leg aching no more, limped after him like a cripple who expected soon to be healed. The joy lasted for the full length of the journey back to Wisbech.

'I got it,' he said to Rosie, 'I got it and I start on the first of the

40

month.' He prayed that she would respond as she had responded to every triumph and tragedy except to the idea that they should move to Worksop. For once in his life, Gerrard's prayers were answered. His wife was her old self, full of hope and unreasonable excitement.

'I've thought about it and I'm glad – glad to start again. I've decided that it's for the best.'

The strange choice of language – more appropriate to voluntary exile than to the start of a great adventure – did nothing to diminish Gerrard's euphoria. He decided to build on her enthusiasm.

'You'll love it there, Rosie. It's a nice little town and we'll have a nice little cottage with a garden.'

The mention of the garden seemed to bring back his wife's depression. But Gerrard was in no mood to notice.

Alice Thomson's baby was born in a bed pushed into the corner of the women's ward and sacrificed, for that purpose, by one of the other inmates. Normally, Alice slept next to her mother and, had the old lady been capable of movement, she would have sat hunched in front of the fire whilst her grandchild came into the world. But on the natal day old Mrs Thomson was too sick to move. The woman who acted as midwife made the sacrifice and added an extra twopence to her professional fee as payment for the provision of special facilities. She warned that she would insist on compensation if, despite the old newspapers with which her bed was covered, the birth resulted in any soiling of the already filthy blankets. The child was a girl and within hours of its birth the mother was talking about 'getting out of this hell hole' as soon as old Mrs Thomson fulfilled the prophecy of imminent death which had been made every day for the previous six months. Alice talked wildly about her sister in Peterborough, a rich gentleman friend in Norwich and her brother, who, she insisted without the support of any evidence, was fishing out of Felixstowe and making a steady living.

For a week, she talked incessantly about leaving, although the women in the ward told her that she was too weak to travel and reminded her that even when old Mrs Thomson died – an event they anticipated each night – it would be a daughter's duty to lay out her mother and attend the funeral three days later. At the thought of staying in the workhouse, the girl was, in turn, abusive, hysterical and violent. Although the workhouse staff tried to avoid any mention of the Thomsons to the master and his wife, the new foreman, who was thought of as the Skinners' eyes and ears, was persuaded to report that Alice was becoming a danger to the whole women's ward. William, who never spoke about her to his wife, decided that her conduct could be interpreted as good news. He broke his usual silence.

41

'If she does go, that will be the end of it.'

'If she goes.' Elizabeth had become incapable of hope.

'The women think she will, after her mother passes on. They're sure of it.'

'Even then they'll remember.'

'Well,' said William, 'I pray for her to go. If we could get rid of her without it being on our conscience . . .'

'Why should she be on our conscience?'

William left the question unanswered and concentrated his mind and will on hoping that she would go. His wish was not granted for over six months. Then, without giving the three-hour notice that the law required, Alice Thomson walked out of the workhouse, leaving her infant daughter hungry and screaming in a bundle of rags on the doorstep of the lodge. Early that evening, her body was found floating in the New Sutton Dock.

Within hours of her corpse being pulled out of the cold grey water, Alice Thomson was famous. In life she would have been a fallen woman – ostracised and cast into the outer darkness of poverty and isolation. In death she was a martyr to man's baser instincts.

The improvement of her status owed much to the circumstance in which she was found. Her body was discovered floating face downwards, with her plain calico Poor Law dress – which had turned almost white with years of wear and washing – spread out around her. Some of the gawping passers-by thought of it as a wedding dress. Others said that it looked like a shroud. Her long fair hair, drifting in the ripples of the water, reflected the sun and looked almost clean. As the children stared in silence and their parents whispered how difficult it would be to pull the body up the steep dock walls, Alice Thomson might have been a Pre-Raphaelite Ophelia. By the time the deckhand on the creosote barge had nerved himself to pull her out of the water with his boat hook, the image of virgin saint was strong enough to withstand the sight of her emaciated, half-naked body and the great purple bruise on her belly where she had hit a piece of floating timber on her way into the water and eternity.

That night, William went to bed afraid of the dark for the first time since, as a child, he had stayed in the workhouse when his uncle, Young Skinner, was master. As he carried his candle up the stone stairs and across the uncarpeted landing, he tried not to look towards the second rickety flight of wooden steps that led up to the attic. He remembered all too well the vast and draughty space beneath the roof beams where he had lain in terror staring through the skylight at the clouds racing across the moon and listening to the eaves creaking in the wind as if the ghosts of a hundred dead paupers balanced on them like pigeons in a loft. Thirty years later, he felt exactly the same chill.

He undressed without making a sound and managed to crawl under the blanket without waking either his daughter or his son. That night, as every night for the previous six months, he thought again that it was time that Anne was moved into a proper bed big enough for her increasingly raw-boned frame. Most of his mind, however, was occupied by the prospect of lying in the warmth which he hoped had already been generated by his wife's body, but the sheets on his side of the bed were like ice. William first shivered and then shook uncontrollably.

'What's the matter?' Elizabeth never allowed herself a moment of half-consciousness between sleep and total command of the sights and sounds around her.

William replied through chattering teeth, 'I'm cold, that's all.'

'That's more than cold. Cold couldn't do that. Stop it. Stop it straight away. You'll be ill.'

'How can I stop it?' William did not share his wife's faith in the indomitable will of man.

'Of course you can stop it. Hold your breath and hold yourself stiff.'

William tried but failed. Instead he pulled his knees up under his chin and folded his arms across his chest in an attempt to touch as little of the cold sheets as possible.

'Stop it. It's nerves, not cold. Just tell yourself to stop it.'

The human ball in bed beside Elizabeth Skinner continued to palpitate. She decided to take command of her husband's body and mind in the way which she still believed – despite the long confinement and longer recovery – she was in charge of her own.

'Turn round. Turn towards the window.'

William obeyed.

'Spoons in a box. We used to play spoons in a box when we were girls at home and couldn't get to sleep for the cold.' But she could not resist adding, 'It's not the cold with you. It's nerves.'

Elizabeth moulded her body against her husband's, pulling up her knees so that they fitted in the angle behind his and pushing her stomach and breasts against his buttocks and back. Gradually he stopped shivering.

'Turn round.' She was clearly enjoying the power she had to thaw his blood. He was pulled close to her again. Her hands were over his cold ears and her warm insteps were pulled up against the cold soles of his feet. For the first time in four years, they made love.

The consensus in the town was that William was innocent but Elizabeth found it almost impossible to believe that there was a single resident who did not adjudge her husband to be guilty. And even when, after a few weeks' malicious gossip, the salacious speculation died down, she remained certain that the whole town still talked incessantly of her husband's alleged adultery. When the butcher boy grinned at her in the way in which he grinned at everybody she was unsure if he was laughing at the thought of William's infidelity or smiling in pity at her betrayal. The text of every Sunday sermon seemed to be chosen either to castigate her husband or to comfort her. Every pregnant woman whom she passed in the street seemed to be asking the silent question, 'Who is the father of Alice Thomson's baby?' She had never been a regular visitor to the shops or the market. Once she became convinced that she was the subject of scandalous gossip, she refused to leave the workhouse grounds.

Unfortunately, the workhouse did not provide a secure refuge for, whilst she believed that she was laughed at in the town, she was sure that she was hated in the wards and work rooms at Lynn Road. In consequence she rarely left the master's lodgings and, in the mornings when paupers cleaned her rooms and made her fires, she cowered in her bedroom holding little Anne too tightly for the child's good and staring blankly into the middle distance.

William was desperate to end her suffering, but he had no idea how to comfort or even console her. The best he could manage was the truth, which unfortunately he did not believe.

'It will pass,' he said without conviction. 'Sooner or later, it will all be forgotten about.'

'It will never be forgotten. Not in this town.'

'Would you like to move? Alfred Ellison asked me to go with him to Lincoln and work on building the city arboretum.'

'Cousin Alfred is just a talker. He probably won't do the job in Lincoln at all and he won't take you with him if he does it. You haven't even seen him on a Saturday afternoon for six or seven weeks.'

It was only five. Alfred Ellison had turned up at the Rose and Crown as usual but William had not been there to meet him. William had spent his Saturday afternoons seeking consolation in his garden. At the beginning of the agony he had hoped to find solace in his son and daughter but his wife increasingly treated them as her own exclusive property. And there were times when he feared that she was attempting to protect both children from his corrupting influence. In the company of his family, he felt even more lonely than when he was on his own. Only his father provided any real help.

'It's no good cursing your luck,' Jacob told him. 'The little hussy said it and it can't be unsaid. And it's no good thinking how can anyone think such things. People do believe the worst and enjoy it.'

'You can't believe it.'

'Of course I don't. Not now. Neither does your brother. Though there's a lot that do. But they'll forget and you will too. You've just got to live through the next few months.'

'You don't think I should move?'

'I can't see how you can. I'll find you a pound or two, and your brother won't complain. Not that I'd listen if he did. But it won't be enough to set you up in anything reliable.'

'Alfred Ellison talked about a job in Lincoln.'

'That's all off. I heard all about the crack-brained idea from Canon Wheatley. The cathedral won't sell the land. Nor the land next door where Ellison wants to build houses. Forget about that. Be a good workhouse master. If it was me, I'd spend fourteen hours a day working until I was too tired to think about it.'

'It's not quite as easy with a workhouse as it is on a farm.'

'I thought you were a reformer, a radical. Why don't you get on with your reforming? You'll have to fight the Guardians – me amongst them – but it will take your mind off all the tittle-tattle.'

William Skinner tried. He began by attempting to exhaust his energies on the subject of workhouse food – prompted by the Report of the Poor Law Board on the Dietary Need of Workhouses and the willingness of Dr Ivor Smith, one of Her Majesty's Inspectors, to attend a meeting and advise on the practice being adopted in other Unions.

William read out the food which had been provided at the Wisbech Workhouse since he had persuaded the Guardians to follow the example of Lancashire and provide meat or soup on each day of the week. 'Dinners. Dinners each day. Sunday, boiled beef. Monday, beef puddings. Tuesday, boiled beef. Wednesday, soup and bread. Thursday, boiled beef. Friday, suet pudding. Saturday, soup and bread.'

The seven dinners were so superior to what had been provided before his appointment that, for the moment, he forgot his troubles and smiled with righteous satisfaction.

To his astonishment, Dr Smith was critical and suggested roast meat or meat pie on two days of the week to provide a more varied diet. The criticism made William think not of his shortcomings as a workhouse master but of his failures as a faithful husband and loving father. He could not concentrate on the discussion about buying a Flavel cooking stove.

His father seemed to read his mind and, after the meeting was over, turned on him with the angry contempt which he remembered from

45

days of misbehaviour in his youth. 'Half of the time, you weren't even listening.'

'I've got a lot on my mind.'

'You're beginning to act as if you did father that bastard. If you're not careful, you'll begin to believe you did!'

'Half the town', he told his wife over breakfast the next day, 'thinks I ruined that poor girl . . .'

'All the town.' Elizabeth had no idea what Wisbech was thinking, but she needed to believe the worst.

William had turned paler but he still proclaimed his calm and confidence. 'As long as you and my father believe that I'm innocent, I can bear it again until it passes.'

'It will never pass now. Even if we live within fifty miles of this place you will be the man who got the dead girl in the family way. We shall bear it for the rest of our lives.'

'If we could find the man. If he confesses . . .'

'If Alice Thomson came back from the dead, confessed her lie and asked you for forgiveness, people would still think that it was you. People are like that. They enjoy seeing respectable families brought down. The spectacle of Jacob Skinner's son fallen low is too enjoyable to be thrown away. Every farm labourer who thinks that your father worked him too hard is rejoicing this morning. Your fall has raised the rest of the town higher. They'll never forget. From now on we're a Punch and Judy show every day of the year.'

'Do you want to move?'

'We have to stay here.'

'We don't *have* to. There are dozens of jobs I could do, all over England. Gerrard Knock got a job in Nottingham somewhere. I could do the same.'

'We have to stay here because, if we left, we'd be admitting that you did it. And I shall never admit that. Never. I know it not to be true and I shall never let anyone say it in my presence.'

William leaned forward and cupped his wife's hand in his. She took her hand away.

'I hate every second of it.'

'And you blame me.'

'Not now I don't. It was all taken out of your hands. When you let that girl stay here to humiliate me every day and to spread the lies and encourage the gossip, then I hated you. Then I blamed you for all my misery.'

'But that's behind us. Now then, don't get worked up about that now. Put it out of your mind. At least she's gone. We just have to live through the next week or two like we lived through the other bad times. Then it won't be so bad.'

'It will for me. Perhaps not for you. But it will be just as bad for me.'

'The baby going away will help.' William had forgotten that his rule of silence about the whole affair had prevented him from telling his wife the welcome news.

'Going? Going where?'

'The long-lost sister turned up from Peterborough. She's taking the baby away, thank heavens.'

'That won't help.' Elizabeth rejected all consolation. 'People will always remember. You mark my words. It will be just as bad wherever the baby is.'

During the next six months there were moments of hope. Thomas Leverington told the Guardians that no son of Jacob Skinner was capable of the base conduct attributed to the master of their Wisbech Workhouse. Canon Winston Wheatley preached a sermon on the text 'Let him that is without sin cast the first stone', and emphasised to Elizabeth after the service was over that nothing he said was intended to suggest that William was a sinner in need of understanding and forgiveness. Jacob Skinner himself again asked his son whether or not the stories were true, significantly adding that it would not be the first time that something like it had happened. Having once more been reassured of William's innocence, he promised to sack on the spot any man who ever spoke of the subject or whose wife and children ever mentioned it. After his father's question had been asked and answered Joshua Skinner said that he had known all along that his brother was a God-fearing, law-abiding man and a loving husband.

The most welcome reaction came from Alfred Ellison who, after weeks of silence, wrote to suggest the renewal of Saturday afternoon meetings with William. The gentle fantasies continued with talk of the Lincoln arboretum, which had moved into the dream world of hopes unfulfilled.

The worst response came from Elizabeth's sister, Beatrice. Mrs Stainton always offered comfort and consolation indistinguishable from pity and sometimes clear evidence of her belief in William's guilt. She actually took the trouble to visit Lynn Road to offer her disturbing solace. 'When I think of you, that day in this very room, having to stand here and listen to what she said, my heart almost breaks for you. However did you stand for it?'

'It lasted about five minutes.'

'But since then, the thought of it! Every minute of the day! I'm glad she's dead. May I be forgiven, but I am. I said to Mr Stainton,

47

I said, "No respectable woman – certainly no sister of mine – should have to face such degradation."'

It was a judgement with which Elizabeth agreed but – as she was not willing to admit her agreement – she stayed silent and let her sister gush on.

'At least she's gone now. That's one good thing to come out of it. You don't have to worry any longer about what's going on. I said to Mr Stainton, "At least my poor Elizabeth will have some peace of mind. That woman isn't under her roof any longer."'

'Bea, I never worried about what William was supposed to have done – if that's what you really meant to say. And you will not be welcome in my house if you talk as if I did. Put that idea out of your mind for good and all.'

'If you say that it wasn't him, that's good enough for me. I said that to Mr Stainton, when he said the story might be true.'

There was only room in Beatrice Stainton's mind for one idea at a time and, when something was firmly lodged in that confined space, it was difficult to dislodge.

'I know that everybody is saying "poor girl" and weeping and wailing about her, but I'm not. It may be unChristian – at least according to the modern view on these things – but I think of it as retribution. It's a woman's job to fight against baser instincts, not pander to them. With men it's natural enough. That's what I said to Mr Stainton.'

'You seem to talk to him a lot, Bea.'

'I do. He is my constant inspiration. Would you like me to ask him to speak to Mr Skinner? It would be a terrible imposition, but I think – good man that he is – he'd do it if I asked him. He could convince your husband that the Lord always forgives.'

Beatrice Stainton did not notice the look of incredulity with which her suggestion was greeted.

'It's four o'clock, Bea. Henry will have finished. No tea tonight. I've got a headache. Walk down the drive with me.'

'Is everything all right?'

'I'm having another baby.'

'Elizabeth, my love! How could he, after all you've been through?'

'That's exactly what he said.'

In fact, William had said the first thing that came into his mind. His study of horticulture had not prepared him for such stony ground to prove so fertile. He was delighted and he hoped for another boy. He was also afraid of the consequences for his wife's life and health. His indecision concerning whether or not to begin a serious conversation about how the ordeal was to be faced was ended by Elizabeth's stern injunction that there were more pressing problems than a birth more than six months distant. The pressing problem was his reputation.

Elizabeth thought it important to repeat to her husband everything that she heard had been said about him in the town. She neither invented nor embellished but she spared him nothing. She believed that it was necessary for him to know what people were really saying and thinking rather than to take refuge in the pretence that the whole sordid business would soon be forgotten. It was essential to her composure – and perhaps even to her sanity – that he understood how she was suffering and would go on suffering for the rest of her life. For he managed to give the impression that he suffered not at all.

Elizabeth's earlier neurosis began to infect her husband. After Alice Thomson's death William was not sure if casual acquaintances treated him differently or if he just imagined that they looked at him with the awe in which the virtuous hold the wicked. Then he told himself that one day the whole story would be forgotten as it had once almost been forgotten before and, as he anticipated the pleasure of that release, the muscles in his stomach began to unwind, the pulse stopped beating in the side of his head and the prickling sensation on the back of his hands began to fade. He tried to convince himself that the prurient glances and the furtive asides were really only in his imagination and that most of the people he met had already forgotten the death and the allegation which preceded it. He had begun to share his wife's obsession that he was an object of universal contempt. But, whilst his wife felt able to exorcise her anguish with complaints about the wicked world and Wisbech, William felt that it was his duty to pretend that he did not notice or, if he noticed, did not mind.

If the looks and whispers were only in his imagination, for weeks he endured repeated slights of his own invention. The paupers remained deferential but, after Alice Thomson's death, they were deferential in a sullen and hostile way – at least, so William Skinner imagined. Shopkeepers took his money without looking him in the eye and paid his change without counting it out in the slow and methodical fashion which was the shopkeeper's habit. William thought they did. The market gardeners and nurserymen behind their Saturday stalls talked to him about the consequences of the summer drought and then, as he passed on, made jokes about him. William assumed that he was the subject of their laughter. He never told his wife about his experiences. Indeed, whenever she described similar incidents to him, he told her how easy it was for false ideas to build up in the anxious mind. He longed to weep with her but he decided that silent suffering was part of his penance.

49

The third baby – a girl christened Agnes – arrived with as little pain and difficulty as her brother Ernest had emerged into the world, but no sooner had William begun to rejoice that he need no longer feel guilty about Elizabeth's labour pains than his conscience faced another crisis. Old Mrs Thomson was at the point of death at last. He struggled not to rejoice. He managed to respond to the news with a decent enquiry. 'Can we do anything for her?'

'They say she'll really be gone by morning.' Not even Elizabeth was sceptical about the latest prognosis. 'I've had her moved into the corner and they've hung a blanket up to separate her from the rest of the ward. She's moaning and raving. You know how upset they get when one of them dies in the night.'

'I don't look forward to my rounds tonight.' William regretted the admission as soon as it was made.

'I shall come with you. Women can deal with death better than men can. You'll have to go. But I shall come with you.'

'I wouldn't dream of allowing it. You'll pretend not to be upset, but you will be. I shan't mind. I can manage.'

'Listen to me. I want to come. I don't want those women to think they can intimidate me. I know what they'll be thinking and what they'll say as soon as we're out of the ward. But I want them to know that they can't break me. No matter how hard they try.'

Elizabeth spoke with a passion of which her husband had thought her incapable. She was hollow-eyed and white-faced, like a woman in a sudden fever. He spoke roughly only because he was frightened.

'It's preying on your mind, proving that you think I'm innocent. You think about nothing else . . . Nobody will have that on their minds tonight.'

'How can I think about anything else? It's all around me, every minute of the day.'

'You've got to think of something else or you'll be ill. You wouldn't have suffered more if I *had* been the father of that woman's child. It's ridiculous.'

Terrified of his wife's response, he left the room before she had time to tell him that she could not have suffered more in any other circumstance or situation. He walked to the women's ward at half his usual speed.

It was a close, still evening, but a fire had been lit in the brick hearth. The older women huddled round it, toasting old pieces of bread and, from time to time, turning the burning logs by poking at them with an iron bolt which had burned off an old door once used for kindling wood. The women sat in groups on the floor or lay, half asleep, on their beds. Nobody spoke.

William drew his usual deep breath before he crossed the threshold and – thus physically and psychologically prepared for a brief expedition to the acrid atmosphere – strode towards the middle of the room. It was the custom – it had once been the regulation – for all the inmates, save the sickest and most infirm, to stand in the presence of the master. That night, the women only moved their heads. One by one, without any plan or co-ordination, they turned to look towards the furthest and darkest corner. The blanket no longer hung from the beams. Instead it covered the bed, which was only just visible in the flickering firelight. Under it were the mortal remains of old Mrs Thomson.

If William Skinner had, at that moment, run from the ward – as every wish and instinct prompted – he would never have been able to face the women again. With difficulty he convinced himself that he was a God-fearing man, a conscientious workhouse master without a blemish on his record or reputation. He began to do his duty.

'Has she gone?' He knew it was an absurd question, but he could think of nothing else to say.

There was a general murmur of assent which echoed around the ward.

'Why didn't one of you come and tell me?'

There was no reply.

'We'll have her in the chapel straight away. Are you to take her or shall I get the men to bring a stretcher?'

Again there was silence.

'Who's to lay her out? It's the usual sixpence.'

Two middle-aged women shuffled forward.

'You're strong enough to carry a little body like that. Get the stretcher from the corridor.'

Shuddering, William hurried out to unlock the chapel door. He would have congratulated himself on the despatch with which he had done his duty had he not been preoccupied with another aspect of the little drama in which he had taken part. From first to last, not one of the women in the ward had looked him in the eye.

'She's dead,' he told Elizabeth, 'dead and laid out in the chapel by now and thank God for it. I've never known them take a death so hard.'

Even as he spoke, William realised the pain he had caused his wife by reminding her that the old lady had acquired the status of saint and martyr. But he stumbled on, so ashamed of his insensitivity that he felt an irresistible compulsion to justify it. He had no way of anticipating the consequences of his folly.

'I wouldn't have mentioned it but for an extraordinary thing the two men told me – the two men who are going to dig the grave.'

'I suppose she's going to be buried with her daughter. That young woman should never have been buried in holy ground. She was a suicide right enough. Canon Wheatley ought to be ashamed of himself.'

William sidestepped the manifestation of what was no more than a subsidiary concern. 'These two men said that the paupers were talking about a headstone for the Thomson grave when it's settled. Those doing extra work have offered to give a halfpenny each to help pay for it.'

Elizabeth smiled – but it was a smile of contempt for her husband. 'Now I've heard everything. Paupers taking up a charitable collection! Why do you repeat such silly stories? They're all so much talk.'

'I thought it was a very creditable notion. I know that they can't do it, but I admired their feelings.'

Elizabeth had driven her husband on to the defensive. Instead of capitulating he mounted a reckless counter-attack. 'I said that, if anything came of it, we'd give a shilling or two.'

'You said *what*?'

'Nothing will come of it. I only said it to show that not all workhouse masters are tyrants and misers. I want them to know that we have feelings too.'

'Sometimes I think you must be mad. You've absolutely no concern for my reputation. But what about our future? What about Anne and Ernest and the baby? What do you think people would say if you bought a headstone for that woman's grave?'

'I'm not going to buy a headstone, I've told you.'

'I despair, I really do.'

William did not believe her. Despair, he told himself with a perverse pride, was alien to his wife's nature. Despair is a sort of surrender and Elizabeth would fight on to the death, never yielding. He was even surprised when she told him, at eight o'clock, that she had a headache and hoped that he would forgive her if she retired early to bed.

He woke before dawn and, as always, lay absolutely still so as not to wake his wife whilst he enjoyed his few moments of absolute silent privacy. Then he gently shook her by the shoulder. Elizabeth sat up. Why, she asked, clearly frightened, was it so dark?

William, unaccustomed to his wife showing fear, felt panic bubbling in the pit of his stomach. 'You're not making sense.' He masked his terror with counterfeit aggression.

'I tell you, it's all dark. I can't see anything. I can't see anything.'

Elizabeth was screaming. During the night, she had lost her sight.

CHAPTER FIVE

Alfred Ellison Sees Justice Done

William Skinner could barely believe that he was standing, half-surrounded by the horseshoe table, and confronting the Board of Guardians of the Wisbech Union as if he were a pauper applying for indoor relief. It was not the full Board that he faced. His father's chair was empty. Jacob Skinner had warned his son of what Thomas Leverington planned – warned him that, since there was no way that he could play the father's proper part, he would have nothing to do with the entire proceedings. But everyone else was there. Only Thomas Leverington spoke.

'I hope you understand that we have no other choice. Our responsibility is to the workhouse and its proper supervision.'

William wished that he could react as Elizabeth would have reacted. Elizabeth would have been respectful without losing her self-respect. No one would have doubted the disdain in which she held the Guardians or her contempt for the decision they had taken and her distaste for the way in which the chairman tried to justify his craven conduct. William certainly shared all the emotions he knew his wife would have felt. But he was incapable of exuding an Olympian disapproval. He attempted a reproof and it sounded like a plea for mercy.

'I trust that I have discharged my duties to your satisfaction. In nearly six years there has never been a time when you thought it necessary to complain of my management. Had you done so, I should have done my best to correct my faults . . .' He knew that the artificiality of his language demonstrated that he was overwhelmed by the ordeal but he was not in control of the way in which he spoke. The voice was his, but the words were the choice of some subconscious personality who believed that a solemn occasion required solemn language. '. . . indeed, if you were to think it right to reinstate me, I should do my best to rectify any shortcomings which you drew to my attention.'

Thomas Leverington lied.

'Nobody's saying that you haven't done a decent job. If you hadn't you'd have heard about it soon enough. But you can't superintend this workhouse with a blind wife sitting at home in your parlour. And that's all there is to say on the subject.'

The other members of the Board continued the concentrated study of the papers which lay on the desks in front of them. William – at a loss to know how to reply – stayed silent and, inadvertently, obliged the chairman to justify a judgement which he would have preferred not to expose to close scrutiny. His explanation swirled slowly on like a muddy river.

'We've always thought that the wife did part of the job. In some Unions they wouldn't have a married superintendent at any price – leastways, they wouldn't let his wife live in the workhouse. But we always saw it differently. It's a job for a married couple, like house-keepers and handymen. You see our difficulty, I'm sure.'

William was too preoccupied with difficulties of his own to spare much time for the Guardians' problems. To his own surprise, his immediate anxiety was not so much the fact of his dismissal as the necessity to report it to Elizabeth. A simple statement of the tragic decision would not satisfy her. She would require a detailed account of his impeachment and his story would be followed by a cross-examination. He decided to avoid, at all cost, telling his wife that the chairman had compared the position of workhouse master to that of a domestic servant. He knew that it was demeaning to plead for a stay of execution. But he pleaded nevertheless.

'She could recover any day, just as quickly as she went blind. That's what the doctor says. There's nothing wrong behind her eyes. It could all come right tomorrow.'

Captain Catling – the longest-serving Guardian – looked up from the fingernail which he was carefully examining and offered an item of inconsequential biographical information. 'I heard it was a stroke.'

The reply was too emphatic. 'It was not a stroke. It was not.'

Arthur, Captain Catling's civilian brother, intervened, as always, with fraternal support. 'How can you be so sure? How can you be sure without looking inside her head?'

'She can speak. She can walk. Her grip's just the same. She can taste and smell. If a spark jumps out of the fire, she can smell the rug burning faster than I can. She still thinks twice as clearly as most men.'

William looked at the Guardians sitting on the other side of the table. Some looked relentless. Others seemed ashamed. He made one last appeal to their reason and sense of justice.

'I could get home tonight and find her right as rain.'

Thomas Leverington's mind was closed for ever.

'You said that straight away after it happened, and that was six months ago.'

William, whilst thinking of all the arguments Elizabeth would have employed to convince them they were wrong, decided to capitulate with the dignity Elizabeth would have employed if she had failed to change the Guardians' minds.

'Gentlemen, it seems that there is little left to be said. I shall be out of Lynn Road by Quarter Day.'

'By the month's end . . . the month's end, if you please.' Thomas Leverington spoke with a slow deliberation, which he hoped hid his shame. 'That is the decision of the Guardians. By the month's end.'

'In which case, there is nothing for me to say except to thank you for your many kindnesses.'

He could not, at that moment, remember what those many kindnesses were but it seemed the proper thing to say and it postponed the awful moment when he would have to sit down again at the horseshoe table and participate in the meeting which had begun with the item, 'Discharge of superintendent'. As he took his place he noticed that the chairman had written 'carried nem. con.' against the first item listed on his agenda. Thomas Leverington turned to William as if the Ordinary Weekly Business Meeting had been concerned with ordinary business.

'Is there a procedural motion?'

'There is,' said William. There always was. Each week the Wisbech Board of Guardians voted on a proposition which was moved by Captain Horace Catling and supported by his brother Arthur. The question was never debated and always defeated.

The chairman read the resolution. 'That the next meeting of this Board shall be fourteen days hence.'

Having once more confirmed that the Poor Law required weekly, rather than fortnightly, supervision, the Guardians moved on to discuss the matters which needed their regular attention. The auditor's report was accepted with satisfaction, it having been noted that thirteen shillings, claimed by the overseer at Tyd St Giles for the conveyance of paupers to Wisbech, had been disallowed. After some discussion it was agreed that the Inspector of Nuisances at Upwell, who wrote to complain that he had received no salary for two years of valuable and loyal service, be awarded an ex-gratia payment of four pounds. In the absence of any other business the meeting was concluded. William did not intend to close the minute book with a bang, yet the pages came together with a noise like thunder. When the sound reverberated around the boardroom, each of the Guardians started as if the whole assembly had been hit by a single shot.

'Thank you, gentlemen. Thank you again.'

He would not have said it had he not been unnerved by the noise he had made in closing the minute book. It was another detail of the afternoon's events which he would not tell to Elizabeth. Were he to report his final words of thanks, she would ask him to list the acts of generosity and friendship which had earned such gratitude.

The chairman interrupted the rehearsal of his homecoming. 'Give your father my regards when next you see him. I well understand why he's not here today. But I hope that next week—'

'I shall see him this afternoon.' It was not William's habit to interrupt the chairman, and his dismissal had done nothing to change his views about the respect owed to seniority and position, but it had seemed that Leverington was about to imply that he and his father no longer met with the frequency proper to loving father and loyal son.

That afternoon, the chairman's greetings were duly delivered.

'I'm finished with the Poor Law,' said Jacob. 'I've been to my last Guardians' meeting.'

'Are you going to resign?'

'What's the use of that? It will only cause another scandal and I'd have thought that we'd have had enough of them.'

As the reference to *another* scandal burned into William's mind his father announced his intentions. 'I've got plenty to do out here and I shall do it instead of wasting my time on the likes of Leverington. I just shan't go to any more meetings. I'll do everything right. I'll send my apologies saying that I'm too busy. More important, what are you going to do?'

'I haven't thought. It's all happened so suddenly. I'd no idea until you spoke to me last Sunday.'

'Well, with a baby and a blind wife, you'd better think damn quick. Do you want to come back here?'

'Is there a job?'

'There is if a son of mine wants one. And there's an empty house at Eastrea. Leastways, there will be on Monday if you want it. You won't do much better. That stiff-necked wife of yours won't like it. But you'll have to put your foot down for once. Tell her that beggars can't be choosers.'

William passed on his father's message in language rather less robust than Jacob would have used.

'We better both sit down. We've got a problem to talk about.'

'Not another girl!'

He took it for granted that she meant another girl making slander-
ous and altogether unjustified allegations.

'Lightning won't strike twice. It's the same one and the consequences.'

'What's happened this time?'

'They've given me my notice.'

'What have you done? What have you done this time?'

'I've told you. It's because of that girl and her baby.'

'But that was more than two years ago.'

'They said it was because of your eyes, that I didn't have a wife to
help me.'

'You don't believe that.'

'Of course I don't. That's what I'm saying. They pretended it was
your fault, that's all.'

'But they're blaming me.'

'They are. It's a scandal but they are.'

It was an unhappy choice of words but William had more to worry
about than one unthinking phrase. He believed that he should have
risked the lie. He should have said, 'Alice Thomson, the Guardians
have sacked me because of Alice Thomson. They came straight out
with it. No apology. No regrets. They sacked me because of the girl
and the baby.' Then Elizabeth would at least have been able to blame
and patronise him. She would have told him that, although they were
ruined, she trusted him and stood by him. By repeating the Guardians' squalid excuse, he had implicated her in the catastrophe of his
dismissal.

'But they're blaming me!'

'They're saying I can't do the job because you're blind. I know it's
not true.'

'So we're on the street. And everybody will say that it's my fault.'

Proper allocation of the blame seemed more important than surviving the punishment.

'Not on the street. I think that the best thing is to go to Whittlesey,
at least for the time being.'

'So, after all this, we end up in a farm labourer's cottage. Is that
what you are saying?'

'I can't see much else for it.'

Elizabeth fumbled with the baby's shawl and it fell from her lap.
William leaned forward from his chair to pick it up but she was too
quick for him. It had fallen across her feet and, being able to locate
it, she snatched it from the floor before her husband could help her.
Her whole being was, at that moment, concentrated on the obligation
to be not pathetic but defiant.

'Do you look forward to being a farm labourer?'

'I am a farmer's son.'

'You're a farmer's second son. It makes a big difference.'

Admiration for his wife's indomitable will began to give way to irritation at her obduracy. It was his nature to face the reality of their new condition. Her instinct was to spit into the wind.

'Well, what do you suggest that we live on?'

'We could go to America. We could stay with Victoria in Boston. She'd put us up. She'd give us a start.'

'Be sensible. You never got on with Victoria, even when you were girls at home together.'

'She's my sister. It's her duty.'

Duty, thought William bitterly, means different things to different people. Victoria's vision of a sister's responsibility might be as idiosyncratic as Elizabeth's view of a wife's obligation. But all he said was, 'She's a sister you haven't seen for five years. She hasn't written to you for nearly twelve months. For all we know her husband doesn't sail out of Boston any more.'

'He's contracted to a fishing company.'

'There are a dozen different fishing ports in New England. Anyway, think of the journey. It isn't practical. It isn't even safe. Not with a baby and you . . . you being . . . you being . . .'

'Me being blind, you mean.'

'Yes, with you being blind. Until you're better, we've got to go steady.'

'That's just foolishness. Talking of me getting better helps no one. We could go to London. Mary's husband got a job in London.'

'Mary's husband is a shipping clerk. I haven't got either the education or the experience. Can you imagine what would happen with a ledger that I had written out? They'd buy tea instead of selling coffee.'

The attempt at humour failed.

'What hurts me most of all is you not caring. Our whole life has been ruined and you don't even seem to mind. And because you don't mind, I feel that I'm facing it all on my own.'

Elizabeth's tone and bearing left no doubt about her ability to carry the lonely burden. It also contributed to William's growing belief that he was a saint. He knew that the years ahead would be more painful for his wife than they would be for him, but he longed for her at least to concede that they were partners in adversity. Since that was not in her nature, he abandoned all hope of comfort for himself and did what he thought would lighten his wife's burden. Although he suffered, he pretended suffering was not justified.

Having decided that he had a duty to hide his heavy heart, he steadfastly looked on the bright side, resolutely avoided meeting trouble halfway, counted his blessings with methodical determination and invariably recalled that worse things happen at sea and that it would be the same a hundred years hence. He would have helped his wife more if he had admitted that he too felt pain. But he thought that he served her best by hiding his anguish. Elizabeth angry – even angry with him – was to be preferred to Elizabeth sad. He suffered and was blamed for not suffering.

'It's no use torturing ourselves. We just have to face it. It won't be all that bad.'

'I'll face it. You know that well enough. But I can't pretend that it won't be bad. It will be terrible, every minute. And it's all for nothing. We're being punished for nothing. That's what I resent.'

William almost shed a furtive tear of gratitude. Never for one moment had she doubted him. Again he misjudged his wife's mood. Instead of silently rejoicing in her confidence he made his last hopeful suggestion. 'There's one thing I could do. I could try your cousin Alfred.'

'What could he do, offer you a job digging ditches or carrying bricks? I'd rather be on the farm.'

'He could lend me enough to start on my own. I've talked to him about a little market garden. He always seemed interested. He might help.'

'He might, but he won't. Nobody has ever known Cousin Alfred do anything except talk. That's why we all hope for something in his will. It'll still all be there in his bank and he'll want to cut a dash after he's gone by spreading it about. Until he's gone, he'll not spend a penny on anything except himself.'

William decided to pass the morning in his garden. He had sworn to himself, out of pride and contempt, that he would do his duty until the last minute of the last day. Duty required him to check the key press and audit the daily inventory of stores before ten o'clock but at that moment he needed his garden.

Whichever pauper had been told to look after the children had left Ernest on the narrow strip of grass which divided flowers from vegetables and he had crawled into the border where he had attempted to uproot a rosebush. Pricked by the thorns, he began to cry and when he rubbed his eyes with earth-encrusted fingers rivulets of mud ran down his face. Agnes, tied into her wicker bassinet beside him, started to sob in sympathy. Then, her stomach having been agitated by the exertion, she methodically dribbled her breakfast down her quilted dress.

'Your mother will be livid with whoever put you here.' William addressed his daughter in the manner that he always employed when speaking to his infant children. Assuming that they could not understand him, he spoke to them as adults because he was speaking to himself.

He dried his son's tears with his handkerchief and then began to wipe Agnes's face with a corner that he had moistened with spittle. She howled.

'Do be reasonable. You've got to be cleaned up. Anybody who saw you now would think that we don't look after you.'

William plucked a sweet pea and handed it to his daughter. Agnes stared blankly at her flower, then put it into her mouth and began to chew. When William tried to take it from her, instead of crying she grinned. The sight of Agnes restored to happiness was immensely reassuring. Pride was reborn. The workhouse master left the garden and began his morning duties.

The news that William Skinner was in trouble reached Alfred Ellison at the end of a confused day. It had begun well enough with the receipt of a letter from Michael Drury, Surveyor to the City of Lincoln, which announced that, the Lincoln Corporation Act having passed into law, the municipal authorities were proceeding with their long-delayed intention of building an arboretum. It would be constructed at Monk's Leys – a site which, in size, slope and aspect, was virtually identical to the land at Brown's Close, on which they had first hoped that the park would be built. All contractors who had bid for the previously abandoned venture were invited to submit new tenders. Maps, further details and application forms were available, on written request to the Lincoln Surveyor's Office. The tender being open and public, a notice containing the above information would also be published in the *Lincoln Gazette*.

A man of different disposition would have been delighted by the news that the dream might yet come true, but as soon as he realised that hope might turn into reality, Alfred Ellison began to worry about practical problems which fantasy did not require him to face. He had no doubt that he would win the Lincoln contract, and he knew that there was great commercial advantage in doing so. Because of Mr Gladstone's Education Act, school boards would soon be competing with churches to demonstrate who was best suited to teach the nation's children. Whoever won would build new schools. With the Lincoln City arboretum to his credit, Alfred Ellison would appear on every tender list in East Anglia. But he was not sure that he could do the job.

First he thought of renewing his offer to William Skinner. At the time when it was made that had also been part of the fantasy. Alfred had enjoyed the pleasure he had given William by describing him as indispensable to his plans but, as the contractor read and re-read the detailed specification set out in the letter, he wondered if the workhouse master possessed any of the skills he needed to employ. He had talked about the job in the firm belief that, in the unlikely event of his ever offering it to William, his friend would not take it. For a moment, he felt a terrible fear that, thanks to Alice Thomson's baby, he might be required to keep his promise.

Then he remembered what William had told him of Elizabeth's determination to stay in Wisbech and convince the doubters of her husband's innocence. He felt like a man reprieved. If he chose to tender, he would not have to decide if William was worth employing. Nor would he have to face the choice between alienating the Lincoln authorities by employing a suspected adulterer and publicly admitting that he did not have the courage to stand by a friend.

He heard that William had been dismissed when Thomas Leverington took him aside at one of his regular Sunday evening soirées and, having made sure that Canon Winston Wheatley was out of earshot, said, 'I'm afraid that your friend Skinner will be leaving the workhouse.'

Alfred Ellison's heart leaped up, for at first he did not grasp the significance of the regret with which the announcement began. It was his nature to assume that news was good – that his dilemma was averted or at least postponed and that his problems had been solved by fate. So, despite Thomas Leverington's long face, he chose to believe that William Skinner had found superior employment and that the Board of Guardians were sad to see him go.

'Well, my word. I saw him last week and he never said a word. Crafty devil. Wherever he's going I wish him well. But he should have told me.'

'He didn't know about it until yesterday. The Guardians hadn't told him then. They barely knew themselves. We only decided just before the meeting on Friday. I wasn't sure, but the Catling brothers were absolutely insistent he should go.'

'You mean . . . ?' Alfred Ellison could not complete the sentence. He found it impossible to express even a second-hand opinion which might disturb the serenity of the world he occupied.

'I mean that he's to be discharged. I feel sorry for the man, myself. But the Guardians were set on it.'

'That's terrible news.'

'You're too tender-hearted for your own good. I wouldn't have done it yet myself. I've got too much respect for his father. But it had to happen sooner or later. Thanks to him, the workhouse has become notorious. Women gossip about it after church. Men joke about it in public houses. That means that they're joking and gossiping about me. And I'll not have that.'

'So you're sacking him because of the girl?'

'We're sacking him because he can't do the job. Not with a blind wife he can't. But you know as well as me that we wouldn't be doing it if it wasn't for all that scandal. He may not be to blame but without him it wouldn't have happened. The talk will go on till he goes.'

'So what will he do?'

'That's not my concern. I suppose he'll work for his father. I told Jacob what the Catlings were up to. I didn't want him to be taken by surprise at the meeting. I went out straight away and told him – as soon as I knew. Unpleasant jobs never improve with keeping.'

It was a sentiment that Alfred Ellison found incomprehensible. He was already working out how he could postpone what he felt might be a confrontation with William yet still maintain his reputation for assisting friends in trouble. He decided to be called away to one of the towns in which he was building houses. If he left early on the following morning, only Thomas Leverington would know that he had been told of William's misfortune and he would not be accused of deserting him in his moment of tribulation. He had work to do which should be done during the early part of the week but the work could be abandoned or postponed.

Had Alfred Ellison been either a pious or a superstitious man, the package which the postman delivered next morning would have been regarded as inevitable retribution for his conduct on the previous night. It contained the tender forms for the arboretum which the original letter had promised would follow at an early date.

Alfred Ellison began to fill them in at once, driven on by the childish pleasure of completing a document of such portentous appearance. It was not a difficult task for, as the Lincoln surveyor had forecast, the new site and the old were almost identical and the careful costing that he had carried out two years before was easily adjusted to fit the new bid. He filled the spaces on the first page with figures which he was sure would undercut any of his competitors and turned to the second sheet. Below the request for further information about estimated dates of completion, there were a number of warnings about penalty clauses which were to be included in the contract. Alfred Ellison liked none of them. And he positively resented the proposed Clause Five which would allow the Corporation to employ an outside consultant if, in its opinion, the company which made

the lowest bid was insufficiently experienced to complete the special-
ised work successfully.

'Impertinence,' he said to himself, 'damned impertinence.' But he
swallowed his pride. They would never impose such an indignity upon
an established builder and civil engineer. He read on. At the bottom
of the page, there was a notice in bold black type.

**The Lord Mayor and Aldermen reserve the right to award
the contract to a company which has not made the lowest
bid if that company is registered in, or carries out business
from, the City of Lincoln.**

Alfred Ellison let the tender form fall on to his expensive Persian
carpet. 'Corruption.' He spoke to himself so emphatically that his lips
moved. 'Legalised corruption. They know who's going to get the job
before the tenders are opened. Money's changed hands. That's what
it is.' He prided himself on knowing the building industry's failings
and foibles. Infuriated but not shocked, he repeated, 'Money's
changed hands.'

He decided, there and then, that the arboretum contract was lost
– lost before he had even filled in the form – unless he could prove
that there had been irregular and improper payments. He rang for
the maid. Reckless of his benign reputation, he shouted at her as if
she had already been slow to carry out his instructions.

'I want my bag this minute. Packed for two days. Both the suits
I've taken out of my wardrobe and the new brown shoes which were
delivered yesterday . . .'

'Now, sir? I thought you were going tomorrow morning.' The maid,
emboldened by years of counterfeit goodwill, did not propose to be
blamed for her master's change of mind.

'Don't argue. Just get the packing done. I want to be in Lincoln by
two o'clock.'

The surveyor was out of the city. But when the town clerk received
Alfred Ellison's card with the message, 'To discuss various frauds',
written on the back, he agreed to see his unexpected visitor at five
o'clock. He listened politely to the allegations. Whenever his accuser
paused to draw breath he nodded politely in a way which might have
signified support and sympathy or could have been no more than a
courteous invitation to continue. It was a technique which always
confounded his adversaries. The irate Wisbech builder kept going for
longer than most complainants managed but after about ten minutes
he too spluttered out like a dying candle.

'Our behaviour, Mr Ellison, has been both legal and professionally ethical. The Lincoln Corporation Act is explicit on the point. Perhaps you overlooked Section Fourteen. It entitles the Corporation, after due notice has been given, to accept the tender which it believes to be in the city's best interest, lowest or not. I'm sure you agree that such a power is both proper and prudent.'

'Is it prudent and proper to accept back-handers from a contractor who wants the job?'

The moment that the sentence was completed, Alfred Ellison regretted having made such an allegation. He waited for the magisterial reproof and tried to decide how he should behave if he was ordered out of the town clerk's office.

'If you have any evidence that such a crime has been committed you will, I know, send it to me or – if you fear I am myself involved – to the police.'

After an agonising silence, Alfred Ellison was put out of his misery as the conversation changed from the challenge to prove illegality to a description of the law.

'Let me tell you how all this will work. You realise of course that I do no more than speculate about the possibilities. Let us assume that there are a dozen tenders, eleven from Lincoln and one, shall we say, from Wisbech. Let us hypothesise that this Wisbech offer was substantially the best. Then I have no doubt that the Wisbech offer would get the contract. On the other hand, were it only a fraction below the Lincoln offers, it is possible – though not certain – that a Lincoln firm would be chosen. And either course would be perfectly proper.'

'Think of how it looks to me, just putting in my bid.'

The town clerk held up an imperious hand and Alfred Ellison heeded his irresistible bidding.

'I had no idea that you were interested – I mean financially interested – in this contract. I assumed that you were a public-spirited citizen anxious to assure yourself of the integrity of this Corporation. Had I realised that you had tendered – or intended to tender – for the work yourself, I would have thought it improper to discuss the subject with you. As it is, other possible contractors may regard my conduct as prejudicial to their interests. I may, myself, have committed an offence. I must bid you good afternoon.'

Alfred Ellison was still pulling on his overcoat as he left the front door of the City Chambers. He knew that he had been totally vanquished. He remained convinced that someone, somewhere in Lincoln, was guilty of corruption but he had abandoned all hope of rooting it out. The arboretum contract, which fate had twice dangled before him, had once more been snatched out of his hands. There was no point in even posting the tender form that bulged in his inside pocket. He could think of only one consolation. He would spend the following morning in the cathedral. Then, his spirit having been revived by its soaring magnificence, he would pass the afternoon in the city's other ancient buildings. But only Wednesday would be devoted to pleasure. On Thursday he would return home refreshed and on Saturday he would spend the afternoon with William Skinner. By then, the young man would have decided to work with his father. And, since there was no longer any chance of his winning the arboretum contract, there would be no difficult question to answer concerning past promises about jobs in that enterprise.

At the door of the Rose and Crown Alfred Ellison exuded the benign concern of a man whose only interest was the welfare of others.

'I cannot say how shocked I was to hear your news. I've told Leverington what I think. Thank God you're not the man to let it get you down.'

'I'm all right. It's Elizabeth who's the problem. She's taken it very hard. Very hard indeed.'

'You've got to count your blessings. You know that.'

'Elizabeth can't think of very many blessings to count at the moment. It all looks black to her.'

'You've got the children. She's got you. And you've both got your father. Jacob won't let you down. He'll find something for you.'

'He has already.'

'Well, there you are then.' William was touched by the obvious relief in Alfred's voice. 'You've got a job to go to.'

'Elizabeth doesn't want to go to it. She doesn't see herself as a farm labourer's wife.'

'Pride comes before a fall, William. Pride comes before a fall.'

William knew that if Elizabeth had been there she would have said that it was easier to extol the virtues of humility from a house in North Brink than from a whitewashed cottage at the end of a muddy cart-track. But, before he decided what to say, Alfred had begun on one of his flights of fancy.

'Did you know that they're going to extend Peckover House? I'm going to talk to Mr Algernon Peckover about how it should be done. I'm sure that I'll get the building work. But I think that he wants to talk to me about the design.'

Depression bore down upon William too heavily to allow him to respond as Alfred required and expected. He was unable to express either delight at the prospect or certainty about the outcome of the

65

Peckover consultations so he remained silent. Another attempt was made to excite his interest and approval.

Alfred Ellison's enthusiasm for the new Peckover House produced a rare feeling of resentment in William Skinner. He was not easily offended but he felt deeply affronted by the way in which the ritual of sympathy had been briefly performed and then abandoned at the first possible moment so that the conversation could move on to more palatable topics. He still believed in Alfred's good intentions. He decided against his normal instinct to shock his mentor into an understanding of the anguish which he and his wife both felt.

'Elizabeth thought you'd help us out in some way.'

'Me?' The return to the real world had been sudden and painful. Alfred Ellison had turned pale. 'What could I do? You don't want to dig ditches, do you? Or carry a hod of bricks? A job on your father's farm is far better than anything I can offer. And there's a house to go with it.'

It was too late to draw back but William could only press on if his wife shared the blame.

'Elizabeth hoped you might help me get started on my own – in a little market garden.'

'How could I do that?' Alfred sounded genuinely puzzled.

'She thought you might lend me enough to put down on a smallholding somewhere – enough to get me the land and see me over the first few years.'

'I only wish I could. But money's very tight at the moment. What I've got is all tied up. Have you asked your father?'

'He doesn't lend. If I ask him I'll be asking him to *give* me money . . .'

'I'm sure that he'd be glad to.'

'If he did it would be Joshua's money he was giving away. It won't be much. Probably not enough.'

'I'd like to help. You know that.'

William, being a simple and trusting man, believed Alfred Ellison and he regretted the distress he must have caused by making the request. He began to apologise. 'I know you'd help if you could. And I'm sorry if I've embarrassed you by asking. You needn't have told me you were having difficulties. If you had just said you couldn't help, I'd have known that you had a good reason. I'm sorry you're in trouble.'

When the request was made, Alfred Ellison's only thought had been of saving both his money and his reputation for generosity. Vague references to his funds being tied up in unspecified projects seemed, at the time, the best excuse that he could invent. But William's interpretation of his explanation was profoundly disturbing. The idea of explaining that a shortage of ready cash was not the same as being in financial trouble did not appeal to him. Although he had no intention of telling the truth under any circumstances, he did not trust himself to invent an explanation which would not reveal some of the tricks of his trade. The best he could do was ask William to keep to himself what he had learned. That in itself would heighten the risk of William thinking him on the verge of bankruptcy. The request would, of course, be scrupulously honoured but he did not relish the idea of even an insignificant Wisbech citizen believing that his business was on the brink of collapse. It was all so unfair. All Alfred Ellison wanted in the world was to be liked and admired without any inconvenience to himself yet fate rained blow after blow upon him. Only that week he had been cheated out of the chance to build the Lincoln arboretum. He could feel the contract in his inside pocket. For all the good it would do him, he might as well have thrown it on the fire.

For a moment he allowed his mind to wander as he imagined the rough slope of Monk's Leys being converted, under his supervision, into the people's park. If only, he thought, there was still a chance of his tender being accepted. Then he remembered that even if a miracle made that possible he would still have the problem of William Skinner on his hands. Indeed, the problem would be worse than the one he faced. William had expected a job with the Arboretum Construction Company – a company which would never be set up. Slowly he drew the tender forms out of his pocket and, with a dramatic gesture, dropped them on William's knee.

'What's in the envelope?' It was not addressed and for a moment William hoped that it was filled with pound notes.

'Open it and see.'

William wrestled with the hard manila paper. Even when he had pulled out the documents it still took him some time to work out what they were. Alfred Ellison was impatient to move back into the dream world of hopes fulfilled and popularity guaranteed.

'It's the contract. It's the arboretum contract.'

'You've got it! I thought that they'd given the idea up. I thought it was all over with.'

'It was and they had. But it's on again.'

'And you've got the contract. Wonderful!' William hoped that it would be wonderful for him as well as for Alfred. He was just emboldening himself to ask about his own prospects when the tender forms were explained to him.

'I've not got it yet. But I shall. I shall put in the lowest price. Have no doubt about that.'

'Is that why your money's all tied?'

'It's why I pretended that it was.'

'Pretended?'

'It was a silly joke. Very thoughtless. You must have believed that your old friend was letting you down.'

The stuttered denial was unconvincing and fearing that William might really believe he had been deserted in his hour of need stimulated Alfred Ellison into new excesses of dramatic affection. He had convinced himself that the story he had invented was true. He turned the tender forms to their last page. 'Only two things to do.' He pointed to the box marked 'Horticultural Adviser'. Then he rose slowly from his chair and led William across to the writing desk in the corner of the room. Theatrically dipping the pen in the half-dry inkpot, he scratched the name 'William Skinner' on to the form. Then he signed it and, pushing it back into the envelope, began painstakingly to write the address of the Lincoln City surveyor. One more flamboyant gesture completed the pantomime.

'I give you the honour of posting it. It's your first job for the Arboretum Construction Company.'

William walked home in a daze. The job that he had been offered was not the job he wanted. But it was a job. He hurried to the first post-box on his route, fearful that, by some bizarre mischance, the letter would go astray. Back at the hotel, Alfred Ellison felt at peace with the world for the first time that afternoon. He had bought time. It would be several weeks before the surveyor was forced to admit that his bid had been unsuccessful. Enough to the day . . . he thought. He was right not to plan what he would do when the reply confirmed that he had been cheated out of the arboretum contract. For when he next heard from the Lincoln surveyor, it was to be told that – having offered the lowest tender price – the work was his.

CHAPTER SIX

Promised Lands

Alfred Ellison leased a house on Lindum Terrace on the crest of the hill on which the arboretum was to be built. He had originally intended to find accommodation which actually overlooked the site but, whilst viewing a set of rooms with the right location, he had noticed the vacant property on the other side of the road. The windows of the house which caught his eye faced nothing more romantic than the fronts of other houses – and modern houses at that, built on parcels of land sold off by Dean and Chapter when there was an organ-loft roof to repair or new vestments to be bought. Yet Alfred Ellison felt an irresistible impulse to sit behind them for they were complicated and he always confused complication with elegance. Had the windows not infatuated him, he would have been seduced by the front door. It was inset behind Corinthian pillars and a Norman arch, and stood at the top of a flight of steps as if to protect the house from the floods of a Tuscan valley. The day after the lease was signed, every room was filled with ornate furniture.

A house was rented for the Skinners at the bottom of the hill in Thomas Street. It was a workman's cottage in a row of workmen's cottages but it was next to the gated entry which ran into the backyard and, since it included the room above the passageway, it was slightly bigger (and, in Alfred Ellison's words, certainly superior) to the houses in the rest of the row. The rent reflected its elevated social position and added to William's conviction that he must begin to keep detailed household accounts. He had lived on his father's charity for the three months before the work began. It had convinced him of the need for prudence.

His salary as head gardener to the recently registered Lincoln Arboretum Construction Company was ten pounds a year more than he had earned as workhouse master – but at Wisbech living had been cheap. At Lincoln there would be no free vegetables dug from the allotment and no cut-price bread baked from workhouse milled flour. Solvency, William decided, depended on the purchase of a penny notebook and the daily entry of each item of income and expenditure. He bought the book but, realising how Elizabeth would resent the necessity of careful accounting, he did not tell her of his intention, fearing that the indignity would drive her to withdraw permanently behind the protective wall of disapproval and disdain. So, since the accounts could not be kept without his wife's co-operation, they were not kept at all.

Elizabeth, William knew, dreaded the move to Lincoln. The idea of living in an ancient cathedral city attracted her and she hoped that William's work with Cousin Alfred would lead to an improvement in both income and status. But she was terrified of moving into the blackness of a place which she had never seen. Temperamentally she was incapable of believing that she would ever see again. William's anxious and hopeful questions about the impressions of colour floating like clouds across her mind's eye were dismissed as pathetic attempts to persuade her that a miracle was possible. And, even when she did begin to detect a difference between night and day, she remained convinced that she would blunder her way through the rest of life. At Wisbech the dark had been familiar. There she could take her bearings from chairs and tables which stood where she had placed them before she was blind. As long as she had remained in the workhouse, she inhabited a world that was mapped out in her mind. Lincoln would be uncharted territory in a strange land. The weeks in her father-in-law's house had taught her the problems of adjusting to new surroundings.

William understood his wife's anguish and the compassion which had allowed him to forgive her so much made him share the agony with her. But he had to struggle hard to avoid a disreputable feeling of relief that his wife would not, at least initially, see the inside of their new home. The house itself was no worse than humble, but the chattels were a shameful indication that, whatever they might pretend, the Skinners had come down in the world. At the workhouse the old, heavy furniture had been the property of the Poor Law Commissioners and was, in one of Elizabeth's favourite words, good. The tables and chairs had been embellished with a minimum of carving, but they were solid oak and, although the wire spring was too recent an innovation to improve the comfort of institutional sofas, their leather covering was intact and the horsehair below them was still more or less in the place which the upholsterer intended. In Lincoln the sideboard was veneer and the easy chairs were made of wicker – the depressing result of a tour of salerooms which William had made in secret one Saturday afternoon. He knew that the wicker chairs would not pass undetected, so he spent more than he could afford on a mahogany console table with tapered legs. He determined to divert the conversation towards it whenever furniture was discussed.

Although Elizabeth dreaded living in Lincoln, the preparations for moving to that city were so traumatic that she longed for the day of her departure to arrive. Beatrice Stainton travelled from March to Wisbech, at considerable and great personal inconvenience, to help with the packing which blindness prevented her sister from carrying out for herself. Beatrice did her duty with a combination of pity and impatience which would have been nearly intolerable to a woman of half Elizabeth Skinner's spirit.

Everything Beatrice did was a trouble. She wrapped the glass and china in newspaper with the air of a woman who had better ways to spend her time and dropped every parcel into the empty tea-chest from a height which signified that the contents had no great value. At least she remained silent about the crockery and china. Her sister's more intimate possessions excited constant comment, all of it patronising and pitying.

Thanks to her husband's private income, Mrs Henry Stainton could afford what she described as 'nice things'. Elizabeth was less fortunate. Beatrice's petticoats had lace at the hem. Her sister's did not. Elizabeth's stockings were darned until the toes and heels contained none of the original wool. Her sister's were not, for her hosiery was given away to the deserving poor as soon as a stitch seemed likely to irritate her delicate feet. The difference in status was too obvious for anyone to miss. Most people would have chosen to ignore it but Beatrice Stainton remarked on the discrepancies time after time. No threadbare bodice was folded and laid in a trunk without an accompanying expression of regret that poverty prevented it from being thrown away. Each scuffed, down-at-heel shoe was identified as possessing a sole which, in more affluent circumstances, would be judged too thin to keep out the rain.

Elizabeth sat on the side of the bed with Ernest playing on the floor beside her and baby Agnes on her knee. She told herself that dignity required each humiliation to be borne with silent fortitude. The baby, who howled every time she was prevented from climbing down from her mother's knee, made the appearance of detached superiority almost impossible to sustain. Anne, sitting across the room on the blanket chest, maintained the poise which her mother had convinced her was the secret of life.

'Shall I take her?' asked Beatrice, reaching for Agnes. 'She may need changing.'

'She's perfectly dry.' Elizabeth clutched her daughter even more tightly and the child howled with renewed vigour. 'At least, I can tell that, blind though I am.'

'I'm not surprised that she's crying. You're crushing her half to death. One of her legs is twisted under her. I do so worry about how you'll manage when you get to Lincoln. The poor little mite . . .'

'I'll help,' said Anne, who, as was only appropriate in a perfect replica, always echoed her mother's opinions.

'She will,' said Elizabeth proudly. 'She's very grown up for her age.'

'Poor little mite.' Beatrice's apprehensions were not specified but it was clear that she had transferred her concern from Agnes to Anne.

Elizabeth, having released the crushed and twisted leg, was in no mood to be lectured about her children's welfare and safety. 'Are you going to finish the packing, or shall we wait for William to get back?'

Beatrice resented the ingratitude, but she had always been afraid of provoking her sister's wrath and, on the threshold of anger, Elizabeth blind seemed barely less intimidating than Elizabeth with sight. Beatrice sniffed and asked a question which she hoped would be awkward. 'What about these funny little boxes? Do you want to take them?'

'Which funny little boxes?'

'The card boxes. There's one with a cribbage board on the back. One is, I suppose, a cigar box.' The doubt was intended to emphasise the absence of cigars and imply that William's professed enthusiasm for a pipe was really the product of his poverty.

'There should be four in all. One made of elm with bevelled edges. The men made them. Made them and gave them to William when he first started the joinery class.'

'Are they yours to take away?'

'The men made them as a sign of respect after he let them work and keep part of their earnings. They were given to William. They're ours.'

'But will Mr Leverington think so?'

'If Thomas Leverington comes here and makes out an inventory, he's not the gentleman that he's supposed to be. Anyway, the boxes belong to William. So does the clock.'

'The clock?'

Although Elizabeth had developed the incredulous repetition of the previous sentence to a fine art, she found the habit infuriating in others. 'That's what I said. The clock. The clock was made by the men at the same time as the boxes. The men gave it to William.'

'But the face? And the works . . . ?'

'Tear it apart if you wish and leave the parts that belong to the workhouse. But we're taking the case. If you don't want to pack it, pass it here. I'll manage.'

'There's really no need to be so touchy – especially when I'm doing my best to help, although I should have been back in March half an hour ago. Take it if you want. It won't be me who is up in front of the justices charged with theft.'

'Don't be so silly, Bea.' Identical advice had been given a thousand times before. It reminded both of them of their childhood and they parted as sisters and friends without Mrs Stainton even expressing her concern that the Skinners were about to begin a life prejudiced by handicap and poverty. As soon as she was out of the door, Elizabeth began to change the baby.

There was no need to perform the difficult task at that precise moment for little Agnes lay, soiled but contented, in her mother's lap. The sensible course would have been to await the return of William and recruit his willing assistance. But Elizabeth was determined to do the job alone. Her husband's esteem was essential to what, in her complex character, passed for happiness. Indeed, the only visible manifestation of affection she allowed herself to display was her unashamed desire for William's admiration. She was strong and won her husband's respect. Had she been weaker she might have kept his love.

Elizabeth, with her daughter held in one arm and the other extended in front of her like an antenna, was led away from drawing room to kitchen by Anne. She searched with her foot for the rug which, as it was rolled up ready for removal, was found only when she almost fell over it. She kicked at the obstacle in her path until it spread out again over part of the scrubbed floorboards. Then she laid little Agnes gently on the rough matting. Elizabeth could sense Anne standing anxious to help, remedy or rescue.

'Please don't get in my way. Go and look after Ernest.'

The little girl ran back to the drawing room and her dolls.

With some difficulty Elizabeth found the basket in which the child's clothes were kept. She sank to her knees beside Agnes, but, unable to judge her distance from the ground, landed with a thud which reverberated throughout the room. She did not pause to rub her bruises, but began at once – working by touch and instinct – to change her daughter, who rolled, without complaint, in whichever direction she was pushed.

The plan worked exactly as Elizabeth intended. By the time she heard the noise of the horse and dray drawing up outside the door, the job was all but finished. As her husband's key turned in the lock, she chased the dirty clothes across the floorboards and just retrieved them in time to make them into a tidy bundle as he walked into the kitchen. She had hoped to be back on her feet, poised and with her

73

daughter on her hip, but she knew that the child, cooing clean on the rug, was almost as good a demonstration of her indomitable will.

'You're ready. You really are a marvel. We can be there before dark.'

She did not smile, for smiling was not her habit, but she enjoyed a feeling of profound satisfaction.

'I thought you'd want to be off.'

To her surprise, William did not reply. He had noticed a brown smear which stretched across the width of the floorboards from the edge of the unrolled carpet to the place where the bundle of soiled clothes lay. Retching silently, he rubbed at the mark with the sole of his shoe and gave thanks that neither Ernest nor Anne was in the room to notice and ask what he was doing.

'Are you still there?'

'I'm here. I'll get your coat from the passage. You take Agnes. Come in, Ernest. Anne, get the baby's shawl.'

'I can manage.' Elizabeth felt her way along the wall and out of the kitchen.

Her husband put a protective arm around her shoulder. She shook it off. 'I tell you, I can manage.'

'I know you can.' He put his arm round her again and, risking the accusation that he was loosening her tightly drawn hair, he kissed his wife on the cheek.

'Careful,' she said, pulling away from him. 'You'll make me drop the baby.'

At Darfoulds, which was no more than a mark on the map, life went on at a pace which many busy towns would have envied. Mr Henry Hodding, whose first wife had died immediately after presenting him with his fifth child, had barely brought his new bride back from the Scottish honeymoon when she announced that she had conceived at a speed consistent with her husband's hectic life. He reciprocated her show of energy and enthusiasm by becoming clerk to the Worksop Corn Exchange Company and, in that capacity, he organised the removal of the cattle market from its old site in the centre of Worksop to a more salubrious location in the quiet meadows at Shaw's Field. He also began to prepare numerous private parliamentary bills for the extension of various Midland and Central railway lines – negotiating one day with a duke for the right to lay track across his land and bargaining with a colliery company on the next for the exclusive contract to carry its coal. Wherever he went, he complained. Most people with whom he did business lacked drive and determination. The local Volunteers trained so infrequently that they failed to remain

74

in a state of constant readiness. The Conservative Party was moribund and his local parish torpid. He often added that both hunts met so rarely that he proposed, one day, to organise his own. It would meet three times a week throughout the season at five o'clock in the morning so that its members could go off to their places of business invigorated by the sound of hound and horn.

The second Mrs Hodding was a widow who found it impossible to avoid comparison between her husband and his predecessor, a man of considerable wealth and slothful disposition. Fortunately, the contrast always favoured Henry, who was articled at fourteen and qualified at twenty, as compared with the late Mr Fergus Mason, who had never done a day's work in his life. Mrs Hodding bored the ladies of the Primrose League with stories of her second husband's triumphs in Chancery Court, concluding with an account of how he had wound up the estate of the late Sir Edward Banks by selling the town of Sheerness to various property developers and had then been thought by his doctors to have put such a strain on his young mind and body that they ordered him to leave London for the more relaxing atmosphere of the country. She always recalled – though never said – that her first husband had been thought to enjoy perfect health, had failed to father a single child and had fallen stone dead when several years younger than the phenomenal Henry Sweet Hodding.

Inevitably, life for the coachman in service to such a paragon of energetic virtue was almost as hectic as that of his master. Mr Hodding travelled on business every day and on business or pleasure every evening. Often he drove himself but Gerrard Knock had, even then, to sit beside him to drive back from the station when the London train had left or in readiness to take over the reins when the solicitor chose to descend into the carriage and read papers in preparation for his next meeting. Rosie was never required to help with the grooming or the mucking out, for Gerrard was never ill, but sometimes, when there was a weekend party at Harness Grove, she worked at table or acted as lady's maid to one of the visitors. She would have gladly worked more often, for she needed the money, enjoyed the men's admiring glances and, most of all, welcomed the company of other servants who lived at Harness Grove.

Gerrard Knock knew that, left alone in the house, his wife was lonely. Indeed, a lively girl of twenty-five could hardly be anything else, living in a cottage with no other building for four miles except the empty replica next door and the great house in the park which she was only allowed to approach when she was invited to skivvy there. But there was nothing he could do to solve her problems for, if he was to remain a successful coachman and groom, he had to work

75

all the hours that God sent and Mr Hodding demanded. He just worried. He had worried about Rosie since the day of their wedding but at Grove Cottage, he worried more than ever before.

At the beginning of their marriage, worry and wonderment combined for, even to him, it seemed barely possible that so desirable a young woman would choose to spend her life with a dwarf whose face looked as if it was made from crumpled brown paper. Then astonishment that she had accepted his proposal changed into apprehension about her continued respect for the vows with which she bound herself to him. Rosie never gave her husband the slightest cause for suspicion. She remained privately passionate, publicly attentive and constantly domesticated. She rarely left the house, always waited up for Gerrard's return, cooked with real enthusiasm and cleaned the house with a manic determination. Yet he still doubted her, for her love for him was wholly unreasonable. So he feared that she would not be unreasonable for ever. But, when he consoled himself with the thought that the evidence made her desertion at least unlikely, he began to worry not about the likelihood of her leaving him but about the abyss into which he would fall if the unlikely horror came about. He began to regret his move to Darfoulds and his reunion with horses.

'I'm off to Lincoln on Saturday. There's talk of a new line from Chesterfield.' He described the latest of Henry Hodding's enterprises with the awe that he felt for his employer's ever-expanding influence. 'I'm sorry, love, but there's nothing to be done as long as I'm coachman.'

'God bless you, I know that, Gerry. I know that you're just working for us.'

'But it's wrong for a young girl like you to be here for days on end with nobody to say as much as good morning to.'

'I've plenty to keep me busy. You shouldn't worry so much.'

'What'll you do on Saturday?'

'I haven't even thought yet. I might go for a walk. I still haven't seen half of the sights around here.'

'You say that every time I go away. But you never leave the house, unless you go into the garden to hang the washing on the line.'

'What would you like me to do, go into one of the gin palaces in Worksop?' Rosie was joking, and there would have been no joke had the idea not been too absurd for serious consideration. Gerrard did not laugh, but his wife threw back her head in a huge – and vulgar – guffaw which revealed the freckles that ran down her full throat and made her curls dance on her shoulders. Gerrard did not even notice. He decided to change the subject.

'I want you to do me a favour.'

''Course I will. What is it?'

'I want you to walk down to Worksop and post me a letter.'

'Can't you post it while you're out with Mr Hodding?' The question was prompted by curiosity alone, and Gerrard knew it.

'I could. But I'd prefer Mr Hodding not to know. He might ask questions.'

'Who are you writing to?'

Correspondence was not a regular feature of life in domestic service. Rosie's temperament protected her from the fear of the family tragedy which the news of an impending letter would have aroused in most working-class women. The secret posting made her insatiably curious about the letter's contents. 'Come on, tell us. Who're you writing to?'

'Mr Skinner, Mr William Skinner.'

Rosie, who was pink by nature as well as complexion, turned white. Gerrard thought that he had put the wrong idea in her head, an idea which could lead only to bitter disappointment.

'Don't think I'm trying for my old job. Don't think that. Anyway, I wouldn't get it. Not from the new man, I wouldn't.'

'What do you mean, new man?' Rosie had turned whiter still.

'Mr Skinner's left Wisbech. Leastways, he's left the workhouse.'

'How do you know that?'

'Mr Hodding told me last night. Mr Hodding wrote to him for a reference. Then he wrote again to thank him for the trouble he'd taken. It came back, weeks later, with "left" written on the envelope. He must have gone months ago – just after us. I told you that he'd got that girl into trouble. He must have admitted it.'

'I don't believe it. I shall never believe it. Never.' Rosie had begun to cry.

'I didn't mean to upset you, love. I never thought that just mentioning Wisbech would set you off like this.' He knelt against his wife's chair, his head barely coming up to her shoulder. Looking up into her face he told her, 'If I'd have known how much you'd hate it here, I would never have come. If I'd only realised how much you liked Wisbech we could have stayed there for ever. Forgive me. I thought that I was doing the best for us both.'

Rosie sniffed. 'I know you were. Thank God we came. Thank God.'

Gerrard often found his wife's opinions incomprehensible. He was not sure whether her sudden enthusiasm for Harness Grove demonstrated fear of serving the Poor Law under a new superintendent or was just another example of her capricious nature.

'It'll turn out all right. I know it will.'

'What you going to write to Mr Skinner for?'

'Just to wish him well. He's been good to me. He made me foreman

77

and he wrote that testimonial to Mr Hodding. It couldn't have been better if my own mother had written it.'

'From what I hear, if your mother had written it you wouldn't have got the job.' Rosie was beginning to recover.

Gerrard reached up and touched her face.

'How will you get it to him?'

'I'll write to his father at the farm. He'll know where he is. Whatever he's done, old Jacob Skinner won't have disowned him.'

Rosie was about to say, 'He's done nothing,' but she had regained enough composure to bite her tongue. So she simply added a note of inconsequential nonsense. 'I wonder if he had much trouble with the move. A lot of things get broken when you move house. They had some nice things. I hope they didn't get broken.'

Alfred Ellison spent the weeks after his move to Lincoln relating the site plan to the site, bidding unsuccessfully for pieces of land on which he had hoped to build houses and arranging his furniture. To his delight the drawing room of his new house was ennobled by a fireplace of the neo-gothic style which might have been the high altar in a medieval cathedral. Every room had beams which bore no load and served no purpose except to act as boundaries between the plaster mouldings which decorated the ceilings. The walls were panelled in oak and the floors were made of polished hardwood blocks on to which he piled as many cabinets, chiffoniers, pier-glasses, tables, chairs and whatnots as could be accommodated and still leave enough room for the nimble visitor to edge across the floor without knocking against a piece of furniture. Every item was highly decorated and it took some time to arrange the rival positions in a way which displayed each ornate scroll and elaborate inlay to best advantage. The work was only completed a few hours before Michael Drury, the Surveyor to the City of Lincoln, arrived to take dinner and to discuss the work to which Alfred Ellison had set his hand.

Michael Drury was a man of exceptional appearance. He was six feet four inches tall and maintained the military bearing he had developed during his years as a cadet at the Royal Military Academy at Woolwich. His fierce moustache and aggressive whiskers, acquired whilst building bridges and canals for the Indian Army, were still jet black. The pockmarks across his forehead and streaks of jaundice-yellow in his eyes confirmed his connection with the Raj. But the city surveyor had put the years of Empire behind him. He regarded himself as a Disciple of Progress and a Prophet of Improvement and boasted a professional lineage which, in his own estimation, went back to Telford and McAdam. It was his passionate conviction that the improvements made possible by science and industry should not be held back by sentimentality, compassion or ancient buildings – a belief that made him supremely unsuited to the position he held in a city with a great cathedral, an ancient castle and innumerable buildings of lesser renown but equal antiquity.

Two years before, when Lincoln's Dean and Chapter had refused to sell Brown's Close to the Arboretum Committee, Michael Drury had denounced the ecclesiastical authorities with a vehemence wholly inappropriate in an officer of the Corporation. When it was suggested that he had spoken with a frankness which had offended his friends and enraged his employers, he answered that he was a scientist and therefore obliged to follow truth wherever it led him. He immensely enjoyed his reputation for speaking his mind. As soon as he had settled down on Alfred Ellison's over-stuffed chesterfield with a glass of whisky in his hand, he began to behave in the way which was expected of him.

'I have to tell you, in all honesty, that I was against you getting this job. I didn't think you could do it. I didn't think so then and I don't think so now. I'd be being less than honest if I pretended anything different.'

'I can do it.' Alfred Ellison was too taken aback immediately to rebut the slander with the vigour that he knew to be justified. 'I've won contracts worth three times as much as this.'

'I don't doubt it. But that's half the problem. It was a mistake to tender four thousand five hundred for setting out the land. None of the other companies got within five hundred pounds of your price.'

'That was the consultant's estimate, the figure he calculated when he drew up the plan.'

'That was two years ago and in any case . . . have you done work for a council before, Mr Ellison? Have you ever been employed by a lord mayor and aldermen?'

'No, I have not. I've built houses, hundreds of them.'

'Working for a council is different . . . different from anything else in the world. Especially when you've won half the work by tender and propose to invoice for the rest.'

'I don't follow you. I've got the whole job.'

'That, again with respect, sir, is because you are an innocent.' The military manner, which he had tried so hard to suppress, burst out from underneath the camouflage of the progressive engineer. 'Problem: to build the pavilion, keeper's lodge, various fences, additional retaining walls. Method: to negotiate individual prices with Mayor and Corporation. Obstacle: the reluctance of said Mayor and Corporation to pay the proper price. Tactic, employed by other contractors but, unfortunately, not by yourself: pad out tender price for the first half and use surplus to make up deficit on second.'

'But how on earth did they hope to get the job, if they all bid too high?'

'Because, my dear sir, it was exactly as you say. They all bid too high. There was a gentleman's agreement to make a detailed estimate and then add seven hundred pounds. Then you came along, all the way from Wisbech, and spoiled everything – and probably arranged your own bankruptcy.'

Alfred Ellison was too stunned to reply immediately. Michael Drury allowed a few seconds for the bad news to sink in and then began to elaborate on his theme.

'My job – I say it with no great pleasure – is to make sure that you don't drag the arboretum down with you.'

'There's no question of that, I do assure you.' The contractor hoped that he sounded certain of his own capabilities and resentful that they were being questioned.

'Of course, I accept the assurance of your good intentions and best endeavours. But I need more reassurance than that. Clause Five of our agreement. I intend to exercise the right to appoint supervisory assistance. It will be Edward Milner of South Norwood. He was consultant landscape gardener to the Crystal Palace Company.'

'I've got a gardener. I've appointed one specially.'

'And the man's name?'

'Skinner. William Skinner. He knows more about horticulture than any man I ever met.'

'What was he before?'

'Before?'

'Before you hired him. My Mr Milner worked at the Great Exhibition. He advised me on the plan for this arboretum. It was his original estimate that you used as your bid to get the job. He's worked at Welbeck Abbey and Haddon and done jobs for dozens of councils. He's a real expert.'

'My man's much younger.'

'Where did he serve his apprenticeship?'

Alfred Ellison could hardly believe that the question was being seriously asked. Stonemasons served apprenticeships. So did glaziers, painters, joiners and tilers. Gardeners grew naturally like the plants and flowers they cultivated. Despite his astonishment, he realised that it was necessary to pander to the surveyor's professional prejudice. He constructed his answer in what he hoped was suitably pretentious language.

'He is entirely self-taught. He was a gifted amateur, a remarkably gifted young man.'

Many of Michael Drury's heroes had been self-taught and he was far too modern a man to believe that every decent landscape gardener had served his time in the livery of one of England's great houses. He was determined to dispel any possible misapprehensions about his willingness to move with the times. 'Nothing wrong with that. What work does he do now? Have you seen anything he's laid out?'

'He was the workhouse master at Wisbech.'

'Well, whatever he laid out there, it wasn't gardens.'

Michael Drury slapped his thigh, leaned back on the sofa, drained his glass of whisky, indicated his wish for a second libation, slapped his thigh again and chortled with childish delight. He made jokes only rarely but when he did, he enjoyed them.

'He can do it, I tell you.' Alfred Ellison was not amused.

The surveyor regained his grim composure.

'Do you know what solifluxion is?'

'Of course I do. I've dug railway cuttings in my time and I've built embankments. And I've seen workmen buried alive because the shoring up was badly done. We called it soil-slip. But we learned about it. We learned the hard and best way.'

'And has he learned? Has your workhouse master ever heard of soil-slip?'

'He will.'

'If he does, he then has to begin to learn which grass binds soil. He has to learn about drainage and the best angle of slope to make sure that the hill doesn't run into the valley on the first rainy day. He has to learn which bushes spread their roots widest and which trees can be transplanted when they're half-grown. Mr Edward Milner knows all these things already. That's why I'm appointing him and that's why you'll do as he tells you. It will cost you two hundred guineas.'

'You're appointing him at my expense?'

'That's what the contract says.'

Before he replied, Alfred Ellison poured himself another whisky. Then he made his last feeble protest. 'He could do it, if we gave him the chance.'

Michael Drury was not in the mood to spare his feelings. Progress rarely came about without pain. His host was about to become one of the casualties in the war for improvement.

'I have to say that your faith in this man does nothing to increase my confidence in either your judgement or your ability. He's clearly not up to the job. Why did you appoint him?'

Alfred Ellison's nerve snapped. He spent half his life building

81

houses and the other half in a fantasy world of dreams which would never come true. In neither part of his existence was he required to do more than give an appearance of courage or loyalty. Terrified that he had lost the surveyor's respect, he decided to offer William Skinner's reputation as a sacrifice to propitiate the Mayor and Corporation.

'He was in trouble, in trouble at the workhouse. Trouble over a woman. He needed to get out . . .'

As he spoke, he lied to himself. It was, he pretended, in William's best interests that he should do everything possible to make sure that the arboretum contract was not cancelled. After all, William could not build houses, as he could. For William, it was the arboretum or nothing. He could not completely exorcise the feeling of guilt, so he spoke up again for William's ability.

'That doesn't mean he's not a good gardener.'

'It means that he can't be trusted.'

'He can be trusted to be gardener in your arboretum.'

'I think not. And Clause Five of the contract makes me the judge. I shall write to Mr Milner tomorrow.'

'That's settled, then. The decision is clearly yours.'

'It is. It is.' The city surveyor spoke with the satisfaction of a man who has successfully concluded the business which he had come to transact. After a moment, Alfred Ellison – speaking like a host who had only just realised that his guest had accepted the invitation for the explicit purpose of bringing bad news – decided that a change of atmosphere was essential.

'If that's your work done, Mr Drury, shall we go in to dinner?'

'I've a couple more items. But we can discuss them over the soup.'

'Dinner can wait.'

'I hope that you're not the sort of man who only likes gossip and tittle-tattle across his table. You'll not find me much of a dining companion if you want to talk about fashion in waistcoats and vintages of wine.'

'You can take your pick.' The subject of the arboretum being temporarily abandoned, confidence was beginning to return. 'Music. Horses. Architecture. Furniture. Politics. I am a passionate supporter of the extension of the franchise and, if you wish, I will argue for more parliamentary reform. I was born in Burnham Thorpe, the birthplace of Admiral the Lord Nelson and I will gladly discuss his plan of battle at Aboukir Bay or his relationship with the Neapolitan Court or his early years on the North America Station. Is there anything there that takes your fancy? I like to amuse my guests as best I can.' Alfred Ellison gambled on none of those subjects – with

82

the possible exception of architecture – being to the surveyor's taste.

'What excites my interest at the moment, Mr Ellison, is the way in which you propose to build the Lincoln arboretum. I am not one of those men who draw a sharp distinction between business and pleasure. And I hope you're not either. I hope you're not saying that we can't discuss business over dinner. That's the sort of silly attitude I can't abide. It's notions like that which drove me out of the army.'

Host decided that guest had gone too far and that a magisterial rebuke was justified.

'I don't think that Clause Five of the contract covers what I talk about at dinner in my own house. That, if you'll forgive me for saying so, is a choice that a freeborn Englishman is allowed to make for himself.'

He was still enjoying the implied distinction between a free Englishman and a Scot imprisoned by the limitations of his nationality when the surveyor replied in unexpectedly conciliatory language.

'I meant no offence and I mean none now, but I must tell you that you're wrong. Clause Five is in the contract in order to ensure that the job is properly done – by you, if possible, and by somebody else if it's not. You're more likely to get it right if you enjoy your work than if you don't. And if you enjoy your work, you'll want to talk about it, wherever you are. I don't have much time for men who work to make money so that they can enjoy themselves at something else.'

'Talk about what you like. But talk about it over the table. The fish is ruined already and the cutlets will be either cold or baked to a cinder.'

So they talked about the arboretum and Michael Drury's plan to make it a pleasure dome of which Kubla Khan would have been proud. But they talked only between courses for the surveyor concentrated on each stage of the meal with manic intensity. He scooped up his soup with a continuous rotating motion which reminded his host of the dredgers that lifted silt from the New Sutton Dock and he cleared his plate of fish before there was time to offer him parsley sauce or salt and pepper. The cutlets were swallowed down whilst he was still being served with peas and potatoes and he had finished his apple pie before the custard was put on the table. It was when he began to hack at the Stilton whilst the cheeseboard was still in Alfred Ellison's hand that silent speculation about the strange conduct became irresistible.

Alfred Ellison first attributed his guest's uncouth behaviour to a well-mannered impatience to finish his food so that he could return to the talk of business without a breach of etiquette. Then, as Drury gobbled on, he decided that he was witnessing nothing more elevated than simple gluttony. Neither explanation was correct. The surveyor was always anxious to complete the task on which he was engaged so that he could move on to his next endeavour. With a meal in front of him, he abandoned all concern for digestion, reputation and tablecloth and consumed it in the least possible time. The future was always full of interest and hope. The next thing always called to him. For that reason, he declined coffee, brandy and cigars. Having satisfied his appetite and said all that he had come to say about Clause Five of the contract, he wished to move on.

'Will you walk the site with me?'

'At this time of night! It's after ten o'clock.'

'It's a clear night. There's a hunter's moon. We'll see as much as we would have seen at noon.'

'I've walked it half a dozen times.'

'But not with me.'

Alfred realised that Michael Drury's enthusiasm was irresistible. He tried to capitulate gracefully.

'I'll find boots.' He was looking at his own embroidered slippers.

'My shoes are stout enough. It's a dry night. But I'll trouble you for the loan of a stick.'

It was Alfred Ellison's turn to be politely dismissive. 'You've forgotten how gentle the slope is. Not more than one in twenty.'

'It's not to lean on. If you'd be so kind . . .'

The two men pushed their way through an opening in the hedge that marked the site's northern boundary in Lindum Terrace and Michael Drury began at once to point out, with his borrowed walking stick, the distant shadows which he identified as pavilions, palisades and promenades. But Alfred Ellison was not listening. In order to squeeze through the narrow gap in the thorn bushes he had turned to face the west and had seen, over his shoulder, the silhouette of Lincoln cathedral, clear and precise against the sky. It seemed that each of its three great towers stretched half of the way to heaven and he was awestruck by the thought that when they had been topped with spires they must have reached all the way to paradise. The gales which had ruined the great central tower he could just forgive. But he thought with a mixture of hatred and amazement of the men who had desecrated the other towers. What sort of savage, he wondered, could commit such an act of wanton barbarism?

Michael Drury noticed that his attention had begun to wander.

'You'll understand better if we start at the bottom where the tea room's going to be. The contract is exact. A tea room, adjacent to the main gate and capable of seating two hundred customers at one time. I take it that you'll build it yourself, not contract it out. You'll build the park-keeper's house as well, will you?'

Before Alfred had time to say that he had no intention of sub-contracting anything, Michael Drury was halfway down the hill, impatient to continue his demonstration. Would it, Alfred wondered, be possible to build a tea room and park-keeper's lodge in the early English style? He decided that he would negotiate his price with the Corporation on that assumption.

'Main gates wide enough to take a carriage. Gas lights on pillars and pedestrian gates on either side. Gatehouse modest but suitably comfortable accommodation for the head gardener. Tea room easily accessible from the road. Nothing too formal or forbidding. This is to be the People's Garden. That is the Council's wish. The whole appearance and aspect must be simple and welcoming – homely even.'

Alfred Ellison had only time to grunt a grudging acquiescence before his mentor continued.

'Another gate here. Nothing like as grand as the main entrance. Dignified but not pretentious. This leads to the lakes. You can decide their exact size and lining. But there must be a bridge. The contract requires a bridge.'

A cloud passed across the moon and Alfred, preoccupied with thought of classical façades and caryatids, did not notice that the surveyor had begun to retrace his steps westwards. When Drury realised that the contractor was fifty yards behind him he shouted over his shoulder into the cold night air. Half his words were carried away on the beginnings of an east wind.

'Got to be hardy but quick growing . . . Edward Milner will advise on that . . . perhaps two bridges. I'll do my best to negotiate a decent price . . . ornamental water . . . keep it shallow . . . Milner will buy plants to keep it clean . . . clean . . . it needn't look like the Crystal Palace. That's just Milner's prejudice. Pavilion design is up to you . . . whatever they'll pay for . . . steps in the middle and at each end . . . the retaining walls . . .'

Halfway up the hill, Michael Drury stopped for Alfred Ellison to catch up with him. He leaned on his stick in preparation for making an important point.

'One good thing about you getting the contract, I can trust you to build the terrace. It's essential to get it right. If that fails the arboretum fails. We need a good, old-fashioned builder for that job.'

Hope sprang in Alfred's heart. He thought of classical proportions, elegant façades, shapes and sizes in harmony with the configuration of the surrounding countryside. The optimism lasted for the few seconds Drury needed to draw breath.

'Don't stand any nonsense from Milner or anyone else about style. The terrace has to be as wide as possible and that means sturdy. On summer Sunday afternoons, there'll be upwards of a thousand people – half of them children – promenading along that terrace. You'll need piers, perhaps a raft to hold it in the hillside. If they make it look ugly, don't worry.'

'Thank you,' said Alfred. It was the best reply of which he was capable.

'Have you seen pictures of Paxton's orangery at Chatsworth? Just like his design for the Great Exhibition. Milner thought of something like that for the pavilion, because it's very light. But we don't have to have a light pavilion if we have a sturdy terrace.'

They were back at Lindum Terrace. Alfred Ellison – who spent much time reassuring himself about his moral courage – decided that if the tour had not ended at that moment he would have put courtesy aside and informed the surveyor that he had grown tired of being lectured to as if he had never taken the arboretum plan from its cardboard tube. Having been saved from that act of conspicuous bravery, he simply said, 'Will you come in for a moment? It's a cold night. You could do with something to warm you.'

'I'll not take another drink, but I'll gladly come inside. We've still got a lot to talk about. We moved so fast that I overlooked half of what I had to say.'

Inside the hall, Alfred Ellison pulled off his heavy boots before venturing beyond the coconut matting behind the door. He could not help glancing furtively at Drury's grass- and mud-covered shoes. The surveyor noticed. 'If you're worried about the damage to your carpets, I'll gladly take them off.'

Alfred decided that he must not allow Michael Drury's boorish behaviour to provoke him into a course of equally uncouth conduct. Builders and engineers could be gentlemen and he determined to prove it. Silently he led the way into the drawing room, trying not to look down at his precious Persian rugs and the marks which Michael Drury's soles were leaving upon them.

'There's one other thing. The plan says box. Mr Milner will want sweet briar.'

'I'm beginning to think that this Mr Milner won the contract.'

'No. You did – despite knowing nothing of landscape gardening. That is why Mr Milner is appointed consultant.'

'At a cost of two hundred guineas to me.' It was Alfred Ellison's one moment of real asperity during the whole evening and he regretted it at once. 'I'm sure that we'll work together very happily.'

'You will if you take heed of his advice on everything except retaining walls. Is there anything left to discuss?'

'I think that you've mentioned everything except grass and flowers.'

'Don't take grass lightly. If you sow the wrong sort, you'll have bare soil by June and if it rains in August there'll be rivulets as thick as your fingers.'

'No doubt Mr Milner will advise me.'

The irony passed unnoticed.

'I'll leave the flowers to you and this gardener that you've hired. I'll trust him with the flowers if I trust him with nothing else and I'll trust you with the walls. For the rest, rely on Milner.'

'I'm very flattered.'

Again the surveyor missed or chose to ignore the sarcasm.

'You shouldn't be. If a builder can't build retaining walls he's out of business and, if you're to be relied upon, you've lasted for nearly thirty years. I trust you to build walls because you're not bankrupt.'

'What a pity walls are so unimportant.'

'I'll tell you once more, for I want you to be in no doubt. If at half-past two on a summer Saturday a retaining wall collapses, twenty children will be buried alive. Ten will be suffocated to death. Somebody will be blamed. I shall make sure it's you. Proper foundations. That's what's needed. Don't worry about the walls at the bottom of the gardens.' He waved dismissively towards the houses opposite. 'They won't carry much of a load. Edward Milner can design them with fancy brickwork. You worry about the others, especially those under the promenade.'

It was Alfred Ellison's habit to fall asleep the moment his head touched the pillow and his nights were normally interrupted only by dreams of Michelangelo, Christopher Wren and William Vanbrugh. But that night he lay looking up towards his ceiling until the small hours of the morning. Then, when at last he slept, he dreamed that he had used the savings of a lifetime to pay Edward Milner's fees and that, despite having taken the consultant's advice in every particular, the retaining wall collapsed and engulfed every child in Lincoln.

The thought of confronting William Skinner was worse than the nightmares. William had to be told that there was no longer sufficient work to justify the employment of a head gardener and that in consequence his status, if not his wages, would have to be reduced. Alfred was pathologically incapable of bearing bad news. He spent the dark hours before dawn thinking of how he could avoid that unpleasant duty.

By six o'clock he had worked out a plan. Although William had become a liability rather than an asset, there was no immediate need to tell him that his services were no longer required. For a week or two he could give him other duties on the pretext that the gardener's job would only begin when the earth was cleared and the footing for the promenade pegged out. William would continue to work for the Arboretum Construction Company until he grew tired of supervising the shifting of soil and found a superior job and alternative accommodation, or until his employer thought of another reason to procrastinate.

As the sun began to force its way round the edge of Alfred Ellison's bedroom curtains, he decided to forget – at least about the previous night's unhappy revelation. It would be several weeks before Edward Milner arrived. Until then it would be unnecessary – indeed it would be positively cruel – to warn William Skinner that nemesis approached, as duly provided for under Clause Five of the contract.

CHAPTER SEVEN

Act of God

Edward Milner left for Lincoln within hours of receiving the city surveyor's invitation. He had intended to enjoy a brief holiday slaughtering pheasant and partridge at Welbeck Abbey and Clumber Park but it was over thirty years since he had walked the lawns of the Great Exhibition with Joseph Paxton and, memories being short, offers of work were not as frequent as they had been during the glorious decade which followed 1851.

Unfortunately, the decline in Edward Milner's income had not been matched by a reduction in his expensive habits or his extravagant tastes. In consequence, he was permanently incapable of living within his means. He only avoided bankruptcy by making periodic raids on the diminishing capital which he had saved during the days when he was in constant demand. A two hundred guinea consultation fee was a bounty to be accepted at once and earned as soon as possible. He caught the first train from Worksop to Lincoln and, immediately he arrived in the cathedral city, hired a hansom cab to take him to the site. The driver agreed to wait in Monk's Road whilst he examined the steep slope on which the Corporation proposed to create the arboretum that he had designed for a different piece of land back in 1868.

To his surprise, the earth-moving had already begun. A team of men was smoothing the slope at the point where, as far as he could judge, the promenade would run along the hillside from east to west. A tall, handsome man with a neat beard was supervising their work. Naturally enough, the consultant assumed that he had found the main contractor. He consulted the city surveyor's letter and, confirming the name of the company which he was to advise, picked his way across the muddy ground with hand outstretched.

'Mr Ellison? Do I have the honour to address Mr Alfred Ellison? My name is Edward Milner.'

The handsome man spat on his right palm and rubbed it against the seat of his breeches. That single gracious action was enough to convince Edward Milner that the Arboretum Committee had engaged a company too small to carry out his grand design. Major contractors did not soil their hands. It was, however, too late to draw back. The handshake was robust and prolonged.

'I'm afraid that Mr Ellison is not here. My name is William Skinner. What can I do for you?'

Edward Milner did not do business with site foremen but he found it difficult to believe that it was such a menial who, a second before, had crushed his fist. The handsome man wore a tweed suit and a soft hat, not the second-hand Sunday best and the almost new bowler that usually marked the uneasy transition from labourer to chargehand. Even more startling were the man's legs. Instead of being tied below his knees and above his shoes with hemp string, they were encased in tall boots which a squire might have worn for his Michaelmas rent collection. Apart from a spattering of the morning's mud, the brown leather glowed with the patina of careful daily cleaning. Edward Milner decided that the man whom he addressed occupied a social position near enough to his own to justify a brief conversation.

'I had hoped to meet Mr Alfred Ellison here. I'd be obliged if you told me where I could find him.'

'Mr Ellison is in Grantham.'

'Shouldn't he be here?'

'Mr Ellison has many interests and this arboretum is only one of them. If you have business here you'll have to transact with me.'

The confidence of the reply convinced Edward Milner that he was speaking to a person of authority – perhaps a member of the contractor's family, a brother-in-law or a nephew by marriage. He adjusted his tone accordingly.

'I'm most obliged to you, sir. You said that your name was . . . ?'

'Skinner, William Skinner.' The hand was extended for a second time, without, to Edward Milner's relief, the initial courtesy of spit and wipe. 'I'm the gardener to the company, the Lincoln Arboretum Construction Company that is, as set up and owned by Mr Alfred Ellison of Wisbech. At least, I shall be when the gardening starts. For the time being I'm just keeping an eye on things whilst Mr Ellison is away. May I ask, since you have the advantage of me, whom I have the honour to address?'

The consultant answered the question in the thunderous tones appropriate to a fellow of the Royal Horticultural Society and author of various works on land drainage, alpine perennials, the transplanting of mature conifers and, most famously, *The Cultivation of Sweet Briar Mazes in Elizabethan England – with original drawings*. His accent grew increasingly imperious as he recalled that, buried in the city surveyor's letter of appointment, was a brief reference to a disgraced workhouse master who had been taken on by the main contractor as an act of kindness. The letter had described the man as a jobbing gardener.

'I, sir, am Edward Milner. I designed the arboretum which is to be constructed on this site and I have been engaged as consultant to the company which employs you.'

The disgraced workhouse master turned jobbing gardener was disconcertingly unimpressed.

'Consultant what?'

'Consultant landscape gardener.'

'There won't be much consulting to be done. We've got it all planned out according to the surveyor's instructions.' William spoke in the apologetic tone of a man who thought he had a duty to give the bad news. He went on to describe the work at Monk's Leys as if, by already having made so much progress, the Lincoln Arboretum Construction Company had taken bread out of Edward Milner's mouth.

'I think', said the consultant, speaking like a man who was not paid by the hour, 'that you'll find that there's plenty for me to do.'

'We thought you'd done it all. I remember your name. Mr Ellison pointed it out to me before we left Wisbech. We've been ordering the plants which you wrote in the margins. Sweet briar for the hedging.' William liked the sound of the words so he repeated them. 'Sweet briar for the hedges. It's all done, I'm afraid.'

'On the contrary, young man. It's only just beginning. Be so kind as to tell me when Mr Ellison is expected back in Lincoln.'

'Tonight,' William told him, trying to sound reassuring. 'Definitely tonight. When I tell him that you were here in person, he'll barely believe me. Have you a business card that I can show him?'

In a better mood, Edward Milner would have been flattered by the idea that his presence in Monk's Leys was incredible. But he was irritated by William Skinner's suggestion that his services were no longer needed.

'Let me assure you that your employer knows full well who I am and why I am here. Mr Drury met Mr Ellison three days ago and wrote to me immediately afterwards. Since he has negligently failed to inform you of my duties, I will repair the omission. In the opinion of the city surveyor, your company is not capable of constructing this arboretum without assistance. I have, therefore, been called in to provide advice and, because of my affection for this city and respect for its surveyor, I have agreed to help. I am, effectively, in charge. Is that understood?'

'I understand what you say. But I take my orders from Mr Ellison. Who he takes his orders from is none of my business. But he pays my wages. Nobody else.'

There was a terrible moment when Edward Milner thought that

the handsome man in the tweed suit was about to offer his hand as if he was in a position to decide that the conversation – a discussion between equals – was over. But the danger passed. He did no more than dismiss the consultant in a couple of sentences.

'Now, sir, if you'll excuse me, I've got work to do. Mr Ellison will not thank me for spending the morning gossiping to anyone who calls.'

The choice of words – 'gossiping' to describe the assertion of the consultant's authority, the reference to his having 'called' as if he were an itinerant evangelist with a tract and a collecting box, and (most offensive of all) his inclusion amongst 'anyone' who might waste the jobbing gardener's time – was, Edward Milner decided, not intended to be offensive. But the use of such expressions, innocent or not, required the consultant to leave no doubt about the power of his position.

'You'll be glad I'm here when you see the figures. Your Mr Ellison got the job by tendering too low. If he's not to lose money he'll need to negotiate hundreds more for labour costs alone. And, without my support, he wouldn't get another penny. Then he's got to work out prices for the extra work. Unless I support him, he'll not get enough to build a decent cattle shed, let alone a tea room and a pavilion. Your Mr Ellison needs me. Never forget it!'

'Thank you. Thank you very much. Shall I tell Mr Ellison that you'll be back tomorrow?'

'Tomorrow at ten o'clock and every day for the next month.'

'You should have told me.' William Skinner – on Alfred Ellison's doorstep before the contractor had finished his breakfast – sounded more hurt than offended. In the dining room his mood changed to reproach that his employer had been so negligent of his own best interests. 'I might have said the wrong thing. Perhaps I did. I had no idea that he could tell us what to do.'

'And I had no idea that he was coming to Lincoln yesterday. I saw no reason to worry you earlier than necessary.'

'Worry me?'

'Worry you that there was no longer a job worth your time and talents.'

Alfred looked up from his haddock kedgeree in the desperate hope that William would take the hint and agree that pride required him to offer his immediate resignation. He then feared that his employee realised how anxious he was to save the cost of the highest wage in the Lincoln Arboretum Construction Company so he lied about his true intention.

'Of course, I want you to stay.' But, in case William took his assurance at its face value, he inserted the idea of self-sacrifice into the conversation. 'Of course, the job – and the salary – is here for as long as you want it, whatever happens. I take it you do want to stay, notwithstanding?'

'With a blind wife and three children, I don't have much choice. I'll think about pride and dignity when I've got some savings.'

'Then you'd better do as he says.'

William Skinner did as Edward Milner said for a full year, and the consultant, true to his word, persuaded the Arboretum Committee of the Corporation to pay for the extra work which could not reasonably be financed out of Alfred Ellison's original bid. On the promise that the pavilion would be designed as a replica of the Crystal Palace, he obtained an extra six hundred and seventy pounds to cover the cost of its construction and the price of the lodge, the tea room and the stout boundary fence which was adjudged necessary to keep cattle off the land. Three hundred pounds was provided, against the inspection of receipts, to build the entrance gates. The consultant's major achievement was the negotiation of seven hundred pounds to cover extra and unanticipated labour costs.

Alfred Ellison decided that he would take no risks and he dug foundations for the promenade deep enough to bear the weight of the whole cathedral. He even ruined the appearance of the smooth retaining walls by piercing it with drainage pipes which, on rainy days, spat out muddy water in the manner of a miniature town sewer. At the top of the hill, the work was delayed. The residents in the new houses insisted that the safety of their gardens be ensured by a buttress of greater elegance than the sturdy structure which held up the soil on the lower slopes. The surveyor told the Lindum Terrace house holders that they should not waste his time in an unfruitful attempt to squander the city's money, but the Mayor and Corporation capitulated and Edward Milner promised to design something suitably delicate.

It took three weeks for the drawings to be finished and almost as long for the burghers of Lindum Terrace to agree to the design. Michael Drury insisted that the best solution was a stout stone and simple mortar. But the householders wanted something superior. In the end, they accepted the design only when Edward Milner provided prints to prove that his proposed pattern of brickwork was based on a form of decorative masonry familiar to anyone who was a regular visitor to Hampton Court Palace.

William laboured at the top of the hill as, during his first year in Lincoln, he toiled at every task to which it was possible to turn his hand. He began work early and finished late in order to compensate for the time he stole by rushing home to Thomas Street to mend the fence, turn the handle of the mangle and make sure that none of the catastrophes which he foresaw – his daughter scalded by water from a cooking pot or his wife falling downstairs – had come about. The other women in Thomas Street all offered help to their blind neighbour. But Elizabeth Skinner was not the sort of woman to be beholden to any stranger and the idea of accepting favours from the working families who lived beside her was not even considered. She felt her way around the house, barking her shins on buckets and coal scuttles, banging against chairs and tables and spilling everything that she carried in a saucepan or jug.

Her sisters never visited Lincoln. Beatrice might have played Lady Bountiful once a month, but Henry Stainton forbade her to travel by train. Old Jacob never moved more than an hour's ride from his farm but he added messages to Joshua's occasional and badly written letters. At Christmas and on the children's birthdays he sent a sovereign wrapped in a piece of old newspaper and stuffed into a match box to deceive feloniously minded postmen. Alfred Ellison still wanted to spend his Saturday afternoons fantasising with William but William thought it his duty to spend his weekends with his handicapped family, and Alfred was either away on business or entertaining influential friends on the odd occasion when it might have been possible to recreate the old intimacy of wishful thinking.

During his first year in Lincoln, William felt more desolate than he would previously have thought possible. Only once, during the whole twelve months, did he enjoy moments of real pleasure. One evening he arrived home to find his wife apparently staring out of the kitchen window. She told him, without emotion or excitement, that when she turned in what she assumed to be the direction of the light, shapes – 'long squirming shapes, like worms' – appeared before her eyes or inside her head.

'I told you.' Doubts rarely afflicted William. 'You're going to be all right. You'll be seeing everything in a week or two.'

'Don't be so silly.'

William was not sure if it was the despair or the contempt which concerned him the most. He pretended that he had noticed neither.

'You'll see. By the time the arboretum's finished you'll be right as rain.'

The work took longer than Alfred Ellison had intended. It was another year before the arboretum was completed and, even when it was done, Elizabeth could not see the full beauty of his work. The park-keeper's house and the tea room to which it was attached were built to Alfred Ellison's own design. The result was a keeper's lodge which began as a half-timbered Tudor tavern but ended as a Swiss chalet with a front door surrounded by classical columns and a Norman arch. The adjacent tea room was partly old English tithe barn but mostly Bavarian beer-hall. The contractor was, nevertheless, congratulated by the surveyor on the stability of the promenade as demonstrated by the sturdy retaining wall and exposed drainage pipes.

The lake, which Alfred Ellison designed and dug, was bigger than the Arboretum Committee had intended and it stretched along almost the full length of Monk's Road. It was, in consequence, necessary to cross it with two ornamental bridges rather than one, but the Corporation refused to make any further contribution to the cost of work which was already twice the original estimate. Mr F. J. Clarke – four times Lord Mayor and inventor of Clarke's Patent Blood Mixture – presented the Committee with a Coade Stone lion. Unfortunately the synthetic stone did not set quickly enough to be in place, at the foot of the central promenade steps, in time for the opening ceremony.

William Skinner anticipated the Grand Opening with mixed feelings. Despite his unexpectedly menial employment he felt a proprietary affection for the arboretum and looked forward to the public admiration which he expected to be excited by trees he had planted, though not selected. However, the completion of the arboretum also meant the end of secure employment. Alfred Ellison had been jovial but evasive when asked how he proposed to keep his promise of guaranteed work and income. William, despite his wife's insistence that the job was beneath him, had applied for the post of lodge-keeper and head gardener. The application was torn up by Michael Drury, who recalled that the unqualified ex-workhouse master had been appointed gardener to the Construction Company after his dismissal by the Poor Law Guardians for sexual impropriety. The position was offered to – and accepted by – Horace Hodson, an elderly butcher who could barely distinguish between a rose and a chrysanthemum but had not been openly accused of adultery. As a demonstration of the way he proposed to perform his duties, he insisted on being sworn constable. He did not intend to stand any nonsense from young men enjoying a day out in the people's park.

The surveyor, motivated part by guilt and part by self-interest, offered to retain William for a further six months if he would supervise the plants taking root and the saplings beginning their slow ascent into trees.

William, his confidence boosted by certainty of six months more employment tried to persuade Elizabeth to make one of her rare expeditions out of house and yard to see the parade which was to mark the inauguration. Inevitably she dismissed the suggestion as if it were intended to humiliate her.

'What good will that be to me? I would feel awful. I wouldn't see

95

anything. People will stare and children will laugh when I look the wrong way. You may like the idea of leading me there like a dancing bear, but I would hate it.'

'You'll see something. You're beginning to see shapes. You'll hear the bands and I'll describe it all to you.'

'I shall stay at home. You take Anne and Ernest, but look after them. Don't go making jokes with your cronies and letting them run under the horses' hooves.'

'There's no danger of that. I thought of finding a quiet spot where you and the little ones could be safe from the crush.'

'Haven't you got a special place picked out?'

'No.'

'The head gardener to the Arboretum Construction Company left to stand on the pavement?'

The incredulity was rhetorical. But it served to emphasise the indignity. Alfred Ellison had been allocated a seat in the stand. So had Edward Milner. But Milner had replied to the invitation with apologies for his unavoidable absence in Bath where he was assisting with the extensions to the botanical gardens in Lansdowne Road. Michael Drury, who had planned the event, was to march in the procession itself, dwarfing the other members of the corporation officers' contingent and demonstrating the military bearing learned in the Royal Engineers. But, for William Skinner, nothing had been set aside. Then, a week before the great event, the city surveyor received a letter from Mr Cyril Pratt, the superintendent of the Derby arboretum. It recommended balloons. 'We find', the letter ended, 'that they always draw well, especially in agricultural districts.'

That night, William Skinner hurried home and asked his wife again, 'Are you sure you won't come?'

'I don't know why you keep asking. It only causes agitation. I've made my mind up and that's that.'

'I've got a special place, a place in the grounds just behind the pavilion. We'll . . . I'll be able . . . There's a perfect view down into Monk's Road. And I'll be able to tell you all about it without worrying what Anne and Ernest are getting up to and you can nip into the back door of the pavilion to look after Agnes if you need to.'

Elizabeth pulled one of her exasperated faces. Then she changed it to calm condescension.

'No. I'll stay here but you take Anne. Ernest's not old enough to trust. I'm glad they've given you a proper place. It's no less than you deserve.'

On the great day William left home at half-past six in the morning and promised to be back to collect his daughter at two. A long morning of hard work lay ahead. Within his railed-off pen, he had to inflate five hundred balloons ready for release when the procession reached the main gate at three o'clock.

Michael Drury planned the parade with the precision he had seen applied to passing-out parades at Woolwich. He prepared for the festivities at the arboretum itself with the methodical care he had employed when the lives of a whole battalion depended on the stability of a bridge built by him across a ravine in Kashmir. He had, at first, resisted the idea of allowing the general public into the grounds on the night before the Grand Opening but he was persuaded by the Arboretum Committee that the deserving poor – who could not afford the full entrance fee and the entertainment it financed – should be allowed in for half the normal admission price on the Friday evening.

During the half-price preview a thousand adults paid twopence-halfpenny to walk the paths and read the notices which identified each tree. Six hundred children were admitted for an entrance fee of one penny. Horace Hodson, who did not hold with such benevolence, retired into his lodge and prophesied rain on the following day.

Everything except the weather had been carefully planned. The Watch Committee issued special by-laws prohibiting traffic on the procession route, forbidding the positioning of flags and banners in places which might prevent the free movement of pedestrians on the footpaths, outlawing the explosion of fireworks in public places and – ambitiously – requiring spectators to remain stationary as the procession passed. The crowd was swelled by day-trippers brought into Lincoln by excursion trains specially arranged by the Midland and Northern Railway Companies. At first it seemed that old Hodson's gloomy prediction about the weather was to be confounded. It was a grey morning, particularly dull for August. But it did not rain.

The dignitaries met at noon for lunch in the Guildhall. The Bishop of Lincoln, in full canonicals, declined to speak except to say a brief grace and commend 'the eloquence of silence'. Colonel George Amcott MP either did not hear or did not accept the episcopal injunction and spent twenty minutes proposing a toast to the city and the health of the Lord Mayor.

Colonel Amcott having spoken, Mr Joseph Hinde-Palmer MP found it necessary to add a word of his own. He described the new venture as an 'instructive means of recreation' for the labouring poor and commended the surveyor's decision to ask specific approval for the types of plants and trees which were planted along the pathways. He was clearly relieved that the labouring poor would not be exposed to flora too exotic for their moral welfare. There was a moment when

97

it seemed that the High Sheriff was about to rise in his place, but Michael Drury rapped the table with his coffee spoon.

'Gentlemen, we must be away. Unless we leave in two minutes, we will be late at the main gate. We don't want a riot on our hands.'

The Mayor led the procession, followed by the aldermen, the councillors and the Corporation officials in strict order of rank, seniority and precedence. Behind them came the band of the First Lincoln Rifle Volunteers whose members had practised every evening for the last fortnight to justify their place of honour. They were followed by a pageant of horse-drawn carts and drays, each one decorated to represent the ancient trades which did business in the city. Halfway down Cornhill, the ostler who was driving the wire-makers' waggon was distracted from the difficult business of guiding his Suffolk Punch by a great banner which had been hung outside the Corn Exchange to advertise Poppleton's butterscotch. As the tail of his tableaux swung wildly round the sharp corner, one of the burning braziers – which gave the ensemble such veracity – fell from the display and scattered hot coals in the crowd. Fortunately, nobody was hurt. There was, however, much screaming on the pavements and the horses which pulled the other floats whinnied, neighed, shied and reared up in a manner which terrified the onlookers. The gardeners, all dressed in green, were thrown in a heap amongst their potted plants and ferns, whilst the tailors – all of whom were working cross-legged on the workbench which had been built to display their ancient habits – pricked their fingers with needles and pins or suffered slight stab wounds from flying shears. The shoemakers, who stood grouped around a vast wood-and-paper last, simply hung on to the symbol of their craft when the cart juddered and swayed. And the stonemasons – the last of the city trades in the procession – held so solid and firm that the drums and bugles of the Royal North Lincoln Militia, immediately behind them, did not even know of the catastrophes which had barely been averted.

Behind the militia, the juggernauts of industrial Lincoln rolled their way towards the opening ceremony – a portable steam engine, a threshing machine with its windmill blades flailing, a road engine and a steam bus bearing the livery of James J. Robey. The band of the Robin Hood Rifles, which marched behind the new and wondrous machinery, could hardly make itself heard above the noise of pistons, driving wheels and crankshafts. Fortunately, the societies following the light infantry felt no obligation to keep in step. The Oddfellows and the Freeforesters – like the Antediluvian Order of Buffaloes and the Rechabites – prided themselves on their essentially unmilitary appearance and bearing. They walked like what they were, respectable middle-aged gentlemen who had banded together for mutual welfare.

The rearguard was formed by the Leeds Model Band, which in normal circumstances would have played far better than the other more martial ensembles. Unfortunately for the Yorkshire musicians, circumstances were far from normal. They had never before attempted to play whilst on the move. Their attempt at mobile performance was wholly unsuccessful and, after various collisions and cacophonies, they decided to abandon the parade. Taking up position outside Clarke's chemist shop, which had been draped for the occasion in scarlet cloth, they gave the crowd a much appreciated but static concert.

It took the procession over half an hour to pass through the triumphal arch of evergreen which had been constructed outside the Blue Boar public house. Inevitably it was late arriving in Monk's Road and the sweep, who had been employed to emerge from a chimney, foaming tankard of ale in hand, almost suffocated before a tap on the roof signalled that the Lord Mayor was approaching and his brief moment of glory had arrived. As the head of the procession passed the forest of flags and banners that had been planted at the main gate, William cut the strings which held the nets of balloons and with an eerily silent certainty the red, white and blue spheres gently rose in the air. As far as he could tell, nobody noticed, for the procession still held the crowd's attention. Taking Anne by the hand, he hurried down towards the terrace. He could not get within fifty yards of the platform on which the opening ceremony was to be held but, sitting his daughter on his shoulder, he patiently waited for the pageant which he knew would follow.

It began with fifty girls, dressed as fairies, dancing from the pavilion in what the programme described as 'The Ballet of Surrender'. Then the fairy queen, a stout lady of mature years, made an exaggerated entrance and ceremonially broke her wand across a buxom knee to signify abdication of her reign. Next a group of elderly men, dressed as monks, handed the Mayor a huge roll of paper which he accepted as the charter by which the City of Lincoln was granted rights in perpetuity over the land. The whole ceremony was ended by the fairies – some thought in retaliation for their expulsion from the land – reciting verse which had been specially composed for the occasion. After they had spoken their lines of doggerel for about twenty minutes, the spectators began to drift away and even the most courteous of the official guests began to make furtive examinations of their pocket watches. The performance was brought to a sudden and merciful end by the vindication of Keeper Hodson's forecast. Without warning, the arboretum was suddenly engulfed in a downpour that drenched most of the crowd in the time it took to run from the open ground around the gate to the shelter of the trees, tea room and adjoining houses. Only the official guests

99

escaped. They hurried from under their awning to the more secure shelter of the pavilion, where tea and entertainment awaited them.

'You've got the girl wet through,' said Elizabeth, fumbling as she attempted to pull off her daughter's sodden clothes.

'What else could I do? It was a cloudburst. One minute it was dry. The next we were all drenched.'

'You must have seen the sky.' Elizabeth spoke as if people lucky enough to possess all their faculties did not always realise the importance of using them.

Anne winced as her mother roughly pulled a dry vest over her head. She said, 'You promised we'd go to see the fireworks.'

Her mother turned in what she believed to be her husband's direction. 'What does she mean?'

'I've told her that there's a fireworks display tonight. I promised her that she could stay up.'

'He did. He promised.'

'It's too late. It begins a long time after you should be in bed.'

Her mother believed that life's lessons – particularly the inevitability of disappointment – should be learned early. One of them concerned her husband's irresponsibility.

'He promised,' Anne repeated doggedly.

'Your father should have known better.'

'Seven o'clock. Six it starts. That's not too late. I hoped you'd walk up with us. There's a space to stand the pram.'

'To hear the noise.'

'You'll probably be able to see a lot of it yourself. You've said yourself you can tell light from dark now. You'll see the rockets at least. You're getting better. You said so yourself.'

'We'd be up to our knees in mud, if the rain's as hard as you say.'

William capitulated. 'If it goes on like this, there won't be any fireworks at all.'

His wife seized triumphantly on his disappointment.

'I can hear the rain on the windows. It's pelting down. There'll be no fireworks tonight.'

'You promised fireworks.'

Anne looked at her father with a reproach that her mother could not have matched. Her mother took her hand and pulled hard to capture her affection. Ernest began to howl.

'It's no good. No matter how much noise you make,' her mother told him, 'you can't stop it raining.'

The rain which rapped against the windows in Thomas Street beat so loudly on the arboretum's glass pavilion that the special guests had to shout their pleasantries to make themselves heard. The string quartet played on, knowing that their music was barely audible, and the soloists looked nervously up at the ceiling as if it might collapse under the bombardment. At the end of the advertised programme, the Lord Mayor announced that the fireworks display was cancelled and that the artistes had generously agreed to continue the entertainment for a further hour in the hope that the downpour would soon abate. Further drinks were served.

Alfred Ellison, standing alone in a corner of the pavilion's *grand salon*, felt profoundly contented. The job was successfully done. Foundations for three rows of houses had already been dug on the arboretum's boundary. In two days he would be home in Wisbech luxuriating in his enhanced reputation. And before that there would be two evenings of celebration, dinner parties in Lindum Terrace at which he would receive the congratulations of the Lincoln quality. He felt especially virtuous about Sunday's gathering, for he had invited William Skinner and his wife despite their lowly position in the city's social hierarchy. Of course they had declined – as he had known they would. But they had been invited.

The rain showed no signs of abating. To those inside the glass pavilion, safe and secure against the deluge but able to see every flash of lightning and hear every clap of thunder, the world seemed wonderful. Sheets of water ran down the sloping glass roof and some of the people beneath it began to wonder if they would ever go home. They chose simply to wait for another glass of hock and oblivion. But a few hardy souls decided that they would brave the storm. Amongst them was Alfred Ellison, who was determined to be home in time to supervise the arrangements for his evening soirée.

As a dozen or so of the Lord Mayor's guests dashed down the hill to the carriages which now awaited them in Monk's Road, Alfred Ellison made his best speed towards the Lindum Terrace entrance and home. As he passed the retaining wall that Edward Milner had designed in the style of Hampton Court, he paused and snorted. The rain ran down inside his collar and he could feel water squelching in his shoes. Not even an earthquake would have stopped him glowering at what he regarded – for no better reason than that he had not designed it himself – as a monstrosity. At first he could scarcely believe what he saw.

He approached more closely and had his first impressions confirmed by the flood of water which splashed across his feet. The wall had cracked.

It was not his wall and it held up nothing more important than a dozen back gardens. There were no children in the arboretum to be crushed to death and he had preparations to make for a dinner party. The wall, he decided, would hold and if it collapsed the blame would cascade down on Edward Milner. Alfred Ellison walked on.

CHAPTER EIGHT

After the Flood

The wall collapsed in the small hours of Sunday morning. The hillside was deserted at the time of the catastrophe, so the devastation was not discovered until one of Lindum Terrace's most influential residents looked out of his back bedroom window to marvel at the ferocity of the storm and found that his back garden had disappeared. He roused his sleeping neighbours, who – despite the day, the hour and the downpour – organised an immediate search party for the missing acres of private property. They found several thousand tons of soil spread neatly across the upper slopes of the arboretum. Its smooth surface was broken only by protruding roots, splinters of garden furniture and the remains of ornamental urns.

The city surveyor was roused from his bed and brought to the site. Being an honourable man, he promised compensation immediately. The residents were not mollified. They demanded retribution, the most strident demands coming from those householders who had suffered the least loss. Michael Drury, who was reasonable as well as honourable, insisted – much to the general dissatisfaction – that the culprits must be discovered before punishment could be meted out. The enraged burghers then recalled that the contractor had rented a house on the other – the unravaged – side of the road. They formed up outside Alfred Ellison's elaborate front door and shouted in the direction of his over-decorated drawing-room window. The miscreant appeared, wholly unaware of the catastrophe which had befallen his callers.

The need to explain the cause of their anger deflected the residents' energy from the task of excoriating the man they held responsible for their predicament. And they were diverted even from that task by the disputes about which of them had suffered worst.

'There's only half of my garden left,' said one.

'Less than half of mine,' said another.

'I'd just had turf laid,' another added.

'My turf had taken root,' insisted the man who had lost half his garden.

Alfred Ellison, still in dressing gown and bedroom slippers, looked on bewildered whilst Michael Drury, who had reluctantly followed the protesters across the road, addressed them in his best military manner.

'Look here, you're probably causing a breach of the peace. You can't invade Mr Ellison's front garden like this. You're behaving like a mob of Chartists.'

Stung by the suggestion that their conduct was comparable to that of men demanding parliamentary representation, the householders from the south side of Lindum Terrace kicked at the gravel on Alfred Ellison's drive and looked up at the clouds which still scudded across the sky. One by one, they turned for home, there to count their losses, confident that a man of the city surveyor's authority would do right by them. Drury walked into Alfred Ellison's hall.

'It's a bad business.' Michael Drury looked grave.

'I don't doubt it, but it's not my responsibility.'

'How can you say that, man? Everything out there was your responsibility.'

'You may say so, Mr Drury, but I doubt if the courts would agree. Edward Milner designed that wall. Fancy brickwork, Mr Drury. In the style of Hampton Court, if you remember. I don't blame him, or you for that matter. The very same householders who are complaining now are the ones who demanded it. But that's what happened. As I recall, he exercised his powers under Clause Five of the contract.'

'Who did the work?'

'My men. Skinner, my man Skinner, supervised it, day by day. But it was Edward Milner's work. Clause Five, Mr Drury, Clause Five.'

'Be serious, man. This could ruin somebody's reputation.'

'Not mine, Mr Drury, not mine.'

'Do you think that this man Skinner did the work as he was instructed?'

'Of course he did. He didn't know enough to go his own way. Yard-deep footings. He had them dug. Double bonding. He saw that the bricklayers did it. That's all he could do.'

'Why on earth did you take him on? Why didn't you get a proper tradesman?'

Alfred Ellison could have told the truth. He could have said that it was all an absurd mistake, that he had only offered William Skinner the job when he thought that the offer was not within his gift, that the whole idea of a workhouse master becoming his horticultural consultant had originally been a dream and that his desire to be loved and admired had trapped him into a series of decisions which he now desperately regretted. But he said none of those things. For there was an easier answer.

'I told you. I told you on the first day that we met. He'd been in trouble. I suppose that I was foolish to trust him. But I wanted to give him another chance.'

'Trust him, Mr Ellison, trust him? What does that mean?'

'He got a woman into trouble. A woman in his care.'

'But, trust him, Mr Ellison. Are you saying that he might not have done what Mr Milner told him?'

Alfred Ellison realised that by doubting William Skinner he might be condemning himself. If the contractor's foreman was guilty, Milner might claim that the contractor was responsible. Just for once in his life, self-interest, honour and the fantasy of his good nature all pointed him in the same direction.

'I've told you. I trust him. He'd do whatever Mr Milner told him to do.'

'We'll have to see what Milner says about it himself.'

Milner had no doubts. He had specified four-foot-deep foundations and had been precise in every detail about how they should be constructed. He had not returned to the site until the footings had been completed. But he had asked for express assurances that his instructions had been carried out. The surveyor congratulated the consultant on his prescience.

'I must say, Milner, if you'd expected trouble, you could hardly have prepared yourself more thoroughly.'

'I hope you're not implying that I was negligent. I've got a professional reputation to protect.'

'Protect it all you wish, Mr Milner. I'll make up my own mind. I'll have all those foundations dug out and find how deep they are. I'll talk to Skinner—'

'You'll match his word against mine! An unqualified workman and a disgraced workhouse master. The man's an admitted fornicator.'

'I like fornication no more than you do. But fornicators can measure and they can dig. I'm a scientist, Mr Milner. It's just not scientific to say that, because a man is an adulterer, he's a bad workman. You will recall that King David built the temple.'

'I didn't know that, Mr Drury. I'm not a Jew.'

'Neither am I, Mr Milner. Just an educated man.'

Michael Drury realised that each man was beginning to say things which, having been said, could never be forgiven or forgotten. He decided to bring the acrimonious discussion to an amicable end.

104

'I'll do the work on the site and I'll talk to Skinner. Then we'll have dinner and decide how to clear up this mess. The important thing is to rebuild those gardens. The committee will worry about who's to blame. But I can persuade them not to do anything foolish. Don't worry about that.'

The effect of his emollience was not what he intended.

'Don't patronise me, Surveyor. And don't suggest – don't even imply – that I am in any way responsible. I have a reputation to protect – a very considerable reputation, if I may say so. And I don't propose to see my good name damaged by a landslip in a little public park. I shall say no more to you on the matter. I shall stay for the next ten days at Welbeck. I am advising on the landscaping of the Abbey water garden. You may address me there, courtesy of the Duke of Portland. Unless I hear from you within the week, apologising for what you have said today, you will hear from my solicitor.'

It was the Duke of Portland's bailiff who called at Henry Hodding's offices in Cheapside. He was an unctuous man, as befitted his calling, and all of his requests were supplications. He seemed genuinely discomfited by the message which he carried.

'His Grace realises that this is not the sort of work that you usually take on. But he feels reluctant to ask his own solicitors to act professionally against the Lincoln Corporation. And this man is agitating. If we don't get it all cleared up, we'll never get the water garden laid out.'

Henry Hodding never turned down work. Assuming that there was a prospect of payment, he would have represented a collier suing his pit for delay in the delivery of his free coal. No apology was therefore needed for a request – made on behalf of the Duke of Portland – for him to act on behalf of a society landscape gardener who believed that he had been defamed by the Lincoln Corporation.

'Send the man to me this afternoon.'

'I think that he rather hoped you would come out to Welbeck. His time is very valuable.'

'No doubt it is. But I'd only go out to Welbeck to see the Duke himself. And then I'd charge more than this man could afford. Send him to me this afternoon. Not before four o'clock and no later than four-thirty.'

Edward Milner arrived at five minutes past four in a carriage with a strawberry-leaved coronet on the door. He had been easily persuaded to leave his drawing board. When he remembered the way in which he had been treated by the Lincoln surveyor he was instantly filled with a righteous indignation which demanded immediate redress of his grievance. Henry Hodding found it difficult to follow the plaintiff's account of events.

'. . . a workman. Not even a tradesman. And this surveyor asked him to verify what I said—'

'And did he?'

'How should I know? I didn't stop to ask. If they won't take my word—'

'Word for what?'

'Word for the foundations which I told him to dig. I told him four feet.'

'And did you check to see that he'd done as you told him?'

'Why should I do that? I'm used to my instructions being followed. Why should I have checked?'

'I can't answer that question until I see your contract.'

'Contract? I didn't have a contract. I'm not a tradesman. I'm a professional man. Michael Drury wrote to me – one gentleman to another – and asked me to advise. I wrote back saying that I would.'

'What did the letter say?'

'I've told you. It asked me to be consultant. Look here, Hodding, I don't expect to be cross-examined by you. All I want is for you to write a stiff note to the people at Lincoln and get an apology.'

'An apology for what?'

'Saying that I was responsible for the wall collapsing.'

'Did they say that?'

'They certainly implied it.'

'When?'

'On the morning after it happened.'

Henry Hodding was losing patience. The Turnpike Trust met in Retford at six o'clock. He could not be late because he meant to leave early for the Volunteers' parade at seven. If he drove himself home to Harness Grove, with Gerrard Knock sitting next to him on the box, trembling every time the coach swayed round a corner, he could be bathed and changed in time to welcome his supper guests. He would have to sacrifice his evening's exercise with the Indian clubs but he would do an extra half-hour with his weights on the following morning. He had no more time to spare on the muddled and imprecise Edward Milner.

'If you want me to represent you, I will. But you'll have to put it in my hands. I shall go to Lincoln next week and see the town clerk. You'd better come with me. One way or another, we'll have it decided on the day.'

'One way or another . . . ?'

'One way or another if we get no satisfaction you will have to take my advice about how to proceed. I can't see this case being worth an action.'

'You mean we wouldn't take them to court?'

'I can't tell you that now, Mr Milner.' Henry Hodding took out his pocket watch, tapped the glass and stared at the face as if he could not believe that the hands had moved so far and so fast since it was last consulted. He already knew the exact time but he was not sure if his visitor understood the relationship between time and money. 'Till next week, then!'

'Till next week,' repeated Edward Milner mechanically.

Henry Hodding assumed such complete command of their relationship that on the following Tuesday he arrived at Worksop station half an hour before the Lincoln train left rather than risk keeping his legal adviser waiting.

Edward Milner had failed to find the letter which had appointed him consultant to the Arboretum Construction Company. He therefore expected that the forty-minute journey would be taken up with an aggressive cross-examination and he determined to hold his own against what – when not in Henry Hodding's forbidding presence – he thought of as impertinence.

The solicitor's carriage pulled up outside the station only a few seconds before the train was due to leave. Whilst Edward Milner fretted and fumed in the waiting room, Henry Hodding leaped across the bridge which connected the platforms. He was followed – at a distance – by Gerrard Knock, a small wizened figure in chocolate-brown livery. The solicitor carried a carpet-bag. His bearer bore a huge bundle of loose papers. By the time the uniformed dwarf reached the carriage door the guard had blown his whistle and waved his green flag. Henry Hodding sat, already comfortable and composed, in a corner seat, holding the door half open ready to receive the documents which his servant flung at his feet, just as the engine hooted and began to move eastwards. Solicitor smiled at client.

'You'll forgive me if I deal with these?'

Systematically but with a speed which made Edward Milner doubt that their contents were being fully comprehended, Henry Hodding worked through the briefs and opinions, tugging at the pink tape which bound them, opening out the stiff legal paper with a flourish which implied impatience rather than the wish to impress, and then piling them neatly on the empty seat beside him. As the train pulled into Lincoln station, the carpet-bag was hurriedly opened and found to be stuffed with books, documents and the spare shirt and extra starched collar which was essential to a travelling solicitor who wished to look as crisp and clean after lunch as before it. Snapping the bag shut again, he spoke his second sentence of the entire journey.

'Do you mind carrying these papers out to the cab?'

Assuming that his wish was granted, Henry Hodding opened the carriage door before the train had come to rest, scattering the passengers who were waiting on the platform. Within five minutes they were in the City Chambers.

Alfred Ellison and Michael Drury were waiting for them in the town clerk's office. Edward Milner shook hands like a man who expected to be affronted. Henry Hodding set out his client's case in the manner of a man who had already wasted too much time.

'Mr Milner has no wish to sue if such unpleasantness and an expensive action can be avoided. But there is no doubt that his professional competence – perhaps his integrity – has been questioned. If you, Town Clerk, make clear on behalf of the Corporation that there is no suggestion of blame attached to him, we can go about our business. I will be frank with you and admit that I advised my client to ask for damages. But, being a gentleman, he is naturally reluctant to enter into litigation. Respecting his wishes, I too hope that it will not be necessary.'

The town clerk was about to reply in what, if his ingratiating demeanour was any guide, would have been conciliatory language. And Edward Milner seemed to be fighting to construct a sentence which would adequately represent his opinion. But Michael Drury's reply pre-empted whatever either of them might say.

'There can be no question of an apology or anything like it. For there is the matter of the fee.'

Edward Milner found his voice. 'Indeed there is. My duties were completed six weeks ago and it has not been paid.'

'Nor will it be,' said the city surveyor, 'until we are certain about liability.'

The town clerk coughed before he addressed the protagonists. Smiling, he turned first to Milner, then to Ellison and finally to Drury. Eventually his glance fell, apparently by chance, on Henry Hodding. Having stumbled across the other lawyer in the room he chose to address his remarks exclusively to his professional equal.

'You will, I know, have read Clause Five of the standard Lincoln Corporation contract and the copy of Mr Milner's letter of appointment. Both of which I sent to you by return of post as requested.' Henry Hodding did not think it necessary to confirm the town clerk's statement. It was a simple reiteration of an established fact intended to convince the laymen present that matters had been dealt with in a proper legal fashion. 'Subsection little c, Roman xi is explicit and referred to in the letter. Any claims for damages incurred by the negligence of the consultant may be met by withdrawing the consultancy fee in whole or part. I fear, Mr Hodding, that restoring those gardens and rebuilding that wall will cost a great deal more than two hundred guineas.'

'Negligence!' Edward Milner repeated the word syllable by syllable as if he were struggling to understand its meaning. His legal adviser grasped the full implication at once.

'How could Mr Milner be negligent in the performance of duties which were not his responsibility?'

'The Lindum Terrace wall was his responsibility. Mr Ellison here, being only a builder, couldn't design anything that looked right. So we asked Mr Milner to take charge. And we paid him for it.'

There were times, thought the town clerk, when the city surveyor's direct manner was a positive advantage.

Alfred Ellison looked as if he had been horse-whipped, and the town clerk added a codicil.

'The surveyor is a most meticulous man. He has a copy of his offer letter, initialled by Mr Milner.'

'Of course I do. We offered an extra twenty guineas in supplementary fees.'

'That', said Henry Hodding, changing his defence without showing the slightest sign of doubt in his case, 'does not mean that my client is culpable of negligence. All we know is that a wall fell down.'

'We know that the foundations weren't deep enough.' Michael Drury had grown tired of the shadow-boxing. 'We were promised four feet and we got barely two. I measured them myself the day after the storm.'

'The implication of what you say . . .' Henry Hodding was not allowed to complete his carefully worded warning.

'That was Skinner's fault.' Edward Milner's indignation was uncontrollable. 'And he's employed by Alfred Ellison, not me. I gave him clear enough instructions.'

'He says otherwise,' said the surveyor. 'And I believe him.'

Henry Hodding stood up, banging the town clerk's desk with malice aforethought. The paperweights and silver-framed pictures danced on the green baize and the cut-glass ink bottles rang in their brass stand like cracked bells.

'We can't remain here whilst my client is called a liar as well as an incompetent. Come, Mr Milner. We will consider further discussions when this . . . er . . . gentleman has regained his manners.'

Solicitor and visibly injured party left the office without a handshake or a farewell. As they walked along the dark corridors of the City Chambers, Edward Milner concentrated all his energy on being offended. Out in the street he began to remonstrate with his legal adviser. 'I am surprised and very disappointed that you didn't demand an apology. An instant apology to follow.'

His face turned pink, red and purple as if the resentment was rising in him like mercury in a thermometer.

'I didn't ask him for an apology in case we couldn't get one. I only walked out because I didn't want you to say any more before I had time to think. I don't like walking out. You only have to walk back again one day. I don't like the sound of things.'

Edward Milner's face turned from purple to white as if all the resentment had run out of him in a single second.

'I tell you that I told Skinner to make it four feet. No court is going to take his word against mine. I know that, for some reason, you're against going to court. But I'm not. Not now. My reputation will be in ruins.'

'It will be if you sue and lose.'

'I was thinking about winning.'

'Don't think about anything until you've told me more about Skinner.'

The reply had to await their arrival at the station. Edward Milner – panting along beside his solicitor and wishing they had not made their dramatic exit from the town clerk's office before their cab had arrived – did not possess enough breath to damn the character of the foreman until he was sitting down in the first-class waiting room. Then denunciation was so comprehensive that it continued, without pause, until the arrival of the Worksop train.

The ever faithful Gerrard Knock – who, knowing his master's habits, had also met the two previous Lincoln trains – was standing at the ticket barrier. He relieved his master of the carpet-bag but he left Edward Milner to carry the bundle of legal papers. Then he followed the two men to the carriage which was standing – with an urchin holding the horse's head – fifty yards down the station approach. Henry Hodding took advantage of the interruption in his client's flow of continuous outrage to ask his first question.

'Tell me again what Skinner did or is alleged to have done.'

'He became involved with a woman. He fathered her baby.'

'So you said. But can you remember no more?'

'It is not the sort of subject on which I choose to dwell. He was taken on by Ellison as an act of charity. No qualifications whatsoever. I know that.'

'So you said.' Henry Hodding hated repeating himself but Edward

110

Milner had complained about the lack of qualifications for most of the journey. 'And you can't recall where it all happened?'

'In East Anglia somewhere. I think that it was Grantham. At least that's where Ellison had gone when I made my first visit to the arboretum site. Ellison and Skinner came from the same town. No qualifications either of them.'

They were back in the carriage and as it turned into Overend Road the solicitor, fearful that he would have to listen to complaints about lack of qualifications all the way back to his office, offered what he hoped was reassurance.

'Well, these details can be found out easily enough. That fact alone is enough to destroy the man's credibility.'

Henry Hodding climbed down from the carriage before it had come to a complete halt outside his office. He shouted to his coachman as he pushed open the imposing door.

'Take Mr Milner to Welbeck and then come directly back to me. Fast as you can.'

As always, Gerrard Knock obeyed his instructions to the last detail. He rattled his passenger up Sparken Hill and raced him through the gates of Welbeck Abbey. He then returned to Cheapside at top pace – even though he dreaded the duty which he knew he had to perform. When Henry Hodding came out of his office, he was surprised to find his driver not sitting on his box but holding the horse's head.

'Could I have a word with you, sir?'

'For God's sake, man, not out here. Not in the road.'

'I couldn't leave the horse, sir. Begging your pardon, sir, but it will only take a minute.'

'I haven't got a minute. But if it's important . . .'

'It is, sir.'

'Then get on with it.'

'I couldn't help overhearing what you were saying to that Mr Milner, sir. What you said as you walked to the carriage.'

'That doesn't matter. You're not a man to eavesdrop on purpose. As long as you keep it to yourself.'

Henry Hodding was about to move towards the carriage door when, to his astonishment, his own coachman placed a restraining hand on his arm. 'Begging your pardon again, sir, but that isn't it. I know this William Skinner, sir. He was the workhouse master at Wisbech when I was foreman. He's the one you wrote to about me. He gave me a good character.'

The solicitor shook himself free. 'It's of no consequence.'

'But it is, sir. He's a good man. He didn't get the girl in the family

111

way. My Rosie's sure of that and she's never wrong about a man's character. If I'm any judge—'

'You aren't any judge. Get up on to that box and drive me home.'

'Yes, sir. But he's an honest man, sir. He deserves a chance.'

'I doubt if I shall be able to give him one.'

The town clerk was surprised to receive so conciliatory a letter. Henry Hodding's client asked for no more than a private apology and the immediate payment of all outstanding fees. The facts were not in dispute. One William Skinner, appointed by the main contractor to supervise the construction, was a man without professional training. His sworn statement that he had been instructed to dig footings to only half the stipulated depth would not be accepted by anyone who knew of his record. It could be argued that Alfred Ellison had been culpably negligent in putting such a man in charge of the work. But the main contractor had been motivated solely by charity and – since he was prepared to accept that his foreman was to blame – the Council would, no doubt, wish to overlook his foolishness.

'I think they're worried,' the town clerk said to his surveyor.

'Perhaps this Hodding man has discovered what a liar Milner is.'

'My dear Drury, you'll ruin the Corporation if you continue to slander respectable citizens in the Council's name. In any case, how can you be so sure?'

'Because I believe William Skinner to be an honest man.'

'I shan't risk proving it. Not with his record.'

'If you sacrifice him, you throw away two hundred and twenty guineas.'

'It's the safest thing. When Milner comes next week, I'll apologise on behalf of us all. That will keep your Scottish pride intact. Skinner will be required to confess on threat of prosecution for negligence. And we'll all live happily ever after.'

'Not everyone, Town Clerk.'

'That's none of your concern. Just do me the courtesy of being here next Wednesday at eleven o'clock. I just want this little drama to be brought to a quick end.'

The dramatis personae all assembled in good time. Michael Drury sat in a distant corner of the town clerk's office with his long legs stretched out in front of him in the manner of a man who thought of himself as a spectator rather than a participant in the events which were to follow. William Skinner, neater and cleaner even than usual, sat next to Alfred Ellison. Both men looked tense but the contractor looked more nervous than his foreman.

Henry Hodding entered the room with his hand already extended.

He did not propose to waste time on prolonged greetings. He was formally introduced to the contractor. The foreman, as befitted his station, was ignored.

The town clerk offered a brief but comprehensive apology. When he emphasised, for the second time, that he spoke for the Corporation as a whole, he turned towards the surveyor as if anticipating at least a nod of agreement, but Michael Drury was staring at the ceiling like a man preoccupied with deep thoughts of his own. Alfred Ellison seemed about to offer his support; but, having leaned forward in his chair, he sank back again without speaking.

'The main contractor accepts that the mistake was made by a man in his employment. But since the man was not under his supervision at the time . . .' The town clerk let the sentence drift away rather than risk inviting speculation about who was supervising the foreman when the footings were dug. Alfred Ellison nodded. He half turned in his chair to repeat the gesture in Henry Hodding's direction but, when he realised that the second act of ingratiation would require him to look William Skinner in the eye, he raised his hand to his mouth and gave an artificial little cough.

'All we now need is for Skinner to say his piece.'

The town clerk believed that the disagreeable work was almost done.

William Skinner stood up. With his hands clasped in front of him and his head bowed, he seemed to embody contrition. Too damn contrite to be genuine, Henry Hodding thought. And too damn well turned out for a building foreman or a jobbing gardener or whatever he was supposed to be. His brown boots shone more brightly than any other boots in the room and his suit, although well worn, had been carefully pressed. Henry Hodding thought of some downtrodden wife heating the flat-iron on the kitchen fire and smoothing out the creases between damp cloth and table.

'Speak up, Skinner,' said the town clerk, staring at the miscreant, who unclasped his hands, lifted his head and stared back.

'Until I got here, I intended to say what you would have me say. And I'm sorry to spring the truth on you unawares. But sitting here I've decided that I won't do it. I was told – told by Mr Milner – that twenty-four-inch footings would do. He told me that we didn't have the rubble to fill deeper foundations and as the wall didn't bear a big load there was no need to wait for the extra stone.'

Only Henry Hodding retained sufficient composure to reply. He did not condescend to speak to William Skinner.

'This man's statement is of no consequence. We all know that he is lying. You must deal with him as you think fit. I doubt if his opinion

113

is likely to prejudice many landowners against the employment of Mr Milner. I'm grateful for your gracious attention. That's all we need.'

'I'm not at all sure it is . . .' Edward Milner had turned purple without bothering to precede his transformation with even brief moments of pink and red.

'Get out of here, Skinner,' said the town clerk.

'Not until he's admitted he's a liar.' Edward Milner had taken on so deep a shade of puce that Alfred Ellison feared that a sudden death was about to be added to the horrors he was being forced to witness.

'William,' he said, 'how can you be so foolish – so foolish and ungrateful? You'll lose the six months' work with Mr Drury . . .'

'I'm not sure that he will.' The surveyor spoke from the back of the room, like a man who had just awakened.

'This is getting out of hand.' Henry Hodding had an edge in his voice. 'You must excuse us for a minute. I want to ask my client for new instructions.'

'For God's sake, William.' Alfred Ellison seemed on the verge of hysteria. 'You said that you'd take the blame. You told me that you would.'

'I did and at the time I meant it.' William Skinner sounded apologetic. 'You are my friend, Alfred.' He paused, astonished by his own effrontery in calling the contractor by his Christian name in front of such elevated company. 'You are my friend and I took your advice. But last night my wife said that I shouldn't do it. And sitting here I suddenly decided that she was right.'

'What on earth is it to do with your wife?' the town clerk asked.

William could not adequately describe his wife's involvement in the matter. So he simply repeated what she had told him. 'She said that I should show some pride and that I should have more respect for our reputation than to take the blame for something that I hadn't done.'

'I understood that there wasn't much left of your reputation.' Edward Milner's face was distorted with hatred and contempt. 'I'd heard that you took this job after you'd been chased out of King's Lynn or Peterborough or somewhere out there – chased out because you're a fornicator. I thought—'

'Now look here . . .' Michael Drury's admonition was unnecessary. Henry Hodding had already gripped his client's arm so tightly that he had frightened him into temporary silence.

'To be honest, sir, that is part of it. My wife said that we'd been treated unjustly once and shouldn't be treated unjustly again. She's a great believer in self-respect and didn't want us to sacrifice any more.'

Edward Milner decided that his own self-respect required him to throw off his solicitor's hand and speak up for himself. 'We! Us! I didn't know that your wife was involved in this. I didn't know that she built the wall or dug the footings.'

'She thinks that any reflection on me is a reflection on her. She thinks that I should have self-respect for her sake.'

'Bravo!' cried Michael Drury. 'You should be proud of her, Skinner.'

Pride, thought Henry Hodding, is playing far too great a part in this discussion. Pride is not a good guide when legal niceties have to be weighed against each other.

'Town Clerk, this cannot go on. We will take our leave of you. You shall hear from me when my client has decided how he wishes to proceed.'

That night, when Henry Hodding arrived home in Worksop, he handed Gerrard Knock his carpet-bag as usual but, instead of stalking off to his carriage without waiting for the limping coachman, he slowed his pace so that they could walk into the station approach together.

'Cost me a lot of money, your old friend William Skinner. I can't see any fees coming my way for this one. Lincoln won't pay me and I can't imagine charging that ass Milner. He's lost two hundred and twenty guineas as the price of his stupidity.'

Gerrard Knock whistled with astonishment.

'He deserved to lose it, Knock. Conceited. Lazy. Dishonest. Not bad qualifications for a professional man. But, if he hadn't been so stupid, I would probably have kept it for him. Learn the lesson. You can get away with most things as long as you are not stupid.'

'Yes, sir.' They had reached the carriage.

'I liked him. I liked your friend Skinner. He seems to have been badly treated, one way and another.'

'Yes, sir, he's a good man. I've often thought that. If you ever want to have another gardener . . .' The impertinence of the suggestion was so great that he could not bring himself to finish the sentence.

'It's his wife I'd like to employ,' said Henry Hodding. 'She seems a marvellous woman.'

Rosie Knock had a favourite saying which she repeated to her husband time after time. 'If you can't say anything good about your fellow men, don't say anything.' Gerrard remembered his wife's advice and opened the carriage door in silence.

CHAPTER NINE

Taking Root

'It is my dearest wish that I never see any of those deplorable people again.'

The town clerk smiled bleakly as he waved a decanter in the surveyor's direction. Michael Drury declined the whisky and wondered if he could also avoid the pointless recriminations which he expected to follow. His first instinct was to grunt and leave. But he suddenly felt an irresistible desire to argue with the self-satisfied lawyer behind the huge mahogany desk.

'I thought that Hodding was very impressive. Kept Ellison on a short rein. Kept control of things. He'll go a long way.'

'Not from Worksop he won't.' The town clerk spoke as if Lincoln were the centre of the universe. 'I know his sort. Railway lawyer. All he knows about is way-leaves. I didn't enjoy doing business with him. Birds of a feather, him and Ellison, if you ask me. How on earth did we come to employ that deplorable fellow?'

'He put in the lowest tender. Lowest by a lot.'

'And what did you think of Skinner? Pretty cool, eh? Especially considering . . .'

'Considering what?'

'Considering what he did. Didn't you know? He got a girl with child somewhere in East Anglia. Not a strong position to be high and mighty.'

'I don't believe it. That was Ellison's story. Ellison's a liar. We know that now. Skinner didn't sound like a rogue to me. He sounded like an honest man who'd been badly treated and decided that he was not going to be treated badly any more.'

'Really, Drury, you have some absurd notions.'

'I have the notions which the army taught me, Town Clerk. One of them is that officers have a responsibility for the men who serve under them.'

'I stand reproved, Surveyor. Have you any other uplifting advice to offer me?'

116

'Not advice. But you might like to know how we're going to pay our debt to Skinner.'

Michael Drury had grown impatient with the complicated rituals of the town clerk's conversation. He did not wait to be asked ironic questions about how the debt had been incurred and calculated.

'I'm taking him on to move the earth back to where it belongs in Lindum Terrace and—'

'You don't mean that you're going to give him the contract? He can't do it. I know it's a small job but he's just a working man. He can't do it. I won't authorise it. I won't sign.'

'I'm not contracting the job out. I'm running it myself. Those Lindum Terrace people have told me that I'm responsible often enough. If I'm responsible for it falling down, I'll take direct responsibility for putting it back. Skinner will be my foreman.'

'I hope you know what you're doing.'

'I'm paying a debt, Town Clerk.' Michael Drury pulled himself up from the sofa and took two long strides to the door. 'And I'm also doing you a favour. I offered Skinner six months' employment keeping an eye on the saplings and shrubs until they are bedded in. That sort of thing. Replacing the shrubs that had died without taking root. He can do that when the soil's moved and the gardens are rebuilt. We don't want him suing the Corporation for breach of contract.'

William Skinner accepted the surveyor's offer with undisguised gratitude but his wife adjusted to what she regarded as a further fall in their status with equally obvious resentment. Almost ten years before, she had accepted the workhouse master's proposal, knowing that she was marrying beneath her and since then every twist of fortune had pitched her another rung down the social ladder. Elizabeth knew that it was her duty to accept fate with resignation and fortitude but she was not capable of hiding her feeling of shame. Since she suffered, she made sure that her husband knew of it.

It took almost a year to rebuild the gardens. The retaining wall – as strong and ugly as anything that Michael Drury had designed for Kashmir or Hyderabad – was put together, stone by stone, under the surveyor's constant supervision.

'This time', the foreman told his navvies, 'we're going to get it right. That's why we're going careful.'

They were just as careful scraping the soil from the crushed grass and shovelling it up from around the bowls of submerged bushes. During the last few days of his back-breaking labour, William Skinner began to look forward to the six months which lay ahead with a mixture of excitement and apprehension. The prospect of devoting his days to the cultivation of trees and plants filled him with delight, but he knew that when his brief stewardship was over he would still have a family to keep – and he had no idea of how he would support them. On the first morning of what he once believed would be six months of bliss, instead of feeling the anticipated elation he looked back with nostalgia on the comparative security of the previous year.

The digging and carting went on during an uneventful autumn and winter and a spring enlivened only by one moment of excitement. At Easter, within a week of clearing and cleansing being finished, William Skinner received a letter from Rosie Knock – addressed care of the arboretum and handed over by Lodge-Keeper Hodson without him noticing that William turned white when he read the name of the sender on the back of the envelope and immediately strode off to the far reaches of the arboretum to read his message in private.

The letter had been written with obvious difficulty and after consultation with Gerrard Knock, to whom reference was made in almost every line. Indeed, Rosie was at pains to point out that the plan – which followed the expressions of regret about the Skinners' continued misfortune – emanated from her husband. Harness Grove's ancient gardener had taken to his bed and gossip from the outbuildings in which the unmarried servants lived suggested that he would not last until the summer. In any event, despite Henry Hodding's notorious kindness, neither his patience nor his pocket was inexhaustible. If that gardener did not die by harvest time, a new gardener would have to be appointed to replace him. The coachman proposed to tell his master where a new gardener could be found. If William was not free – or not willing – to take up such an appointment, Rosie asked that he write at once to spare Gerrard the disappointment of backing a horse that would not run.

William read the final page for a second and third time just for the pleasure of repeatedly visualising the establishment Rosie Knock described.

There is a walled kitchen garden to the side of the house which is all herbs and a kitchen garden round the back but no root vegetables. These are grown on the home farm. There are lawns in front and ponds with lilies and two big cypress trees. The flower beds under windows are overgrown because the old gardener had been sick for so long. There are raspberry canes and strawberry beds round the back and rockeries from the gate up the drive with many foreign plants both from Italy and Switzerland. I think there is an orchard behind but that is not the gardener's business.

It was all too good to be true and, in William Skinner's unusually pessimistic judgement, the product of Gerrard Knock's wishful thinking. William could visualise him, exhilarated from a day with the horses, stimulated by several bottles of stout and suddenly moved to tears by a fit of maudlin concern for the bad times on which his old friend had fallen. Then he imagined what Elizabeth would say if he told her that Knock – once his workhouse foreman and, in her estimation, a household servant – was trying to rescue him from unemployment. He decided that it did not matter. He would not tell her. Courtesy required him to answer Rosie Knock's enquiry. He would truthfully explain that he would gladly work at Harness Grove. And that would be the end of the episode. It was all wishful thinking. He would, he decided ruefully, not hear from Rosie again.

Rosie Knock read William Skinner's reply with an anxiety which rendered her almost illiterate. First she practised the pronunciation of each word silently inside her head, picking them out one by one with her finger to assist her concentration. Then, still stumbling over every sentence, she recited the contents to her husband in a voice and manner which she thought appropriate to the importance of the occasion.

'Speak normal,' said Gerrard Knock. 'Speak normal. It's just a letter, not a Royal Proclamation by the Queen.'

His wife blushed. But her vocal cords would not produce their usual tones. She still sounded like a publican's wife at a church tea party when she declaimed the dramatic conclusion.

'"... and would, therefore, be glad to consider such a position." Will you mention it? Will you mention his name to Mr Hodding?'

'I will not.'

'You owe him that, Gerry. You really do. He helped you when you were down.'

'It's no good, Rosie. I wish I hadn't agreed to you writing. I can't do it. No matter how you go on, I can't. It wouldn't be right. It's not in my place to do no such thing.'

'You're always telling me of the talks you have with Mr Hodding. Only last night you told me that he'd talked to you all the way to Chesterfield about how wicked Mr Gladstone is. And you told me that you spoke up for Mr Gladstone as if you were in the Marquis of Granby.'

'And so I did. But that's different. Mr Hodding started it off. "Knock," he said, "Knock, this Mr Gladstone looks like coming to Steetly." Then he tells me about a clergyman from Southwell who saw Mr Gladstone in London to tell him about rebuilding that old chapel . . .'

119

'I know,' said Rosie, 'you told me.'

But Gerrard was not to be denied another recital of his story.

'Then he says, "You can go and see him if you want to, but I won't, good manners or no good manners." And I said that I would and he started to go on as usual about him being a Tory renegade and I said—'

'If you could say all that, why can't you say that you know a man who'd make a good gardener?'

'Because it's more than my job's worth and I should have said so before. You think that Mr Hodding is a very friendly sort of gentleman. And so he is when he's of a mind. But some days he bites my head off if I say one word out of place. I can't do it, Rosie. So don't go on about it.'

'Then I'll wait till I get a chance and I'll do it myself.'

Gerrard Knock choked, coughed, swallowed and tried to speak all at once for he feared that his wife might be as good as her word. It took him several seconds to regain enough composure to make his threat seem credible.

'You do, my lady, and there'll be hell to pay in this house. Letting me down to the master. I won't stand it. No man would.'

'Then act like a man and speak to Mr Hodding.'

'Why should I? All he did was employ me and I always gave him a good day's work in return.'

'How can you say such a thing? He made you chargehand and then foreman. He gave you a good character when you got this job here. If you don't help your fellow men, you can't expect your fellow men to help you.'

Rosie had a home-made homily to suit every situation. Her husband usually admired her brief excursions into moral philosophy, for he thought that a woman who held any opinion on such subjects must be a character, but he was not in the mood to be chivvied about his obligation to help William Skinner.

'Just don't let me hear that you've been talking to Mr Hodding, that's all. Don't let me hear that, my lady, or I'll want to know the reason why.'

At the time, Rosie meant to obey her husband. And she genuinely tried to accept that the idea of William Skinner becoming the gardener at Harness Grove and living in the cottage next door was no more than a dream which helped her to survive the days of loneliness and the evenings of despair. Then, early one bright May morning when engaged in nothing more miraculous than sweeping the steps that connected her little front garden to the Chesterfield Road, she briefly believed that the dream might come true.

Rosie did not see or hear the approach of Henry Hodding until he rode up so close that the shadow of his great bay mare fell across her. He had ridden silently along the swathe of grass that skirted the road and she had been concentrating on removing the last remnants of fallen leaves and faded petals from the corner of the steps. Suddenly she could feel the horse's breath on her face and smell the sweat which had turned into foam along its flanks. Fearing it would brush against her she stepped back with a start and Henry Hodding boomed down from high above her in the saddle.

'I'm sorry to startle you, Mrs Knock.'

'It's my fault, I'm sure, Mr Hodding. My thoughts were a thousand miles away.'

Hodding was not the man to pursue the apology, even though Rosie had blushed scarlet and held one hand to her palpitating heart.

'Has Knock come back yet?'

'Yes, sir. He's been and gone. Had his breakfast more than half an hour ago.'

'No matter. I only wanted him to walk Sweetwater back to the stable, whilst I looked inside the empty cottage.'

'Shall I hold her, sir?'

'She'll get cold standing. It can't be helped, I'll come back later.'

Henry Hodding pulled the mare's head round and touched his hat without looking back at Rosie. She was a woman and therefore deserved some form of salutation but she was a serving woman and did not, therefore, warrant the added courtesy of a backward glance. Had she been forced to confront him face to face, Rosie would not have dared to ask the question. But looking at his broad back she felt bold enough to ask her question. It was prompted as much by fear as by hope. 'Are we to have neighbours?'

The bay, which had only just been urged forward, was pulled to a halt and Henry Hodding turned in his saddle with surprise. There was a pause before he gave the answer.

'Just looking,' he said. 'Empty buildings get neglected. We don't want it to fall down, do we?'

He spoke to the coachman's wife as he would have spoken to an impertinent child. Her sin was innocence, so there was no need to tell her that whoever lived in the cottage next door was none of her business. A gentle pat on the head was sufficient to remind her that serious matters were the concern only of those who were qualified to deal with them. Henry Hodding turned for home again. Amazement replaced surprise when his coachman's wife engaged him again in conversation.

'I thought it might be the new gardener. We heard you were looking for one. We know someone, someone who might . . .'

She did not have the nerve to go on, afraid that her behaviour was so brazen that Mr Hodding would choose not to speak of it even to his servant who was her husband. But although she was too afraid to finish her story, she was glad that she had begun it. She believed there was a chance – a slight chance but a chance nevertheless – that the immense figure which again towered over her would bend in its high saddle and, leaning down, tell her that he was indeed looking for a gardener and that he would welcome the advice of his coachman and his coachman's wife about where one might be found.

Henry Hodding kicked his heels into the horse's flanks and, without speaking, trotted back to the stables where Gerrard Knock was mucking out.

'I told you to wait at the house.'

'I thought I'd better get on with the clearing up, sir, if we're off to Newark at nine. I told one of the girls to run out and fetch me when she saw you on the drive.'

At that minute, the terrified parlourmaid appeared in the gate of the stable yard and, discovering that it was too late to give her warning, fled with a shriek.

'I meant at your house, not this house.'

'I'm sorry, sir. I misunderstood you.'

'You don't listen, Knock. That's your trouble.'

'I heard you, sir. But I didn't understand. You said meet at the house, sir. This is the house. I call my place a cottage.'

The description of Henry Hodding's occasional bad temper which the coachman had given his wife was wholly accurate. Indeed, sudden flashes of anger were so frequent that it was strange that Gerrard Knock had never learned to deal with them.

'Are you being impudent, Knock?' The parlourmaid halfway back to the kitchen could hear the roar across the stable yard. She strained to hear what followed but could only just make out the occasional word. What she heard was enough to justify her running on breathless into the kitchen. For amongst the words which she did identify were 'wife' and 'intolerable'.

'I'm truly sorry, sir,' said Gerrard Knock. 'She means no harm, but she's rash. The man she spoke about has fallen on hard times. And he was once very kind to me and her. She'd like to repay the debt.' Embarrassed, he let his apology run on for too long. 'She means well, but she's no idea of her place.'

'She'd better acquire one.'

'Acquire one, sir?'

'She'd better learn. Learn her place.'

'Yes, sir. I'll see that she does. I told her weeks ago that she shouldn't mention the gardener.' As soon as he made the admission, Gerrard Knock knew that it was a mistake for he humiliated himself by acknowledging that his wife did not respect his wishes and he revealed that Rosie had planned and plotted to make their family friend the gardener at Harness Grove.

'Who the hell is this paragon?'

'This what, sir?'

'This man who does you so many favours that you think that he ought to replace poor old Withington.'

'You know him, sir. Leastways, you've met him. He's called William Skinner.'

'I've never met anyone called Skinner in my life.'

'Begging your pardon, sir, but you met him in Lincoln almost a year ago. There was trouble over the arboretum. He worked for the company that built it. I told you I knew him and you said that he'd stood up for himself very well.'

'Good God. The man with the beard who looked like the Prince of Wales. His wife told him to behave like a man.'

Gerrard Knock was not sure if his employer meant to make a comparison and if the comparison was intended to be a rebuke. He thought that he ought to explain why William Skinner was particularly responsive to his wife's advice.

'She's blind, sir. She woke up one morning and couldn't see.'

Henry Hodding felt threatened by the obligations of compassion. He knew that his coachman did not possess the guile intentionally to pluck at his heart strings, but fate might be about to take advantage of his good nature. He decided to end the potentially dangerous conversation. 'Well, I'm not in the market for a gardener. I shan't turn Withington out. And until he passes on, the rest of you will have to help discharge his duties. When the time comes, I may ask you about this Skinner man. But tell your wife to keep clear of things that don't concern her.'

'I will, sir. Believe me I will.'

Gerrard Knock kept his promise as soon as he walked in the cottage door.

'You've fair let me in for it, you have.'

'What have I done now?'

'You know very well. Speaking to Mr Hodding about the gardener. *And* I'd told you not to. That's what hurts. Your own husband tells you not to and you take not a blind bit of notice.'

'It just slipped out.'

'Don't be so soft.'

'It did, I swear it.'

'Anyway, my lady, he gave me a rare dressing down. I'm lucky to keep my job.' The coachman was keen to express his anger more forcibly but he could not put the words together.

'And have they got a new gardener?'

'That's not the point.'

'But have they?'

'No. And they won't get one until old Withington passes on. Till then, we've all got to lend a hand.'

'And what when he does?'

'That's none of your business. You could have got me sacked this morning, and where would we be then? I'm serious, Rosie. Forget about it.'

She forgot about it until the day old Withington died and from then until the funeral in Whitwell churchyard she thought of nothing else. The old gardener had hung on into the last months of William Skinner's employment at Lincoln arboretum.

As the Reverend David Wolstenholme threw the second handful of earth on to the coffin Rosie still had no idea how she could force the issue to some conclusion. Beyond the churchyard gate, her husband stood holding the head of the horse which had drawn the Hodding carriage. Throughout the graveside ceremony, he never took his eyes off his wife, for he feared that in a moment of madness she would leap forward and claim the gardening succession for William Skinner.

Rosie's only indiscretion was to leave the churchyard before the Hoddings. As she saw the vicar turn from the grave, she took advantage of her humble position in the back ranks of the mourners to dart out of the gate before the slow ritual of handshaking and regrets began. Gerrard ignored her as she dashed past him, but despite his show of disapproval he felt relaxed for the first time that afternoon. Rosie was out of harm's way and, as her figure bobbed away into the distance, relief reawakened his old admiration for her rebellious spirit and devoted housekeeping. She would be back in Darfoulds before he had rubbed down the horse and his tea would be ready when he got home. He smiled at the thought that she was his. When Mr and Mrs Hodding got to the carriage he had to remember not to smile as he removed his bowler hat.

'I'm sending for that friend of yours, Knock – the gardener from Lincoln.'

The coachman was too astonished to reply.

'He made a very good impression on me. Very straight, he seemed. Very smart-looking man. I've written to the Lincoln surveyor to find out where he lives.'

Gerrard Knock did not volunteer the information. He knew that Henry Hodding had begun to believe that the idea of appointing William Skinner was his own exclusive initiative.

'The vicar recommended a man from Clowne, an old soldier he wanted to help. But the man's only got one leg.' The temptation to smile became almost irresistible, but no humour was intended. 'You'd think he would have realised . . .'

Henry Hodding was in the coach and too busy spreading the rug across his wife's knees to bother finishing the sentence. At the door of Harness Grove, he turned to Knock as if his sentence had not been interrupted by a five-mile drive. 'Man with one leg's no good. Don't you go telling this Skinner that I want to see him. None of your business or your wife's. Anyway, it's only right to wait for Withington to be cold in his grave.'

Gerrard Knock, still shivering from the freezing hour he had spent outside the Whitwell churchyard, thought that it would not be long before the old gardener was in a state suitable to the appointment of his successor.

In the belief that it was best for gentlemen to do business with gentlemen, Henry Hodding wrote to Michael Drury informing him that William Skinner would be interviewed for the post of gardener at Harness Grove. The letter was composed in language which allowed no discretion to the candidate. Skinner was to be bundled up like a parcel and posted from Lincoln to Worksop. There was no mention of such tedious topics as wages, conditions and accommodation, which the employer intended to decide as and when appropriate.

The interview would take place at nine o'clock on the following Saturday morning – a time which required William's journey to begin at half-past five, but enabled Henry Hodding to fill the time between breakfast and his departure for a meeting of the Turnpike Trust. Elizabeth, who did not want her husband to become a gardener but looked forward to being a pauper even less, contented herself with criticisms about his appearance and detailed arrangements for his journey. She had a genius for disputing detail.

'It can't take that long.'

'I don't want to risk being late. The next train doesn't get to Worksop till after eight.'

'It won't take an hour to walk there from the station.'

'What if the train's not on time? Anyway, I want time to smarten up.'

Elizabeth gave one of her knowing looks.

'I see. You're going to have breakfast with the Knocks.'

'I'm going to smarten up. Nothing wrong with that, is there?'

'Nothing at all. I just wish that you'd tell me the truth.' She leaned forward and stared into his face.

'Go to a barber and get your beard trimmed.'

'No need for that. It's a waste of money.'

'It's very uneven at the sides.' William had noticed the same thing in the mirror that morning and had decided to make the necessary adjustments before he went to bed that night. If Elizabeth could see that his whiskers were uneven, her sight had improved more than either he realised or she admitted. He noted the fact with profound satisfaction. When Elizabeth could see again, some of the burden of guilt would be lifted from his shoulders.

'I shall do them myself.'

'Of course, if we can't afford twopence . . .' Elizabeth turned away, bumping against the table in a way that was wholly inconsistent with her ability to detect an unkempt beard.

'Of course we can. If you think I should get it done properly . . .'

'It's not what I think, is it? I thought if you were going to see the Knocks you'd be going out of your way to look your best.'

Gerrard Knock was waiting to greet him, already dressed in his coachman's livery. Rosie was frying sausages in the kitchen.

'We thought you might like a bite, Mr Skinner.' Knock retained the manner of a workhouse labourer speaking to master. 'It's just sausage and fried bread. But we thought you might welcome it.'

In the doorway of the living room, Rosie gave a half-curtsy as she carried in the hot plate, protecting her hand by holding it between the folds of her apron.

'How's Mrs Skinner?' she asked.

'She's doing very well. The sight's coming back, bit by bit. She told me my whiskers needed cutting this morning.'

'That's wonderful.' Rosie blushed to think that she might have endorsed Elizabeth Skinner's judgement on William's appearance. 'How are the little ones?'

'They're a handful. But Anne's a great help now. Very grown up in her ways – a regular little mother to the other two.' William smiled at the thought as he touched his beard to make sure that it held neither crumbs of bread nor drops of fat. 'I ought to go out the back and have a wash. I don't want to keep Mr Hodding waiting.'

He reached the top of the long drive by ten to nine, meaning to follow Gerrard Knock's instruction and take the path round the back of the house to the servants' entrance. But Henry Hodding was standing outside his front door, already changed from riding clothes into business suit and anxious for his working day to begin. As always he had no time to spend on pleasantries.

'You got a good character from Mr Drury, Skinner. But he didn't say anything about your gardening. Come with me.'

They walked together round the corner of the house and Henry Hodding took up position between the two great trees which Rosie had called cypresses but which were, in truth, yew. He pointed to a bush in a flower bed at the foot of one of the mighty trunks.

'What's that?'

'Ribes,' William answered.

'What?'

'Ribes.'

'Heavens, man! It's the flowering currant! Everybody knows that.'

William Skinner did not even think of explaining that Ribes was the name that was used in the botany books. It would not have mattered. Henry Hodding was incapable of being patronised.

'What's this? Try a name I've heard of.'

'Aubrietia, sir.'

'Right. Tell me about it.'

'It's named after a gardener called Aubrey.'

'What's that to me? Tell me about what it looks like, grows like.'

'In the spring the leaves have a greyish look. It has a little purple flower.'

They walked on past the delphiniums and peonies, the spiraea and garrya, which William was careful to call tassel plant. His only mistake was berberis, which he correctly identified but went on to classify as *Thunbergii atropurpurea*.

Henry Hodding opened the door which led through the brick wall surrounding the herb garden. William followed him inside.

The garden was badly neglected. It was divided into square beds by gravel walks which ran from wall to wall and crossed each other at right angles, but the once precise boundaries – where boards had been sunk into the earth to separate path from bed – were overgrown and, in places, resolute herbs had pushed their way up through the gravel. Mullein and lady's mantle leaned so far across the paths that it was impossible to walk their length without pushing them aside. Bronze fennel, rue and catmint had almost completely taken over a bed which was the rightful home of rosemary. A terracotta pot sprouted thyme. Variegated sage, mint and lamb's ear grew in between and over the blocks of granite which had once been stepping stones, placed along the deepest border to allow the conscientious gardener easy access to the wall that caught the sun and held up apricot branches. Calendulas and giant poppies grew by what had once been a lily pond but had been colonised by reeds and bulrushes. And a sprinkling of wind-borne seeds had dotted the garden with local weeds. Across one corner, where the high north wall was green with moss and lichens, there was a wooden seat. Henry Hodding sat down. William stood at a respectful distance amongst the lavender.

'Where did you pick up all this knowledge?' The question was meant to sound aggressive. Henry Hodding was not the man to be intimidated by learning.

'At the arboretum, sir. We labelled everything with its Latin name.'

'Well, there won't be any Latin here. Here you'll be bending your back all day, mostly in the kitchen garden.'

'I'm not afraid of that, sir. I was the working foreman with a gang of navvies.' He held out his hands, palms upward. They were covered in hard brown calluses.

'What do you think of this?' Henry Hodding waved his hand in a wide arc from golden marjoram to silver artemisia.

'It'll take a lot of work to get it back to its original state.'

'Will you enjoy doing it?'

'To tell you the truth, sir, I like it as it is. No doubt you do too. That's why the seat is here.'

Henry Hodding was impressed – not by the proof of physical labour or by the botanical knowledge but by William Skinner's manner. It was attentive without being obsequious, respectful but not deferential. Skinner, he decided, was the sort of man who would do an honest day's work unsupervised and at the end of it have the nerve and the sense to speak up if there were problems that needed the master's attention.

'You'll start at the month's end. Do you want to see the house?'

'If I may, sir.'

'You can't miss it. It's on the Chesterfield Road. Your friend the coachman lives there now. But he'll have to move next door to the small place. He's no children. You've got four, haven't you?'

'Three, sir. Big girl and two smaller. One's a boy.'

'It's all the same. You'll still need Grove Cottage. Next door there's only one bedroom. Knock will take the dray to Lincoln for your furniture.'

William walked off with a heavy heart to the cottage, which he had already seen. He had every intention of taking the job and devoting the rest of his life to the berberis, aubrietia, peonies and delphiniums.

128

And, of course, he would take the house which went with it. Neither his employer nor his wife would allow any argument on that score. But he dreaded seeing Rosie again now that he knew that because of his arrival at Harness Grove she would have to leave her cottage and disturb the measured calm which he hoped had come to their marriage. For a moment he thought of only pretending to visit Grove Cottage, walking straight past as he trudged back to the railway station. But Henry Hodding's passion for organising every detail allowed no such deception.

'The quick way's down the back. Round the front of the house. Follow the path through the field. Then there's a gate at the far end.'

The new gardener hurried off, worrying every step of the way but determined to get the meeting over as quickly as possible. Only Rosie was at home. No sooner had he stepped inside the door than she threw her arms round his neck. The deference had disappeared.

'William! It's lovely to have you back after all these years.'

CHAPTER TEN

The Price of Democracy

Despite the brevity and informality of the interview, there was only one question which Henry Hodding regretted failing to ask his new employee. He was not to be blamed for the omission, for at the time of interview in the overgrown herb garden the information he needed but lacked was of no consequence. But at the beginning of William's second year in his employment events in the world outside Darfoulds made it essential for the master of Harness Grove to know the political inclination of all his servants.

There was to be a by-election in the Bassetlaw Hundreds and, for the first time in thirty years, the Conservative candidate was to face a Liberal challenge. That should not have surprised the grandees of the local political establishment, for manhood suffrage had come to North Nottinghamshire and the old electorate of barely two thousand prosperous burghers – who had regularly returned the Tory nominee – had been augmented by six thousand new voters of unknown allegiance and dubious social origin. The grandees' response to the crisis was the appointment of Henry Hodding as Conservative agent.

The new agent did not intend to be embarrassed by his own employees talking seditious Liberal nonsense in Worksop public houses. Gerrard Knock had already been told to keep his opinions of Mr Gladstone to himself and had announced without conviction that he no longer admired the Grand Old Man. On the first morning of the campaign, William Skinner was summoned to the back door of Harness Grove to be instructed about his political duty.

'What are your politics, Skinner?' Henry Hodding believed in coming straight to the point.

'I haven't thought much about it, sir.'

'Think now.' Evasion was not to be tolerated.

'I really don't know, sir. My father always voted Tory but I've never voted.'

'No doubt. But I shall expect you to do the same if you ever get the chance.'

130

'I'm sure I shall, sir.'

'I'm pleased to hear it. In the meantime, you can help me in the poll here.'

William Skinner first looked blank and then nodded enthusiastically.

'You can start tomorrow, as soon as you've washed yourself after work. There's going to be trouble in this election. Half the riff-raff in the country are going to vote. Colliers are going to vote. I could do with a second man sitting up on the box with Knock.'

For the first week of the campaign there was only trouble in the Liberal Party Committee Rooms at the Bull Hotel in Worksop. Five days before nominations closed, Lord Edward Clinton, that party's first choice as standard-bearer, withdrew from the fight. The great Liberal families – Saville, Foljambe and Devonshire – were approached in turn. None could provide a younger son to carry Mr Gladstone's banner. An invitation was sent to Mr Joseph Garside of Sheffield, who first said that he would and then that he would not. At last, and with only hours to spare, Edward Bristowe of Leicester was persuaded to allow his name to go forward. A Conservative wag composed a derisory lyric which, sung to the tune of 'Ten Little Nigger Boys', heaped scorn on the radicals' scramble for a candidate.

> Ten Little Yellow Boys started out to dine
> Lord Edward wouldn't come, then there were nine

It was printed on a thousand handbills for distribution in the constituency. Henry Hodding read the ten verses with meticulous care but without a smile. He could not imagine why anyone could think them amusing. But it was extremely gratifying. The Liberals were already in disarray. He was, he decided, a first-class election agent.

The Liberal campaign never recovered from its uncertain start. Indeed, it was so lacking in spirit that at first it failed even to generate the hooliganism that Henry Hodding feared, and, a full week before polling day, William Skinner was released from his duties as bodyguard. On the morning of the ballot, bent over his spade, he felt real disappointment that he was to miss the day at the hustings for which Gerrard Knock was preparing by decorating the carriage with blue ribbons. He watched wistfully as the last streamer fluttered out of sight round a corner of the drive.

The road outside the Lion Inn, the Conservatives' Worksop headquarters, was packed with a singing, swaying, boisterous crowd. Gerrard pulled the carriage to an enforced halt and Henry Hodding, who had begun to enjoy his brief excursion into the turbulent world of politics, opened his window and leaned out to offer a word of encouragement to the men who had clearly come to pledge their allegiance to his cause. He was immensely gratified to hear one man cry, 'It's old Hodding,' for he had discovered that to be described by the public as 'old Hodding' was an indication not of age but of fame. He waved in the direction from which the compliment came.

A tomato splattered against the side of his carriage. A rotten apple flew over his shoulder and, hitting the folded silk above his head, burst and fell in a dozen juicy fragments on to the floor. A turnip dislodged, but did not remove, Gerrard Knock's bowler hat and a potato – which bounced from the shafts – set the harness jingling. The horse whinnied and tossed her head. The coachman pulled gently on the reins and made reassuring noises in his throat, but the mare was not reassured. She began to rear up.

'Hold her, man!' Henry Hodding shouted through the trap-door. 'Hold her!' Outside on the box, as he dodged the flying fruit and vegetables, the coachman felt deeply aggrieved. He was doing his best to hold her, yet from the safety of the coach Mr Hodding bellowed at him as if he had fallen asleep.

Henry Hodding climbed out on to the road. It was surprise which made the men around the carriage door stand back. There was a chorus of hisses and a whole symphony of boos. But there were no more missiles. As the Conservative agent took hold of the horse's bridle, he was gently jostled, but as he led her towards the inn yard, the crowd parted. Gerrard Knock's relief at being safely inside resulted less from his fear of the mob than from his shame at sitting useless, whip in hand, whilst he was led into the livery stable by his own master.

'Look after her,' said Henry Hodding. It sounded like a reproof delivered to a coachman who could not be trusted to do his duty without explicit instruction. 'They're cowards with drink inside them. But she doesn't know that. Keep her warm. She's badly shaken.'

Gerrard Knock, who was at least as badly shaken as the horse, lowered himself to the cobbles with difficulty. The rungs, which were built into the coach to assist in his descent, seemed to have been moved from their usual position. He had to feel for each one by exploring the smart paintwork with the toe of his boot. He had no doubt that his master was noting every scratch.

'Take her out and put her in a stall. I'll walk for the rest of the day.'

'Am I to stay here, sir? Or shall I go and get Skinner to give us a hand?'

'I've told you. Stay with the horse. Keep her quiet. I don't want her prancing about in the stall and breaking a leg whilst I'm in there.'

132

He jerked his finger contemptuously in the direction of the hotel's back door. Politics had suddenly lost its charm. The hope of winning an election was, on his scale of values, not to be compared with the fear of losing a horse.

There was panic inside the inn. A messenger from Blythe had brought news of early-morning fighting in the streets and the looting of a grocer's shop. The report from Retford was that the public houses had been open since dawn and that a brass band – playing with increasing gusto but in diminishing harmony – was leading a column of drunken Liberals round and round the market place. Honest citizens were afraid to approach the stalls and stall-holders dared not leave their wares unattended.

'It's the colliers,' said Mr Denison, the Conservative candidate. 'They've come in charabancs from miles around. A man who was arrested for being drunk and disorderly in Blythe says that he came from Carlton.'

'Are they still drinking outside?' The candidate's wife hoped that, by some miracle, sobriety and tranquillity would return to Worksop.

Henry Hodding had no comfort to offer. 'They were when I came. I could smell beer as soon as I got out of the carriage. Half the men had bottles in their hands.'

'The public houses ought to be closed at once.'

Mr Denison looked out of the window with the despair of a Bourbon watching the mob approach Versailles and realising that they have been incited to riot by the palace guard. The publicans were the backbone of the Tory Party.

'The crowd's getting bigger by the minute. They'll start battering on the door soon.'

'We can't close licensed premises without the Riot Act being read.' The agent remembered more than the law. He recalled that, acting in his professional capacity, he had applied to the licensing justices for the opening hours to be extended. Mr Denison had intended to float to Parliament on a tide of alcohol.

'Where are the policemen, the extra policemen?' Mrs Denison was becoming hysterical.

Henry Hodding, although perfectly calm, took up the same theme. 'They certainly ought to be here. The town's paying enough for them. I've never known special constables being paid like regulars before.'

At that moment – as if to stifle criticism – the sound of a police whistle hushed the crowd and Mr Denison looked out of the window with the gratitude of a garrison commander who believed that the siege was about to be lifted. At first, all he saw was a single uniformed figure pushing his way through the crowd. Then he noticed that a civilian walked imperiously, two paces behind the officer, trying – as best he could – to avoid the handshakes and backslaps of those members of the crowd who recognised him. Henry Hodding identified the approaching relief column.

'It's Bleasdale and that rogue Tylden-Wright.'

Charles Tylden-Wright owed his popularity partly to his status as Liberal member of the County Council but mostly to his agreement, as chairman of the licensing justices, to the public houses being opened all day. Henry Hodding's Conservative contribution to that happy event had been overlooked by his political opponents, who began to cheer as Superintendent Bleasdale, the commander of the local force, beat on the inn door with his staff and demanded entry for his distinguished companion.

'Everything all right in here, Hodding?' Tylden-Wright asked.

'You can see very well that it isn't.'

'Where are the police?' Mr Denison demanded to know. 'The police that we're paying for.' His concern was not solely the result of anxiety to save expense for the ratepayers.

'They're out at the polling stations.' Superintendent Bleasdale was not accustomed to having his instructions challenged even by the man who was expected to be Bassetlaw's next Member of Parliament. 'And out at the polling stations they are going to stay. You asked for the extra boxes, Mr Denison. My first duty is to guard them until they're sealed and delivered to the Corn Exchange.'

'And what about us?' Mrs Denison's voice rose an octave between the beginning and end of the sentence.

'What about you, dear lady?'

'It's not a joke, Charles. For God's sake!' Henry Hodding quickly became impatient with games. 'That mob of yours is preventing the proper conduct of this election.'

'It's not my mob, Henry.'

'You're councillor for this ward. Those who've got votes, vote for you. Go outside and tell them to go home.'

'That's a perfectly good-natured crowd out there. I walked through them five minutes ago and I understand that you did exactly the same – unmolested – a few minutes earlier. There's a bit of high spirits. But it's polling day. A bit of fun is only to be expected. They're not vicious. You walked through them.'

'Well, let's see if I can walk through them again now. I'm going to Eastgate polling station to do my job.' He turned to Superintendent Bleasdale. 'I leave Mr and Mrs Denison in your charge, Sergeant. They won't leave this hotel today. You make sure that they're safe.'

'I'll walk with you part of the way,' said Charles Tylden-Wright.

'Bleasdale will see us through the crowd and then he'll do what's needed to reassure these good people.'

Led by the superintendent, who blew his whistle with extra vigour to prove that he was not a sergeant, the two men made stately progress through the crowd, accompanied by nothing more menacing than a few catcalls directed at the Tory and the occasional complaint to the Liberal about the company he was keeping. Back at the Lion Inn, the doors were locked and the window barred. Every able-bodied man armed himself with a stick or cudgel, meat-cleaver, toasting-fork or carving-knife. Constant estimates were made of the size of the crowd, which was said to grow at each inspection. When yellow flags and bunting appeared outside shops which were known to be owned by Conservatives it was assumed that they had been occupied by the enemy. Then, half a brick came through the window of the hotel dining room.

Charles Haywood of Potter Street, a cattle merchant who had been doing innocent morning business at the Lion, decided to make a dash for help. The back door of the inn was swung open and the brave volunteer flung himself into the lane that led to freedom and rescue. He had made about fifty yards when the rioters at the front of the hotel saw him and he covered about another twenty before he was brought down by a flying tackle. The first kick split his head open. The second removed four teeth. Mr Haywood crawled home to Potter Street and, before collapsing on to his parlour couch, locked and bolted his door.

Two hours later, Joe Makin – gamekeeper to Mr Balchin of Gateford, who had been sent by his master to Worksop to run errands in the Tory cause – offered to brave the crowd. It took him some time to persuade Mr Denison to open the front door. When he squeezed through the narrow gap which was all that was allowed him, he was immediately engulfed in a whirlwind of flailing fists. Sydney Smith of Burnt Leys, who had hoped to spend the day chaperoning Mrs Denison through the shopping streets, seized his walking stick, plunged bravely into the screaming mob and dragged him back inside. The two men sat bruised and bleeding on the bottom steps of the inn's main staircase when Gerrard Knock, at last convinced that the house was calm, came in from the stable in search of food.

'Is Mr Hodding back yet?' the coachman asked innocently.

Mr Denison did not like to tell him that his master was dead and that every Conservative in the Lion Inn would soon follow him to a meeting with their Maker.

In fact, the agent was still making his methodical way through the more remote parts of the Bassetlaw constituency. It was in the rural areas where Conservative support was strongest, and the agent was determined to deliver the vote and return his candidate to Parliament –

135

whatever little disturbances were making Mr Denison's heart flutter in the Lion Inn.

It was another three hours before Henry Hodding, his rural work completed, turned back towards Worksop. The discovery that the Conservative headquarters were still besieged filled him with as much guilt as astonishment. The crowd was, he decided, more drunk and dangerous than when he had left in the late morning. It took him five minutes to reach the Bridge Street police station and almost as long to attract the attention of the half-dozen officers who were on duty.

'Find me a justice,' he said in a tone calculated to freeze the heart of the sergeant who sat at a high desk.

'Councillor Tylden-Wright is at the Bull,' a young constable told him to the obvious consternation of the more senior officers.

'Then he's near enough to know what's going on down the road. Go and get him.'

The young policeman was sent running to Liberal headquarters. Whilst he was gone, Henry Hodding took a sheet of paper from the sergeant's desk without asking permission. By the time Tylden-Wright arrived he had already written out the message. No justification was necessary.

'Send it,' he said. 'Send it now. Before someone gets killed, if it hasn't happened already.'

Tylden-Wright handed the note to the sergeant.

'To the Commanding Officer at the Sheffield Barracks, if you please. Be sure to write "Justice of the Peace" by my name.'

Without comment, the sergeant began to tap the letters into his telegraph machine:

WORKSOP IS IN STATE OF RIOT! I REQUIRE YOU IN HER MAJESTY'S NAME TO SEND A FORCE OF SOLDIERS HERE.

No one spoke or moved until the keys had stopped clattering. Then Henry Hodding issued his third curt order.

'I shall need all your officers to help me back into the Lion.'

'Is that wise?' asked the sergeant.

'It is necessary. It is where I should be.'

They pushed their way down the street and, although the constables received frequent blows, Henry Hodding, within the tight circle of their protection, suffered nothing worse than a ruined hat and a couple of kicks on the shins. He was greeted with amazement inside the Lion. Even without the added status which came from resurrection, Henry Hodding would have taken instant command. Because of his enhanced authority, the assembled company waited in complete silence for his instructions. He demanded the immediate cutting of sandwiches and dispensation of whisky in medicinal-sized drams. The clear implication of his orders was that, in his absence, no one had thought of eating or drinking. A tablecloth was torn into strips and Mrs Denison, who was already whiter than the napery, was instructed to replace the bandages which had been wound round Joe Makin and Sydney Smith only a few minutes earlier. When Gerrard Knock reported that the horse was safe and well, his master announced, in a tone which implied a threat rather than gratitude, his intention of visiting the stables himself. No one, he announced, was to leave the inn until the crowds dispersed or the soldiers arrived. He added that boards should be found to cover the broken windows. It had begun to rain and the velvet curtains would be ruined by exposure to a prolonged downpour.

Fifty-three officers and men of the Prince of Wales' Own left Sheffield's Victoria station at five minutes past nine and arrived in Worksop at a quarter to ten. Superintendent Bleasdale, who met them on the platform, found it difficult to keep up with their light-infantry pace as they marched to the scene of the riot. The rain had already done their work. The colliers had climbed into the charabancs and returned to the pit villages and all but half a dozen of the local drunks had been put to bed. By the time the first ballot box was opened the light infantrymen had been unnecessarily reinforced by a hundred and fifty fusiliers who arrived from Newark by special train. Every man obeyed the order to show no emotion when the returning officer announced the result. Mr Alfred Denison had been elected to represent the Bassetlaw Hundreds by a majority of one hundred and eighty-seven votes out of the seven thousand that had been cast. After he had made a halting acceptance speech, the crowd called for the agent.

Henry Hodding spoke in the appropriate third person. 'Mr Denison wants to give his particular thanks to his friends in the country areas, who turned out in such good numbers and made up for all the nonsense in the town.'

There was, the new Member of Parliament decided, a clear implication that the agent had spent the day securing the vote in the wild rural parishes whilst the candidate had languished in the comfort of the Lion Inn.

The news of the riot took several hours to reach Harness Grove and, since it was brought by the Whitwell curate who had seen Henry Hodding ride through his parish during the late afternoon, was received with composure. As long as her husband was safe, Mrs Hodding did not care if Worksop was razed to the ground. Indeed, her opinion of that town was so low that she had long expected it to suffer the fate of Sodom.

A passing tinker, who called at the servants' quarters and asked for water, told the cook that the Lion Inn had been besieged, occupied and set on fire. When the butler enquired of his mistress if she had heard of a disturbance in town, she assured him that the master was safe, without condescending to explain from what he had been saved.

Sensation was rare at Harness Grove and the maids determined to make the most of their excitement. It was, they decided, their duty to visit Rosie Knock and Elizabeth Skinner with warning or condolences as necessary. For, if they had ever known, they had forgotten that the gardener had not ridden off that morning on the box next to the coachman.

The Knocks' cottage was dark, and repeated hammering on the door provoked what they first thought was movement in the bedroom, but then there was nothing except stony silence. The girls decided that the brief sound of life was only in their imagination and that Rosie was either seeking comfort next door or – the explanation favoured by the romantically inclined – searching the rubble of Worksop for her husband. They moved next door to Grove Cottage. That was dark too, but they could not believe that Mrs Skinner was out so late. After much knocking on door and windows, they let themselves into the kitchen. Doors were not locked and bolted in Darfoulds. It was a community of friends and neighbours.

Elizabeth Skinner was making her careful way down the steep stairs. She carried no candle, for her eyesight had still not sufficiently returned to give flickering light any purpose.

'Is that you, William? You'll wake the baby. I've had a terrible time with Ernest as it is.'

'No, mum, it's us.' The housemaids treated Mrs Skinner with a deference inappropriate to her station.

'Is it my husband? Has something happened to him?' She tried not to sound anxious but she found it difficult to hide her agitation.

'We hope not, mum. But there's been a riot in the town. We know that the master's safe . . .'

'Then my husband must be safe too. He's with him, isn't he?'

'We hope so, mum. But we thought we ought to see if you were all right. You having difficulties and all. It's the Liberals that have caused all the trouble.'

'When is Mr Hodding expected home?'

'We're not sure, mum. Mrs Hodding said that it'd be late. Perhaps early tomorrow.'

'Well, then,' said Elizabeth. 'Let's all go to bed and get some sleep.'

Crushed and denied their moment of drama, the girls retreated from the cottage. But Elizabeth did not sleep. First she was kept awake by Agnes, who whimpered as she dreamed on the other side of the lath-and-plaster wall which divided the bedrooms. Then Ernest woke and, as always, howled with rage when she refused to let him climb into her bed.

Elizabeth lay staring sightlessly into the dark, wondering how long she could avoid feeling her way into the bedroom and frightening her children into silence, and praying that Anne would subdue her brother and sister before it was necessary for their mother to mount a punitive expedition against them. The prayer was answered but still she could not sleep. No matter how hard she tried to compose herself, her mind was filled with irrational fears for her husband's safety. For more than an hour she imagined that he was the victim of all sorts of mob brutality. Then – still surprised by her own lack of control – she tiptoed into the next bedroom and silently shook her elder daughter by the shoulder. The child woke without a sound as she had woken a hundred times before when her mother needed help with one of the younger children.

Out on the landing, Anne was given her instructions. 'Go and see if Mrs Knock knows what's going on.' She could not resist a criticism. 'She's probably been up at the house gossiping with the servants.'

'Is Mr Knock back?' Anne was tying her shoes. She had pulled her topcoat over her nightdress.

'I don't think that he can be. I've not heard the carriage go up the road. But Mrs Knock might know something.'

Anne lifted the usually noisy latch with both hands and stepped out into the damp, cold night. Like the servants who had called two hours earlier, she thought that when she rapped on the Knocks' back door there was a sudden noise from the room above her. But, like them, she received no answer. She did not want to beat on the door in case the hammering wakened the sleeping children in the next cottage, so she turned the knob and walked into the kitchen as she had walked into it a hundred times before. She was about to call up the stairs when she heard a voice from the bedroom.

'It's nothing. We would have heard the carriage.'

The reassurance was followed by Rosie Knock's unmistakable laugh.

'Anyway, it's time to be off. He'll be out there at half-past six tomorrow no matter how late he's back. And he'll expect to see me with my back bent.'

There was more laughter and much rustling of clothes.

'Tell me something before you go,' Rosie demanded.

'I love you.'

At last Anne recognised the voice that she strained to hear through the miasma of cold and sleep. The man upstairs was her father.

139

CHAPTER ELEVEN
In the Cold

There was no doubt that William loved Rosie Knock. But he did not love her with the total passion that she felt for him. Rosie made him happy. Just being with her made him forget past failures and fears for what lay ahead. In moments of anxiety and doubt, he always told himself that there could be no more certain sign of love than that. He never felt guilty about the constant deception of his wife. Nor did he doubt that he was a good husband. He knew that he did his best by Elizabeth and that the family balance sheet showed her to be in his debt. But he did sometimes fear that what he owed Rosie would never be repaid.

He promised, and she expected, nothing. So when she talked of her cousin in Sligo running away to America with his brother's wife, he knew that she was not thinking about doing the same. But he wondered – though he dared not ask the question – if she longed to run away with him. Sometimes, because he dared not ask and did not want to run away himself, he felt demeaned by loving her in a way which was not complete.

On Sunday mornings when he walked to church with Elizabeth and met Rosie hurrying home from mass, he felt ashamed of greeting her as if she was just a neighbour, and he hated, but could not resist, making comparisons between the two women in his life – one strong but the other tender, one brave but the other kind. And he always admired most the virtues possessed by the woman who was not with him. He decided that he loved Rosie more than he loved his wife but that he admired Elizabeth more than he admired his mistress. He often suspected that he betrayed himself as well as her by keeping the woman that he loved for the spare moments of time. Then they would meet and make love and, instead of increasing his guilt about keeping her for a part of his life, he would note that what they felt for each other was pure, perfect and indestructible.

They made love with a fierce determination which William had never felt before, working at each other in a single-minded pursuit of shared pleasure. Once she had asked him if he still made love to his wife and he had lied and said he did. When he asked her if she still made love to her husband, she had lied and said she did not.

Only on the night of the Worksop riots were they ever in danger of being found out. Elizabeth's blindness and Gerrard Knock's demanding employment ensured that their secret was safe. After work, William could walk towards home and make a sudden diversion into the next-door cottage without fear that his wife would see him as she stood in her kitchen window or that Knock would return unexpectedly early from one of Henry Hodding's visits to railway company, Turnpike Trust or Territorials. William always planned his assignations with impatient care. He agreed to call round only on days when he knew that Hodding's last appointment was on the Worksop side of Darfoulds for that ensured that as he and Rosie lay together, they would hear the Hodding carriage clattering along the Chesterfield Road on its way back to Harness Grove. It took the coachman an hour or more to get the horse out of its harness, rub it down and lock it away in its stable. The gardener could be dressed and out, back in his cottage in ten minutes.

William never even knew that, one late night, his own daughter had heard and recognised his voice coming from Rosie's bedroom. For despite her innocent immaturity, Anne chose silently to leave the cottage and pretend that, having received no answer to her call, she had been afraid to shout loudly in case Mrs Knock's sleep should be disturbed. Her mother, always ready to complain and, on that night, agitated as well as bad-tempered, had told her that she was a silly and disobedient girl. But just as her mother's wrath escalated from scolding to banishment upstairs, the sound of Hodding's carriage changed anger into relief.

'Your father will be home in ten minutes. You can stay down and see him.'

William walked through the door as his wife spoke. But Anne turned on her heel and climbed the stairs to bed.

'Is she all right?' William asked. 'Has she been sick or something?'

'She was worried about you. I told her you'd be back as soon as Mr Hodding got home. But she wouldn't listen.'

'Then why didn't she wait to see me?' William walked towards the stairs to call up to his daughter.

'Leave her alone. She's in one of her moods. She'll be normal in the morning. It's time we were both in bed. No doubt Mr Hodding will still expect you in the garden at seven o'clock.'

'He will,' said William. 'No doubt about that.'

William felt safe again. Life was back to normal. Breakfast, the next morning, would be like every other breakfast.

His optimism was not wholly justified. Elizabeth clattered the pots in the usual way and urged her children to sit up straight, chew their food thoroughly and refrain from talking with their mouths full. Ernest and Agnes, as always, obeyed when they believed that their mother was watching them and defied her instructions when they thought that they could escape detection and punishment. Anne sat white and silent.

'You don't look well,' her father told her. 'Perhaps you should stay at home today.'

'She'll do no such thing. Just because she's—' Elizabeth was interrupted by her daughter before she had completed the contradiction of her husband and the admonition of her daughter.

'I don't want to stay at home. I'm off now.'

Anne left the table without finishing her breakfast or asking permission to get down. She was out of the kitchen door before her mother could complete the usual inspection of hands and face or make sure that her coat was fastened on every button.

'I'll have a word with that young lady when she gets home.' Elizabeth spoke as if her husband needed reassurance that she would be sufficiently severe.

'It's just her age. All girls are like it when they're half children and half grown up. She'll grow out of it.'

The changes in character which her father anticipated did not come about. In appearance, she grew more and more like her mother – tall, stiffly erect with white skin drawn tightly across her sharp jaw and angular cheekbones. Elizabeth's pride in Anne did not allow her to recognise that her daughter's behaviour had become a caricature of her own. Anne could not bear to be touched, washed obsessively and busied about in the kitchen in a way which invariably inconvenienced the rest of the family more than it helped her mother. She was happiest cleaning the living room with a zeal that required her father to move from chair to chair as she banged her brush against the furniture and shook the rugs as if her intention was to punish, rather than remove, the dirt. She went to church twice on Sunday – first to matins with her mother and father and then alone to evensong – but she did not enjoy those devotions with anything like the pleasure she experienced at Sunday school, where, as the oldest girl in the class, she was required to impose rigorous discipline on the smaller children.

Anne performed all her duties in a manner which made clear that she was a martyr who enjoyed her martyrdom. Self-sacrifice became her way of life. At teatime, she was always the last to reach for the bread and butter and if Ernest took all of the jam before the dish was passed on to her she accepted the deprivation with a stoic smile.

Her father recognised how strange she had become, but was frightened to speak about it even to her mother – who exhibited nothing but admiration for the daughter whom she described as 'old before her time' and 'wise beyond her years'. The Reverend David Wolstenholme – vicar of Whitwell and incumbent at the newly restored Steetly chapel – said that the precocious child was a gift from God, specially designed to help her mother bear the burdens which Providence had heaped upon her. For, although Elizabeth's sight had improved, it was not fully restored and nobody, least of all Elizabeth herself, believed that it ever would be. It was not the last example of the whole series of misfortunes which she regarded as conclusive proof that Providence was prejudiced against her.

Agnes was six when she caught what her father immediately identified as rheumatic fever. William had been struck with a similar sudden illness at Agnes's age. At first, Henry Hodding refused to accept the diagnosis of his own doctor for he had personally driven all such dread diseases out of the Worksop area by his introduction of a sanitary water system. But as the pain persisted and the flushed child lay hot and irritable for almost a week, it was generally admitted that the symptoms were too plain to allow any room for argument. Inevitably, Hodding switched to the opposite extreme. Despite the doctor's assurances to the contrary, he persisted in the belief that the disease was contagious and attempted to have the patient moved into quarantine in a Harness Grove attic. Elizabeth Skinner, notwithstanding the respect which was properly due to her husband's employer, dismissed the idea out of hand. The prospect of an epidemic sweeping through Darfoulds was of no consequence when compared with the risks of a blow to her pride. If she needed assistance in the nursing of the invalid, it would be provided by Anne. To accept outside help would be to admit that the family was not sufficient unto itself.

Throughout the long weeks of Agnes's painful illness and slow recovery, Anne was the devoted nurse that her mother knew she would be. She stayed up late into the night, sitting at her sister's bedside long after the patient had fallen asleep. She ran upstairs to answer calls which the rest of the family had not heard and she kept Ernest in a state of absolute, if rebellious, silence whenever he was in the house. When, at last, Agnes recovered enough to walk up to Harness Grove and thank Mrs Hodding for the soup and fruit, it was Anne's privilege to take her. By then, the young nurse's devotion had become such a legend that the forced conversation was more concerned with the older girl's virtues than with her sister's health. Agnes sat in the window seat and looked absentmindedly out into the garden with its lily pond and borders kept neat by her father. Anne, erect on a hard chair, stared attentively at her hostess.

'I do not know what your mother would have done without you.' Neither did Anne, but proper reticence prevented a reply so Mrs Hodding continued uninterrupted. 'How old are you now?'

'Twelve, mum. Thirteen in February.'

'And what are you going to do after you finish school?'

'I don't know, mum. My mother hasn't told me yet.'

'What would you like to do?'

'Whatever my mother wishes, mum. I don't think she'll want me to leave her.'

'Would you like to come and work for me?'

'If my mother wanted me to, I'd like it very much.'

Mrs Hodding had grown tired of the catechism and Agnes was pulling dangerously at the tassels on the window-seat cushions.

'Cook is going to take you into the kitchen for tea. You tell your mother that next spring I shall need a new kitchen maid. You'll have to live in, but you'll be able to see your mother on your afternoon off and you'll get news about her from your father. Tell your mother from me that you can start on May Day.'

Anne, grave and without any sign of feelings of her own, reported the conversation to her mother almost word for word. Instead of the gratitude which Mrs Hodding expected, the offer of employment as a kitchen maid provoked barely suppressed fury. 'You'll do no such thing. The very thought of it . . . Going to skivvy in the Hoddings' kitchen – or anyone else's for that matter. She should not have talked to you about it in the first place.'

'Then I'm not to work there?'

'You are not. It's all very well for Mrs Knock to wash up in that kitchen but no daughter of mine is going to do it. We'll both walk up to the house tomorrow and tell that cook she'll have to find somebody else to clean up after her.'

The cook, who resented the gardener's wife's pretensions, said that nobody had told her that Anne was to be employed in her kitchen. The butler, loitering with intent to find out the intruder's business, expressed the opinion that the mistress would never have made such a suggestion – just as the mistress herself bustled into the kitchen and, ignoring both of her senior employees, announced, 'If you want your daughter to start in April, she can, Mrs Skinner. That silly girl Phyllis says she's going to go in May. But the master says it's best to start and finish things with the financial year.'

Neither Anne nor her mother exhibited any of the triumph they were entitled to feel. Indeed, both looked nervous.

'It's not that I'm ungrateful, Mrs Hodding, but I don't think it's

144

right for her. Thank you very much. I came to tell Cook that Anne doesn't want to do it.'

'That's up to you, Mrs Skinner. Plenty of girls will be pleased to take the job. Do you need her to stay with you?'

'I can manage now, thank you. It's Anne. She needs something that she can rely on – rely on in the future.'

'She'll be married in ten years, just like that stupid girl Phyllis.'

Mrs Hodding was distracted by the memory of the ingrate whose old job was on offer. Jealous of her dignity, she hoped that she had not seemed to care whether Anne Skinner worked for her or not. She turned to the cook with the intention of discussing the lunch menu as an indication that the conversation was over.

'Not Anne.' Elizabeth was emphatic. 'Anne won't be married in ten years. Anne wants something better than that. And I'm going to do my best to see that she gets it.'

'What', asked Mrs Hodding with heavy irony, 'had you in mind?'

'Sewing,' said Elizabeth Skinner in a desperate invention. 'Sewing of some sort. Tailoring. Dressmaking. Something like that.'

All Henry Hodding's servants believed the gardener to be a snob. The maids admired his grave good looks and the butler was unashamedly covetous of his Sunday suit. The cook felt sorry for him and argued that anyone who bore his burdens was likely to keep himself to himself. The boot boy objected to labouring for him in the autumn when the digging had to be done and was driven to near rebellion by the condescension of his temporary superior. But they were united in their resentment of his bland refusal to take part in any of their social activities.

At Harness Grove the servants made their own amusements. They might have enjoyed the weekly church dance three miles away at Whitwell, or have explored the varied delights of Worksop, which was four miles in the other direction, but in the tiled kitchen which the butler called 'the servants' hall' they could organise convivial diversions of their own. The butler was a beery baritone. The boot boy played a concertina and the cook had a fund of stories from her days in better service. When the master and mistress were out for dinner and the children had been fed and sent to bed, they would often push back the table from the centre of the tiled floor and enjoy themselves in a way they thought scandalous. Sometimes even the nanny and the housekeeper came downstairs and joined in. Rosie Knock sang too loudly and clapped with too much gusto whilst her husband watched with undisguised if misplaced admiration. But William Skinner said openly that he did not enjoy that sort of thing so when a party was arranged to celebrate Phyllis' translation from domestic service to married servitude there was doubt about whether he should even be invited.

'He won't come,' the boot boy said. 'What's the point? It's a waste of time.'

'It's only manners,' the butler told him. 'If we're asking Knock and his wife, we've got to.'

'Poor man's too busy looking after his wife and children,' the cook added. 'But we ought to show him that he's wanted.'

'Not by me he isn't,' the butler told her. 'But we've got to ask him, notwithstanding. It's only manners.'

To the servants' surprise, William accepted their invitation and, to their astonishment, he came. It was Gerrard Knock – after a few drinks, the Irish life and soul of the party – who was missing. He had been required to drive Henry Hodding to a Volunteers' dinner in Newark and Rosie had been warned that he would not be back in Darfoulds until after midnight. She complained about his absence, more loudly than a servant's wife should, saying that there was a perfectly good train service and that she would never understand why the master would not travel in his uniform, which she thought to be most becoming.

The cook calmed her down. Whatever her justification, there was no sense in saying something that she would regret afterwards – particularly in the presence of the housekeeper, who might report it to Mrs Hodding. The cook proved so persuasive that Rosie recovered enough composure to dance, first with the other maids and then with each of the men who bowed and asked her. Accompanied by murmurs – first of amazement and then of disapproval – she had no sooner been escorted back to her chair by the sweating butler than she walked boldly across to William, who was standing by the fireplace pretending to drink a glass of beer. A hush fell on the room as ears were strained to catch what she said. Nobody was sure that she asked him to dance and everybody felt certain that he did not ask her. But they stepped together into the middle of the tiled floor and followed the rhythm of the boot boy's concertina in perfect unison.

'Just showing off,' said the butler.

'He must have been a lovely dancer once . . . before the disaster.' It was not clear if the cook referred to Elizabeth's blindness or William's marriage.

They danced together for almost an hour and when the butler announced that the time had come for a sing-song, they parted without a word. The cook, who believed herself to be a contralto, gave such a moving performance of 'In the Gloaming' that Phyllis and her husband-to-be wept openly at the idea of lovers being forced to part. The butler called for a chorus of patriotic ballads, but Rosie astonished everyone for a second time that night by volunteering a humorous monologue which she performed with zest. To nobody's surprise, William slipped away at the end of the second verse.

'Not refined enough for him,' said the boot boy, embittered by his failure to provide an adequate accompaniment.

'She enjoyed that,' said the cook. 'She's one of those who likes performing. I never like to have that sort working in my kitchen. Always cause trouble.'

It was assumed by the butler, who shared her prejudice, that the cook's wise words had carried as far as Rosie herself whilst she was being congratulated by the more generous spirits amongst the maids, for she too left the party without thanks or farewell. She ran across the field that separated house and garden without even pulling her shawl across her shoulders. As soon as she closed the cottage door behind her, she reached for William.

'Let's go straight upstairs. We haven't got long. Gerry won't be away much after midnight.'

'Perhaps I shouldn't stay.'

'If you don't want me . . .' William feared that her laughter would echo through the wall and wake Elizabeth.

He watched her undress, as enthralled by her abandon as by her body.

'Did you enjoy tonight?' he asked.

'Lovely. It was lovely. Didn't you?'

Before he had time to say that he was not sure, she was all round him and there was time to think of nothing except being engulfed in her. Then there was no time to think at all. She was still lying on top of him when Henry Hodding's coach clattered past the window.

There was a full moon. William hurried home in the shadow of the two cottages. He lifted the latch without a sound and prepared to tiptoe across the kitchen. Sitting under the window in a pool of silver light, Anne was struggling to take up the hem of a coat which she was to pass on to Agnes. She looked, her father thought, less like a girl than one of the children in the old paintings which hung on the vicarage wall – small adults with faces already lined with sorrow.

'What on earth are you doing up at this time of night?'

'I'm finishing the coat. I've got to finish it by morning.'

'She doesn't need it tomorrow. You'll ruin your eyes. Off to bed with you.'

'I like doing it. I'm going to sew for a living. Mam wants me to.'

'That doesn't mean you have to work until midnight. Your mother would be furious if she knew.'

'But you won't tell her, will you?' Anne rethreaded her needle.

*

147

Anne thought of little except sewing. It was, she knew, her destiny to sew. Her mother's announcement of that vocation allowed no other possibility. For her last few weeks in the school which Mrs Hodding had set up in Darfoulds, her entire interest and energy were concentrated on patching dresses, darning socks, repairing tears in her father's working trousers and cutting down clothes for her brother and sister. She did not hem and pleat because her mother demanded it. She sewed away because, believing that it was her mother's wish for her future, hemming and pleating was all that she wished to do. Her commitment to a career in tailoring or dressmaking was so complete that Elizabeth Skinner began to wonder how she could explain to her daughter that the whole idea was an invention, made to see her through a moment's uncertainty. Then Anne saw the advertisement in the *Worksop Guardian*.

The Skinners did not take a paper and the copy which blew against the front-garden hedge was a week old, but when her father sent her out to remove it from the privet, the classified columns were still clearly readable and the words 'seamstress apprentice' were printed in bold type. Instead of screwing the crumpled page into a ball and putting it in the dustbin, she ran into the kitchen and, before her mother could prevent it, spread out the paper on the table and began to read aloud: 'William Allen, Tailor and Dressmaker of Bridge Street, Worksop, have a vacancy for a young lady of industrious disposition to be apprenticed to a tailoress in the company's workroom . . .' Anne read on with mounting enthusiasm, which even the phrase 'living in preferred' did nothing to dampen. Only when she reached the last line did her voice drop with disappointment. Even then, though audibly subdued, she read on: 'Wages five shillings and sixpence a week. Security bond, twenty pounds.'

She was unsure what a security bond was, but she had no doubt that the money had to be paid by the apprentice to the company which employed her rather than the other way round. And she was sure that twenty pounds was beyond her parents' means.

'Would you really like it?'

'I would, Mam.'

'It might have gone. They might have taken somebody on last week. And even if they haven't, they might not want you.'

'I would like it.'

'Living in?'

'I'd rather live here with you,' Anne remembered her destiny, 'and look after you.'

'You might have to live there. I'd manage.'

'I'd still like to do it.'

'I'll talk to your father.'

The promise filled Anne with alarm. She was well accustomed to her father being consulted on matters of family finance and management, but all of the consultations seemed to end in disagreements, with William begging his wife to be reasonable and Elizabeth demanding that her husband understand how she felt – shocked, demeaned or resentful according to the nature of the sacrifice she had to make. Anne was too young to realise that the bitter little battles always ended with her mother getting her own way.

Anne's future was discussed that night, as soon as the children were in bed, the supper pots were cleared away and washed, the table set in preparation for the next morning's breakfast and William settled in his chair with a seed catalogue.

'Anne wants to be a dressmaker.'

'How has she got that idea into her head?' Before the question was complete, he was back amongst the sweet peas.

'She's seen an advert for a firm in Worksop.'

The child's fantasy having turned into potential reality, William reacted with the proper concern of a caring father. 'It's terrible hard work. All day for a few pence. It'd kill her.' He turned back to his catalogue, certain that the idea would come to nothing.

'It's twenty pounds.'

William thought that his wife had started out on a new tack which held no interest for him. He grunted. He hoped the noise would pass for a response.

Elizabeth persisted. 'Have we got it?'

'Got what?'

'Twenty pounds.'

'What for?'

It was Elizabeth's turn to be impatient. 'For Anne's security bond. She wants to be an apprentice. I think we should let her. If we can.'

'We can't. You know that. It's almost every penny we've got in the world.'

'We'll not find a better use for it.'

'What if you're ill again? What about doctors' bills?'

'You know that I'm as strong as an ox. The eyes have got as much better as they're going to get.'

'What about Agnes, then? What about Ernest?'

'Ernest won't need doctors' bills. He's never had a day's illness in his life.'

'You know very well what I mean.'

'I only know what you say.'

'What I say is, we'll need it for Ernest's apprenticeship.'

'That's years away.'

149

'We won't have saved enough. Not fifty pounds by the time he's ready.'

Elizabeth decided that she had endured enough disputation. 'I want it for Anne.' She hoped that there was no more to be said and accepted her husband's silence as agreement that their life's savings should be spent on their elder daughter's security bond.

'I want to tell Mrs Hodding. She's shown a real interest in Anne. It's only polite.'

'Will we get any of it back?'

'Half if we're lucky. She won't spoil much work.'

'Only half?'

'Half at best.'

Next morning when Elizabeth told Anne the good news, Ernest asked, for the first time, what job he was going to do.

'What do you want to do?' his father asked him, desperately playing for time.

'I want to be a joiner.'

There was a long silence before William decided to do his duty. 'I wouldn't set my heart on it. We'll apprentice you if we can. But it costs money. We'll have to pay a security bond when Anne starts dressmaking. We may not be able to manage two of you.'

'But I'm the man,' said Ernest. 'I've got first call.'

William not knowing how to reply, the kitchen fell silent again.

'Anne needs it,' Ernest's mother told him. 'We've all got to look after Anne.'

That night, when Ernest got home from school, he went up to his bedroom and took his most prized possession from its place of honour on top of his chest of drawers. It was one of the cigar boxes which the Wisbech paupers had made for his father and at a time of particular poverty it had been given him as a birthday present. Both his mother and father had told him how valuable it was and why he must look after it with especial care. The box contained all his treasures — a soldier's button that he had found in Steetly churchyard, a feather which he believed had come from an eagle, a shell which reminded him of the sea he had never seen, a blue-veined stone, a champion conker, a penknife and a French five-centimes piece with the head of Napoleon III embossed upon it. He tipped his favourite things on to the bed and carefully examined all the wonders of the box that his father had pointed out to him so often in the past. He ran his fingers along the dovetail joints to remind himself that they fitted too perfectly to be detected by a touch and he opened and closed the lid to confirm the precision of the bevelling that made top join bottom so exactly that the key always turned in the lock. Then he dropped the box on the floor and trod on it. He imagined that he could feel, under his sole, the two tiny brass hinges which had once been so carefully inset.

He never mentioned joinery again, but accepted that – since he would be spared the colliery – his fate would be to work in the quarry which had been dug so near to Steetly chapel that the recently renovated Norman church was rocked each day by dynamite explosions. If he was as clever as the teacher said, he might work in the office. Otherwise he would shovel limestone for the rest of his life.

Ernest accepted his obligation to look after Anne and forced himself to rejoice when she was bound apprentice to a tailoress at William Allen of Bridge Street. She got the job largely because Mrs Hodding wrote to Robert Allen, the son of the firm's founder, and recommended her gardener's daughter in language so strong that the proprietor took it as an instruction. Mr Robert, as the proprietor was known, discharged the girl whom he had originally appointed and agreed – in deference to the last paragraph of Mrs Hodding's letter – that the new apprentice could choose to live in or travel to work each day from home. To his surprise, she chose to live in.

Life at William Allen's was hard – far harder than Anne could ever have imagined and harder even than her father had feared. There was much talk about her looking and behaving like a lady, but she was required to work like a convict committed to penal servitude. Reconciling the obligatory appearance with the necessary effort was a particular burden. She enjoyed wearing the compulsory black dress – for, although it was more appropriate to a woman four times her age, it matched her personality and added to her conviction that she was a small replica of her mother – and every morning, as she took her place in the crowded workroom, she looked at herself in the long mirror and confirmed that the dress was spotless and without a single visible crease. But when her day was finished, ten hours later, and she was almost too tired to eat, the thought of sponging and pressing her one dress before she went to bed was almost too much to bear.

The dormitory above the Bridge Street shop was cold and draughty but Anne found physical conditions less unpleasant than the company of the other five girls who endured them with her. Eating with young women whom she barely knew was so unpleasant an experience that, for the first few weeks of her apprenticeship, she hardly ate at all. She could not, however, avoid undressing in their presence. Each night, she volunteered for last use of the ironing board in the hope that her colleagues, having made their dresses fit for the following day's hard labour, would collapse into bed and fall asleep before it was necessary for her to prepare for the morning in nothing more than her long bloomers, woollen spencer and linen petticoat.

151

Three of the girls who bent over the workroom table were apprentices. The others did not aspire to acquiring more skill than was needed to sew hems and buttonholes for a few years before they went off to marriage and a different sort of drudgery. In the workroom, the apprentices were afforded a variety of courtesies which were denied the seamstresses but in the dormitory the order of precedence was reversed. Out of working hours, the young women who expected soon to become wives and mothers felt, and acted, like superior beings. They treated their colleagues, who expected to devote their lives to making other people's clothes, with pity, contempt and occasional hostility. Anne Skinner – because of her forbidding appearance and uncompromising manner – was spared the worst of the working girls' aggression. Her portion of scorn was diverted to the apprentice who occupied the next bed. Charlotte Harthill, an orphan from Peterborough, was indebted for her twenty pounds security bond to a distant uncle in Grantham. He believed that his gift had totally discharged his duty towards his dead sister's daughter. Charlotte attracted particular scorn because she had nowhere to go on Sunday.

It was not compassion that made Anne take Lottie Harthill under her wing: she needed to have someone in her life who was dependent upon her. Lottie fulfilled Anne's compulsion to guide the future of another human being – the task for which years of assistance to her blind mother had prepared her. And Lottie needed help. Her work was superb, but that only deepened the prejudice that the other girls felt against her because she was small, timid and alone in the world.

The bond between them was strengthened by Charlotte's occasional Sunday visit to Grove Cottage, where she sat silent in the corner of the living room, but it was not until the fourth winter of Anne's long apprenticeship that they were bound together with hoops which were never to be broken.

On the Monday before Christmas, the William Allen girls woke up to find Worksop covered in snow. The sight of the great drifts, blown against the walls of Bridge Street, filled the girls with delight. Despite the cold, they crowded to the frosty windows and discussed how they would spend their brief holiday. They imagined themselves taking on the personae of the line-drawn ladies who illustrated the winter pattern books – fur muffs in place, astrakhan collars turned up, coat hems almost touching the ground and queues of moustachioed young men waiting to help them on with their skates or buy them roast chestnuts from the barrow on the frozen lake shores. They also looked forward to shouting, shoving and screaming when they were snowballed by passing workmen and delivery boys. In their excited minds there was no incompatibility between their imagined appearance and anticipated behaviour.

Then the most junior girl – in William Allen's employ for less than a year and therefore good for nothing except running errands, heating irons and retrieving pins from finished work – returned to the dormitory with the news that the tap was frozen and there was no water for washing. There were several minutes of consternation before Anne Skinner had the idea of breaking the ice on the water butt in the yard and several more before the most junior girl could be bullied into dipping the great iron kettle into the freezing water. By the time the kettle was ready for the fire, it was too late to wait for it to boil. The girls were left to choose between washing in cold water or not at all. They completed their toilettes in haste and in bad temper. The energy which they had employed in contemplating the joys of Christmas was diverted into general dissatisfaction with everything around them.

They became particularly dissatisfied with Charlotte Harthill, the usual butt of their bad temper, who caused special offence. During the morning inspection only Lottie's appearance was judged up to the standards expected of a William Allen employee. In vain did the girls explain about the problem of the water and the rush in which they had been forced to dress.

'Charlotte Harthill managed,' said the supervisor.

Adverse comparison with the least favoured apprentice in William Allen's employ drove even the junior girl into a rage she could barely suppress. The three seniors snorted with such open anger that the supervisor warned them to mind their manners if they wanted to escape twopence being withheld from their Christmas wages in addition to the penny they had already lost. Anne accepted both reproof about her appearance and the prospect of punishment with her usual stoical bitterness. She had developed her mother's talent for conveying her feelings in a look and she stared at the supervisor with bleak contempt. Work began with the warning that hair would have to be tidied during the lunch break and, if the renovation left no time for the usual soup and cheese, the miscreants had only themselves to blame.

Lottie sat on her stool waiting for the other girls to rebraid, replait, reroll and replace the buns worn variously in the nape of the neck, on top of the head and over the ears. It was the junior girl who pulled the first hairpin out of Lottie's hair. Then the seniors joined in. In a few seconds the victim was in tears. When fear turned to anger and she tried to defend herself, they began to pull at the strands and wisps that hung out of place over her eyes. One gave a particularly vicious tug and told her, 'Think about me when you're here on your own on Christmas Day.'

'She's coming home for Christmas with me . . . and leave her alone, or you'll have me to deal with.'

Anne had no idea what terrible vengeance she was threatening, but she knew it was the sort of thing which her mother said with invariably stunning effect. She was not surprised when Lottie's assailants slunk towards the end of the workroom in which the soup and cheese would soon be deposited.

'Let me help. You'll take all day if you go on like this.'

'You'll miss your lunch.' Lottie's snivels had turned into tears.

'I'm not hungry.'

Together they began to pin Lottie's two tight buns back into place. Before the job was half done, Anne had taken over completely, gently imprisoning the loose hair and then wiping the tear-stained face with her own handkerchief. When she had finished, she stroked Lottie's face.

'Come on. You've got time for a drop of soup. I'll come with you.'

'Am I really going home with you for Christmas?'

'If you want to.'

'What will your mother say?'

'She won't mind if I ask her. I'll write a postcard tonight.'

'And what about your dad?'

'He won't mind either. Anyway, it's Mam who decides.' In the years since she left home, Anne had begun to understand the strength of her mother's character. 'If she says it's all right, it will be.'

The workroom was silent all afternoon except for the sound of pounding treadles and the occasional noise of clicking shears. Supper was eaten in sullen resentment. By bedtime the snow had begun to fall again, but the joy of the morning was not renewed. One by one the girls undressed and crept, shivering, into their chilly beds and the candles were blown out. Lottie, her feet like ice, felt too cold to sleep. When Anne slid silently in beside her she felt more contented than she had ever felt before.

Elizabeth Skinner was not so welcoming as her daughter had believed that she would be. She was courteous enough in front of her unexpected guest, for she felt genuinely sorry for the girl and always appreciated an opportunity to patronise someone less fortunate than herself, but she did not want her daughter to doubt that Lottie's presence was an inconvenience that she alone would have to bear. Late on Christmas Eve, whilst she and Anne were washing the supper dishes in the kitchen, the problems were all set out.

'I haven't got much of a present for her. Just some ribbons and pieces of lace I had about the house.'

'That sounds very nice, Mam.'

'And we can't move Agnes out of her bed, or she'll never sleep. You'll have to push your bed against the wall and both of you manage in that as best you can.'

'We'll manage, Mam.'

'And she'll have to go home early on Boxing Day afternoon.'

'Oh, Mam. Does she have to? Can't she stay and go back with me after supper?'

'Be thankful she's here at all. The trouble I had – and the expense – cooking the extra food. She'll just have to go after Boxing Day dinner.'

'Why will she?'

'Because I say so. And because we're all going to Beard's Mill. Your dad's going to help with the skating, sweeping the ice and doing I don't know what and I've promised to go with him. Heaven knows, I don't want to go. But Mr Hodding will be offended if I don't.'

'Can't Lottie come too?'

'She hasn't been invited. Only the servants and the servants' families have been asked.' Elizabeth pronounced the word servant as if she felt a duty to remind her daughter of their humiliating station.

'Do I have to go?'

'If you stay here you do. If you go off back to Worksop that's a different matter. Do that if you want. We'll do nothing at Beard's Mill except watch Mr Hodding perform and try to keep warm.'

Boxing Day was the warmest day for a week – so warm that the Hoddings feared the ice on Beard's Mill dam would melt, and certainly warm enough to allow Elizabeth's thoughts to wander from the misery of cold face and numb fingers. She thought instead of the indignity of standing with the Hodding servants watching the family and its Christmas guests make fools of themselves on the frozen pond. The ladies giggled and pretended to be afraid, the young men attempted to carve complicated patterns on the ice and fell flat on their backs and the middle-aged couples glided hand in hand for a few yards and then staggered on to the bank with cries of triumph. Only Henry Hodding circled the frozen pond with poise and confidence. He tried nothing elaborate, but methodically made five anti-clockwise circumnavigations before he stopped, turned and made exactly the same number of clockwise circuits. He skated with his arms folded and his gloved hands tucked securely under the folds of his ulster so as to allow not the slightest suspicion that he was prepared for a fall.

Each time he changed direction, he told his wife how many laps he had completed and explained to her that he was being careful to avoid the dizziness which would prevent him from completing the hour's continuous activity which he regarded as essential to his health.

The servants' families stood at a respectful distance and applauded their master's achievement, marvelled at the daring of the young men

155

and gasped artificially if one of the young ladies ventured on to the ice. Gerrard Knock fed a bonfire. The butler dispensed hot rum punch, tepid coffee, warm mince pies and badly burned chestnuts. William Skinner, with sacking wrapped round his boots to give him a firm foothold, swept the ice clean of tiny frozen particles which the skaters had cut up and which might, in retaliation, have impeded their progress. At four o'clock, Henry Hodding, having broken the previous year's endurance record, announced that it was thawing and skating must stop. The servants were welcome to stay and finish what was left of the food and drink.

Elizabeth Skinner stalked off home to her daughters after warning Ernest not to snowball and giving notice to William that, if their son disobeyed her instructions, she would want to know the reason why his father had been party to the mutiny. The butler packed up the plates and glasses, Ernest and the serving girls ate the mince pies, Gerrard Knock made the fire safe. Rosie, with exaggerated bravado, drank the few remaining drops of rum punch.

When the various tasks had been completed, the butler asked for help in carrying the boxes and the baskets back to Harness Grove. When William Skinner bent down to pick up a hamper, Rosie bent down with him. Their cheeks rubbed together and her hands, reaching for the leather handles, touched his. He stood up with a start. Rosie slowly straightened herself and took hold of his arm. 'Come and have a slide on the ice.'

'You heard what Mr Hodding said. It's begun—'

'I'm not afraid of a dipping. Are—?'

'Don't be so silly.' The butler, who was paid to be pompous and usually exceeded his duties by also being stupid, realised that a scene was developing.

'Look here, Mrs Knock. If you want a slide, you slide with your husband and leave Mr Skinner to get home to his family.'

'My Gerrard's lame. My Gerrard couldn't slide to save his life. But Mr Skinner could. Fit as a flea is Mr Skinner.'

'I'm sorry.' Gerrard was addressing the whole company. 'It's the rum punch that's talking. She's not used to it. Come on, Rosie. Home and bed for you.'

'Home and what?'

'Home.'

'But I want to slide. Ernest will slide with me.'

She ran at Ernest and Ernest did nothing to defend himself. Rosie seized his hands and dragged him down the bank and, miraculously, they glided together towards the centre of the pond.

'You see, it's easy. Just like dancing. Your dad's a great dancer.'

Rosie put her arm round Ernest's waist and – holding him far more tightly than would be allowed in a respectable ballroom – bent and braced her knees again and propelled them another six feet across the ice.

'Again!' she cried, and they moved another yard with Ernest enveloped in the folds of her cloak and in her arms.

'Again.' Ernest emerged, flushed and infected by her enthusiasm. He pushed in one direction and she pushed in the other. With a scream and a squeal they fell and landed in a heap on the ice. Rosie's skirts flew up about her waist. There was a horrified pause before anyone rushed forward. Then the ice cracked and woman and boy both sank, without a struggle, into the cold water. They were still holding hands.

Despite his limp, the coachman was first down the slope and into the dam. The gardener was only a few seconds behind him but, by the time William plunged in, Rosie had appeared through a patch of ice vomiting water, rum punch and her half-digested Boxing Day dinner. Ernest surfaced a few second later, shaking with cold and gasping for breath. For a moment, there was more concern for the rescuers than for those they had tried to save. Then they too splashed their way up through the pieces of floating ice and, together with Rosie Knock, scrambled out on to the bank, turning the snow around them from pure white into dirty grey. Ernest, too weak to reach safety himself, was dragged out of the water, wrapped in the butler's greatcoat and carried up the long hill to Harness Grove.

'Where's Knock?' asked Henry Hodding, watching the water spread across the terracotta tiles of his kitchen floor.

'At home changing his clothes and looking after Mrs Knock,' said William as he tried to pull off Ernest's sodden trousers.

'Good God!' Henry Hodding rarely blasphemed. 'Did they fall in as well?'

'They all did,' said the butler vacuously, holding out the old clothes which William and Ernest were to wear.

'Go and get him. Give Skinner the towels and go and get him. Tell him to take the carriage to Worksop and bring the doctor back here.' He looked first at Ernest – still shivering and fighting for breath – and then at the boy's father, who was himself shaking with cold and fear. 'Unless I'm much mistaken, this young man will be dead before morning.'

CHAPTER TWELVE

Thoughts of Death

By next morning Ernest had completely recovered. But Rosie, who had spent Boxing Day evening subdued, though hardly repentant, woke early on the following day with a pain in her back. Although she felt cold, a rivulet of sweat ran down between her breasts. When she tried to sit up, her head swam and her husband, serenely asleep beside her, seemed to be a distant blur. An hour later she felt better – well enough to insist that, although she needed to stay in bed, she would have completely recovered by the evening.

When Gerrard got home from work, his breakfast plate and mug were still on the kitchen table and he could hear his wife fighting for breath in the bedroom upstairs. Her hair was matted and the bed-clothes were soaked with sweat, but she insisted that she did not need a doctor. Her husband chose not to argue with her for he preferred to believe that she was not seriously ill. Twice during the night the panting stopped so suddenly that Gerrard was woken by the silence. But, after a few minutes' peace, it began again. At six o'clock on the morning of the Feast of the Holy Innocents, Rosie lay so still and cold beside her husband that he was afraid she was dead. She was only unconscious.

Elizabeth Skinner came round from next door, diagnosed pneumonia, prescribed hot poultices front and back and said that permission must be sought to send for Mr Hodding's doctor. By the time the proprieties had been completed and the doctor approached, Rosie was conscious again and so hot that she tried to throw off the blankets and sheets. When the doctor arrived she was comatose again.

The doctor confirmed pneumonia and added pleurisy. He complimented Gerrard on the hot poultices and suggested they be continued with mustard added to the boiling water in which they were heated. He said that medicine would be ready in his surgery if the coachman cared to call for it after six o'clock. Having repeated the firm instruction to 'keep her warm', he ended his visit with a question. 'Are there any children to look after?'

'No, sir. Is it catching, sir? I'd like the lady from next door to keep an eye on her whilst I'm at work. But if it's catching . . .'

'That's not why I asked. The medicine will last for a week. If you need any more like that, let me know. The instructions are on the bottle. You can read, can't you?'

Rosie died before the bottle was empty. Only once during the six days did she say anything that her husband understood. Smiling a pale version of her old smile, she whispered, 'What a nuisance I am. But then, I always was.'

Gerrard, who had spent the time he was allowed away from work silently mopping her sweat and pulling the bedclothes over her, began to cry. 'I'm sorry,' he said, 'I know what it's been like and I'm sorry.'

He was greatly comforted by all the other servants. Even William Skinner, who nobody imagined would have thought of such things, sat with the widower on the nights before the burial. At the funeral, the gardener stayed by the coachman's side to the very end. Even when Gerrard lingered by the grave, William stayed with him until the thud of clay on the coffin was too much for the coachman to bear.

William did not stay with Gerrard Knock because he felt sympathy or compassion. He stayed because, standing by the coachman's side, he came as close as he dared to proclaiming his own loss. As they left the churchyard together, he felt only hatred for the widower – a hatred based on a perverse mixture of envy and self-pity. Gerrard Knock was allowed to grieve and was comforted in his grief by mourners who believed that Rosie loved him as he loved her. Yet William, who had loved her more and was loved by Rosie in return, received not a word of consolation. He was paying the last penalty of a secret liaison.

It was at the funeral that Henry Hodding first described young Ernest Skinner as 'the boy who nearly died on my kitchen floor'. Ernest did not think of himself as a boy of any sort for he was fifteen and had worked for two years at Steetly Quarry, where he sharpened the picks and carried cold tea for the men who cut the stone. Then – his grave manner and conscientious habits having been noted – he became assistant to James Sewell, the chargehand at the dynamite hut. After six months, Ernest had so impressed his superiors that he had been given permission to issue fuses on his own authority. Having acquired a position of such responsibility, he thought of himself as young no more.

But Mr Hodding persisted in his description and Mr Hodding, being the squire of Darfoulds, was entitled to call anybody anything that took his fancy. So, when Ernest was summoned to Harness Grove one Monday night, he changed immediately into his Sunday suit

159

and gritted his teeth in preparation for patronising reference to the dramatic events of Boxing Day. A tall man in tweeds sat on the sofa in the Hodding drawing room. His right foot was encased in a carpet slipper which had been split up the front to reveal a bandaged toe, and his left arm was suspended in a silk sling. A malacca cane rested across his knees.

'This,' said Henry Hodding proudly, 'is the boy who almost died on my kitchen floor. Ernest, this is Mr Arnold Hirst.' He pronounced his visitor's name in a way that suggested he was taking something of a risk by having such a man under his roof.

'Evening, si',' said Arnold Hirst.

Ernest had never been addressed with such respect before and the greeting, which he felt to be wholly inappropriate, bewildered him.

'Speak up, boy,' said Henry Hodding.

Ernest could think of nothing to say except a repetition of what had already been said to him and that seemed an impertinence. So he mumbled.

'Don't like boys who don't speak out plain,' said Arnold Hirst.

'He usually does,' Henry Hodding told him, as if Ernest were not there. 'I can't think what's come over him.'

Arnold Hirst tapped his leg with his malacca cane in the manner of a conductor rapping the baton on the music stand in order to obtain the full attention of his audience. The sharp noise that resulted suggested that the shin was in splints.

Before he had time to begin his performance, Henry Hodding took over. 'Mr Hirst has had an accident.'

'An athletic accident,' the temporary cripple added.

'He fell off bars in his gymnasium.'

'Rings – my hand slipped out of one of the rings as I was practising somersaults.'

'No matter.' The details of the catastrophe did not concern Henry Hodding. 'You will see that Mr Hirst is not permanently incapacitated.'

'Though it happens quite often.' Arnold Hirst smiled with pride at the thought of his medical history. 'I've broken eleven bones in thirty years – not to mention dislocations. Gymnastics. Wrestling. Rock-climbing. One day I'm going to Switzerland to try out this skiing thing.' He described his ambition as if its chief attraction was the new opportunities it provided for fractures. 'Look at the nose.'

Hirst half turned his head so that his profile was in sharp relief against the autumn sunlight that streamed in through the french windows. It seemed to be a nose of no particular interest.

'Straight as a die. Ears too. Perfect. Yet I've boxed since I was ten.

Still do at forty-five. Don't mean to boast. Hate boasting. Just wanted to show what you can do if you keep in trim. Do you box, si'?'

'No, sir.' Ernest was careful to pronounce the whole word.

'You should. The noble art of self-defence.' He spoke each word of his romantic definition as if the phrase was poetry and he struck a pugilistic pose that caused the malacca cane to fall from his knee. Ernest, anxious to make up for previous infelicities, darted to pick it up.

'Leave that there.'

As Ernest cowered back, Arnold Hirst picked up his stick with difficulty and, twirling the silver knob, drew a sword blade from within the hollow cane. He parried and slashed the air, producing a sound which he visibly enjoyed.

'Fencing don't make you fit. But you need to be fit to fence. Indian clubs are the best. It's our Christian duty to keep fit. I'll give you a pair of clubs when you come to work for me.'

Henry Hodding's patience, already stretched almost to breaking point, snapped.

'For heaven's sake, Hirst, let's get down to business. The young man doesn't know what you intend for him.'

Arnold Hirst drew breath in preparation for setting out his proposal. But it was too late. Henry Hodding was in full flow.

'Mr Hirst needs someone to help him – at least until his bones mend. And, no doubt, when he breaks some more. The two lads he's tried already didn't suit—'

'Very puny. Couldn't climb the rope in my gymnasium. No strength in the arms.'

'Being a timber merchant, he needs someone who is good at figures. Multiply nine and a half by fourteen.'

'One hundred and thirty-three,' said Ernest without blinking.

'What did I tell you, Hirst? And this boy almost died on my kitchen floor.'

'Divide nine by eleven.'

'It won't go, sir.'

'Never mind, Hirst. He can learn fractions later.'

The clue having been given, Ernest picked it up and rectified his mistake. 'Nine-elevenths, sir.'

'Very good. The question is, do you want to work for Mr Hirst here?'

Ernest's confidence, which had been severely damaged by his confusion over the proper manner of introduction, had been restored to robust health by his arithmetical success. 'I've got a job already, sir.'

'I know that. But this is a better job.'

Ernest was deeply offended. 'I work with dynamite at the quarry. I'm in charge of the fuses. That's a good job.'

'Not as good as this one,' said Hirst, easing his broken arm in its sling. 'Particularly if you can box.'

'I'd better talk to my mother about it.'

Ernest did not quite understand his own emotions, but he knew that he felt both desperately anxious and desperately reluctant to take on a job which required him to work with wood.

'I thought you said he was your gardener's son,' said Arnold Hirst, who – not believing that women should normally be consulted about such matters – assumed that the boy had no father.

'Mr Hirst will want to know very quickly. He'll want you to tell me what you've decided tomorrow night. You'd be a young fool not to take it. Tell your father I said so.'

William Skinner was inclined to take his master's advice. He was anxious for Ernest to escape from the quarry and the dynamite store. He had spent too many mornings listening to the distant blasts and expecting some awful tragedy. He did not think of himself as a friend to his son and, since Ernest did not share his obsession with plants and flowers, they talked to each other only about the trivia of family affairs – Elizabeth's eyesight, Anne's job, Agnes's health and the importance of keeping clean and tidy. But he liked the idea of having a son who everybody said looked like him and he felt guilty that the boy had not been apprenticed to a decent trade. Working for Arnold Hirst seemed a job with prospects. He was sure that Ernest should take his chance.

Ernest's mother was not certain and she asked her son a number of detailed questions which she hoped would help to make up her mind. Each one increased Ernest's annoyance for he knew none of the answers and did not enjoy admitting ignorance even to his own family. There was a moment of crisis when his mother actually announced that she would accompany him on his return visit to Harness Grove and discover the details on which the final decision would be based. But his father summoned up enough courage to intervene on behalf of the rights of man.

'You can't embarrass the lad like that. If anyone goes, I'll go.'

That solution was dismissed in silent contempt. 'We'll work out the questions and he can ask them for himself.'

So, much to Henry Hodding's impressed surprise, Arnold Hirst was cross-examined about wages, security and prospects. The replies came not from the prospective employer but from his friend and solicitor, who invented them on the spot. Initially Ernest would be paid two shillings a week more than he received at the quarry. For a young man of talent and ambition, Hirst's timber yard was the gateway to success. The employment would be permanent. In the unlikely event of Mr Hirst avoiding injury for more than a few weeks, alternative work would be found.

'Where would I work?'

'In Retford, of course.'

'That's what my mother said. How would I get there?'

'Dear me, if you don't know that I'm not sure you can do the job.'

'I do, sir. That's the trouble. I'd have to go by train and it would cost half my wages.'

'Move into lodgings,' Henry Hodding suggested. The whole subject had begun to bore him. 'You're old enough to leave home.'

'That'd take half my wages too.'

'Perhaps Mrs Hirst will put you up in the servants' quarters.'

Ernest was not sure that Arnold Hirst was even listening. He thought, My mother wouldn't like that. But he said, 'How much would that cost me?'

'How should I know? Mrs Hirst will tell you that.'

'I might be worse off than at the quarry.'

Henry Hodding would have preferred the boy who almost died on his kitchen floor to have thought of nothing except the glorious prospect of working his way to the top of the timber business. He decided that what Ernest lacked in ambition, he made up for in caution. If Arnold Hirst expanded into the funeral business, as he intended, he would have a man with the imagination of an undertaker already in his employment. Having pioneered the idea of Ernest working in the Retford woodyard he was not prepared for anything to stand in the way of its fulfilment.

'I'm sure that Mr Hirst will see that you're not out of pocket.'

'Then I'd like the job, please, sir.'

'You don't seem very enthusiastic.'

Nor was he. Ernest would have preferred to remain at the quarry where, thanks to Anne's permanent employment at William Allen's, he could become the centre of his mother's attention. The Skinner family never discussed their feelings for each other, but Ernest – who was too young to understand the complexities of married life – sensed that, if his parents loved each other at all, it was a different sort of love from that which held together other married couples. He could not recall his father ever touching his mother or commenting on her appearance. They never went out together except to church and, even then, Elizabeth never held William's hand as they walked through the old gravestones to the church door. He had no doubt that, some-

163

how, his father had shut the light out of his mother's life. He thought that he could provide the affection which she had been so long denied. On the night before he left for Retford, he confessed how little he wanted to go and wallowed in his mother's comfort.

'But you will come home on Sundays.'

'Anne said that. But we hardly ever see her at all.'

'Anne's doing very well for herself. And that makes me very happy. She'll set up on her own one day. There's no reason why you shouldn't do the same. And I'll be very proud of you.'

'You don't sound as if you'll even miss me.'

'Of course I shall. So will Agnes. That's why you ought to come as many Sundays as you can.'

'I shall,' said Ernest, and he meant it. He did not miss a Sunday at Grove Cottage in two years.

It was duty, not desire, that brought Ernest home for he developed an almost immediate passion for the timber business, which was so strong that it overcame his original horror of working amongst joiners without being one himself. He loved the smell of new wood, the sound of the circular saw cutting planks out of logs, the feel of hard oak and soft sawdust and the sight of great trees crashing down through neighbouring branches. He devoted his life to becoming an expert on floorboards, roof beams and the door panels which Hirst's of Retford sold to builders all over Nottinghamshire. He enjoyed learning what he believed to be the technical language of his trade and, before his first week was ended, he was talking about 'three by two' as if he had described timber by its size since he was a boy at Darfoulds. Most of all, he loved walking in the woods with Arnold Hirst and marking the trees to be felled during the following week.

The ritual of selection was mysterious and complicated. Hirst would march through the woods like a man who knew his exact destination. Then, in front of the oak, ash or elm which had merited his attention, he would go through a methodical routine. Scraps of bark were pulled from the trunk and examined. He tapped the trunk with his folding ruler and, with his head held on one side like a thrush prospecting for worms, listened intently to the sound he had made. An exposed root was pierced with a bradawl that he carried especially for that purpose. Calculations were made, to Ernest's surprise, not in his head but in a small black-backed notebook. Then, after a long period of quiet contemplation, Arnold Hirst would cry, 'Let's have him!' as if he had sighted a fugitive grouse or partridge that had to be brought down with a single shot. Ernest's duty was to dart forward and, with an agility denied to a man with fractured bones, draw a chalk line round the chosen tree and scrawl 'H' on the bole to confirm that it was to be felled and taken to Hirst's timber yard.

It took two months for Arnold Hirst's bones to heal, and during the weeks of incapacity Ernest began to feel an admiration which came dangerously close to idolatry. Ernest admired Arnold Hirst because he represented, with ferocious energy, a set of values to which the young man was instantly attracted. He believed in duty and discipline, playing the game, soldiering on, shaving twice a day and always raising his hat when he passed a lady in the street. Ernest determined to live by Arnold Hirst's code of chivalry.

When there were no fractures to impede his progress, Hirst spent most of his Sundays walking in what had once been Sherwood Forest. Ernest came to believe that he used these excursions for the preliminary reconnoitre of the trees he would mark for felling the following week. But on Sundays he never touched bradawl or notebook. That would have been labour and Arnold Hirst was a strict Sabbatarian. One weekend when he asked Ernest to join him on a tramp to Bawtry he forced the young man to face the first conscious moral dilemma of his life. Had the excursion involved work, Ernest would have accepted without hesitation, but since it was for pure pleasure he realised that it was his duty to decline and visit his parents instead. He desperately wanted to spend the day with Hirst. The anguish he felt at the prospect of missing so glorious an opportunity convinced him where the path of virtue lay. He already believed that suffering was an essential part of the good life.

'I don't think I can. I'd like to. But I don't think I can. My mother expects me home on Sundays.'

He longed for Hirst – acting under the powers which Ernest's esteem conferred upon him – to say that, on this special occasion, his parents could be forgotten. But he had become a disciple of a stern, unbending creed.

'Then you must go home. Your first duty is to your family.' It was a belief that Arnold Hirst held with absolute conviction, despite having formed the habit of communing with nature each Sunday as a way of escaping from the wife he detested.

The judgement having been handed down, Ernest would no more have neglected his weekend at Darfoulds than he would have failed to exercise with his new Indian clubs each morning and evening, taken strong drink or neglected to trim the incipient moustache which he was growing in tribute to his mentor. He spent each Sunday at Grove Cottage, neither enjoying himself nor bringing enjoyment to his family, but sitting at the table in a corner and wallowing in the pleasure of his self-sacrifice. His mother always asked him how he was. He always assured her that he was well and then fell silent. His father then took up the conversation and enquired about his prospects. Ernest invariably replied that he was doing well but intended to do better, before he sank back into his own thoughts. They ate dinner. Agnes asked for second helpings – to the delight of William Skinner, who saw it as a sign that the rheumatic fever had left no permanent scars, and to the dismay of Elizabeth, who believed it to be the symptom of a new wasting disease. Soon after the meal was over, Ernest left for Retford and evensong at St Paul's Church, where the vicar was an adherent of the doctrines of Pusey and Keble.

A hundred such Sundays passed before a conversation of any significance took place. Then his mother asked him if he would walk with her to Steetly chapel before he left. She asked her first anxious question before they were down the garden path and on to the Chesterfield Road.

'Have you noticed Agnes?'

'I thought she looked very well.'

'She's marvellous. It's a miracle. She's almost a grown woman. If she goes on like this, she'll outlast your dad and me.'

'Why shouldn't she?' Ernest could think of no better answer.

'Because she had rheumatic fever. You never quite get over it, whatever your dad says. She's going to grow up but she's going to grow up wilful. She'll need keeping out of trouble and then looking after when she gets in it.'

'That's years away, Mam.'

'Perhaps it is. Let's hope so. But what happens if I drop dead tomorrow? These days I can't help thinking about it! I've got the idea in my head that I shan't make old bones.'

'Don't say such things.'

'But what if I do?'

'Dad'll look after her.'

'Your dad would be married again in six months.'

Ernest was scandalised. But curiosity overcame outrage. 'Who would he marry?'

'Somebody. Anybody. I don't think that he has anyone in mind. But he won't stay on his own. Your dad isn't cut out to look after himself.'

'He'd still look after Agnes.'

'I think he would. But we can't be sure. I want you to promise me that you'll look after her if she's on her own or if she's ever in trouble.'

'Won't she get married?' Ernest sounded nervous.

'Of course she will. But that might not be an end of her worries. It might be the beginning. Think of what life would have been like for me if your father had been a different sort of man. I've been lucky. Let's hope she's the same. But marriage isn't all comfort and joy.'

'But she's not going to go blind, Mam.'

'Promise me you'll look after her.'

Ernest accepted his second burden, and, being a young man of solemn propriety, felt the weight of his new responsibilities descend upon him as he spoke.

'Your dad says that she's grown into a good-looking young woman. I can see her now, but not very distinctly. He says if we lived in Worksop, lads would be round every night.'

'It's because of her complexion. And her red hair.'

'Auburn,' corrected her mother. 'Auburn. Funny, isn't it? We've never had auburn hair in our family. Nor your father's to my knowledge. It's just like Rosie Knock's hair was.'

'How's Mr Knock?' Ernest was anxious to change the subject. 'How long is it since Mrs Knock died? Do you know, I haven't thought of her for years.'

'I have,' his mother told him. 'I think of her every day.'

They had reached the churchyard gate and Rosie's grave, with its still-new headstone, stood out amongst the dark-grey crosses and the broken columns which had been aged by sun and rain. Ernest lifted the latch.

'Let's go home,' his mother said. 'I want to make sure that Agnes and your dad are all right.'

CHAPTER THIRTEEN

In Sickness and in Health

Elizabeth Skinner's premonitions about early death were wholly unfounded. She was, as she told her husband when their savings were spent on Anne's apprenticeship, as strong as an ox – healthy in every way except for her eyes. Her sight, which after the sudden Wisbech blindness had gradually improved, was never fully restored and, after ten years in which she peered at a world which was blurred but visible, darkness gradually engulfed her again. At first, she lived in nothing worse than twilight. Then dusk turned into a moonless night. She stumbled about Grove Cottage, colliding with the furniture, burning her hands on the hot oven and knocking pots off the dresser. When she scalded herself by pouring the kettle over her feet instead of into the sink, William decided that help was necessary. He wrote to Anne at her Worksop lodgings and told her that she must come home.

Anne was twenty-two and full of ambition. She shared lodgings with Charlotte Harthill and devoted herself entirely to the hopes which drove the two women on. They always appeared at William Allen's shop at twenty-five minutes past eight and were in their places at the workroom table exactly five minutes later. They left together at precisely six-thirty and hurried home to Gateford Road, where they invariably arrived well before seven o'clock. In other women such a determination to deny their employers a minute's unpaid labour would have been regarded as mutiny, but Anne and Lottie were special. In a bare day they finished more work than their colleagues could complete with the help of three hours' overtime and Lottie's dressmaking – like Anne's tailoring – was always of the highest quality. They were respected in the workroom for their talent, and their status was further increased by the mystery which surrounded them. Apart from occasional sightings on their way to and from church on a Sunday morning, the young women were never seen outside working hours. Whilst their colleagues talked incessantly about husbands and fiancés, weekend walks and evening outings, pets, furniture and the births, marriages and deaths column in the *Worksop Guardian*, the two friends kept their secret. Had the way in which they spent their time in Gateford Road been known to Mr Robert Allen, they would have been dismissed on the spot – despite their undoubted skill and industry. For the Misses Harthill and Skinner were taking in work on their own account and saving the profit in preparation for the day when they could set up their own business. Returning home to look after a sick mother did not feature in Anne's plans.

'What are you going to do?' Lottie looked up from over the letter which Anne had handed her across the breakfast table. She was concerned not to sound as anxious as she felt.

'I'm going to talk to Ern first. He'll know what's right.'

'And will you do what he tells you?'

'I didn't say that.' There was a note of bad temper in Anne's voice. She did not like being cross-examined, even by Lottie.

It was just as well that Anne had not planned to follow her brother's advice. She had hoped that he would say it was important for her to work and build a business, and advise her to salve her conscience by making a small weekly allowance to her parents. He urged her to do quite the opposite.

'Of course you must go home. It's a daughter's duty. When I think of the way she always looked after you. You can still work at Allen's. The walk will do you good. And you'll save money living at home. Of course you've got to go back.'

'Why can't Aggie look after her?'

'She's not old enough.'

'Of course she is. I was living away from home when I was no older than she is now.'

'Well, Mam doesn't feel safe with her. Thinks she's flighty. She wants you, Anne. That's clear from the letter.'

'What about you?'

Ernest looked blank.

'Yes, what about you moving back?'

'It's not for me to move back. It's a daughter's job. You ought to think yourself lucky that you have a job and a trade that you can keep up. Most unmarried women never leave home at all and are left with nothing when their parents die. You ought to be glad to move back.'

'So you'll not lift a finger?'

'Don't say that. I go every Sunday. You haven't been for months.'

'I work on Sundays.'

'I don't believe you.' The explanation was too shocking to be true.

'We do ten hours every Sunday. Both of us. Mostly hemming and pleating. Seamstresses' work. And we put every penny we earn away.'

'What for?'

'For our own business, that's what for. Skinner and Harthill,

Ladies' Tailors and Dressmakers. We'll be ready in a couple of years.'

'So you won't go back to Grove Cottage?'

'I never said that. I've got to think about it and I've got to talk to Lottie.'

'What's it to do with her?'

'The business. I've told you. We were going to open a business together.'

'You can still do that. I'll lend you the extra money. I'll start saving money soon.'

'The money's not the only thing I promised her.'

'You're not married to her, you know. There aren't any vows to be broken. I don't understand you. I thought you were so close to Mam. I thought she was the only person who mattered to you.'

It took Anne several seconds to answer. Then she replied with a calm certainty that added to Ernest's mistaken conviction that all his sister wanted in the world was to grow up in her mother's image. 'I shall think about it. I shall talk to Lottie. Then I shall go to Grove Cottage next Sunday and see what things are really like. I shall see for myself.'

'If you don't believe our father's letter . . .'

'Don't be silly, Ernest. I want to see for myself. Will you be there?'

'I'm there every Sunday, aren't I? It's not a great event for me to be there.'

'We'll talk to Dad.'

Talking to Dad was difficult, for it was a cold Sunday and they could not sit out in the garden. So, although Elizabeth Skinner spent most of the afternoon clearing up the debris of dinner and preparing tea, they had to ask furtive questions during the moments when their sister disappeared into the kitchen to offer her help. She was never away for long for family mythology insisted that exposure to the steam of washing-up water or the chill of an open back door might well prove fatal to a young woman whose system had been weakened by rheumatic fever. Ernest took the initiative when Agnes bounded out of the living room with a napkin which her father had dropped and left under the table.

'How is she?'

His father seemed not to understand the need for brief and immediate answers.

'How's who? Your mother or Agnes?'

Agnes reappeared in the doorway. 'I'm very well, thank you very much.'

She sat on the arm of her father's chair and he stroked her long auburn hair.

'We can't help worrying. She won't look after herself. On the go all the time.'

'I'm not an invalid but they won't believe it.'

'Get off the arm of that chair, young lady.' It was her mother's turn to make a sudden entry. 'It'll break off under your weight. You talk about being a grown woman often enough. It's time you started to behave like one. The weather's warm enough for you to go for a little walk if you wrap yourself up. You'd like to go for a walk with her, wouldn't you, Anne?'

'I'm off in half an hour.'

'What about you, Ernest?'

'I'm walking into Worksop with Anne.'

'Get your coat,' said Elizabeth. 'I'll go with you myself if nobody else will. Put the kettle on, Anne. That is, if it's not too much trouble. We'll have a cup of tea when Agnes and I get back.'

'I don't want a walk, Mam. I'm halfway through my story.'

'You read too much. You'll have eyes like mine if you go on like this. It's a walk for you.'

'Listen to your mother. A walk will do you good.'

William spoke with genuine concern for his daughter's welfare. Anne and Ernest nodded in emphatic, though bogus, agreement with his judgement. Agnes, overwhelmed by the weight of opinion, led her mother into the cubby-hole under the stairs where the coats were kept.

'I didn't realise,' said William in a half-whisper, 'that you were asking about your mother. She's managing very well. She ought to let Agnes do more to help her. The girl's willing enough but her mother won't let her do anything. Your mother's well enough in herself but the sight's no better.'

Elizabeth, whose hearing had improved as her sight deteriorated, shouted through the thin board wall of the cubby-hole, 'I'm blind. That's how I am. Better to call it what it is. But I'm managing. I'm managing perfectly well, thank you very much.'

After Agnes, swathed in thick coat and woollen scarf, had led her mother out into the watery sunlight, Anne decided to approach the subject directly. 'It's your letter. We weren't sure what to do about it.'

'I knew it was that.' Father looked at daughter without malice. 'I knew something special must have brought you all this way. Do you know, we haven't seen you for three months.'

'Ten weeks,' said Anne sharply. 'Ten weeks. I've kept count.'

'It doesn't matter.' Ernest wanted decisions taken before the walkers returned. 'We have to decide how she's going to be looked after.' After a pause, he added, with obvious disapproval, 'Anne works on Sundays and says she can't really move back home.'

171

'We can manage all right. Your mother does wonderfully well, considering. If only she'd let me and Agnes do more, there'd be no bother. But she will do everything. If I wash a pot, she washes it again. And she treats Agnes as if she'd melt in the rain. But we'll manage. You've got your own lives to lead.'

'But what about the letter?' Anne had it with her in the inside pocket of her best handbag.

'Oh, the letter! I shouldn't tell you, but your mother asked me to write it. Don't let her know I've told you. She'd die rather than you found out.'

Anne's heart sank. If her mother had been so desperate that she had asked her husband to write such a letter, there could only be one answer to the plea he had made on her behalf. Christian duty demanded that she return home. Ernest would prod and prick her conscience. Even Charlotte, to whom she felt an allegiance far stronger than that which she owed to her mother, would say that she must pack up her belongings and leave Gateford Road. She tried not to think of the years of lonely drudgery which lay ahead. Charlotte would find another ladies' tailor to become her partner . . .

'There's no need to take any notice of the letter.' William seemed amused by her mistake. 'She doesn't really want you to come home. In that minute – the minute when she made me write it – she just wanted to feel that you would come if she needed you. You forget how close you used to be. She's frightened of losing you.'

Anne was numb with relief. Ernest could not quite believe his good fortune.

'What will you tell her?' Anne asked.

'I shall tell her the truth. If you came back home tomorrow, you'd be no help to your mother. She wouldn't let you be. You'd just be two more mouths to feed and beds to make. You wouldn't look after her. She'd look after you. That's her nature. I shall tell her that you both offered, which I trust you did—'

Anne said, 'Yes,' before Ernest had the chance to argue.

'—and I shall say that I told you it was best not. That will convince her that you care about her. And that's what she wants. And it'll fit in with her ideas about me. I don't care about anything as long as tea's ready.'

'Don't you care about anything?' Ernest's question sounded like an accusation.

'Don't you even care what Mam thinks about you?' Anne had inherited her mother's concern for respectability and reputation.

'I care. But I suppose that I don't care enough. A long time ago, I made a terrible mistake. I couldn't decide between doing what was right and doing what I wanted. So first I did one and then the other. It's a sure way of getting things wrong. Now I live from day to day keeping as happy as I can and making your mam as content as is possible.'

'What would you do if you had your time over again?' Anne asked him.

'I'd do what made me happy. I wouldn't try to act like God and choose—' He had been jolted back to reality by the sound of footsteps on the path and he grinned at Anne as if he enjoyed the prospect of witnessing his wife's anger. Outside the window, Agnes was confirming her mother's fears that the paint was peeling off the sills. William's mood had changed. 'You'll be in real trouble if the kettle's boiled dry.'

The kettle had not even been filled. Anne rushed into the kitchen to make sure that it was at least on the fire when her mother came in. There was no water in the pitcher on the table and she had to go out into the yard to fill another bucket. Over the sound of the clanking pump she could just hear her father asking Ernest for help.

'She takes notice of you. Far more than she does of me. Try and persuade her to let Aggie do a bit from time to time. It would be a help to her and it's only right for the girl. It's time she lived a normal life even if the rest of us—'

William Skinner fell suddenly silent. Anne dropped the pump handle and carried her half-filled bucket into the kitchen. Her mother, having exhausted her examination of the peeling paintwork, was back in the living room.

Anne and Ernest Skinner prospered, though they did not prosper at quite the speed for which they had once hoped. Anne and Charlotte worked each evening until their fingers were too stiff to hold their needles, and worked on Sundays for as long as their eyes would focus on the material that they cut and stitched. But, after a year, the tin box under the bed which they shared contained less than twenty pounds. They looked forward to two more years of hard labour before they would be able to set up business on their own.

Ernest continued to fetch and carry for Arnold Hirst with the loyalty of a cocker spaniel and was rewarded with suitable signs of his master's approval. He was first given his own plumb-line, bradawl and then, with due solemnity, his own brass sovereign scales. Ernest assumed that the gift of sovereign scales presaged the assumption of real responsibility, for the only use to which he could possibly put them, as Arnold Hirst always confirmed, was to check that the builders who brought the firm's timber had not filed gold dust from the coins they gave in payment. But, although he expected each week to end with the request to settle up the bills himself, he continued to

173

spend his Fridays doing no more than carrying the Gladstone bag in which the money was brought home.

Arnold Hirst persisted in taking an aggressive interest in Ernest's health and leisure life. Careful check was kept on what progress was made with the Indian clubs. Once a week he would be asked to give an exhibition of his latest skills and as he developed greater proficiency he was given heavier and more highly decorated clubs to swing. His first pair were described as 'Harrow size' and were made of plain varnished wood. But on the day following the demonstration of the 'blind double-hander' – both clubs rotated in opposite directions behind his back – a new pair, twice as heavy as the old, were waiting for him as he left the house for work. They were painted in a red, white and blue diamond pattern, to which Arnold Hirst affectionately referred as 'Harlequin'.

Socially, master kept man at arm's length. Only once in the first year of his employment was Ernest asked into the Hirst dining room. Then he was called down from the servants' quarters by the valet in a manner which suggested that a trial was imminent and conviction certain. Arnold Hirst sat at one end of his table finishing his breakfast. His tiny wife, covered in curls and lace, sat at the other staring silently at the world over a plate of untouched scrambled eggs. The valet pointed to a chair in the middle of the table and a maid poured out a huge cup of thick black coffee. Ernest was bracing himself to drink it when Hirst spoke.

'Settin' up a boys' club at St Paul's. Lots of louts about and I'm going to get 'em off the streets. Want you to help.'

Ernest took a great gulp of coffee. It tasted better than he had anticipated.

'You'll teach the clubs and how to fence—'

'I can't fence, sir.'

'I'll teach you and then you'll teach them.' The plan seemed obvious enough to Arnold Hirst. 'And we'll have boxing. The noble art of self-defence.'

He clenched his fists and menaced Ernest across his toast and marmalade. Then, dropping his guard, he ran his forefinger along his nose, to remind himself that it was still straight, and felt his ears to confirm that they bore no resemblance to cauliflowers. 'We'll have some jolly good scraps.' He swayed his head from left to right and flayed the air in the great void between him and Mrs Hirst. 'What do you think of that?'

Ernest thought very little of it. Indeed, he was not in the slightest degree attracted by the idea of standing toe to toe with a young man of approximately his own age whilst Arnold Hirst encouraged them to punch each other. But he realised that ambition required him to feign enthusiasm.

'I'd like it very much, Mr Hirst. I think it's a grand idea.'

'Knew you would. Mondays, Wednesdays and Fridays. Straight after work.'

'I go to the Institute on Mondays, Mr Hirst.'

'The what?'

'The Mechanics' Institute. I learn draughtsmanship. You told me that it would come in handy.'

'I did?'

'You gave me two shillings for the entrance fee.'

'Good Lord! Well, I wasted my money. Get along perfectly well without draughtsmanship. Boxing for you on Monday nights. Enjoy yourself for a change. Hardly ever out of your room after work.'

It was true. Ernest had no capacity for friendship and no enthusiasm for what other men of his age would have called pleasure. He spent his evenings in a solitary contentment which he mistook for happiness. As soon as he arrived home, he changed out of his suit. It was the only good suit he possessed and at Grove Cottage he had kept it for best, but Hirst's timber yard had become the centre of his life and therefore warranted, each working day, the care with his appearance which had previously been taken only on Sundays. On his visits home he wore ancient tweeds which he had inherited from his father years before. Anne had mended one knee so well that the patch could hardly be seen but it was clearly an old suit. He felt guilty about relegating his mother to the second rank of importance, but he consoled himself with the thought that she could not see how shabby he looked. In any event, there was nothing else he could do. Work came first and he owned only one good suit. He put it on each morning immediately before he left the house and took it off immediately he returned. Even before he pulled on a pair of corduroy trousers which were a relic of his time at Steetly Quarry, he hung his best jacket on a hanger and stretched out his best trousers under the mattress on his bed in the mistaken belief that his weight would press out the creases overnight.

He ate his evening meal in his room, for, since he did not think of himself as a servant, he did not choose to eat with the servants downstairs. It was always bread and cheese, cut with his pocket knife because the possession of table cutlery might have revealed the secret of his suppers. Ernest spent ten minutes on his food – preparation, consumption and the removal of every crumb from the carpet. Then he turned to his secret vice. It was fretwork.

It was a passion which he pursued on every evening of the week except Sunday, when, no pastime other than reading being permissible, he read stories of adventure in the colonies. Captain Marryat was a particular favourite and he possessed his own copies of *Midshipman Easy* and *The Phantom Ship*. They stood on the mantelshelf in his room like ornaments, with the pictures which celebrated heroism on their cloth bindings facing the bed. They were the only possessions he had on display, for Ernest had no doubt that fretwork – like eating – was forbidden in the servants' bedrooms.

He had almost forgotten that once he had hoped to be a joiner, and on the rare occasions when he half remembered his old ambition to shape wood he felt no regrets about having abandoned the trade. He made entries in ledgers and counted coins and therefore knew himself to be socially superior to anyone who used plane or saw. But, although he gloried in earning his living whilst wearing a three-piece suit, he still felt the need to make something with his hands. Fretwork, being no more than a hobby, did not compromise his professional status.

He took his fretwork, like he took every part of life, with a solemnity which, in a less serious young man, would have been incompatible with pleasure. Each joint had to be perfectly cut, each corner perfectly square, and the complicated twirls and curves which decorated each piece of bric-à-brac had to be perfectly symmetrical in design and execution. He sandpapered each plywood surface until it was smooth as glass and then stained and polished it until the patina was perfect. Although he did not know it, day after day he laboured to produce work as fine as that which he had crushed beneath his foot on the day when his joiner's destiny was denied him.

The finished work went home to Grove Cottage and, since he thought of each gift as a work of art, he saw nothing strange in making letter racks for a woman who had not received a letter in ten years or in giving half a dozen different pipe-holders to a man who possessed only one pipe. Experience and success made him ambitious. He designed and made, section by section, overmantels which might have been intended for Welbeck Abbey or Thorsby Hall. He smuggled each bracket, shelf and candle-holder out of his lodgings and gradually assembled them on the wall above the fireplace at Grove Cottage. His father watched with a mixture of admiration and concern about the legality of making such fundamental changes to Henry Hodding's property. His mother felt each new extravagance and marvelled at complicated shape and perfect finish.

When the overmantel was made and hung, Ernest began to decorate it with fretwork for fretwork's sake – miniature rocking chairs, minute wheelbarrows, tiny towers with Norman arches above the windows and Saxon arches over the doors, windmills with sails that spun at the touch of a finger and haycarts with wheels that turned on

176

their fretwork axles. Elizabeth felt each one and marvelled. William saw the fruits of his son's labour and rejoiced. Agnes saw them and giggled with a combination of sisterly admiration and girlish frivolity. Her father reported her admiration to Ernest.

'Can you make her something? Something special of her own? She doesn't have very many nice things. Make her something she'll like having.'

Ernest wondered if Agnes would prefer a letter rack or a toast rack. His father had a better idea.

'She'd like something to keep her bits and bobs in. A box. Make her a box. It's six weeks to her birthday. You could make it by then.'

The idea of making a box did not appeal to Ernest. He knew what proper boxes should be like – made of oak or elm not plywood, and fastened together with complicated joints which fretwork did not allow. He had no intention of making a second-rate box.

'What about a pen-holder?'

'I don't think she'd like that. Can you do something to do with books? She likes books.'

'I'm not sure that I could make a book stand. It needs a solid base.'

'Think of something that a young woman would like.'

'She's not an ordinary girl, Dad. You know that. She doesn't see very many people and she reads. That makes it harder.'

'She's more ordinary than your mother makes out. She went to a dance in the parish rooms at Shireoaks last week with the housemaids. Your mother tried to stop her going and then fretted all night. But she came back lively as a cricket and looked at herself in the mirror—'

'A mirror. I could do a surround for a mirror. If I could buy an old one to build it round.'

William Skinner gave his son a shilling and Ernest bought an old mirror in Worksop market. He broke off the rotting oak frame before he got it back to his lodgings for he was afraid that the woodworm would infect the plywood sides of the tea-chests that he kept under his bed. He carried the oval glass back to his lodgings without scratching a fragment of quicksilver from its back. Surrounding it with a fretwork wreath became an obsession. He had borrowed a history of wood carving from the Mechanics' Institute and he set out with his single saw to create a garland of which Grinling Gibbons would have been proud. When it was finished – leaves, flowers and ears of corn stained mahogany and embossed against a background of intricate trelliswork – Ernest looked forward with impatient pride to seeing his achievement hung on his sister's wall.

Carrying it from Worksop station to Grove Cottage was agony for so many petals and fronds protruded from the edge of the frame

177

that it was impossible to hold it under his arm without risking his masterpiece being broken and defiled. Holding the chain by which the mirror would be hooked to the wall, Ernest marched down the Chesterfield Road as if he was protecting his lower abdomen with a brown-paper-covered shield. His arms began to ache before he reached the bottom of the Station Approach but he dared not lay down his burden in case the buds and ears of wheat were damaged by contact with the tarmacadam road.

He staggered into Grove Cottage and recklessly hung the mirror on one of the hooks in the alcove where the coats were kept. He knew that if his mother found out what he had done she would complain bitterly about the risk of damage to his father's ulster and the nearly new plaid cloak which Anne had bought from the Duchess of Portland's lady's maid to become the pride of Elizabeth's modest wardrobe, but he could bear the weight no longer. He flexed the muscles which his Indian clubs had not prepared for such an ordeal and examined his scarred palm. William was gratifyingly impatient.

'Let's see. It's very big. Much bigger than I expected.'

Ernest tore at the top of the paper and then paused. 'Where's Agnes?'

Before his father could answer, his mother appeared in the kitchen doorway. She was drying her hands on her apron as if to prevent any suggestion that she had not been hard at work.

'I didn't hear you come in.'

Almost everything that Elizabeth Skinner said sounded like a reproach. Ernest rushed to move the mirror.

'What are you up to? This room's too small to run about in.'

Relief that his sin was undiscovered turned into dejection that his mother had forgotten that it was the day on which Agnes was to receive her gift. His father had to explain. 'He's brought the mirror for Agnes.'

'Where is she?' Ernest had grown impatient again.

'Didn't you see her as you came up?' asked William.

'She wasn't there. The chair's on the path. But Agnes isn't there.'

'Perhaps she went round the back. I didn't hear her pass the window. But I might have been chopping the parsley.'

Ernest went through the kitchen and into the back garden. There was no sign of Agnes.

'Back round the front,' his father suggested.

The chair was still empty. Agnes had disappeared.

CHAPTER FOURTEEN

The Windows Open

Despite her blindness, Elizabeth Skinner organised the search party from a vantage point on top of the front steps. Opinion about Agnes's fate was divided. William believed that she had gone for a walk. Elizabeth was sure that she had been abducted. Ernest was certain that, whatever had happened to his sister, he would never forgive her for ruining the morning on which he had brought the mirror home.

William's suggestion that his daughter might have walked up 'the back way' across the fields towards Harness Grove was treated with contemptuous incredulity by his wife. Wherever she had gone, she must have gone by the Chesterfield Road. The two men set off to reconnoitre – William towards Worksop and Ernest in the direction of Steetly. Within twenty minutes both returned to report failure. Ernest had hurried as far as the crossroads at Abraham's Farm and, since he was unable to decide which of the alternative trails to follow, had then abandoned the chase. William's search was more leisurely. When he got to the wall of Worksop Manor he could see almost a mile ahead down the straight road. The only sign of life was an elderly woman walking in his direction. She had passed no one except a courting couple sharing a bicycle.

Elizabeth accused William of abandoning the search for his daughter.

He remonstrated gently, 'She couldn't have got that far. I could see halfway to Worksop. It would take half an hour to walk it. Five minutes before Ernest came in she was in the front garden.'

'She must be in one of the fields.' Elizabeth was becoming increasingly distraught. 'Go back, both of you, and look in the fields.'

'She couldn't have got through the hedges, Mam. And there's a ditch right down to the manor wall.'

Ernest chose to argue and therefore became the new object of his mother's displeasure. 'There are two gates on the way to Steetly. Did you look in the fields? Did you look up the drive? She might have gone the front way to the house.'

'I did, Mam. I looked inside both fields. Nothing there. You could see every bit of grass. She wasn't there.'

He lied unconvincingly. But, before he could be challenged, his father – whose interest had suddenly been caught by movement along the Chesterfield Road – asked Ernest, 'Can you see that man? Is he drunk or what?'

'Has he got Agnes? Tell me quick. Has he got Agnes?'

'No, love. It's just a man wobbling about on a bicycle, down the road.'

'I'd have thought even you would have had more sense. Are you worried about your daughter or are you not?'

William did not reply.

The man on the bicycle was within sight of Grove Cottage and William could understand why the cyclist rode standing on the pedals like a boy who could struggle uphill only by loading all his weight on to every thrust of his foot. Agnes, her auburn hair streaming out behind her, sat on the saddle. Her skirts were pulled up almost to her knees and her legs were spread out straight and wide so as to keep well clear of pedals and the pedaller. When William realised why a grown man found such difficulty in cycling along a flat road, intrigue turned into outrage.

The cyclist stopped at the bottom of the flight of steps which led into Grove Cottage's front garden. It took all his strength to keep the bicycle and its passenger upright. Agnes squealed and held on to his waist even more tightly as the wheels skidded sideways. Elizabeth, who had been bewildered by the moments of silence, gave a little scream of her own.

'Is it Agnes? Somebody tell me. Is it Agnes? Is she all right?' Mother moved instinctively towards the noise of her daughter's sudden shout. Only Ernest's restraining arm saved her from falling down the steps.

Agnes looked up.

'I'm all right, Mam. I'm sorry if you've been frightened. I didn't think.'

'Of course she's been frightened.' Her father was at the beginning of one of his rare rages. 'What do you think she's been?'

'Will somebody please tell me what's happening?' Elizabeth had still not regained her composure. 'You'd think that you'd have more consideration – all of you.' She began to feel her way down the narrow steps, staring sightlessly in the direction of the cyclist who stood silent and still, apparently neither afraid nor ashamed. Ernest did his duty.

'She came back on a bicycle, Mam.'

Elizabeth knew that he could not be joking, for her son did not make jokes. Had he, she wondered, gone mad? Or was she losing her mind as she had lost her sight?

'For heaven's sake, William. What's happening?'

'A young man brought her back, sitting on the saddle of his bicycle.'

'He was pedalling,' added Ernest, who did not want his mother to think that Agnes had endured the intimacy of leaning against him as he pushed her along with one hand on the handlebars and the other brazenly under the saddle.

'And what have you got to say for yourself?' William demanded.

Ernest was astonished that, despite the obvious signs of his father's growing anger, the young man answered calmly, without a hint of guilt or shame. 'I took her for a ride, that's all. She said that she'd never been on a bike and I offered to hold it whilst she had a try and then I brought her back. That's all.'

'Who's *she?*' asked Elizabeth. 'A young man with any respect wouldn't call her *she.*'

'I don't know her name,' said the young man.

'How did it all happen?'

'Don't worry, Mother. It's all over.' Ernest was afraid that there would be a scene.

'I want to know.' His mother thought that a scene was called for.

Agnes giggled. 'He was going past and asked the way from Steetly to Worksop and I told him.'

'And then what?' Her mother was determined to be spared nothing.

'Then he was going past the other way and he asked me the way from Worksop to Steetly.' Agnes, laughing too much to be sure of her balance, half fell, half climbed off the bicycle.

'Inside,' said Elizabeth, outraged by Agnes's frivolity.

Agnes shuffled a few paces in the direction of the steps.

'She'd better wait for a moment, Mother. We need to get all this cleared up.'

William was reasserting his rights as a father. The young man had a military bearing. He was well over six feet tall and his curly chestnut hair was cut short. There was something sinister about his long jaw and the air of menace was dispelled by neither his ruddy complexion nor his luxuriant moustache. William feared that he was a soldier.

'And what's your name? It's about time that you spoke up and accounted for your conduct.'

'My name is Brackenbury. Ernest Brackenbury.'

'My brother's called Ernest. But I call him Ern.' Agnes was still laughing.

'There are a lot of Ernests about. I'm called Brack by most people.'

181

Everybody except Elizabeth was cowed into silence.

'And what do you do, Mr Brackenbury? What do you do for a living?'

'I'm a policeman . . .'

Ernest Skinner – Ern, as he permitted himself to be called – allowed incredulity to overcome his inclination to take no part in the unseemly wrangle.

'You're a policeman and you don't know your way to Steetly – or to Worksop?'

Agnes almost laughed again.

'I'm not a policeman round here. I'm a policeman in Sheffield.'

The laugh subsided and Agnes asked her first question. 'Then what are you doing round here?'

'These days, my father has a smallholding at Thorpe Salvin. But I went back to Sheffield. I was born and bred there.' He did not feel any duty to add that he had been estranged from his family for almost five years.

'I don't want to see you hanging around here again, Mr Brackenbury.'

Even as he spoke, William had understood how silly he sounded. Agnes stood by the side of the road flushed with excitement, her long Titian hair dishevelled in a way which was never allowed at home and clearly savouring her brief experience of sin. Ernest Brackenbury kicked the wrought-iron gate that was always propped open. One of the hinges had snapped in two.

'It's rusted right through. I could do it in ten minutes if you'd let me take it away. I was 'a blacksmith before I was a policeman.'

It was not an offer that Ernest Brackenbury expected to be accepted so, without another word or glance in Agnes's direction, he climbed back on his bicycle and pedalled off in the direction of Worksop.

Throughout the autumn and early winter, the long-jawed man on the bicycle was never mentioned in Grove Cottage. Each of the Skinners decided to pretend that he had never pedalled his way into their lives – Ernest because he was ashamed that his sister had fallen so low, William because he knew that to mention the incident was to revive tension and disharmony and Elizabeth because she felt that it was the first dangerous sign that one day her daughter would want to be free. Agnes herself was also afraid to remember her few moments of liberty. For she knew that the more she thought of the world beyond Grove Cottage, the more she would long to live outside her mother's jurisdiction. And she knew that her wish could never be granted. So although she thought about the policeman with the chestnut hair and sometimes dreamed that she was riding on his bicycle, half leaning against his shoulder to preserve her balance, she did not mention his name until the New Year's Eve of 1899.

It was William who suggested that the family should see in the new century together, and Elizabeth, despite her prejudice against celebration, agreed in the hope that Anne would come home. Anne came and brought Lottie Harthill with her and Ernest walked with the two young women from Worksop as protection against early-evening revellers. He did not yet possess a swordstick of the sort with which Arnold Hirst had so often swished the air, but he had made himself a 'loaded cane' by pouring molten lead into the top of an old curtain rod and binding it fast with a piece of leather cut from a worn-out glove. He swung it ferociously as he marched out along the Chesterfield Road but, to his disappointment, neither his sister nor her friend noticed that he was specially armed for the occasion. Indeed they seemed to notice nothing but each other. Throughout the whole journey they spoke barely a word to their escort. They were engrossed in their private world of prints, silks and pattern books, bias binding, button cards and London fashions. Throughout the dying hours of the nineteenth century they maintained their exclusive intimacy. Gerrard Knock had been invited from next door because, although he was not family, it would have been wrong to leave him on his own. He tried to make conversation by asking Anne about the Prince of Wales's trousers, which were creased down the front rather than the sides.

'We don't know about men's clothes.'

Gerrard was shocked by the contempt with which she dismissed his question. It was as if she was affronted by the thought of fly-buttons, turn-ups and inside-leg measurements – and performing any sort of service for a man.

She leaned back over the pamphlet that she and Lottie were examining. It was called *Health and Beauty in Dress*. In it, Ada S. Ballin preached the gospel of wool, a material particularly suitable for clothes worn whilst participating in energetic activity. Dr Jaeger's Sanitary Woollen System was, by Anne's standards, progressive to the point of impropriety, but Lottie, whose frivolous nature she indulged, took an interest in such things. Anne closed her eyes and tried to concentrate on her partner's reading.

'"Every garment worn whilst cycling should be of a flannel or woollen material without any added mixture of cotton or linen in any form. Sore throat is often to be traced to the linen band which so many tailors and shirtmakers will fit round the neck of a flannel shirt, whilst there is often in addition a little square of

183

linen marked with the maker's name and address which, when it is damp, can be readily felt . . .'''

Lottie did not notice that Anne was half asleep. She read on.

'''. . . for female bicyclists I recommend neat dark cloth lined with woollen material and the ideal way of wearing them is with woollen combinations—'''

Anne woke up with a start and glanced furtively round the room to see if any of the men showed signs of having heard the forbidden word. Lottie realised that she had made an inexcusable *faux pas* and tried to cover her confusion by pointing to Miss Ada S. Ballin's illustrations.

She read from the caption. '''The skirt can be unfastened for riding. When it is buttoned up the bows hide the slit.'''

Anne looked at her partner in a way which suggested that Lottie had not made amends for her original lapse of taste. The pamphlet fell to the floor with a thud and the whole family turned and stared at its open pages.

'Are you taking up cycling?' asked Agnes. 'I went for a ride on a bicycle last summer.'

'Didn't you fall off?' Lottie had no sense of place or occasion.

'I was held on, wasn't I, Ernest?'

For a moment, Ernest thought of saying that he had given Agnes her ride. Then he realised that his mother would know that he was lying and would not regard chivalry as sufficient excuse for deceit. Gerrard Knock, puzzled by the silence, made his second attempt at polite conversation. 'And where did all this happen, then?'

'On the road right outside. I went all the way down to the manor gate and back.'

'Without falling off? I don't believe you,' said Gerrard.

'A man held me up on the way down. Then I sat on the saddle on the way back. He was a policeman.'

Before he could express his incredulity a second time, Gerrard was offered a glass of luke-warm punch by William, and Ernest had seized him by the elbow to ensure that he diverted his entire attention from the subject of Agnes's cycle ride.

'Well, what's it going to be like?'

'What's what going to be like?' Gerrard asked in reply.

'The new century. Nineteen hundred.'

'Better than the old, I hope. Better than the last ten years, anyway.'

'Do you know him?' Agnes interrupted the speculation.

Gerrard had not prepared himself for a night devoted to conundrums and he could only feebly reply, 'Know who?'

'The policeman who gave me a ride. Mr Brackenbury.'

'I don't know a policeman of that name. But I knew a farrier called Brackenbury.'

'That's the one,' said Ernest, forgetting himself for a moment. 'He said that he used to be a blacksmith.'

William Skinner copied his son's bad example. 'How do you know him?'

'He's shod at races I've been at. He was one of them blacksmiths who travelled round the courses. Wonderful smith. Real way with horses, he had. There'd be a horse kicking up and prancing about and he'd have a new shoe on before it noticed. And he was just a lad then. But better than men twice his age.'

'So why did he give up and become a policeman?' Ernest was particularly interested in the ways in which young men furthered their prospects.

Anne and Lottie continued the examination of their pamphlet. Elizabeth – who, until then, had been rocking in her chair and pretending not to hear what the men were saying – decided that it was time to change the course of the conversation. 'I don't see why we're all so interested in this young man. He was very rude and Agnes was very silly. But it was all a long time ago and it's best forgotten. I'd have thought that we had better things to talk about.'

William and Ernest fell immediately silent. But Gerrard Knock was not to be denied his knowing moment. He had not been broken by Elizabeth Skinner's will. He had a story to tell and, since he had no doubt that it would hold his audience in thrall, he intended to tell it.

'They say he tampered with a horse.'

'Tampered . . . ?' Anne looked up from her reading, ready to be horrified at a story of unnatural cruelty.

'A horse went lame five furlongs out. It was the favourite. When they looked at it afterwards the shoeing was wrong. They said that a novice blacksmith wouldn't have made such a mistake. So they decided that Brackenbury must have done it on purpose.'

'Why should he do that?' Agnes seemed to resent the allegation.

'He's a gambler. At least he was. Gamble on anything. Horses, prize fights, cards, anything. Couldn't help himself, they reckoned. You know what horse-racing men are like . . .'

'We don't.' Elizabeth was scandalised. 'William's never had a bet in his life.'

'What are they like?' asked Agnes.

'They like to keep things quiet. I daresay he got a good hiding.

Paid for by some of the men who'd lost money on the nobbled horse. But then he was just warned off. They wouldn't go to the law. Just warn him off. So he ran off to Sheffield. I suppose he thought they wouldn't dare come after him if he joined the police.'

'Didn't he need a reference?' Ernest prided himself on knowing the ways of the professional world.

'I don't know about that. But he was a good farrier. That's certain. I heard Mr Hodding say so.'

Even Elizabeth was impressed. 'What had Mr Hodding to say about him?'

'It's that Mr Robinson . . .'

The news that a laundry owner from Newark was in the market to buy Worksop Manor had been the weekly preoccupation of the local papers since November. Anne and Lottie, who thought it profession-ally necessary to keep informed about the local gentry, had already speculated about the number of senior female servants who might be brought with him. The thought of a new cook, housekeeper and lady's maid in search of coats and dresses added to their regret that they still did not have enough capital to set up on their own. As usual, Anne spoke for them both. 'Is he definitely coming?'

'I don't know, do I? All I know is that he saw Mr Hodding twice in a week. Just before Christmas.'

Agnes, who had been listening with undisguised excitement, could contain herself no longer. 'But what about the young man on the bicycle? What's he got to do with Mr Hodding?'

'When Mr Hodding brought Mr Robinson to the door and put him into my carriage, they were talking about hunting. Mr Robinson hunts with the Rufford. I knew his old groom. Helped me to get this job, God rest his soul. Came from my village.'

'Yes,' said Agnes, 'but what about the young man, the young man on the bicycle?'

'Well . . .' Gerrard Knock paused to emphasise his resentment at being rushed, '. . . well, as I was saying. When Mr Hodding brought Mr Robinson to my carriage, they were talking about hunting and Mr Hodding said, "There's no good farrier in Worksop now. Got to go to Newark." And Mr Hodding said, "There used to be a young man called Brackenbury from Thorpe Salvin."'

'It's five to midnight,' said William.

The Skinners, Gerrard Knock and Lottie Harthill turned with proper determination to the serious business of greeting the twentieth century, and even Agnes forgot about the mysterious young man with chestnut hair when her father began to organise the ritual of seeing the old year out and the new year in.

When the time came to hold hands, Anne and Lottie would not let Ernest come between them and Gerrard Knock cried during the singing of 'Auld Lang Syne'. But nothing, not even Ernest's suggestion of a moment's silent prayer for the defeat of the Boers and the safe return of our soldiers, could dampen Agnes's spirits. When her mother whispered that since it was past midnight bed should not be delayed, she pretended not to notice and made Ernest dance with her across the living room even though neither of them knew any steps. And when the quarryman from Steetly came first-footing to the door, he was greeted like an old friend. Nobody went to bed until, at two o'clock, Ernest began to calculate how many hours' sleep the various revellers would enjoy before their several duties required them to face the first working day of 1900. Only Agnes was allowed to lie late in bed. She slept until ten o'clock, when she was awakened by the noise of Ernest Brackenbury knocking on the front door.

'Yes?'

It was Elizabeth Skinner's invariable greeting and, combined with her practice of counterfeiting a fixed stare in the direction of the person to whom she spoke, it often allowed her a few moments' grace before her blindness was recognised.

'You won't remember me.' He did not mean it. It was the bogus self-effacement of a man who was wholly preoccupied with himself and believed that he was blessed with a striking appearance. To his surprise, he was right.

'No. I can't say that I do. What can I do for you?'

Even if she had been able to see her visitor, she would not have recognised the cyclist whose unwelcome intrusion into her life had lasted for only a few minutes. For he was no longer an immaculate Lothario. He had not shaved that day, and although his hair was still a pattern of chestnut waves, every other part of his appearance was dishevelled. His dark suit, shiny with age before he put it on, was dappled with recent stains. His collar was limp from a night's soaking in sweat. A handkerchief was wrapped round his hand.

'It's the gate, missus. When I was here last I noticed the gate. The top hinge had gone. I wondered if you'd like it mending. I'd do it for one and sixpence.'

'My husband deals with that sort of thing. You'd better come back in a couple of hours when he has had his dinner. I shouldn't think he'll want to bother. That gate's been propped open for a year or more. Ask him if you want to. Are you a gypsy?'

It was then that Ernest Brackenbury felt certain that Elizabeth Skinner was blind. For no one who could see would have mistaken

187

him for a gypsy – even after a night spent playing cards in the stable behind the White Hart. He had lost every penny he possessed and, when the tapman had refused his IOU, he had cut his knuckles on the scoundrel's teeth to teach him how to recognise a gentleman. But dirty, dispirited and stained with the tapman's blood and vomit though he was, nobody with sense and sight could confuse him with a dirty tinker who lived in a caravan and poached rabbits.

'All right, missus. I'll come back.'

He walked down the path as far as the gate, kicking at the gravel as he went, to make sure that the sound of his departing footsteps followed Elizabeth Skinner back into the cottage. As soon as the door closed behind her, he grasped the top wrought-iron rail and heaved the gate off its one remaining hinge and out of the weeds which had already grown over its lower bars. It was too late to save his suit so he hoisted it on to his back and marched towards Steetly. There was, he knew, an easy way to climb the wall which surrounded the quarry's offices and workshops, for he had played late-night cards in every empty outbuilding in the area. He was tired and his burden was heavy, and he pulled himself over the crumbling stone with difficulty. Once inside, he darted across the empty yard into the smithy.

'Bugger me,' said the blacksmith's striker. 'Look what the wind's blown in. It's Brack.'

The bellows boy, sensing that he was in the presence of a celebrity, touched his forelock and waited to hear what the smith had to say.

'Out!'

'Give us a chance. I need a favour. I need it bad.'

'Out! There's trouble wherever you go. It follows you.'

The blacksmith motioned in the direction of the striker. 'I've not heard a word of language out of him for two year or more. But in you come and he's cursing and blinding. In front of the boy, too.'

'All I want is this gate in the fire for ten minutes and a lend of your anvil. It'd be a Christian act. I'm doing a favour myself. But I need a bit of help from you.'

'You a favour?' The striker laughed theatrically.

'I'm mending this gate for the blind woman who lives in the cottage on the Chesterfield Road.'

The blacksmith was, for the moment, impressed. By showing interest he was lost. The hard edge of outright rejection had been softened. 'How do you come to know Mrs Skinner?'

'I did a favour for her daughter in the summer. I said I'd mend the gate and I went and got it just now. All I want is ten minutes in the fire.'

'And what if the manager comes in?'

'Tell him you're doing a favour for a poor blind woman.'

The smith agreed. He lent the fire, his anvil, his striker, his bellows boy, his five-pound hammer and his skill. Brack watched whilst a new iron bar – the property of the Steetly Quarry Company – was heated and then rolled up to form the hinge that would swing from the gatepost's bracket.

'Best to make a good job of it,' said the smith, rasping the rust from the gate's bottom bars. 'Proper gentleman, Mr Skinner. Pleased to help him and that poor wife of his. Take it back with my compliments.' He dabbed the patches of bright metal with an old paintbrush. 'It'll need another coat straight away. Don't forget to pay my respects to Mr Skinner. Though no doubt you'll tell him that you did all the work yourself.'

'He wouldn't believe it. He knows I did a better class of work. He knows that I shod horses.'

'Less said about that the better. And the sooner you're out of here the better pleased I'll be.'

Having achieved his object, Brack left without a word of thanks or a second thought about the smith's opinion of his conduct and character. He was back at Grove Cottage before William Skinner had finished his dinner. As soon as the gate was hung back in its place, he beat a triumphant crescendo on the door.

'Who's at the front at this time of day?' William asked the question in the hope that he would not have to part the velvet curtains, draw back the two bolts, open the two locks and release the chain to find out. Elizabeth, deciphering the coded message, wearily stood up. Agnes laid a restraining hand on her arm.

'Save your legs, Mam. I'll go.'

'Better not. It's probably the gypsy.'

'What gypsy?' asked her husband.

'He came round this morning wanting to mend the gate for one and sixpence. I told him to see you.'

William snorted in irritation and decided that it was his duty to send the man on his way. He did not recognise Brack beneath his stubble and inside his stained suit. Nor did he notice the mended gate swinging securely on its new hinge. All he saw was an obvious ruffian standing on his front doorstep.

'What can I do for you?'

'I've brought the gate back.'

'You're not a gypsy.'

'I think the lady of the house mistook me for the man who came round sharpening knives. I'm the one she told to mend the gate. She promised me two shillings.'

189

'Don't try that with me.' William knew his wife too well to be deceived into believing that she would squander so much money on so pointless an enterprise.

'You're trying to cheat me out of my money. The lady – the blind lady – promised me two shillings. I've done the work. Look.' Brack waved towards the gate – first with his right hand and then with his left. 'Look. I took all the skin off my hand doing it.'

It was William's turn to lie. 'Get out of this garden or I'll call my son from inside and we'll throw you out.'

Agitated by the raised voices, Elizabeth had joined her husband at the door. She stood resolute behind his shoulder. Agnes, although forbidden to leave the kitchen, had crept upstairs to the bedroom and watched from the window with excited disbelief as the drama unfolded below her. She, at least, had recognised the young man who began to plead with her father and she believed every word he said. Her parents, in their adult wisdom, knew it all to be lies – even though Brack's last desperate gamble was to tell the truth.

'Please, governor. If I'm not back in Sheffield by nine o'clock tonight I'll lose my job.'

'Then you'd better get on your way,' said Elizabeth.

'It's my bicycle. I need it and it's in pawn. I need one and . . . two shillings to get it out. I need it to get about. I've done the work and it's worth the money.' William was about to reach into his purse and offer the young man sixpence. He could feel Elizabeth's disapproval radiating from behind him but he would have risked his wife's wrath had Brack not persisted in calling Elizabeth a liar. 'And, whatever she says now, she told me to do it. She promised me two shillings.'

The door slammed shut in Brack's face. He walked desolate down the path, trying to decide if it was worth the effort of carrying the gate down the road and throwing it over a hedge. Then he heard an upstairs window creak open. Agnes leaned over the sill. She was holding the tin pillar-box in which she kept the few shillings that she called her savings. It had been prised open along the joint which divided the V and R of the royal cipher. A badly aimed florin landed on the patch of grass that separated cottage from road. Brack picked it up quickly and ran down the road without looking back.

CHAPTER FIFTEEN

Doing Business

The arrival of John Robinson at Worksop Manor was greeted at Harness Grove with mixed feelings. Henry Hodding looked forward to the frequent company of a fellow Conservative and huntsman, but Mrs Hodding worried about the social competition that Mrs Robinson would provide. The Hoddings lived only on the fringes of real Dukeries society and Mrs Hodding accepted that status without complaint or resentment, for her husband advised the Manverses and the Cavendish-Bentincks and, although she felt a commoner in the country, she behaved like an aristocrat in town. John Robinson's decision to rebuild the dilapidated manor and fill it with his extensive family and large household threatened her supremacy in the one area where she reigned supreme. She particularly resented the idea that she should be toppled from the pinnacle of her little world by a man who had made his fortune out of brewing beer and washing other people's dirty clothes. She complained so regularly to her husband that he began to fear for the state of her mind and for the peace of his own home. Mrs Hodding's only consolation was hunting and even in the season she could hunt only two days in each week.

The idea of founding a new hunt had been in Henry Hodding's mind for years, but it was Arnold Hirst who suggested that it should be done at once as a distraction for the increasingly gloomy deposed queen of Worksop society. The timber merchant was an expert in founding things: he had set up numerous boys' clubs, fencing societies, chess circles and boxing associations. None of them had lasted long. Even his great Christian crusade to take the lads of Retford off the streets – for which Ernest Skinner had sacrificed the Mechanics' Institute draughtsmanship course – had been abandoned after a few weeks. But one collapse never prevented Arnold Hirst from looking forward to the next creation. Setting up was an object in itself. He was particularly good at new names.

'The Grove Hunt. Call it the Grove Hunt. Meet here at Harness Grove.'

191

'I've thought about it for a long time,' said Henry Hodding. 'Legally it's easy enough to do but it would cost a pretty penny. Hounds. Huntsmen. Kennels.'

'Twenty members at ten guineas a year. Cover it easily.'

'I need to think about it. I never do anything without thinking about it first.'

He might have added 'unlike you', for he had just completed a complicated legal action to extricate Hirst from an unwise investment. The woodyard had been mortgaged to cover the losses and Hirst, much to his solicitor's chagrin, seemed to believe that he had escaped from his folly completely unscathed.

Ernest Skinner, who had been encouraged by his employer to put money into the same dubious scheme, had not been so lucky. He had borrowed twenty pounds in the belief that, by the end of the year, it would be worth two hundred. After six months it was worth only five and his creditors, whose interest he had intended to pay out of his profits, called in the loan.

Ernest could think of no one to ask for help except Anne. She thought in silence for what seemed a lifetime and then replied slowly. She found it almost impossible to say the words.

'Between us – Lottie and me – we've got thirty-seven pounds. If you really need it – really, life and death – you can have my half. All of it, if you have to. If you can manage with less . . .'

'I can't. I need more than that. I need twenty-one pounds, nine shillings and sixpence. Twenty-one pounds—'

'Well, I've not got that. So you can't have it. And I'm not asking Lottie for a lend of hers. It's bad enough as it is. We could have set up this year. I wouldn't blame her . . .'

The sentence was too frightening to finish. Anne lived in constant terror of Lottie finding a new partner but it was something of which she never even spoke to Lottie herself. She was afraid that, by talking about her nightmare, she might make it come true and believed that by admitting to the weakness of worrying she would undermine the admiration of strength that made lion lie down with lamb. Lottie, Anne first thought, would expect her to make the sacrifice, for she spoke in awe of her dedication to duty. Then Anne changed her mind: Lottie might think of the sacrifice as an excuse to end their partnership.

Ernest disturbed her agony. 'Do you think I can get the rest from Dad?'

'He hasn't got two pennies to rub together.'

'Don't be so sure. Didn't he get anything when our grandfather died?'

'He got some bits and bobs to remember him by.'

'Well, it's worth a try. Will you come with me on Sunday? We'll get him on his own and tell him that you're giving me—'

'Lending you.'

They got William on his own but as soon as he discovered that they wanted to talk about money he insisted that Elizabeth join them. Agnes was, for once, sent off to wash up in the kitchen.

'How have you got yourself into such trouble? That's what beats me.' Elizabeth had always believed her son to be a sensible young man.

'It seemed right enough when I did it. Mr Hirst said that it couldn't go wrong and when I asked the Penny Bank for the money, they lent it me as soon as they knew that Mr Hirst had recommended it.'

'He's got a lot to answer for, has your Mr Hirst, if you ask me.' Elizabeth was in a mood to broadcast blame. 'If he was a gentleman he'd accept his responsibility.'

'It's no good saying that. He's not going to.'

William's reproof of his wife shocked Anne. She was not accustomed to their father taking command. She attempted to turn the conversation back to awful reality.

'I'm lending him eighteen.'

'Isn't that your business money?' asked Elizabeth.

'It's all I've got.'

'What will you do?'

'I'll go on working at Allen's. The business will have to wait.'

Elizabeth turned on Ernest. 'You're not going to take all Anne's savings! I can't believe it.'

'What else can I do? I've already been summonsed for not paying on time. If I don't pay up next week, I'll be in court.'

'Can't we sell something, William?'

'We've got nothing worth five pounds. All we own isn't worth twenty.'

'What about writing to Wisbech? Your brother wouldn't miss it. Ask him.'

'I could ask him, but I know what the answer would be. He's a farmer!'

'Mam, it's got to be my savings. There's no choice. But Ernest needs another three pounds odd. That's what we've come to talk about.'

'When I was a girl at home, I wouldn't have believed that I'd ever be in such trouble.'

'You're not in trouble, Mam.' Anne spoke with no conviction. 'None of us is. Ernest needs another three pounds, that's all. There's no need to upset yourself. If worst comes to the worst, we'll go to a money-lender.'

'Listen to me!' For a moment, William was almost imperious. 'There is one way to save you both.'

Normally Anne would have resented the equation of her sacrifice with Ernest's foolishness but she had room in her heart for no other emotion except the agony of faint hope. Her father seemed to be proposing the impossible but, whilst she could not believe in salvation, she could not resist planning how salvation could be celebrated. If, by some miracle, she woke up next morning with her savings intact, she would tell Lottie that the time had come to make the great leap. Then, together, she and Lottie would give notice.

'Borrow it from Mr Hodding.'

'Mr Hodding wouldn't lend me twenty pounds.' Ernest did not want to relax his emotional grip on Anne's savings. 'How could I pay it back? I couldn't promise anything definite.'

'Don't be so stupid, Ernest. He won't lend it to you but he will to me. I'll borrow it. I'll pay it back. At least, I'll take the responsibility. You'll all have to help. Might as well get on with it and put your minds at rest. Going up there won't get any better with the keeping.'

Despite his conversion to Sabbatarianism, Ernest made no objection to the business being done on the day of rest. His father who, as always, had taken off his best suit between church and dinner, went upstairs to put it on again. Then, for the first time in all his years of service, he set off for Harness Grove without having made an appointment.

William Skinner stood in the kitchen for almost an hour before the butler said that the master was ready to see him in the study – a room into which William had never been before. Henry Hodding sat behind a mahogany desk wrestling to keep alight the remnants of a cigar. He did not ask his gardener to sit down.

The cigar emphasised the social gulf between them. That William understood and accepted. He was not, however, prepared for the memories which the study's furniture raised in his mind. The green baize, the brass drawer handles, the bookcases with folded canvas behind the glass in the doors – they were all disturbingly reminiscent of the boardroom in the Wisbech Workhouse. Standing, at first ignored, as he had stood at the Guardians' horseshoe table, he felt again the old anguish of undeserved disgrace. He was about to beg his employer for money.

Henry Hodding succeeded in getting his cigar to draw.

'Nothing wrong, I hope, Skinner. Nobody ill or anything?'

'No, sir. Not really, sir.'

'Good. I thought it might be Mrs Skinner's eyes. Or even young Agnes. When I heard that you'd come up to the house—'

'I'm sorry about that, sir. But it couldn't wait till Monday.'

'Not giving notice, are you? You'd be a fool if you did. I know the wages aren't much by today's standards, but I don't work you to death, do I? You'd be a fool to leave.'

'It's not that, sir. It's Ernest.'

'That boy nearly died in my kitchen. In some sort of trouble, is he?'

'He's in debt, sir. He's put borrowed money in a company that isn't any good.'

'Something in South America, is it? Hardwood? Mahogany? That sort of thing?'

'Yes, sir.'

'How much does he need?'

'Twenty pounds and some coppers.'

There was a long pause. Then Henry Hodding opened one of the desk drawers and took out a steel cash box. It was decorated with red and gold initials which William did not recognise and, for a moment, he was distracted from his anxiety by the attempt to identify the letters.

It took Henry Hodding some time to find the right key. As he waited, William knew that he should feel nothing but gratitude and relief at his employer's instant generosity. But he felt angry that he was required to stand in silence and watch the act of charity take place without being told that help would be provided. If Henry Hodding had agreed to lend a thousand pounds to a friend, he would not have counted out the money in silence. Four five-pound notes were laid on the green baize.

'You can find the coppers yourself.'

'I don't know how to thank you, Mr Hodding.'

'Do you know how to pay me back?'

'It'll take years. Perhaps I ought to have said. We'll all chip in, Anne, Ernest and me. But it will still only be coppers a week.' He paused before he made the last, dreadful confession. 'I shall be in your debt for as long as I work here and perhaps afterwards.'

'I was just thinking about that. You can work most of it off. What about young Agnes working in the kitchen?'

'Her mother wouldn't want it. I don't mean to sound ungrateful, but the girl isn't strong.'

'Then you'll have to do it yourself.'

'Do what?' William was so apprehensive about the tasks which Mr Hodding might have in mind for him that he addressed his master man to man.

'I'm starting a hunt. Mrs Hodding will be master. But, naturally, I shall run it. There'll be all sorts of jobs to do. The huntsman will be half-time. Retired man from the Rufford. So there'll be hounds to feed and clean out. You can look after them before you start in the morning. We're going to buy a couple more horses so there'll be more tack to clean than Knock can manage. He'll teach you what to do. I'll tell you when you've worked it off.'

William's spirits were not even lifted by Henry Hodding's benediction.

'Look here, Skinner. I know it's Mr Hirst's fault. And I respect you for not putting the blame on him. I'll remember that when I'm working out how long it will take to pay me back.'

William should have laid the twenty pounds on the kitchen table with an air of triumph but he could not even pretend pleasure. Ernest and Anne mumbled 'Thank you' and then sank back in silent relief. Nobody asked him how the money was to be repaid. You would think, he told himself, that country squires were in the habit of lending money to their gardeners.

'By the way,' he added as an afterthought when the money had been counted for the third time, 'I'm going to give a hand with the new hunt.'

'What hunt?' asked Agnes, who was interested in such things.

'The new hunt here at Harness Grove. Mrs Hodding's going to be Master of Foxhounds.'

Ernest's reaction was, by his standards, shamelessly frivolous. 'Anne won't like that. She thinks fox hunting is cruel.'

'It doesn't stop her sewing fox heads on muffs and making collars out of fox tails,' said Agnes, intending to provoke her sister.

'Stop it,' said her mother. 'Stop it. I don't want you arguing this afternoon. Thanks to Mr Hodding we can hold our heads up again.'

'And thanks to Dad,' added Ernest.

Everybody, including William, looked surprised.

Anne did not wait to take off her hat and coat before she announced the news. 'Tomorrow. We're giving notice, tomorrow.'

It was not Lottie's way to argue. But, during the long years of dreaming about a business of their own, one of her greatest pleasures had been the enjoyment of Anne's description of how the great day would dawn. On a succession of Wednesday afternoons, they would tour the salerooms of Worksop and Retford, looking for second-hand sewing machines, tailors' dummies and the pink chaise-longue essential to a genteel fitting room.

The vital purchases having been made, they would warn their landlord of their intention to carry out a tailoring and dressmaking business from their rooms. When furniture had been moved around,

196

what had once been their bedroom would be redecorated in striped green-and-silver wallpaper. A white rug would cover at least part of the stained-oak floorboards. Pattern books and perhaps a bolt of cloth would be kept on a low table, and a long cheval mirror would be placed where it caught the light. Finally, a Grecian urn (filled with flowers according to season) would crown a tall wicker stand. Then, the fitting room would be ready. They would live, sleep, eat and sew in the larger room across the landing. When the rooms were ready, an advertisement would be placed in the *Worksop Guardian*. But, until then, the secret could be kept. Anne always said that it would be silly to sacrifice a week's wages before there was work of their own to be done.

With so much of Anne's wisdom to rely on, Lottie was able to question the sudden decision to leave William Allen's at a moment's notice. She was able to argue with the announcement and still do nothing more rebellious than demonstrate how clearly she remembered every word of Anne's previous pronouncements on the subject.

'Aren't we going to get the things first?'

'The machines we've got will do for a start.'

'Don't you need a treadle?' Lottie's disagreements were always expressed in the form of questions. 'Won't it be too hard sewing heavy cloth on a hand machine?'

'I can do it if I have to. Anyway, we can see what's for sale on Wednesday afternoon, after we've put the advert in. We might buy one then.'

'When will it be in the paper?'

'Saturday.'

'Can't we give notice on Friday? Don't you want us to get another week's wages?'

'If we don't do it straight away we'll never do it. Tomorrow. Tomorrow, first thing.'

Lottie might have invented more questions had she not been headed off with demands for tea.

'Bring the pot in here. I'll write out the advertisement.'

The sound of pleasure that greeted the suggestion confirmed that the diversion had been successful.

Drafting the advertisement proved more difficult than the partners had anticipated. Anne could not decide if it was important to identify the individual trades or if a generic description of the business would be enough to attract the customers they needed. In the end the dilemma was solved when Lottie noticed a price list on the back page of that week's *Guardian*. Anne seized the paper from her hand and announced that the message had to be compressed into thirty-five words, including a maximum of ten in heavy type.

197

We are pleased to announce that
Mesdames SKINNER AND HARTHILL
(Late of William Allen of Bridge Street)
have set up business as
LADIES' HIGH-CLASS DRESSMAKERS AND TAILORS
at 39 Gateford Road, Worksop
Satisfaction Guaranteed

The final promise was Lottie's idea and Anne pandered to her silliness because they still had words to spare. The advertisement was copied out neatly and the result was examined with a pleasure that was in no way spoilt by the anxiety which realism would have prompted. They had only one worry. Anne added more water to the teapot and, wagging her finger at the world, enquired, 'What shall we do if somebody comes on Monday morning, before we're ready?'

'Even Saturday,' Lottie added, taking on Anne's mood, as was her duty.

'We'll have to work hard, my word, on Wednesday.'

'Oh Lor'!' said Lottie. Even in her excitement she remembered not to pronounce the final letter and offend Anne with her blasphemy.

There was more time for preparation than either of the women had anticipated. As soon as they announced that they were leaving, Mr Robert Allen dismissed them on the spot without notice and required them to leave the work room on the instant. Their departure was momentarily delayed by a dispute over a pair of deckling scissors which Lottie said were her private property.

'Don't demean yourself,' Anne commanded. 'We can manage without a pair of old scissors.'

Lottie obeyed and the two women swept out, followed by catcalls from their erstwhile colleagues which included the hope that they would be happy together and requests for invitations to the wedding.

It took all week to collect what they needed. They could afford only one treadle sewing machine so it was important to find one which was more or less up to date and in good condition. Lottie had doubts about buying a modern Singer because the golden sphinx had been almost worn off the black-enamelled chassis. But Anne dismissed her objections and returned to the examination of dressmakers' dummies. Having found one without tear or stain, she began to question the proprietor of the saleroom about its origin.

'How do I know where it came from, lady? I've bought half a dozen this year. What's it matter, anyway?'

'Bugs,' answered Anne. 'Bugs. Black-clocks. Cockroaches. Silverfish. I want to make sure that it came from somewhere clean.'

'All my stuff's clean, madam. And I'll ask you not to suggest otherwise. Tell you what. I'll knock off a shilling to pay for fumigation.'

The offer was ironically made and accepted at its face value. In retaliation, the saleroom owner refused to take any responsibility for delivery so the two women were obliged to push the dummy through the streets on its castors. After a moment's dispute, Anne agreed to leave it at the bottom of the stairs until Ernest arrived in the evening to help with the rearrangement of the furniture.

At ten past five – almost an hour before her brother was expected – Anne heard climbing footsteps. The tap on the door was too tentative for Ernest's heavy hand. Lottie fumbled with the knob and discovered, standing on the landing, a young lady who was, as she repeated time after time on the following day, 'dressed in the height of fashion'.

Lottie had never seen such clothes before. But she recognised, from pattern books and ladies' magazines, every detail of her complicated wardrobe. The visitor was, in the language of the popular newspapers, 'a Gibson girl' and, in consequence, had contorted herself into what she believed to be the shape of a swan. The transformation of her human form had been achieved with the help of a bosom corset, probably the patent 'Neena Bust' which the makers claimed to be modelled on the Venus de Milo. She also wore 'fitted hips', which served to emphasise the curves above and below her waist and stretched tight the top of a skirt which then fell to her feet in graceful folds. It ended in a wide swirl which must have caught every dusty step on the three flights of narrow stairs.

The skirt was purple and the blouse above it – pouched in the latest style and pulled down in front below the waistline – was mauve. Over the blouse she wore an embroidered bolero jacket, which, under its gold and black silk fleur-de-lys, was a shade of purple lighter than her skirt. Her yellow, wide-brimmed hat was piled with so many velvet violets that the peeling landing wallpaper was only just visible behind her.

'Is this Skinner and Harthill?'

Lottie still could not believe that the young lady had found what she was looking for. 'Who do you want? There's only us up here at the top.'

'Are you Skinner and Harthill?'

'Yes, we are.' Anne was at her partner's shoulder. 'What can we do for you?'

'I'm in trouble. Can I come in?'

Anne was reluctant to expose the chaos in the half-cleared living room to so sophisticated a gaze. 'We've only just moved in.' It was the truth, but it was intended to deceive. 'There's nowhere for you to sit down.'

If the young lady heard, she did not understand. For she advanced through the doorway like a man-o'-war in full sail. Even Anne retreated in the face of her irresistible self-confidence. With an unerring instinct for the piece of furniture most suited to her elegant posterior, the uninvited guest removed a pattern book from the chaise-longue and carefully lowered herself into as comfortable a position as the wire and whalebone would allow.

'I'm in such trouble. And I've tried everyone else.' Realising that the truth might cause offence, she added a little conscious charm. 'Now, I know why nobody had ever heard of you. You've only just moved in.'

'Today. Only today,' said Anne, anxious to establish the reason why the brass bedhead stood in one corner of the room and the blankets and pillows were piled on the table. 'Did you see our advert?'

'My maid saw it. She showed me barely an hour ago and I got ready straight away and came right round from Sparken Hill. Nobody knew about you.'

Anne looked at the skirt. 'You've walked from Sparken Hill?'

'My father brought me. He owns the livery round the corner.'

Lottie could scarcely believe her. She had assumed the unexpected guest to be at least the daughter of a duchess. She knew that Sweeting's Livery Stable did well but the young lady must be wearing . . . As she made the silent calculation, her lips moved with the effort of the mental arithmetic . . . Two pounds for the shoes. Pound for the gloves. Blouse, skirt and jacket, twenty pounds. Petticoats and stockings not less than two pounds ten . . . The total had reached twenty-four pounds, ten shillings before Anne interrupted her inventory.

'How can we help you?'

'I need a motor-car coat. I need it by ten o'clock on Wednesday morning and no one will make me one on time. I've tried all day. I've telegraphed London. You're my last hope.'

'We'll make you one.' Anne was already reaching in the table drawer for her tape measure.

'By Wednesday at ten?'

'If that's what you want, that's what we must do.'

Lottie gasped. 'Have you got your own material?'

'I hoped you'd have it in stock. Linen. I'd like cornflower-coloured, but beige would do, or cream. Cotton lining. Big pearl buttons. Let me see what you've got in stock.'

'Our cloth hasn't got here yet.' Anne decided that the lies no longer

200

mattered. She returned to Lottie. 'Do you think it will get here first thing tomorrow?'

'I don't know.' It was the best that Lottie could manage.

'It probably won't. I'll nip round to our wholesalers first thing so we can get started early. Cornflower cambric. That should be all right. First fitting at two o'clock? I'm afraid the fitting room isn't ready yet. We'd better measure you in here.' The tape measure was already at work. 'Loose, I take it, with enough in the skirt to wrap round over your knees.'

Anne cried out the measurements and Lottie wrote them down whilst Miss Lucy Sweeting described her recent vicissitudes. She had no idea when she arrived from London that her father had bought a motor car but truth to tell she was not very close to him. Indeed, her mother – who never spoke his name – did not approve of her annual visit. But he was, after all, her father.

'Buttons on the cuffs to keep out the dust?'

If she had even suspected that her father had bought a car, she would have had a proper coat made there and then at her proper tailors. Not least since the car had been specially bought for her – to show off or to show her off in. The shame of having to sit there in an ordinary coat! She had begun to hope that under the goggles nobody—

'Slit at the back with buttons and plackets?'

Without looking at the fashion plate which Anne waved before her, Miss Sweeting nodded and went on to explain that the motor car was chocolate brown, which was why the coat had to be cornflower. Anne decided that it would be sinful to allow such an opportunity to pass her by. 'Perhaps I should have said earlier. We'll have to charge a little more for a rush job like this. I'll put our best girl on the seams and buttonholes – I wouldn't trust anyone else – so she'll have to work over.' She tried desperately to calculate a price that would take full advantage of her first customer's gullibility. Fortunately, no figure was required.

'Of course, whatever you say. Just have it ready for Wednesday at ten.'

For safety's sake, Anne led the way down the narrow stairs and Lottie, who had not spoken for half an hour, followed behind holding Lucy Sweeting's full skirt as if it were a train to protect it from the dusty carpet. She was still playing the part of page when the trio moved out into the road, where they were greeted with astonishment by Ernest. He was carrying a fretwork letter rack with the words 'Home Sweet Home' burned on it in pokerwork. Anne decided, there and then, that it would not be kept in the fitting room.

CHAPTER SIXTEEN
Tally Ho!

There was more for Vincent Sweeting to boast about than the mere possession of a chocolate-coloured motor car. Henry Hodding had invited him to become joint master of the Grove Hunt. He kept his good news to himself until he sat with his daughter in the back seat of the Daimler travelling through Sherwood Forest at fifteen miles an hour.

He announced his great social achievement like a conjurer producing a rabbit from a hat.

'Vincent Sweeting, MFH. Not bad, eh?'

When he received no immediate response, he drove the importance of his message home. 'What would your mother think about that, then?'

'She hates horses. Like me.'

'What doesn't she hate? That's what I've always pondered.'

'She likes going to galleries and exhibitions and listening to chamber music and reading. And she likes telling Grannie what a rotter you are.'

'Does she say that I provide every penny that she spends, her and her mother?'

'And me, Daddy.'

'I didn't mean that. Truly I didn't. You know it's a pleasure to spend money on you.'

Lucy was almost touched. 'She never says you're mean. Never.'

'I should hope not, indeed. And if she does, I hope you'll call her a liar.'

'Yes, Papa.' She shuddered under her muslin veil and repeated the promise. 'Yes, Papa. I'll call her a liar.' 'Papa' was the form of address which she reserved for moments when she despised her father even more than usual.

'Will you come when the season starts? Will you come and hunt with the Grove?'

'Certainly not! I'm not going to gallop about on a great brute horse.

I hate riding. I'd break my neck at the first hedge and what would dear Mama have to say about you then?'

'There'd be no need to ride very far. Just trot with us for a couple of furlongs. I know you've ridden in London. We'd start out over flat country. Down to Stubbin's Meadows.'

'What if the fox didn't want to go that way?'

Vincent Sweeting laughed nervously. He loved his daughter to be clever at other people's expense but it seemed unfair that she should treat him so badly when all that he wanted was for her to be happy and proud of him. 'You'd look lovely in your riding clothes.'

'I don't have any. I gave them away last year when I promised myself never to sit on a horse again.'

'Have some new ones made. Have them made here. Those two treasures that you found on Monday could make them for you.'

'What! Have you seen this coat?' Lucy plucked at the skirt and pulled at the collar. 'Davidson gets this the moment we're back at Sparken Hill. She's so ugly it won't matter. You can tell a mile off that it's not made in London. Those two are after the servant trade. Servants' topcoats and widows' weeds. I don't think I'll even give this to Davidson. She'd be insulted.'

'You look very nice to me.' The last feeble attempt to ingratiate himself with his daughter had hardly provoked a snort before Vincent Sweeting had thought of another way of capturing her interest.

'I met an old friend of yours last week.'

Lucy was just capable of forcing herself to play the game. But she insisted on playing according to her rules. 'Am I to guess who it was?'

'You are.'

'Well, I can't.'

'It was Brackenbury.'

'The blacksmith?' She was anxious to emphasise the boredom, so she yawned behind her hand before she added, 'I thought he was in prison.'

'Just the opposite.' Sweeting wriggled in his seat with delight. At last he was going to score a point. 'Just the opposite. He's a policeman. At least he was last week. He's going back to smithing.'

Sweeting warmed to his subject. One of his great joys was telling his daughter stories about men he believed to be infatuated with her – especially if they were so much beneath her station in life that they were forced to worship from afar without any risk of diverting her attention from him. 'I used to watch him eyeing you up and down when he came round to shoe the horses.'

'He never even noticed I was there. That was the only interesting thing about him. That and getting warned off at Doncaster.'

'Wetherby.'

'If he was banned, how can he be blacksmithing?'

'He's not shoeing racehorses. Or horses of any sort now. He's doing monumental work. He told me he was doing the new altar rails for Thorpe Salvin. But you can't believe a word he says.'

Lucy Sweeting, her eyes half shut, was dreaming of the house on Sparken Hill and a bath and the end of the purgatory she had to pay for the good things in her life.

Her father continued his monologue. 'Mind you, he'll be back in racing. John Robinson will see to that. He owes it to him. I wonder why he left Sheffield so quickly? I'll tell you this. He had his eye on you. I warned him off once or twice.'

Lucy woke from her reverie with a start. 'Oh, Papa, you do so embarrass me sometimes. You really do. Please stop.' She leaned back in her seat. She remembered Brackenbury vividly. Tall, curly hair, moustache and imperious manner that was wholly inappropriate to his station. What was it, she wondered, that attracted her to uncouth young men? She decided that it must be the charm of the unusual.

The first meeting of the Grove Hunt was adjudged by all who took part to be a wonderful success. The hounds, although unable to pick up a scent, bayed with immense gusto, and terrified the local poultry so comprehensively that there was not a duck or a hen on the Derbyshire–Nottingham border which would not have preferred to be left to the mercy of the foxes. Gerrard Knock wore his top-hat as a sign that he was senior to the part-time huntsman.

At John Robinson's invitation Brack came over from Shireoaks, where he had rented a squalid room over the baker's shop. He replaced a couple of loose shoes as if he had never left smithing. It was the first time in three years that he had shod a horse but if he was moved by the smell of hot iron burning into hoof or the hollow sound of hammer on shoe, he showed no sign of it. He collected his dues from each of his customers, touched his forehead and retreated to the back steps where he sat, waiting for more work and tossing a penny in the air. He gambled with himself that it would come down tails more often than heads. For once he won.

Agnes Skinner, against her mother's wishes, stood underneath the yew trees watching the hunt assemble without realising that the recipient of her recent generosity was sitting round at the back of the house. She knew – for both her mother and Anne had told her – that it was wrong to kill God's creatures for pleasure but she was entranced by the sight of the scarlet coats, gleaming top-hats, sleek hunters and panting hounds. She waved to Ernest but her brother ignored her.

The turn-out was far better than the joint masters had expected. Samuel Beard, the miller, was there with his son-in-law Joseph Anderson, who had set up practice as a family doctor in Cheapside. Arnold Hirst had brought a second horse in the confident expectation that he would exhaust the coal-black mare on which he began the day. He had not, however, brought his wife. Mrs Hirst did not ride and she declined the joint masters' invitation to drink the hunt's health and see it on its way.

To the delight of one joint master and the distress of the other, Mr and Mrs John Robinson agreed at the last minute to join them. As late as the previous evening, they had feared that courtesy required them to stay at the Manor with their weekend guests, Mr and Mrs William Anson of Newark. But Mr Anson, who had made his fortune from meat and devoted his time to racing, announced that he would like to 'give hunting a try'. So, dressed in borrowed clothes which strained across his bulging belly, he weighed down John Robinson's second-best hunter.

Lucy Sweeting had been lured up from London by the hope of an increased dress allowance. She waved prettily from the steps and said, through clenched teeth, how much she was looking forward to the dinner which her father was giving that evening.

'And I', cried Vincent Sweeting from the saddle of his chestnut gelding, 'am looking forward to having such a beautiful and charming hostess by my side.'

Lucy's smile reminded Dr Anderson of rigor mortis.

The temporary hostess of Rock House, Sparken Hill, spent most of the day agonising about the *placements* for dinner. She had no problem about determining the proper social precedence but she had the greatest difficulty in deciding which of the guests she would least dislike sitting next to. In the end she decided that the older men would probably be the least tedious so she bowed to convention and put Henry Hodding on her left and John Robinson on her right.

Arnold Hirst was at one end of the table but it did not prevent him from entering into animated conversation with Dr Anderson, who was at the other. 'Know anything about fractures?' Dr Anderson gave a self-deprecating Edinburgh shrug which encouraged Hirst to improve the general practitioner's experience. 'I've had eleven.'

'Perhaps,' said Lucy, from her position opposite her father, 'we should keep you in a bottle.'

Vincent Sweeting roared with laughter. John Robinson smiled and Arnold Hirst cried, 'Beg pardon? Didn't quite catch.'

'I said that I'd never heard of so many broken bones before. How did you come by them?'

The usual litany of athletic endeavour lasted for several minutes. Then, as was Arnold Hirst's habit, he went on to urge his own eccentric habits on his fellow guests.

'What do you do for exercise, Miss Sweeting?'

'I'm not sure that it is proper for you to ask such an intimate question.'

Her father rocked with laughter.

'I only ask it because of concern for your welfare.'

'Since that is your reason, I shall tell you. I rise. I bathe. I dress. I find it all an immense physical effort.'

'You ought to ride,' said John Robinson.

'Horses', Miss Sweeting told him, 'are things of the past. Soon we shall all have motor cars.'

'You won't get much exercise from them.' Because of his recent financial difficulties, Arnold Hirst had been prevented from purchasing a Wolseley.

'On the contrary,' Dr Anderson's Scottish accent added to the authority of his professional opinion, 'the jolting which occurs when a motor car is driven at speed produces a healthy agitation.'

'It certainly has that effect on me.'

Mr Sweeting almost choked with delight at his daughter's apparently endless fund of repartee.

'I meant it acts on the liver.' For a moment the physician was carried away by his enthusiasm for his profession. 'I don't mean nerves, Miss Sweeting, I mean peristaltic movements.'

'Bowels.' Arnold Hirst knew that he, as the only person in the room who took an interest in physiology, would have to translate the diagnosis into layman's language.

'I think', said Lucy Sweeting, 'that we had better leave the gentlemen to their port and cigars.'

In the dining room the talk – horses and Consols, Balfour, Campbell-Bannerman and the new King – dragged on for nearly an hour. But, when gentlemen and ladies were reunited, Arnold Hirst resumed the pursuit.

'Motoring won't do, you know. Need something else. Ever thought of Indian clubs?'

'No, Mr Hirst. I have never in my life thought of Indian clubs.'

'Tennis?'

'I have given some thought to tennis and rejected it.'

'Fencing?'

There was a pause and Arnold Hirst knew that he had struck home. 'Fencing, dear lady. The foil, the sabre and the épée. In your case I would recommend the foil.' He parried an imaginary opponent's blade and then, with a triumphant cry, thrust for the heart.

'Hamlet,' said Lucy Sweeting, 'Hamlet and Laertes. I saw them fence at Drury Lane last year.'

'There's a great deal of it in Shakespeare.' He tried hard to remember if he had fenced whilst playing Bottom at school.

'And Beatrice. I believe Beatrice fences with Benedick.'

'Believe she does.' Arnold Hirst was out of his depth.

'What sort of clothes should I wear?' It was the preoccupation of Lucy's life.

'Sporting clothes. Tennis sort of clothes. Cycling sort of clothes.'

'Not men's clothes? I think Beatrice wore men's clothes for fencing.'

Arnold Hirst's unconventionality only went so far. The conversation was getting out of hand. He decided to bring it to a sudden end. 'There are fencing masters in London who would be delighted to teach you. I'll send your father a note with suggested names. Send it tomorrow.'

He looked round in desperate search for a lady who would join them. It was impossible to leave Miss Sweeting standing alone in the middle of her own drawing room. He failed to attract Mrs Anderson's attention. Mrs Robinson was engrossed in chatting with Mrs Beard. Mrs Hodding was nowhere to be seen. And, had he not known her better, he would have sworn that his own wife was being careful not to catch his eye. His worst fears were realised.

'Why don't you teach me? I've got another five days to pass before I go home. Your wife told me that you have a gymnasium in your house. Why can't you teach me there?'

'My dear young lady, I have a company to run. Couldn't spare all that time.'

'You assume that I would be a dull pupil. Perhaps you are wrong. Surely you could spare me an hour?'

'Take far longer than an hour. Should be a lifetime.'

'If you were not a married man, I should believe that you were proposing to me.' To Hirst's relief, Lucy Sweeting turned towards his wife.

'Isabel, your husband refuses to teach me to fence. And you said that he was such a gallant.'

For some reason, the discovery that the two women were on Christian-name terms was particularly disconcerting. 'You know how busy I am. Tell Miss Sweeting all the things I do.'

'You could spare a couple of hours, surely?'

'No, I could not. But there's one thing I could do. Young man who works for me. Teaches fencing to the local lads. I'll tell him to do it.'

207

Lucy had become bored with her game. The mouse was no longer of any interest to the cat so she parted her paws and let it scamper back to its conventional little hole. There was, however, time to fill before she could escape to London.

'The young man will do very well.'

'I will send him round tomorrow.'

'Shouldn't I come to your gymnasium?'

'It would be best here. If you had the dining room cleared . . .'

'Four o'clock, then.'

'I thought of early evening after work.'

'No, four o'clock after my sleep. That's when I'm at my most energetic.'

'I'm sure he'll be delighted.'

'I'm sure he will.'

Out at Harness Grove, the hunt servants were having a party of their own. The butler and the part-time huntsman sat aloof in the pantry reminiscing with each other about bigger hunts and better families they had served and the housekeeper had retreated to the no-longer-needed nursery to drink genteel port and lemon with the no-longer-needed nanny. But in the kitchen three housemaids and the boot-boy, who called himself the valet, were entertaining. Ernest Skinner had been invited but evensong in Retford had forced him to decline with thanks. After much debate an invitation was also sent to William but the middle-aged gardener, knowing that the young people had asked him out of courtesy, decided that the rheumatism which had stopped him running errands in the damp morning grass must also prevent him from sitting by any hearth other than his own. After much argument, Agnes, who had not been invited, was allowed to take her parents' apologies.

Sitting in the best chair – the place of honour intended for William Skinner – was Brack, the hero of Agnes's bicycle ride. He was trying to insulate himself from the merriment which filled the rest of the kitchen, for he had come to Harness Grove for the single purpose of playing cards with the boot-boy. Whilst he was prepared to wait patiently until his victim grew tired of flirting with the housemaids, he had no intention of joining in the jollity surrounding him. He had, in his own estimation, fulfilled all the obligations of courtesy by accepting a glass of beer and evading a number of questions about the Sheffield police force and his reasons for leaving it. He sat silent and self-confident at one end of the room whilst Agnes stood, speechless and bewildered, at the other. At first she worried that he would not recognise or, if he did remember who she was, choose to pretend

208

that they had not met. Then, at last, he risked having to exchange another round of silly banter and looked up. As soon as he saw Agnes he beckoned her towards him, without moving from his chair or putting down his glass. He did no more than lift one hand and curl one finger. Agnes, more self-conscious still, pushed her way between the servants and stood beside him. Then, still without getting up, he put his hand into his pocket and took out a florin. 'I'd better pay my debts. I'm very grateful.'

'No, keep it. That's all right.'

'Don't be silly. Take it. I'm sorry that I didn't thank you at the time but I thought it best to be on my way. Your father said that he was going to set your brother on me.'

'My brother was in Retford.'

'Lying old bugger!' Agnes had never heard the word before. She blushed and drew in her breath. Brack did not apologise. 'Well. I'm very grateful, anyway. Gate still on its hinges?'

'It's very well, thank you.'

'That's all right, then.'

There was a long pause for Brack thought that the conversation had ended and Agnes believed that it had only begun. He looked into the bottom of his empty glass. She examined the florin as if it might be counterfeit. Inevitably, her nerve gave way first. 'Would you like another drink?'

Brack handed Agnes his glass without a word and she scurried across to the sideboard and the pitcher of beer. He nodded his thanks.

'Have you still got your bicycle?'

'I have.'

There was another long pause. Then, at last, Brack showed interest in the conversation. 'How old are you?'

'Twenty.'

'Get away. You're no more twenty than I'm eighty.'

Agnes blushed again, partly from embarrassment and partly from anger. There was a long pause.

'Can you play cards?'

Agnes was delighted by the question.

'Of course I can.'

'At your age? Cards is said by some to be sinful. How has a child of your age got corrupted so quick?'

As she turned away, almost in tears, Brack reached out and caught her by the elbow. She shook him off.

'You've got to learn to take a little joke.'

'Why have I?'

'If you're going to play a hand of cards with me you have.' He took a pack of cards out of his pocket and, although it was old and curled at the corners, shuffled it with the ease which comes from years of practice. The maids, who had heard of his reputation, watched furtively in the hope that he could perform with the flashy skill of a fairground conjurer. But he did not spread the cards up his arm, pass them from one hand to the other like the bellows of a concertina, or spread them out in the shape of a fan. He shuffled like Agnes shuffled before playing snap or patience, but he did it at twenty times the speed and with the look of a man who was fulfilling his destiny. 'What can you play?'

'Rummy. I can play rummy. And I can play whist.'

'Have you ever played brag?'

'I've never heard of it.'

'If you can play whist, you'll pick up brag in five minutes.'

Agnes knew nothing of men and the ways of the world but she sensed that Brack wanted to teach her – and her instincts insisted that he wanted her to be an unreceptive pupil who learned slowly under his stern guidance. But she could not bring herself to pretend that she was dull-witted and in awe of the mighty intelligence who dealt the cards. The boot-boy, who was at last ready for his game, approached with the announcement that he had never before seen Brack play without money on the table. He watched silently throughout a whole hand.

'It's a good job you're not playing for money. You'd be skint.'

'I'll be ready in a minute.'

'I'm not sure that I wouldn't rather play her than you. She'll give me a game. You wouldn't, playing like this.'

Brack did not look up. 'I shan't play like this against you. When I play you, I'll be trying.'

Agnes lost the last four tricks. It was, she decided, time to go home.

But Brack had still one favour to ask. 'Are you off?'

'I might be. I might not.'

'Well, I'm going out into the stable to teach this young man how to play cards – and some manners. I shan't want to break off. In an hour, if he's not come back, bring me another glass of beer. We'll be in the tack room.'

'Does Mr Knock know?' Agnes was suddenly afraid that her mother would find out how she had spent the evening.

'Knock's at home feeling sorry for himself,' the boot-boy said. 'That's his business, not ours. What the eye doesn't see . . .'

Agnes stood about, occasionally speaking to one of the maids and pretending to drink lemonade, for another forty-five minutes. When the clock on the mantelshelf struck ten she could wait no longer. She filled a glass with beer and ran out of the kitchen, stumbled across the cobbled yard and rattled open the stable door. The hurricane lamp, which gently swung from the roof beam, cast a circle of light on the tack-room floor. Brack and the boot-boy sat cross-legged at its circumference, their feet and legs clearly illuminated but their heads and bodies in the shadows. Agnes peered forward to make sure which was Brack and, having identified him, put the glass down by his side.

'Watch out, for God's sake!'

The glass had toppled over. She had placed it on the pile of coins which was his winnings.

Agnes ran from the tack room and out into the yard. She did not stop running until she reached Grove Cottage. Her father was sitting in his usual chair attempting to rub wintergreen on his shoulder without removing his long-sleeved flannel vest. When his daughter dashed in through the back door, he pulled his hand from inside the neck in the guilty manner of a man discovered in an indecent act.

'Where've you been? Your mother's been worried to death.'

'You know very well where I've been. You could have come yourself if you'd wanted to.'

'I almost did. I almost came up to fetch you an hour ago. Your mother wanted me to.'

Even though she had been spared the humiliation, Agnes felt sick at the thought of what might have happened. Her mother's voice called down from the top of the stairs.

'Is that you, Agnes?'

'Yes, Mam.'

'Are you all right?'

'Of course I am. I've only been up at the house. You know where I've been.'

'But you shouldn't stay out so late. It isn't good for you. If only you were sensible, like . . .' The denunciation was abandoned in mid-sentence when Elizabeth Skinner remembered that Ernest was sensible no more.

'It's Home Sweet Home!' Lucy Sweeting greeted Ernest Skinner with an intentionally bad imitation of a joyous reunion. Ernest was bewildered and her father, who was preparing to make an over-formal introduction, waited to hear his daughter's undoubted witticism explained. 'It is, isn't it? You are the boy with the carved wood, aren't you?'

Ernest did not reply.

'What fun! Papa, when I went to see those two funny women who made that awful motoring coat, this boy came calling.'

'Don't you remember?' Vincent Sweeting could not believe that anyone who had met his daughter could possibly forget the experience.

Ernest remembered. He had recognised Lucy as soon as he walked into the Sweeting drawing room but he had hoped that she had not recognised him. From the moment of their first meeting on the pavement in Gateford Road, he had realised that he was not equipped to deal with such a young lady. He had therefore made up his mind to dislike her – but he had taken that decision in the belief that he would never see her again. At the moment of their second meeting, he stared into the middle distance and cursed his luck.

'Well, I remember him. He was carrying this wooden thing. It had "Home Sweet Home" written on it in scorch marks.'

'Pokerwork.'

Vincent Sweeting, having decided that his daughter had enjoyed another triumph, turned to the business of the day. 'This is the boy who is going to teach you how to fence.'

'How delicious. Have you brought swords?'

The first lesson was, by every reasonable test of success and failure, a total disaster. Lucy agreed to wear the fencing mask only after her father – in a rare exercise of paternal authority – had pronounced her eyesight more important than her coiffure and announced that unless her face was protected he would cancel the lesson. The quilted chest-protector was buckled on with the comment that it was the only corset she had ever seen designed to be worn over rather than under day clothes. The risk of being exposed to more dubious language having suitably terrified the men, Lucy plunged her hand into the gauntlet – and withdrew it with a shriek when she discovered that it was damp from the combined sweat of a dozen other duellists. Ernest's shame at having simultaneously to face so many facts of physical life was increased by the whole sordid business being transacted in the presence of a lady. He was made more uncomfortable by the discovery that pupil and master were almost equally ignorant about fencing. Lucy had seen plays and read books. Ernest had only taken lessons from Arnold Hirst and had, in consequence, learned more about human vanity than the foil and the épée.

Lucy, to Ernest's astonishment, judged the first encounter a great success. She seemed particularly to enjoy the moments when, abandoning technique and etiquette, she slapped him on the side of the head with the flat of her blade, painfully trapping his ear between his skull and the wooden frame of his wickerwork fencing mask. Pride prevented him from complaining. But, despite his sore head and loss of dignity, Ernest felt only relief at the announcement that Lucy would expect him at the same time next day. He certainly disliked her. But it was a sort of dislike which he had never felt before. After the second meeting, his passion to avoid sight and sound of her changed into an obsession to be the undisputed victor in each passage of arms. After the third joust he borrowed a manual from Arnold Hirst and spent the evening studying its diagrams instead of varnishing a watch-holder which he had designed for the table at the side of his father's bed. He did not learn enough to prevent Lucy Sweeting from penetrating his guard at will.

'Look here, Home Sweet, I've got an idea.'

Ernest was too breathless to speak. So he simply looked at Lucy in apprehensive enquiry.

'Why don't I teach you to fence?'

'Because you can't fence yourself. You don't know a thing about it. You just prod and swipe. That's not how it's done.'

'If we'd had real duels, I would have killed you ten times over.'

'But that's not the point. You might as well say that a wrestler could strangle a boxer to death. There are ways of doing things. Fencing is an art—'

'Oh, Home Sweet! You are so pompous. You talk like a fifty-year-old vicar. How old are you?'

Ernest blushed but did not answer.

'It doesn't matter.'

'I'm twenty-three.'

'I meant that being pompous doesn't matter. I think it's one of the things that I like about you.'

The compliment, although clearly qualified, gave Ernest immense pleasure. He was delighted by the implication that Lucy was impressed by more than his pomposity alone. He was desperately anxious to win her respect, though he still did not understand why her opinion of him was so important. In so far as he thought about it at all, he told himself that he was determined to prove that he was her equal. The idea that Lucy was attracted to him because she felt superior in every particular was beyond his comprehension.

'I'm serious, that's what I am. Call it pompous if you want. But I can't afford to be silly.'

Lucy touched his moustache and pretended to be hurt when he flinched away from her fingers. 'You have a very serious moustache. The moustache of a serious middle-aged man. And a serious hair cut.' She patted the neat crown of his smooth head as if he were a dog to be complimented with a touch. 'If you shaved off that thing on your top lip and moved your parting to nearer the middle you might be quite good-looking.'

When Lucy touched him, Ernest felt the shock waves from the top of his head to the tips of his toes. He was scandalised by her behaviour, and he could not prevent himself from thinking of how shocked his mother would be were she – improbably – to be watching from the other side of the room. But he was undeniably excited by the experience. Lucy, he told himself, represented the contempt for respectability that riddled the worthless world of wealth and sophistication. Though touched by pitch, he would not be defiled.

'You want to make me feel ashamed of being sensible.'

'I shan't even try. But I will teach you how to fence – if you want me to, that is.'

'Are you trying to say that you want a lesson again tomorrow?'

'I'm saying that if you'll come here each night, I'll pretend that I'm killing you every night for another week.'

Ernest tried not to look puzzled. He was afraid that Lucy constructed her fanciful questions with the intention of making him admit that he did not understand. He would deny her that satisfaction. So, by remaining silent, he provided her with an opportunity to patronise him.

'Let me put it simply – you being proud of being a simple as well as a sensible man. I'd like another week of thrusting and parrying.' She giggled, as far as Ernest could make out, pointlessly. 'So, if you're available, I shall stay to keep my grey-haired old father company. No doubt you will need to ask that absurd Mr Hirst.'

'No, I shan't,' said Ernest, deciding that he would seek Arnold Hirst's permission that evening.

Ernest Skinner's infatuation with Arnold Hirst was over. It had ended with the investment catastrophe. He had learned from a Mechanics' Institute pamphlet that buying and selling shares was a hazardous business – no better than betting on the horses, as his mother had described it when he dropped his guard one Sunday afternoon and revealed his interest in the stock market. He did not regard one error of financial judgement as proof of a permanently flawed character. Indeed, he would have admired Hirst's calm acceptance of his losses as a sign of nerve and character had Ernest's own twenty pounds not been written off with similar equanimity. He did not share his mother's view that his employer, having advised him to take the risk, ought to pay off his debt, but he did think that Arnold Hirst ought to take an interest in his predicament. When three months had passed without the subject having been mentioned, Ernest identified, for the first time, his quaint employer's principal eccentricity. Arnold Hirst believed that the world existed purely for his own amusement.

The discovery inevitably resulted in a new comparison being made between the two middle-aged men in his life. During his early days at the timber yard, Ernest had often wondered what sort of a man he would have become had he been born a Hirst rather than a Skinner. He had usually concluded that he would have been suave, dashing and, most important, rich. After Hirst had left him weighed down with debt, he felt grateful for the parents which fate had provided. His father was no more than a gardener, but he possessed a courage and understanding that would have done credit to a prince of the blood – and was certainly beyond the capacity of a timber merchant. The reassessment of the relative merits of father and employer did no more than rehabilitate William Skinner in his son's mind. It made Ernest determined to uphold the honour of the line of humble heroes from which he sprang. He could not bring himself directly to ask Mr Hirst's permission to continue with Miss Sweeting's entertainment but, knowing that if the amusement was to be provided in working time permission must be obtained, he decided to announce his intention and hope that there would be neither refusal nor reservation.

'Not sure. Not sure at all.'

Ernest was defiant. 'I've told her that I will as long as you agree. She'll know that you've ended it. So will her father.'

'Not sure that her father wouldn't expect me to stop it. Save him the trouble. Wouldn't be surprised if he wanted it ended.'

'He came in on the first day and said how pleased he was that Lucy—'

'There you are. It's Lucy now. Last Monday, I'll warrant it was Miss Sweeting.'

'I was going to say "Sweeting". But you stopped me.' Ernest had still not acquired the confidence to accuse Hirst of interrupting. 'You stopped me. I was going to say "Lucy Sweeting". That's her name.' He sounded unconvincingly emphatic, although what he said was true.

'Be that as it may, I see nothing but trouble. Dang me, sir. Nothing but trouble.'

It was clear, even to innocent Ernest, that Arnold Hirst was finding it unusually hard to express himself.

'Young woman. And very attractive. Not a thing I enjoy saying, but flighty by all accounts.'

Ernest could think of nothing to say. And by saying nothing he made Hirst's task infinitely more difficult. Another salvo of incoherence was launched into the silence.

'Wrong ideas. Don't want any wrong ideas. Very attractive young woman. But . . . also a very rich young woman. Only daughter. Heiress. Apple of her father's eye. Spoilt, they say.'

Suddenly, Ernest understood the message which was being sent to him with such difficulty. It was anger which caused the ambiguity in his reply. He was, however, careful not to give offence by his choice of names. 'Miss Sweeting would never think of such a thing.' Realising his error, he added with a speed that emphasised the afterthought, 'And neither would I.'

Arnold Hirst, believing that his duty had been done, pronounced himself satisfied. 'Sure you wouldn't. But a word from a friend. Don't forget the differences between you, the differences in class – even if she does.'

Back in his bedroom, Ernest tried, in his usual methodical way, to unravel his thoughts. He deeply resented the reference to his inferior social standing, even though he accepted that an unbridgeable gulf separated the Skinners and the Sweetings. When he thought about the divisions in society, he regarded them as right and necessary. He just preferred not to be reminded that he was near to the bottom of the heap.

Considerations of social class were not, however, at the forefront of Ernest's mind as he slowly removed his office suit and pulled on the workman's corduroy trousers in which he spent his solitary evenings. But that night the saws and the plywood remained hidden whilst he sat on the bed and attempted to put his thoughts back into their usual prosaic good order. The unaccustomed turmoil was not simply the result of righteous indignation. He had lived for more than twenty years without making more than a casual acquaintance with sexual desire so he was genuinely astonished by the allegation that either romantic or carnal inclinations might lie hidden under the irritation that Lucy Sweeting caused him. No such thought had ever entered his mind – until Arnold Hirst put it there. For a few lewd moments Ernest imagined himself, épée in hand, forcing himself upon her. Then he pulled himself together and attempted to turn his mind to nobler things. He found it difficult to concentrate on *Marquetry* by A. F. Williams-Burrows BA. He endured the unusual experience of a disturbed night and felt debilitated throughout the following day. At four o'clock he left for Worksop with a reluctance that he tried to attribute to lack of sleep.

'Are you sick or something?' It was not Miss Sweeting's habit to spare feelings.

'I worked until three o'clock this morning.'

'Good Lord! Whatever were you doing?'

'A special costing job for Mr Hirst. Half an acre of standing timber. Elm mostly. I had to calculate what it was worth.'

'Do you want the night off?'

For one reckless moment, Ernest considered turning on her and announcing that he was not a paid servant to be granted or denied little favours according to his employer's whim. But he contented himself with a brusque dismissal of the offer.

'I feel perfectly all right. I often do it, stay up all night on some job or other. Unless you don't feel up to it . . .'

'Well, thank you very much. I was going to suggest a little walk up to the Lion Gates and something to eat when we got back. You look as if you haven't had a good meal for a week. But if you want to fence . . .'

'I do.'

Ernest defended himself determinedly and the night ended with his ears almost intact.

'Did you ask Mr Hirst about next week?'

'I didn't need to ask him. I told you it's up to me.'

'Well, are you going to come?'

Ernest paused before he replied and, when Lucy seemed about to repeat her question, he feared that she would either say that she was not begging for favours or offer to arrange payment for his time and trouble.

'I suppose so.' He sounded more grudging than he intended but Lucy did not take offence.

'Good! I'll be able to give you a hiding every night.'

Ernest thought that she would be as good as her word. But it was not only concern for his ears which filled him with foreboding. The more he thought of Lucy Sweeting, the more she frightened him. Everything she did made him feel nervous and uncertain. He blamed her for the humiliating talk with Arnold Hirst and for the shameful thoughts which it had stimulated. Throughout the weekend, no matter how hard he tried to concentrate on the finer things of life, his thoughts kept returning to his evenings at Sparken Hill. He repeated the words of their inconsequential conversations in his mind and he saw, in his memory, her face smiling with scorn as she rejoiced in her superiority. By Monday morning his insecurity had grown so great that he decided he would stay in the woodyard and enjoy the thought of her amazed frustration as she waited in disbelief that he would let her down. Then he feared that she would attribute his absence to apprehension, anxiety or lack of breeding. Because he knew each accusation would be true, he would face the ordeal bravely.

When he arrived at Sparken Hill, Lucy Sweeting was standing in

217

the drive beside her father's motor car and he briefly believed that Providence had delivered him from his tormentor. But Providence, as he was beginning to learn, had a bad habit of letting him down. The car pulled away from the porch leaving Lucy waving a feeble goodbye.

'God!' she said. 'We've just got back from lunch with some hideous people. He made me go. You'll have to wait while I get changed. It'll take ages without a maid.'

Ernest's gratitude that she had not yet called him 'Home Sweet' was not great enough to prevent him from grasping at straws which floated before him. 'It's probably not worth it, then. I've got to be off before five.'

'You're so sweet, Ernest.' It was also the first time that she had ever called him by his name. 'So charming. So gallant. So suave. I'll warrant that you sweep the village maidens off their feet.'

'I'm just trying to be sensible.'

'I know. You're a sensible young man. Far too sensible to want to spend time with me.' She turned her back on him. 'If you undo those buttons it will save me ten minutes twisting and turning in front of the mirror.'

It was, Ernest knew, a challenge designed to expose his working-class prudery. He knew it was important to complete the task without his hand shaking and he had managed twelve buttons out of the twenty before his fingers touched her skin. She turned, as he knew she would, and reproved him in exactly the way that he expected.

'There's more to you than I realised. I'd better do the rest myself.'

Holding the dress around her neck with an altogether unnecessary determination, she swept up the stairs. Ernest, although fascinated by the pink back above the lace of her petticoat, congratulated himself on neither apologising nor explaining that he had touched her back by mistake. It was almost half an hour before she returned.

'I decided that it was safest to do the buttons up myself.'

'Put your mask on.' Ernest had endured enough.

There were complicated curls and ringlets to be protected so, as always, fitting her head inside the helmet took several minutes of careful manipulation. The visor was barely in place before Ernest struck her across the left cheek.

'What in God's name are you doing?' She reached instinctively for the bruised spot even though she could not touch it under the wicker-work mask.

'On guard.'

Although the second assault was preceded by the usual formalities, Ernest slashed again before the last syllable was pronounced, narrowly missing the fingers which Lucy still held to her face.

Lucy Sweeting tore off her helmet without any concern for the curls and coils of hair which spilled out on to her shoulders. Ernest was afraid that she was about to run screaming from the room like a child with a grazed knee. First, she hurled the foil. It missed him by a yard. The gauntlets, which followed, hit their target. Then she threw herself at him.

The force of her body knocked him to the ground, where he lay for a moment stunned and winded. He fully regained his senses only when she struck him across the face. Then, still inside her quilted fencing guard, she used her weight to hold him down as she punched and pummelled at every part of his body that she could reach. Fear more than strength eventually enabled him to throw her off. Parted, they both crouched on the floor, eyeing each other like angry dogs in opposite corners of the same kennel.

'You stupid bitch.' Ernest could taste blood.

'Serve you right. I won't be hurt. I can't stand pain and nobody hurts me, *ever*.'

'You're lucky that I didn't hit you back.'

'You just try.'

'Don't worry. I'm too much of a gentleman.'

Lucy laughed. 'You can't be pompous with your nose bleeding.'

'Oh, God! And you've cut the inside of my mouth.'

Lucy bent over him and Ernest thought she was going to inspect his wounds. It was because he was surprised and unprepared – no less than because he had never kissed a woman before – that their teeth ground together in a way which made Lucy draw back for a moment. Then her tongue was back inside his mouth and Ernest hoped that she would not be disgusted by the taste of blood.

'Help me out of this ridiculous armour.' There were no jokes about Ernest's roving hands or inexperienced fingers, just a single-minded will to wriggle free of the fencing guard. She pulled her tweed jacket off with the padding and the next time she kissed Ernest, instinct made him push his hands inside the bodice of her petticoat. The whalebone which held her figure in its artificial shape bent and cut into her breasts. Instead of complaining about the pain, she wriggled free.

From then on it was as if there were two Ernest Skinners in the room. One made love to Lucy Sweeting on the floor of her father's drawing room. The other watched, amazed that such a thing could happen, astonished that it should be so pleasant and, above all, astounded by how simple it all was. After delight had turned to guilt and shame, Lucy pushed him off her and sat up.

'Now that wasn't so bad, was it?'

219

CHAPTER SEVENTEEN

Reluctant Candidates

'I plead no excuse for coming forward. Perhaps you would have found a better candidate than me if you had been successful in inducing Colonel Rolleston to come forward. But that gallant officer was too unwell to enter upon such a contest. I shall make a good fight of it. You all know what my politics are. All my family were Tories and I assure you that if successful I shall be a firm supporter of Lord Salisbury's Government. It would be a sad thing for this country if the settlement of the South Africa question passed into other hands than those of Lord Salisbury. No greater calamity could happen.'

John Robinson sat down with obvious relief and to polite rather than enthusiastic applause. He was not a natural orator. Indeed he was no orator at all. Such political talents as he possessed were best suited to the office of county alderman, which could be occupied without the inconvenience of contesting elections. From the moment that he agreed to stand for Parliament he had regretted his decision. But it had seemed to be his duty. As he left the platform he furtively took out his pocket watch.

'Just a few people to meet. Only half a dozen or so.' The chairman had noticed the candidate's concern about the time.

'I need to be in Worksop by ten.'

'You'll do that easily,' said the vicar of Arnold, who was hovering in the background, anxious to witness a child of his parish return in triumph but determined not to be closely associated with the doomed Conservative cause.

The vicar's estimate was wrong. It was nearer eleven when the candidate got home. The butler was waiting in the hall. 'Your visitor's here, Mr Robinson. I put him in the drawing room. I hope that was right. He seemed to expect it.'

'I've no doubt he did.'

John Robinson was an old-fashioned man and he furnished his drawing room in an old-fashioned style. Every window had several sets of curtains, and brocade draperies decorated each alcove. All

220

the flat surfaces were crowded with vases, classical statues, silver candlesticks, brass carriage clocks, urns, busts, porcelain dishes, china figures and marble obelisks. At one end of the room a long low table was covered in row after row of framed photographs dating back to when photography was a new science and young Jack Robinson had prided himself on being up to date. Many of the photographs were of Robinson himself, dressed for the many parts that he played in local life – town councillor, sheriff, huntsman, steeplechaser, brewer, race-horse owner and squire. There were portraits of his father outside the Manor House at Arnold, of his brother (with whom he had founded the laundries and breweries which made his fortune) and of Sandford, his only son. The pictures, in their ornate frames, proclaimed John Robinson's success and echoed the message of the whole room. It was a shrine dedicated to progress, prosperity and wealth.

The guest, who sat upright and unblinking on one of the sofas that ran out from the fireplace, was an incongruous figure to find in such a setting. He was dressed in a respectable blue suit which might have marked him out as anything from solicitor's clerk to prosperous publican but the hand which rested on the arm of the sofa was hard-ened with calluses.

'Hello, Brack. I'm sorry I've kept you waiting.'

'It's been a long time, Mr Robinson.' Brackenbury rose very slowly and then offered his hand with an altogether inappropriate familiarity.

'I'm sorry. Adoption meeting in Rushcliffe.' Robinson, who prided himself on his courtesy, gave Brack's hand a perfunctory shake and marvelled at his willingness to apologise for a second time.

'I didn't mean that, Mr Robinson. That's all right. I meant it's been a long time since we met. Three years? Anyway, a lot's happened.'

'A bit less, I think. Was Sandford still alive?' John Robinson measured time from the death of his son.

'I'm sorry. I didn't mean that either. I meant you coming here. And I'm told you're a justice of the peace now and an alderman.'

'The Duke of St Albans' old seat. I was appointed when he died.'

'But the horses haven't done so well.'

'Sit down,' said John Robinson. 'Sit down and have a drink.' He moved across towards the whisky on the sideboard.

'Not for me, thanks.'

'Still not?' There was a chink of decanter on glass and the gush of a soda syphon.

'It's my upbringing.' Brack did not smile. 'Methodists abjure strong drink.'

John Robinson sat down facing his guest and, putting his glass on the table which separated the two sofas, leaned forward with unashamed excitement. 'Can you still shoe horses?'

'You know I can. You've been out to Harness Grove when I've smithed for that tinpot little hunt that Hodding's set up.'

'But can you shoe racehorses?'

'I can, given a chance and given a week to get my hand back in.'

'I'm starting a stud here.'

'And you want me to come and work for you?'

'Steady on. One fence at a time. It's not all decided yet. I've bought two good brood mares and I'll buy a couple more, if all goes well.'

'Meaning?'

'I think . . . indeed, I know . . . the Duke of Portland is going to lease me Raeburn and Donovan.'

Brack whistled. 'Keeping or selling?'

'I'll keep anything that looks sharp. Do you want to work for me?'

'I can't see how I can. At least, not at race meetings.'

'That can be arranged. As long as you've not been in any trouble since. I can arrange it.'

'You got me warned off. You should know how to get me back.'

'It was the best thing, Brack. Better a quiet word than an official enquiry. Once it got official we couldn't have kept the police out. Better a quiet word.'

'Better than two broken legs at any rate. And that was what the bookmakers were offering.'

'I thought I acted most generously.'

'You did, Mr Robinson, you did. Seeing that it was your horse that I nobbled.'

'And might have crippled.'

'Never that, as you well know. I knew too much about my trade for that. That's why you want me back now.'

'It'll be three months before we get things started here.'

'Don't make it any longer. I'm near enough to Carey Street as it is. There's no money in ornamental work. It's all paid for by public benefactors such as yourself. They grind you down to the last farthing.'

'Your troubles haven't made you any more respectful to your betters. I would have thought the police would have at least taught you to mind your manners.'

'I learned a lot in the police force but not that.'

'And you didn't get into any trouble?'

'No, Mr Robinson.'

'Nor married?'

'No, Mr Robinson.'

'Good. Good on both counts. Travelling round race meetings and bloodstock sales is no life for a married man. Three months, then.'

Ernest had regarded the fencing lessons as inherently ridiculous from the first time he had taken guard in front of the fireplace in Lucy Sweeting's drawing room. Initially he had continued to make what he knew to be an exhibition of himself because he was fascinated with Lucy Sweeting. Fighting with her, even in the absurd mock combat, excited him in a way that he had never experienced before. He longed to see her again, but dreaded returning to the scene of his barely believable sin. Instead of keeping their next assignation, he sat at home. He felt relieved at having avoided another meeting but he agonised about missing an opportunity to share her company. He had no idea how to respond to Arnold Hirst's complaint.

'Don't understand you. Really don't.'

'I didn't feel very well on Tuesday.' As he made his excuse, Ernest knew that he spoke like a sickly child, but he was unable to behave like the club-swinging, coffin-board-estimating, fretworker that he prided himself on being. 'And on Wednesday it just slipped my mind.'

'And never even sent a message. Seemed all right to me on Tuesday.'

'I felt terrible.' He decided not to add that he still felt no better.

'Sweeting says his daughter complained all Tuesday evening and sulked all day Wednesday. Promised him you'd go today. Better apologise straight off.'

Ernest hesitated for only a second. The idea of returning to Sparken Hill terrified him but he was delighted that he was being forced into facing the terror again. He carefully considered whether or not he had a duty to offer a formal apology for what he had done – sometimes concluding that no other course was open to a gentleman and sometimes deciding that a gentleman would pretend that the incident had never happened. Blocking it out of his mind was made all the more difficult by his wish that it should happen again. Arnold Hirst's instructions tipped the balance between the desire to hide and the temptation to wallow in his own wickedness.

He expected Lucy to look visibly undone and was almost disappointed to discover that in appearance at least she was still the expensive and extravagant young woman whom he had despoiled. To his astonishment, she spoke to him in exactly the same manner as that which had so irritated him at their first meeting.

223

'Home Sweet! Where were you yesterday? Making another wooden thing? "Bless This House" this time?'

She might at least, Ernest thought, have suspected him of seducing a Harness Grove housemaid.

'I wasn't very well.' As soon as Ernest made his apology he bitterly regretted defending himself with such a pathetic alibi. But he still hoped that, by introducing so basic a topic as health into the conversation, he had opened the way for reference to even more carnal subjects.

Lucy was no more sympathetic than Arnold Hirst. 'You look all right to me.'

'I am now.'

They pulled on their armour. Ernest was so shamed by the pantomime that he could not bring himself to cry, 'On guard.'

'God Almighty! You're fierce today.' Ernest had driven Lucy across the room by the sheer energy of his assault. He had abandoned his pretence at technique and had laid into his opponent with a passion that Lucy found difficult to distinguish from fury. For the first time in months, she felt frightened.

'That's enough for a minute. Let's have a drink.' She moved to pull the bell rope.

But Ernest was back in the caricature of the position which he believed to be the formal prelude to a duel. He squinted at Lucy above his outstretched arm. 'I've come here to fence. That's why I'm not at work. Let's get on with it.'

'Dear, dear Ernest. You really are full of charm. You really are. A young lady offers you a cup of tea or a glass of lemonade and you say—'

'I thought you wanted to fence.'

'Well, at this moment I don't. I want tea or to talk. Is that idea totally repugnant to you?'

'I come here for these fencing lessons.'

'To give or to take?'

Lucy was back on her old form. It was beyond Ernest's endurance.

'I've got to get back. I told Mr Hirst I'd get back as soon as I could.' He was already half out of his quilted jacket.

'Think kindly thoughts of me,' said Lucy. She had said it a hundred times before as the suitable prelude to a hundred different sorts of farewell. But to Ernest it seemed like a special message. Doubts about its meaning were dispelled by the addition of Lucy's usual postscript: 'If you think of me at all.'

Terrified that she was bidding him goodbye for ever, he asked, 'Are we fencing tomorrow?'

'Whatever you like.'

Ernest fled.

When he returned the next day, Lucy refused outright to consider a pretence at fencing. Ernest agreed, with what in him passed for grace, to walk up to the Lion Gates and trespass in Welbeck Park. As he was cross-examined about his life, he contemplated attempting to kiss her, but that, he decided, would be even more outrageous than what had already happened. Kisses he believed to be signs of affection and, since Lucy was his social superior, the suggestion of decent feelings would be a greater presumption than expressions of animal desire.

When they got back to Rock House Lucy did not ring the bell, but turned her own key in the lock and strode into the hall. She pulled off her coat before Ernest had closed the door behind her and threw it to him. As he caught it, she bent her head towards him. He kissed her instinctively and all thoughts of the gulf between them were driven from his mind. He actually led her into the drawing room where – since he lacked both imagination and experience – they made love for the second time in exactly the same way and on exactly the same spot.

On the following day – Lucy's last in Worksop – there were no preliminaries. As soon as he had been assured that there was no one in the house, Ernest walked into the drawing room and began to undress. As they lay together in the warmth of the fire, he really believed that he and Lucy would be together for ever. He wondered if he ought to talk about their future or vow his eternal fidelity and he was just bracing himself to tell her he loved her when she jumped up from the floor.

'I'm baking,' she said, pointing to a red mark on the back of her thigh where she had caught the fire.

Ernest had never looked at her naked before. When they had made love she had either been half dressed or too close for him to see her body, and when they had finished he had always averted his eyes in the foolish belief that she did not want him to look. But when she was burned by the fire, he simply turned over on his side and gazed at her. She was not in the most romantic of positions – half bending down in an attempt to examine the pink patch of flesh below her left buttock – but he thought it was the most beautiful sight he had ever seen. He decided to propose there and then. Before he had formed the sentence, Lucy was on her feet complaining.

'God,' said Lucy. 'Just look. I'm off to put something on this and you'd better be on your way. The maid will be back in quarter of an

225

hour.' She picked up her clothes and, carrying them in a bundle, rushed from the room, leaving Ernest to remember that she could not stand pain. He dressed in five minutes and waited for another half hour in the hope that she would reappear. Then, slowly, he returned to Retford.

It was almost three months before Lucy Sweeting realised that she was pregnant and almost another full week before she told her mother. She did not break the awful news until she had decided whether or not to divulge the father's name.

Ernest Skinner was not Lucy Sweeting's first lover, and as soon as she was certain that there was to be a baby, she consoled herself with a wonderful weekend in the country which she dedicated to the notion that, since she was a fallen woman, she might as well enjoy some of the pleasures of her new status. But her brief and generally unsatisfactory liaison with the timber-company clerk was the only encounter which coincided with the beginning of her pregnancy. She was amused by the absurdity of ruining her life in such a ludicrous adventure, though she was cheered by the thought that the father of her child was, at least, not a man whom her mother would expect her to marry. It was to prevent all talk of weddings that she decided to identify the culprit as soon as his name was demanded. At first, her mother took the news calmly. It was not the first time that such a thing had happened in her circle of acquaintances. Her lip only trembled when she asked the crucial question.

'Is the man married?'

'No, Mama. He is not.'

Mrs Sweeting's relief demonstrated a high regard for convention and a low opinion of her daughter's morals. She was about to embrace her daughter when Lucy dropped the stone into the pool.

'I can't marry him.'

'Why ever not? Of course you will marry him. We'll make him marry you whoever he is. You're good enough for anyone. The man will marry you. Don't you worry about that.'

'Mama—'

'You ought to have more respect for yourself.'

'Mama, listen. The father of my baby is a clerk in a timber yard. His father's a gardener for a little country squire. I suppose that he can read and write, but I've seen no evidence of it. He makes wood things for a hobby. The first time I saw him he was carrying a box he'd made as a present for those two terrible dressmakers. He'd burned "Home Sweet Home" on it.'

226

'My God!' Mrs Sweeting's elation at the news of Ernest Skinner's bachelor status had turned to despair at the discovery that he was penniless. 'My God! How did it happen?'

Lucy wondered if the truth would be entirely incredible. She cast about for a convincing lie.

'Did he rape you?'

She decided on the truth. 'If it was rape, he was the victim.'

'How can you say such things? This is not a time for jokes. It's jokes that got you into this trouble. Your father won't think it funny when I write and tell him.'

Vincent Sweeting, far from seeing the humour of the situation, found it difficult to accept the basic fact which the letter described. He left at once for London to hear the terrible story from his daughter's own lips. To his profound distress it was identical to the one set out by his wife.

'But you can't have . . .' he spluttered. 'Not in my house. Not upstairs in that bedroom that I had redecorated when I knew you were coming to stay.'

'No, Papa. *Not* up in the bedroom, down in the drawing room. On the floor. On the floor in front of the fireplace to be exact. I remember rolling against the coal scuttle.'

'It's you I blame for this.' Vincent Sweeting was unable to suppress his disgusted rage but was incapable of venting his anger on his daughter. 'It's the way she's been brought up. What have you done to this girl? God almighty! Who could have believed that a daughter of mine could talk like that.'

'If it had only been talk, Papa, we wouldn't have a problem. You've just got to face facts. And we've got to decide how we deal with them.'

'We have no choice. You've got to marry him.'

'Didn't Mama tell you? When she wrote the letter describing my misdeeds and their consequences, didn't she tell you who the man was?'

'She did not. Some young fellow who's not done a day's work in his life, I suppose. Has he got any money?'

'Papa. It's Home Sweet Home. It's the fencing boy. It's Master Skinner. It's the woodyard clerk. All we have to decide is whether we keep it or give it away.'

For the first time in his life, Vincent Sweeting hit his daughter. She staggered back, knocked off balance as much by surprise as by the blow across her head. She was hurt but not intimidated.

'Papa. Let's get one thing clear. I'm not going to marry him.'

'Don't be so bloody silly. Of course you're going to marry him. At least you are if it's his baby. Or are you pretending it's his to protect one of your gentleman friends?'

'How could you suggest such a thing about your own daughter?' Mrs Sweeting knew the answer. She had left him because of the invincible vulgarity which prompted the question.

'How could she get in the family way on the carpet in my drawing room? You brought her up, not me.'

'For God's sake, stop arguing about who made me a bitch. Now you know it's Skinner, you realise marriage is out of the question. Don't you?'

Her mother answered. 'I don't want to take her part against yours, Vincent, but can you imagine what her life would be like? A young woman of her upbringing and intelligence living with a man like that?'

'For God's sake, woman. She was happy enough to copulate with him.'

'I'm not going to be bullied by your foul talk. For once, once in thirty years, I'm going to stand up to you. It's her life. She's not going to spend it with a man she's nothing in common with.' Mrs Sweeting warmed to her subject. 'An oaf, an ignoramus, a man with rough hands and vulgar habits.'

The meaning was not lost on her husband. 'Who's going to keep her then? Not *this* oaf. Not *this* ignoramus. Not *this* man with rough hands and vulgar habits who's kept her since she was born. Not unless she marries that man, he won't.'

'I don't believe you.' Lucy was still smiling her superior smile.

'Then I'll have to convince you. I'll begin by asking this young Mr Skinner what he thinks should happen. After all, the baby's his as well.'

'Do you really want a scandal? Do you really want jokes to be made about your daughter in public houses?' Lucy, who knew she would die if her father ever told Ernest Skinner that it was his duty to marry her, elaborated the picture of ridicule and humiliation. 'And about you. You'll look ridiculous to everyone who hears about it.' Ridiculous was Lucy's adjective of the moment. 'You'll be the ridiculous father who invited in the young man who seduced his daughter on the drawing-room floor. The best thing for us all is for me to go away, quickly, and have the baby in the country somewhere. Then farm it out to a decent family so that I can reappear in London.'

Vincent Sweeting was sweating. Lucy mistook anger for anxiety. 'Please, Daddy. Please. I know it will cost a lot of money. But you have so much and I'm in such trouble.'

After an obvious effort of will her father began to stutter out his

228

answer. 'If . . . you want my money . . . you'll have to take it on . . . on . . . my terms. Just for once. It may be your son . . .' Lucy prevented herself from saying that unfortunately there was no doubt about it. '. . . but he's also my grandson.' It was almost as difficult not to say that it might be a granddaughter. 'As far as I can make out . . . the only one I'm likely to have. He's going to be . . . be . . . be . . . brought up properly. Marry that young man, or marry somebody else. But marry somebody quickly. And look after that boy. Then I'll . . . look . . . after . . . you.'

'You don't think that I know anybody else who would marry me – anyone who'd like to marry me and is still single?'

Vincent Sweeting struck his daughter again. Her bravery did not survive the second blow. She first screamed and then stood openmouthed and staring blankly into the distance. He hit her a third time and would have gone on hitting her had his wife not grabbed his arm.

'Don't you dare. She's having a baby.'

Lucy came back to life, giggling at the absurdity of her mother's defence. Her father dropped his hand and turned from scarlet to white.

'The jokes are over. Do as you're told or out on to the streets, where some fathers would say that you belonged. I mean it. The sooner you understand, the better for all of us.'

Vincent Sweeting, overcome by a combination of guilt, anger and bewilderment, promised before he left for Worksop that he would not tell Ernest Skinner that Lucy was expecting a baby. As soon as he was settled in the corner of his railway carriage, he began to compose the letter with which his promise would be broken. He made several attempts to set out the basic facts in simple language but he found it impossible. Three times he wrote out the stark first sentence. And three times he tore the paper into pieces and threw them out of the window. As they blew across the line he felt an irrational fear that someone might piece the fragments together and read his terrible story. Telling it felt like a betrayal.

He decided that the proper course would be to send for Ernest and inform him with proper solemnity that he was about to become a father. Back on Sparken Hill, he was so anxious to catch the last post that he wrote his message on a black-edged condolence card. When Ernest received it next morning, although he did not take it at its face value, he feared that it was an augury of impending doom. He tried his best to concentrate on his day's work, but had to recalculate half the estimates. He arrived at Sweeting's servants' entrance twenty minutes before his appointed time but was shown straight into the drawing room. Vincent Sweeting had decided to get the ordeal over as quickly as possible.

'Is something wrong?' Ernest spoke first not because he was brave but because he was afraid.

'There is. There is indeed.'

The pause which followed was agony to both men.

'Is it Lucy?' Ernest prayed that she was not dead and that, if his prayer was answered and so was no more than mortally sick, she had asked for him to come to her bedside. 'Is there something the matter with her?'

'There is.' Sweeting swallowed, licked his lips, swallowed again and, with an obvious effort of will, spoke the terrible words. 'She's having a baby. Your baby.'

Ernest's first reaction was astonishment at his own composure. Had he anticipated the answer he would have expected to be immobilised by shame. But he scarcely felt embarrassed. Gradually he realised why he was so calm. He was pleased. The anxiety which he also felt was submerged beneath excitement. He and Lucy would be reunited and would spend the rest of their lives together making love on carpets in front of drawing-room fires.

'What have you to say for yourself?'

Ernest was about to say that he would do the right thing when Sweeting's temper snapped. 'Right here. In my house. Behind my back. I could hardly believe it when she told me. You dirty little bugger. I can't get over her doing it with you. I ought to have you locked up for assault. I can't get over—' A shaft of hope suddenly pierced Sweeting's suicidal anger. 'It was you, wasn't it? She says it was, but . . .' He almost blurted out, 'But looking at your rough hands and ready-made clothes, I can't believe it and I want you to say that you never touched her so that I can find the proper gentleman who is the father of her child and must become her husband.'

'Yes, it's me. I'm the father.'

Vincent Sweeting had never really doubted it. He had noticed his daughter's weakness for well-set-up young working men. No doubt the rough hands and the shabby suit had been part of the attraction. 'So what are you going to do about it?'

It was the wrong question. If the father of Lucy's baby had been one of the rich idlers with whom she spent her time in London, it would have been sensible to demand that he behaved like a gentleman. But that was not to be expected of Ernest Skinner. He did not have the breeding. Perhaps that did not matter. But he did not have the money either. And that did. Vincent Sweeting demanded an acceptance of responsibility because he could not think of anything else to say.

'I shall marry her,' said Ernest in the manner of a man who felt that a duke could not have made a more handsome offer. The condescension in his tone infuriated Vincent Sweeting into telling the truth.

'But will she marry you? That's the question.' Ernest winced like a man who had been punched in the stomach and Vincent Sweeting decided to hit him again whilst he was down. 'She says she'd rather go on the streets. She said she'd rather—'

'Why did you send for me, then?' It was desperation, not logic, that prompted the question. 'Why did you send for me, if she won't marry me? You needn't have told me about the baby at all.'

'I'll tell you why. She says she won't marry you, but I say she will. I didn't send for you to ask favours. You're here so that I can tell you what you're going to do. What do you earn?'

'Two pounds ten a week, Mr Sweeting.'

'I don't see our Lucy living on that. You'd better come and work for me. You'll both be living off me, so I might as well get some value for my money.'

'We can manage. I can get another little job at night.'

'Don't be so bloody silly. You don't know what she spends. You'll come and work for me. And you'll come and live here, at least at first.'

'When do you think it will be, Mr Sweeting?'

'Just as soon as I can get some sense into her head.'

'So I ought to tell my mam and dad straight away?'

'Tell them whenever you like. It's going to happen. Tell them now if you fancy it.'

'What shall I say?'

'That, young man, is your concern. But I advise you not to tell them the truth. They won't believe it. No decent person would. Tell them something near the truth.'

Encouraged by the warmth of his welcome into the Sweeting family, Ernest constructed a story which was far enough from the truth to be credible but near enough to what had really happened to be disreputable. His father was surprisingly calm.

'And you got friendly because of this fencing, did you?'

Ernest nodded.

'And one thing led to another?'

Ernest nodded again.

'Did you do anything else together?'

'No, Dad. Nothing except. . .'

231

'Well,' said William, 'it's too late for tears. But I hate to think what your mother's going to say. Shall we tell her together?'

Ernest accepted gratefully.

'She'll ask you the details, because she won't know what else to say. When's the wedding going to be? Soon, I expect. Will it be in London?'

'I suppose it will. I didn't ask.'

'So we won't go down.' William had never been to London and longed to go.

Elizabeth expressed her shame in a couple of simple sentences and then confessed to a deep sense of guilt. The son of a decent mother would not have behaved in that way.

'Will we go to the wedding?' William asked.

'Of course we won't.' The quality of Elizabeth's contempt had not faded with the years. 'Gardener and his blind wife. I can't see us fitting into that sort of society. Nor will you, Ernest. Mark my words, you're in for a hard time, my lad. But you've made your bed and you've no choice but to lie on it. There's nothing more to be said.'

'We could say "Congratulations",' William suggested. 'After all, our only son is getting married.'

'I'm worried about telling Agnes and Anne.'

'Agnes will be excited,' her father promised.

'Agnes doesn't understand about these things. What she knows about life she's learned from books. Anne understands and she will be disgusted.'

CHAPTER EIGHTEEN

Growing Up

It took three visits to Worksop and a couple of temporarily cancelled bank accounts to convince Lucy Sweeting that her future lay with Ernest Skinner. The meetings between the happy couple were as bewildering to the young man who was to be her fate as they were to her parents, who never left the couple alone, despite, as Vincent Sweeting tastefully put it, 'the damage being done'. Sometimes it seemed that Lucy loathed Ernest with a passion which required her to belittle him at every opportunity. Then, at the next moment, it was clear that she was attracted to him like, in her father's delicate phrase, 'a bitch on heat'. Ernest's emotions, though no less painful to behold, were at least more consistent. He was entranced.

He was entranced by everything about her – her clothes, her manner of speech, her interests, the little scraps of knowledge that she tucked away for sudden use when it was necessary to surprise or impress, her table manners, her expensively shod feet and most of all her body. He was even infatuated by her brazen manner, her sophisticated dress and he had fallen truly in love with what he believed to be her pilgrim soul. He believed, not entirely without justification, that she was daring and brave. Others might have described her as reckless and wilful. But for Ernest she possessed another virtue which transformed all her other qualities into characteristics of sanctity. She was his.

He believed that she had given herself to him on that first evening like a bride, and because he thought he possessed her his life was changed. The reasoning, given the social assumptions on which they were based, was wholly logical. Lucy Sweeting was magnificent. She had chosen to make love with him. Therefore, there must be something about Ernest Skinner, gardener's son and timber-yard clerk, which was attractive and admirable.

Armed with a new confidence he came to a second and less rational conclusion. In spite of the taunts and the abuse, she wanted to marry him. The bullying and the baiting were no more than manifestations of a generally headstrong character which caused her to behave with almost equal contempt towards her parents. The conclusion to which he came was right. But it was more the cancelled bank accounts than the visits to Worksop and the physical attractions of her bridegroom that made Lucy eventually agree to the wedding. When she had solemnly promised her father that she would become Mrs Ernest Skinner, the lucky man was sent for by his prospective father-in-law.

'I have decided,' Sweeting told him, 'that your request for my daughter's hand in marriage shall be granted.' It was the sort of speech which he had rehearsed in his head a thousand times in preparation for welcoming a baronet into the family. Ernest replied no less inappropriately.

'I know that I can make her happy. I *know* that I can.'

His fiancée, wholly without impatience or anxiety, was waiting alone in the morning room.

'You better go in and see her.'

Ernest politely offered precedence to his father-in-law.

'Nay. Go in by yourself. You don't need me for this. Mrs Sweeting'll be down in a minute. Go in and tell her, whilst you've got the chance.'

The door having banged shut behind him, Ernest approached his bride. She was reading a magazine with genuine detachment. Despite the absence of the slightest encouragement, he fell down on one knee. He was about to make a proposal as he knew proposals should be made. But the bride spoke first. 'Do get up, you silly boy. Come here and give me a big kiss. I've not had a proper cuddle for months. Quickly, my mama will be here in a minute.'

Lucy had barely disentangled herself when Mrs Sweeting confirmed her daughter's judgement. Ignoring her daughter, she spoke to Ernest with a sensitivity of which few of her friends would have thought her capable. 'I know you would like to buy Lucy an engagement ring. But I hoped that she'd wear my mother's.' She looked accusingly at her husband. 'I have never had one. But if you'd take this one instead of buying one yourself, I'd be very grateful.' She took a large diamond ring from her finger. 'It's not what you'd choose. But you'd do us a great favour if you'd take it and give it to my daughter.'

Ernest accepted the offer with gratitude and prepared himself to make insincere pleasantries, but his contrived contributions to the conversation were not needed. What followed was a business meeting at which he was an observer, not a participant.

'Your father's wired to London. The first banns will be read on

Sunday. That's better than a special licence. A special licence would only attract attention.'

Lucy patted her still inconspicuous belly. 'I'll attract attention anyway.'

'No, you won't. As long as we get on with it now. Anyway, in London—'

'Why London?' Ernest was emboldened by his newfound self-confidence and his longstanding tribal affection for his family. 'If it's in London none of my people will be there.'

'It has to be in London, Mr Skinner.' Lucy's mother acknowledged his participation in the ceremony for the first time and simultaneously demonstrated her conviction that he was not and never could be a full member of the family. 'It has to be in London because London is the home of the bride's mother.'

'And', Lucy added, 'because in London nobody will make a fuss about the baby. Up here in Worksop everybody would know and everybody would see. But in London we'll be able to rush in and out of church without anybody noticing that I'm four months gone.'

'But what about my mother and father?'

'There are trains, Mr Skinner, and there are hotels. They will be very welcome at the church. That goes without saying. And they will be very welcome at my house afterwards. Whether they come or not is for them to decide. In any case, it's going to be a very quiet affair.'

'Very quiet. Very quick and very private,' Lucy added. 'Rejoicing will be kept to an absolute minimum. Joy will be strictly confined.'

Her father tried to look disapproving, but failed. It was left to Mrs Sweeting to insist on the questions of propriety being treated with suitable sobriety.

'Don't be silly, Lucy. You're getting married. It's no laughing matter. Your father and I simply want to arrange things as discreetly as possible, for your sake. Afterwards – when the baby's arrived and Mr Skinner has got used to our ways – we'll have a real party. A christening party. That would be the thing.'

'In the meantime a quiet wedding and a full frock with pleats and panels and no waist.' Lucy seemed almost to be enjoying her notorious condition. 'Guests not welcome. I'll be lucky if the bridegroom turns up.'

'I'll turn up,' said Ernest. 'Of course I will. How could you suggest such a thing? In front of your mother too.'

'I was wrong.' Lucy pinched his cheek in a show of mock affection. 'I'll be unlucky if the bridegroom turns up.'

*

At first Ernest discouraged the idea of his parents attempting what he told them would be an arduous journey. Then a week before the great day, he changed his mind. 'I'll feel lost if you don't come. There'll be nobody there I know.'

'Except your wife,' said Elizabeth, who was not in a mood to spare her son's feelings.

'You know what I mean. I'll be like a stranger in that big house.'

Ernest had only to wait a second for his father to respond with the sentimentality for which he had hoped.

'Of course we understand. Couldn't leave you on your own. I've always thought we should go. Mr Hodding's offered me the time off. He says it's an easy enough journey. It takes three hours and only one change. We'll talk about it, won't we, Mother?'

'We might, if we'd been invited.'

'I've told you, Mam.' Ernest was exasperated. 'Nobody has. It's to be very quiet.' He spoke in Mrs Sweeting's unmistakable middle-class patois. 'A large wedding wouldn't be appropriate. I doubt if there'll be a dozen there, even if you come.'

'So it won't be like a proper wedding.' Elizabeth was suffering and she was determined that she should not suffer alone.

Agnes spoke up for her brother. 'It won't be like a real wedding, if we're not there, Mam. Anne says she'll make you a coat. My Christmas coat will do for me. I can't bear to think of Ernest down there without anybody to look after him.'

'You're not thinking about Ernest. You're thinking about a new coat. You're—'

'That's not fair, Mam. I said a new coat for you. I said I'd manage—'

'If you're not thinking about the coat, you're thinking about the excitement. All you're after, my girl, is a trip to London. You're thinking about yourself, as usual.'

Normally, William would have allowed the bickering to ebb and flow around him but on that evening he decided to defy his instincts. 'Well, I'm thinking of Ernest. I've lived for the best part of sixty years without seeing London and I dare say that I could live without seeing it for a good deal longer. But if Ernest really wants us there . . . Your mother and I will talk about it.'

'It's no good you saying that. It's no good getting their hopes up. How could I go to London?'

'We'll look after you, Mam. Dad and me. And,' Ernest added, 'Mr Sweeting will put you up somewhere. He said so.'

'If we go, we'll pay our own way. We've got a few pounds left, haven't we, William?'

'We've got enough for this. It would be a poor look-out if we couldn't find enough to get to our only son's wedding.'

Elizabeth was not ready to capitulate. 'I'll need to sleep on it. I don't know if I can face it.'

Ernest, to whom a nod was never quite as good as a wink, was about to plead with his mother not to leave him in suspense all night. But William put his forefinger to his lips in a gesture of silence which even his son recognised. It was time to go home. As he pulled on his coat Ernest remembered that the patience his father urged upon him was not practical.

'How will I know? I need to know tomorrow if you're coming. I need to know by the time the post goes. I've got to write and tell Mr Sweeting.'

'I can't help that. I'm not making up my mind until I've slept on it.'

'I'll go and tell him, Mam,' Agnes offered. 'I'll go to Retford tomorrow when you've made up your mind.'

'If we go. If, mind. You can take me into Worksop and leave me at Anne's while you get the train. How long will it take?'

'An hour altogether. Train, walk to Hirst's yard, everything.' Ernest had temporarily abandoned his standing objection to his family visiting him at work.

'Anne can measure me for the coat . . . that's if I go. And I haven't decided yet.'

Agnes, who did not believe that she could survive a whole night of hope and anxiety, went late to bed and did not fall into a fitful sleep until after midnight. After six hours of tossing and turning, she heard the rattle of the kitchen door-latch. It was, she assumed, her father making his usual desperate attempt to be at Harness Grove by seven o'clock. Usually, she lay quiet and still until she was sure that the frenzy was over but believing that her hopes of a visit to London would be turned into certainty, she decided to brave the demands to find studs, pass collars and replace broken shoelaces. She leaped down the last three stairs and charged into the living room.

The kitchen was quiet but not calm. Her father, still wearing his nightshirt, sat hunched over the table. Behind him, Elizabeth was pushing at his shoulders as if she were kneading dough.

'What's the matter?'

'Your dad's rheumatism's come back. He can't move his head.'

'Won't we be able to go to the wedding?'

William tried to look at her, but he was unable to turn his head in her direction. He groaned and returned to his close scrutiny of the tabletop. Her mother, being mobile, was able to turn in her direction with uninhibited anger.

237

'You shouldn't even be thinking about such things when your father is sitting here in agony. No, we won't be going to the wedding so let's not hear any more about it.'

'It might be better by Friday.' Agnes knew that she was clutching at straws.

'If he can't go to work on Monday, he can't go gadding off to London on Friday. I've told you. Forget all about it.' She turned back to her husband. 'You ought to see a doctor. You're sweating with pain. It's not just ordinary rheumatism.'

'I couldn't get there. And I can't send for him because I've got a stiff neck.'

'Agnes, stop looking as though you've lost a shilling and found a penny! Run up to the house and tell them . . . anybody in the kitchen . . . tell them that your dad won't be at work today.'

Elizabeth stood up and felt her way from the back of her husband's neck to his waist. She tugged and he groaned.

'I'm going to get you back upstairs. You'll feel better lying down.'

Agnes, delayed by disappointment, had only half pulled on her coat when her mother turned on her. 'Before you go running off up there, give me a hand with your dad.'

As wife and daughter pulled and pushed him upstairs, Agnes whispered to her father, 'Would we have gone? If it hadn't been for this, would we have gone?'

Her mother heard and answered, 'How do I know? I've not had time to think about it. I've been up half the night, pushing your father's back.'

William collapsed on to the bed with a groan and, although unable to turn his head in his wife's direction, spoke to her with an obvious and new anguish. 'She's like a child. She's a woman and she still talks like a girl of ten. It's the way we pamper her. We've made her peculiar. I'm in agony and she's still talking about going to London.'

The outburst convinced Agnes that her father was seriously ill. She could not recall him ever having spoken about her in such a way before. His unkindness could be explained only by the pain he was suffering. She had never experienced anything like it and, because her father's conduct was strange as well as cruel, she felt profoundly insecure. Her mother's accustomed bitterness was a welcome reassurance that life in Grove Cottage was very much as it had always been.

'She'll have to be sensible if you're in bed for long. I can't do everything. I know everybody thinks I can, but I can't. I can't carry meals up those stairs. She'll just have to help for a change.'

'Mam! It's not me who wants to sit out in that garden in all weathers with a blanket wrapped around my knees.'

'I don't want you to sit out there. I'm afraid that you'll get your death of cold. I just bring the blanket.'

William tried to sit up, but fell back with a grunt. Reminded of her husband's existence, Elizabeth abandoned bickering and resumed her traditional role of saint and martyr. 'You ought to be ashamed of yourself, arguing about such silly things when your father is lying in bed with heaven knows what. Anyway, you'll have to help whilst he's lying up here whether you like it or not. I can't do it all.'

Agnes – as if to demonstrate her maturity – decided that there was no point in trying to right the wrong she had been done and began to help her father wriggle into a comfortable position.

'What are you doing now?' her mother asked. 'I told you to go up to the house twenty minutes ago. It must be nearly seven. They'll think your dad's still coming.'

As she ran over the fields that separated Grove Cottage from Harness Grove, Agnes decided to turn that day from a girl into a woman. She made that change by acting as she believed her mother would have behaved in her place. She boiled kettles, filled hot-water bottles and carried them upstairs without considering either the risk of scalding or the patient's wish to be joined in bed by boiling hot earthenware. She insisted on making the invalid's bed at inconvenient times and cooking him food that he had no wish to eat. But, as well as imitating her mother, she tried to keep her father amused by reading to him.

William's concentration was not sufficient to sustain his interest in long passages from the classics and Agnes judged that since the stories from the weekly magazines were too trivial for her liking, they would be far too frivolous to hold her father's attention. So she read him poetry. She had been introduced to verse through the works of Ella Wheeler Wilcox – a poet from whom her mother quoted copiously on friendship and forgiveness. But, undaunted by that unhappy initiation, she had explored Keats and Shelley in two battered volumes which she borrowed from the vicarage, and had loved them from the start. She moved on, with some difficulty, to Browning and Byron and assumed that she knew all there was to know about poetry. When her father mentioned Alfred, Lord Tennyson, she was as mortified by her own ignorance as she was astonished by his erudition. She promised that if he was still in bed at the weekend she would search the Mechanics' Institute for a copy of *Idylls of the King* and read him the stories of Arthur and Guinevere.

'How do you know about them?' It was not a flattering question.

'A long time ago I knew a man who wanted to be an architect, wanted to build great castles and palaces.' Agnes sat, entranced.

239

'King Arthur had something to do with the sort of buildings he liked. I can't remember exactly what. It was over twenty years ago. We were full of ideas that now seem very silly. Dreams.'

Agnes never got the chance to read to her father from *Idylls of the King*. On the day before Ernest's wedding, William Skinner made a miraculous recovery. He awoke, still aching but in obviously better spirits, and, as the morning went on, he shouted downstairs at five-minute intervals with news of relaxing neck muscles and loosening joints. By midday he was demanding to be helped out of bed and in the early evening he visited his garden.

As Agnes watched him bend down with remarkable agility and pull weeds from between the strawberry plants, she abandoned her speculation about how handsome Ernest would look in the new suit Vincent Sweeting had bought him and turned to her mother.

'Isn't it wonderful that Dad got better so quickly?'

For the first time Elizabeth Skinner spoke to her daughter like one woman sharing intimacies with another. 'Do you think that your dad's back has really stopped hurting?'

'He says it has. He says it's perfect.'

'It's a bit quick. A bit sudden for a real recovery.'

'He wouldn't pretend it had got better. Not if it hadn't.'

'What if he pretended in the first place? What if it never hurt at all?'

'He wouldn't do that. Why should he?'

'Not to go to London. Because he didn't want to go.'

There was a time when Agnes would have thought her father incapable of such a deception and believed her mother above such base suspicions. But that evening she only wondered if it was possible to sustain so convincing an act for four days and nights. Why, she wondered, was the idea of the trip so intolerable that the boredom of bed was to be preferred to a visit to London? She decided that duty, if not conviction, required her to rally to her father's defence.

'Dad wouldn't do that. Not m'dad.'

'Don't you be too sure. He's a good liar when he wants to be. If you're so determined to be grown up, you'd better start learning a thing or two about your father.'

Ernest Skinner spent the night before his wedding in the Grosvenor Hotel. Vincent Sweeting, who occupied a suite close by his single room, led him down to the huge pillared dining room and, rightly assuming that he would be awestruck by his surroundings, ordered a simple meal for them both. He felt suddenly paternal towards the awkward young man, who looked and felt out of place and failed hopelessly in his attempts to hide his anxiety and appear at home. He did not, however, feel sorry for Ernest for he was about to acquire an incomparable pearl. However, Vincent Sweeting felt immense anxiety about the priceless jewel which was about to pass from his own safe keeping into the possession of the pathetic and wholly unsuitable timber-yard clerk. Most of all he felt pity for himself. Not even the thought of the pain that his wife was suffering was much consolation. He had hoped to see his daughter married to a real gentleman, ideally one so short of money that he was prepared to devote his life to the livery stables and the collection of rents. By a supreme effort of will, he abandoned all thought of what might have been and turned instead to his duty.

'You told me . . . told me when we first talked about marrying her . . . that you'd make her happy.'

'I will, Mr Sweeting.' Ernest spoke with the simple conviction of a man who had not examined his assertion in any great detail.

'I'm sure you mean what you say. But it won't be all that easy.'

Ernest nodded in simple-minded agreement.

'You'll have to try and change your habits to be more like hers. You'll have to change for her, 'cause she won't change for you.'

'Change in what way, Mr Sweeting?'

'Money, first of all. Money. We've got to get straight who pays for what. I'll not be ungenerous. I promise you.'

'You've been very generous already. You pay me far more than I'm worth. Just sending out accounts isn't worth much.'

'Sometimes I think you don't enjoy working for me. You'll get used to it. And there's prospects for my son-in-law. There were no prospects in that woodyard.'

'Wood's my business, Mr Sweeting. That's what I know about.'

'Perhaps it is, but it won't keep my daughter. And try to look cheerful. Tomorrow ought to be the happiest day of your life. Of course, I realise that in your case you've already—'

'I am cheerful. Leastways about marrying Miss Sweeting, I am. And it will be the greatest day of my life once the wedding's over and we're on our way home. It's London that makes me miserable. I can't abide it.'

'You've not seen it.'

'I know it's not Retford – Worksop neither.'

'That's the sort of thing I mean. Lucy loves London, she'll be back down here given half a chance.'

Ernest smiled for the first time that day. 'Not when she's settled down with me she won't.'

Vincent Sweeting despaired. 'Anyway, try and look cheerful tomorrow.'

Ernest tried. He assumed a fixed grin as he stood before the altar of St George's Church, Pimlico, waiting to be married with the full benefit of clergy but without the support of a single member of his own family. The only resemblance to the sort of wedding for which Mrs Sweeting once hoped was the immaculate morning suit worn by the bride's father. And that was a betrayal of the agreement that the whole ceremony would be conducted with minimal formality. Instead of bridesmaid and best man, Lucy's uncle and the one friend she felt would be neither patronising nor censorious acted as witnesses. After a hasty glass of champagne at Mrs Sweeting's house in Warwick Square, the happy couple were hurried towards Marylebone and Worksop.

A whole first-class carriage had been reserved on the train. As a posse of porters carried the trunks, portmanteaux and hat boxes along the platform, seven men who were distant acquaintances of the Sweetings nodded to Vincent and raised their hats to his daughter. He consoled himself with the thought that Lucy had laced herself so tightly that no one could possibly suspect she was pregnant.

Ernest slumped in a corner seat and prepared himself for the next ordeal. That night he and Lucy would share a bed in Vincent Sweeting's house on Sparken Hill. The idea of lying next to Lucy excited him so much that he could feel a pulse tapping away inside his temple but the thought of living in the unaccustomed splendour of her father's house made him feel like an orphan who had been adopted by rich foster parents. Foolishly, he had hoped that immediately the train pulled out of the station he would feel all the pleasures of a man going home. But as he thought about his new job and the daily routine of his new life he wondered if he would ever feel at home again. Bravely he decided to raise a subject which, he had been promised, would be discussed immediately the wedding was over. He coughed nervously to catch the attention of his father-in-law, who was sound asleep, and his wife, who seemed fascinated by the squalid north London landscape that was scuttling by the window. Vincent Sweeting awoke with a start and Lucy slowly turned her head in his direction and fixed him with a challenging stare.

'We really ought to talk about lodgings. I mean lodgings for when the baby comes. I ought to be looking around now.' He hoped that, by ending with a half-apology for his own inactivity, he would both avoid the impression of making unreasonable demands and sound like a good husband.

'Lodgings?' Lucy asked, spreading the syllables over a hundred yards of track.

'There's nothing to decide for a bit,' Vincent Sweeting told him. 'Then we'll find a house.'

'I said after the baby comes.' Ernest meant to concede his father-in-law's point.

'You don't really expect me to live at Sparken Hill for nearly a year, do you?' Lucy sounded genuinely distressed. 'You just said so to tease Mama.'

'It's no good trying on your tricks.' It was always a shock to Ernest when Vincent Sweeting was angry with Lucy. 'We've decided. You agreed as well as your mother. There's nothing more to be said.'

'But . . . God!'

'And you'll have to improve your language. In Worksop we're not used to women blaspheming. We'll talk – we'll all talk – about another house after the baby's born. We'll all talk about it then.' He nodded his head in Ernest's direction in much the same way as he would have told an ostler which was the next horse to be fed and watered.

'You can't really mean that the baby—'

'Don't say it. Stop now. It's all decided and you know it. Your mother's coming up. It's all decided.'

Lucy giggled. 'Perhaps there'll be a romantic reunion.'

Vincent Sweeting guffawed at his daughter's witticism. Lucy preened herself like a matador who has despatched a tiresome bull and Ernest turned away, for their bickering demonstrated an intimacy between father and daughter greater than that between husband and wife. The idea of living at Sparken Hill frightened him more and more. But he was not sure how he could escape if, as he must, he was to take Lucy with him. Clearly all the details of his future had been decided without it being thought necessary to ask his opinion. He was trapped. On the other side of the carriage the argument squabbled on.

'I'm not going to trail round with you to see all those dreary people.'

Ernest had never felt so lonely in his life.

'Then what will you do all day?' Vincent Sweeting asked.

Lucy laughed without humour. 'I shall stay at home and fence with my husband.'

It was time to make a great leap for freedom and self-respect.

'I want my mother and father to come round.' Ernest could hardly believe that it was his voice that echoed across the compartment, almost drowning the noise of the wheels. 'I want them to come round to tea, quite soon after we get back.' His voice grew stronger.

Suddenly he was shouting. 'Sunday. Next Sunday. Agnes, I want Agnes to come as well, and Anne, if she's free.'

Lucy bent her head so that she could see her husband without interference from the swoop of ostrich feathers which were fastened to the crown of her hat but curved down across and beyond the brim.

'About time you suggested something like that. You shouldn't have hidden them away for so long.'

Ernest was about to protest but Lucy was in mid-flow and not to be interrupted.

'I suppose that really you've kept me hidden from them. I suppose I'm the first fallen woman they've ever met. They'll just have to make the best of me if I'm going to be mother to their grandchildren.'

Ernest thought of nothing except Lucy's assumption of several pregnancies. But Vincent Sweeting thought he ought to tell his daughter to calm herself. He did not like the idea that the baby would have other grandparents than him. But Lucy barely paused for breath.

'I don't know why you didn't let them come to the wedding instead of inventing that absurd story about your father being ill. Anyway, next Sunday. And dinner not tea. You've got to learn to do things properly.'

She slid into the middle seat of the carriage and, leaning against the arm which Ernest had pulled down to separate him from the rest of the world, kissed him on the cheek.

'I knew you'd come to life before we reached Worksop. Why do I have to keep telling you to cheer up? Papa says that you've promised to make the best of things.'

Ernest, who had flinched and, as she moved towards him, turned, had tears in his eyes. 'I love you,' he said, hardly noticing and certainly not caring that Vincent Sweeting was fully awake and looking at him with undisguised hatred.

Elizabeth Skinner had to be persuaded to accept the invitation to dinner at Sparken Hill. She said that she did not possess the right clothes, would not recognise the appropriate knives and forks and could not imagine what she would find to say. Agnes said that she wanted to go, but pleaded for her wish to be granted in a way which suggested that its denial might be a relief. Anne dismissed the idea of her joining the party with a combination of incredulity and contempt. She had an order to finish by Tuesday morning. She and Lottie (there was heavy emphasis on her commitment to her partner) would be sewing all Sunday evening and probably into the night. In the end, reason – as represented by William Skinner – prevailed.

244

'We've got to decide if we're going to cut ourselves off from him altogether or if we're still going to treat him like our son.'

'Of course we're not going to cut him off.' Elizabeth was offended by the suggestion.

'You say that. But if we won't go and see him . . . in his new home.'

'I just won't feel comfortable in that big house. I would have done once. But I won't now.'

'And you won't invite them here in case his . . . his wife . . . doesn't feel comfortable in this cottage.'

'It's true, isn't it? She won't.' Elizabeth seemed to be enjoying herself. 'You can't deny it.'

'Well, if they don't come here and we won't go there . . .'

'I didn't say that I wouldn't go.'

They went. And they devoted all of Sunday morning and afternoon to preparations for their ordeal. Agnes prepared with genuine enthusiasm.

'Just keep hold of me and I'll lead you.'

'Like a performing bear?'

'Now, Mother. You know that the girl is only trying to help.'

'I only meant showing you where things are.'

'Perhaps you ought to cut up the food on my plate. Or you could feed it to me with a spoon! You just leave me to look after myself. I can manage. You know that well enough. All I need is for your father to show me my place and sit me down like any gentleman would do for a lady.'

William was unable to obey his instruction for Vincent Sweeting was eager to fulfil the obligations of the perfect host. Indeed, in order to demonstrate his manners, he offered his arm to Elizabeth with such a flourish that he elbowed her in the ribs, thus enabling his guest to locate exactly where her arm was to rest. She accepted his invitation and walked into the dining room with the confidence of a woman who could see all the obstacles in her way. Host and husband almost collided in their attempt to move Elizabeth's chair and, once it was pushed against the back of her legs, she sank gracefully down on to the seat, confident that there was only one more ordeal to face. She had to locate the cutlery. Her fingers felt their way along the table-cloth. Knife. Knife. Spoon, knife. Then only damask. The trial was over. She would work her way inwards as the plates were put before her.

Suddenly, a foot to her right, there was a crash of breaking glass and across the table a little yelp of anguish from Lucy. Elizabeth took it for granted that she was responsible. Then Lucy said, 'It doesn't matter. Just leave it.'

Years of blindness had made her sensitive to sounds and she judged that Lucy was speaking to someone further down the table. Ernest, she knew, was on her left. Either William or Agnes had caused the catastrophe. There was the sound of napkins being dabbed on the table and then, a second crash – far bigger than the first – seemed to shake all the china and rattle every piece of cutlery.

'I told you to leave it.' Lucy sounded more contemptuous than concerned.

Agnes was simply agitated. 'Careful, Mam. It's going to drip on to your dress.'

Agnes's voice was coming from the other side of the table.

There was more mopping with napkins and the table shook again as somebody, pushing a chair back from the table, bumped against a table leg.

'God,' said Lucy. 'It's an earthquake.'

Elizabeth thanked Providence that she could only imagine the distress which her husband, the only possible culprit, must be suffering. She blamed herself. If she had put her foot down William would not have disgraced himself in front of the Sweetings.

'It might be easier, Agnes,' Lucy was taking command again, 'it might be easier if you helped your mother back from the table for a moment while we mop up.'

'It's stopped dripping.' It was William who was speaking – speaking without an apology and apparently unabashed. 'Not all that much spilled.'

Elizabeth marvelled at her husband's continued effrontery.

Vincent Sweeting spoke for the first time. He seemed to be addressing Elizabeth but he was too agitated to aim his remarks in one particular direction. 'Are you sure you're all right, dear lady? I cannot apologise enough. Your first visit to our house . . .'

'It's nothing,' said Elizabeth, deciding not to add that there was only a small damp patch on her dress above one knee. Perhaps she should express the regrets of the whole family. She prayed for William to apologise. She could hear him clearing his throat as he always did in preparation for saying something controversial.

'Let's just forget about it. We can't let a drop of water spoil our evening. Agnes, put your mother's serviette over the wet bit in the cloth.'

'Quite right, Mr Skinner.' Lucy rang the silver bell which stood on the table in front of her. 'Let's hope the soup isn't cold. We all know that Papa's clumsy. It's because he's grown so fat. But I still love you just as much as I always did.'

Elizabeth sighed so loudly with relief that the maid, hurrying

246

through the door with the soup, wondered if the stiff lady in the black dress was yawning with impatience to be served.

When supper was over and the Skinners had left for home Lucy plucked at her husband's sleeve. 'I like your father. I hope you grow up to look like that. But your mother's a Tartar. She thinks Papa's a real oaf. He is, of course, but she needn't have been so snooty. Bit of a snob, your mama.'

'It's time for bed,' said Ernest with the full authority of a husband. He took his wife's hand and led her towards the stairs.

'Don't,' cried Lucy, 'you'll embarrass Papa. Dragging me to bed.' Then, in case her father had either not heard or not comprehended, she shouted again, more loudly, 'Ernest, you shouldn't drag me off to bed. Not in my condition!'

Ernest took no notice.

CHAPTER NINETEEN

Something to Look Forward to

The suspicion that William's rheumatic pains were no more than a pretence persisted for almost three months after Ernest's wedding. Throughout that time the sudden but brief attacks of pain came and went in a way which always suited his convenience. He was incapacitated on the day before the funeral, in Wisbech, of a sister whom he hardly knew, and the spasms struck again as he was about to leave home to assist with the decoration of the Skinner and Harthill fitting room. Elizabeth gave no sign of doubt until the evening of the party which had been organised by the Harness Grove servants to celebrate the thirtieth anniversary of Henry Hodding's residence in Darfoulds. The butler had prepared a suitable speech. Gerrard Knock and William were required to decide between themselves who would second the loyal address and who would actually hand over the silver salver, the cost of which had been met by the servants with varying degrees of resistance and resentment.

'Well,' asked Knock, who had called round at Grove Cottage an hour before the party was due to begin, 'which do you want to do? If I'm to make a speech I need to turn my mind to it now.'

'Whichever you like,' said William. 'Either way, I need to be getting ready.' But instead of levering himself out of the chair he pushed feebly on the arms and sank back with a groan. 'Would you believe it? My back's gone again. You'll have to do both.'

'I suppose he believed you.' Elizabeth had been careful to ensure that the coachman gave her husband's sincere apologies.

'Can't see why he shouldn't.'

'Let's see how it feels tomorrow morning.'

The recovery was, as usual, miraculous and William prepared for church with his customary meticulous attention to the details of his appearance. Throughout the service he sang with the gusto of a confirmed believer who was in robust health. No one could doubt, as he knelt for the final prayers before the recessional hymn, that he was looking forward to joining in Advent's impatient demand 'O Come,

O Come, Emmanuel'. There was the familiar coughing and clearing of throats as the congregation rose from its knees and waited for the vicar to announce the number of the hymn which they had already read on the noticeboard and found in their hymn-books. In the moment of silence that preceded the organ's first notes, William Skinner gave a cry of pain and gently subsided on to his chair. Then, clutching his back, he rolled on to the chapel's cold stone floor and lay there moaning. In that minute every suspicion was removed. Everyone knew that, no matter how great the horror that a pretence of pain might avoid, William Skinner would never willingly make such an exhibition of himself.

The sidesmen carried William out into the porch and laid him on the stone bench which thoughtful Norman craftsmen had constructed for such an emergency. After the gasps of shock and cries of sympathy had died down, the congregation demanded the ransom of captive Israel. Henry Hodding, sitting in the front row, hardly turned his head until the service was over. Then he took command. The gardener was to be driven at once to Dr Anderson's surgery in Cheapside.

It was a painful journey. Elizabeth sat nervously in the consulting room listening to her husband grunt agreement and groan dissent.

'How long do you think he's had pains, Mrs Skinner?'

'About two years, Doctor. He had back attacks when he was a little boy but he grew out of them. Perhaps a little longer.'

'Yes, that's what he says. And has it always gone away in a couple of days?'

'It was longer once. Once it was nearly a week.'

'How long ago was that?'

Elizabeth could remember exactly. 'Nearly three months. That's the only time that it was as bad as it's been today. I didn't realise that rheumatism could be so bad.'

'I doubt if it's rheumatism. I think it's Still's disease.'

'Is that bad, Doctor?'

'It's not a good thing for a gardener to have. It's a sort of arthritis. The joints seize up. If I'm right, it's not going to get any better and it will probably get worse. I'd better ask Mr Hodding if there's any other job he can do. He'll have pain bending.'

'He wouldn't want any other sort of job. He's a gardener.'

'Mrs Skinner, he won't be able to garden if his joints stick together like bricks and mortar. And the more inflamed they get the worse he'll be. He must be in pain most days as it is. He only tells you when it's very bad. Even if he struggles on, he'll only be able to garden for another year or two.'

'Is there nothing to cure it?'

'No.'

'Doctor, he's not yet sixty. How are we going to live?'

'Your son's done very well for himself. He'll help you, surely?'

'My husband wouldn't think of such a thing and neither would I. Ernest has got to make his way. We're not going to hold him back.'

All that Elizabeth could think of at that moment was the embarrassment with which William had received the outstanding repayment of Ernest's twenty-pound loan – an embarrassment so great that it was several days before he could bring himself to pass it on to Henry Hodding and reveal that he was already, indirectly, in receipt of Vincent Sweeting's charity.

William Skinner was put to bed in Grove Cottage and left to contemplate his future alone. As the pain in his neck radiated out along his shoulders and down his back, he feared that he would never work again. For all his adult life, he had made the best of things – accepting, with good grace, less than he hoped for and less than he believed he deserved. He had done all he could to protect his family from hardship and had even shielded them from his own suffering. Until that day, he had even avoided self-pity but that morning he had nothing to look forward to, no hope that eventually there would be some sort of reward. Tomorrow would just be one day nearer to permanent infirmity and the poverty which would follow.

All that was left to him was the enjoyment of his suffering so he concentrated his thoughts on how really desperate the rest of his life was likely to be as it moved full circle from workhouse master to pauper in receipt of indoor relief. When he heard a knock on his bedroom door, he would not have been surprised if the unusual courtesy had been performed by the grim reaper complete with scythe and hour-glass. Indeed, he would have welcomed such a visitation. It was Henry Hodding, making the first visit to Grove Cottage that his gardener could remember.

'Sorry to hear about this, Skinner.' He waved an opened envelope in the invalid's direction. 'Dr Anderson sent me a note. It sounds pretty painful.'

'It's very good of you to bother, sir. I don't feel too bad.' William did not even try to sound convincing. 'I'll be up and about again in a day or two.'

'That's not what the doctor says. He says it's permanent. "Steady deterioration", he says.'

A little of the quiet indomitability had survived the trauma of the doctor's surgery. 'Well, sir – begging your pardon and his – I'll have

250

to prove him wrong. I can't afford to be an invalid, whatever the doctor says.'

'You can afford it for a day or two. That's what I've come to say. I shan't expect you at work for at least a month. I'll send the wages down each Friday morning. Then we'll see.'

William could not make up his mind if he was being threatened or reassured. He struggled to choose the optimistic alternative. 'It's very good of you, Mr Hodding. But who will do the work until I get back?'

'When the old gardener was ill the others did it. But he hung on for months and they all grumbled to each other behind my back and caused trouble. This time, I'm going to set somebody on.'

The appointment of a new gardener was, William decided, confirmation that he had another month to work at Harness Grove. He was still speculating about whether the weeks in bed would be counted as notice when his successor was named.

'I'm going to set on that blacksmith who shoes for the hunt. He's lost his job again, or given it up, and Mr Robinson wants to find him something for a week or two. As soon as you're able, I'll expect you to keep an eye on him and make sure that he doesn't lean on his spade all day.'

'But he's not a gardener, sir.'

'He can dig. He can burn leaves. He can drain the lake and clean the muck out. That's all I need at this time of year. Anyway, you ought to be pleased that I'm having a blacksmith. You've no need to worry about losing your place.'

Even the comforting reference to the prospects of continued employment could not ease the pain in William's back and neck. He changed the subject by saying the first thing that came into his mind. 'I'll worry about the garden.'

'You worry about it too much. It's time you started to worry about yourself and your family. You've got to think of Mrs Skinner now. And young Agnes.'

That, William felt sure, was a definite hint that he would not be at Harness Grove by the end of the year. Then it seemed that Henry Hodding was referring to an even more dismal prospect.

'I suppose Ernest will look after them . . .'

Gloomy though he was, William thought not of his imminent death, but of the constant assumption that he would spend the rest of his life taking money from his son. 'Ernest will be a father in a week or two. He's got responsibilities of his own.'

'Well then,' said Henry Hodding, halfway to the door, 'you've got something to look forward to . . . whatever happens.'

*

Mrs Sweeting arrived in Worksop several weeks before either she or her daughter's baby were expected and immediately attempted to assume command of the house on Sparken Hill. She was allowed to take decisions concerning menus, the decoration of what was to become the nursery and the contents of the layette. But she felt, and was, no more than a visitor. For a bond had grown up between Lucy and Ernest which was as close as it was peculiar. Vincent Sweeting watched the development of the strange relationship with a mixture of astonishment and paternal satisfaction. His daughter was clearly contented, more contented than she had ever been. Nothing had ever given her the pleasure she derived from poking fun at her husband. And Ernest, although continually harassed, never appeared to mind. Vincent Sweeting, joint master of the Grove Hunt, compared their feelings for each other with the relationship between fox and hounds. One enjoyed hunting, the other enjoyed being hunted.

Ernest gloried in being the butt of his wife's wit. He joined in the laughter with which his father-in-law greeted every sarcastic assault and even sometimes recognised cruel humour in asides which Vincent Sweeting first thought to be no more than the small change of conventional conversation. At times, Ernest seemed to be creating opportunities for his wife to laugh at his expense. The cradle was a continual source of amusement for the whole family.

Ernest originally intended to make it from plywood. He first made a perfect model based on a picture he had found in a book of Elizabethan furniture. Lucy, caught off guard early one morning, so forgot herself that she expressed obviously genuine admiration for the careful workmanship. Then she noticed the rockers which curved under its head and foot.

'It swings the wrong way.'

'What do you mean?' asked Ernest.

'A baby has to be swung up and down, not sideways. This is like a hammock. Any baby in this would be sick in a minute.'

'Don't be silly.' Mrs Sweeting had bustled in. 'Cradles always rock that way. Anyway it doesn't matter. I've ordered a proper cradle. It will be here in plenty of time.'

She was about to add that Ernest had made a toy which some child – she meant some poor child – would cherish when her son-in-law took the model from her.

'I'm going to make one full size.'

'What size is full size?' Lucy asked. 'I'm only going to have a baby-sized baby.'

'No grandchild of mine is going to sleep in a home-made cot made out of an old packing case.'

252

'Let him make it.' Lucy grinned at her husband. 'He's nothing to do in his spare time at the moment.' Ernest grinned back.

Mrs Sweeting, hearing her husband's chesty cough approaching down the hall, prepared to appeal to his sense of right and wrong.

'Have you seen it?'

'Indeed I have. I saw it this morning before the last coat of varnish was dry. A real little work of art. I wish I could make things with my hands.'

His wife did not share the enthusiasm. 'He's made dozens of things like it before. Their room's got them in the places where ornaments should be. What's so special about this one?'

That one, Vincent Sweeting should have said, was special because it was the beginning of a father's first gift to his unborn child but he could not bring himself to speak to his wife in such sentimental language. He said what he believed but what, in comparison, seemed to him to be of secondary importance.

'It's a real little gem. First-class craftsmanship. Hours of loving work went into it.' It was as near as he could get to the expression of emotion.

'And do you expect Lucy's baby to sleep in a thing like that, a thing made out of matchwood?'

'Plywood.' Despite the sophistication of his new life, Ernest remained obsessed with detail.

'No, I don't.' Vincent Sweeting was sufficiently emphatic to dismiss all thought of any sort of inferior material. 'Indeed I don't. It should be made out of solid oak. And I've arranged it all for tomorrow morning. It should be here by ten.'

'What should?' Lucy feared tragedy or ridicule. 'What *have* you done?'

Vincent Sweeting smiled in triumph and laid one great arm along his son-in-law's shoulder as a tangible sign of the ties which bound them together. Their common purpose was the worship of Lucy and the glorification of her imminent child. Sweeting's mind was filled with confused thoughts of carpenters and kings bringing gifts to celebrate the birth.

'I've bought a work bench and a vice, half a dozen saws, a plane and three chisels . . .' The inventory ran on and on. 'I took advice from Arnold Hirst and he recommended half-inch oak. Though he thought that you might need thicker for the rockers. We'll set it all up in the summer house. Get anything else you need from Hirst's. You've got an account there now. Just think of it. Six months ago you sent the bills out. Now you send the orders in.' He squeezed Ernest's shoulder with delight. 'Get it finished in time. Come into work when you feel like it. It's a wonderful gift to be able to use your hands like that.'

Ernest toiled in the summer house for nearly a month. Several times he almost abandoned his labour of love altogether for half-inch oak was not worked as easily as plywood and the tenon saw was more difficult to handle than the thin fret blade. He did not even aspire to dovetailing but he chopped the mortice joints out with reasonable ease and three times reached the great moment when the cradle was to be assembled. Three times he fitted the pieces loosely in place in preparation for boiling his new glue pot and fastening the parts so tightly that the cot would bear the weight of the bonniest baby and a succession of subsequent brothers and sisters. Three times he glumly took the unglued sections and tried to pare down their edges and corners in the hope of making them fit together in something like the proper oblong shape. But the right-angles never joined together at ninety degrees. After his third attempt at what he knew real joiners called 'bodging', he bought new wood. His next effort was squarer but it still looked as if, after being perfectly made, it had been crushed out of shape. The baby was due within a week. It was, he decided, too late to start again. It had to be his fourth attempt or nothing. It was another fiasco, but he decided that anything was better than no gift at all.

To his distress, Vincent Sweeting organised a ceremony in the drawing room. There was champagne and a lace-edged cloth under which the cradle was to be hidden until the moment came for its spectacular exposure. Lucy snatched the covering away before her mother was properly settled. But, even halfway down on to the sofa, Mrs Sweeting recognised the inadequacy of Ernest's offering. She gave a startled cry and appealed to her husband. 'You can't let the baby sleep in that. It's all higgledy-piggledy.'

Vincent Sweeting looked apologetic. 'It isn't quite what I imagined.'

Ernest trembled at the thought of what his wife would say.

'We might have a crooked baby,' she said. 'Anyway, it won't notice for a week or two – as long as it doesn't fall apart that is.'

'It won't do that,' said Ernest gratefully.

'Then bring it across here.'

Lucy was lying on the couch and the cradle was placed, as instructed, on the floor beside her. She leaned down and rocked it from side to side. 'The poor little mite will go straight in here.'

Ernest took his wife's hand and looked at her with blind devotion.

'It's all very well behaving like that now. I hope you love me as much when the baby comes and I'm driven out of my mind with boredom and—'

'I will,' said Ernest. 'I will.'

The baby became the family's exclusive preoccupation. Lucy hated the restrictions that pregnancy placed on her and could hardly bear to wait for the load to be lifted from her belly and her spirit. Ernest waited for the arrival with apprehension and an inclination towards resentment. He had survived one earthquake and begun to love life amongst the shock waves that still radiated from his wife. He did not want the earth to open up beneath his feet again and he was afraid that the intrusion of a baby – even Lucy's baby, which he was proud to have fathered – might disturb the precarious balance of his married life. Vincent Sweeting felt all the anxiety about blood and pain that his daughter had managed to put out of her mind. He was terrified by the thought that, somehow, he would be required to witness his daughter's birth pangs – that he would hear her screams through the thin bedroom wall or be called to her side at the moment of delivery to perform some task which would expose him to the full horror of her human birth. Mrs Sweeting was simply a fireside obstetrician who talked continually of breaking waters, bearing down, contractions and afterbirth. Sometimes she reminded her son-in-law of Arnold Hirst coaching a young man in the use of Indian clubs. The graphic descriptions usually ended with Vincent Sweeting announcing that he could stand no more and his wife reminding him that, bad as the thought of the delivery might be, the reality would be far worse. There was mutual, though unspoken, agreement that the baby could not come too soon, then general and openly discussed worry that its arrival was so long delayed. Dr Anderson was called and, after he had examined Lucy in her bedroom, he submitted himself to cross-examination from her parents. He tapped the tweed pocket in which his stethoscope bulged.

'I could hear a very clear heart beat – very strong and very regular.'

'That's all very well,' said the expectant grandfather. 'That's all very well as far as the baby is concerned. But what about my daughter? She looked very pale this morning and drawn.'

'It's a strain, Mr Sweeting. Having a baby's a strain and waiting is an additional strain. But she's very well in herself and the baby—'

'Damn the baby. That's what caused all the trouble.'

Lucy and her mother shuddered in perfect unison and Ernest pursued his close study of the ceiling. Dr Anderson steered the steady course expected of a medical man.

'Believe me, Mr Sweeting, if the baby wasn't well, there'd be real

255

reason for concern about the mother. As it is, mother and baby—'

Lucy, who had been affecting lack of interest in the whole subject, came to life.

'I don't blame Jonah for not wanting to come and live here. I didn't want to come and live here. Mama didn't want to come and live here. Nobody—'

'Who's Jonah?' her father asked.

Lucy patted her belly. 'It's the little man living inside this great whale. Don't I look like a whale? I certainly feel like one.'

'You look lovely. Doesn't she, Ernest?'

The proud husband nodded vaguely in his father-in-law's direction.

'I told Dr Anderson that I'd spend tomorrow morning jumping up and down. But he says that's the way to stop babies, not to make them come.'

'I said no such thing.'

What passed in Lucy for a sense of humour was not instantly recognisable as wit to Scottish general practitioners.

'A fall now, indeed any sudden shock, would be most undesirable. It might start the labour. But it would start in quite the wrong way. We must all wait patiently.'

'That's easier for you than it is for us, Doctor,' said Mrs Sweeting.

'No doubt. But you must try to take her mind off it. I'm sure Mr Skinner will do all he can. Read to her, Mr Skinner. Nothing more soothing than reading aloud.'

Dr Anderson was not a man to take elaborate leave but even the few seconds that he spent on the doorstep were enough for a ripple of cool night air to penetrate as far as the Sweetings' drawing room. Mr Sweeting liked to keep his house warm. No window had been opened since the day it was built and the atmosphere was heavy with the smell of burning coke and escaping gas.

Lucy sniffed at the fresh air in what she believed to be an amusing imitation of a hound scenting a fox. 'I'm going for a walk.'

'At this time of night?' It was eight o'clock and Mrs Sweeting believed that the country was unsafe after five.

'Ernest will go with you,' Vincent Sweeting decreed. 'But not too far. Just a little stroll up the road.'

'Well, I meant to go as far as the Lion Gates and walk on the grass in the park.'

'You'd be trespassing,' said Ernest. 'It's not a right of way up the main drive. The path is further up, the public footpath.'

'You don't have to come if you don't want to.'

'You won't go on your own.' There was panic in her mother's voice.

'I won't go at all. I shall sit in this stuffy room and twiddle my fingers. Then I shall go to bed and try and arrange this cannonball in my stomach in a way that lets me go to sleep.'

'Dr Anderson gave you something for the insomnia.' Mrs Sweeting believed in medicine.

'No, thank you. I will just lie there and wish that I was somewhere else or, better still, someone else.'

Lucy went upstairs at ten o'clock. Half an hour later she heard her father stumble to bed and so fail in his attempt to close his door in silence that the sound of the slamming shook the house. When the distinct sound of Ernest's slippered feet pattered along the landing, she closed her eyes and lay still so that if her husband came into her room he would believe her to be asleep. At first she had hated sleeping alone and argued that it was not even necessary during the final few nights but for once she was glad to lie cold and lonely between the cool sheets. Her mother did bustle in – and peered so closely at her that Lucy felt the anxious breath on her cheek – but, convinced by her daughter's carefully modulated breathing, she decided all was well and passed on to bed.

When the house was finally still, Lucy tried to settle down for the night. Since she could lie only on her side, she had no real hope of a good night's rest. She tried to shift the weight in her stomach by hitching her hips first to the left and then to the right. Then she stretched out her legs until she could feel the tendons pull tight in her calves and gave a little cry of pain as the cramp ran up the back of her thighs. An attempt to bend her knees was quickly abandoned in favour of rotating the feet. She became conscious of her arms, which got in the way of every movement she tried to make. Folded across her swollen stomach, doubled under her head or laid limp by her side, they were always an encumbrance.

By midnight the pillows were her principal enemy. They were pulled, pummelled and rolled up in turn. First they were too high. One was thrown on the floor. Then, since Lucy was sure that she lay too flat, the bolster was doubled up and she half lay and half sat as she stared disconsolately into the dark. Through a gap that the maid had left in the curtains, she saw a single star. Lucy stared at it for almost half an hour before she felt her careful way across to the window. Instead of opening the curtains, she held them round her like a cloak and, with the heavy velvet warming her shoulders, pressed her nose to the cold glass. It was a cloudless night.

Lucy had no real wish to go for a walk. It was not the stars or the new moon or the clear night that excited her but the idea of defying the representatives of staid respectability. On a bright spring morning she would have found little charm in Sparken Hill, the Lion Gates and Welbeck Park, which lay beyond them. In the middle of a cold winter night they had no attraction except the opportunity they provided to defy and offend. It had to be Sparken Hill, the Lion Gates and Welbeck Park, for that was the route which had provoked so much outrage and anxiety.

Despite the difficulty of dressing in the dark, she did not light the gas. She had decided to leave the house in absolute silence and return in such secrecy that she could tell the story of her escape over breakfast the following morning. Her mother would give a little shriek and tell her not to invent silly stories. Then she would find the muddy shoes and wet hems scattered on the bedroom floor and pretend to faint at the thought of what might have happened. As Lucy lowered her swollen frame downstairs and rattled the great Japanese vase that stood by the bottom step, she almost wanted to be caught for the hysteria which followed would be a welcome distraction. But, although the dried bulrushes rustled and creaked, there was no sound from the floor above.

Her feet were wet before she got to the road, for she had walked across the lawn so as not to crunch the gravel on the path, and she was tired before she got halfway to the Lion Gates. But she pressed on: to turn back and creep silently into bed would have been to concede victory to her parents. Inside Welbeck Park the ground was soft and the fronds of dead bracken clutched at her ankles. Fifty paces, she thought, and then I can turn back. She began to count them off.

The lodge-keeper who found her thought that Lucy was dead. She lay in a gulley next to the log over which she had fallen, embracing it with one arm as if it were the lover with whom she had spent the night. She had turned towards the rough bark and when the man rolled her over to look at her face, he saw the blood and the little hand of her baby pushing out below the hem of her torn skirt. Then Lucy gave a great sigh and the lodge-keeper – despite being a countryman who had seen death and nature since he was a child – turned and ran to his house shouting for his wife.

The woman told him to turn away whilst she lifted Lucy's skirts. There was much running backwards and forwards with blankets and water and a last desperate dash for help. Then the blanket was pulled over Lucy's face and the lodge-keeper's wife rubbed her hands clean on the rough grass as she asked her husband, 'Who do you reckon she is?'

'I reckon she must have been running away from the Abbey. Don't know who's been staying there.'

'She must be somebody, wearing clothes like that. Is she married?'

258

'She's wearing a wedding ring.'

The lodge-keeper and his wife agreed that one of them must take a message to the house but neither of them wanted to be left alone with the bodies, though both knew that proper respect required somebody to stand guard. Their dilemma was solved by the appearance of a distraught young man who, although he wore no greatcoat and the grass was stiff with frost, sweated like a navvy on an August afternoon. He knew, without pulling back the blanket, what lay against the log. He took command.

'Go and get a cart. She's laid here long enough.'

The lodge-keeper recognised the voice of authority and hurried off down the driveway to obey his orders.

'Shall I stay with you?' The lodge-keeper's wife had noticed the wild look in the young man's eyes. She was afraid to stay and afraid of what would happen if she left.

'I'll need your help when the cart comes back.'

Comforted by so rational a response, she risked more questions. 'Are you the husband?'

Ernest nodded.

'I'm very sorry.'

'I knew she'd be here.' Ernest was in command no longer – in command neither of the situation nor of his own emotions. 'I knew when we got up and she'd gone that she'd be here.' He began to cry. 'I knew her. I was the one who understood her. I should have known that she'd come here to spite us.'

The lodge-keeper's wife told him not to upset himself, and Ernest sniffed and continued his monologue in a voice too calm for the message it conveyed.

'It's all our fault. We should have guessed and should have gone with her.'

The lodge-keeper's wife looked nervously in the direction of the house. Her husband had not yet disappeared round the corner into the stables. It would be fifteen minutes before he got back with the cart.

'She shouldn't have been out at all in her condition. You were right to tell her to stay in.'

'You didn't know her. Telling her was no good. She just did what you told her not to.'

To the relief of the lodge-keeper's wife, an elderly man staggered through the Lion Gates. He saw the couple standing by the log and, waving his arms wildly, began to shout, 'Is it her? Is it our Lucy?'

Ernest had still not drawn back the blanket and he did not reply until his father-in-law was near enough to hear what amounted to no more than a whisper.

'She's dead. She came here last night.'

'God almighty! Last night! How do you know? She couldn't have.'

'She did. I know. I should have known last night.'

An hour seemed to pass before the lodge-keeper returned with the gardener's cart. It was no more than a flat board with two badly fitted wheels at its centre. But it was high off the ground, high enough to be pushed by a man walking upright. Ernest took charge again.

'Hold that end,' he told Vincent Sweeting. 'Hold it tight or it'll tip up.' He bent down beside the log.

'Better let me,' said the lodge-keeper's wife.

Ernest took no notice and began to tuck the blanket under Lucy's head. For a second the side of her face was exposed. Her clear blue eyes were still open and her skin was the cold milky white for which she had once struggled with so many boxes of powder and bottles of cream. Vincent Sweeting cried out and turned away.

'I'll take her feet.' The lodge-keeper's wife bundled the baby inside Lucy's long skirts and, when Ernest gave the word, lifted mother and child from the grass.

When Vincent Sweeting heard the thud and felt the weight of his daughter and her baby land on the cart, he almost relaxed his grip on its handle, and the lodge-keeper, afraid that the body would slide back on to the ground, rushed forward to hold it steady.

'I better come with you,' he said. 'Where are you going?'

'Halfway down Sparken Hill,' Ernest told him.

They set off with Ernest and the lodge-keeper at each end of the makeshift bier. Vincent Sweeting walked at the side like a pallbearer, holding the blanket in place over his daughter's corpse.

Sparken Hill was still asleep so only a few servants at upstairs windows saw the cortège pass. For the last steep half-mile, Ernest and the lodge-keeper struggled to hold the cart against gravity, and Vincent Sweeting feared a dozen times that the blanket would slide from Lucy's face, but they arrived outside Rock House with the dignity appropriate to death. Mrs Sweeting, wearing an unbecoming nightcap and a shawl which did not match her dressing gown, was standing on the gravel drive.

'Is it Lucy?'

It was not really a question and no one felt any obligation to answer.

'And what about the baby?'

'Dead,' said Ernest. 'Dead as well. He's with his mother. We killed them both.'

'Now then,' said Vincent Sweeting, carefully staring at the gravel. 'There's no cause for you to believe that.'

'I should have known what she'd do and I should have stopped her. I was the one who knew what she was like.'

Mrs Sweeting was too overcome with grief even to resent his presumption.

Lucy Skinner was buried with little more ceremony than had accompanied her marriage five months before, though the party at the graveside included William Skinner, who insisted that pains in his back could not prevent him from supporting his son at his moment of grief. There was no funeral tea and Mrs Sweeting left straight from the churchyard for London. The carriage which took her to the station went on to deliver William back to Grove Cottage.

Back in Sparken Hill, Vincent Sweeting – being a businessman – decided that it was best to close the books at once. He offered his son-in-law whisky, but Ernest, who had become a teetotaller again, declined. Sweeting tried to be tactful.

'I've been thinking what's best to do ever since the . . . ever since. No doubt you've done the same.'

Ernest nodded in a way that made plain that he was not telling the truth.

'It's best to clear things up straight away.'

'Yes, yes, it is.' Ernest answered without conviction.

'There's a pair of houses that I've built on Overend Road opposite the station. I'm going to give you one.'

Sweeting expected instant gratitude. After several minutes of silence, when he had not even received cursory thanks, he could not resist – despite the sad solemnity of the day – showing his anger. 'You didn't expect to stay here, did you?'

'No,' said Ernest, speaking with sincerity for the first time. 'I didn't expect and didn't want.'

'And I'm going to give you six months' wages.' He took a huge roll of bank notes out of his back pocket and, licking his forefinger and thumb, began to count the money on to the table.

'Lucy would disapprove.'

Even as he spoke, Ernest knew that if Lucy had been alive and in the next room he would never have said such a thing.

'What do you mean?'

'She'd say that it was vulgar, flashing cash about like that.'

'But she'd have taken the money all the same.' Vincent Sweeting was weeping.

'And so will I. I can't afford style. I have to be sensible. I've got a

261

sensible haircut. Lucy used to say so.' Ernest was weeping too.

'What will you do now? Go back to Hirst's?'

'I will if he'll have me.'

'It would be no good staying on with me. You didn't—'

'No. Rents and cabs are not in my line. I want to be back with wood.'

'Well, Arnold Hirst will jump at having you back. He'll treat you like a gentleman now. You being my son-in-law, so to speak.'

That, Ernest knew, would have made Lucy laugh out loud. It was not the right moment to say so.

'No hurry. Take your time. But don't go into the livery. Best to make a clean break there. Somebody else can collect the rents till I get things sorted out. Me, if necessary. But take your time moving out of here. Next week'll suit me fine.'

'I'm going tomorrow, Mr Sweeting. I'm going home to Grove Cottage. I'll stay there until I've got some furniture for Overend Road.'

'Is there anything you want to take?'

'I'd like that cigar box.'

The wedding gifts had included numerous cigar boxes in a variety of shapes and sizes and, to allow no misunderstanding, Ernest waved in the direction of a large walnut casket, bound with brass. It contained a complicated system of drawers which pulled out, swung round and doubled back on themselves when the lid was lifted.

'You're not thinking of starting smoking?' It was Vincent Sweeting's unsuccessful attempt to lighten the mood and he regretted it at once.

'No, I'm . . .'

'I know you're not. Stupid of me. I should have realised. Sentimental value, is it? Given you by somebody special?'

'I don't know where it came from. It's the workmanship. It's near perfect.'

'That's very nice, Ernest. Very nice. I've always admired your interest in wood. And your talent with your hands.' He paused, struggling to say what was in his mind. 'And there's another thing.'

'Yes, Mr Sweeting.'

'I don't blame you for anything . . . You've nothing . . . nothing to reproach yourself for.'

'No, Mr Sweeting. I don't believe I have.'

'And another thing.'

'Yes, Mr Sweeting.'

'You're young. Your life's ahead of you. You'll start again one day and put all this behind you.'

'I know, Mr Sweeting.'

262

Ernest knew that he would not. But he lacked the energy to argue with his father-in-law.

Brack began work at Harness Grove two full weeks before William Skinner was allowed out of bed, so for a fortnight there was no one to supervise his digging and the burning of leaves. But, even without a real gardener to guide him, he dug and raked with a methodical determination that belied his reputation as a man who could not be trusted. Henry Hodding called to him from the drawing-room window whilst he was shovelling the stinking mass of rotting weeds from the bottom of the lily pond.

'Rotten job. Still, it has to be done.'

'Yes, sir.' He barely looked up.

'You've done very well. Skinner will be delighted when he sees how much has been done. Make sure to have a word with me before you finish.'

'Yes, sir. Thank you, sir.' Brack did not even straighten his back.

William hobbled out into his garden after almost a month of rest and warm, expecting to complain that the winter's work had not been done. The bare earth, where soon hardy annuals would grow, had been turned over in such immaculate furrows that it looked as if it had been ploughed, not dug. The wistful smell of burning leaves was still in the air but the previous day's bonfire had been carefully stamped out and the ash piled against the wall and protected by a wind break of recently cut logs.

'You've done a lot.' William poked at the logs with his stick.

'I'd like to have done more. There's plenty to do.'

'Did you cut the logs?'

'Why? Shouldn't I have done?'

'It's usually done by the boot-boy or one of the casual men. It's not gardener's work.'

He meant no offence, though his manner was made aggressive by anxiety. Offence was, however, taken.

'I am a casual man, Mr Skinner. I don't pretend to be a gardener.'

'Well, you've turned over those flower beds as if you were.' William wanted to make amends but Brack did not understand.

'You needn't worry. It'll all be ready for you when you come back. Better than when you left, I shouldn't wonder. The cold frames are falling to pieces. I'll mend them before I go. And the tools are in a right state. I thought gardeners looked after their tools. You can't close the shears. I've put some oil on the screw but it still won't budge. I'll clean the tools up ready for you.'

William Skinner straightened up with difficulty. Even when he had

263

pushed on his sticks with all his might, there was still a curve in his back. But he was no longer bent. 'You will not', he said, 'touch any of my tools. Ever.'

Brack's expression did not change. Indeed, it seemed that when he spoke only the long jaw moved whilst the rest of his face remained still. 'If I can't touch your spade, how can I dig the rest of your garden?'

'Of course you can use a spade.'

William was going on to explain that the spades were not his personally, that all the spades in the hut hung there for the use of the casual men who came in to lift potatoes or landscape the new gardens between the house and Hub Wood, that his own spade was clean and bright in his shed at Grove Cottage. But Brack spoke first. 'What about the rakes? Can I use the rakes? There's still leaves to be collected near that plantation.'

'Be sensible, man. Use what you need to use but don't touch anything that's none of your concern.'

He knew that he had chosen exactly the right words, and he believed that he had spoken them with authority. Brack touched his brow to signify acceptance of his instructions. But William was mortally afraid — afraid for his job in particular and afraid of Brack in general. As he turned and hobbled for home he could feel the menace follow him over the bridge that crossed Darfoulds Dyke. He did not even feel safe when he was back in his own chair in front of the Grove Cottage fire. Brack was lodging with Gerrard Knock next door.

The arrangement had not turned out to be the pleasure which the coachman had anticipated when it had been agreed that Brack could move in during his brief tenure as temporary gardener. Brack was an accommodating lodger who was always prepared to do more than half of the jobs which, they both knew, were really women's work, but he was not a talker and Knock had invited him there to talk. He was not even a listener of the quality for which his temporary landlord had hoped. He simply sat on a hard-back chair, silent and impassive except for the occasional grunt of agreement. He should have talked about horses. The offer had been made in the belief that he was knowledgeable on the subject and would want to exchange stories with a fellow enthusiast. Knock did not surrender his disappointment without a fight.

'I was thinking today . . .'

Brack showed no sign of having heard.

'. . . thinking of big Hervey. You know, Mr Hodding's big black gelding. I passed you when I was walking him out this morning.'

Brack made a noise which might have been no more than the

264

clearing of his throat. He was thinking but not thinking about Hervey, the big black gelding, for horses did not interest him. Shoeing interested him because he was a farrier by trade and he was proud of his craft. Racing interested him because it provided a chance to gamble and gambling was the preoccupation of his life. He made himself an authority on form, a student of stud books and an expert on the going at a dozen courses. But horses which were not registered at the Jockey Club were of no concern.

'William Skinner came to see me this morning,' Brack said.

'I didn't know he was out of bed. You know the horse I mean. You couldn't miss him. Great black gelding more than seventeen hands. Head like a bulldog.'

Brack was not to be deflected.

'Tell me about him, your man Skinner.'

'He's not my man.'

'Didn't you get him his job?'

'And he got me mine three years before that.'

'Well, he doesn't like me. That's sure enough.'

'Then you're the first one. I thought he liked everybody. He even likes his wife and anybody who likes her must be a saint.'

'I don't want any trouble. Tell him he's nothing to bother about with me.'

'It's only natural.'

'That's as maybe. But I've done nothing to encourage her. She hangs around without me asking. I'm not interested. Tell him, will you?'

'Lord bless us and save us! Are you talking about . . . ?'

'I'm talking about his daughter. She turns up wherever I go – kitchen garden, orchard, everywhere.'

'You mean little Aggie?'

'She's not so little. She's turned twenty. And she's a good-looker – I'll grant her that – but I'm not interested.'

'Good God, man. That's not what worries him. He thinks you're after his job.'

Brack was neither flummoxed nor amused by his mistake, only categoric in his denial.

'I'm no more after his job than I'm after his daughter. I couldn't afford to do it for long. If Robinson doesn't come up with something soon, I'm going to try the pit. Tell Skinner, will you?'

CHAPTER TWENTY

Out of the Nest

Brack left Henry Hodding's employment after two months' hard labour. William Skinner, who never received the reassuring message, was far from ready to resume his normal duties but he told them that he was 'on the mend' and began to grunt and groan his way around the garden. Ernest Skinner spent a month at home with his parents and then, having been reinstated at Hirst's woodyard, moved into his own house in Overend Road. He took with him almost all the fretwork bric-à-brac he had made as a present for his mother.

Skinner and Harthill, the partnership, had begun to prosper and Charlotte Harthill and Anne Skinner, the partners, decided that they could afford an addition to their family. They bought a mongrel bitch from the farmer who delivered their milk and began at once the frantic activity which was to occupy the small part of their time which could be spared from sewing: the protection of bitches on heat from the attacks of rapists and the guiles of seducers.

Only Agnes was less than contented. She rebelled against her inactivity and her father supported her in the rebellion.

'She's a woman now, Elizabeth love. It's only right that she should do something.'

'I'll not have her in service. And what else can she do?'

'There must be something. She reads enough. In the old days she could have helped in the school. But now . . .'

'She ought to keep house for Ernest. But she doesn't want it and I don't think he does either.'

'You'd think there'd be something she could do to help Anne.'

'Well, there isn't. Anne's not a charitable institution. She's got her own living to earn and I'll not have her held back.'

'We'll have to find something else. Because, if we don't, heaven knows what she'll find for herself. She's got her mind set on working. And we should encourage her. We'll not be here for ever. Sooner or later she'll have to earn something.'

'I shall ask Ernest,' said Elizabeth. 'He'll know what to do.'

Ernest knew what to do. Since Lucy's death, Ernest had become certain about everything. He had made a brief excursion into the world of excitement and romance, and it had ended in pain and guilt. He did not propose to travel such unpredictable roads again so he decided that his life would be guided by caution and certainty. He had no doubt what Agnes's future should be. She ought to work in one of the shops from which he had collected rent when he was Vincent Sweeting's assistant as well as his son-in-law. He would choose the shop himself and he would choose it with care.

After much thought and some investigation, he approached Mr Walter Ashton, Worksop's largest and most distinguished grocer, who – wishing to buy his freehold and not realising that Vincent Sweeting and his son-in-law were estranged – agreed at once. Ernest was quite sure that, at first, it would be best if Agnes worked for only half a day and suggested mornings. He could not have been blamed for not knowing that the bookkeeper – who also worked for only the first half of the day – was a bookmaker's runner.

Ashton was more than the 'grocer and provision merchant to the gentry' he claimed to be on the signboard along the full length of his double-fronted shop. He was confectioner, tea merchant, drysalter and occasional purveyor of dairy produce to aristocracy. There were days, in almost every week, when a servant from Welbeck Abbey called in to buy a pound of caramel creams or a box of crystallised fruit, and Mr Ashton felt no obligation to enquire if they were required above or below stairs.

In appearance, the shop certainly justified the strawberry-leaf coronet which was embossed on its windows to signify the Portlands' patronage. It had all the appendages of high class. A gallery, in which the more exotic merchandise was displayed, ran the full length of one side of the shop and was approached by a cast-iron spiral staircase. A cashier sat in a glass booth in a distant recess, beyond the chests of tea and the sacks of sugar, and received the cylinders of bill-wrapped money which whizzed towards him along overhead wires for return to the assistants at their counters bearing receipt-wrapped change. There were canisters of coffee beans as big as the pots which held the forty thieves, glass jars filled with sweets which demanded to be weighed out in the gleaming brass scales and, immediately behind the left-hand window, the butter counter.

The butter counter was the pride of the shop, not because of the quality of the produce – which was excellent – but because the performance of the man who sold it was extraordinary.

The shop assistant on the butter counter was less a grocer than a juggler. Each order was beaten into perfect shape – square, oblong or circular, according to the customer's taste – by wooden paddles which the butter magician held in each hand and manipulated like diabolo bats. The butter flew through the air above his head and between the bats until it was ready for wrapping. Then came his *pièce de résistance*. He tossed the pat particularly high whilst he picked up, from the marble top of his counter, the instrument with which the job was finished. It was a bat on which was embossed the letter A. Every pound of butter which left Ashton's grocery was monogrammed with the proprietor's initial. Casual passers-by stopped in the street to see Ashton's butter prepared. Farmers who made their own butter in ancient churns bought half-pounds of Lightly Salted from Ashton's just for the pleasure of seeing it weighed out. Half of the customers who visited the shabbily refined tea room under the cashier's eyrie lingered over cold second cups to see another pound fly through the air.

Ashton's was not the sort of shop with which Agnes was familiar but it was, her brother felt certain, a suitable establishment for the employment of his sister. It was arranged that she should dispense tea – a commodity she could handle without overtaxing her system, particularly since she promised to rest for an hour in Anne's workroom before she made the arduous thirty-minute journey back home.

Agnes waited, impatiently, to start her new life. She believed that on the day her job began she would be free.

It was during the last morning of her first week of liberty that Brack appeared in the shop and began a close examination of the currants, raisins, figs and dates. His deep interest in dried fruit lasted for several minutes. Then he was diverted by the shelves of cocoa and tobacco. The beverages being in close proximity, he was near enough to Agnes for her to attract his attention. When he seemed about to move on to glacé cherries and caramelised fruit, she was more frightened of missing the chance of renewing their acquaintance than she was of making a show of herself.

'Hello, Mr Brackenbury.' She thought he would be startled, but he nodded as if he had expected to see her there. 'Doing a bit of shopping?'

'I'm looking for Mr Jameson, Harry Jameson. Has he gone yet?'

Agnes had worked at Ashton's for less than a week and the book-keeper only came in on Wednesday and Friday mornings.

'Does he work in the yard at the back, a little fair man?'

'He's the bookkeeper. He comes in to do the accounts on Fridays.'

'I don't know him, Mr Brackenbury. Shall I go and ask for him?'

'No need for that.'

'Or perhaps I could serve you with something?'

268

'Thank you, no. It's a personal matter. Mr Jameson has something that belongs to me and I've come to get it, that's all.'

'Shall I tell him?'

'You can give him a note. Can you come into the tea room for a minute?'

Agnes beamed. 'I've finished. I finished just before you came in. I've just got to get my coat.'

'I'll see you in there. What would you like?'

'Tea, please. Tea and a toasted teacake.' The reply was immediate and instinctive, the result of a week of mornings spent just outside the tea room reading the bill-of-fare which was imprisoned inside a box-wood picture frame.

'Unless that's too much.'

'If I can catch Jameson, it will be the best investment I ever made. Quick as you can.'

Agnes did not even stop to fasten her coat. By the time she had joined Brack at his cast-iron table, he was in deep conversation with a small, bald man whose face was scarred by two blue weals which ran in parallel lines down the length of his left cheek. She hovered, nervous and ignored, for a few seconds and then perched on the edge of the empty chair.

'How long have you been waiting?' Brack asked.

'A fortnight,' said the bald man with the scarred face. 'He swore he'd bring it last Friday.'

'It's only a week with me but that's enough. More than enough.'

'Does the young lady know if he's here?'

'She doesn't know him.' Brack spoke as if Agnes was not there.

'We'll have to go round to the house.'

The waitress arrived and forced the two men formally to acknowledge Agnes's presence. Brack pushed the pots in her direction. It was taken for granted that she would pour the tea.

'This is Mr Bailey,' he said. 'He wants to see Mr Jameson too.'

Mr Bailey's brow furrowed as he struggled to think of something to say.

'I'm surprised that a young lady like you didn't choose an ice.' Leaving Agnes to ponder whether she had been paid a compliment or offered a reproof, he turned his back on her and continued the sort of conversation in which he felt at home.

'I heard you were back down pit. Why did you go to Shirebrook?'

'I needed the extra money.'

'You'll need it if the roof falls in.'

'That's all nonsense. Roof's as safe there as it is in any pit. That was all talk to get the wages up. It's having to use a fork I can't stand.

They only have to hear the noise of a shovel and they sack you. You cut tons of coal and because you leave it lying on the floor you don't get a penny. If only I could get hold of that bloody—'

When the waitress came with the bill, Brack gave Agnes a florin and told her to take it to the young lady at the table by the door. 'Whilst you're there, ask her if the bookkeeper's in today.'

Agnes returned in triumph to report what she had found out. Jameson was still in the office but he was not coming down. A pot of coffee and a piece of seed cake were to be sent up at one o'clock. Brack thanked her and asked a second favour – though it sounded more like an order than a request. She performed her second duty with the same willing enthusiasm with which she had discharged the first and returned, as instructed, with a piece of paper. Brack had hoped at least for smooth greaseproof from the cheese counter, but she brought rough manila from herbs and spices. Bailey snorted in amusement but Brack simply licked his stub of indelible pencil and began to write in a surprisingly elegant hand. 'I were promised today. Leaving now. Working 2 to 10. Back tomorrow same time. If I don't get it then, I'll be at Clowne on Sunday. Brack.' The bookmaker's runner was a sidesman at Clowne Parish Church. So Brack assumed that, spurred on by the fear of exposure, he would make sure that the winnings were available next day. He folded the paper double, then folded it twice more.

'What does it say?' asked Bailey.

'It said I'd be round at Clowne on Sunday if he didn't dish out tomorrow.'

'*We* would be round at Clowne,' Bailey corrected.

'No, just me. I wasn't sure you'd come. And it's no good making promises like that if you don't keep them.' He turned to Agnes. 'Put this into Mr Jameson's hand. Tell him I just came in and asked you to deliver it.'

'What if he asks about you?'

'He knows me. When he's read it, he won't ask nowt.'

Almost before Agnes had reached the tea-room door, Brack was on his feet and ready to leave without another word. But Bailey followed him between the tables. 'Good-looking young woman that. And sweet on you. Hangs on every word.'

Brack replied without turning round. 'I'm old enough to be her father.'

'Don't talk so daft. She's twenty if she's a day. You're nearer her age than mine.'

'Well, you're not sweet on me, are you?'

'I wouldn't miss the chance of that one if I were single.'

'I did nearly take her out once, just to spite her father. But then there was a cock fight at Shireoaks. I lost twelve shillings.'

'Well, I wouldn't complain if there was a well-set-up young woman who thought that the sun shone out of my backside. If that roof falls in one day, you'll need somebody to look after you. I'd think about it if I were you.'

'I've told you there's nowt wrong with that bloody roof. It's all talk.'

Brack did not think about the risk of the roof collapsing at Shirebrook pit. He had a letter in his back pocket which promised that, as soon as the Manor Stud and Stable was set up, he would be the farrier. The letter was signed by John Robinson himself and, although Brack was neither easily impressed nor instinctively trusting, the postscript had convinced him that the promise would be fulfilled. The postscript was an apology for the delay. Brack, who himself apologised rarely and then only with difficulty, had no doubt that if John Robinson was prepared so to demean himself he must be anxious to secure the services of the best racing farrier in the district. So he expected to be out of the pit within months. After that, whether the roof fell in or not would be no concern of his.

Although he did not think about a crushed leg or broken back, he did think about growing old. He was almost thirty and in the years since the end of his apprenticeship he had seen more of life's troubles than many men of sixty had endured. All the troubles had been of his own making and most of them had been caused by gambling. He had interfered with John Robinson's horse at Wetherby because he needed the bribe that he was offered to pay his debts. He had been dismissed from the Sheffield police force because he was seen at the racecourse in Doncaster when he was supposed to be in bed with influenza. He had stolen the scrap iron from the Whitwell blacksmith who employed him because he knew that with a pound in his pocket he could make a fortune playing dominoes against the Irish navvies who had come to sink a new pit shaft. The time had come to settle down. He would, of course, continue to place the occasional bet and he would sometimes play a hand at cards. But he was beginning to think of a more comfortable life than was possible in the cold room above the baker's shop in Shireoaks. He would like to come home to cabbage and boiled beef.

The idea of cabbage and boiled beef – combined with clean shirts, darned socks and regularly made beds – so appealed to him that he invited Agnes Skinner to a dance at the Miners' Welfare. To his astonishment she declined – declined with obvious regret, but declined

271

nevertheless. She had been promoted to confectionary and was weighing out sugared almonds when he asked her and he noticed how her hand shook when placing the brass weights on the scales but that was little compensation for rejection. When he visited the shop a month later – once more in pursuit of the bookkeeper and another unpaid debt – he chose not to speak to her. When Agnes saw him she wanted to run across the shop and explain that she had wanted to accept but had known that her mother would never have let her go. And she might have done it had a lady not asked for half a pound of treacle toffee. Agnes slammed so hard with her little steel hammer that jagged fragments flew at the customer like shrapnel.

It was another month before she saw him again. By that time she was an accomplished confectioner who could tip up a glass jar at an angle so exact that a quarter pound of peppermints would fall into the scales without one sweet bouncing on to the counter or falling to the floor. She was just as adroit with every form of jar – fat-bellied and leaning menacingly towards the customers like a Chinese mortar, squat and expansive in the style of a brick kiln, or so tall and elegant that it was impossible for even her small hand to reach inside. Success and freedom had made her calm and confident. The next time that Brack pushed his way through a crowded shop she did not hesitate to pull at his sleeve and tell him that the seam, under his armpit, had split. Brack was not in a good mood. The bookkeeper had again failed to pay his winnings.

'I know,' he said. 'It's been like that for a week.'

'It looks terrible. If you wait till I've finished, I'll sew it for you. It'll only take a minute.'

'I've told you. I know about it. It doesn't matter.'

'Suit yourself. But it makes you look like a tramp.' She grinned but the grin turned into a laugh, not a giggle. 'You look just like you did that day when you mended the gate. Like a gypsy.'

'I can't come back. I'm working.'

'Well, I can't do it now.'

'Can you do it on Sunday?'

'Where?'

'I'll walk past your house at eleven.'

Part of the reason why he agreed to do Agnes the favour was the kindness she had shown to him when first they had met but he also allowed her to sew his seam because he had developed a sudden desperate desire to be looked after. Her impertinent references to her mother's mistake about the gypsies almost hardened his heart but he was a proud man who took pains with his appearance and he could think of no other way of getting his jacket mended before he went to the boxing in Sheffield on Monday night. He wanted to be there smart, and in person, to collect his winnings.

Sunday morning was a blissful success. Agnes's announcement that she was 'slipping out for a breath of air' was greeted neither by suggestions that she should take her mother nor by demands that she should stay in and clean the house. Brack arrived on time, wearing his best suit and carrying the split jacket. They walked half a mile down the road and sat on the grass in Stubbin's Meadows whilst the sewing was done. Brack, who had trousers to patch, cuffs to turn and buttons to replace, asked her again if she would go with him to the Miners' Welfare Dance.

'M'mam would never let me go.'

'You're a grown woman.'

'I'm a grown woman who lives at home. She'd make my life a misery if I just went without asking her . . . I could go to the dance in Whitwell church hall.'

Brack hesitated only because his widowed mother had moved to Whitwell to live with her sister and he owed them both money. But he looked at Agnes's pink complexion and auburn curls and thought of the working trousers which he had torn on a nail.

'I'll see you at nine o'clock outside the church. Under the lychgate, if it's raining.'

He did not walk her home, for he played cards at noon each Sunday in a deserted hut down by the canal. Agnes watched him walk a few paces towards Worksop, then turned and ran towards Grove Cottage. It was not the giddy canter of an infatuated girl but the determined gallop of a woman who knew exactly how she was going to spend the rest of her life.

Agnes arrived home outwardly composed, but secretly enjoying an elation she had not previously experienced. Her feelings were in stark contrast with the mood of her family, who sat in the living room at one moment restless with apprehension and the next immobilised by despair. Henry Hodding had sent a message to warn William that he proposed to call on him that afternoon.

'After all this time,' said Elizabeth. 'And after all you've done for him. I think it's disgraceful.'

'We've got to admit it isn't as it should be. It's not like it was last year at this time. Brackenbury did the rough work, but since then I've done very little.'

'You won't say that to him when he comes, I hope.'

Ernest had become a man of affairs. He had invested Vincent Sweeting's gift in gilt-edged Chesterfield Corporation Stock which guaranteed a net yield of one per cent. Combined with the occupation of his own desk in the timber-yard office, the possession of capital reinforced his feelings of authority.

'Admit nothing. Tell him that you think the garden looks as well as it has ever done.'

'I can't say that because it's not true. Mr Hodding will think that I've gone . . . soft in the head as well as crippled, if I say that.'

'Say that you're getting it back to normal, bit by bit.' Elizabeth was keen to preserve her reputation for uncompromising probity. 'It is. I wouldn't ask you to say so otherwise. But it is.'

The gloom, although it had spread to Agnes, had not quite extinguished or obscured the glow which had warmed her ever since Brack had agreed to meet her at the Whitwell dance.

'We'll manage between us.'

'Easier said than done.' Nothing had happened that morning – or indeed for the last thirty years – to make her mother's heart leap up.

'I've got a job. Ernest's got a house. That's a bit of luck.'

'It is in these circumstances.'

'Anne's working.'

'We're not going to sponge off Anne.'

Why, Ernest wondered, was it Anne who always had to be protected? It was a daughter's duty to look after her sick and elderly parents. Yet his sister had done nothing. It was not as if she were married. For the first time, he thought how like a married woman . . . how like a married man . . . She took all the important decisions that were properly the husband's part. His reverie was interrupted by a knock at the front door.

'It's him,' said Elizabeth, pulling off her apron and stuffing it under one of the covers. 'I thought he'd be more considerate. The girl said three o'clock.'

'I'll leave you to it,' said Ernest, disappearing into the kitchen.

There was a second and more impatient knock.

'Shall I go, Mam?'

'Just wait one minute.' Elizabeth was, haphazardly, sticking extra pins into her hair in the vain hope that the disintegrating bun at the back of her neck would be stabilised by weight of numbers. William, bending with difficulty, was attempting to brush ashes and coal dust into a neat heap in one corner of the brass fender.

The door rattled for a third time.

'I'll let him in.' William took down the walking stick which he had hooked on to the mantelshelf and hobbled towards the door.

It was a maid – not the parlour maid who had been sent to act as herald of Mr Hodding's arrival, but a new girl from the kitchen with

274

blacking still on her hands and face from the morning assault on the grates and fireplaces. Her hand was already raised to rattle the knocker a fourth time.

'Does Mr Knock live here?'

'No, my girl, he does not. Mr Knock lives next door. But I doubt if he's in at this time on a Sunday morning.'

'I've got to find him straight away. Where is he?'

'What's your business with him?'

'It's the master. He's fallen off his horse. They think his back's broken. They daren't move him. Mr Knock's to go and get the doctor.'

CHAPTER TWENTY-ONE

Breaking Out

Henry Hodding had not broken his back. But he had fractured his pelvis and cracked several ribs. A bed was set up in his study and, in the moments when the pain was too great to allow concentration on his legal papers, he looked out of the window at a corner of his garden and felt reassured that at least one part of his establishment was prospering without his personal supervision. He never actually saw his gardener at work but the weeds he noticed one day had disappeared by the next, the edges of the beds and borders seemed to straighten themselves and, although he never heard the sound of shears, when the first shoots of spring began to blur its sharp line the privet hedge was silently trimmed. He was so pleased with the way in which the work was being done that he sent William Skinner a note congratulating him on both his industry and his recovery. When William showed it to his son, Ernest almost smiled.

Only the most favoured of Henry Hodding's clients were allowed to journey out to Darfoulds and be given audience at Harness Grove. The most regular visitor was John Robinson, whose ostensible business was the formation of a charitable trust to finance the building of almshouses dedicated to the memory of his son. Discussion of rules of management and eligibility for tenancies was usually brief for Henry Hodding regarded the examination of a trust deed as barely worth his attention, and John Robinson had created so many memorial institutions that he was an expert on their constitution. The discussion always worked its way slowly towards subjects in which the lawyer was genuinely interested. It would move from the disposal of the trust's income to the investments by which the income would be produced. From there it was an easy leap, via the prospect for Consols, the size of the national debt, the burdens heaped on the middle classes, to the cost of keeping horses. Once horses had trotted into the conversation, the two men settled down for the evening.

'I could have told you', said Henry Hodding, 'that the Duke would

276

prevaricate. Prevarication is in the blood. The turnpike. Land for the railways. Even the water supply. Took his father months to decide. Then months before he signed the papers. How long have you waited?'

'Nearly a year.'

Brack had waited just as long and with greater impatience. He had laboured for weeks in the Harness Grove garden and had sweated for months back in the Shirebrook pit – sustained by the hope that he would become a racing farrier again. He believed himself to be the best collier who had ever cut coal, and he certainly worked with a manic intention to fill more tubs in a day than had ever been filled before. For he needed the money and he enjoyed proving that he was the strongest and most determined man underground. But he was a blacksmith by trade and it was the thought of shoeing horses – so near to owners, trainers and jockeys that he was tipped a winner every day – which sustained him through the long shifts of hacking away at the coal face and clearing away the loose coal, not with a shovel but a fork.

He earned eight and sixpence a day, worked five shifts most weeks and, by the standards of most Derbyshire miners, was counted comfortably off. Only the strongest men went underground so often, and few of them could move sufficient coal to earn a bonus. Yet on most Wednesdays he was reduced to borrowing coppers from his workmates.

Brack's betting was based on a simple rule. As long as there was money in his pocket, he went on gambling. If, on Friday night, he beat the checkweighman at dominoes, he staked his winnings in a Worksop card school on Saturday. If he ended Saturday better off than he was when the day began, he wandered the countryside on Sunday looking for bare-knuckle boxing matches, cock fights and gypsy pony races. On Monday morning whatever he had left was handed to the local bookmaker with complicated messages about how his winnings were to be wagered again if there was 'anything to come'. On the rare occasions when he got to Tuesday with cash in hand, he took the day off from the pit and visited the nearest race course. Because he went on gambling for as long as he had any money left, he went on gambling until he had nothing. He was usually broke by Wednesday.

Whitwell Church held its dances on Wednesday evenings but it was a lucky week for Brack and he arrived outside the church at nine o'clock with fourpence in his pocket. It was drizzling and he stood in the cover of the lychgate with his jacket turned up against the cold night air. Agnes, it seemed, was late, so late that he began to believe that she had changed her mind. Then, just as he had decided to walk back to Shireoaks and spend threepence on a fish supper, she suddenly appeared – not along the road which he was anxiously watching but from the direction of the lighted church hall. She wore a pale-blue silk dress which suited neither her complexion nor the colour of her hair and it was clear, even to Brack's unpractised eye, that it had been made for an older and bigger woman. The sleeves were the right length and the hem brushed her instep at the point of fashionable respectability, but it sagged at the shoulders and the complicated embroidery on the bodice had clearly been designed as a tribute to middle age. To Brack none of that mattered. She had already been inside and he would not have to pay for her ticket.

'You haven't been in already?' It was a remarkably good imitation of genuine resentment.

'I had to. I couldn't wait at home until half-past eight. They'd have wanted to know why. I had to walk up with the maids from the house and wait for you here.'

'So you've been in there for nearly two hours.' It was no longer necessary to counterfeit the reproach in his voice, but it was lost on Agnes.

'And I've danced nearly every dance. I've got a book at home and I've been learning all the steps.'

'Whilst I've been stood out here in the rain.'

She gripped his arm. 'I'm sorry. I didn't know what time it was, not till the interval. I thought that you'd wait under the lychgate.'

They hurried together towards the welcome light of the open door. Agnes showed the torn cloakroom ticket as proof that she had already paid and Brack handed over two bright new pennies. To his relief the interval was not yet over.

'I should have said. I should have said before. I don't dance much.'

'I'll show you.' Agnes was already moving from foot to foot. 'Don't you dance at the Welfare? You invited me to the Welfare dance.'

'At the Welfare most of the men just stand at the back. There are some real fancy dancers. But mostly. . .'

'You stand at the back and drink.'

'Not me.' He was pushing his way towards a quiet corner. 'I'm not a drinker. Two half-pints at most.'

'I'd like a drink now.' Agnes settled down on a rickety orchestra chair and carefully arranged her faded dress to make sure that it was clear of the patch of floorboard that had been polished with french chalk. Brack fought his way back across the hall to the trestle table

278

near to the door where lemonade was on sale at a halfpenny a glass. To his relief there were a couple of familiar faces in the little knot of men which hovered half in and half out of the dance.

'Didn't think you were a dancer, Brack.' It was the lamp boy from Shirebrook pit.

'I'm not.' Brack pushed his way back towards Agnes, concentrating hard on not spilling the lemonade.

'Thought you could do anything,' said the lamp boy's father. Brack looked back over his shoulder and decided that the man was only trying to be friendly. The man who looked after the pit ponies gave him a friendly wink.

Brack swallowed the whole glass of lemonade in two gulps and Agnes took his thirst as a sign that he wanted to dance as soon as the three-piece band began to play. Her drink was still not finished when the pianist began to examine his music and the fiddler started to adjust the spotted silk handkerchief that protected his Sunday suit from the back of his battered violin. But she led Brack on to the dance floor and, after a moment of confusion, began to push him around the hall approximately in time to the music.

They did not sit down for an hour and Brack hated every minute. He was younger than half the men at the dance but he felt the oldest man in the hall. Worse, he felt the most ridiculous for, although he could not recognise the incompetence of others, every one of his own mistakes was marked by a little squeal from Agnes as he stepped on her toe or by the angry glare of couples who blamed him for a sudden collision.

Agnes wanted to exhibit her delight. She applauded when there was the briefest pause in the music and shouted 'Encore!' when she feared that the band was about to take another rest. At last she felt tired and Brack, prompted as much by relief as by chivalry, offered her a second glass of lemonade. She accepted with enthusiasm. 'And can I have a penny rock cake?'

He walked slowly towards the trestle table, thinking that if Agnes Skinner was sickly, as some people said, her condition affected neither her appetite nor her self-confidence. The lamp boy and his father were still by the door.

'So you can dance, then,' said the lamp boy.

Brack took the remaining penny out of his pocket. It too was mint new and, lying in the open palm of his hand, it shone in the gas light like gold. He smiled without humour at the lamp boy's father and spoke to the pony man. 'I'll toss you for it. Double or . . .'

The man pulled out a leather purse and, tipping its contents forward so that he could identify each copper, selected four ancient black farthings and covered the gleaming penny in Brack's palm. 'Give it me back on pay day. If you won, it would spoil my evening. If I won, it would spoil yours. Anyway, we don't gamble on church premises.'

Not at all abashed, Brack closed his fist and pushed to the front of the little crush of hot and breathless dancers which had formed in front of the trestle table.

Brack did not walk Agnes home, for Shireoaks was in the other direction, but he waited until the maids were ready to go back to Harness Grove and made sure that she went safely on her way in the giggling company. As they parted, the maids turned away in mock respect for their privacy.

'Next week?' To Agnes's delight, Brack spoke loud enough for the maids to hear.

'Nine o'clock again?'

'Can't get here earlier.'

'Then come straight in. I'll see you inside.'

They met in Whitwell on the next five Wednesdays. And on Sunday mornings, after church had ended and before the card schools had begun, they walked in Steetly Woods and along the footpaths and bridleways which joined Darfoulds to the surrounding farms and hamlets.

It took six weeks for him to persuade her to go to a dance at the Miners' Welfare. She began to relent only when he told her that the men at the pit had heard that he took her to the Whitwell dances and wondered if she was too good for the company of colliers. And she did not finally agree until he convinced her that the next dance was special. It was to mark the opening of the Miners' Welfare Branch Library at Rhodesia – two rows of desolate coal-company cottages which had been renamed to reflect the Empire's glory. Agnes told herself that if the dance was at a library it must be respectable – or at least her mother would believe it to be so.

They met at the Methodist chapel and Brack walked her to the Welfare, where he paid sixpence for two tickets. She wore, as always, the one dress that she thought suitable for such an occasion and at first saw no significance in the song which the miners whistled as she walked past them. It was 'Alice Blue Gown' and, after she had heard it blown tunelessly through a dozen pairs of pursed lips, she realised that they were making fun of her. Most of the miners had never seen her before. So Brack must have told them that she owned only one frock. 'I once had a gown, it was almost new.' Agnes remembered the words. 'It wore and it wore and it wore, till it went and it wasn't no more.' Suddenly she seemed to be surrounded by jeering miners with pint glasses in their hands, whose wives and sweethearts all wore brand-new dresses.

By biting her bottom lip and holding her breath she managed to walk out of the library hall without crying. But she was barely down the steps before the tears came. Once in the road, she ran towards Holme Car and the path home. Brack caught up with her before she had got twenty yards.

'What the bloody hell's the matter with you?'

'They were all laughing at me because of you.'

'Talk sense, woman. Who was laughing at you?'

'All your friends were, your butties as you call them. You heard them. "Alice Blue Gown". Only one dress and it's almost new. You must have told them that.'

'Don't be so bloody soft. Do you think I spend my time talking about you?'

It was, Agnes thought, exactly what her mother would have said in rather different language. 'Why did they do it, then?'

'They do it every Saturday. Any girl in a bright blue dress gets the same treatment. If there's a couple together, they whistle "Two Little Girls in Blue". They hope that somebody will be daft enough to run home crying. And tonight somebody fell for it. I'll have something to say to them at t'pit on Monday.'

'I don't believe you.'

'Suit yourself.'

'Well, I'm not going back there.'

'Nobody's asking you to. I wouldn't go back myself. I'd feel too bloody silly.'

'Don't you swear at me.'

They walked on in silence over the footbridge across the river and along the path which had been worn into the grass alongside the railway line. They walked slowly and it took them more than half an hour to get to Darfoulds but Agnes was still home long before the time that she had promised so they stood, uneasily, at the bottom of the steps which led up to Grove Cottage. It was early and the only possible reason for her to end their evening together was distaste for Brack's company and she longed to be with him more than anything else in the world. She leaned on the gate which he had offered to mend on the day of their first meeting. It swung on hinges which had rusted again since that fateful New Year. The hinges creaked.

'Shush,' said Brack. 'They'll hear us inside.'

'What?' Agnes was thinking of the dishevelled young man who had begged for two shillings. Now she knew why she had prised her money box open and thrown the florin out of the window.

'What?' The question rang out louder than before.

'Shush,' said Brack again and he leaned down and kissed her.

It was not the sort of kiss that her reading of Browning and Byron had led her to expect. But Brack had kissed her and she had no doubt that he would kiss her again.

As she waited and hoped, the front door of Gerrard Knock's cottage opened and, framed against the background of a fluttering candle, the little coachman began to hobble towards them. 'Mr Hodding's been down to see your dad. His second time out. I've just driven him back, less than twenty minutes since.' He spoke in an urgent whisper to emphasise the serious import of his message.

'Has he been sacked?' Agnes asked.

'I don't know. He said nowt to me.'

She touched Brack on the hand. 'Front gate of the house at eleven tomorrow.'

It was her command and he agreed to obey. Without looking back, she darted up the steps and through the front door, which was never locked. Her father was alone in the living room, bracing his shoulders and turning his head from side to side in the hope of easing the pain in his neck.

'Has Mr Hodding been down?'

'He has.' Her father affected calm.

'And what did he say?'

'What do you think he said?'

'I don't know.' She feared that she knew very well, but she dared not put it into words.

'He said that he was going to take on an assistant gardener to do the heavy work. He said that Ernest couldn't be expected to come up here and work at night for very much longer and that we'd been lucky to keep the secret for a week, let alone months. He knew all along. And he said that we should be proud of Ernest, that he was a credit to his upbringing and that he had nearly died on the kitchen floor in Harness Grove.'

Agnes had no doubt that Brack would marry her. She believed the kiss to be a compact, a proposal as binding as anything which might have been begged on bended knee or requested in a formal interview with her father. The assumption was absurd but it was also justified. Brack did not kiss girls for pleasure: he, too, regarded the kiss as a clear statement of his intentions.

For years he had thought of women as a handicap – lead weights which were hung on to his saddle to slow him down to the speed of his rivals. He had always considered that courtship would leave too little time for gambling and that marriage would prevent it altogether. But Agnes, by everything she had done from the moment she had thrown him the florin from her bedroom window, had behaved as if with her he could live like a single man and still enjoy the comforts that a wife existed to provide. He knew that in some things she would seek to rule him. She would want to dress him up and show him off and she would expect him to perform the little courtesies which made her feel loved and protected. But he had decided, long before the evening in the Miners' Welfare Library, that the hand-holding, the fetching and carrying would be a small and diminishing price to pay for a comfortable home and a warm bed.

The warm bed he thought of as little more than the chance to sleep in comfort. His mind regularly turned to what the colliers called tupping but he regarded it as something which, in youth, was got over quickly under a hedge or behind a wall so as to make no more than a brief interruption in life's serious pleasure. He had therefore confined his passion to ladies – often a good deal older than himself – who, for one reason or another, would make no demands upon him when the brief liaison was over. He accepted that, at some time in his life, a more permanent sexual relationship might be necessary for the production of children but, although he was belatedly prepared to consider the advantages of becoming a husband, he put the thought of becoming a father firmly out of his head. The object of marriage was to be looked after. A baby might deflect his wife from that essential task. When, during their Sunday walks, he pricked his finger on a bramble or caught his hand on a stinging nettle, he always cried out so loudly and complained for so long that Agnes told him he was a baby. Even if she had realised how apt that description was, she would still have wanted nothing else but to marry him.

They both took the future for granted – a year of unsuccessful attempts to save, a rented house in Worksop and then a quiet wedding. On the rare occasions when they talked about their lives together, it was always Brack's hopes and prospects they discussed. He told her how wonderful life would be when he became John Robinson's farrier and, though he never went into details about the ways in which it would be wonderful for her, she listened with unqualified delight. All she hoped for was to be with him. As long as he talked about sharing the years ahead, she did not care what her share of their life together would be. Although she rarely cried out when she was hurt or complained about inconvenience or lack of consideration, emotionally Agnes was a baby too.

Her first task was to create some sort of relationship between Brack and her family – all of whom disliked him for different reasons. To her mother he was the scoundrel who took her daughter on the scandalous cycle ride and to her father he was the impostor who had tried to take his job. To Ernest he was the criminal who had been warned off race courses for nobbling horses and to Anne he was a man. Although Brack seldom talked to Agnes about his intentions, her family discussed them interminably.

'Are you sure that he really means it?' asked Ernest, who had come to regard himself as an authority on the ways of the wicked world. 'Men like him . . .'

'Men like what?' asked Agnes amiably. One of the new features of the Skinners' Sunday conversations was her invincible serenity. However great the family's wrath, Agnes turned it away with a soft answer built on the confidence she felt about her love for Brack.

Ernest was not, however, prepared to be put off. 'Men with no roots, who've been cut off from their families. Men who keep changing jobs.'

William, who hated trouble, was sure that his daughter would say something about pots criticising kettles but to his relief, and Elizabeth Skinner's fury, Agnes simply replied, 'I'm going to be his family now. He won't cut himself off from me. I hope you're going to be his family too. That's why I want him to come here for tea.'

'Of course he can come for tea,' said William. 'This is your home and, if you want somebody to come for tea, they must come.'

'But not next Sunday,' Elizabeth added. 'Anne's coming next Sunday. They might not get on.' Agnes beamed and her mother, sensing how happy the promise had made her, decided that she was too happy for her own good. 'But don't think that we approve. We never will.'

'We'll not get married for at least a year, anyway, so you've got a year to get to know him. When you do, you'll like him. Everybody does.'

'I shan't like him until he gets a steady job.' Ernest congratulated himself on his cunning in not promising that he would like him even then.

For almost a year, Brack went to Grove Cottage on every Sunday when Anne was too busy to spend the afternoon at home. But Agnes's prediction that they would learn to like him did not come true. Elizabeth did not even try, and even when his sister announced that Brack was at last out of the pit, Ernest continued to mutter about getting and keeping a good steady job. William tried to be friendly, for he was friendly by nature, but the more he reached out to Brack, the more Brack backed away.

'Do you think he's shy?' he asked Elizabeth after one difficult afternoon when Brack had answered all his questions politely but failed to initiate any conversation of his own.

'I think he's peculiar.'

'A cold fish.' It was one of William's favourite expressions and his least favourite type of person.

'Calculating,' said Elizabeth. 'More calculating than cold. He's scheming all the time.'

Ernest was almost encouraged. Perhaps this Mr Brackenbury would scheme himself to some great success. 'Agnes was on again all afternoon about him meeting Anne.'

'Well, I don't want him here next Sunday. I've not seen Anne for three weeks.'

'They'll have to meet sooner or later.'

'Why will they? Nothing will come of it and we don't help Aggie by pretending that it will. He'll get tired of her soon enough.'

'That's wishful thinking. I tell you, they'll get married.'

'You say that . . .'

'And so does Aggie.'

'He never does.'

'That's because we make sure he doesn't. When he's here we talk about anything and everything except him and Agnes – the pit, politics, the garden, anything. Try him next Sunday.'

'Not when Anne's here.'

Anne's note, confirming her Sunday visit, ended with the news that she was bringing Lottie. The message filled her mother with despair. Elizabeth had planned to make another doomed attempt to recreate the intimacy of the years before Charlotte Harthill first attracted Anne's sympathy and then her love.

'If she's coming, I might as well let Agnes bring that man.'

Elizabeth could never bring herself to pronounce Brack's name but she always spoke of him with a bitterness which left no doubt about whom she meant. Brack was to be invited to punish Anne, to ensure that everybody's Sunday would be as unpleasant as Elizabeth's and to cause Lottie Harthill the greatest possible discomfort.

When Anne came to tea, preparations began on Friday with the boiling of ham and the pressing of tongue. On Saturday, cakes were baked, jellies, fruit trifles and blancmanges were made and Sunday morning was devoted to the preparation of fresh bread and warm scones. Sunday dinner was neglected – even when Ernest was there – for Sunday tea with Anne was not just a meal. It was a festival.

When Lottie came, Anne always behaved strangely. She echoed her friend's fear that she had no appetite. Then, whilst Charlotte Harthill nibbled on a sandwich, Anne ate more than anybody else explaining, as she leaned across the table to reach for another piece of pork pie, that she would force it down out of respect for her mother. When only the family sat round the table, they enjoyed inconsequential conversation which was only rarely disturbed by Ernest's profound pomposity. But when Lottie was there Anne talked all the time, contradicting her father, sneering at her brother and treating Agnes like a child. On the afternoon when she met Brack, she launched at once into a diatribe against horse-racing, which she denounced as cruel. When she paused to consume a pickled onion, Agnes spoke up.

'Brack and I are going to get married on Leger Day.'

A terrible stillness fell on the room, interrupted only by the sound of Anne swallowing a half-masticated onion. Then Lottie gave a little yelp of consternation which, since she was not a member of the family, Ernest resented as an intrusion.

'Why Leger Day? Why do you have to get married on a race day?' Elizabeth asked.

'That's the day we get one of Mr Robinson's houses,' Agnes told her. 'Renting it cheap as well. We want to go up to Whitwell and see the vicar. Will you come?'

'We're going to church at Steetly,' said her mother as if that little chapel was being abandoned and betrayed. But Agnes's high spirits were irrepressible.

'Walk on with us to Whitwell. Serve Steetly right for not marrying people.'

Ernest thought that a walk to Whitwell would be very nice, and Lottie, who had seemed in a trance, mused wistfully that she had not been to Whitwell for years. Anne, fearing an outbreak of independent thought, announced without explaining why that she must be home at six o'clock. Then Ernest – being a man of the world who had been married and knew how to behave – leaned across the table and offered Brack his hand.

'So that's it then, is it?'

'What do you mean, Mam?'

'I mean that it's all decided. No asking your father. No talking to me. We're just told.'

'I've tried to talk about it, Mam. But you wouldn't. I told you a year ago that we'd get married.'

'You told me you wanted to. And I knew you were moonstruck. But that's different. What about you, Mr Brackenbury? You've not said a word.'

'There's enough talking going on without me joining in.'

*

Brack's failure to avow eternal love across the fruitcake and over the jam tarts convinced Anne that the betrothal was a fantasy which existed only in her sister's imagination. But, although he sowed seeds of doubt in all the family's minds, the preparations went ahead as if the wedding were a certainty. Lottie measured Agnes for a dress. Bits and pieces of furniture were bought in salerooms. Mr Hodding was respectfully notified that his gardener's daughter was to wed.

Even when the banns were read in Whitwell, Anne remained convinced that Brack would change his mind or, more likely, just disappear, and when Henry Hodding offered the use of his carriage to convey William to the ceremony in comfort and Agnes in style, there was an argument about the wisdom of spreading the anticipated humiliation from the cottage up to the house. As the wedding day approached, Anne's suspicions spread to the whole family. By the morning of the ceremony they had convinced themselves that the only reason for its arrangement at three o'clock in the afternoon was Brack's determination to have a whole day in which to effect his escape. Much as they worried about the consequences of the marriage, they worried more about the shame of it not taking place.

At half-past two, the horse and cab arrived to carry Elizabeth and Ernest to Whitwell. They should have left at once but Elizabeth insisted on waiting until Agnes and her father were ready to follow them.

Gerrard Knock, without justification or permission, wore his best livery and his top-hat with the emerald cockade. He had trimmed the coach with white ribbon and tied roses in the horse's bridle. As William, bowed but elegant in a new suit, made his way carefully down the steps to the road, the coachman, holding his whip like a lance, stood to attention as he waited to hand Agnes into the coach. Her wedding dress was second hand but it was, according to Lottie, better than anything new that she could afford and it had been altered with more care than had been thought necessary for the blue party dress.

Ernest fretted all the way to Whitwell. He lived in perpetual fear of being late and in consequence kept his pocket watch ten minutes fast and usually arrived five minutes early. The hired cab pulled up outside the church at exactly three o'clock and the bride arrived three minutes later.

Before Gerrard Knock had time to climb down from his box Ernest had reappeared, agitated and gesticulating, in the church porch. He rushed down the path, waving his arms and crying out that the carriage door must not be opened.

'He's not here. He's not turned up. What did I tell you?'

Agnes's face appeared at the carriage window. 'It's not yet five past

287

three, Ern. He's just a bit late. Go back inside and look after Mam.'

'He won't come. The best man just told me. He went to Doncaster last night. You won't see hide nor hair of him today.'

'We'll just have to see which of us is right. Dad and I will just wait.'

'You go and look after your mam.' William was holding Agnes's hand. 'We'll be all right here for a bit.'

Ernest looked after his mam inside the church until three-fifteen. Then he reappeared and told his father, in desperation, 'It's no good. She won't stay inside any longer. She's coming out to take Agnes home.'

'I shan't go. You run back and tell her I shan't go. Tell her to wait till half past. If he's not here by then, we'll all go home.'

At half-past three, Gerrard Knock climbed down from his box and tethered the horse to one of the pillars of the lychgate. His little face barely reached as high as the carriage window.

'I don't like to say it. It's no good waiting any longer. It's what he does all the time. Goes to a big race and loses every penny. Then he's not seen for days.'

'Come on, love.' William turned to his daughter. 'Let's go home.'

CHAPTER TWENTY-TWO

Against the Odds

Agnes was not convinced so she sat, looking first at her lace-gloved hands and then at her silk-slippered feet. She had promised to leave at half-past three but she concentrated her energy on willing her father not to speak, her mother not to come out of the church and Brack to appear over the horizon. At a quarter to four her nerve snapped.

'You go,' she told her father. 'Mr Hodding might want the carriage. I'll stay here. You take Mam back home with Mr Knock and get warm. I'll wait in the gate till he comes.'

'Don't be silly, love. You can't stand there in your wedding dress. If you stay we'll all stay.'

'I'm staying here. I'm staying till he comes.'

It was then that the hansom cab appeared. Hansom cabs were a rare sight in Whitwell and it was reasonable enough to assume that it bore Brack to his wedding, but it approached at so slow a pace that Agnes could not believe that it carried the bridegroom, for she had expected him to come to her at a gallop like a Lochinvar made all the more eager by delay. But before the cab had drawn up to its agonisingly slow halt she saw Brack's face behind the moist window. She did not see it clearly and she feared that he would climb down dirty and dishevelled as she had seen him on that first day. But he stepped out immaculate in his best suit. He wore a bowler hat and, to Agnes's amazement, lilac gloves.

'You've done it this time, you bastard.' It was Brack's composure that had made Gerrard Knock lose his temper. 'That poor little girl . . . And him all screwed up with his back pains . . .'

'Has the vicar gone?'

'It'll be a bloody miracle if he hasn't. I'll tell you what—'

Brack did not wait for the end of the reproof but strode off down the church path.

'Don't get out yet.' Gerrard Knock shouted through the trap-door between coachman and passenger. But Agnes was already in the road

289

and helping her father down beside her. Ernest, red with exertion and embarrassment, ran down the path towards them.

'It's all right.' He spoke as if they had not taken part in the drama of Brack's arrival. 'Walked in as cool as a cucumber and said to the sidesman, "We're under starter's orders". Then the best man says—'

Agnes was already halfway to the church, a full pace ahead of her father.

'Help him,' Gerrard Knock commanded. 'His joints have set, sitting in the cold.' Ernest was just in time to catch the church door and stop it both striking William Skinner and clanging closed with a crash that would have sounded like the last trump.

'Who gives this woman to be married . . . ?'

William Skinner stood in the aisle, a yard behind the wrought-iron rails that Brack had forged and wondered why there were never proper weddings in his family. Why had his son and daughters thrown their lives away, instead of living, happy-ever-after, as he had once hoped? Plants, he thought. Plants. Plants and people are just the same. All you can expect from a rose bush is a rose. If Agnes has children, they – God help them – will be the same. They, too, will grow in stony ground.

When the service was over and the bride and groom turned to walk down the aisle, Agnes tried to hold her husband's hand but he pulled it away and she could do no more than take his arm like an elderly dowager at a christening.

'Where've you been?' she hissed. 'My dad thought you weren't coming.'

'I'll tell you in the carriage.'

'Tell me now.'

'I've been working.' He whispered out of the corner of his mouth, but one of the wedding guests heard and laughed.

They said no more until they were outside the church and then there was only time for groans and giggles as the maids from Harness Grove bombarded them with rice. Brack protected his new wife's face with his bowler hat and the more conventional onlookers all remarked on the old-world gentility of his lilac cotton gloves.

Inside Henry Hodding's carriage, Agnes did not even wait to wave or to pick the rice from her hair.

'Tell me now. Where have you been?'

'I've told you. I've been working.'

'I don't believe you.'

'Suit yourself.'

'Where have you been working?'

'I shod Mr Robinson's horse at Doncaster this morning. And I

290

earned an extra dollar. If I could get my hand into my pocket, I'd show you.'

'I still don't believe you.'

Brack pulled back the glove from his wrist. Beneath it there was a bandage. He lifted the edges and Agnes saw the suppurating corner of a red, raw burn. 'If I haven't been working, you better tell me where I got this.'

'Why didn't you say?'

'I meant to tell you after.'

'But why didn't you say before you went and did it?'

'Because you would have fussed. You'd have told me not to go. If it hadn't been for the accident I would have been at Whitwell at three and I would have told you after. If the fire basket hadn't broken, I wouldn't have burned me hand and I'd have had the shoes on in half the time. And if I hadn't missed the train, I would have been at Whitwell by three. I was just unlucky.'

'Does your hand hurt? It looks awful.'

'Not now. It did at first, a bit. Not now.'

'Let's hope your bad luck hasn't lasted all day.' Agnes had moved close to her husband. Because she dared not touch his hand she put hers on his knee.

'Hope not. I put two bob each way on Mr Robinson's horse and I had to leave before the race. Funny feeling, not knowing if you've won or lost.'

Brack lost his bet but for the first week of his marriage he had no doubt that the luck which had deserted him in Doncaster had returned. There was no honeymoon, for honeymoons were not the habit of his class, but there were three days alone with Agnes in their new home, during which he discovered that making love to his own wife in his own bed was an altogether superior experience to cold copulation with a housemaid behind the Miners' Welfare, not least since it could be accompanied by little luxuries. Most of them involved Agnes running up and down stairs with food and drink.

His good fortune persisted until the following Sunday afternoon when he won two pounds in the card school and walked back to his new home thinking how he could have turned it into two hundred by backing all of the winning horses at Worcester on the following day. He toyed briefly with the idea of telling Mr Robinson that he was ill and taking the day off. Then he decided that the odds of discovery were too great even for him to risk. Somebody – probably the bookmaker he bankrupted – would split on him. The bets would have to be laid in Ashton's High-Class Grocers.

Tea was waiting for him. It was only a poor imitation of a Grove Cottage tea and it was considerably less appetising than it had been two hours before when it had first been set out on the table. The thin slices of bread and butter had dried and curled at the edges and the meat jelly between the pork and the pie crust had started to melt and spread across the plate from the cut that Agnes had made when she had her own tea at six o'clock. Brack did not seem to mind. He sat down, not so much at the table as by its side, with his long legs crossed and one elbow on the white cloth. He grunted a sort of greeting, cut a piece of pie and ate it out of his hand. Then he took the *Sporting Life* out of his pocket and spread it over the table, covering the bowl of trifle, the cheese dish and the jar of pickles. 'Is there any tea?'

'Are you all right?'

'Of course I am. But I'd be better with a pot of tea.'

'I've been worried to death.'

'Pour it out, love. I'm dying for a drink.'

'I'm waiting for it to mash. I was worried about you.'

'Worried about what?' He was marking the Worcester race card.

'Because you're two hours late. You should have been home at five.'

He put down his pencil and looked at her for the first time since he had got home. Then he picked up his cup and saucer and held it towards her. She poured the tea and watched as he added milk and stirred in sugar without putting the cup back on the table. He gulped down a long noisy drink before he spoke again.

'Not late.' He spoke very slowly. 'Not late. There's no time when I should have been here. This isn't work. It's home. I come and go here as I please. Not late.'

As he spoke he leaned towards her and cupped his hand round the back of her neck. She expected him to pull her face towards his but he did no more than gently increase the pressure. Although she could feel his fingers and thumb pressing into the flesh under her jawbone, there was no pain. Yet all that Agnes could think of was poachers silently killing the rabbits they had trapped – killing them by squeezing the base of the skulls until their spines snapped.

'Pour us another cup of tea, love.'

He spent the next hour writing complicated instructions on the back of an envelope. As he struggled to form the necessarily small letters, he licked the point of his pencil and intoned strange incantations. '. . . anything to come, Ashanti Warrior to win in the two-thirty . . . anything to come, New Century in the three o'clock.'

The writing done, he emptied his back pocket on to the table. Agnes thought how Elizabeth would have shuddered to see the broken matchsticks, fluff and particles of indefinable dirt spread across the cloth with the silver and copper coins. She was astounded by how much money he had and watched, fascinated, as he counted out two pounds and put it in the envelope. A shilling and two sixpenny pieces were left on the table.

'Careful it doesn't spill.' He handed the heavy package to his wife. 'Take it t'shop tomorrow, will you, and give it to that bookkeeper.'

'You don't mean that you're going to gamble away all that money? It's more than I can earn in a fortnight.'

'If I win, I'll have more than you can earn in five years.'

'But you won't win. You're throwing it away. When I think of all the things we need.'

Brack reached out and cupped his wife's head in his hand again. As his fingers pressed into her neck for the second time, he pulled her towards him until their faces almost touched. When he was so near that she could feel his breath, he tightened his grip. For a moment, she thought that she would faint with the pain. Then he let her go and spoke very slowly and very quietly.

'What I do with my money is my business. We'll get on a lot better if that's understood. Now do as you're told. You take that envelope and give it to that Mr Jameson.'

Harry Jameson took the envelope without looking at it and put it in his pocket so quickly that no one in the shop noticed the transaction. When Agnes asked for a receipt, he gave her the huge wink of a man who appreciates a good joke.

Next morning when Mr Jameson came into the shop, he pretended to examine the lemon drops whilst he renewed his acquaintance with the young Mrs Brackenbury, who, he had decided, was a wag.

'Nothing to pay. So I shan't need a receipt.'

She did not smile.

'You hardly expected it. Not from an accumulator. Thank God I've never had one come up. Not very likely, is it? Winner in all six races! Cor blimey Charlie.' He passed on to keep his respectable books.

It was more than a year before Brack had another big win at the Sunday card school and dreamed again of turning it into a fortune. Agnes, still luxuriating in the pleasure of Saturday nights, never asked him about the success of his Sunday afternoons. But, whenever he concentrated intently on the *Sporting Life*, she prayed that he would not ask her to take another accumulator to Harry Jameson.

The royal visit to Worksop and Retford, though no more than a brief diversion on a journey north, was anticipated by the burghers of those loyal towns with a proud enthusiasm which would not have been

293

inappropriate to the announcement that the court was moving permanently to north Nottingham. For years both towns had felt intentionally slighted by the house of Saxe-Coburg-Gotha. Edward – both as Prince of Wales and as King – had been a regular visitor to the area, but he had seen no more of the district than the road between Lord Saville's seat at Rufford Abbey and the Doncaster race course. In the autumn of 1905, the Court Circular announced that on 12 December the great wrong was to be righted.

In Worksop, stands were erected along the royal route and places were allocated to local schools and the pensioners in Mr John Robinson's almshouses. Mr Robinson himself paid for a triumphal arch of autumn flowers which was built across Sparken Hill, where the procession turned off through the Lion Gates into Welbeck Park. It was crowned with a mighty E made entirely of golden chrysanthemums. The *Worksop Guardian* predicted that the royal route would be lined with loyal citizens waving the paper Union Jacks that it offered to its readers at a nominal price.

Agnes Brackenbury was determined to be amongst them and entirely to her surprise Anne Skinner and Lottie Harthill announced their intention of closing their business for the afternoon and joining her on the pavement edge. Such was Anne's enthusiasm that she asked Agnes if her husband could be persuaded to approach John Robinson with the suggestion that their parents be allocated places in one of his stands. He refused. It was then that Ernest had his brilliant idea.

Hirst's woodyard overlooked the station at which the Great Eastern Royal Saloon was to draw up at a quarter-past three on the day of the visit. During that time the Mayor and town clerk of Mansfield would be presented to Their Majesties, an arrangement facilitated by Ernest, who had supervised the removal of a fence which separated the platform from the woodyard so as to accommodate the band of the 4th Notts and Derbyshire Regiment. After some persuasion, Mr Arnold Hirst had agreed that Ernest could put chairs out on the flat roof of the saw shop and use it as a grandstand from which to watch the great event.

'It won't be as good as Worksop with the carriages and yeomanry and all that, but Dad will be able to sit down and Mam won't think that everybody's looking at her.'

'They'll never go,' said Agnes, desperate not to miss the opportunity to see the King and Queen in comfort. 'Not all the way out to Retford.'

'Let's try.' Ernest, by his own initiative and efforts, had obtained for himself the prospect of a half-day's privileged status. For once the whole world (or at least a substantial part of Retford and Worksop) would wish that they could do what he was doing. He did not intend to give up his moment's superiority without a fight.

'I'd like to go,' said William. 'If I can manage it. Tell me again about the stairs.'

Ernest explained that the roof was easily accessible from his office window and that the window was high and wide, the sill low and that stepping out of it would be no more difficult than stepping into the zinc bath his father had not been able to use for more than a year.

'I'll come, if your mother will.' He turned to his wife. 'Aggie will tell you what's happening. And you'll hear the band. It'll be a day—'

'You've no need to go on about it. I'll come. I've always wished that I'd gone to that opening of the Lincoln arboretum. Do you know that your father built it, Ernest? There was a great march with the Mayor and the Bishop and your father had a special place to stand . . .'

'We'll have a special place this time, all of us.' William was overcome by his wife's unexpected tribute.

The great day was bright and cloudless, and all over Worksop men, women and children who, out of sheer exuberance, had put on their Sunday clothes as soon as they got up began to worry about them becoming dirty or damaged between breakfast and the King's arrival. Then a special edition of the *Worksop Guardian* reported the awful news that the monarch had been struck down by some mysterious bowel disorder. Anguish and despair swept through the town until, one by one, Edward's desolate subjects read in the Stop Press column that Queen Alexandra was to make the visit alone. Had that been the first news they received, they would have thought the presence of the consort little consolation for the absence of the King. But, having feared that breeze flapped bunting in vain, most people agreed that a queen was better than nothing. John Robinson typified the indomitable spirit by personally supervising the conversion of the chrysanthemum E, on top of the arch of flowers, to an A.

Agnes – having cooked the breakfast, cleared out the grate, laid the fire for the evening, filled the copper in preparation for a disgracefully late day's washing on her return and peeled the potatoes to make sure that supper was ready at its usual time – left home for her morning's work before news of the King's illness was abroad in the town. Just as he was leaving for Worksop Manor and the Robinson Stable, Brack had given her a sealed envelope. It was covered in cryptic messages and weighed so heavy in her hand that she calculated its contents to be at least two pounds in copper which, she had no doubt, was intended for another doomed accumulator.

At Hirst's woodyard it took William ten agonising minutes to climb the stairs and, with Agnes pushing and Ernest pulling, another five to negotiate the window sill. He dropped exhausted into his chair just as the band struck up the national anthem and steam from the royal train curled up into the sky above the houses of East Retford. The Mayor and the town clerk took up their positions at the edge of the platform. Behind them, the aldermen and borough councillors formed up in parade-ground fashion. Ernest, who had an eye for such things, noticed with surprise that there was no red carpet on the platform.

The Great Eastern Royal Saloon, distinguished from the other carriages only by the two extra lines of gold piping on its maroon livery, stopped exactly opposite the welcoming party and the spectators on the roof saw the top of a compartment door open and the plume of a high busby bob as its bearer bent to alight. Two little girls, both carrying flowers, emerged from the station manager's office and disappeared between the welcoming party and the train. The band played the national anthem for the second time and the Great Eastern Royal Saloon glided slowly on its way to Worksop.

'Is that it, then?' Anne could not believe that it was all over.

'Nobody told me that she wouldn't get out of the train. They just said she was coming. I thought at least she'd get out and walk about the platform.' Ernest was almost in tears.

'What happened, then?' Elizabeth did not realise that nothing had been described to her because there was nothing to describe.

'She stayed in the train, Mam.' Agnes sounded scarcely disappointed. 'It was all over in a couple of minutes. But I'm glad we came. It's been a lovely day altogether.'

The royal train arrived in Worksop at exactly twenty-six minutes to four and Queen Alexandra and Princess Victoria stepped out on to the platform. As they took their seats in the Duke of Portland's postilion-drawn carriage the guard of honour sprang to attention and the escort – a hundred officers and men of the Sherwood Rangers Imperial Yeomanry – wheeled into position for the trot through the town.

The whole route to Welbeck Abbey was decorated with flags and flowers and the pavements were packed. In its report of the great day, the *Worksop Guardian* boasted that every man, woman and child had enjoyed a perfect view of the Queen and her daughter and that special arrangements had been made to ensure that all the old and infirm, whether or not they were residents in the local almshouses, were able to watch in comfort and safety.

John Robinson, having completed the necessary alterations to his arch of flowers, told his men that they were free to join him at the corner of Bridge Street and Watson Road where his own private stand had been erected under the archway which led into Ashton's yard. Brack walked back into Nottingham with an intentionally obvious reluctance and, when the other men scrambled for the seats behind the Robinson family, hung about, hands in pockets, outside the grocery so that everybody would understand that he was no more impressed by queens and princesses than he was by brewers, launderers and racehorse owners. As the clatter of the Yeomanry foretold the arrival of the royal procession, the shop assistants – pulling off their aprons and dusting flour from their clothes – rushed out into the street. Harry Jameson, still wearing his sleeve protectors, panted behind them. When he saw Brack he lost all interest in the royal family.

'I didn't expect to see you.'

'I didn't expect to be here.'

'I bet you didn't. But now you are, what about it?'

'What about what?'

'You know bloody well what I mean. The three quid you owe me. You make enough fuss about your winnings.'

'Haven't you got it?'

'Don't try that with me. You know bloody well I haven't.'

'I sent it with Agnes this morning. Didn't she give it to you?'

Harry Jameson turned his attention to the disappearing procession. Concentrating on the hindquarters of the last two Yeomanry horses, he spoke to Brack over his shoulder.

'I'm not buggering about any more. By the end of the week or you know what.'

297

CHAPTER TWENTY-THREE

Shapes and Sizes

Brack liked to eat his breakfast in silence. Sometimes he read the *Sporting Life*. Occasionally he turned the pages of the *Worksop Guardian*. But usually he stared into the middle distance and chewed methodically on the streaky bacon with which he began each day. When the conventionally edible parts of each rasher had been carefully cut into four precise pieces, speared on his fork between egg and tomato and washed down with sweet, strong tea, he turned to the rind which remained. He sucked each strip until only the hard, hairy skin was left. The sight always reminded Agnes of a giant starling consuming a worm.

If Agnes spoke during the early-morning ritual, Brack first ignored her and if she spoke a second time made a noise intended to indicate his wish not to be disturbed. On rare occasions when she persisted, he told her that he expected 'a bit of peace and quiet in my own home'. The admonitions rarely needed to progress past the grunt but there were mornings when Agnes could not contain her enthusiasm for trivial conversation.

'We must have had a better view than anyone.'

Brack looked at his wife over his paper. She took his silence as encouragement to continue.

'We had such a lovely day. I do wish you'd been there.'

To Agnes's delight, Brack carefully folded his newspaper and laid it down on the table. She noticed that one corner rested on the butter and that a greasy stain gradually engulfed the advertisement for 'H. W. Fox. Turnip, Swede, Mustard and Cole Seed Merchant, Market Place, Worksop', which was printed alongside the masthead. At last, he spoke. 'I didn't miss her, I saw her in Worksop.'

'Why didn't you say? Why didn't you say when I talked to you about it last night?'

'There would have been too much fuss. I knew that you were making it up when you went on about her brown dress.'

'I did see her. I did. I saw her on Retford station.'

'Then she changed her frock before she got to Worksop. She changed in ten minutes. When I saw her, it was blue.'

'So you let me make a fool of myself . . .'

'I let you tell a pack of lies. I didn't want you blubbering and inventing more daft stories. I wanted my tea on the table. It was late as it was.'

'I saw the top of her head. I did see that. I saw her hat, her brown hat.' Agnes gambled on her husband not remembering the details.

'Well, I saw all of her in Bridge Street.'

'What were you doing there? You were supposed to be at work.'

'I was working. Otherwise I wouldn't have bothered. I got marched off by Mr Robinson after we'd rebuilt that bloody stupid arch on Sparken Hill.'

'I'm glad you saw her, anyway.'

'I was too busy to take much notice. Too busy talking.'

His wife, fear mixed with relief, was concentrating on buttering a slice of bread. She took bread and butter seriously and she became quickly preoccupied with making sure that a corner of crust was not left naked. She did not take Brack's bait, so he fished for her again. 'I was too busy talking to your Mr Jameson.'

Agnes's head jerked up so quickly that he knew she was caught.

'You know who I mean?'

''Course I do. The bookkeeper at our shop.'

'The bookies' runner.' It was the only thing that Agnes had not wanted him to say. 'The man you gave the money to yesterday. You did give it to him?'

'First thing yesterday. As soon as he came in.'

'What did he say?'

'Same thing as last time. A joke about not giving receipts. Said he wouldn't want one from you if you won. And he laughed.'

Brack hit her across the side of the head with the flat of his hand. He did not strike her hard and it was surprise as much as the weight of the blow which knocked her from the chair to the floor. As she fell she clutched at the table. But she managed only to catch hold of the cloth and pull it on top of her with a crash of cutlery and a clatter of broken crockery. She lay on the pegged rug in front of the fire and began to whimper. The tea, which had drenched her as the teapot fell from the table, was no more than warm and the plate which had glanced off her forehead as it fell to the floor had done no more serious damage than deposit a crust of bread in her hair but she feared that she had been cut and scalded. As she reached up to feel what she imagined to be a gash on her brow, her hand brushed against the

299

sharp edge of the broken milk jug, and she cried out, sure that she had slashed her palm.

Brack watched without speaking as she struggled to her knees. As she pulled herself up on the table he asked her, almost casually, 'How much is left?'

She half fell on to the chair and, head in hands, began to cry.

'I asked you, how much is left?' Brack leaned forward and shook her by the shoulder. 'I'll not ask you again. How much is left? Did you spend it all yesterday when you were supposed to be in Retford?'

'It's all there. I didn't even open the envelope.'

'Then where is it?'

'Down the back of the sofa.'

The crying had turned to sobs. She lay sprawled across the bare tabletop with her head buried in her arms and coughed and spluttered as she choked on her tears. Brack brushed past her as he walked over to the sofa. He tried to push his hand between the back and the seat, but he could do no more than squeeze the tips of his fingers into the join. He turned and gripped her shoulders. 'If you're lying again . . .'

'I've not lied. I've not. Sit on it. Then you'll get inside.'

Agnes was sobbing no longer. Terror had driven out hysteria. She knew that she had hidden the money down between the springs, but she was suddenly overcome with the irrational fear that it was no longer there. 'Sit on it and you'll get your hand inside.'

Brack put one knee on the sofa and pressed down. Then he tried again to slide his hand between back and seat. After a struggle it disappeared and he pushed on until his sleeve rolled up almost to his elbow. He ran his fingers along the hessian at the bottom of the sofa as he searched with increasing urgency. His thumb caught on a nail which stuck out from one of the laths. He cursed and searched on. Suddenly, he let out a great sigh of satisfaction. 'Good job for you that it's here.'

It was obvious that the envelope had not been opened but he picked up a knife from the floor, pushed it under the flap and cut a jagged, greasy gap along the back. Then he tipped the contents on to the tabletop. Agnes watched as he counted the coins. When he had made sure that every coin was there, he turned again to his wife.

'Are you going to work today or not?'

Agnes bit her lip. She knew that, if she spoke, she would start to cry again.

'Because, if you are, you'd better start cleaning up this mess. And you'll need a bit of cleaning up yourself. There's butter in your hair and tea-leaves all over your frock.'

She bent down to start picking up what was left of the breakfast pots and her husband slapped her on the bottom. Agnes knew that his only intention was to humiliate her.

'I want you to do a little job for me.' He did not wait for her to ask what it was. 'I want you to take this envelope to Mr Jameson. It's what I owe him. It's my losings.'

'He doesn't come in today.' She wiped her eyes on her apron. 'He doesn't come in till Friday.'

'You look after it, anyway. Look after it till then. I'm sure you can be trusted. Hide it somewhere. You're good at that. I've left the envelope open. I know I can trust you to give him every penny safe and sound.'

That afternoon, Agnes went home to Grove Cottage. She intended to tell her troubles to her mother. But, before she could begin, her mother began to describe troubles of her own. 'It's your dad, he can hardly move in the morning. He's trying to work but he can hardly move.'

'Will he have to give up the job?'

'I wish he would. He could finish tomorrow if he wanted to. Mr Hodding's promised him a pension and we can stay in the house. Gardeners don't want to live in these days. But you know how stubborn he is.'

'Perhaps that's just as well. Perhaps if he gave in . . .'

'You haven't seen the pain he's in. It's terrible to watch.'

'What does the doctor say, Mam?'

'He says it'll never kill him. But I'm not so sure. A man can't go on suffering pain like that day after day. I'm frightened, Agnes. I never thought that the day would come when I'd admit it, but I am. Frightened for him and frightened for me.'

'It won't come to that, Mam. But, if it did, we'd look after you.'

'You don't understand. I don't mean I'm afraid of the workhouse or living on my own. It's just that I can't imagine living without your father. I've got used to him. It's being blind, I suppose. It's him I want to look after me. Not that anyone else would bother.'

'We would, Mam.'

'We. Who's we? Not your sister. She's not interested in us any more. I hadn't seen her for six weeks before yesterday.'

'She was here two—'

'She's all caught up in that Lottie Harthill. I've never seen two young women so friendly.'

'It's the business, Mam. That's all. Anne's doing what you always wanted, that's all. She's getting on in the world. It was just like old times yesterday. All of us together. Ernest was so—'

'And poor Ernest. He can't look after anybody.'

301

'Ernest's all right. Good steady job. House of his own. Money in the bank. I wish I was so well off.'

'Don't tell me you've got troubles.' Elizabeth spoke in a way which made the idea seem incredible. 'I was only saying to your dad last night that at least you were settled. And he tried to stop you! Now you have a little place in Newgate Street.'

'It's not much, Mam.'

'We can't all have big houses given to us like Ernest did. I can think of dozens of young women who'd give the world for what you've got. Your husband's got a good job – just as good as Ernest's, even though he does get his hands dirty. Nothing wrong with that . . .'

It was the approval of dirty hands which let Agnes know that her mother was lying. Elizabeth would be contemptuous of manual work until she died. Agnes could not imagine when her mother had suddenly decided to affect an unconvincing sympathy with the disadvantaged and the dispossessed.

'As long as you keep your health and don't start a family too early and lose those few shillings that you earn from Ashton's, you'll be all right. I told your dad last night, "At least we don't have to worry about Aggie," and he agreed. It's a miracle. You once being so delicate. Do you know we thought you'd not live to be a grown woman?'

'Where is he? Up at the house?'

'He's in bed. He has a sleep in the afternoon most days. You can take him a cup of tea and keep him amused like you used to.'

Her father, propped up against his pillows, looked so warm and comfortable that it was impossible not to envy him the advantages of being an invalid.

'Well, this is an honour. Didn't expect to see you two days in a row. Nothing wrong is there?'

She could not bring herself to tell him. There was no doubt in her mind about how he would respond: he would be entirely sympathetic and wholly on her side; he would offer what he believed to be useful advice and try, to the full extent of his limited ability, to help her. But she could not bring herself to disturb the strange tranquillity of the airless room. The soft pillows, the patchwork quilt – even the walking stick propped up by the bed to be used for rapping on the floor when her father wanted help, refreshment or company – all conspired against describing the harsh reality of her marriage.

'I'm fine, Dad. But I'm worried about Mam.'

As soon as she said it, Agnes regretted having risked worrying her father by blurting out the first words which came into her head. She need not have worried.

'Your mother's fine. Never enjoyed herself so much in her whole life.'

Sympathy for her father began to evaporate. 'But all this trailing up and down stairs. She's not a young woman. And being blind . . .'

'I know it's hard work. She likes me being dependent on her. She certainly doesn't want me to fuss and ask her how she is. Sometimes I'd like to give her a hand in the house but I know that she wouldn't let me. It's best to let her feel a martyr.'

'But don't you want her to know that you worry about her? If she thinks that you don't care, she'll think that you don't love her.'

'Your mother hasn't believed that I love her for more than thirty years and it's too late to start convincing her now.'

'She's worried about losing you.'

Agnes no longer cared about the pain she caused her father.

'That does her good as well. Me dying will be the last thorn in her crown. All her life's been a sacrifice. This is not the right time to change all that.'

'Don't you want her to think that you love her?'

'I want her to think what keeps her happy. If she manages best on bitterness and regret, it wouldn't be right to try and end the one thing she relies on.'

'But you do love her?'

'If you were a bit older and a bit wiser, you wouldn't have to ask. Love comes in a lot of different shapes and sizes. If you're lucky you catch the sort that they write about in story books. One man and one woman. Can't stand a moment out of each other's sight. That's the best sort and it's the easiest sort. Take my word for it. But sometimes love isn't that easy. I hope you never find out what I mean.'

'I'm very happy.'

'I'm pleased to hear it. Your mother was against you marrying him. If he started beating you, I'd be held responsible.' He did not laugh at the joke.

'Why do you say that?'

'Because I'm not stupid and I'm not blind like your poor mother. I know men like him and I can see the mark on your face. You didn't trail up here two days running without some reason. Do you want to talk about it?'

Agnes shook her head.

'I won't tell your mother – unless you want to leave him and come back here.'

'What if I did?'

'I'm old-fashioned. I think a woman's place is with her husband for better or worse. That's what I believe. And I've told you, love

303

comes in different shapes and sizes. Some wouldn't agree, but I reckon that you'd be happier with him – whatever he does – than leaving him. Your mother wouldn't understand. She'd weigh up respectability against black eyes. At first she'd say you've got to stay for fear of what the neighbours would think. Then she'd say you'd got to leave because of the pain and the indignity.'

'And you . . . ?'

'I wouldn't say stay for respectability's sake and I wouldn't say leave because of dignity. If you love him, struggle on somehow. If you don't, be off and keep house for Ernest. You're lucky. You've got somewhere to go. Most women who get beaten haven't.'

'I'm going to stay,' she said. 'Stay put for a bit, anyway, and see what happens.'

'And don't let anyone else poke their noses into your business – your mam, Ernest, Anne. Especially Anne. Me neither, for that matter. You better go downstairs. Your mother will wonder what we're talking about.'

'You spent a long time with your dad.' Elizabeth sounded both suspicious and resentful.

'We didn't talk about anything much,' said Agnes. 'Daft little things. Nothing that you'd think very interesting.'

She meant it.

When Anne Skinner had a problem she usually consulted her brother. She rarely took his advice for she only thought of him as a sounding board against which her own ideas could be tested. Lottie always interrupted with silly questions but Ernest sat still and silent – his brow furrowed with the effort of concentration – and then, when he was sure that she had finished, he warned her to be careful. The tone of the discussion was set, and the nature of the relationship revealed, by the way in which it was arranged: when Anne Skinner had a problem she did not go to Overend Road to see her brother, she sent him a message saying that he must come to her.

Whenever the summons came, he always assumed that he was to be told of a family tragedy, so when he got home and found the instantly recognisable note lying on the coconut mat beneath his letter box, he rushed straight out without changing his work clothes. Only rarely was his conversation with his sister anything except an anticlimax.

'I want your help, Ernest. We both do.'

He inclined his head in a way which he believed would convey both sympathy and perception.

'Are you listening?'

'Of course I am.'

'We're thinking of buying a house.'

'What?' Ernest could not prevent himself from interrupting. Anne felt no obligation to confirm what she had already told him.

'We want you to look over it for us, you knowing about this sort of thing – wood rot, rising damp.'

'Death-watch beetle,' said Lottie from her seat in the corner.

'We'd like you to look at it this weekend, if possible. We want to sign the papers on Monday.'

Ernest waited for the details to spill out, but his sister sat in triumph waiting for his reply.

'Of course I will. Where is it?'

'Newcastle Avenue. The corner of Newcastle Avenue and Brook Passage.'

'It's called Brook House,' Lottie added, clearly proud that she was going to live at a name rather than a number.

'Why Brook House?'

'There's a stream.' Brook was far too romantic a word for Anne to use. 'It runs all along the garden by the side of the house. There's a long strip of garden to the side of the path. Then the stream and our fence at the top of a bank.'

The brief acquaintance with draughtsmanship which Ernest had made before he abandoned his set-square for a rapier had not equipped him to visualise the layout his sister described. But his association with builders had taught him to be wary of water. 'How near is the brook to the house?'

'Ten yards.' Anne answered with a certainty which came from years of measuring cloth.

'It's a bit near. Is there a cellar?'

His sister assured him that there was not, in a manner which suggested that the absence of a cellar solved the problem of the stream.

'That's a bad sign. I'll take a couple of floorboards up and—'

'We want it.'

He had never heard Lottie speak with such authority.

'Not if it's got water in the foundations.' He looked to Anne for reassurance and support.

'It's just the right house for us. Goes back a long way. We'd have the fitting room in the front and two big workrooms upstairs.'

'Two?'

'We're going to take on two girls. We've more work than we can manage. It's just the right size. Four machines. Perhaps six.'

'And there's the bridge. That's why I want it.'

305

It was obvious, even to Ernest, that his sister did not want Lottie to explain her enthusiasm for the bridge and it was equally clear that Lottie was not to be prevented from describing why the bridge was crucial to her future happiness.

'You can get underneath it by climbing down from our garden.'

Ernest decided that the bridge must be a structure of unusual architectural beauty which was seen to particular advantage from below. He was surprised and impressed that Lottie took aesthetic considerations so seriously but he was not so impressed that she was prepared to recommend purchase of a house with water in its foundations – just for the privilege of having a noble stone arch outside the gate.

'They fish from it. Little boys. And they climb down on to our bank and fish from there. Sticklebacks and tadpoles. Little frogs. Minnows. Newts. Even beetles. They scoop them up in their nets and put them into a jam jar. And they die. They take them home and they die in a day. And snails. The snails on the leaves. We're going to stop it. Aren't we, Anne?'

Anne, thinking that her brother might not take their purchase seriously, made a quick choice between praising the house and defending Lottie. 'It's her nature. We'll never change her. She can't stand the thought of anything being hurt.' She turned and smiled at her partner. 'Gentle. She's too gentle for her own good sometimes.'

Encouraged by Anne's support, Lottie warmed to her theme. 'We're going to stop them. We're going to have the fence rebuilt at the top of the bank and have spikes put on top. And barbed wire. That'll cut their hands to ribbons if they try to climb over and we'll put tar along the wall thing on the bridge. Tar with broken glass along the . . . what's it called?'

'Parapet,' said Ernest, swept along by her malicious passion.

'Yes, the parapet. We'll have tar with broken glass in it and that'll have their knees raw if they try to get over.'

'What if they come under the bridge, climb down the other side and come through?' There was no irony in Ernest's question.

'They don't fish under the bridge. It's dark and the little boys are afraid. It's courting couples down there.'

'And we'll think of ways to stop them,' Anne added. 'That's if we buy it.'

There was a foot of water in the foundations, but, despite the stern warnings against purchase, Lottie and Anne bought Brook House. Ernest supervised the removal from Gateford Road, and the gloomy prophecies with which he accompanied every instruction to carry a chair upstairs or leave a sewing machine in the back room did not quite manage to destroy all the pleasure they felt in moving into a place of their own. Agnes came in the afternoon and attempted to lift boxes and packing cases which could only be easily moved by two strong men. Ernest agitated about arranging a visit for his parents. The partners waited impatiently to have their home to themselves. Lottie fretted silently, adjusting curtains when no adjustment was necessary and picking imaginary specks of dust from the antimacassars. Anne dropped hints about having to get up early the next morning to finish orders of unusual urgency and eventually Ernest realised that she wanted him to go home but when he put on his coat and asked Agnes if she wanted hers, his sister shook her head. 'I've got to talk to Anne.'

'Won't Brack expect you home?' Ernest asked.

'He's out. Out working. He won't be back till after midnight. It's that I want to talk to Anne about.'

Anne had no doubt that, once Lottie was in bed and Ernest was on his way to Overend Road, her sister would pour out her heart. She expected a full account of Brack's vices. She knew, as everybody knew, that he was a gambler. She also suspected, without cause or justification, that he was lecherous, drunken and workshy. She had tried to say as much when the idea of marriage had first been mentioned but nobody had listened. She determined not to recriminate, but simply to offer what comfort and support she could reasonably provide.

'And I'm going to move away. Out of Worksop altogether.'

Anne decided that her judgement had been vindicated. Agnes was going to leave her husband. The shame that she would bring on her family was best not mentioned for the moment, for nothing should be done to encourage the continuation of the unhappy marriage. God worked in convenient, as well as mysterious, ways. The end of the unfortunate union had come at just the moment when her sister could be usefully employed at Grove Cottage or looking after her widower brother.

'There's no need to leave Worksop. Come here. Come here tonight. Stay now. I'll go and get your things tomorrow. I'm not afraid of him. He won't dare to come here and fetch you back.'

'Do you mean Brack?'

'Of course I do. He won't come here.'

'You didn't think . . .'

'No, I didn't. I never thought that it would bring you anything except unhappiness. I blame myself for not saying so at the time.'

'Anne! Listen to me. I'm not saying that I'm leaving Brack. I don't know how you could think such a thing. I'm going with him to Shirebrook. He's starting a business of his own. He's rented a shop in Main Street and he's going to sell bicycles.'

'Bicycles!'

'It's the coming thing. He says he'll make his fortune. He's rented a shop from Mr Hardstaff, who used to be estate manager for Mr Robinson.'

'So you're not going to leave him!'

'Of course I'm not. How could you think such a thing? He's my husband.'

'And you're happy with him?' Anne did not easily let go.

'Of course I am. We've had our ups and downs. Everybody does.'

'Lottie says he hits you.' Anne played her trump card. 'She says that in the summer she noticed a big bruise on your arm and then at Christmas there was another on your shoulder. You leaned down to pick up a present from under the tree and she saw a bruise as big as a man's hand between your shoulder and your collarbone.'

'You two must have enjoyed yourselves. I can just imagine the two of you lying in that little bedroom and telling each other about the way he beats me.'

'Aggie! I only wanted to help. I've been waiting for you to tell me. I didn't like to raise the subject myself in case you were offended.'

'Well, I'm offended now.'

'He gambles, doesn't he?'

'He has a few coppers on big races. Horse-racing is his one pleasure. He doesn't drink. He works all the hours that God sends. I know that we were brought up against it but other people don't think it's so bad.'

'And he hits you.' It had turned from a question into a statement.

'He's my husband, Anne, and I love him.'

'You'll learn,' said Anne. 'You'll learn. And we'll be here when you need us.'

'For God's sake, don't be so smug. You couldn't understand. All that concerns you is that wretched little business. You've never loved anyone and you never will.'

'I'd never love anyone who hit me.'

'More likely no one would ever love you.'

Anne put on her martyred face and Agnes thought how like their mother she looked.

'Whatever you say now will be forgotten and forgiven no matter how cruel you are. When you need us we'll be here – Lottie and me. Don't forget that. There'll always be a home for you with us.'

'Both of us?' Agnes asked. 'Both of us? Me and the baby?'

CHAPTER TWENTY-FOUR

A Moment of Happiness

Agnes had not rushed to her husband with the joyful tidings that she was pregnant, but had broken the news – with great reluctance and after much procrastination – as if she were confessing a misdemeanour. Her husband received the information with what anyone who did not know him would have taken to be modest pride and genuine pleasure. Agnes did not believe that his good humour would last. But as the weeks went by she was forced into the unlikely conclusion that Brack liked the idea of becoming a father and felt grateful to her for being a party to his achievement. Gratitude bred a tenderness Agnes had previously not known and generated concern for her welfare. Brack did not look after her but he was prepared to let her look after herself by sacrificing time and energy which she might have devoted to him.

He continued to gamble but he gambled little more than was the general practice amongst the miners and the railwaymen of Shirebrook. He put coppers on horses with the local bookmaker and he played dominoes in the Manvers Arms and cards in the Miners' Welfare – where, betting being against the rules, he could do no more than slide halfpennies across the table. The old rage to wager every penny he possessed seemed to have died. Agnes longed to attribute Brack's redemption to a belated interest in family life, but she was aware that the real cause of the change in his conduct was the cycle shop.

The cycle shop prospered. Cycling was in fashion and Shirebrook, at the centre of ideal touring country, was within easy pedalling distance of the cycle race track in Langwith. Miners cycled to work at the pits and railwaymen cycled to engine sheds and sidings. On Saturday afternoons, the colliery manager and his family visited local beauty spots on Singer Safety Bicycles, and on Sundays enthusiasts from miles around made for the Portland Hotel at nearby Cresswell, where the proprietor advertised 'Cyclists and visitors generally will find every accommodation . . . private sitting rooms . . . large and small parties catered for . . . on the shortest notice'. On the advice of Mr C. Hardstaff, landlord and sometime land agent to John Robinson and honorary secretary of the Cyclists' Union (North Nottinghamshire Branch), Brack set out to be indispensable to the cyclists of the area, whether they were groups of Fabians in search of fresh air and uplifting conversation, harassed husbands who had found a new excuse to spend weekends away from home or honest workmen who had bought an ancient boneshaker and used it for no more than their daily journey to and from work.

He was lucky if he sold one new bicycle in a month for a new bicycle, with free-wheel and pneumatic tyres, cost more than six pounds. But there was an insatiable demand for cycling's bits and pieces, and an unquestionable thirst for cycling gossip and authoritative opinions on the new obsession. Brack set out to meet all the needs.

The buying and selling of second-hand bicycles engrossed him. Each Friday afternoon he studied the To Be Sold columns of the *Worksop Guardian* with a passion he had once reserved for the *Sporting Life*.

'Cycles – a number of good second-hand LADIES and GENTS'.' A dealer. No profit to be made there.

'Bicycle – Rudge Whitworth – for sale: first-class condition: 22in frame. CHEAP'. Rudge Whitworth was cycling's thoroughbred. But even second-hand cycles of that make were beyond the pockets of his clientele.

'Lady's Cycle (Campion) good condition, exceptional bargain, 45/ – also gents for reasonable offer. Allison, Junior, Gateford Road, Worksop'. With any luck Allison would be very junior indeed and Brack would be able to knock him down to three pounds for the pair.

Having identified his quarry, he set off with a glint in his eye, which Agnes had only previously seen on those terrible mornings when her husband had convinced himself that he was about to bankrupt the bookmakers. Before he left the house, he always consulted notes on the back of an old envelope and muttered to himself as he had once muttered about accumulators and each-way bets. 'Lady's Campion, say thirty-five bob . . . if it's clean. Should make a dollar on that. Thirty if it needs new tyres . . .'

Agnes rejoiced that the buying and selling of second-hand bicycles occupied a place in her husband's heart and mind that had previously had room for nothing except betting. Then she realised that the calculation of the cost at which he could sell a Rudge or a Raleigh was, like the haggling over the price that he paid for a Humber or a Hercules, simply a different sort of gamble. But she rejoiced still, for

310

when he pitted his wits not against bookmakers but against miners and engine drivers with old bicycles to sell, he usually won.

Even so, the income from the sale of second-hand bicycles was far exceeded by the profits made from selling the accessories of his business. Brack did a roaring trade in brake blocks and handle-bar grips, carbide lamps, oilskin capes, spare mudguards and replacement tyres. He also mended cycles – tightening loose spokes, replacing worn cotter-pins and straightening front forks and drop handlebars which had been bent by late-night accidents and collisions with walls and kerbstones. Punctures were mended free as an encouragement to future business, but Brack did not mend them himself. Puncture mending was Agnes's work.

Each weekday, as soon as the breakfast pots had been washed and dried, the enamel bowl was filled with water from the butt outside the door and carefully placed on the kitchen table in preparation for her special contribution to the success of the shop. After a couple of days, the whole operation – holding the inner tube under the water and squeezing it, inch by inch, until the tell-tale bubbles pinpointed the tiny lesion – became second nature, a task which she could easily perform whilst thinking about the shopping to be done, shirts to be washed, dinners to be cooked, clothes to be mended and beds to be made. She never learned to enjoy sticking the patch over the puncture – the glue always leaked out from between rubber inner tube and rubber patch and, after drying on her fingers, had to be peeled off like dead skin – but she rejoiced at the thought that she was helping Brack and delighted in the new chivalry with which he treated her. No matter how many customers waited to be served, he never expected her to take the wheel out of the frame or prise the tyre from the rim. He always delivered the inner tube into her hand like a knight errant laying his sword on the altar.

Brack's job, she knew, was in the shop for half of the sales were made to men who rattled the bell above the door for no better reason than to talk to the proprietor. He was regarded in Shirebrook, and far beyond, as an expert on all matters appertaining to cycling and cyclists. Brack worked assiduously to maintain that reputation. He stole from Charles Hardstaff a cardboard copy of the Cyclists' Touring Club Badge and hung it in his window like a royal warrant. He joined the Cyclists' Union, obtained a copy of its standard letter on the proper procedure for sending bicycles by rail and nailed it to the counter as if he had been appointed special agent by the railway. Most important of all, he talked – with a mystery which generated extra excitement – of his days in cycle racing. Nobody knew where he had raced or how many races he had won but every customer

311

understood that he preferred flat cinder tracks to the banked tarmac-adam which had been introduced to protect the new generation of cowardly riders. Brack's talk was of sprint finishes and malicious collisions. It was worth the cost of a box of valve rubbers any day. Indeed, it proved so popular with men who had never sat astride a saddle that he added putty and cobblers' wax, brass screws and linseed oil to his stock to provide an excuse for lifelong pedestrians to call in the shop for cheap conversation. After six months in business, he decided to branch out into three-speed gears. On the morning that the baby arrived he was studying a leaflet on how Bowden brakes were fitted when he heard first a cry and then a crash from the kitchen. He found Agnes leaning against the table drenched with water from the enamel basin which she had dropped as the contractions began. When he carried her upstairs, she did not mind that he banged her feet first against the doorjamb and then against the banisters. She was afraid. But she was also happier than she had ever been in her life.

It was an uneventful birth. At first, Agnes was sorry that the baby was a girl, for she was sure that Brack would have preferred a boy, but he pronounced himself satisfied to the point of expressing hope that she would be as pretty as her mother. Anne and Lottie brought large quantities of unsuitable baby clothes and Ernest, who had performed the heroic task of shepherding the glowing grandparents from Worksop to Shirebrook, stared at his niece in awed fascination.

When they had all gone home Agnes told Brack, 'It's nice to be quiet. Nice to have the house to ourselves again.'

Brack sat on the side of the bed with his arm along the pillows on which Agnes rested her head.

'We'll never be quiet again. Not for a year or two, anyway. This one makes enough row to keep all the street awake.'

'And when her brothers and sisters come along . . .'

'Steady up,' Brack said. 'We've only had her for a couple of days and we don't know what we're going to call her.'

'Ernest wants to call her Elizabeth.'

'I wouldn't mind.'

'I would.' Agnes looked down at the baby. 'Too much of a mouthful.'

'Just the sort of thing your brother would like.'

Agnes grinned, though she knew that she was betraying her mother and brother with a single smile. 'He's had a hard time, Brack.'

'No harder than dozens of others. It's his nature. I've never known such a solemn sod. How you two come to be brother and sister . . .'

'You don't think I'm solemn, then?'

'No. You'd enjoy yourself given half a chance.'

'I used to like going out. I liked those dances.'

'It's about time you started enjoying yourself again.' When he said it, he meant it so sincerely that he went on to describe the delights he proposed. 'We'll take the babies for walks. And we'll go to the whist drives. And there are still dances at the Welfare—'

'I'd like that.'

'—and concerts. We'll go to the races. We can take . . . Elizabeth.'

'We're not going to call her Elizabeth. I tell you what I'd like. There's a long poem about King Arthur—'

'We can't call her Arthur.'

Brack rarely made jokes so Agnes laughed as loudly as she could to acknowledge the rare and welcome event rather than in tribute to the quality of the wit.

'In the poem, there's a girl called Enid. She's the kind one. She's helpful.'

'And beautiful?' Brack asked.

'I think so. They all were at King Arthur's court.'

'All right, Enid. Enid Anne, to keep Worksop happy.'

Brack squeezed his wife's shoulder and offered a huge index finger to his two-day-old daughter. Agnes flinched.

'What's the matter?'

'I've got a pain in my shoulder. I've had it ever since the baby – since Enid – came. I must have twisted something.'

Agnes was back mending punctures within days of Enid's arrival – sharing the kitchen table with Brack, who had bought his first three-speed and was learning how to fasten it to a back wheel. A sudden gust of rain splashed against the window.

'What time is it?' Agnes had made one concession to her condition: she worked sitting down and, reluctant to push herself out of the chair, she asked Brack the time rather than walking into the hall to consult the clock. He pulled out his cheap pocket watch.

'Eleven. Plenty of time before dinner.'

'Mrs Waldron won't be back until twelve. If it rains any more, the washing will be wetter than when she hung it out.'

Brack was concentrating hard on his three-speed gear.

'Next week I'll be back doing it all myself.'

'No, you won't,' said Brack. 'No washing for a month. She's coming next week and the week after. She's been paid.'

The sudden gust had turned into a steady downpour. Encouraged by Brack's concern for her welfare, Agnes was emboldened to suggest

313

the unthinkable. 'Will you get them in, Brack? They'll be soaking in five minutes.'

Even as she asked the question, Agnes knew what a terrible mistake she had made. She had attempted to take advantage of Brack's good nature and she would have nobody to blame except herself if he was angry. Taking the washing from the clothes line was woman's work. Her husband could not be expected to stand in full view of the neighbours picking off clothes pegs, folding the sheets and piling the shirts and socks into the wicker basket. She waited for the explosion.

Brack slowly stood up. 'I'd better get some of this muck off my hands first.' He walked across to the sink. As he passed Agnes he menaced her with his oily hand. She cowered back in mock terror and gave a little theatrical scream. Then she looked with genuine anxiety towards the sofa where Enid lay asleep.

'You've done it now. You've woken her up. No peace until dinner time.' Brack was searching under the sink. He turned on the tap. 'You'll never get it off just using cold water.'

'I can't find any soap.'

'There'll be a new bar in the washhouse.'

Brack retreated from the sink, shaking his hands to remove the water that clung in globules to the grease on his fingers. He crossed the kitchen towards the little hall which led to the shop and the stairs.

'Where're you going now? The washing will be drenched, if you wait much longer.'

'I'm not going out without a coat on. I'll get drenched as well.'

Agnes gave a grunt of exasperation and dried her hands on the threadbare towel which hung beside the sink. She could hear Brack cursing as he struggled to find his topcoat under the old jackets, tattered shawls and battered hats.

'You'll get grease on everything with those filthy hands.'

'Then how can I get my coat?' He sounded as aggrieved as he was puzzled.

'I'll go myself.' There was no attempt to disguise the exasperation. 'It's easier. They'll all be wet through if we leave them any longer. If you want anything doing properly, do it yourself.'

'Suit yourself.'

She tiptoed across the muddy yard thinking that a little help was worth a lot of pity and reached up to unpeg a linen petticoat which flapped wet in the wind. Before she pulled the petticoat free, she touched its deep hem. Water dropped on to her fingers. With the pegs still on the clothes line, she rolled up the skirt and twisted it between her hands as if she were wringing out a face cloth. After half an hour in the rain, the petticoat was as wet as if it had never been through the mangle. Agnes decided to leave the clothes on the line. She stretched up again to wring the water out of one of Brack's flannel shirts.

It was the noise, reverberating from her neck and rattling down her backbone, that frightened her. There was no pain to speak of. A dull ache spread out from between her shoulder-blades and down her arms, but, to a woman who had given birth hardly a week before, that barely qualified as discomfort. And even that passed before she realised that she could not lower her arms from above her head.

The paralysis lasted for barely a minute. And then, without understanding how she knew that she was free, Agnes realised she could move again. The real agony that ran from the base of her skull to the bottom of her spine began only when her arms were down by her side. Slowly she lifted them again, hoping that some bone or muscle would slip back into place and end her suffering. But, no matter how she bent her elbows or twisted her shoulders, the pain persisted. She stood in the garden with rain and tears running down her face until Brack, his chin smeared with oil and his topcoat over his shoulders, came out into the yard.

'What the bloody hell are you up to? You're soaked. You'll get pneumonia.'

Agnes stumbled towards him. 'I've got more than that. I can't move. I'm paralysed.'

'Don't be so soft. Of course you can move. You're moving now. You walked across this yard.'

'I can't move my head. You've got to believe me. I can't move my head and I can't move my neck. And I hurt. I hurt all down my back.'

Brack led his wife inside. He took the threadbare towel from the hook by the sink and, without a word, began to dry her hair. Agnes screamed – not in pain but from fear that he did not believe her.

'Don't you understand? I can't move my neck. I'm paralysed.'

'Let me rub it.' He reached forward, but Agnes screamed again and, in her anxiety to avoid his touch, staggered against the sink. Instinctively she reached out to save herself from falling. When she screamed a third time, it was a scream of agony. Brack needed no more convincing.

Dr Anderson said that rheumatoid arthritis had complicated causes. Agnes had not been infected by blocked sewers or poisoned by contaminated meats. The disease was not carried by air or water, rats, beetles or flying fish. Her father's related condition might have been a contributing factor but there was no scientific certainty that it could

315

be inherited. It just happened. She was just unlucky. One day medical science would find the cause and then discover the cure. But for Agnes there could be no remission and recovery. Gradually, one by one, her joints would atrophy. She might walk for another five years and feed herself for another ten, but she would end her days as a cripple. It went without saying that there would be no more children.

Neither Anne nor Ernest accepted the doctor's diagnosis. They did not quarrel with his prognosis that their sister would live in immobile misery. But they both challenged his analysis of the malady's origins. Ernest attributed it to Brack's conduct and hinted at beatings and manual labour beyond the endurance of a woman with child. Anne had no doubt that Agnes was paying the price of her husband's lust. To her it was obvious that the paralysis was the consequence of childbirth.

'Who's going to look after her?' asked Lottie.

'She can manage on her own for a year or two,' Anne assured her. 'By the time she's bedridden all the work will be done by poor little Enid.'

She had begun to talk of 'poor little Enid', not because the baby was in any way unwell, but because she believed that the child had been sent to punish her parents for the sins of the flesh and would carry the guilt for the rest of her life.

'It's not going to be easy for Brack.'

'He's made his bed and he's going to have to lie on it.'

'Do you think he'll be kind to her?'

'She won't see much of him. He'll be off every night, drinking with his cronies.'

Ernest, who had arrived for his regular nightly visit, corrected her. 'Off every night gambling. He doesn't drink much. He gambles.'

'Poor little Enid,' said Lottie.

CHAPTER TWENTY-FIVE

Poor Little Enid

Poor little Enid prospered to an extent that outdid even the success of the cycle shop. The maudlin aspect of Brack's nature – which for years had been submerged beneath the layers of selfish arrogance – pushed itself to the surface of his character as he shamelessly, in the neighbours' words, 'doted on his daughter'. Agnes, despite her gradually growing paralysis, looked after Enid with a thoroughness which owed something to her natural instincts but more to the fear that by the time the baby became a girl her mother would no longer be capable of providing proper maternal care.

Brack's enthusiasm for his daughter went further than the constant purchase of expensive and unsuitable presents, boasts about her prodigious intelligence and the identification of admirable characteristics which she had inherited from him. As well as manifesting his affection in all those dubious ways, he exhibited a real desire to behave like a good father should. He enjoyed first watching and then amusing the child whilst her sick mother took the frequent rests which the doctor said were essential to her continued mobility. He carried her upstairs to bed each night and, without being asked, increased the housekeeping money so that Agnes need no longer push the pram from shop to shop in search of cheap meat and cut-price groceries.

The parents argued about their daughter's upbringing only when Brack wanted to put Enid on display in a way her mother thought demeaning or dangerous. There were constant though amicable disputes about the child sitting on the edge of the shop counter, or being carried to the Miners' Welfare on her father's shoulders, or being pedalled around the village precariously balanced between his knees on the handlebars of his bicycle. The arguments always ended with Brack coyly stating that he 'didn't want a row' because 'she understands every word that we say' or Agnes capitulating because of memories of her first bicycle ride along the Chesterfield Road to Darfoulds.

Anne could never be convinced that Agnes and her daughter were

317

living in anything except abject poverty. Because Anne believed it, Lottie believed it too. A chill invariably descended on the shop whenever the door bell announced that Anne and Lottie had come to call. For Anne and Lottie could hide neither their feelings nor their suspicions.

'Are you all right?' It was Anne's invariable greeting.

In the back room, Brack – carrying Enid under his arm like a sack of potatoes – pulled a sour face. Enid gurgled with pleasure as Anne repeated her question.

'Are you all right?' Anne seemed to expect a gloomy answer. She looked pityingly at Enid, who – still gurgling with delight – had been dropped into her wicker bassinet together with a whole flock of plywood sheep, a rag doll with china head and arms, a miniature concertina, a humming top and the pencil with which Brack had been drawing animals, theoretically for Enid's amusement but – as she was too young to identify the shapes – in practice only for his own pleasure. Agnes picked up the sharp pencil without even looking in her daughter's direction. As she put it out of harm's way on the mantelshelf, she answered her sister's question.

'I'm fine. My wrist's a bit sore but my back's much better today.'

Enid began to shout from beneath her covering of toys. To her aunt's surprise she shouted not in pain or hunger but in something approaching elation. The child's mood was so incompatible with her aunt's mission that Anne decided to ignore her altogether. Lottie could not, however, contain her feelings. She reached down into the bassinet, rattled the tin bells which hung from its hooks and began to coo.

'What a happy little girl. What a lovely baby.' She dug Enid in the ribs and Enid stopped shouting and began to coo.

Anne coughed menacingly.

'Are you sure you're all right?' She stared at Agnes to emphasise the special import of her question and spoke the words slowly and with equal stress on each syllable.

'I'm as good as you can expect. And she's marvellous.'

'She's as strong as an ox,' Brack added. 'Let her hold your finger. She'll pull it off.'

'What about the walking?' asked Anne. She knew that the walking had been a problem.

'She's staggered a step or two but she's very heavy.'

'She's not fat,' her father explained. 'Very healthy, a bit of weight at her age.'

'And you're managing all right?' Anne was sure that if she asked the question often enough, she would get the right answer.

318

'Apart from the wrists.'

'I thought so.'

'But they're much better than they were last week.'

'Your fingers look puffy.' Anne was not prepared to accept good news without a fight. 'Here, let me look.' She seized Agnes's hand and held it before her like an anatomical specimen. 'You flinched. I felt you flinch. It hurt, didn't it?'

'Of course it hurt. You can see the inflammation. But luckily it doesn't get wrenched like that very often.'

'The joints are all swollen,' said Lottie. She was genuinely concerned about Agnes's health and obviously anxious to show her sympathy.

'The woman's got rheumatoid arthritis,' said Brack. 'What do you expect? Her feet are worse. Would you like to look at them as well?'

He might have added that her back had kept her awake for half of the night and that every time she had turned and groaned – either because of the pain in her spine or because of the prospect of another exhausted day – he had woken too. Had he told them that each time she woke she had demanded that he rubbed her shoulder or pushed at the point beneath her shoulder-blade where she believed that the ache began, they might have understood his real feelings. But Brack would not condescend to curry his sister-in-law's favour so they believed that his refusal to be patronised was proof of his callous contempt.

When the door bell rang and Brack bustled back into the shop to serve his customer, Anne began to talk to Agnes in riddles.

'Everything? You know?'

'I've told you, we're fine.'

'But really? I thought you might have some plan you didn't want to talk about . . . before.'

'What sort of plan?'

'We thought, Lottie and me, that one day you might pack up and . . .'

'Why should I do that?'

'We were wondering', Lottie found the truth irresistible, 'how we would manage if you suddenly arrived one day.'

'Why should I want to go to Worksop?'

'For a bit of peace.'

Lottie contributed with a combination of concern and emollience. 'At least, if you came for a day or two you'd get some rest and some good food inside you.'

'How dare you! How dare you come here like Lady Bountiful and

319

'. . . and . . . We can afford to eat. I don't need a rest.' She broke down in tears.

'You don't have to pretend with us,' said Anne. 'We only want to help.'

'But we've got to think about things,' Lottie added. 'Anne's very worried about the business. How we'd manage if we had an invalid upstairs and a baby to look after. For very long, that is. A week or two wouldn't be so bad.'

Lottie thought that she was being no more than sensible but the explanation of Anne's motives turned Agnes's resentment into fury. 'You didn't have to worry. Whatever happens, we won't be a burden to you.'

Anne gave one of her triumphant looks. Agnes had confirmed that she was near to breaking with Brack. Lottie, who assumed that she had provoked nothing more than injured pride, tried to promote reassurance.

'Nobody would be happier than us,' said Lottie, 'if you were really all right, if he was really looking after you.'

'He was up half the night looking after me.'

Anne smiled incredulously. She had developed her mother's talent for conveying disagreement by carefully composed looks and glances. At the suggestion that Brack had allowed his sleep to be disturbed for no better reason than to help and comfort his sick wife, she put on her contemptuously sceptical face. She dared not ask her sister not to insult her intelligence with such an invention. But that was the message her expression conveyed and Agnes knew it.

'He was. He was. He rubbed my neck and pushed under my shoulder-blades. Three times I woke him and he did it each time.'

The description of Brack's attempts at first-aid confirmed Anne's suspicion that her sister was lying.

'I've told you. You don't have to invent stories for us. You can be yourself with us. We keep everything you say between these four walls. I don't even tell Ernest—'

'Why don't you go home?'

'Because you need us. And we've come to help. We need to sort things out before there's a crisis that we can't manage.'

The shop door clanged its bell again. The three women froze into silence.

Brack returned to the kitchen, not to talk to his visitors, but to amuse his daughter. As he made a bee-line for the bassinet, he noticed his wife's tear-stained cheeks. 'Are you all right?'

'Don't you start. Don't you ask the same silly question. Of course

320

I'm all right. Or I would be if you all stopped asking me the same stupid question.'

The gloom was infectious. Enid threw the rag doll out of the bassinet and began to cry.

'Bloody hell.'

'Don't you swear at me,' said Anne.

'I'm not swearing at you. I'm swearing at the baby.'

'Poor little mite. You shouldn't swear at her. You shouldn't swear at all,' Anne told him.

'I'll swear at you as much as I like if you come here and upset everybody. I don't know what all the fuss was about, but I know that things were fine until you came.'

Anne was not satisfied with pulling exasperated faces. The sharp intake of breath and the sigh which followed were indications that her patience was totally exhausted. 'Come, Lottie, we'll not stay where we're not welcome.' She turned to Agnes. 'It's you I'm sorry for, you and the baby. We won't come here again. But you know where we are if you need us.'

She began to unpack the Gladstone bag which, throughout the argument, she had clutched in front of her. As Agnes tried to comfort and quiet the baby, her sister methodically banged on to the kitchen table a baked custard still in its oven-blackened tin, a stone jam jar with beef tea leaking from under the greaseproof paper tied across its top, a pressed tongue bulging out from its basin and a half-pound of home-cured ham.

'Ern bought the ham.' It was Anne's valediction and final rebuke. She swept from the kitchen and through the shop with that ultimate reproof still hanging in the air. Lottie followed a pace behind looking apologetic.

When they had gone, Agnes sat down on the hard chair at the head of the table and began to rock Enid on her knee. Brack walked towards her.

'Don't. We might as well use it. They mean well, really they do. Anyway, I don't want to clean it all up.' She was mistaken. He wanted to do no more than stand in front of her, with his hands on her shoulders and their daughter sandwiched between them.

'I think that sister of yours is off her head.'

'I'm sorry. I am really sorry. I don't know what got into her.'

Brack took the baby from his wife. 'Get some bread and butter. I'd love a bit of this tongue with a pickled onion.'

Anne Skinner did not keep her word. She continued to visit Agnes in the unshakeable belief that only her visits, and the gifts of food which

321

accompanied them, stood between her sister and lonely starvation. Naturally enough, Lottie trailed along behind, wanting to help out but apprehensive about the disruption of her safe little world. There was one terrible moment when Anne told her that the weekly errands of mercy were doing so much harm to their health and damage to their business that she would have to think of a way of dispensing charity which did not require all of Thursday to be devoted to good work.

'We could walk,' said Lottie. 'That would be the healthy thing.'

'Six miles each way? With our three baskets?'

'We could do it.'

'The train isn't so bad.'

'It's terrible. It takes so long. And it never goes at the right time. And it is so dirty.' Lottie so forgot herself that, for once, she contested Anne's argument, rather than supported it.

Desperation inspired invention. Anne had actually opened her mouth to insist on travelling by train when an original thought forced itself into Lottie's mind. 'Bicycles.'

'What do you mean?' Anne was bewildered.

'I mean we could go to Shirebrook on bicycles. A lot of ladies ride them now. We must have made a dozen split skirts this year.'

'We couldn't ride. We couldn't balance.'

'Of course we could.' Lottie's desperation made her sound enthusiastic. 'It would be good for us.'

'I don't know . . .'

'We could try. Next Thursday we could try one of Brack's bicycles.'

'Why Brack's bicycles? I can see him laughing at us.'

'I'd rather him laugh at us than a man from a shop in Worksop.' Lottie agreed that whoever gave them lessons would find their antics ridiculous.

'You'll have to ask him,' said Anne.

'I'll ask Agnes to ask him.' Fear had made Lottie devious.

Brack was delighted. He calculated that, even with bicycles to bring them, Anne and Lottie would visit Shirebrook no more frequently but with proper persuasion they might spend as much as ten pounds. No sooner had Agnes, giggling, told him of their interest than he began to dismantle his window in order to display a Raleigh – the twenty-two-inch safety model with chain guard and handlebar basket which might have been designed for carrying alms.

Anne volunteered to try first. She took up such an upright position that the handlebars had to be pulled higher. Showing a surprising knowledge of elementary mechanics she carefully confirmed that they were screwed firmly back in place before she stepped decorously over

322

the pedals and settled herself in the saddle. Remembering her pre-occupation with respectability, Brack stooped and held the cycle frame just above the back mudguard. The pupil placed her left foot on the pedal and, with no more than a brief glance behind her, pressed down hard. She pressed down so hard that Brack could not retain his grip. Cycle and rider careered down the road for a couple of yards and ended up in a heap in the gutter. Agnes, who had not been allowed to watch, heard the cry and the crash and hurried out. By the time she had got to the end of the passage, Anne was up and back in the saddle, muttering, 'I'm not going to let this thing beat me.'

It took her an hour to learn how to balance. After she had learned to cycle in a straight line, she began to teach herself how to turn corners. She fell off twice more before she handed the Raleigh to Lottie. 'Your turn. If I can do it, you can.'

At first Brack thought Lottie was a natural. She possessed an almost perfect sense of balance. But the mechanics of the machine were beyond her. 'When you brake, stop pedalling,' Brack shouted. Lottie stopped, as instructed, and lifted her feet in the air. 'It's all right. It's a free wheel.'

'What's that?'

'Just keep your feet on the pedals. Keep them still and they won't move.'

The idea unnerved her. Every time she thought of the pedals remaining still as the cycle moved forwards, she lost her nerve and her balance. Brack tried to explain the principle by showing her an elderly fixed-wheel model. Lottie insisted on riding it and all her natural talent was again revealed.

'I'll have this,' she said, 'if it's for sale?'

'It ought to be in a museum.'

'So should I. We'll go well together.'

Brack was not the man to miss a sale. The two bicycles were sold for nine pounds. As Anne handed the money over he calculated how many brake blocks and brake cables he would sell during the next eternity of Thursdays.

The bicycles were, from Worksop's point of view, a great success in all but one particular. The journey from Worksop covered undulating ground. Both women were unable to pedal up the hills and Lottie was unable to freewheel down, so she cycled for only a third of the journey and pushed her elderly boneshaker on every incline. At the bottom of each slope, Anne waited for her to catch up with a patience which confirmed that she was loved and understood.

Once at Shirebrook, the routine was always the same. Anne never missed any detail of her sister's deterioration. Each newly swollen

323

knuckle was a subject for concerned comment. If Agnes listened to what she had to say without looking her straight in the eye, she expressed anxious sympathy about the increasingly paralysed neck. Agnes took everything in good part except the criticisms of Brack and the implication that Enid was being neglected. After two years in which Enid learned to walk energetically and talk incessantly, Anne still talked of the pretty pink child as if rickets and melancholia could not be long delayed. Whenever Anne Skinner visited Main Street, Brack carried his daughter out of the kitchen and into the shop, where he attempted to teach her conundrums which were beyond her comprehension and tried to coach her to recite nursery rhymes which were too complicated for both her infant vocabulary and her piping voice.

Usually Anne complained that her niece was being kept from her. Agnes denied the accusation and then proved it to be true by having to make several dashes into the shop before she emerged with Enid. Brack always attempted to lure his daughter back by announcing, at the top of his voice, that Little Bo Peep had lost her sheep and urging Little Boy Blue to blow his horn. Often Enid's return to fairyland was accompanied by tutting and outraged intakes of breath. The idea that Anne might one day welcome the child's passion to be with her father seemed so unlikely that, when it happened, Agnes asked her sister to repeat what she had said.

'I'm glad to have a quiet word,' she nodded in the direction of the shop. 'Just you and me. You, me and Lottie, that is. It's really Lottie who ought to tell you.'

'Tell me what?'

'We want you to come to Worksop.' Anne made the suggestion during every visit. Agnes could not understand why Lottie had been deputed to make the regular suggestion.

'Is that all? You know the answer. My place is here and this is where I want to be.'

'We just want you to come for the day.' Lottie was insistent. 'Just for the day out.'

'That's lovely. But there's the journey. The journey would take a lot out of me. I can't come on the crossbar of your bicycle.'

'We'll arrange for a car.'

Agnes's suspicions were confirmed. Anne did not normally make such expensive offers.

'What are you up to, Anne?'

'There's somebody Lottie wants you to meet. She's staying with us for a week or two.'

'For heaven's sake, Anne, just tell me what you want.'

'It's my sister,' said Lottie. 'She's called Ginny.'

'Your sister! How long have you had a sister? I thought you were an orphan. Anne always said that you had nobody else in the world.'

'That's what I thought. So did she. We were both wrong.'

'And she's at Brook House?'

'In bed,' said Anne gloomily. She waited for Lottie to paint the whole picture.

'She was a nanny for a big family in Glasgow. She was grown up and away from home in service when I was born. That's why I didn't know about her until now.'

'How did she find you?'

'She knew I'd been an apprentice at Allen's and the family she worked for wrote there, when they wanted to turn her out. Allen's sent the letter on to Newcastle Avenue.'

Anne added with stoical resignation, 'Now she's in the back bedroom pining – pining for children.'

Lottie explained. 'She's spent all her life with children and she misses them now. That's why we'd like you to bring Enid to see her.'

Enid did not want to leave her dad. But after a great deal of persuasion, considerable bribery and a few threats she agreed to put on her velvet dress and her best patent-leather shoes. Persuading her to have her hair brushed was more difficult but eventually she succumbed to flattery and, repeating almost word for word her mother's description of how the curls would sparkle and the ringlets shine, she submitted herself to the brush. Once she was settled in the deep padding of the Austin, she began to enjoy herself. She waved regally to the neighbours who were peeping from behind their curtains at the unusual sight of a motor car in Main Street and said that she would like the journey to go on for ever. It lasted for half an hour – at the end of which Enid was bored and bad-tempered. When the driver opened the car door, she leaped down into Newcastle Avenue without waiting for her mother and, whilst Agnes was still making her slow and painful descent, gambolled off – as if by instinct – in the direction of Darfoulds and Grove Cottage.

She returned whimpering to her mother when, entreaties and warnings having failed, Agnes limped down the Brook House path and out of sight with the threat that she was such a bad girl that she was to be abandoned. Confronted by her aunts, real and adopted, she first turned shy and then demanded that they come out into the garden and show her the stream.

'It's the journey,' said Agnes, by the way of apology, 'she's all excited and silly.'

It was then that the dog came out on to the path.

The dog was neither big nor beautiful. Indeed, it was his spectacular ugliness which had endeared him to Anne. After years of providing protection for bitches, she had become the owner of a predatory male, simply because she believed that no one else would love him. The original owner could only have chosen to call him Prince as a cruel comment on his essentially plebeian appearance. He was not the first dog that Enid had seen but in the few days of her cosseted life he was the first one that had been allowed to lick first her hand and then her face. Enid shuddered and stood with eyes closed, every muscle tense and her arms rigid down her sides.

'Prince is kissing you,' said Anne.

Agnes thought that he ought to be stopped, but was reluctant to antagonise her sister within minutes of arrival. She bent slowly down to stroke the dog and distract his attention. Prince turned and began to lick the hand that scratched beneath his collar and behind his ear. Enid howled.

'It's mine. It's mine. I want it back.' She stamped her small foot in passionate frustration.

'I'm sorry.' Agnes was genuinely embarrassed. 'I don't think she's very well. The journey must have upset her.'

Enid screamed on.

Agnes grasped her daughter by the shoulder and – either forgetting her recent diagnosis of Enid's condition or deciding that a slap was the best cure for hysteria – slowly lifted her rheumatic arm. Anne, without the handicap of swollen joints and aching muscles, swept up her niece and hugged the child to the cold folds of her bombazine skirts. Prince, wholly unaware of the emotional turmoil he had caused, loped off. Enid looked at the world through one tearful eye. She began to scream again.

'She likes the dog. You shouldn't scold her for that.'

It was difficult for Agnes to believe what she had heard. Anne, the apostle of discipline and of Elizabeth Skinner's stern belief that all children's natural instincts should be suppressed, was speaking up in favour of a tantrum. She was defending a rebellious little girl who, even as her aunt spoke in her defence, was kicking at her champion's shins in her attempt to break away and follow the dog.

'Want the dog. I want it.'

'Well, you can't have it.' Agnes made the great effort and, seizing Enid by the shoulder, began to shake her.

'Agnes!' Anne felt too strongly to convey her disapproval by looks alone. 'How could you? The child only wants to be with the dog.'

'The child wants her own way and she can't always have it. I'm surprised you encourage her, Anne.'

'I'll certainly encourage her to love dumb animals. There are too many people about who—'

Anne's excursion into moral philosophy was interrupted by Lottie. 'Come inside. Ginny's awake. I'm just going to give her a little wash. Come up in five minutes.' Lottie disappeared in the direction of the stairs, carefully holding a towel under the damp flannel she was carrying. She knew that Anne would be angry if it dripped on the floor.

It took considerably longer than five minutes to prepare Enid for the audience. Even when she had been calmed and quietened by the craven expedient of dragging Prince back into her presence there was much restorative work to be done before she was returned to the state of pristine respectability in which she had arrived at Newcastle Avenue. When she was cleaned and polished to her mother's satisfaction, Agnes told her what a pretty girl she was and almost added that it was a pity she was not so nice inside. Then she remembered Anne's brief departure into tolerance and decided against provoking a pointless argument with her sister. The wisdom of her decision was confirmed when Anne promised that Prince would be eagerly waiting in the kitchen to be reunited with his new friend.

Enid mounted the steps carefully, balancing both feet on each tread before she ventured any further upward. Her mother followed so close behind that she pressed against Enid's back. Agnes was unable to hold her daughter safe, but she was determined that if the child missed her footing she would not totter back down the stairs. Anne, bearing a glass and a soda-water syphon, preceded Lottie, who formed the rearguard and carried a quarter of boiled sweets which she was going to give to Ginny for Ginny to present to Enid. When they were all assembled on the landing, skirts had been smoothed down and collars straightened out, Anne tapped on the bedroom door. A deep voice bade the visitors enter.

Propped up in bed between a half-dozen pillows was a woman of such enormous size that Agnes feared to look at her in case she betrayed her amazement. Everything about the invalid was huge. Her massive face was crowned with a mane of hair that seemed to be arranged into every style of which hair is capable. It hung white and straight over her shoulders and was piled in a faded, tawny coil on the crown of her head. It was curled grey and tight in a bun over each ear. The bang which stood up from her forehead was matched by a fringe which flopped down over her brow. It was hair of such diverse abundance that it should have dominated the features which it surrounded. But they were so big that the hair seemed no more than their natural accompaniment. The vast nose, long and bulbous at the end, protruded from between immense and rosy cheeks. It was separated by a wide mouth with full lips from a whole series of chins which cascaded down on to the red-flannel nightshirt that covered the vast bosom. The face, unadorned, would have been memorable. But it was made wholly unforgettable by two giant, hairy moles – one above the left eyebrow and the other on what would have been the point of the first chin, had Ginny's anatomy boasted anything that was not round and soft. The huge face split open in a benevolent smile, revealing two gleaming white teeth the size of modest gravestones. Enid screamed and threw herself at the door which, fortunately, Lottie had shut behind her.

'Hello, my little darling.' Ginny spoke in a deep voice which, seeming alien to the body from which it came, made Enid scream even louder and throw herself once more at the door.

Ginny either did not notice or she decided, as a matter of professional judgement, to ignore the tantrum. Agnes grasped her daughter by the shoulder and shook her for the second time in ten minutes. As Enid gasped, her mother realised with shame that she was intentionally digging her fingers into the soft flesh below her daughter's neck.

'I'm sorry, Miss Harthill. She's in a funny mood today. I don't think she can be very well.' Agnes was trying to pull Enid towards the bed.

'Is she an only one?' boomed the baritone voice from the bed.

Agnes nodded. The question made her feel guilty. She would have begun to make excuses and give explanations had not Ginny warmed to her subject.

'Only children are always difficult. They get too much attention.' The mighty frame hitched itself up the bed and a hand the size of a leg of mutton emerged from under the bedclothes and beckoned in the agonised mother's direction. 'Come here, my dear. Come here where I can see you. Leave the child. She won't do herself any harm screaming for a little while.'

It was too late. Agnes had already hobbled across the room and grasped Enid by the arm. She opened the door in preparation for hustling her daughter downstairs.

'It's home for you, young lady. I don't know what's got into you today.'

'She's always the centre of attention, that's the problem.' The voice of professional experience reverberated around the room in a bass so profound that it gave it extra authority. 'Take my advice and get her a little brother or sister. Two aren't much more trouble than one. I've looked after dozens and I know.'

Agnes, who had begun to resent the remorseless analysis of Enid's tantrum, was about to insist that her daughter usually behaved impeccably and that all Shirebrook marvelled at her dignified self-composure, but the unnoticed arrival of Prince made the defence of her daughter's character unnecessary. Enid sat on the floor in the corner of the room feeding the dog boiled sweets which had fallen from the bed. Ginny prised herself up in order to deliver her opinion of the child's shortcomings.

'They'll make him sick,' said Anne. 'Take them off her.'

'Let her come and sit with me,' said Ginny, encouraged by Enid's contented smile. 'You can never be sure with dogs. I remember a little beagle puppy at Dalemny—'

'Prince is very friendly,' said Lottie, coming as near to contradiction as she was capable. 'And always very good with children.'

Despite Lottie's assurance, Agnes lifted Enid up and sat her on the bed. She feared that, parted from the dog, her daughter was about to scream again, but at least she was safe. Enid turned to Ginny and bit her on the arm.

CHAPTER TWENTY-SIX

Charles Hardstaff Comes to Call

Six months passed before the idea of another visit to Worksop was seriously discussed in the Shirebrook cycle shop. Anne's regular visits continued unabated. But apart from doing her duty by asking anxious questions about Agnes's health and welfare, she avoided contentious or potentially divisive subjects of conversation. Her comments about Enid were limited almost exclusively to requests for reassurance that she was being properly fed and favourable references to her instinctive enthusiasm for dogs.

Enid herself behaved as if the awful episode had never happened – save only for the way in which she threw herself with indiscriminate abandon on every passing dog. Agnes, despite knowing that she had a duty to apologise for her daughter, never spoke of that shameful afternoon. But she thought of it continuously. It was not the memory of Enid's deplorable conduct or Ginny's extraordinary appearance that kept her awake at night. It was the fear that there might be some truth in what she had been told about the consequences of Enid remaining an only child.

Her real concern was less for Enid than for herself. She desperately wanted another baby and Ginny's opinion of Enid's conduct and character only added to the obsession.

It was a passion of which she never spoke. It was certainly not the sort of subject which Agnes thought it right to discuss with her husband. But she knew, or thought she knew, that he would not be sympathetic to the idea. Since the beginning of her illness he had barely touched her. She had convinced herself that the estrangement was the result of concern for her health rather than distaste for her swollen joints and revulsion at the sight of her increasingly crooked body. But even that counterfeit conviction served to confirm that there would be no return to the real marriage which had been such a joy to her. Nor would there be a second baby. For six months she brooded. When Anne again suggested that she should visit Brook House, Agnes considered the invitation with considerable foreboding. It had nothing to do with fears about Enid's conduct. Agnes did not want to be told that she ought to have a second baby.

The idea of the visit was unrelated to Ginny's needs and interests. Elizabeth and William Skinner were anxious, indeed desperate, to see their granddaughter again but neither of them was capable of making the journey from Darfoulds to Shirebrook. Elizabeth thought that the solution to their dilemma was obvious: they must all meet in Newcastle Avenue. She felt particularly resentful that she had had to suggest the idea herself.

'I would have thought that Agnes would have wanted it. She must know that you want to see little Enid. Doesn't she want to see us? You'd think that knowing . . .'

'The journey's more difficult for her than it is for us.' As always, William offered the most charitable explanation possible and as usual Elizabeth rejected it.

'When she wanted to go to Worksop to see Lottie's sister, she hired a car.'

'She didn't. Charlotte Harthill paid for it . . . Either her or Anne.'

'Anne wouldn't. She wouldn't pay for Agnes to go and see this Ginny before she came to see me.'

'I'll speak to Anne.' William simply wanted the argument to end.

'Don't tell her I asked you. I don't want them to think that I'm begging them to come to Worksop.'

'I've told you. I'll speak to Anne.'

William spoke to his daughter. She told him what she believed to be the truth. 'Enid's a very difficult child. She's a terrible handful for her poor mother. I could manage her but Agnes can't . . . or won't. She's let her turn into a little terror.' Anne paused, then added, 'She likes dogs, though.'

Encouraged by Anne's conversion to the belief that there was some good in everyone, William pressed his argument. 'I'd still like to see her. Little terror or not. And if the truth is known, your mother feels very neglected. Though she won't say so.'

'I'll speak to Agnes.'

Anne spoke to her sister. Agnes told her what she knew to be lies. 'We've never known her behave like that before. You've seen her often enough. I can't remember when she last cried.'

The bite was not mentioned. Agnes hoped that it was forgotten or overlooked as a momentary aberration.

'Will you come?' Anne seemed almost importunate. 'We'll send a car again.'

'You must be doing well.'

'Ernest's offered to pay. He's got money in the bank and you know how he is about Mam and Dad and their little fancies. It being nearly Christmas, he wants us all to get together. He's spent months making bits and bobs. He wants to hand them out. We thought a week on Saturday.'

'A party!' Agnes's description was as much hopeful as ironic. 'I've not been to a party for years. Brack will come. He'll cycle there when the shop closes.'

'He'll be very welcome, I'm sure.'

'Enid's much better when he's there. He spends his time keeping her amused.' Agnes regretted the admission as soon as it was made, but at least it provoked the response for which she hoped.

'She doesn't have to go upstairs and see Ginny. If Ginny frightens her – by being an invalid and bedridden that is . . .' Anne had intended to do no more than avoid the suggestion that Enid had been frightened by Ginny's grotesque appearance. She had forgotten that her sister would, one day, be a bedridden cripple herself. 'Do you really think Brack will come? I can't see it myself.'

To Anne's admitted astonishment, he came, and to Agnes's undisguised relief Enid behaved impeccably. Her infatuation with Prince had not diminished with the passage of more than half a year: she followed the dog from room to room, falling upon him when he sank down in a corner and setting off again in affectionate pursuit as soon as he grew bored of being hugged and searched for peace and solitude behind a chair or under a table. After half an hour of patting and stroking, it was clear that Enid's attention had become unwelcome but Prince remained good-natured, reinforced in his tolerance by Anne's constant assurances that he could be trusted.

Only when Prince left the house, closely followed by his new friend, was there any misgiving. Lottie called, 'Keep to the path!' and Anne cried, 'Keep off the garden!' and they both rushed to the door to warn of the risk of death by drowning in the brook. But the alarms – and the excursions which followed – were nothing new. A similar crisis occurred even on days when Enid was not at Newcastle Avenue and Prince ventured near the stream alone.

Agnes could not remember when she had last been so happy. Brack was thoughtful and attentive. Her mother and father sat side by side on the chaise-longue (now covered in cream and lime-green stripes) which had been dragged out of the fitting room. It was, Agnes recalled, the most uncomfortable piece of furniture on which she had ever sat but her parents seemed entirely contented. Ernest distributed fretwork objects. None of them was attractive and some were impossible to identify. All were welcome to their recipients. Anne presided with a benign authority and Lottie, although forced to run up and down the stairs in order to keep Ginny fed and entertained, remained cheerfully fey. Surrounded by so much goodwill, Agnes could hardly feel the pain in her back and shoulders and barely thought about the second child that she would never have. Then Enid asked about the old lady in the bedroom.

'What about her?' Lottie replied cautiously. She did not want to suppress the child's compassionate instinct, but neither did she wish to risk a repetition of the previous catastrophe.

Enid ran across the room to the chaise-longue where her grandfather was half asleep. With a shameless determination to ingratiate herself with the old man, she laid her head winningly on his shoulder. 'Can I go and talk to her, Grandad? She likes little girls. Auntie Anne said so when we came before.'

'What about that?' her proud father asked. 'Best part of a year and she still remembers the talk from the last time she was here.'

Anne, who wondered if Enid remembered everything from her first visit, suggested that Ginny might still be sleeping but her stratagem was immediately destroyed by the sound of gale-force coughing and thunderous sneezing which emanated from the floor above.

'I'd better go up,' said Lottie nervously.

'Can I come too?' Enid asked.

Her father, although not entitled to answer the question, gave his permission. 'Of course you can. The lady likes good little girls – good little girls who love their dads.'

Lottie led the way and Enid followed with her mother once more behind her. Anne decided that it was her duty to stay downstairs and intercede, whenever necessary, between her parents and Brack. She listened apprehensively for sounds of trouble above.

Ginny – in Agnes's estimation even more vast than when they had met before – gave no sign that she recognised her assailant or even remembered the assault. Enid, unusually subdued, left her mother in no doubt that she recalled her last visit to the bedside had ended in tears. But she clearly felt neither the fear nor the revulsion which the sight of the invalid had once produced. She stood by the bedroom door, twisting the hem of her dress in her hands.

'Come here, little girl,' Ginny commanded. 'What's your name?'

Enid neither moved nor answered.

'Come here.'

Ginny patted the bed. Agnes looked again at the mighty hand: it had been the sight of that huge fist which had brought on hysterics during Enid's last visit. But the child remained calm and walked slowly across the room and stood beside Ginny's heaped pillows. She stared at the giant head as it turned towards her.

'What's the matter? Cat got your tongue?'

It was a kindly question and Enid knew it. She smiled, giggled, kicked her feet, examined one corner of the pillows. But she did not talk.

'Can't you talk? A big girl like you must be able to talk.' Ginny turned to Agnes. 'Is she shy?'

'A bit. I think it's all the excitement. All the people downstairs.'

'Is she an only one?' She had forgotten that the question had already been asked and answered. Agnes nodded.

'That's what does it. That's what makes her withdrawn. I've seen it a dozen times. Take it from an old woman. She needs a brother or a sister. Better still both.'

'Agnes isn't well, Ginny.' Lottie looked at Enid to see if she had understood a conversation which she should not have overheard. 'Usually she's a great talker.' The attempt to change the subject failed.

'Then you ought to adopt one. The orphanages are full. The work-houses are full. You ought to give a poor child a good home. Is your husband in work?'

At the mention of her father, Enid came to life and from then on there was no way in which she could be silenced. She asked Ginny about her hair, her bedjacket, her red cheeks and inevitably, in the end, her moles. Everything she said confirmed the conviction that the child was shy because she was lonely.

Agnes returned to the living room, her mind filled with a single idea. 'It's been lovely, Dad. And a lot easier than I thought. We can get to Darfoulds. Brack will hire a cab. We'll come up next week. It's been so long since I was home and I've got a lot to talk to you about.'

Agnes knew that she ought to have talked to Brack about adopting a baby before she talked to anybody else but she half convinced herself that it was more sensible first to find out how the task could be accomplished and then persuade him that Enid needed a brother. As soon as Enid followed Elizabeth into the Grove Cottage kitchen she began to cross-examine her father about paupers.

'Thank heavens, I haven't seen the inside of a workhouse for thirty years. And I hope things have changed since then.'

'But what happened then? What happened when someone wanted to adopt a child?'

'I can't remember it happening. Perhaps it did. I can recall one or two single girls having babies . . .'

'They do arrange adoptions though, don't they?'

'I suppose they do. Workhouses round here are full enough these

334

days. But I don't know what happens if somebody wants to adopt an orphan. Anyway . . . why do you want to know?'

The pause gave her away.

'I can't believe it. I can't believe that you could be so foolish. What does Brack say?'

The second silence was as revealing as the first.

'You don't mean that he doesn't know what you're up to? You don't mean . . . !'

'I'm up to nothing, Dad. I'm just asking. And I thought you'd understand. It's not like you to be so nasty.'

'It's your arthritis that I'm sympathetic about. How could you look after another baby on your own? Not properly, you couldn't.'

'I'm not on my own. Brack will help like he helps with Enid.'

'It sounds like you're on your own to me. Otherwise you would have talked to him about it.'

'I tell you, I'm just finding out.'

'Well, all I know is that the workhouses round here are full. There are a lot of miners near to starvation these days. And the children are mostly sick. Rickets. Ringworm. Consumption. It would be wicked to have one of them behind your shop with Enid. Think about her. She's a grand little girl. Concentrate on her.'

'Will you believe me – I'm not saying that I'm going to do anything. I'm just finding out. Will you listen to what I'm saying?'

'I'll believe you when Brack knows. And if you don't promise me you'll tell him, this minute, I'll tell your mother what you're up to.'

In the face of such an awful threat, Agnes had no choice but to accept her father's terms of surrender. 'Very well. I'll tell him tonight. I'll tell him as soon as I get home. I promise.'

Agnes did not keep her word, for when she got home, the whole idea seemed no more than a dream and the real world was Brack – huge, intimidating and concerned solely with himself and his only daughter. But although she did not speak of adoption she brooded. She brooded for so many months that the idea became an obsession. Time after time, she determined to tell Brack of her longing and time after time she lost her nerve. Then, one day in the park, she knew that she could stand the frustration no longer. She decided that she would walk into the shop and just speak the words before she could feel afraid.

Agnes entered her home the easy way, through the front door. Brack was standing in front of the counter next to a fair middle-aged man with whom, until the shop bell had disturbed them, he had clearly been in animated conversation. When Enid ran towards her father, he bent down and picked her up with his usual pride and pleasure. But, although his behaviour was exactly what Agnes would have expected, she detected something shifty in his demeanour. Brack was, his wife decided, feeling guilty. The fair-haired man was clearly a bookmaker. She prayed that Brack had not lost more than he could afford and prayed even harder that he had not again succumbed to the desperate compulsion to gamble away every penny that he owned. The fair-haired man turned in her direction. 'Well, if he won't introduce me, I'll have to introduce myself. My name's Hardstaff. I'm your landlord.'

Agnes only just resisted the temptation to hug him with relief. 'Has my husband offered you a cup of tea, Mr Hardstaff?'

'To tell the truth, we've had a drop of something different.'

He tapped his hip pocket. It gave out the hollow sound of an empty metal flask. Brack looked so guilty that even the landlord noticed.

'He tells me that he doesn't normally touch it, Mrs Brackenbury. He certainly didn't when he smithed for Mr Robinson. But we've broken the rule tonight, just for once. We've been celebrating.'

'Celebrating what?'

Enid was whispering confidently into her father's ear so Agnes assumed that it was his preoccupation with his daughter that prevented Brack from answering her question.

'A new lease,' said Charles Hardstaff. 'We've signed a new lease today. We both signed not ten minutes since. But I didn't think that I'd have the pleasure of meeting you and the little girl.'

There was no time to insist on making a pot of tea, for the landlord, without even a glance at his tenant, picked up his bowler hat from the counter, fitted it carefully on his head, tipped it to Agnes and slid out of the door.

'What's been happening, then?'

'Enid wants taking down the yard. I'll tell you all about it when you come back.'

Brack did not, as Agnes had hoped, launch into his story straight away. Instead he asked her inconsequential questions about her visit to Darfoulds. Concern about her father's health, her mother's temper and the little adventures and inconveniences of her daily life was not a regular feature of her husband's conversation. Indeed, usually he spoke only to convey brief messages concerning subjects of interest to him – his admiration for his daughter, his need for food and drink, his concern about the weather and the speed with which it was necessary to complete the repair of a punctured inner tube. Unnerved by Brack's strange behaviour, Agnes babbled on about the holly being in full berry and the twenty pounds of jam her mother had already made. Brack was clearly not interested in her replies but as soon as she finished one answer, he demanded more details of her day. After half an hour her powers of invention were exhausted. As much out of fatigue as curiosity, she tried to change the subject. 'I didn't know the lease was up.'

'We've got a new'n now. Did you see Mr Hodding whilst you were there?'

'Where would I have seen him? He doesn't come round calling to Grove Cottage. I thought we were here for as long as we wanted. How long is the new lease for?'

'I just thought that you might have seen him, that's all.'

'Everything's all right about the lease, isn't it?'

''Course it is. You heard him say. We signed a new one. That's what he was here for.'

'You're sure?'

'Why shouldn't I be? I can't think what's got into you.'

Brack turned to Enid who, kneeling on the rug in front of the fire, was drawing her grandfather. Her chalk scratched on the slate. 'Your mam's got one of her worries again. If she had something worth worrying about she wouldn't make such a fool of herself.'

It was the sort of casual brutality which had once been a regular feature of her marriage. But, during the years when Brack had mellowed, such attacks had become so rare that an act of wanton aggression caused the special pain that came with surprise. Agnes bit her lip and remembered that, unlike their early years together, a single assault would not inevitably lead to the sustained abuse of which she had been so afraid. She looked gratefully towards Enid, working away at her picture, completely unaware that she had changed her father's character and her mother's life. The chalk scratched on the slate again.

'For God's sake stop that bloody racket.' Brack snatched the chalk from Enid's hand and threw it across the room.

'Leave her alone. Just because you're mad with me for some reason. I don't understand . . .'

Enid stood open-mouthed in amazement. She had never before seen or experienced her father's violence. She was too startled to cry.

'It's all right, Enid. Dad doesn't like that scratching noise. Get the chalk and be careful not to do it again.'

'I said stop it. And I meant stop it.'

Brack stood up and took a sudden, huge step towards the fireplace. Agnes was sure that he was going to strike the child. If she had been capable of sudden movement, she would have tried to force herself between father and daughter. He raised his hand but then he paused. As Agnes struggled to lever herself up from the chair, he brought the heel of his boot down on the slate. It cracked into a dozen pieces and the wooden frame, with which it was surrounded, split at each of its carefully jointed corners. Enid ran sobbing to her mother whilst Brack rested against the mantelshelf like an exhausted man.

'Dad didn't mean to frighten you. He just didn't like the noise.'

An hour after she had been carried upstairs Enid lay in bed, still white and shaking. 'Is he coming up to kiss me goodnight?'

'Do you still want him to?'

'Don't you dare try and turn my child against me.' Brack was at the bedroom door. He spoke to Agnes but he looked at Enid.

'She's still very frightened. Don't make things any worse.'

'I've been all round Shirebrook and there aren't any shops still open. At any rate, not shops that sell slates.'

'Uncle Ern will make you a new slate. There's no need to waste money on buying one.'

'We can manage without Skinner charity.'

Agnes was afraid to leave Enid alone with Brack for fear of the child saying something which provoked him, but she was even more afraid of staying in the bedroom, for her presence was clearly an incitement to Brack's violence. She hobbled towards the door. 'Don't keep her awake too long. She's had a tiring day.'

'I'll come down when I'm ready. Nobody tells me how long I can stay with my own daughter.'

Agnes sat in her rocking chair for an hour, listening to the noise coming down from Enid's bedroom. Brack shouted. Brack sang. Brack clapped his hands, stamped his feet, fell on to his knees with a thud and on to the bed with a rattle of castors and a shudder of springs. Whatever he did, Enid screamed with delight.

'She'll never sleep tonight,' Agnes said to herself. 'She'll never sleep and it'll be me who has to get up in the night to make her a drink and sing to her until she dozes off again.'

By the time Brack came back into the kitchen she had worked herself up into such a frenzy of resentment that she could not contain her indignation. 'I'm not having it. I stood it once. But I shan't stand it again.'

'What will you do then? Run away to sea? Work on the railway? Go down the pit? If you don't have this, what will you have – have for your supper and your breakfast?'

It was the old, cruel Brack – coldly mocking the weak and glorying in his power and strength. It was a Brack she had not suffered for years.

'What's got into you? I don't understand you. I really don't. What's happened to make you like this?'

338

'If you want to know, I'll tell you.' He handed her a letter.

It was signed by Charles Hardstaff and concluded: 'In the light of your continued failure to reply I must give you notice to vacate the premises by 1 January 1912, if by that time you have not paid off the arrears in full.'

Agnes wanted to ask how it had all happened and why she had not been warned but wisely she did no more than make a meek enquiry. 'Do we have to go? Are we really being turned out?'

'You've read t'letter.'

'But isn't there anything that we can do? I'll try to borrow something from Worksop, if you like. They'd help. They helped Ernest when he got in a mess.'

'I might have known I'd get no sympathy from you.'

'I only said I'd try to get Worksop—'

'You said we were in a mess. And we aren't.'

'It seems like a mess to me.' She regretted having said it before the sentence was finished. But Brack, instead of reacting with the violence which she feared, smiled indulgently.

'We were in a mess. But I've got us out of it.' He spoke as if he was announcing a triumph. 'He came to chuck us out but we've got a new lease. So there's no mess and no need to go running, cap in hand, to Worksop.'

'So what's happening, then?'

'We've got to pay more money for a week or two – until the arrears are paid off. We might be tight for a week or two.'

'How much? How much more?'

'We'll manage. It won't be easy, but we'll manage.'

'How much? I said, how much more?'

'Twice as much.'

'We'll never pay that. He might as well have chucked us out tonight. We'll never pay that.'

'We will if we go steady. And we'll have to. We've no choice. We'll be all right as long as they don't have this bloody strike. It's because of the sackings and the short time that we've got into this state. Do you know how much we've taken since summer?'

'I think you've gambled it away.'

It was the first time that Brack had hit her for more than four years. He bent down over her and, as she looked up at him from where she lay, spoke very slowly. 'I've not bet more than a couple of coppers on a race since that little 'un came along. You ought to know that. You're usually only like this when you've been with those two old cows at Worksop. I know what they think of me. And they don't think much more about Enid.'

'They think enough about her to worry about her being on her own.' Agnes pulled herself up to her knees.

'What do you mean by that, for God's sake?'

'They think I should adopt a baby, so she's not a lonely only child. So she's not spoilt.'

'Silly bitch.' Brack hit her again.

An anxious Christmas turned into a desperate New Year. The Derbyshire miners, showing little or no concern for the commercial prospects of the Shirebrook Cycle Shop, voted by a majority of two to one 'In favour of giving notice to establish the principle of an individual minimum wage for every man and boy working underground'.

Brack cursed and read aloud with murmurs of vicious disapproval from the editorial in the *Derbyshire Times*:

The tail is wagging the dog and the motive power of that tail . . . has been largely provided by the socialist element which has been insidiously capturing the miners' lodges in this country for some time.

There was confusion about the day on which the strike would begin for the notices to terminate employment stipulated the end of February as the final working day, and it was leap year. So a few men turned up at the pits on the twenty-eighth of the month whilst those who possessed a calendar did not. The incompetence of the miners' leadership was no consolation to Brack. He gloomily read the considered conclusion of the *Derbyshire Times* and nodded his agreement:

A month's stoppage of the coal supplies of the county would lead to absolute chaos, not to say anarchy.

As the bell over the shop door rang less and less frequently, the strike increasingly obsessed him. Everything that the miners did enraged him. The colliers who stayed at work to feed the ponies, man the pumps and repair the pit roof were accused of feathering their nests. When the more benevolent mine owners gave permission for their striking employees to pick coal from the slag heaps, he said that the weak-minded employers deserved all the trouble that they were going to get. And when a few hard-hearted managers refused to supply the free coal to which their men were legally entitled, he applauded their courage and wondered why the police did not arrest the leader of the Chesterfield lodge, who protested the breach of their members' contracts. But most of all he objected to the marbles.

Marbles had become a mania with the striking miners. Casual games were played on every street corner and leagues were organised in pub yards. Shops which had once sold six for a farthing to the occasional little boy, doubled the price and did business with their usual customers' fathers. And when the supply of real marbles ran out – rolled down drains, flicked into hedgerows and thumbed into ditches – ginger-beer bottles were smashed to retrieve the green glass balls within their necks.

'You'd think that they had more sense, grown men.'

Agnes thought that Brack spoke of the bottle-smashers and echoed his criticism. 'There's a ha'penny back on some of them. Paying a ha'penny for a marble! They must be mental.'

'They must be bloody mental to play the game at all.' Brack's language had badly deteriorated since the strike began. 'But then they must be bloody mental to be out on strike.'

'Seven and six doesn't seem much to me. Not for a full day down the pit.'

'It's more than I've taken in that shop today.' He anticipated what he believed his wife was about to say. 'And don't talk to me about hard work. I've worked down the pit. It's not the hard work they make it out to be. So don't pretend it is.'

'I wasn't going to pretend anything. I was going to ask you if we'd be able to manage.'

'Manage?'

'Pay the rent and buy the groceries.'

He handed her three florins and a sixpence. 'Here. I don't want Enid to go without.'

Everything that the miners did offended him. The discovery that they were invoking divine support drove him into a lather of righteous, if hardly characteristic, indignation. He did not love God, indeed he did not believe in His existence, but he hated the miners so he was particularly severe on an impertinence which he described as coming as near to blasphemy as you could get.

'What's a bishop doing preaching at their service, that's what I'd like to know?' He had seen the headline in the *Derbyshire Times*.

'He doesn't seem to agree with them.'

Agnes had read on. The full text of the Bishop's sermon was set out beneath the headline. She did not understand it fully but it was clear that it was an awful warning against a strange new vice. She wondered why no one had ever told her of it in Sunday school.

There are forces at work today which may oust your leaders and introduce a system of new leaders; a system which I dare proclaim is wicked, cruel and criminal. I mean the system which goes by the name of syndicalism. The men are being used as pawns in the game of war.

After reading the peroration twice and still not understanding it, Agnes read it aloud to Brack.

'Quite right. Give the bastards what for. Quite right.'

'I don't understand what it means.'

'It means that it's all politics. Revolution like the French Revolution. It means that they're not interested in this country – in honest, hardworking folk like you and me. They want revolution.'

Agnes marvelled at her husband's erudition, trembled at the thought of the miners' real ambition and wondered what the answer was to the only question which really interested her.

'Are we going to manage?'

'God knows. It depends on how long this bloody strike goes on and how much damage it does. One thing's certain. There's no money to spare to spend on bicycles.'

Within the next week, the railway began to lay men off. Short of coal, it had to restrict passenger services and cancel half of the goods trains. The Chesterfield tramways ran for only half a day and the gasworks published notices in local papers warning its customers to expect sudden reductions in pressure.

Soup kitchens were opened by the Catholic Church and the Methodist missions. The Sheepbridge Coal and Iron Company closed down its steelworks and offered free midday meals to its laid-off employees and their families on the strict understanding that they would repay the full cost once coal supplies were restored and work began again. The workhouses were full for the first time that century and whilst fully paid-up members of the Derbyshire Miners' Association survived on strike pay, the hundreds of colliers who had allowed their membership to lapse – or who had fallen behind in the payment of subscriptions – struggled, with their families, to survive.

Brack read the report in the *Derbyshire Times* with grim satisfaction:

Living as many always do, literally from hand to mouth, the deadly struggle, brief though it has been, has brought too many families almost to the last extremity.

'Serve the buggers right,' he said. 'Serve the buggers right. They deserve all they get. Only trouble is, if this bloody strike goes on much longer, they'll drag me down with 'em.'

*

The strike ended on 9 April. The militants argued that the miners had little to show for six weeks on strike and the moderates insisted that the new Minimum Wage Act, although only half a loaf, was better than either no bread at all or the continuation of a bruising fight that the miners could not win.

'We've managed,' said Agnes. 'We've managed, and it's all over.' Her back had been particularly bad all day and she was looking for a reason to rejoice.

'I wish to hell it were over. But it isn't. Not by a long chalk.'

'But the paper says they're going back to work.'

'It says they've voted to go back. That's different. There's arguments now about how much they'll be paid when they start. And half the bloody pit has fallen in. Christ knows when they'll be back at work with money in their hands. And when they are, it'll all go to the pawn shop to get back their Sunday suits. They won't be doing much bicycling for a bit, I'll tell you that.'

Brack seemed to delight in his despair. Agnes sensed that he was in a mood to reveal the full extent of their peril.

'How much did we take last week?'

'If you really want to know, I'll tell you. We didn't take enough last week to pay the rent.'

'Let me ask Worksop. You know very well that they helped Ernest. Why shouldn't they help us?'

'Because I'm not Ernest, that's why. I don't do fretwork and I don't play with Indian clubs. I don't skate. And I don't ask for favours.'

'I'll ask them. I don't mind.'

'You're my wife and you'll do what I say. You won't ask for charity.'

'If I have to go to the workhouse with you, that'll be charity.'

'It won't be Worksop charity. Anyway,' for a moment he sounded genuinely hopeful, 'we're not done for yet. There are still ways. There's still ways round it.'

'What ways? There's no way of paying bills when you don't have any money.'

'Hardstaff hasn't asked me for a penny this month. He knows I'm tight but he daren't foreclose. He'll give me time. He daren't kick me out and lose his rent for good. Nobody else could make a go of this shop. He doesn't want to chivvy me so he hasn't even been round.'

It was not until an hour after Agnes had gone to bed that Charles Hardstaff arrived. He did not waken her by knocking on the door or clanging the shop bell for, at midnight, Brack was waiting for him on the pavement. There was a brief, and apparently amiable, conversation. Then the two men disappeared into the passageway that led to the yards at the back of the Long Terrace. It was after two o'clock

343

when Charles Hardstaff left. He walked with the jaunty air of a man well satisfied with his night's work. In the bedroom above the shop, Brack lay in the darkness unable to sleep. He was kept awake not by fear, but by excitement.

CHAPTER TWENTY-SEVEN

Comings and Goings

Agnes woke as usual in the small hours. As always she struggled to relieve the pain in her shoulders and the ache in her back without waking her husband. She turned on to her back and stretched her arms down by her side. Then she gently turned her head, first to the left and then to the right. All the unsuccessful exercises were conducted at the edge of the mattress in the hope that they would be completed and she would fall asleep again with Brack still undisturbed.

There were nights when the agony was so intense that she had to shake him awake and ask him to rub her neck or push at the point of her spine which she believed to be the centre and the source of her paralysis and he responded with a kindness and sympathy which would have astounded Anne and Lottie. But she always, at least, tried to let him sleep on through her tribulations and, on the night when the memory of his assault was still the first thought in her waking mind, she bent her swollen joints with particular care.

The eiderdown had slipped to the floor and, fearful that her husband would shiver himself awake, Agnes dangled her hand over the side of the bed as if she were lying in a sailing boat and testing the temperature of the water in a pond. She found the eiderdown, pulled it back on the bed and with great stealth and considerable pain began the slow process of sliding it over her sleeping husband. Gently she reached out to find exactly where he lay. Brack was not in the bed.

Agnes sat up in panic and began to run her hands along the mattress to make sure that he was not rolled up like a hibernating hedgehog in one of its corners. When she was certain that he was not there, she eased herself on to the strip of carpet which ran alongside the edge of the bed on the bare floorboards. There was no candle in the room so she had to feel her way through the darkness to the door.

'Are you there, Brack? Are you there?'

She called out in a sharp whisper which she hoped was loud enough to wake her husband if he had fallen asleep in his chair but low

345

enough not to rouse Enid in her bedroom above the kitchen. When there was no response of any sort, she bit her lip and with a great effort of will climbed on a chair and lit the gas.

Relief that Brack was not lying dead in front of the fire turned into fear that he was lying injured behind the counter, the victim of a stroke, heart attack or, more likely, burglary. What she saw in the shop confirmed in her mind that there had been a burglary. The shop window was a shambles. The cut-out cardboard figure which advertised Raleigh bicycles lay on its back, staring up at the ceiling through a litter of empty boxes. What had once been a pyramid of oil cans had collapsed into a heap and the sou'wester which was once the companion of a yellow oilskin lay lonely and neglected on a pile of mudguards. The oilskin itself was missing. So was what had been the centrepiece of the window display since Anne had bought the Raleigh – a green Singer Safety Bicycle, with saddle bag, handlebar basket, Bowden brakes and three-speed gears on the back wheel. The thieves, Agnes decided, had stolen the bicycle and abducted its rightful owner. Then she realised that, if Brack had been kidnapped, whoever took the Singer had carefully locked the shop door behind them.

She went back into the kitchen and sat down, frightened and bewildered. Her washing basket was upside down against the kitchen door. The day before it had contained shirts which, too dry to iron, had been rolled up to await dampening and smoothing on the following morning. The shirts had gone, so had the socks which had been left to dry on the fireguard. She went into the pantry. The bread pancheon was empty and there was no cheese under the wire-mesh dome.

It was still almost impossible to believe that Brack had left without excuse or explanation. Then she saw, folded up on the floor behind the door, a piece of paper which he had obviously dropped as he silently edged out into the night. Slowly she opened it out on the sideboard under the gas jet. It was a page from the *Sporting Life,* a newspaper which she had almost forgotten existed. The headline read 'Racing at Derby' and below it was printed the list of runners and riders.

She was almost relieved by the discovery for it seemed at least to confirm that Brack would be back in a couple of days – penniless and in despair, but back home with her and Enid. A terrible thing had happened that night but it was not so terrible as she had initially feared. He had not run away to another woman who could be his healthy, proper wife. He had left her for nothing more threatening than a racehorse.

It was still only half-past five and she knew that it was wrong to

346

wake the child. Nevertheless, once she had remade the bed she fumbled her way through the darkness and into the box room. She just managed to lift Enid out of bed and drag her, still half asleep, across the landing. They spent what was left of the night together.

For three days, Agnes assumed that every ring of the shop bell and every sound of footsteps in the yard meant that Brack had come home. So, when the kitchen latch was lifted without a warning knock, she pushed herself off the sofa and was halfway across the room before the door opened. A Catholic priest stepped inside. He noticed her surprise. 'You'll forgive me, Mrs Brackenbury.'

Agnes was astonished by his voice. She had seen him pottering in the garden by the side of his strange little church and padding along the footpath as he visited his few parishioners. But she had never heard him speak. Agnes knew little of the Catholic Church. She believed that its adherents worshipped statues and that its priests were all Irishmen with red faces and impenetrable accents. The priest who stood inside her kitchen door spoke in the tones of an English gentleman.

'You must forgive me. Walking into houses is one of the bad habits which priests acquire – like smoking, drinking and, I fear, an enthusiasm for horses.'

'I'm afraid we're a bit untidy. I was just getting the child's dinner and I've not had a chance to clear up.'

Agnes had no time for the Church of Rome. But her uninvited visitor wore a clerical collar and so qualified for some of the respect which was properly due to a real clergyman from the Church of England.

'It is I who owe you the apology for calling unannounced and walking in. We do it with all our people to remind them of our authority. If we stood outside their doors and knocked, they might begin to think that they were our equals.'

Judging, correctly, that the ice would have been more easily broken by a formal introduction, he held out a small white hand. 'My name is Froes. I'm the priest across the road at St Joseph's.'

'Thank you very much, but I'm Church of England. My husband's a Methodist. I'm grateful for your interest, but my little girl's already christened. At Steetly.'

'Believe me, I've not come to baptise you into the one true faith, although it's my bounden duty to attempt to save your soul by that certain method . . .'

The irony was lost on Agnes. 'I'm afraid I'm very busy at the moment. If you could call back at a more convenient time . . .'

347

'I hoped that your husband might spare me a minute.'

'Is it bicycles?' Agnes felt the relief appropriate to escape from forcible conversion. 'I'm afraid that he's out. Can I help you?'

'He seems to have been out for several days.'

'Can I help?' Agnes decided that it was best to avoid comment on the length of his absence. 'I look after the shop when he's away.'

'I'm afraid that it's not bicycles either. When he gets back would you tell him I called and say Edge Hill Lad. He'll know what I mean.'

'Edge Hill Lad?' For the first time since they met, Agnes understood something that the priest had said. 'Edge Hill Lad? Is it a racehorse?'

'Edge Hill Lad is, indeed, a racehorse and a rather good one at that. Your husband was kind enough to put a bet on it for me. As I told you, racing – perhaps I should have said gambling – is one of the priest's original sins. As always your husband placed my bet and, as very rarely happens, the horse won. Unfortunately, the whole business seems to have escaped his—'

'At Derby last week?'

'Yes, he came round to look at my *Sporting Life*. I wouldn't have bothered you if I'd known he was still away. To be honest, I wanted to place another bet. I wouldn't have mentioned that either but you're clearly not the sort of woman to be bothered by these things.'

'How long have you been betting with my husband?'

'Two years or more, on and off. Ever since I discovered the existence of a kindred spirit in the area. This is only my second win.'

Agnes hated Father Froes. And because she hated him she would not be in his debt. 'How much does my husband owe you? He'd want me to pay you.'

'Fifteen shillings.' He pronounced the words with the slow and careful deliberation of a man whose only object in life was the recovery of his money.

'Fifteen shillings!'

Father Froes could not have failed to recognise the anguish but he stood immobile, impassive and waiting to be paid.

There was three pounds, seventeen shillings and sixpence halfpenny in the tea caddy on the mantelshelf. Agnes knew the amount exactly. When Brack left there had been nine and twopence. Then she had pulled the purse from inside the sofa's springs and added the furtive savings of five years. That had increased her capital to over four pounds. In three days she had spent twelve and ninepence before she had decided that the indignity of credit was better than sacrificing her only source of ready money. Now she was being asked to throw away fifteen shillings. She was outraged. But she could not stand out against the priest's determination. She counted out six half-crowns into the smooth palm. Father Froes handed one back.

'If you see him before Tuesday, would you be so kind as to say, "Charity to win in the three o'clock at Doncaster." I couldn't resist Charity. It sounded like a message.'

'I may not see him.' There was not the slightest hint of the wish to help.

'Well, then, just ask the little girl to run across to the presbytery.'

For the first time in four days, Agnes felt more angry than afraid – angry with the priest who suggested such a thing but more angry with Brack, who had brought this shame upon her. 'I shall do no such thing. No daughter of mine is going to be a bookies' runner.'

'Quite so. You are perfectly right and I should not have asked it.' He backed towards the door. 'If your husband has not returned, keep it until he does. There will be other occasions for its use, I'm sure of that.' For the second time Father Froes lifted the latch, without invitation. 'God bless you, my child.'

Agnes waited for another week. She had no trouble buying groceries, for her credit was good. Nor did she have the problem with Enid which she had first anticipated. There were questions – 'When is Dad coming back?' and 'Is he coming back tomorrow?' – but they were turned aside by a stiff answer – 'Soon' and 'Perhaps.' But it was a desperate seven days. She took Enid for her walks and did her shopping almost hysterical with the hope that he would be there when she got back and nearly incapacitated with the notion that somebody would ask her about him when she was out. When Mr Hardstaff approached her on the recreation ground, she did not recognise him.

'I'll walk home with you. I came to see Brack.'

She put on a brave face. 'I don't think he'll be there. I doubt if he'll be back.'

'I know he's not there. I've been round already. No wonder he's going bankrupt, shutting the shop on a Wednesday afternoon. When will he be back?'

'I don't know. I really don't know.'

'Well, where is he, then?'

'What business is it of yours?'

'I'm his landlord. Your landlord for that matter. It's my business when he owes me rent.'

Mercifully, at that moment, Enid called from the far end of the shale path. 'Mam, I've got a stone in my shoe. Come and get it out. It hurts.'

'I'll have to go and look after my little girl.'

To Agnes's immense relief, Enid – who was limping along the path – had begun, uncharacteristically, to cry. It was shameful for a mother to be so pleased by her daughter's distress but she could not help feeling that a relief column was about to lift her siege.

'He's run off, hasn't he? Run off and left you.' Mr Hardstaff seized her arm and she winced with pain and surprise.

'Don't you dare say that. And take your hand off me.' She was afraid to shake herself free. 'I think you'd better be on your way, Mr Hardstaff. I dread to think what my husband will say when I tell him.'

'It's no good being high and mighty with me—'

'Mam, I can't get it off.'

'You can see that I have to look after the child.'

Enid, despite her protestations, had pulled off her shoe. She had also broken the patent-leather strap which stretched across her instep. She held the shoe in her hand as she trod delicately on the gravel path, shouting for help each time her stockinged foot touched a sharp stone.

'I don't mean to be rude—'

'Put the shoe on and come and sit down on this bench.'

'I can't, it's broken.' The foot was back inside, but the broken strap flapped the threat that it would be out again at any second.

Mr Hardstaff took a handkerchief out of his pocket and bound it round Enid's instep. 'There, we've bandaged you up. Now run up the bank and play whilst I talk to your mam.' Enid gambolled off, affecting a grotesque limp. 'Before you complain about my presumption, Mrs Brackenbury, take my advice and listen. There are things you need to know.'

'I'm not going to listen—'

'I've not come all the way from Worksop to tell you tittle-tattle about Brack. Do you know how much your husband owes me?'

'That's his business, not mine.'

'Perhaps it is and perhaps it isn't. It'll be your business if he's away somewhere when you get evicted from that shop.'

'Is that what you're going to do to us, the little girl and me?'

'Not unless I have to. If Brack had seen reason six months ago it wouldn't have come to this. I could have got him a part-time job smithing, until he got over the bad patch. But he wouldn't have it. I don't want to turn you out. I don't want the shop to stand empty for months. I told him all that. But that was before . . .'

'Before what?'

'Before he borrowed ten pounds on the security of the stock and then took the bicycle. That bike was worth the best part of five pounds.

350

And don't tell me that he hasn't taken it, because I know he has. I looked in the window when I called round. It's gone. So don't tell me any fairy stories.'

Agnes knew that loyalty should make her reticent but she was also desperately insecure. She needed to know whatever Mr Hardstaff could tell her about Brack's prospects. And he seemed such a kind man. She stayed and braced herself for the next revelation.

'Five pounds that bicycle was worth and, if I know him, he'll have sold it for a quid or thrown it in a ditch.'

'Of course he won't. He'll need it to come back on.'

'And what makes you think that he'll come back?'

'Because the shop is his home and I'm his wife. That's his daughter running about up there with your handkerchief tied round her foot. He'll not leave her.'

'I hope you're right. I hope it for your sake and I hope it for mine. Because if I do ever see hide or hair of him again, I'll get some of my money back – if I have to skin him alive and tan him. And I can't wait for ever. That wouldn't do at all. If I got a reputation for being soft with bad payers, half of Mansfield wouldn't pay their rent. Have you got any money now?'

'How much does he owe you?'

'I didn't mean that. He owes me a lot more than you can find. I mean, have you got any money for groceries?'

'Of course I have.'

'I don't believe you.' Mr Hardstaff took out his purse and began to search amongst the silver.

'Put that away. We owe you enough already. How much is it? Tell me.'

'With the ten he borrowed, it's nearer eighty pounds than seventy.'

'We'll never pay that off!'

'I'm sorry for you and the little girl but there's nothing that I can do. If you take my advice, you'll start making plans.'

'What sort of plans can I make?'

'Have you got a mother and father still alive? Brothers or sisters? You're going to need somewhere to live.'

'That's not a matter that need concern you. But, rest assured, wherever I live it will be with my husband.'

'I hope we don't meet again, Mrs Brackenbury, but I fear that we will.'

Mr Hardstaff left without reclaiming his handkerchief, and Enid and her mother began to limp back to the shop together.

'Would you like a little holiday?' Agnes asked.

Enid was not sure what a holiday was, so she made no reply.

'Shall we go and see Auntie Anne?'

'And Prince?'

'And Prince.'

Agnes walked on home wondering how she would manage to carry her luggage from the shop to the Shirebrook railway station.

Anne was not at all surprised to see her. Had a whole month of daily letters and a week of constant telegrams warned of the arrival of her deserted sister she could hardly have been more prepared. She offered a less than ecstatic welcome.

'You'll have to go up into the attic. It's warm and aired. I'm sorry, but with Ginny being in the back bedroom . . .'

Agnes said that the attic would suit her perfectly and that Enid, although too excited to sleep, ought to be put at once to bed.

'Can't she stay up to see her uncle Ern? Ernest will be round at about seven. He'd like to see her.'

The giant maw had opened ready to swallow up both mother and daughter. Imperceptibly and against the wishes of both victims and abductors, Agnes and Enid were becoming part of 'Worksop'. To Anne, Brack was already part of the fantasy life in which she had never quite believed. Reality was Newcastle Avenue, Overend Road and Darfoulds. Her sister and niece existed in limbo and came to life only when they crossed its boundaries into her real world. One of the rules of life in that little universe was proper respect for Ernest.

'He comes most nights. He likes to have his supper at home at Grove Cottage. Then he walks round for a talk – mostly a talk about old times.'

Anne talked about her brother as if he were an ancient with a whole life to look back on. Agnes remembered that he was not yet forty but had already been sucked into the Worksop world of memory, disappointment and regret.

'We'll only be here for a day or two.'

'We're glad to see you,' added Lottie. 'Glad to see you safe and well.'

'Why shouldn't I be safe and well?'

'No need to worry about that now. You're here, that's the main thing.' Lottie's reassurance was interrupted by the sound of Ernest at the front door. Apart from Ernest, only customers were allowed entry through the fitting room and it was too late for a customer. He registered a moment's surprised delight at the sight of his sister, ignored his niece and proceeded to fit a new washer on the dripping scullery tap with the promise that they would all 'talk later'. With Enid tucked up in bed, the conversation began.

'First of all,' said Anne, 'you mustn't worry about money. We're doing quite well. I'm not saying that there's money to throw about. But you mustn't worry.'

'We hardly notice that Ginny's here,' added Lottie, as much out of self-vindication as in an effort to make Agnes feel at home.

'Stay here. Go to Grove Cottage. Come to me. It's entirely up to you,' Ernest insisted.

It was clear to Agnes – though she was not sure why – that, despite the protestations, they all waited for her to say that her visit would be brief. She obliged.

'I only want to stay here just for a few days until Brack gets back.'

'I know,' said Anne. 'But we still have to decide where you'll be happiest. There's plenty of space at Overend Road. It's not country like Darfoulds but it will be better for Enid's schooling. There's a school called Ashleigh House that we've seen advertised in the *Guardian*.'

'It's up to you,' Ernest repeated. 'But I reckon Overend Road would be best.'

'Not that you're unwelcome here,' Anne insisted. 'Make up your own mind. It's a big decision for a woman on her own.'

'Listen.' Agnes was too exhausted to be exasperated. 'Listen, will you. I'm here for a day or two. Don't talk as if I've left Brack.'

'We know you haven't,' said Anne. 'But, if you have, Overend Road would be best, especially for Enid.'

'You'd be able to look after Ernest,' Lottie added.

'It's for you to decide,' said Ernest, looking like a man whose guilty secret had been revealed too soon.

'Then I'll stay here for a day or two.'

'Good.' Ernest sounded genuinely pleased. 'And go out to Darfoulds and see Dad and Mam whilst you're here. They'd love to have Enid.'

Ernest's idea worked out in a way that he could not have foreseen. After almost a week at Brook House, Agnes and Enid spent a weekend in the spring sunshine at Grove Cottage. Enid showed every sign of liking her grandfather almost as much as she liked her aunt's dog and she returned to Newcastle Avenue with great regret and temporarily unquenchable tears.

On the day of her return, Anne decided that a definite decision had to be made about Agnes's future. She had no doubt that, for as long as her health permitted it, her sister should keep house for Ernest. It was the sensible way to solve all the problems. The front door rattled earlier than usual. Anne waited for Ernest to appear and make the suggestion with the special impatience that comes from anticipated success.

'Didn't you unbolt it, Lottie?'

'I thought I did.'

'You couldn't have done. Run along and do it now. Ernest's standing on the step.'

The door was already unbolted, so Lottie pulled it open. It was not Ernest who stood on the step, but a collier, covered in coaldust from head to foot. It was several seconds before Lottie realised that it was Brack.

CHAPTER TWENTY-EIGHT

Blood Sports

'Is she here?'

'You'd better come in.' Lottie looked up and down the road in the hope that none of the neighbours had seen her visitor.

Brack leaned his Singer Safety Bicycle against the wall and removed his cap in an act of unusual courtesy. A band of clean skin gleamed white below his hairline. The rest of his face was black with coaldust.

'Is she here?'

Lottie did not reply, for she was not sure which answer Anne would want her to give. She turned and led Brack through the fitting room. As he negotiated the padded dummies, the chaise-longue, the tall vases filled with rushes and the piles of pattern books, he asked her again, 'Is she here?'

To Lottie's relief, Anne appeared in the kitchen doorway and, after only a momentary shudder, answered the question. 'She's out. Won't be back till late.'

'It's near six o'clock.' Brack sounded scandalised.

'She'll want Enid in bed by seven. She might let her stay up for a treat but she'll want her in bed by seven.' Anne saw no reason to mention that Agnes was at Grove Cottage. She took great pride in the ability to deceive without lying.

There was a terrible moment when it seemed that he was going to announce his willingness to wait. But he twisted his cap and, with considerable difficulty, left his emollient message.

'Will you tell her I'm back. I can't stop now. Not like this. But will you tell her I'm back.'

Convinced of his resolve to go, Lottie offered him a cup of tea and Anne, staring at her partner with undisguised fury, only just managed to spread a newspaper on the couch before he sat down.

'Are you working down the pit?'

It was, thought Anne, exactly the sort of question Lottie could be relied upon to ask.

355

'Warsop Main.'

'Why there?' Apprehension, not curiosity, prompted the question. Anne was sure that Warsop Main was not the nearest colliery to Shirebrook. She had assumed that Brack had returned at least to live over the cycle shop. If he had moved, there was a risk that he had moved closer to Worksop.

'It was the only job I could get. And I had to take that at seven shilling a day. But it's a job.'

'What's happened to the cycle shop?'

'It's finished. The strike saw to that.' He picked up his cap from the hearth. It had left a thin coating of coaldust on the tiles. 'I'll thank you for the tea and be on my way. Just tell her that I'm back. The sooner she comes home the better.'

'I can't believe it,' said Lottie the moment the front door shut behind him. 'Never said he was sorry. Never asked how she was. Never even asked about poor little Enid. He's a brute. The thought of Enid having to go back to him . . .'

'Why should she go back to him?'

'She'll want to.' Lottie had no doubt about Agnes's reaction to the news of Brack's return.

'Not until she knows that he's back she won't.'

'But you've got to tell her.'

'On Tuesday I have. On Tuesday when she gets back. But a lot of water will flow over the dam before then. For one thing Ernest will go and see him and find out what's what.'

'What good will that do?'

'It depends on what he finds.' Anne could not wait to tell her brother where his duty lay.

Ernest arrived at the back door of the bicycle shop as early as the first Sunday train from Worksop could get him to Shirebrook. He had accepted his assignment with an enthusiasm that neither timorous Lottie nor determined Anne had expected and he meant to carry it out with conspicuous success. He was not prepared to risk Brack having left before his arrival.

He knocked before Brack was even out of bed. He beat three times on the door before there was a movement in the bedroom. Then Brack's head appeared at the window. Ernest's first reaction was disbelief that hair could be so neat above so unshaven a face. Then he called up, 'It's Ernest. Ernest Skinner. Can I come in?'

'Has something happened? Has there been an accident?'

'Nothing like that.' Ernest sounded positively jovial. 'I've just come round for a bit of a chat. Come down and let me in.'

Ernest had expected to find a shambles. And he was deeply impressed to discover the kitchen in near-perfect order. He was a single man living alone and he knew how easy it was to collapse into squalor. But in the kitchen behind the cycle shop clean dishes were piled in the sink, the fire was laid and a neat white tablecloth was already spread across the table in preparation for breakfast. At first Ernest thought that there must be a woman in the house. Then he decided that Brack was far too composed to allow for such a possibility. He looked at him with a new respect and Brack understood.

'It's best to keep things tidy. Else you get into a right mess.'

'How long have you been back?'

'A week. A week yesterday. Sit down. I'll put t'kettle on.'

Brack, who was preparing to rebut Ernest's uplifting advice and reject his proposals for a new and better life, could not help feeling a grudging admiration for his brother-in-law's nerve in turning up at all. He watched, fascinated, as his uninvited guest pulled off his woollen gloves and carefully put them in his greatcoat pocket. Having made sure that the pocket flaps were in their proper positions, Ernest removed the greatcoat itself and folded it into a neat bundle in a way which suggested that it was to be wrapped up in brown paper and sent through the post. He placed the putative parcel on the sideboard. Finally, he unwound the long knitted scarf from around his neck and rolled it into a soft grey cylinder which he balanced on top of his now cubic coat. Brack decided that a man who took his clothes so seriously had to be reckoned with. He put two more rashers of bacon in the frying pan.

'Is she not coming back, then?' He seemed to ask the question almost casually.

'She'll come back. She'll come back as soon as she knows that you're here.'

'Bloody hell! Haven't you told her?'

'We haven't seen her. She's at Grove Cottage. Expected back on Tuesday.'

'But that Anne Skinner said—'

'I know. I'm sorry.'

'The bloody liar.'

'If you speak about my sister like that . . .' For a moment memories of his chivalrous past flooded through Ernest's mind. Then he remembered that the days of chivalry were over. 'She didn't lie. She'd be very careful not to. She just didn't tell the truth.'

'Will she tell her on Tuesday?'

'I shall. She's your wife and her place is with you, however you treat her. But I wanted us to talk about—'

'How I treat my wife is none of your business.'

'I'm not saying that it is. I'm here to talk about business, not what goes on between you and Aggie. If you wanted to go back to smithing, I'd set you up. Strictly business, of course. I'd expect paying back.'

'Is that what Miss Skinner sent you to say to me?'

Ernest ignored the question. It was impertinent, perceptive and incapable of being answered in a way which was both honest and convincing.

'I'm not interested in smithing any more.'

'Why on earth not? It's a danged sight better than being a collier.' Ernest, having approached as near to bad language as he ever got, immediately regretted his vehemence. 'At least, I'd prefer it.'

'Smithing is finished. Horses will be a rarity in twenty years' time and I never did like gates and railings.'

'What about the railway? They have blacksmiths on the railway. If you don't want to risk it on your own, try the railways.'

'I could. And I could try the pit. They have blacksmiths there an' all. But I'll tell you something, Mister Skinner – something I wouldn't tell everybody and I'm surprised that I'm telling you. To me, smithing is horses. I'm a farrier by trade, not a blacksmith. If I go back to smithing, I'll be back at the gambling. I'll be surrounded by people who think of nothing else except handicaps, hard going and starting prices. I want to put all that behind me.'

'You're giving up gambling!' Ernest announced the triumph with the air of an evangelist who had just made a convert.

'I didn't say that. I'm giving up big gambling. I'll put sixpence on now and then. But I'll never go mad again like I did at Derby. I've learned my lesson.'

Ernest longed to know what had happened at Derby. But to ask was the certain way to make sure that Brack did not tell him. He remembered Brack's favourite phrase. 'Suit yourself.'

'Derby changed everything. I learned my lesson. I learned it just in time.'

'I'm pleased to hear it.'

'Do you know what happened?' Brack did not wait for an answer. 'I had a system – terrible things, gambling systems. They make you think that you can't lose.'

'I don't even know what a system is.' Ernest sounded apologetic, though he had no doubt that he was entitled to be proud of his ignorance.

'Well, I'll tell you. A gentleman – an educated gentleman – helped me to plan it. Look at any race card. It's a racing certainty that a favourite will win before the end of the meeting. Well, nearly certain, at any rate.'

Ernest forced himself to look impressed.

'So I went to Derby. You've got to be at the meeting to follow on one bet with another.'

There was no need to counterfeit bewilderment.

'So I borrowed a bit and took what was in the till. I was sure that I'd win enough to get straight again. I bet five pounds on the first race – five pounds on Merrymac, the favourite at seven to two. If I'd won, I'd have taken my seventeen pounds and just watched till the next day. Well, I might have put a shilling . . . Anyway, I didn't win. It came in third.'

Brack went on to describe, race by race, the intricacies of the multiplier bet. It was, he assured Ernest, the sure way of making money – as long as the punter had sufficient funds to gamble on until a favourite won and he both recouped his previous losses and made his planned profit. 'It's a perfect system, if you've got the cash. Bookmakers use it and make fortunes. Only I ran out of money.'

'So what did you do?'

'No good betting what I'd got left on the favourite. I put it on an outsider at eleven to one. If it had won, I'd have solved all my problems.'

'But it lost.'

'The favourite came in. Goes to show. To them that have shall be given.'

'You don't sound as if you've got over it to me. It's still in your blood.'

'But I can keep it under control. And I can tell you how I know. When I lost in the third, my first idea was to pawn the bicycle. Pawn it or sell it to somebody on the course and put every penny on a horse in the four-thirty. But I didn't. I had more sense. I stopped myself. I knew I wanted the bike to get home on.'

'You didn't come home. Not for nearly a month.'

'I did bits of jobs. I was ashamed. And I didn't want to see Agnes and tell her what had happened.' Brack grinned for the first time. 'And I didn't want to see the landlord neither.'

'So you left Agnes to face him.'

'I knew you'd preach me a sermon before long. I'm not interested. Just tell my wife I'm back. If she wants to be a collier's wife, she's welcome.'

There was, Ernest decided, reason for hope. Brack had refused the offer of a return to smithing because he wanted to avoid temptation. What was more, he was washing the greasy breakfast plates, within minutes of leaving the table. A man who kept his house clean and tidy must have a lot of good in him.

'I'll lend you something if you like. I'll want a proper agreement and proper security. But I'll set you up again.'

'The shop's finished. No good pretending otherwise.'

'It's a genuine offer.'

'I'd be grateful if you'd lend me enough to pay off the landlord. He's been very reasonable. But sooner or later . . . I need this place for when Agnes and Enid come back.'

'You think they will come back, do you?'

'I do. And I'd like to get a new place. I can manage the rent, but not much more.'

'It'll have to be a business deal, mind. Like I offered for the shop, a proper agreement written down.'

Ernest began the long and careful process of putting on his outdoor clothes. He felt proud of the way in which he had faced and overcome the family crisis. Having decided, long ago, to protect himself against the pain of human emotion, he would have much preferred to pretend that Agnes and Brack lived in perfect harmony. But he had done his duty. He pulled his muffler tight around his neck, carefully buttoned his greatcoat and eased on his gloves with a sense of profound self-satisfaction. Thanks to him, the world would soon be as it was before. Brack's aberration had disturbed the calm water of life in Worksop.

Agnes knew that the old times had gone for ever. She would never trust Brack again. No matter how happy the day and enjoyable the evening, she would always wake up on the following morning worrying if Brack was still by her side. Had she not enjoyed those four peaceful years, it would have been possible to struggle on, hoping and pretending that one day she would enjoy the security which she once thought that marriage would provide. That hope had died on the morning Brack left for the Derby races, and his return did not bring it back to life. The good years seemed no more than a sham, the time when she was not loved but tolerated. Brack was coming home to take her back on sufferance. It was the only way that he could be with Enid again.

She gave no thoughts to Brack's feelings and the sudden violence which she had provoked by her suggestion of adopting a second child seemed no more than a terrifying revelation of his true character. The joys of their physical union were forgotten so she did not recognise the new barrier which had been built between them. When Brack left home, they were separated by Brack's distaste at the thought of making love to her. When he returned they were divided by his enthusiasm for making love to someone else.

Agnes liked the new house in Austin Street, but she did not like

360

Jack McGovern, the cobbler who had moved into the shop in Main Street and seemed, mysteriously, to be part of the deal that Brack had done with Mr Hardstaff. He had become a close friend of Brack within weeks of moving to Shirebrook and she knew that it would be wise to like him. But, no matter how hard she tried, she could feel nothing except fear and loathing whenever she met him. She was ashamed of her feelings because she attributed them to Cobbler Jack's most conspicuous attribute. His face seemed almost split in two by a hare-lip.

Jack McGovern, who came round every evening in the generally unrealised hope of supper, made her feel uneasy. Whenever he and Brack were together she felt that they were laughing at her – not because of her increasing infirmity, her girlish optimism or even her prudish habit of blushing when she heard bad language, but because of something she did not know which was all the more frightening because it was a secret. She tried to convince herself that her fears were all imaginary and were based on a childish revulsion at the gash which divided his top lip and crumpled his nostrils.

No matter how much she told herself that it was wicked to hold a man's deformity against him, she could not clear her mind of the thought that he was evil. He looked like one of the gargoyles whose open mouths spouted water from Steetly chapel roof on rainy days. They were, she knew, representatives of the devil – condemned to look out of the church and never in. Jack McGovern spent too much of his time looking into her house.

Jack McGovern seemed to be part of everything Brack did.

'If you hadn't come back so quick, I'd have had some furniture in that front room. Jack knows a place where chairs and stuff are going cheap.'

'We can't afford it, however cheap it is.'

'Oh, yes, we can, I've come into a bit.'

'How?'

'Checkweighman's bonus. We're better off than I thought.' He felt in his back pocket again and, after a good deal of searching, brought out two sovereigns. 'Here. Buy something for Enid. And buy yourself something. You don't want to wear Worksop's cast-offs for ever.'

Agnes knew it was betting money. She could tell by the way he felt in his pocket that there were more sovereigns in there – sovereigns he did not want her to know about, far more sovereigns than could possibly have come from any checkweighman's bonus. She was not even tempted to confront him with the truth. Her only feeling was bewildered despair that after so long the big betting had started again

– bewildered despair and a deadening regret that she had agreed to return.

'I shan't get home till late for the next night or two. I'll be busy. I'm going to help Jack McGovern with a bit of decorating.'

The idea was so absurd that Agnes was caught off guard. 'I don't believe you.'

Even that did not disturb his amiable equilibrium. 'I am. It's God's truth. I'm going to paint and paper. He'll pay me a quid or two. He's got a bit has Jack. That's how he got the shop. Paid a big lump sum down.' Brack felt in his pocket again and withdrew a five-pound note. 'Send this to your brother for me. First repayment on the loan he kindly made us. Earlier than expected. He won't half be surprised.'

Within the week, Brack was as good as his word – at least as far as the furniture was concerned. A cheap three-piece suite – covered in mottled brown American cloth – was delivered on what, when on normal duty, was clearly a coal lorry. It returned with a walnut sideboard which was really too big for the room but would have been a credit to a boarding house. A butcher's boy brought a bright nickelled horn and metal handle, and explained that the gramophone itself was too big to carry in his bicycle basket.

Enid leaped on to the sofa and bounced up and down on the noisy springs. She knocked to the floor the patent ashtray which was fastened to a strip of American cloth draped like a waiter's napkin over the sofa's wooden arm. When her mother told her to stop at once, she ran to the sideboard and wrenched open one of its doors. Inside there was an old copy of the *Derbyshire Times*. A ring had been drawn around one of the classified advertisements – half a dozen wicker-backed orchestra chairs.

Whilst Agnes was still wondering when the chairs would arrive, Enid began to explore the far recesses of the sideboard. She found two brand new packs of playing cards, the seals on their boxes still unbroken.

'Put them back. Put them back this minute.' Her mother could not have sounded more agitated if her daughter had run in from the washhouse with a packet of rat poison in her hand.

'When do you open?' Brack said.

The cobbler's shop looked almost ready for the night's entertainment. 'As soon as the chairs come. And when you've brought the bloody whisky inside. It's been in the yard half the afternoon. It's a miracle it hasn't been pinched by one of those bloody Irishmen. Get it in for Christ's sake.'

'Don't be so rude about the bog-trotters. Aren't you one yourself?'

'That's why I know what fucking thieves they are.' He hissed his affectionate contempt through his tattered mouth. 'I'm telling you, get it carried in. What do I pay you for? Jesus Christ!'

'Better not let the priest hear you talk like that.'

'The priest can fuck himself. He knows my opinion about church and religion.'

'How do you come to know him, then? I thought you were one of his flock.'

'Well, you thought wrong. I used to be. But not now. I only know him because he had a bet with me and lost. It was when I was shoeing in Nottingham and just making a bit of a book. I've done business with him ever since. Christ knows why. He's a terrible payer.'

'Hard up. It's well known. Catholic priests always are. They take vows of poverty as well as not to have women. When I took bets to the pits for him, he was always quick to come for his winnings. He's hard up. That's all.'

'He's got a fortune locked away in the bank. Left to him by an uncle or cousin. But he's as mean as buggery. Rich sods often are. I'd gamble he's worth ten thousand pound.'

Brack looked sceptical.

'Didn't you know that he paid for the church?'

'Paid for the church?'

'Paid to have it built. Paid out of his own pocket. That's why he's parish priest. He went to the Bishop in Nottingham as bold as brass and said that if they'd make him parish priest he'd pay for a church. He didn't see himself as a curate. And the Bishop prayed and the Virgin Mary appeared and said, "Send him unto Langwith Junction and Shirebrook where he may save the soul of all the Paddies who sink the new mine shaft." And here he is, saving their souls except on days when there's racing at Newark and Doncaster.'

'You don't believe all that, do you?'

'Of course I don't believe it, you silly bastard. They believe that the statues in their churches come to life and bleed. Do I look like a man who believes that sort of shit? But I'll tell you, I don't mind providing a little entertainment for those who do. It gave me a very good life in Nottingham, whilst it lasted. And I shall do better here. I shan't be too greedy here.'

'Why did you decide to come here? Was it the priest?'

'Not likely. I've meant to come here for years.'

He took a thick leather wallet out of his inside pocket and began to search in the compartments into which the silk lining was divided. First he pulled out a pair of postage stamps and laid them on the seat of the chair beside him. Then he found two or three links of silver

363

chain. Eventually he retrieved a folded piece of newspaper. It was brown with age and he had to open it with care. He coughed theatrically before he began to read: ' "*Derbyshire Times*, 4 May 1901. Raids on Shirebrook shebeens . . . time after time the police . . . made big hauls and the justices imposed exemplary fines." Didn't you know about that? In those days, Shirebrook was the place to find a woman, any time of night or day. I decided then that I'd come here and set up a card school.'

'It's not like that now.'

'I know it's not. But I'd got the idea into my head. So I came. I never thought that I'd meet somebody like you to give me a hand. When Froes told me you were a bookies' runner and in need of a quid or two, you could have blown me over with a fart.'

The customers arrived at eight o'clock. By nine, the air was so thick with cigarette smoke that Brack could barely make out the cobbler's bench against the wall opposite the door. Jack poured whisky into cracked glasses and chipped cups and dealt on to the table around which the gamblers sat. Nobody seemed to find the slightest pleasure in their evening's entertainment. They cursed when they lost but when they won they scraped their winnings from the table without a smile. Jack took his percentage and kept the bank with the precise vigilance of a church warden counting the evening collection. At ten o'clock, two ladies edged their way through the gloom towards the table where the drinks were kept. Neither was young or beautiful. Both wore dresses which were significantly too tight. Brack noticed that they were down at heel but doubted if they had come to have their shoes mended.

Jack McGovern stood up. 'I'm shutting shop. You can take your pick. Sport with them tonight or sport with me tomorrow.'

'What sort of sport?' Brack asked.

'A sing-song and a rabbit run. That's all.'

'I've not seen any coursing since I was married.'

'There's plenty if you know where. And I do. The yard behind the King's Head at Clowne.'

'Must be a big yard.'

'Little rabbits.' McGovern laughed humourlessly. 'Dogs get 'em too quick. That's the only trouble. You get a lot of betting, but dogs get 'em straight away. Sometimes you can't be sure which one got first nip. I've seen terrible rows about that. And then some of the dogs start fighting . . .'

'What time do we go?'

'We'd better set off at six. It's a good hour's walk.'

The start of the coursing was delayed for almost an hour. The organisers were short of rabbits, for the men who had been sent to catch them at Cresswell Crags had returned with only three and one of those, on being tipped out of the sack in which it had been brought to the inn yard, was found to have a broken leg. It was hit on the head, cut into bloody pieces and fed to the dogs to ensure their continued enthusiasm for the taste of raw meat. Men were sent out on to local wasteland, set traps and returned with another four rabbits more or less intact. The first run began at half-past eight.

Jack McGovern offered evens on Hewitt's Smoker. Dabber's Diner was second favourite at seven to four, with Middleton's Luce at five to two and all the rest at three to one. 'Trouble is,' he confided to Brack, 'I've not heard of half these bloody dogs. For all I know, one of 'em's red hot. It only needs a couple of quid on one quick bastard to bust me. For God's sake keep your eye on the bloody rabbit. Sneeze and it'll be all over and some six-foot collier with six pints inside him will claim his dog won and try to shake the money out of me.'

There was no disagreement about the winner of the opening course. A torn-eared cross between whippet and Alsatian, called Marshall's Beauty, won by a clear snarling length. Despite its ferocious appearance, it took so long to despatch the rabbit that the more fancied dogs all got a bite before the rabbit was torn apart and the owners recaptured their favourites. Nobody disputed the judge's decision. Fortunately, Marshall's Beauty was unknown not only to McGovern. The punters were all equally ignorant of the bitch's potential. So was the owner. He only backed her with a shilling – explaining afterwards, with the coarse wit of a man who considered himself to be a character, that he had bought her only the day before and had thought her to be no more lively than the bitch he had married.

'That's a bloody good start.' McGovern shovelled up what was left of the rabbit's entrails to make sure that they were not a distraction to the dogs during the second course. He kicked sand on to the patch of blood which marked the spot where the competition was won.

There was half an hour's pause whilst new odds were called and bets laid on the second course. Marshall's Beauty was promoted to joint favourite, closing at three to two on. The owner himself wagered a pound which Jack McGovern at first tried to refuse with the uncharacteristic explanation that it was more than the punter could afford. There was general agreement that it was really nervousness at the prospect of losing so much money. His judgement was immediately vindicated by the owner's fumble with the buckle at the moment of the dogs' release. Nobody expressed, or felt, any sympathy. As well as losing his pound, he had lost the numerous smaller bets put on by the miners and railwaymen who crowded the yard.

365

McGovern did little better than break even on the rest of the night's races but he walked home in high good humour. To Brack's surprise, John Marshall walked home with them. When they were half a mile from the King's Head, McGovern gave him thirty shillings. 'We won't be able to risk that one again, John.'

'We will if we travel a bit.'

'Nay. It's too risky. You might be able to choke her again when you're slipping her collar. Mind you, that won't work too often. But she'll never be an outsider again. You're too well known. At least you are in the colliery villages.' He turned to Brack. 'You know who this is, don't you?'

Brack confessed his ignorance.

'This is John Marshall of Alfreton – big union man. He was the first miner to stop work in 1912 – leastways the first to come up. Have you heard of him now? He's famous for it.'

When Brack shook his head, McGovern decided to cause a little trouble. 'He was against the strike, John. It bankrupted his cycle shop.'

'You'd not understand, Mr Brackenbury, not being a miner yourself,' Marshall said.

'But he is a miner, John. They've taken on new men. Had to with so many of the regulars like you being blacklisted. Tell him how much you earn, Brack. Five bob a shift?'

'I've been a miner before.' He sounded strangely apologetic. 'I was down the pit at Shirebrook.'

'Tell him how much you earn, Brack.'

'I'm a checkweighman now. But started at seven bob a shift.'

Marshall was moved to speak at last.

'Fuck me. Do they make fucking blacklegs checkweighmen these days? They must be off their bleeding heads. They were half starved for months and then they make a bastard who signed on for seven bob a checkweighman. They deserve all they get.'

'You didn't do so badly out of it, you cheeky sod.' McGovern had decided to switch his attack to Marshall. 'What did you charge, John, five pounds a night?'

'Five pounds a night!' At last Brack recalled the extraordinary story. 'Are you the John Marshall who went on to the music halls and made an exhibition of himself?'

'I was the first man up and I appeared as the first man up. That's how they advertised it. I was proud of it. But then I'm not a bloody blackleg.'

'Blackleg be buggered. I've more respect for myself than to parade about on stage with me face blacked like a nigger minstrel.'

366

'I put my pit clothes on. And I carried my pick and my lamp. I were proud to do it. I were proud to be black. You get black down the pit.'

'Getting mucky doing t'job is one thing. Dressing up's another. You ought to have more self-respect. All those London toffs laughing.'

'They were clapping, cheering sometimes.'

'They were laughing at you, you silly sod. I'd have been ashamed. Ashamed to do it and ashamed to see you.'

'Boys! Boys!' McGovern had begun to fear that his joke had gone too far. 'Let's not get heated. We've had a good night.' He handed Brack a pound.

'Here, he's made more than me. And it was my bloody dog.'

'But he's my partner, John, a regular thing.'

They were back in Shirebrook and Jack McGovern said that if his furniture had arrived he would have invited them into the cobbler's shop for a drink. After the apology had been made a second time, Brack realised that he was supposed to suggest that they all went to Austin Street. John Marshall – as offended by Brack's opinions as he was outraged by McGovern's meanness – declined without thanks.

Brack and McGovern made their noisy way through the kitchen. There were no mantles on the gas brackets and there seemed no point in finding and fitting them so they settled down with a candle. McGovern provided a hip flask and Brack, although he never drank spirits, provided the tea cups.

'Your wife not back, then? I thought you said she'd be back by eight.'

'She's back. Her coat's hanging up. And the kid's doll is in the back. She'll be in bed.'

'Doesn't she wait up when you're out? Doesn't she wait up in case you want a bite of something?'

'She's sick. She's got rheumatoid arthritis.' Brack was not so much making excuses for his wife as apologising for not being master in his own house.

He sat in glum silence. So he heard Agnes make her slow way downstairs.

'Where on earth have you been? I've been worried to death.'

'I've been out with my friend here, Mr McGovern.'

'You might have left a note. You knew we were coming back today. It could have been an accident at the pit or anything.'

'I don't have to account to you for my comings and goings. I do what I want in my own house.' He knew that he was doing what was expected of him and he was sure that he could do better. 'Mr

367

McGovern and I are starving. Stop your daft questions and make us a couple of sandwiches.'

Agnes turned to go and do as she was told. But Brack had not quite finished. 'And when you've done, bring Enid down. I want Mr McGovern to see what a treasure I've got.'

'It's after midnight!'

'Bring her down. I shan't tell you again. Bring her down now and get the sandwiches after.'

CHAPTER TWENTY-NINE
Faithful Service

It was Elizabeth who persuaded William Skinner to retire. He had done no gardening for years but he persisted in hobbling between the flower beds and along the rows of beans and Brussels sprouts, hampering the work of the man who had waited to replace him and in the meantime was called the under-gardener. Henry Hodding wanted him to go and offered him Grove Cottage rent free to go with his pension but William hung on. He had hung on all his life and the habit was hard to break. Elizabeth broke it by convincing him that he was going to die.

He had developed all the old man's side-effects of Still's disease. His eyes were dry and inflamed. Bad circulation made his fingers cold and blue. When he coughed – and he coughed a lot – the pain in his chest might have been tuberculosis or pneumonia.

'Unless you stop bending and walking about in the cold you'll be in Steetly churchyard before the summer's out and, mercy me, you'll go before I do. That's what the doctor says and I can't understand why you don't take any notice.'

'He hasn't said it to me. Anyway, if I give up work, I might as well be in Steetly.'

'Of course he hasn't said it to you. They don't do that. He's told me. Told me so that I could prepare myself.'

William took his wife's hand. 'It may not be fair, but it's natural. I've had my three score years and ten. And I've not had a bad life. Another couple of springs and summers and I'll have nothing to complain about.'

'But I will. I'll be here on my own. I don't know how I'll manage without you.'

'Anne—'

'Anne will look after Lottie and their business.'

'Ernest, then. Ernest's all on his own. You can move in with him.'

'I don't want to go to Worksop and Ernest won't want me. If you go, I'll have to look after myself. And it's all so unnecessary. All I

369

want is to keep you warm – warm and alive. And you won't even do that for me. You must really hate me to want to die rather than let me look after you so that you can look after me.'

It was the sort of appeal that William was not equipped to resist. He insisted on walking up to Harness Grove so that he could give his employer the news himself. The butler told him that he was invited into the drawing room. It was the first time he had been shown such respect since the day of his cross-examination about Ernest's debt. The courtesy was as near as Henry Hodding ever came to sentimentality. His attempts at nostalgia were not a success.

'And all your children were born down in the cottage.'

'No, sir. I brought them with me. Agnes, my youngest, was not much more than a baby.'

'And now she's got two children of her own.'

'One, sir. Enid. She's nearly eight.'

'Her husband shoes horses, doesn't he?' Henry Hodding bravely persisted in his attempts at casual conversation.

'He's a collier now, sir. He tried to start up a business, but it didn't work. He's been down the pit getting on for two years.'

'I'm sorry to hear that. He was a damn good farrier. Did we decide on a pension?'

'Yes, sir. We did, sir.'

The subject embarrassed William. Since he was not going to work, he could not believe that he deserved to be paid. He would accept whatever Mr Hodding gave him, for neither he nor his wife could live without it, but he had no doubt that he would live for the rest of his life on charity.

'I'd like to give you something, a little keepsake to express my gratitude.'

'There's no need for that, sir.'

'Nobody says there is. If there was a need for it, I wouldn't want to do it. Take it with good grace, Skinner. I'll arrange some sort of a ceremony. I'll talk to Knock about it. He's your friend, isn't he?'

'He is,' said William, but he thought, Gerrard's just the man for this. This is the job for a Catholic. If we're going to have a wake, he'll know the way it should be organised.

William hoped that the party would be held in the house – ideally in the drawing room, which he thought was the proper place for parties to be held and would therefore be the location which confirmed that, for once, he was being treated as an equal.

Henry Hodding, believing that he had a sense of occasion, decreed that it should be in the garden. A marquee was hired in case the weather was inclement but Hodding prayed for the autumn evening

370

to be fine, for he wanted to say his formal farewell in the herb garden where Skinner's obvious affection for the unkempt flower beds, the overgrown paths and the tousled terracotta pots of ancient plants had first won him the job. His prayer was answered.

In more than thirty years, the herb garden had not so much changed as intensified. The thyme, the rosemary, the calendulas, the sage, the lamb's ears and the Lady's mantle were all still there. Indeed, if anything they grew in even greater mixed profusion than on the day of William's arrival at Harness Grove for he had allowed, indeed encouraged, them to scatter their seeds across the whole garden. When he started, it was at least possible to recognise which pot had once been marjoram's exclusive territory and which bed had been originally intended for mullein. When he left, there were no boundaries.

A new bench stood across the sunnier corner of the high brick wall. The old wooden seat on which Henry Hodding had sat to interview his applicant gardener had rotted away into firewood before the turn of the century and had been replaced by a wrought-iron tribute to Victorian England. When William Skinner appeared, leaning on his wife's arm and guiding her towards their host, the knot of guests parted so that he could make his way to the place that had been prepared for him. Elizabeth was invited to sit at his side. Inevitably, she argued and, equally inevitably, she agreed.

Mr Hodding thought that Skinner's children should be posed around him. Anne sat by his side, resenting being put on display but proud to be seen as a replica of her straight-backed mother. Ernest stood behind, his left hand resting lightly on his father's shoulder. Agnes, now able to walk only with the aid of a stick, limped up and hovered on the edge of the group. Her father tried to make room for her on the bench, but she said it was easier to stand.

'Where are the grandchildren?' Mr Hodding demanded.

The only grandchild was holding her father's hand and ostentatiously smelling the chrysanthemums.

'Over here, Mr Hodding.'

'Well, bring her up. You too, Brackenbury. All part of the family. Stand at the back next to your brother-in-law.'

Anne looked apologetically at Lottie whilst Enid was squeezed on to the seat in the space that had been intended for her mother. The child beamed like a fashion plate. Henry Hodding junior emerged from the black cloth behind his mahogany camera and instructed them all to smile. The spectators all applauded when the magnesium flare exploded and Henry Hodding shouted to them that they must quieten down. He then approached the tableau and picked up a card-

371

board box which had been hidden behind a terracotta pot of opium poppies. From it he took an object which different observers identified in a variety of ways.

Anne thought it was a communion chalice and toyed, for a moment, with the idea that it was to be presented to Steetly chapel in tribute to her father in the way that benefactors bought stained-glass windows or pews and labelled them with the names of those they wished to be remembered. Then she recalled that such gifts were made only to commemorate the dead and she decided that even Mr Hodding – notwithstanding his brusque practicality – would not anticipate the unhappy event so publicly. Brack thought that the object might have been designed as the trophy for a steeplechase and almost asked Gerrard Knock if his employer had bought it second hand from John Robinson. It reminded the maids of a massive egg cup and the butler believed that it must be a huge silver goblet from which to drink the old gardener's health. It's just an ornament, thought Anne – just an ornament and no use for anything practical. She was still estimating how much it had cost, and which objects of greater utility could have been bought for the same price, when Henry Hodding completed his brief speech by reading the words engraved on the grail.

'Presented by H. S. Hodding to William Skinner in remembrance of his faithful service at Harness Grove.'

The applause, only slightly less enthusiastic than that which had greeted the magnesium flash, was the sign for William to push hard on the seat of the bench in a noble effort to rise to his feet.

'Sit down, Skinner. Sit down. You're all right where you are. Anyway, there is another presentation still to come.'

Gerrard Knock stepped forward, carrying a second cardboard box. It was wrapped in identical paper to that which had covered Mr Hodding's gift but was scarcely half the size of the first. Lottie, who was used to buying expensive accessories in better shops, decided that both presents had been bought at the same jeweller. The old coachman removed the lid and fumbled with the tissue paper in which the contents were wrapped. After an agony of clumsy confusion, he pulled out a silver cream jug which Anne decided cost at least five guineas and would never be used for cream. He did not attempt a speech but read from the jug's curved belly.

'Presented to W. Skinner by his fellow servants at Harness Grove.'

William forced himself to his feet before Henry Hodding had time to prevent him. 'I want to thank you all but, most of all, I want to thank Mr Hodding. I hope he won't think that I presume upon his good nature if I say that he's been a good friend to me over these

372

many years. I hope I've served him well. I've loved his garden. And I hope that he'll allow me still to walk in it, when I can. He's been kind enough to let me keep Grove Cottage and I hope some of you will come to see me . . . I'm not much for oratory. So that's all I have to say . . . But thank you . . . It's been a wonderful evening.'

The other servants crowded round to examine the gifts.

'Not a word,' said Anne to Lottie, 'not a word about mother. You'd think he'd lived there all alone these thirty-odd years. It's shameful. She must feel humiliated.'

'I feel humiliated,' said Elizabeth to Ernest. 'He didn't want to *presume* to call Mr Hodding a friend. He hoped he'd be *allowed* to walk in the garden – allowed to walk in the garden that's broken his back. No wonder they called us servants on that thing that Gerrard Knock gave him. What was it?'

'A cream jug, Mam. A silver cream jug. It was very nice.'

'That's as may be. But don't expect me to use it. Don't expect to find it on the table.'

Gerrard Knock and Brack talked in a confidential whisper in a far corner of the herb garden. When Agnes first noticed them, she feared that they were engrossed in a discussion of horse-racing. Then she saw Brack smile and knew she need not worry, for it was not a topic in which he ever found joy or amusement. But she would not let Enid run to join him. 'Leave him alone for a minute. For goodness' sake, let him talk to Mr Knock without you interrupting all the time.' She held on to the back of her daughter's dress. Words alone would not keep Enid from her father.

'You've become a real family man.' Gerrard Knock felt no malice towards Brack but he could not resist the chance of annoying him. 'Your old friends wouldn't recognise you, standing there with the Skinners.'

Brack only grinned.

'And old William talks about you as if you were his own son. You're a butty now.'

'Checkweighman.'

'God almighty. They trust you with their earnings?'

'They trust me to make sure they get all that they've earned. That's different.' Brack was still grinning.

'So you're doing very nicely.'

'Not so bad. We've moved out from the back of that bloody shop.' He did not add that the move had been made possible by the loan from Ernest Skinner which had enabled him to pay off his debt to Mr Hardstaff. 'We've gone round the corner to a nice little house in Austin Street.'

'Your father-in-law says that nobody could have made a go of the cycle business.'

'It's going to be a cobbler's shop now, a man called Jack McGovern. I can't see him doing much.'

'I shouldn't think that many miners take their boots to be mended.'

'And they don't buy much leather. They pinch bits of driving belt, like I do. Jack will make his living on the side.'

It was time for more presentations. Mrs Hodding, who had seen silver-framed photographs of royalty at Welbeck, had produced a picture of her husband in hunting pink waiting to lead off the Grove. Its pewter frame would, she had no doubt, not look out of place in Worksop Manor. If William had not known him better, he would have believed that Henry Hodding was blushing. Gerrard Knock was about to return to the fascinating subject of Cobbler Jack's subsidiary earnings when there was a scream from the other side of the garden. Enid had wriggled free from her mother and in her mad dash towards her father had slipped on the loose gravel path and fallen into a bed of marjoram. Brack reached her in two strides and hugged her to him like a parcel that he was afraid would be snatched from him. One of the maids – the nearest woman to the catastrophe – carried out a cursory examination and announced 'no damage done'. Agnes, who hobbled to the scene of the accident as quickly as she could, confirmed the diagnosis. She took Enid kicking and screaming out of Brack's arms and stood her on the grass. The pain of her journey across the herb garden combined with self-consciousness to shorten her temper. What began as an attempt to smooth down the child's dress ended as a severe shaking.

'Be quiet. There's nothing wrong with you. Be quiet. Anyway, it's your own silly fault for running across here when I told you not to.'

'She was running to me.' For Brack that was justification enough.

'Well, she shouldn't have been.' Agnes gave her daughter another shake. 'Be quiet or you'll spoil Grandad's party.'

'She had a right tumble, it's shaken her up.' Brack bent down and was about to pick Enid up again, but Agnes snatched her away.

'Be quiet or I shall give you a smack.' The warning had its predictable, rather than its desired, effect and the howling reached a new crescendo. The smack was duly administered.

'You bad-tempered bitch.'

Everybody in the garden heard what Brack said to his wife and everybody turned and saw him pick Enid up and march out of the garden with her sitting triumphantly on his arm as she rubbed her wet cheek against his rough face.

*

'I don't believe you're going to leave her alone with him.'

The party broke up only slightly earlier than Henry Hodding had intended and the family made their way back to Grove Cottage.

'He is her father, Anne. And I don't see me travelling back to Shirebrook at this time of night, any more than I saw myself running after him.'

'But will he look after her properly?' William was going to suggest that Ernest escorted his sister home.

'He's marvellous with her. The only danger is that he'll feed her chocolate biscuits and ginger beer all night. I'm whacked. He starts afternoons tomorrow. As long as I get there before dinner time, it won't matter. But I want to get off home first thing or he'll think that he's got an excuse for missing a shift. No talking tonight.'

Agnes talked, first to Anne and Lottie and then – after Anne and Lottie had left – to Ernest. When Ernest went home she talked to her mother and father until her mother announced that it was time for bed. Then, since William seemed reluctant to end the evening, she stayed downstairs and talked to him.

'I'm sorry if we spoilt it all, Dad.'

'You didn't. She's just a little girl. Little girls behave like that sometimes. You certainly did.'

'I don't mean Enid. I mean him.'

'He does seem fond of her.'

'He is. He's daft about her. I know he'd have liked a boy but he wouldn't have doted on him any more than he dotes on Enid. And she worships the ground he walks on.'

'You ought to be glad.'

'I am, Dad.' A change of subject seemed essential. 'Anyway, what about you? It's been a long day for you. How do you feel?'

'Not so bad. Better than I expected. I've had a bad week. I could barely get out of bed at all last Monday.'

'You look very well now.'

'It's my colour. I always look well. It comes from working outside. But I'm not getting any better. I'll tell you that. When I said about visiting the garden to Mr Hodding, I thought that I'd never be able to do it.'

'Is Mam managing to look after you?'

'She's managing marvellous. She's as fit as an ox really. I've told you what worries me is how she'll get on when I'm gone.' He leaned forward. 'You will look after her when I'm gone? She'll be lost. She won't admit it, but she'll be lost.'

'It's not going to happen for years.'

'But promise that when it does.'

'I promise.'

Agnes kissed her father on the brow and began to climb the stairs – more concerned about how early she had to get away than about his familiar talk of death and his continued anxiety that she should take responsibility for her mother. She fell asleep at once, surrounded by the comfortable reassurance of her old room. But when she was woken at three by the sound of a bird in the eaves, her first thought was of her father's failing health. She almost crossed the landing to his bedroom to make sure that the shudder which ran down her aching spine was not some sort of premonition. She lay awake for almost an hour and then fell into a fitful sleep. When she woke again she was half conscious of shouting from across the landing. When her name was called a second time, she was relieved to recognise her father's voice. To her astonishment, he appeared in the half-light of the bedroom door.

'Come and look at your mother. Come and see.'

Elizabeth Skinner had died peacefully in her sleep.

Mr Hodding sent Gerrard Knock to Newcastle Avenue in the Harness Grove carriage and, as soon as they had drawn the curtains in the fitting room and sewn black crêpe bands on to the arms of their autumn coats, they travelled back to Darfoulds. William needed both his daughters to stay at Grove Cottage, so Ernest was sent immediately to Shirebrook where Brack, after twelve hours of his daughter's exclusive company, was, as Agnes had confidently predicted, more than willing to release Enid into her mother's care. He did, however, delay her departure until he had told her the news of her grandmother's death to comfort her as necessary. She said that she was sad and asked Ernest if he had brought Prince with him. Brack did not ask how long Agnes was likely to be away.

William was taken to Brook House where, Ginny Harthill having been transferred to one of the attics, he was offered the back bedroom for as long as he wanted it. He wanted it for less than twenty-four hours, after which he began to complain about the draughts, the light, the damp, the dark and the cold. Agnes, sharing the smaller attic across the landing with Enid, told Anne that he would never settle.

'He's pining for Grove Cottage already. He thinks he's lost Mam and the house.'

'I think she's right,' said Ernest. 'He's afraid that Mr Hodding will have it off him if he doesn't live there.'

'We'll take him back in a couple of weeks. And we'll look after him up there. But we can't do anything until the end of the month.' Anne sounded unusually apologetic. 'We've got so many orders to finish.'

376

'Couldn't you go back with him, Agnes? Just for the first day or two until Anne's not so busy?' Ernest had begun to enjoy setting the family to rights, so he did not consider the problem of a married couple, whom he had recently joined together, being so quickly rent asunder by his next response to a clear call of duty.

'How can I? I've got a husband and a new house in Shirebrook.'

'It will only be for a week. No more than a fortnight, anyway,' said Lottie.

'Lottie, it's not possible.' But even as Agnes said she could not, she knew that she would. She would take her father back to Grove Cottage, not out of love for him or out of concern for her overworked sister but in order to escape for a few days from Jack McGovern and all that he stood for.

'A week then. Ten days. No more.'

CHAPTER THIRTY

Enid Begins Her Education

Agnes and Enid lived happy and almost undisturbed in Worksop for over two years. Annie and Lottie encouraged them to stay with genuine, indeed passionate, enthusiasm. Europe was at war and, in Newcastle Avenue, the conflict between the great powers was judged entirely in terms of the threat posed to life in Brook House. Ernest was too old for conscription and had no inclination to volunteer. Brack, like all miners, was exempt from Kitchener's call. The drawings of heartless Huns bayoneting Belgian babies did not disturb the calm tranquillity of life in the Brook House fitting room. Nor did the prospect of a blockade cutting off the supplies of tea and sugar essential to the good life. The one real worry was the prospect of billeting – British soldiers sleeping in the attic above Ginny's bedroom or across the corridor from Anne and Lottie themselves.

Enid giggling on the landing was bad enough but it was not to be compared with the noise of hobnailed boots on the stairs, the smell of cheap tobacco in the air and the sight of young, red-faced, rough-handed men in the kitchen and perhaps in the fitting room itself. It was a real threat, for half a dozen territorial battalions were constantly in camp in Welbeck Park in transit to France and Flanders and billeting officers were continually sighted in north Nottinghamshire, requisitioning the spare bedrooms of innocent householders. Enid and Agnes, as long as they remained in residence, were protection against such ravages. In consequence even when they were not needed in constant attendance at Grove Cottage, their status was changed from burden to saviour.

Agnes made the best of her new popularity at Brook House for six days of each week and spent most Saturdays at Grove Cottage, where Enid talked incessantly to her grandfather, who sat outside on sunny afternoons and by his fire on all but the warmest days. Agnes spoke, for respectability's sake, of 'looking after her father' or 'giving Anne and Ernest a rest', but the joints in her neck and shoulders had set harder and her back had begun to bow. She could do little more than make him cups of tea and pick up the books that he had dropped on lawn or carpet. And that she only did with difficulty.

Life at Brook House was crowded but unusually secure. Ginny slept her time away in the attic. The work room accommodated Anne and Lottie, two recently recruited seamstresses and the clatter of their sewing machines, which sometimes rocked the whole house. But the noise they made at full treadle was the sound of prosperity. Although Ernest insisted on contributing to Agnes's upkeep – as he contributed to his father's – Mesdames Skinner and Harthill, Ladies' High-Class Tailors and Dressmakers, did not find the burden of Agnes and Enid more than they could bear. Indeed, they insisted on incurring extra and unnecessary expenses. Enid was not allowed to attend the local elementary school. Instead she was sent to Ashleigh House, which offered 'separate schools for boys and girls' and 'moderate terms'.

For the first few weeks of their second separation, Agnes had waited in daily terror for the arrival of a vengeful Brack. Ernest had told her that he would not come, for Ernest, whose wisdom neither of his sisters overrated, had gone to Shirebrook to collect clothes and he had judged that Brack would let his wife and daughter be. Ernest, being a man of ostentatious honesty, had refused to take Agnes's key and creep into Austin Street when Brack was down the pit. He had chosen instead to knock on the rarely opened front door at a time when he knew that Brack would be at home, even though that required him to risk being watched as he took from the dressing-table drawers items of ladies' clothing that a gentleman should never touch. The deserted husband had let him in without a word and declined his offer to carry a message to the errant wife. Despite her brother's assurances, Agnes never quite believed that Brack would not, one day, hammer on the Brook House door. She was afraid of him coming. But she wanted him to come.

At first, Enid constantly spoke of her father and asked not when she was going home to Shirebrook to see him, but when he was coming to Worksop to see her. After a few weeks, the longing passed and she became absorbed in the new loves of her life. To Prince and her grandfather was added reading. Ashleigh House introduced her to books. Her mother encouraged the acquaintance and the whole family benefited. On Saturday afternoons Enid read her school books to William, who expressed astonishment at her accomplishment. In the kitchen at Newcastle Avenue, she sat on the horsehair sofa either reading silently to herself or entertaining Prince with *Lamb's Tales from Shakespeare*, Grimms' Fairy Tales and, as the months went by, any book, paper or magazine that she could lay her hands on. Agnes

379

remembered when she had been the same, and hoped that in the new tranquillity she would regain the habit.

Only once during those two peaceful years did Shirebrook reach out towards Worksop. One morning in the autumn of 1916, Lottie Harthill answered the Brook House front door and found, to her horror, that the caller was a Catholic priest. He asked for Agnes. She was not at home, for it was the day on which the memorial service to Lieutenant John Hodding RNVR was being held at Steetly chapel and William Skinner's two daughters sat on each side of him at the back of the church as the parish paid its respects to old Henry's grandson – lost, presumed killed, in Gallipoli, whilst serving with the Naval Brigade. Lottie explained the reason why the priest's request to see Mrs Brackenbury could not be granted.

'These are indeed terrible times.' Lottie was impressed by his impeccable manners. 'Six lads from Shirebrook were killed in the summer. Two from one family. Please God it will soon end.'

'I don't understand these things,' said Lottie. 'I just want it all to be over.' She did not like keeping her visitor on the doorstep but she would not have felt comfortable inviting a Catholic priest into the house. 'Is there any message?'

'I shall call again,' the priest said. 'God bless you.'

Lottie reeled back affronted and found it difficult even to report the event to Anne. There was general consternation when she revealed that the priest came from Shirebrook.

'You don't think that he's turned Catholic as well as everything else, do you?' Even Ernest, who had tried to see the best in Brack ever since the discovery of his tidy habits and neat disposition, could not forgive him that.

'I know he's friendly with the priest. But I thought that it was just the racing.' Agnes still hoped that the friendship was based on gambling, not religion.

'He didn't sound like a priest,' Lottie told them.

'I thought that when he first came round to see Brack. I don't think he's Irish. He sounded educated.'

'There you are, then.' Ernest could find no more excuses. 'He's got in with Catholics.'

'If he's turned Catholic . . .' Anne believed that no wound should be left without salt. 'If he's turned Catholic, he won't believe that he's even married. He won't recognise a wedding in one of our churches.'

'They have churches,' said Lottie.

'Exactly.' Ernest was pleased to explain the point. 'And they don't believe in anything that goes on in anybody else's. He won't believe that Enid's been christened. So she won't go to heaven.'

380

'She will!' Agnes said emphatically.

'It all goes to prove that you're both better here.'

Anne believed that she had finally resolved the moral dilemma which they had all faced since Agnes's arrival. She had no doubt that marriage was folly but it was also highly respectable. Once the act of madness had been committed, a wife's place was undoubtedly with her husband – especially when the more conventional customers of Skinner and Harthill were in the fitting room and likely to ask questions about the fatherless child in the kitchen. There had been times when she had thought of suggesting that Agnes should try to end the embarrassment by finding out if life was still intolerable in Shirebrook. But that was before the threat of billeting hung over her and in the days of innocence when Brack was thought to be nothing worse than an obsessive gambler and a wife-beater. Now that he was suspected of Catholicism, a reunion was out of the question.

'I hope he's all right.' Everyone looked at Agnes. It was the first suggestion that the priest had come for anything except to claim Brack's wife and children for Rome. To suggest an alternative theory was regarded as family treachery.

'Of course he's all right. If he hadn't been, the priest would have said. I gave him plenty of chance.'

'Anyway,' added Ernest, 'we would have heard.'

If Anne recognised the illogicality of her brother's comment she only chose to reinforce the prejudice which prompted it.

'You're right. He would have been round here. Or he would have sent somebody. He'd have been after money.'

It was the first time that anyone had heard Agnes say anything critical of Brack. It was, Anne told Lottie in bed that night, the turning point. They were safe for the duration.

'Have you thought any more about what we discussed yesterday – about a clean break?' she asked Agnes next morning.

Her sister remembered only a brief discussion about reading aloud. 'I'm going to begin with *A Christmas Carol*,' she said.

The reading aloud was not a success. Enid could read more quickly than her mother, even when Agnes read in silence. So when Charles Dickens's words were carefully articulated, with pauses for breath and corrections of mispronunciations, she leaped ahead. And sometimes, to demonstrate her frustration, she leaped ahead out loud. Her mother was disconcerted but never angry.

Agnes had decided that her daughter was a prodigy and, since all she knew about such rarities came from books, she took it for granted that the phenomenon to whom she had given birth must be either a consumptive or an ingrate and was glad that Enid was incorrigibly superior rather than terminally sick.

Ashleigh House, the private school to which Aunt Anne insisted on sending her niece, was more equivocal in its attitude towards the pupil who shared her mother's view that she was the star of the establishment. Having at last, after several years of troubled existence, been recognised by the Board of Education, it took great pride in the 'testimonials from successful pupils (home and abroad)' which it offered to prospective parents, and the 'individual attention' it lavished on the children within its care. Enid showed every sign of becoming a successful pupil but she was too enthusiastic about receiving individual attention – ideally, from her point of view, the attention of the entire school directed towards the one individual in whom she seemed interested.

Enid was a strangely pretty child – thinner than Agnes (with her preoccupation with wasting diseases) would have had her be but, because she had been spared puppy-fat, possessing an elegance which was strikingly unusual in one so young. She had clear, piercing blue eyes which were wide set in a face that combined high cheekbones and a broad brow. It was generally agreed she would grow up to be a raving beauty, and generally regretted that she looked forward to that desirable state with such undisguised satisfaction.

Mr Alwyn Parry – the principal of Ashleigh House – devoted most of his teaching time to the boys' department but, after Enid Brackenbury's arrival at the school, he was constantly required to give his wife advice about how to deal with a pupil who insisted on picking and choosing from the syllabus. Enid's enthusiasm for books was not matched by her interest in any other aspect of the curriculum. She sewed badly and therefore treated needlework as an activity beneath her dignity. She added and subtracted only with difficulty, and therefore avoided adding and subtracting whenever she could. As the Allies fought in France to defeat the Kaiser, the little time that Ashleigh House had previously spent on history and geography was extended to accommodate stories of Britain's glorious past and accounts of the nourishing foods grown by and exported from the Empire. Enid liked tales of military valour and descriptions of waving wheat only if they were offered her in the form of narrative fiction. Nobody doubted her patriotism. She was violently angry when she was forbidden, because of her tender years, to sell flags on behalf of good causes in the market square.

Her refusal to concentrate on subjects which did not inspire her became so disruptive to the school as a whole that Mr Parry called round to Brook House to discuss his wayward pupil with her mother.

Aunt Anne dominated the conversation, but not to the headmaster's satisfaction. She complained about novels being allowed in the school at all, insisting that she had never read one because she regarded truth as superior to invention and suggesting to Agnes that the child be removed from the influences of such dubious teaching methods. Since Anne would not tolerate credit, Ashleigh House's 'Moderate Inclusive Terms' were paid in full and in advance. Mr Parry made a quick adjustment to his opinion of Enid and announced that if, together, they encouraged her to work harder, she would go far without the aid of literature. Agnes said that she had no objection to novels in moderation.

Enid's wilful neglect of subjects which did not take her fancy infuriated the stern unbending Mrs Glenys Parry almost as much as her haughty disdain bewildered the other little girls in her class and offended more senior pupils. She made no friends and, knowing that she was unpopular, insulated herself against the dislike of her schoolmates by affecting a feeling of superiority which was even greater than that which she felt. Because she held herself at such a distance, she was rarely taunted about the peculiarities of her family life. Then Alice Moore told her that she knew her uncle, Ernest Skinner.

'My dad collects the rent for Mr Sweeting. He says your uncle Ernest used to do it, that he worked for Mr Sweeting full time.'

'He never did.' Enid had never heard of Lucy Sweeting and was not sure how long full time was, but she felt certain that she had to deny the allegation. 'You're talking silly. He works at Hirst's woodyard in Retford.'

Alice did not return to the subject again for a second time until more than a week had passed. Then she made an even more extraordinary allegation.

'My dad says you're related to Mr Sweeting. Ernest Skinner was married to his daughter.'

Enid began to hope that a great mystery was about to unfold. She had just – surreptitiously – read *Jane Eyre* and the thought of her uncle as a fretworking, club-swinging Mr Rochester so intrigued her that she could not avoid showing interest.

'Walk home with me,' said Alice. 'My dad's there. He'll tell you all about it.'

Home was a large house in Gladstone Street which opened directly on to the pavement. A notice hung in one downstairs window. It read,

Joshua Moore, Rent and Debt Collector
Accounts Got in Quickly
Nine Years' Experience.

Joshua Moore was at home, as his daughter had promised. He was nursing a headcold and the debris which blocked his nasal passages combined with his thick Birmingham accent to make everything that he said almost unintelligible to Enid. Alice, in the artificial accent she had learned at the Ashleigh House elocution classes (optional and additional charge), demanded that her father repeat and confirm his story about Uncle Ern.

Joshua Moore turned on his daughter with what even his ten-year-old visitor could recognise as outrage. 'You didn't ought to have told her that.' He sniffed, swallowed, blew his nose and repeated with increased passion, 'You didn't ought. That was just talking at home.' His denunciation was interrupted by a giant sneeze.

'I just told her what I'd heard you say.'

Moore, his face buried in a great spotted handkerchief, replied between sneezes. Enid was able to follow only the drift of what he said. He was clearly not denying the truth of what his daughter claimed but merely complaining that she had repeated his story. Enid had been excited by the idea of Uncle Ernest's mysterious marriage but the rent collector's reaction to the revelation made her begin to suspect – and hope – that there was a deeper mystery than the marriage itself.

A sneeze having been contained, Moore turned on his daughter again. 'You've no business telling things like that. Them was family matters. It's not your business to tell her things what her mother hasn't told her.' He turned to Enid. 'Now be a good girl and run along home. I'm a bit poorly. Don't bother with things that don't concern you, there's a good little girl.'

Joshua Moore could not have said anything that was less likely to slake Enid's thirst for the story of her uncle's past. She decided, there and then, that it involved something far more dramatic than a forgotten marriage.

'Please tell me, Mr Moore. I know my mam won't mind. Perhaps she doesn't know. I won't sleep all night unless you tell me.' She stared at him without blinking, deepening the silence which followed her entreaty and itself pleaded for reply.

'If your ma wants you to know, your ma will tell you.' Another giant sneeze gave Moore time to realise the foolishness of what he had said. If Enid went home and told her mother what had happened, he might have Ernest Skinner to reckon with. A reputation for spreading tittle-tattle was not an asset to a debt collector and he could not afford a scene or scandal. He revised his opinion. 'You just forget all about it and run off home. It was just grown-up talk that Alice earwigged. Be a good little girl and forget all about it.'

It was the third time that he had called her a little girl and Enid's resolve to find out the truth was hardened by the repeated insult. She was not wise enough to realise that she could blackmail Moore into telling his story just by threatening to ask her mother the questions which he refused to answer, but she was old enough to suspect that, if the thought of speaking about her uncle's past caused the debt collector so much anguish, Ernest Skinner must have done something which was discreditable, dangerous or romantic. An early death, which was a common feature of marriage amongst Enid's neighbours, would not in itself have justified such a fuss. Joshua Moore began a succession of sneezes, each one louder than the last. Enid should have stalked menacingly home, pausing at the door in order to allow an opportunity for Joshua Moore to plead with her to stay whilst he told the whole story. Instead, she pleaded with him.

'I've come all this way for you to tell me. Alice promised. I can't stand not knowing things.' She rubbed her nose violently and hoped that her eyes would fill with tears.

Foolishly, Moore tried to change the subject. 'How's your dad? I've not heard about him since the accident. Is he better? I've not heard.'

Memories which had been almost obliterated by the years of separation came flooding back. Enid was too distressed to react calmly. 'Where is my dad? Where is he?'

Joshua Moore looked hopelessly at his daughter. Enid, finding his failure to reply intolerable, leaped at him and, pounding him on the chest, began to shout, 'Where's my dad? Where is he? Tell me! What's happened to him?'

Sniffing, Joshua Moore turned to his daughter and held Enid's wrists as she tried to kick his shins. 'Is she all there?' He tried to hold her at arm's length. 'What's she on about?'

'I don't know, Dad. I've never seen her like this. Stop her before she hurts you. Give her a smack. She's gone mad.'

Enid stopped kicking and sank sobbing into a chair. Moore bent over her. 'How old are you?' She did not answer. 'She's not normal. Is she peculiar at school?'

'Yes, she is. She reads books all the time. Grown-up books.'

'Where does she live?'

Enid answered, 'In Newcastle Avenue.' She had rolled into a ball in the armchair.

Joshua Moore bent over her again. 'You're coming with me, young lady. I'm taking you home.' He turned to his daughter. 'And you're coming an' all. We'll try to mend some of the damage you've done, you silly little bitch.'

There was silence from the chair. Enid was enormously encouraged

385

by Moore's announcement. She might not discover either her father's whereabouts or the state of his health, but she felt certain that she was going to discover at least the secret of Uncle Ernest's fascinating past.

They walked from Gladstone Street to Newcastle Avenue at a pace which put unreasonable pressure on Joshua Moore's inflamed mucus membrane. The rent collector held on to Enid's wrist with the iron grip he sometimes employed when marching persistent defaulters to the county court. But his prisoner had no wish to escape. She trotted along at his side with an enthusiasm to reach Brook House which he did not share and only shied away when he cleared his throat and spat into the gutter or held his nose between finger and thumb and blew green slime on to the pavement. To her relief, he prepared himself for the meeting with her mother by liberal use of his spotted red handkerchief.

'I'm afraid I've upset your little girl.'

It was Lottie who had come to the door and Moore had made the obvious assumption. Enid ran down the hall and into the kitchen where, without a word, she sank dramatically by the side of Agnes's chair and buried her head in her mother's lap.

'What on earth's the matter? Don't be so silly.'

Before Enid had a chance to reply, Lottie arrived with Joshua Moore. When Agnes saw Alice, a step behind them, she gave a start and almost stood up.

'Is something wrong at school? Tell me.' She assumed Enid was in trouble. 'Tell me what you've done.'

Anne, who had recognised the male footsteps through the floor-boards of the first-floor work room and over the noise of her treadle sewing machine, pushed her way between Alice and Lottie. 'What's happened? Is Auntie Lottie to send for the police?' She pulled Enid to her feet. 'Are you hurt? Has something happened to you, something nasty?' She looked accusingly at Joshua Moore.

The rent collector, who had not been bracing himself for the ordeal of addressing so large a gathering, decided that he had better speak up at once. 'I'm afraid that I upset her by saying something about her dad. You see, I didn't know.'

'Didn't know what?' Anne asked the question in a tone which was intended more to intimidate than to encourage an answer.

The nuances of her intonations, like the subtleties of her glances, were lost on Moore. He answered her directly. 'I didn't know that you and Mr Brackenbury were separated.' He had still failed to identify the dramatis personae in the little drama.

'This is Mrs Brackenbury. And she is not separated from her husband. They are temporarily living apart. My sister is an invalid . . .'

'For heaven's sake, Anne. This gentleman – whoever he is – clearly knows what's going on. What can we do for you?'

'He's come to ask about Uncle Ernest.'

'Don't be silly, Enid.' Agnes rattled the dog's lead that was hanging over the arm of her chair and, as she intended, the dog to which it was regularly attached leaped up from where it had been lying on the rug in front of the fire. 'Take Prince for a walk in the garden. He has been waiting for you to come home. Take this little girl with you.'

Enid refused point blank.

'Please,' said Lottie.

Enid clenched her teeth, looked at her feet and, unusually, remained silent.

'If she was mine . . .' Anne left the terrible consequences of that condition to the general imagination.

'If Enid chooses to be silly, just ignore her. She's too big a girl to behave like this. But if she acts like a baby we'll have to treat her like one.'

Joshua Moore took Agnes's declaration as permission for him to say his piece.

'I'm afraid I put my foot in it with the young lady. I mentioned her father. Not in any disrespectful way. I just asked how Brack was and your daughter had a right fit. Kicked and shouted like a right little Tartar.'

The idea of Enid behaving in such a way was so unlikely that all three women assumed that the story was an invention.

'How do you know my husband?'

'I'm a debt collector, missus.' Moore took a card out of his pocket and handed it to Agnes as if he were hoping for her custom.

'Was my husband in debt?'

'No, missus. Never. I just collected his rent on behalf of Mr Hardstaff. I collected it last summer when Mr Hardstaff was on holiday. He went away for a full month. I got to know Brack, Mr Brackenbury that is, quite well. He was never in debt even though he wasn't working.'

'Not working!' Anne repeated the condemnation. The news that Brack was idling at home came as no surprise to her.

'After the accident. After the roof-fall at Warsop Main.'

CHAPTER THIRTY-ONE

Moving On

Agnes knew that she must go home but she had no idea if she was responding to the demands of love or the call of duty. She still loved Brack. Of that she was certain for at least most of the time. But it was a love so unlike her early passion that sometimes she wondered if it was love at all. The admiration, which had once amounted to idolatry, had turned into the fascination of the rabbit for the stoat. After the two years of separation, what she remembered best about him was the contempt in which he had held the world when first they had met. In the early days of their courtship he had seemed to look out on life from behind the protection of plate glass and she had marvelled at his self-contained detachment. Now he seemed simply alien to every aspect of her life but she was still fascinated by him. She went home after telling Anne that she had no choice, but she did not explain that she was drawn irresistibly back by the continuing strength of an old passion.

'You look awful.'

It was not how she had expected to greet him. Anne and Lottie had exchanged meaningful glances and told her to prepare for the worst but she had chosen to believe that they spoke of his health and reminded them of Joshua Moore's assurance that her husband had totally recovered. She had neither expected nor wanted a romantic reunion but she had assumed that they would begin with a few seconds of bogus sentimentality. She had imagined him saying that he knew she would be back before long and had planned to reply that the important thing was that she was back now. But he was so pale and drawn that she could not bring herself to tell him, as she had intended, that he looked as well as Joshua Moore had predicted.

'You don't look so clever yourself.'

Brack was doing more than reply in kind. He had not seen Agnes for more than two years and she had changed more than he would have thought possible. Her hair was no longer auburn but a strange tawny brown with streaks of grey and white running from her temple to a tight bun at the back of her neck. It was clear from the hunch of her shoulders that her back was bent even when she was not leaning on her sticks. Brack looked at the gnarled hands and could barely believe that he was married to a woman who looked so worn and old.

'You better come in for a minute.'

Agnes had not expected to be invited into her own home as if she were a visitor but she pulled herself up the two steps and flopped on to the kitchen sofa. 'Can I have a drink, a drink of water?'

Brack turned on the tap and reached for a cup.

'Let it run. Let it run for a bit.' He remembered that she had always believed that water, left in the pipes, was stagnant and poisonous.

'I'm surprised they let you come.'

'Lottie came with me. She's waiting at the railway station. I told her I wanted to see you on my own first.'

'I meant that I'm surprised they let you come at all.'

'They couldn't have stopped me. Once I heard you'd been hurt, I decided. Anyway, they didn't try. Once I heard—'

'How do you mean, once you'd heard? It was more than a year since.'

'We only heard yesterday. You should have told us.'

'I tried. The priest went all the way to Worksop. Went on the day they took me to Chesterfield. He saw that Miss Harthill and she said you weren't there. He meant to go back, after he'd been to see me in the hospital. But I told him no.'

'Why did you do that?'

'I couldn't see any point in your knowing. I wasn't going to die and I'd have nothing to leave you if I had. I didn't want to see you and I doubted if you wanted to see me. I couldn't see the use of pretending.'

'As long as you know that nobody told me.'

'Now that they have, what do you want?'

'What do I want? I've come home to stay. Lottie's at the station with my suitcase—' He was about to interrupt her when she finished the sentence, '—and Enid.'

'God almighty! You've not left Enid standing about in weather like this? You must be off your bloody head.' Brack was already struggling into his jacket. 'I'll go and get her.' He was halfway through the door before he asked, 'Can you still manage to look after her?'

It was the first sign of reluctant reconciliation. Agnes knew that, whatever the truth, there was only one answer that she could give. 'With a bit of help, I can. Enid's wonderful for a girl her age. I'll get more and more stuck but, as she gets older, she'll do more and more. She's very willing.'

'Well, you needn't worry. Jack McGovern fixed me up with a sort of housekeeper. If you want, I'll keep her after you come back. She's only a lass, but she's a hard worker.'

Brack hurried off to the station, drawing deep breaths in order to convince himself that the broken ribs which had taken him to Chesterfield hospital were healed. He could hardly believe that he had been so stupid. At the end of the happiest year of his life he had sacrificed the prospect of pleasing himself for ever. And he had done it for no better reason than the discovery that Enid was sitting in the cold waiting room at Langwith station. He had thought that he would not mind never seeing his daughter again. It had taken more than a year to persuade himself that she no longer mattered but in the end he was convinced. Now, because she was only half a mile away, he had decided to endure the purgatory of having her mother back under his roof. He was desperately impatient to see Enid again. But he did not go straight to the station. First, he called in at Cobbler Jack's. He had to warn his sort-of-housekeeper that Agnes had come home.

Agnes sat in Austin Street certain that she had made a terrible mistake. Brack did not want her back. She was the price that he had to pay for Enid's company. Had she been able, she would have limped away from Shirebrook and hobbled out of her husband's life for ever. But he was already on his way to the station and Enid. Soon he would bring his daughter home. Agnes was trapped.

Lottie left as soon as the joyous reunion was completed, and Agnes began to adjust to being back home in a house which had changed only in little ways. There were, to her surprise, new curtains in the front bedroom and new crockery in the cupboard by the side of the sink. Brack himself laid the table for supper and, as soon as the bread was cut, launched into a graphic account of the accident at Warsop Main. Enid hung on every word that her father spoke and refused to go to bed. Brack, ignoring her mother's advice, said it was her first night back and she could stay up for as long as she liked. But at nine o'clock her mother insisted. Enid was made to wash in the kitchen and driven up the steep flight of stairs that began right behind the third door in the living room.

'I shan't sleep a wink,' Enid said. 'And you wouldn't let me bring any books to read.'

'I've got some books,' her father said proudly. 'I read books now. They're in the front bedroom next to the bed.'

Enid was not impressed and climbed the stairs with bad grace. She examined the books piled on the floor at the side of her father's bed and to her surprise could not understand any of the titles. When she pulled the bedclothes up around her neck, she wondered for a moment if her father would come upstairs to tuck her in and kiss her goodnight. She determined to stay awake for a full hour to give him every chance to do his duty. She was asleep in five minutes.

Downstairs, Agnes began to cross-examine Brack about the accident. 'Did it hurt a lot?'

'Like the very devil. Arthur Ellis never felt a thing, never has. But I get a couple of broken ribs and it's bloody agony.'

'Who's Arthur Ellis?'

'He lives four doors down. Broke his back working the same stall as me. He's got a bed down in the living room. Can't move a muscle but hasn't felt a bloody thing. I go down and see him most days. He just lies there. But all that ever happens is that he gets his head propped up so that he can look out of the window. I only just missed that.'

'How long did you have to wait till they got you out?'

'Half an hour, they say. I can't remember much about it. I heard the crack, then I woke up with half a ton of rock on my chest. I was bloody terrified. When I knew they could get me out, I wasn't bothered until I started spitting up the blood.'

Agnes shuddered.

'That's what kept me in Chesterfield General. Might have done for me. Would have killed some men, punctured lung. But panel doctor says I'm ready to go back down t'pit. And it's only a year.'

'You're not going? Not yet?'

'I'm not going at all. I'm starting my own business again. I'm buying the old smith, in Langwith Road.' The pause did not produce the anticipated gasp of admiring astonishment or even the apprehensive sigh which would have been almost as gratifying so the narrative continued. 'I've made a bob or two since you left. Not down t'pit. Doing odd jobs of one sort or another. And I've saved most of it.'

At last Agnes was visibly agitated. 'You seem to see a lot of this priest, you're not—'

'Not likely. He likes to throw his money away on slow horses and Jack and me are happy to take it off him. But I wouldn't give twopence for all that bloody nonsense that goes on inside his church. I learned better when I was in hospital.'

Relief at the reassurance that her husband had not been seduced by the Whore of Rome was quickly replaced by the fear that Brack was embarking on another doomed enterprise which could end only in bankruptcy and eviction. 'Is there still work? You don't see as many horses about as you used to. Ernest says that the war proved the value of the internal combustion engine. It's motor cars now. It won't be long before they're all over the place. Motor cars and lorries.'

'For once brother Ernest is right. And that's what I'm going to sell in Langwith Road. I'm buying a dray, a motor dray. I'll do deliveries. Heavy stuff. Coal in particular.'

'Don't most people round here get cheap pit coal? It's mostly colliery cottages. They get coal free or for next to nothing.'

Agnes had not changed. She still always expected the worst. He could think of no reason why he should explain his plan to buy, for a few pence per hundredweight, the free coal which was delivered to every miner and then sell it, at well under the commercial price, to houses in suburban Nottingham and Derby. He remembered from his days as checkweighman that selling free coal was a sacking offence. But he also recalled that desperate colliers were always looking for customers. Thanks to the lorry he meant to buy, he could match supply to demand. He judged that it would be best not to explain the secret of his success to Agnes. So he boasted on. 'Then I'll buy cars. Second hand at first. But new before long. We'll hire them out, sometimes with me driving, sometimes without. And we'll sell them.'

'Can you drive?'

The question illustrated Agnes's inability to live up to her husband's aspirations. He had described to her the prospect of prosperity and success and she had responded with demands for irrelevant detail. When he had told his tale to the housekeeper that Jack McGovern had found him, she had demanded to sit with him in the cab when he took his first ride. Thinking of the girl – and how she had cried when he had said that his wife was coming home – he almost told Agnes, there and then, that she had chosen to leave and could not walk back into Austin Street as if she had never been away. Then he thought of Enid asleep upstairs and he talked of hopes he expected even a stupid woman to understand.

'There's a house with the old smithy. It hasn't been lived in since before the war. I meant to move in right away before you came back but it wouldn't be suitable for Enid. I'll get the work done, quick. Then it'll be just right. We can have a bedroom each, so you can stretch out.'

Agnes had not stretched out for years, but she believed he meant well.

'And the girl can have somewhere to sleep.'

'The girl?'

'I've told you. The housekeeper. Jack McGovern found her for me. She's called Betty Smith. Used to work for him. She'll save you doing all sorts of things.'

'Can we afford all this, Brack?'

' 'Course we can.'

'Worksop will go on paying for Ashleigh House.' Agnes hoped that she was making a vicarious contribution to the respectable new life which they were to live together.

'What's Ashleigh House?'

'It's Enid's school in Worksop. She's doing ever so well.'

'You don't mean she's going to stay there, stay with them?'

'They've offered. Monday morning till Friday night. It'd be a shame to stop her. She's doing ever so well. There's a Miss Foster there who says—'

'And what about you?'

'I'm stopping. I'm stopping with you. I'm back and I'm here to stay.' She sounded as if she might add, 'Whatever you want or whatever I prefer.' But she just returned his bleak stare with the steady gaze of determination. It was too late to turn back. All that was left was doing what was best for Enid.

'It's right to get Enid some education. I know that's not as important for her as if she was a boy with his living to earn. But, Brack, she's as bright as a button. Listen to her talk about Dickens and Walter Scott. She's just read *Ivanhoe*. Read it herself from start to finish. She can tell you all about knights and crusades and Jews lending money. It would be a terrible shame to stop her now.'

'I don't want her stopped.'

Agnes found it difficult to change direction. She had spent so much energy dragging Brack towards her hopes for Enid that she could not quite believe that she need tug no longer. 'It'll stand her in good stead. I know she'll get married.'

'Marriage', said Brack, 'is servitude for women.'

Even if Brack had spoken in his usual voice, Agnes would have felt uncomfortable to hear him talk so strangely. As he offered his opinion in the artificial accent of a neutered church deacon, stressing every syllable with often misplaced emphasis, she felt frightened as well as bewildered. It was as if some alien spirit possessed him and addressed her through her husband's body in its own strange words and vowel sounds.

'What do you mean?'

'Karl Marx says that marriage is no better than prostitution.'

'Brack! How could you say such a thing?'

She had never heard the word spoken before. She could not focus on the idea that what had happened to her in Whitwell parish church was in any way related to the lives lived by those women in Market Street. She felt insulted by the subject being mentioned in her presence.

'How could you use such a word in our own house with Enid asleep upstairs?'

'I was only saying what's true. Marriage is bondage. Slavery for both man and woman. When the millennium comes—'

'I'm not going to listen to any more of your nonsense.'

'If you only knew, I'm speaking up in your defence. In defence of you and all womankind.'

'Who are you defending me from? Where have you picked all this up? I don't understand you.'

'Down the road, if you want to know. This is what we talk about with Arthur Ellis.'

'You talk about marriage . . . and slavery?'

Brack decided that his wife was no more equipped to share his new ideological interests than she was to appreciate his commercial acumen. Enid would be different. She would stand side by side with him in the battle for socialism and female emancipation.

'Make us a cup of tea.'

Agnes pushed herself up with difficulty and hobbled out into the kitchen. Her crooked hand clutched the tap like a claw. 'I can't turn this thing,' she shouted. 'I can't get it to budge.'

Brack stretched his long legs across the hearth. 'It's just a bit stiff. Try turning it with the dishcloth.' Listening to the gratifying sound of water splashing against the inside of the iron kettle, he decided that next morning he would begin to convince Enid of the need to fight for women's rights.

Four houses down the road, Arthur Ellis approached his twenty-seventh birthday in a contraption which Brack always thought of as a cross between a baby's bassinet and a coffin. It had been designed to hold Arthur Ellis's rigid body without taking up too much space in the back room of his miner's cottage. Its front wheels had obviously begun life on a baby's perambulator. Those at the back had clearly been designed for a bicycle. As a result of the discrepancy in their size, Arthur Ellis lay at an angle which enabled him to see as much of the world as was visible through the back-room window. Since it opened out on to the yard, beyond which was a water closet, a brick wall and a lean-to shed, the view did not afford him much entertainment.

Neither did Sally Ellis. When he married her she was a jolly girl with big hands, a red face and an enthusiasm for physical contact. She poked Arthur in the chest to make sure that he was listening, elbowed him in the ribs to convince him that she had just made a joke and struck him on the back as a sign of her affection. In those days she laughed a lot. She was still only a girl but she was jolly no more. Arthur had not heard her laugh since they brought him home from Chesterfield General Hospital.

It was not only grief that had broken her spirit. On the evening of the accident at Warsop Main, she had been told that her husband's spine was fractured and that he would be dead before morning. If she had known then that the doctors were wrong and that he had the chance to live for years, she would have fallen on her knees and given thanks. But now, with him lying in a living death under the back-room window, she sometimes wondered if the first diagnosis would have been best. She tried to put the thought out of her mind for she was mortally afraid that her real concern was not so much for her crippled husband as for herself. In little more than a year, work had turned the big hands bony and the round cheeks pale.

Arthur was not an exacting patient but, although he did not demand it, he needed constant attention. Sally prided herself that he wanted for nothing. She kept him dry and thanks to the constant application of surgical spirit he had not suffered a single bedsore. She had achieved that by regular lifting and turning, and often – just as she had rolled her husband on his side or pulled a clean sheet halfway underneath him – she would have to leave the job half finished and run into the front room. Their house had been turned into a general store and she could not afford to miss the sale of one pound of sugar or a single packet of salt.

Sally Ellis tried not to resent the nightly procession of visitors that passed through her kitchen door, padding in mud from the backyard on to the linoleum and letting the warmth of the overheated kitchen escape into the cold evening air. Although she was grateful for the time they spent in entertaining Arthur, she wished that they would show a little more thought and consideration. Father Froes only upset her husband by urging him to make sure that she went to mass each Sunday. Ernest Brackenbury gave Arthur racing tips and encouraged him to place bets that he could not afford. Worst of all, Owen Ford stayed long into the night, reading, reading, reading and Sally could not go to bed until the reading was over and she had made the preparations for the cripple's long lonely night.

It would have been different if she had liked Owen Ford but he was an official of the Miners' Association and a socialist, and all his ideas – and the books from which they came – were anathema to her. Sally Ellis was a good Catholic. She spoke to Father Froes about barring the Anti-Christ from the house.

'It's all talk,' the priest told her. 'If it amuses Arthur I wouldn't bother. Brack takes it all with a pinch of salt. I'm sure that Arthur does the same.'

Father Froes was behind the times. Brack's first reaction to Owen Ford had been contemptuously hostile. On his more emollient days he had dismissed the ideas of Marx and Engels as a bad joke. At more aggressive moments he had denounced the death of the Tsar at Ekaterinburg and the closure of his cycle shop in Shirebrook with equal passion and left no doubt that Owen Ford was personally responsible for both atrocities. But gradually the communist began to win him over.

Brack was not attracted by the analysis of capitalism's inherent contradictions or the certainty of the proletariat's ultimate victory but he was immensely moved by the stories of struggle and sacrifice. It had been the same during the early years of the war. No miner was more likely to shake hands with a soldier on leave from the trenches. The martial enthusiasm had worn off, but whilst it had lasted it was genuine enough. The stories of Peterloo, the Chartist Riots and Bloody Sunday stimulated similar emotion. Brack was able to identify with those glories without being expected to risk being shot at in France or Flanders.

His romantic enthusiasm was buttressed by a more practical calculation. Owen Ford, although described by his detractors as a communist, was a stalwart of the Independent Labour Party. The ILP was winning seats on local councils all over the Derbyshire and Nottinghamshire coalfields and Brack saw himself as an ideal councillor. Election would bring customers to the haulage business. It would give him the social status he deserved and it would provide endless opportunities to impose his opinions on other people. So he encouraged Owen Ford to conduct his classes in politics across Arthur Ellis's paralysed form. Each evening Owen entertained anyone who would listen with readings about the working-class movement and its historical struggle. Sometimes they read from Fabian pamphlets or tracts from the Social Democratic Federation. Occasionally they turned to more modern writers. One day, when Owen had caught Sally looking bored, he had offered to bring a copy of George Bernard Shaw's *Intelligent Woman's Guide to Socialism*, which she could read in her spare time to improve her understanding.

When Father Froes found a copy of *Merrie England* lying on the sideboard he had denounced Robert Blatchford as an Anti-Christ whose work would be thrown on the fire in any proper Christian home.

'Don't do that, Father,' Arthur had told him laconically, squinting at the priest over the side of his wickerwork sarcophagus. 'Don't do that. It cost fivepence, secondhand, and we still get free coal.'

Father Froes turned to Sally and asked her, as if he suspected that she was to blame, 'Where in heaven's name does Ford get such things?'

Arthur told him. 'Owen's brother's got a stall full. He's got a book-stall on Chesterfield market. Books and foreign stamps.'

'I warned you, Father,' Sally told him, 'but you wouldn't believe me. You said it was all play acting.'

'I still can't take it seriously. He doesn't really believe any of the wicked rubbish, does he?'

Father Froes found it easier to conduct his conversations with Arthur Ellis through Sally. He could look at her and guess, from the expression on her face, what effect the pastoral advice was having. Arthur simply stared at the ceiling. A pulse throbbed in his neck. But not a muscle moved in his face and his unblinking eyes seemed to be focused on something high above the roof tops of Austin Street. However, whilst none of the priest's questions were asked directly of him, he always answered for himself.

'I believe that we're exploited. I believe that what's rightly ours is taken by the employers.'

'He really mustn't let the accident make him bitter. He mustn't brood. He . . .' Father Froes could not think what else Arthur ought to do.

'All the accident's done is give me time to think. And thanks to Owen I'm thinking about something sensible.'

'We must find other things to interest him. I'll bring him my old copies of *Sporting Life*. He does have a little flutter from time to time, doesn't he?'

'More than from time to time.' At last, Sally answered one of the questions. 'Most days.'

'Well, there you are, then. There's something to hope for. If he takes an interest in horses, he won't have any time for all this socialist rubbish.'

'Brack has.' Arthur was no longer trying to look over the side of his cot. The disembodied voice rose from behind the wickerwork, sharp and ironic. 'Brack's got time for it. And, as you well know, he likes the horses does Brack. I'll tell you this, Father, there's nothing like a ton of rock fallin' on you to make y'take an interest in politics. That and fifty quid compensation.'

'Are you telling me that Brack sits here and listens to that Owen Ford reading from tracts and pamphlets?' The priest had been panicked into speaking directly to his parishioner. 'I don't want to call you a liar, Arthur, but I can't see it. I can't see it at all.'

397

'I'm not saying that, Father. But I'm saying that he's a socialist.'

'I can't believe he knows the meaning of the word.'

'You should hear him talk,' said the disembodied voice. 'I'm not saying he reads much. He doesn't study like Owen does. But he knows which side his bread's buttered. And talk . . .'

'Talk the hind legs off a donkey,' Sally added. 'You should have heard him going on against the war.'

Father Froes was a patriot. 'It's always the men who've stayed safe at home who talk about the Germans winning. Defeatist talk is as bad as shooting our boys in the back. It's always the same. It's the men who stay at home who want to sue for peace. There are older men than him in the trenches. How old is he, anyway?'

'Brack's not a pacifist, Father, nor a defeatist either,' said Arthur. 'He doesn't want us to surrender to the Germans or sue for peace. He'd like the same thing to happen here as happened in Russia. He'd like the workers to take over.'

'May you be forgiven.' Father Froes was so breathless with shock that he could barely speak the words.

'Arthur's just trying to cause trouble, Father. Take no notice.'

Sally began to smooth her husband's pillow. As she bent over him, she knotted her brow and pursed her lips. If Arthur realised that she was pleading for no more provocation, he took no notice.

'I'm not saying that I believe in it. I am a pacifist. I'm just telling you about your mate Brack. Doesn't he tell you about these things when you call round with the bets? I'd have thought you'd discuss these things. You being an educated man.'

'I certainly don't discuss Bolshevism with anyone. Or syndicalism, which will be the death of this coalfield if it's not stamped out.'

'Don't ask me to worry about that,' said Arthur. 'The coalfield has been the death of me.'

Sally Ellis bit her lip and Father Froes began to unfasten the little leather case which he had grasped with increasing anxiety during the discussion of the Russian Revolution. As he looked at the chalice, the flask of wine and the silver box which contained the wafers he wondered what he would do if Arthur refused the sacrament. His hand trembled as he kissed his scapula and hung it round his neck. He was afraid to go on, but he knew that he must, for all the village knew that Arthur Ellis might die any day. The medical gossip was unanimous. Suddenly, as Sally was feeding him or turning him over for another rub with surgical spirit, what was left of his spinal cord would snap. Father Froes could not take responsibility for Arthur's soul being stained by sin at the moment of the final fracture. Were that to happen as a result of his priest's negligence or cowardice, they might both spend eternity in torment.

He knelt by the side of Arthur's litter and waited. After what seemed like an hour he decided that he would prompt what ought to have been the spontaneous beginning to the act of Grace. 'When did we last do this, Arthur? When was your last confession?'

'Two weeks ago, Father.'

'And what have you to tell me?'

There was another long pause.

'We're on our own, Arthur. Sally has gone into the kitchen. I know you want to make a confession.'

It seemed that more help was needed.

'Think, Arthur. Have you had any improper thoughts?'

'Dirty thoughts, Father?'

'Carnal thoughts, my son.'

'No, Father.'

'Then blasphemous thoughts? Have you ever doubted God's love? Have you ever despaired of redemption and salvation?'

'No, Father.'

'In nomine patris et filii et spiritus sancti.'

When the time came, the priest broke off a thin corner of wafer and put it between Arthur's lips. He watched anxiously as a small movement of the neck confirmed that it had been swallowed successfully.

'Misereatur vestri omnipotens Deus, et dimissis peccatis vestris, perducat vos ad vitam aeternam.'

Father Froes rattled chalice against flask as he packed them away. He dropped his bag on the linoleum with a thud and intentionally kicked a table leg as he moved to pick it up. Halfway through the eucharist, his tranquillity had been disturbed by the thought that he should have invited Sally to join them. He wanted her to know that she was welcome to return to her own back room. The door shook as she pushed it open with her knee. She was carrying a tray.

'Father.'

'Yes, Arthur?'

'Just a minute before you go.'

'Of course, Arthur.'

'There's something I should have told you.'

'Tell me now.' He waved away the cup of tea which was offered as an accompaniment to the revelation.

'I should have told you during confession.'

Sally put down the cup and saucer and returned to her kitchen.

'I bore false witness.'

399

Father Froes reached for his scapula.

'I told you that Brack was a Bolshevik. That he wanted revolution. It's all just talk, Father. He's got a big mouth but he doesn't mean it. He doesn't understand either. Not like Owen Ford does. He just likes the sound of his own voice. I want to confess again, Father. I don't want—'

'Arthur, in heaven's name! That was just a joke. You don't have to be sorry about that.'

'I'd rather. If it's all the same to you.'

As Father Froes began to prepare for a second act of absolution and contrition, he comforted himself with the thought that, although he was being kept from the comfort of his presbytery for another fifteen minutes, the young man's determination to go through it all again proved that the True Church did not easily let its prisoners escape.

CHAPTER THIRTY-TWO

A Little Learning

Arthur Ellis survived for so long that his house in Austin Street became one of the sights of the north Nottinghamshire coalfield. Miners who passed by his window peered furtively between the faded curtains in the hope and fear of seeing a man who had survived for so long with a broken back. Jack McGovern had several times offered to gamble on the date of Arthur's death but Brack, who was famous for betting on everything from the winner of the Grand National to the number of wasps caught in a pot of jam, refused. Agnes never visited the crippled miner but she constantly cross-examined her husband about Arthur's health and state of mind.

'Why are some days worse than others?'

'Don't know. Today was a bad 'un. That was plain enough. Could barely move his head at all.'

'How does he take it? In himself, I mean.'

'He never seems miserable, I'll tell you that. Very quiet. Especially today, being a bad day. But he never seems upset. You'll have to go and visit him. He loves company. It's a bit funny talking to him when he's lying flat on his back. But you get used to it. He understands every word that you say. He likes a good talk.'

'No, I don't want to. I wouldn't like it. I wouldn't know what to say. I just wanted to know what it was like.'

'What what is like?'

'Lying there. Not able to move.'

'You could have guessed that. It's bloody terrible. You take my word for it.'

Agnes could walk only with difficulty. The rheumatoid arthritis had reached her knees and had locked them at an angle which allowed her only to shuffle along like a manacled convict.

'It's wonderful that he keeps cheerful,' she said.

'Owen Ford says that there are thousands like him. Crippled by the war. He says that they were pushed through Chesterfield in bathchairs at the end of the Armistice parade.'

'I don't want to talk about it any more.'

'Suit yourself.' Brack resented his wife's attempt to dictate the topic of conversation. To Agnes's surprise, he leaned towards her and, giving her thigh a friendly though agonising slap, enquired, 'Do you want to talk about tomorrow's trip? Do you want to talk about the outing?'

'It's not an outing, Brack, whatever else it is. Anne and Ernest will never forgive me if I don't go. They're unhappy enough as it is about Dad not being there. You'd think they'd understand that he'd go if he could. I've got to go.'

'Of course you have. I really ought to go myself. I would if there wasn't so much work to do. I'm not grumbling. But it's got to be done. We can't have a lorry and a couple of motors standing in the yard and not earning. But you go and enjoy yourself.'

Agnes took some time to adjust back to Brack's benevolence and to the idea that she might enjoy herself at a funeral.

'He was so good to Dad. That's why I've got to be there.'

'I'm telling you go. And don't wait till Wednesday. I'll take you tomorrow. We'll set off early enough to take Enid back to Ashleigh House. And I'll come and fetch you back on Friday.'

'It's a lot of trouble for you.'

In another mood, Brack might well have told her – calmly and without apparent malice – that, if she wanted to save him trouble, the longer she was in Worksop the better. On that evening he merely encouraged her to go. 'I'll be all right. Enid's been on all weekend about a tennis racquet.' He took a roll of bank notes out of his pocket and peeled off two pounds. 'Is there a shop that sells them in Worksop? If not, tell her we'll get her one on the way back. We'll come home through Chesterfield. Don't worry about me. I'll look after myself for a bit.'

'Betty will look after most things. She'll get your dinner and tea. She'll do the washing as usual tomorrow. If there's any darning needs doing that can wait.'

'Oh, aye. Betty will be here. I'd forgotten that. She'll keep an eye on things.'

Agnes felt only a moment's surprise that her husband had over-looked the existence of a maid who lived in for five days a week.

'If I go tomorrow, Anne'll be able to take my black coat in. I've lost pounds since she made it for me. I don't want to go there with it hanging on me like a skeleton.'

'You'll not take Enid, will you?'

'Yes, I shall. Why not?'

'Funerals are no place for children.'

'She's got to learn about these things sooner or later. Anyway, she's fourteen. There's plenty of girls out scrubbing floors at her age. It's no good trying to keep her a child. That's what Mam tried to do with me.'

'I don't mean that. I meant making her stand there and listen to all that rubbish. "I am the Life and Resurrection," saith the Lord! "Death, where is thy sting?" I don't want all that nonsense drilling into her.'

'Brack, that's blasphemous! I hope you don't say such things in front of her.'

'And I hope you don't tell her lies about getting her rewards in heaven. That's all lies invented to stop working men from worrying about getting their proper reward on earth.'

'I don't feel well enough to argue. If you don't want her to go to Mr Hodding's funeral, I won't let her. But she'll want to go. She'll want to see all the gentry dressed up in mourning. She'll be real disappointed. If she's got to stay in Newcastle Avenue you can tell her when you're driving us to Worksop in the morning.'

Brack told her that he was letting her go to the funeral only to look after her mother and that she must not believe a word that the vicar said. Agnes did not argue. Nor did she tell her husband that Ashleigh House promised in its brochure an act of Christian worship every morning and a lesson devoted to religious instruction each day. He need not have worried. Throughout the service, from the arrival of the choir singing 'Peace, Perfect Peace' to the performance of Rachmaninov's 'Prelude' in C Sharp which accompanied the departure of the cortège, Enid's mind was firmly fixed on the wonders of possessing her own tennis racquet.

The service was held at St Anne's, the church built in Newcastle Avenue by John Robinson as a memorial to his wife. For Steetly chapel was too small to hold the congregation which everyone agreed would assemble to pay their last respects to Henry Hodding. The family, led by the widow and the two surviving sons, filled the first four rows of pews. Then came the representatives of town and country, bar and bench, Church, territorial army and turf. Each of the hunts to which Mr Hodding rode was represented by its master. Every firm of solicitors who practised within the county sent its senior partner. The Harness Grove servants were crushed against the font at the back of the church.

The walk from Brook House took Agnes longer than she had anticipated and when she arrived at St Anne's – as the service was about to begin – every seat had been taken. The old butler hissed a message along the pew and two of the younger maids stood up with bad grace and offered their seats to the unknown cripple and gaunt lady on whose arm she leaned. Lottie, Enid and Ernest stood against the table, which was covered by religious tracts and missionary pamphlets. As the coffin was carried out of the church, it passed within a yard of Ernest's professional eye. He gasped with admiration. 'Look at that,' he said in a whisper so loud that the mourners in the back pew all turned startled heads in his direction. 'Just look at that. Unpolished oak. Not a blemish.'

The Skinners and the Brackenburys held back in proper deference as the Hoddings, the Humble-Crofts, the Robinsons, the Andersons, the Hancocks, the Longbottoms and the Kemps followed the body out into the snow, hurriedly buttoning up their coats and wondering if proper respect required the gentlemen to keep their heads uncovered until Henry Sweet Hodding was in the hearse and on his last journey to Steetly churchyard.

By the time Agnes and Enid escaped into the cold afternoon air, the cortège had moved off. The old butler padded across towards them, holding on to convenient gravestones to make sure that he kept his feet.

'It's a sad day, Aggie. I was looking for Ernest.'

'He's already gone on to Steetly. He's going to the churchyard. So is Anne.'

'Do you want to come in the dray? The little girl as well if you want. There's plenty of room. Not as many servants as there used to be.'

'No, thank you. I'm going straight to Grove Cottage. My dad's very upset and I want to keep an eye on him. Anyway, it's too cold for me. I missed Mr Knock. Will you give him my best wishes? He went round to see Dad yesterday and—'

The old butler turned and steadied himself against a weeping angel. 'Haven't you heard, Aggie? Gerrard died in the night. Died in the stable whilst he was getting the harness ready for today. Mrs Hodding told him to leave it to one of the lads. Should have given up years ago. He was older than your dad. We all told him to give up, but he wouldn't listen. Never would. They found him this morning, lying in the mucky straw.'

'I bet you that bugger Brack doesn't come round tonight.'

'What's it matter? We can manage without him.' Owen Ford leaned back in his chair so that the light from the gas mantle illuminated the book in his lap. Half of his face was in darkness. Along the cheek which caught the light, a long blue scar proclaimed his years in the pit.

'It doesn't matter to me. But there's them to who it does. First Wednesday for months he's not been here.' Arthur Ellis gave what sounded almost like the laugh of a man who hugged a secret to himself.

Owen Ford was not amused. 'Well, I'm glad he's not here. He never listens. He sits there pretending to take it all in, but just waiting to start spouting.'

'You don't need to worry, he won't be here tonight.'

'Do you want me to read this book or not?'

'Not if it's the same as Monday. I couldn't understand a bloody word.'

Owen Ford snapped shut his brand-new copy of *The Acquisitive Society*. He was deciding whether or not to attempt *New Fabian Essays*, when Brack came through the door which joined the back room to the shop. He was carrying a two-pound bag of flour and a jar of treacle.

'Who is it?' Arthur asked from inside his wicker cage.

'It's me. I'm only putting my head round the door, to see if you're all right.'

'You should get those at Co-op,' said Owen. 'Arthur knows that comrades we may be, but I'll not patronise his private enterprise when I can go to the Co-op.'

'Don't be so bloody silly. You get your living from a private enterprise. Your brother's a bloody capitalist if ever I saw one. Communist or not, you hired a van from me to shift the furniture when your mother died.'

'There was no socialist alternative available.'

'You big pompous sod! If you were a right friend you'd do all your shopping here, instead of just reading them books for your own bleeding amusement. Anyway, there was no alternative available to us. We'd run out. The Co-op'll be shut by now.'

'Planning, Brack. Planning. It's the essential weapon of socialism. Since I've been looking after myself, I've sat down every Sunday and written out a list—'

'The only list Brack ever wrote out is runners and riders.' It was the voice from the invalid carriage. 'What surprises me is that he's come out shopping himself. Female emancipation is it, Brack?'

'My wife's away with her sister.'

'She's ill, Arthur. She's got arthritis. That's why she never comes round.' Owen Ford had an irresistible compulsion to educate.

'I know that. One cripple knows about another. I know more than you'd think, just lying here. I know what Brack's been up to tonight.'

'Well, you know more than me.' Innocence was an essential ingredient of Owen's philosophy.

'I thought everybody knew. Everybody except his wife. It's all they talk about in the shop. Sally comes in here as red as a beetroot.'

'What's he on about, Brack?'

Brack did not answer.

'He knows what I'm on about. I'm on about him tupping that housemaid of theirs. That's right, isn't it, Brack? She's been in the family way and he paid to get rid of it.'

Owen Ford bravely edged between Brack and the wickerwork coffin.

'Brack, he's not worth bothering about.'

'Bothering about! He's a bad bastard. Lying there festering.'

He pushed Owen Ford aside and leaned so low over the cot that Arthur Ellis could feel spittle splattering against his face. 'You bad bastard. If you weren't a fucking cripple . . .'

'What would you do, Brack, break my back?'

It was not within Arthur Ellis's power to flinch and the sight of him lying absolutely still broke Brack's nerve.

'I'm getting out of it.'

Owen Ford followed him into the cold night.

'You've got to understand . . .'

'He's an evil little runt. That's what I understand.'

'He's dying, slowly. He can't move a muscle. He just lies there and thinks.'

'He can think what the hell he likes in future. Don't expect me to come round and amuse him.'

'I'll talk to you about it. Are you still going to Worksop on Saturday?'

'Saturday or Sunday. One or t'other.'

'I'll talk to you when you get back.'

Enid and Agnes spent Thursday and Friday at Grove Cottage. Agnes had wanted to come back to Brook House but her sister had been emphatic.

'You ought to take the chance whilst you can. It can't be so long before . . .' She gave one of the significant looks which she had learned from her mother. 'Enid can help. She's a big enough girl to look after you now. Sooner she learns the better. She won't have a maid to look after her.'

'She ought not have two days off school.'

'Two days won't hurt, Mam.'

Usually Enid could not wait to get to Ashleigh House but the idea of forty-eight hours at Darfoulds had two incomparable attractions. She loved her grandfather's company – he told her stories of Wisbech and Lincoln as if they were twin Edens from which he had been expelled after a youth and early manhood spent in innocent grace. And at Grove Cottage she could read her latest book. She had discovered *Wuthering Heights* and could have devoured it in a week had Aunt Anne not detected it under her bedclothes and forbidden her ever to open it again. Indeed, it would have been burned on the spot had Enid not explained that she could sell it back to Owen Ford at the weekend.

'His brother sells books. He'll give me something in exchange. Perhaps money as well.'

'Mind you do give it back. And get something suitable in its place. Promise.'

'Promise, Auntie. What shall I get?'

'Don't ask me. I don't know anything about books. I don't like made-up stories in particular. I like truth, not invention.'

Sustained by her aunt's peculiar school of literary criticism, she felt just able to postpone her next visit to the Heights and the Grange until Saturday. At Grove Cottage there would be no censorship. Her mother would encourage her to read anything and everything and her grandfather would sit in front of the kitchen fire and listen to her recount the tales she had read. She had buried Cathy and Heathcliffe by early Friday afternoon and had begun *Tess of the d'Urbervilles*.

'Are you going up to Steetly, Aggie?' For more than a month, William Skinner had left the house only for brief and uncomfortable visits to the midden. The Hodding funeral had concentrated his mind on churchyards. 'Somebody ought to go. That grave hasn't been looked at since October.'

'Mam can't go. Anyway, Uncle Ern says he'll go next week with the Christmas wreaths.'

'Somebody ought to go.'

'I'll go,' said Enid. 'I'll tidy it up. Then somebody will have been there.'

'Now, before it's dark,' her mother told her.

But she was warm and sitting on the pegged rug in front of the fire, roasting chestnuts on a wire toasting fork and waiting to tell her grandfather of Tess's terrible fate and the horrors of Stonehenge. When her mother pulled herself upstairs for a 'lie-down', Enid made no move towards the coats which hung behind the door.

'You're a great reader, Enid. Just like your mother was once.'

'I've not much else to do.'

'What are you going to do when you leave school?'

'I'm staying on another year.'

'What are you going to do then, get apprenticed to your Auntie Anne?'

'I'd like to be a school teacher or work in a library.'

'Don't you want to get married?'

'I suppose so.'

'Don't let them turn you against it, Annie and your mam. Your mam's had a hard time, one way or another. But she'd marry your dad again if she had her time over. How old are you?'

'Fourteen, Grandad.'

'It's old enough to understand. Loving somebody – properly. That's the most important thing. More important than your books or money or anything. Just because it doesn't always happen right is no reason to turn people against it. Don't let your mam and dad—'

'They don't, Grandad. They never talk about it.'

'Loving and looking after, that's the important thing. Wanting to look after somebody. It's more important than somebody wanting to look after you. And wanting . . .'

'Wanting what, Grandad?'

'. . . and not just wanting. If you really love somebody you don't let anything stand in your way. You . . .'

'Is that how you felt about Grandma?'

Before William Skinner could answer, his daughter's voice called to Enid from upstairs. 'If you're not gone this minute, you're not going at all. It'll be dark in an hour.'

When the verger of Steetly chapel arrived to lock the great iron-studded church door he saw what he assumed to be a body lying under one of the ancient gravestones which stood alongside the churchyard path like a giant granite tabletop balanced on four carved legs. It was too cold even for a tramp to find rest on the patch of grass which the gravestone sheltered from snow. Some desperate vagrant, the verger decided, had crawled under the great stone slab in search of protection from the morning's storm and there he had died. The body lay too still to encourage hope that it still drew breath.

Death was not a stranger to the verger. He had put his spade through many a rotting coffin lid and seen the decomposing face of a husband whose grave he was opening in preparation for the reunion of a man and wife, and he had unceremoniously bundled dozens of still-born babies into the unmarked earth, so he thought of the corpse as no more than an inconvenience. It was not until his boots were within a foot of her face that Enid Brackenbury even noticed him. For she had become Catherine Linton, lying in the quiet earth and –

true to her grandfather's vision of uncompromising love – waiting for Heathcliffe to join her.

Worksop did not boast a tennis-racquet shop but Enid's disappointment was soon dispelled by her father's offer to drive her to Chesterfield, where, it was universally agreed, tennis racquets were to be found in abundance.

'And we'll call in the market and see this brother of Owen Ford's. It's about time you had some books of your own instead of borrowing all the time. Some good books, properly bound.'

The spire of Chesterfield parish church was not as Enid had imagined it. It was not crooked like a corkscrew, but twisted like a poker which had been caught in the bars of a fire and bent out of its true shape. As the battered old car pulled slowly up the hill to the centre of the town, the weathervane on the top of the steeple seemed to be pointing into the sky immediately above the travellers' heads. When Brack turned the wheels and edged into the market square, the weathervane followed him and appeared still to reach to heaven over Enid's shoulder. Even when they turned a second time and drove up to the door of the covered market, the top of the spire still inclined towards them. It was the first miracle of the afternoon.

The second cause for wonder was the covered market itself, which shone in the winter dusk like a cavern of light. It was lit by every sort of illumination. Gas jets flared gold and warm at either side of the door. Electric bulbs hung from the ceiling on twisted cords. Gas mantles glowed along the walls. On each stall Christmas candles flickered amongst the fruit and vegetables, the cheap children's clothes, the cut-price cutlery and the workmen's shoes. Sides of beef and whole sheep's carcasses hung, like meat curtains, from hooks at the front of the butcher's shop. The greengrocers' counters were piled high with the special treats of the season – pineapples, tangerines, dried figs and dates, crystallised fruit, brazil nuts and bananas. The drapers had brought out all the children's party frocks and labelled them as special offers available to lucky customers at give-away prices. The ironmongers had filled their glass cases with fancy scissors and penknives which boasted more blades than a schoolboy could ever hope to use, and the shelves of the general dealers were heaped with clockwork trains, humming tops, 'Little Carpenter' and 'Little Nurse' sets, teddy bears, lead soldiers (singly and in boxes of eight), brightly coloured rubber balls, dolls' tea services and jigsaw puzzles made from pictures of the King and Queen in their state robes and the Prince of Wales in naval uniform.

The market buzzed and rattled with the collective noise of five hundred shoppers, and, above the hum of their conversation, the sudden cries of traders promoting their wares were occasionally audible but always too indistinct to understand. The sounds were as exciting as the sights and they combined to make Enid want to stop at every stall. But her father hurried her on. He had the idea of books in his mind and he had no thoughts to spare for anything else.

The stall which was rented to Percy Ford – 'Books (new and second hand), Stamps (British, colonial and foreign) and Picture Framing' – was, by comparison with the rest of the covered market, a drab disappointment. It consisted of two long counters, running back to back down the centre of the market hall, which ended in a tiny wooden office. Furthest away from the office, the cheaper second-hand books were thrown in an untidy heap of broken spines, torn bindings and missing pages. Then there were neat tightly packed rows of old, but less battered, stock. Most of the old books were stirring tales of British heroism in foreign parts, with cloth covers decorated with line drawings of Scottish soldiers shooting mutinous sepoys and rebellious Boxers being suppressed by gallant Blue Jackets. Beyond the adventure stories were bound volumes of the *Boy's Own Paper*, the *Magnet*, the *Illustrated London News* and *Punch*. Then came the serious novels – Dickens, Thackeray, Scott, Trollope and Hardy – all bound in sensible, hard-wearing imitation leather. Next was a section devoted to modern authors – Edgar Wallace, Ian Hay and John Galsworthy. The classics, bound in real leather and sometimes even illustrated, were only one partition away from the office. In the place of honour, piled with love and care, were the political texts. They were the books which Percy Ford read most and sold least often.

The office windows – and the glass pane in its door – were filled with displays of postage stamps. Some sheets were decorated with small squares of russet red, Prussian blue and mauve. On others triangular reproductions of garish Old Masters were stuck side by side with oblong pictures of castles and cathedrals in Eastern Europe and South America. Below them were strange messages – 'Chile 7 cents. 1917. Perf.'

Brack began to riffle through the classics. 'This one looks nice – have this. It's Shakespeare.' He handed Enid a large leather-bound volume with the word 'Comedies' embossed on its decorated spine below the immortal name.

'There's three, Dad. I'd have to have three.'

'Don't be greedy, Enid,' said Agnes.

'I wasn't being greedy, Mam. I just said that there were three books in the set. I didn't ask for them. I just said there were three. I'd like novels. I like novels best.'

Before Brack could leap in the direction of his daughter's preference, Owen Ford appeared from inside his brother's office. The sight of the Brackenburys seemed to fill him with resentment. 'You didn't tell me you were coming to Chesterfield. If I'd known you were coming, you could have had a lift.' Owen, in his resentful agitation, had confused passenger and driver.

'I didn't know I was coming m'self when I left Shirebrook. This one made me.' Brack grasped Enid's knitted woollen beret and, using it like a floor cloth, gave an imitation of scrubbing the top of her head. 'She said we'd got to come, so come we did. I told you she was a great reader. We've come to get her some books.'

'Come inside,' said Owen.

The office was so small that, even had there not been piles of books in the corners and picture frames propped against the walls, it would have been difficult for five people to inhabit it with comfort. The stock of Percy Ford's trade littered the floor, and the Brackenburys had to edge inside one by one and stand at whatever angle to each other and the merchandise that allowed them to keep both feet on the floor. The introductions were, therefore, carried out with some difficulty and an embarrassment which was intensified by Percy Ford's infectious diffidence and extraordinary appearance.

Percy Ford did not look like a bookseller. He was a giant and, since his arms had been designed for an even bigger man, his hands reached almost to his knees. Although he was of wholly pacific disposition he possessed the face of a pugilist. He had been born with cauliflower ears and a nose which seemed to have been flattened to his face by a lifetime of straight lefts and right jabs. In his early thirties he had suffered a nervous breakdown which had resulted in the loss of all his hair but even that unhappy experience had not branded him as sensitive. The smooth pale pink skin, stretched tight over his skull, added to the impression that he fought in fairground boxing booths.

He held out a huge hand. Enid, whose attitude to giants had been determined by her first meeting with Ginny Harthill, recoiled and knocked over the *Waverley Novels*.

'I am', said the monster in the tones of a stage aristocrat, 'most extremely sorry. I tell myself to tidy up the place, but I never find time to do it.'

The apology was greeted with universal disapproval. His voice reminded Agnes of the vicar who preached the sermon at Mr Hodding's funeral. Brack had no time for anyone who talked la-di-da. And Enid was simply overwhelmed by the effort of relating sight to sound.

'Keeping this place tidy is near impossible. Never mind. It's the books that matter. What can I do for you?'

411

'Novels,' said Enid quickly. 'I'd like to buy a novel.'

'Jane Austen?' Percy Ford enquired hopefully. 'I wouldn't try George Eliot quite yet.'

'I want Sherlock Holmes.'

'Goodness gracious me.'

'I read part of a story in an old *Strand* magazine at Grandad's. It was lovely.'

'It's all right with me,' Brack said. 'Whatever she wants. It's her treat.'

They edged out of the office and Percy Ford began to search amongst the better second-hand books, muttering 'Doyle. Doyle, Arthur Conan,' as he turned over or picked up what he hoped would be *A Study in Scarlet* or *The Hound of the Baskervilles*. 'I suppose that you particularly wanted Sherlock Holmes? Conan Doyle wrote other stories.' He seized, in sudden triumph, a book to which half of the paper dustjacket still clung. Enid noticed that although most of the title had been torn away, 'Exploits' was still clearly visible. She hoped that it referred to the genius of Baker Street. 'You'd like this. It's about a French officer in the Napoleonic wars. Very exciting and very funny.'

'It's no good,' said Agnes. 'Once she's got her heart set on something, there's no changing her mind. If she wants Sherlock Holmes, that's what she'll get.'

'I just don't have no Sherlock Holmes.' Percy Ford was becoming exasperated and the careful grammar – like the cultivated accent – began to break down. 'They're very popular. They're in great demand.'

'What about *The Scarlet Pimpernel*?' Enid seemed willing to compromise.

'I saw one of them, just a minute since . . . just a moment ago.' He was beginning to sweat. 'If you'd only told me when it was on top.'

He began to dig again and Brack started to dig with him. Enid casually examined the books which they cast aside in their frantic search. Agnes edged her bottom against the counter and sighed as the weight was lifted from her feet.

'I wouldn't mind *East Lynne* . . . Mrs Henry Wood. Who's Rosa Carey? Do you know what she writes about? How do you say this name? Hoffnung? What's *The Amateur Cracksman*? What's a cracksman, Dad?'

'I've got it!' cried Brack. 'I've got—' It turned out to be *The Scarlet Letter*.

'I know there's one here somewhere.'

'Here's another amateur,' said Enid. '*The Amateur Gentleman* by Jeffrey Farnol. What's that about?'

'I've read that,' said her mother. 'I read it when it first came out. I read it when we lived behind the cycle shop. You won't like it. It's a romance.'

'I will,' said Enid, for no better reason than that her mother had prophesied the opposite. 'I like romances.'

'It's just a woman's story.' Percy Ford could make no more damning criticism. 'Shop girl's stuff. It's all about love.'

Enid hoped that by love he meant something improper. 'That's what I want. Here's another one by the same person. *The Money Moon*. Can I have them both?'

'Have whatever you want.'

'It's all right,' Agnes told her. 'But you won't like them. You like more sensible books.' She turned to Percy. 'She'd really like a Sherlock Holmes.'

'I'll send you a postcard when I get one in.'

'I thought that you'd want to have something better.' Owen Ford lifted his eyes from the Fabian tracts and looked accusingly at Brack. 'I thought you'd encourage her to read something more serious.'

'I've told her. I've just offered to buy her Shakespeare.'

Determined to demonstrate his enthusiasm for serious literature, he reached again for the complete works in three volumes. He opened the comedies at random and thrust an illustrated page under his daughter's nose. She read the caption with unusual difficulty. 'Miss Glynn and Mr Hoskin as Isabella and Lucio.'

'It's expensive is that.' Percy Ford lifted the leather to reveal the marbled endpapers and flicked the corners of the pages to make the gilt flash and shine in the gaslight.

'We'll have it. And the other two.' Brack was reaching into his back pocket. 'And the Sherlock Holmes.'

'*Scarlet Pimpernel*.' The bookseller meant to correct him.

'Aye, that an' all.' Brack pulled out a roll of pound notes. 'Then we better be on our way. We've got to buy a tennis racquet before the shops shut.'

As Agnes limped out of the covered market she turned to Brack and asked him anxiously, 'Can we afford all this?'

''Course we can.'

Before she had a chance to answer, Owen Ford had caught up with them. 'Can I have a lift back?' His tone made clear that he still resented the Brackenburys travelling to Chesterfield without him.

'You can if you trust my driving. We've got another call to make. But if you can wait, you're welcome.'

'It's easy enough, isn't it? Just like riding a bicycle, they say.'

'It's all right once you get the knack.'

Brack swung the starting handle and climbed in behind the steering wheel. The car bucked and juddered before it moved forward. Agnes shut her eyes tight and waited until she was steady in her seat to ask the question which had worried her ever since she met Percy Ford.

'How long's your brother owned the bookstall?' What she really wanted to know was how could a man who looked so rough speak like a gentleman.

'Ever since he came back from Oxford University.' Owen Ford waited for his audience to be astonished. He was not disappointed.

'Go on,' said Brack. 'You don't mean real Oxford?'

''Course I do. Ruskin, the working-man's college. The Association paid for him. He were supposed to come back to work for them. Then Hicken got elected and wouldn't have him. Hicken's a local preacher. Leastways, he was until he got into Saltergate. Percy's bitterly against chapel and church. Used to preach against religion outside St Mary's. Hicken wouldn't have that. Seems a pity all that money spent on Ruskin going to waste.'

'What's Ruskin?' Enid had woken up as the car pulled up outside the sports shop.

'Do you want this racquet or not?' Brack led the way into the shop, already an expert on lawn tennis.

'Off you go,' said Owen. 'I'll tell you next week. Come round to our house with your mam and I'll show you the picture of Percy at Oxford with the students.'

When they returned with the most expensive racquet that the shop stocked, Owen continued the conversation as if it had never been interrupted.

'Hicken will never be half the man that Haslam was.'

'Nor Hancock.' Brack had barely met the senior officers of the Derbyshire Miners' Association and he knew nothing of their conduct and character but that did not prevent him from passing judgement on all the officials whose names he could recall. 'That Spencer's all right. He's the old school. Isn't looking for trouble all the time.'

'I'm not sure.'

'What about Barnet Kenyon, then?' Brack had played his last card. If Owen had nothing to say about Barnet Kenyon, he would have to switch the conversation to another topic. By mentioning the Association's general agent, he had exhausted his sum of knowledge on the miners' leadership.

'He asked for all he got.'

Brack grinned his agreement, despite knowing neither what Barnet Kenyon deserved nor what he had received.

'Rules are clear enough. Once he got into Parliament, he lost his retainer. Wouldn't be reasonable to get double pay. Especially when he were doing nothing for the Association. He knew that well enough.'

'Quite right.' Brack turned to his daughter in the back seat. 'Look, Enid, Bolsover Castle.'

Enid was asleep again. And when she was wakened by the car's sudden swerve, they had passed the castle and narrowly missed a courting couple who – walking hand in hand along the road ahead – had escaped Brack's notice.

The gate which led into the Brackenburys' muddy yard was swinging open. As Brack drove between the potholes, half a dozen chickens, which ought to have been in the hen coop at the bottom of the garden, flapped squawking into the air.

'Give us a hand getting these buggers back.'

Owen Ford, who gladly accepted an invitation to supper, seemed less enthusiastic about chasing fowls. By the time he was out of the car, Brack had started running round the side of the house. He ran in long desperate strides like a man who ran because he was afraid. Owen followed. The air smelt of burning paint.

By the side of the house – on the patch of undulating tarmacadam which had been laid straight on to the soft earth – Brack's lorry and the wedding car stood side by side in the yard. The long saloon was no longer white. What little paint remained was scorched into black and grey patches which stood out like scabs on the smoke-stained naked steel of the rest of the bodywork. The front nearside tyre was still burning and the heat of the fire had cracked the windscreen. The ashes of what was left of the dray's smouldering wooden platform smoked between the girders of the chassis. Inside the cab, flames still flickered from the charred driving seat. As Owen Ford stumbled towards Brack he kicked against an empty petrol can.

CHAPTER THIRTY-THREE
Fact and Fancy

There was, Brack decided, no convenient alternative to telling the truth. It was not his natural instinct and he knew how easy it would have been to confuse the explanation which Agnes already believed – an explanation which would have caused her far less distress than admitting what had really happened. But the truth would, he believed, shock his wife into total silence.

Agnes suspected that the fire was the work of an impatient bookmaker. Had he confirmed her suspicions she would have complained for weeks, despite his insistence that he was the victim of atrocious luck and that he had finally learned his lesson, but she would not want to talk to him, or anyone else, about what had really happened. He was reassured by the thought that it was really all her fault and, it was necessary to his undisturbed peace, he could tell her so.

He meant to begin his honest explanation after Enid had gone to bed. But as soon as they got in the kitchen Agnes noticed the red weal on the back of his hand and insisted on poulticing it with a patent ointment which she applied hot to congested chests and cold to burns. As she ministered to him, she expressed her admiration for his courage. It was, she kept repeating, impossible to imagine why anyone should wish to set fire to the lorry and motor car. He was so irritated by her concern that he decided to answer her unspoken question there and then.

'I know who did it.'

At that moment, Agnes thought she knew too. She waited for the description of bribed jockeys, doped horses, falls at the final fence and going heavier than anyone could have reasonably expected. She was telling herself that she should have realised it was all the outcome of an unpaid gambling debt when Brack took a deep breath.

'Betty. Betty did it and ran off. Look in her room. You'll see that all her stuff's gone.' He had already prepared his answer to the next question.

416

Agnes did not disappoint him. 'Why should she do such a wicked thing?'

The explanation came rushing out as if it were a single word. 'Because-she-expected-me-to-marry-her. That's why.'

'What! How could you marry her? You're married already.'

The absurdity of her response was obvious even to Agnes. But she felt absurd and could not help showing it. Brack felt no sympathy for her bewilderment. Indeed, it infuriated him. The simple statement of Betty's expectations should have answered all her questions. Any normal woman would have realised that he had told the girl that his wife had left for good. But, he reminded himself, any normal wife would have realised that he had slept with the maid from the first night that she moved in.

'I gave her to believe . . .'

'Gave her to believe what?'

Brack believed that his wife was being intentionally obtuse. No one could be so naïve. Agnes had chosen to make it difficult for him to explain. This was her revenge – the humiliation of explanation. She was enjoying making him confess the sins for which she was to blame. Hard questions, he decided, warranted harder answers.

'I told her that I'd kicked you out. She wasn't surprised. She'd expected me to do it for months. Being a normal young woman, she couldn't understand why I'd stuck it for so long.'

'Perhaps she thought you'd "stuck it" because of Enid.'

Brack continued to set out the bitter truth as punishment for his wife's persistent cross-examination.

'She did. She did at first. That's what I told her. But after a bit it wore thin.'

'And you told her I'd left you.'

'I told her I'd kicked you out.'

'Then this morning . . .'

'This morning I told her that I hadn't.'

'What did you expect her to do?'

'Cry a bit. Come back to work as usual on Monday morning. I didn't expect her to do this, I can tell you that. I didn't expect her to go off her bloody head. If one of them petrol tanks had been full the lorry would have gone up and she'd have gone up with it.' He paused to consider the consequences of such a catastrophe. 'And that would have got into the papers all right.'

'It'll get into the papers now.'

'No, it won't. Why should it?'

'Because if a car and lorry get set on fire people talk about it.'

'Owen won't say owt.'

417

'Perhaps he won't, but what happens when you can't do your work on Monday?'

Brack spluttered with the beginnings of an answer. He was almost relieved when his wife turned on him.

'Not that I care. I don't care what they say. They've said too much already for me to mind any more. They've seen the bruises where you've hit me.'

'They never have.' Brack could not hide his outrage. 'They've never seen any such thing.'

'Oh, yes, they have. They've seen them when I've been out in Shirebrook. They'd all know about you and that girl.'

'Why should they? You never have.'

'Oh, yes, I have.'

'You're a liar. You didn't know till I told you. You're so peculiar you didn't even think that I'd want to behave like a real man. I suppose you're going to go running back to Worksop now.'

'And let that girl move in here? I'll stay in this house if it's the last thing I do. You'll have to put me out to get rid of me. And the neighbours would find out about that.'

'Don't talk so bloody silly.'

'If you're so keen on talking sense you can tell me this. What are we going to live on? I know you don't care, but I've got a young daughter to think of. Thanks to you, we'll all be out on the street.'

'I've not had time to think. You've been going on about that bloody girl all the time. I suppose I'll go back down the pit. At least till I can get a bit of money put together.'

'Won't any of your friends help you out?'

'It's hundreds of pounds. Who do I know with that sort of money?'

'Worksop would help. But you're too stupid to take it.'

'I might. I'm getting too old for the bloody pit. Would you ask them?'

'Don't think I'd do it for you. You're not worth it. You aren't worth anything. I'm doing it for her.' Agnes inclined her head, as far as the paralysis allowed, in the direction of the bedroom. 'Drive Enid and me to Worksop tomorrow and we'll talk to them.'

'What'll you tell Enid?'

'I'll tell her the truth. I'll tell Worksop too.'

'No, you won't. I'm not having Enid know. I don't give a bugger for Worksop, but I'll not have Enid knowing.'

'Better to hear it from me than from somebody in Shirebrook. Anyway, I want her to know what sort of father she's got. She worships the ground you walk on. It's about time she found out what sort of man you are.'

*

418

Only Lottie seemed scandalised. Agnes would have preferred to speak to Anne and Ernest separately and alone but her brother was visiting Brook House for Sunday tea and there was no alternative to facing them together whilst Enid was sent out in the garden.

'I'm not surprised,' said Anne. 'Not surprised at all.'

She spoke in disturbingly matter-of-fact language. She would have sounded much the same if Agnes had told her that, at last, a crumbling drain had fallen in. The implication of her tone was clear: anyone who had failed to take sensible advice about early renovation should not complain about the stench.

'Anyway, the lorry's no good. And even if the motor car can be made to work, it will need pounds spending on it.'

To Agnes's distress, they did not take the bait. Had she not known her brother so well, she would have believed that he condoned Brack's conduct.

'He's probably learned his lesson. It's a terrible thing to have done. I'm not saying it isn't. But I can't see him doing it again. Perhaps the shock will do him good. Perhaps he'll settle down now.'

'Ernest's right,' said Anne. 'When you came in I thought that you'd left him for good.'

'Do you think that's what I should do?'

'Perhaps you ought to stay here for a bit.' Lottie blushed as if she had said the wrong thing.

Anne made no attempt to disguise her annoyance. Although she spoke to Agnes, her anger was clearly directed at Lottie. 'You can't keep bobbing backwards and forwards. You have to make your mind up to stay with him or make a break and get a home of your own for you and Enid.'

'What on earth would I live on? He wouldn't pay a penny.'

'We'd help,' said Ernest. 'Anne and I have talked about this many a time. We'll both help and Enid can get a little job.'

'That's another thing.' Anne decided to get all the unpleasantness over at once. 'It's time Enid started work.'

'But she's doing so well.'

'I know.' Ernest tried to sound benign. 'We're all very proud of her. She's a very clever girl. But what's the point of it? Another year at Ashleigh House, then she'll be looking for a job. Let's sit down with a piece of paper.'

Ernest was already licking the point of his pencil. He took the little notebook out of his pocket.

Lottie tried to make amends for her earlier mistake. 'We've still got the figures you worked out last time she was here,' she said. Obligingly she reached behind the clock on the mantelshelf.

'Do you mean . . . ?' Agnes was too upset to finish the sentence.

Agnes stared at Ernest, willing him to take command of the conversation. He rose to the occasion magnificently. 'We had a little talk weeks ago. That's all. We'd have liked you here. Anne just can't manage everything. There's Ginny upstairs . . .'

'Ginny's not her sister.' Agnes was in tears.

'She's Lottie's sister,' Anne reminded her, 'and Lottie lives here too. Then there's Dad, coming down here every time he's out of sorts, and he needs looking after even when he's at Grove Cottage. Your Enid's a handful. I don't mean that she's a naughty girl. She's just full of life. But what with her and the business . . .'

'I didn't come here to stay. I'm staying in Shirebrook. I decided that last night. I came to beg you to lend us money – enough to set us up again. Whatever you say about him, Brack's a hard worker. He's done well. If we get over this . . .'

'You should have said.'

Anne was more resentful than sympathetic. She clearly believed that she had been trapped into sounding selfish by the pretence that Agnes and Enid were coming to stay.

'Don't worry,' Agnes sniffed. 'I won't ask now. Brack'll go back down the pit.'

'There's no need for that.' Lottie was at her most disarming. 'All we said was that we couldn't manage with Enid any more. Lending you something is different.'

'I wouldn't take it.'

'Yes, you would,' said Ernest. 'Come with me into the fitting room and let's talk about it quietly.'

He stood up – grey and grave, the epitome of middle-aged respectability – and pushed open the fitting-room door. Nobody except Lottie had ever before invaded its privacy without first asking Anne's permission. He set out his scheme to Agnes, which she did not understand but which she accepted in every detail except one.

Ernest was unable to persuade Agnes that it was right and sensible for Enid to leave Ashleigh House so he left it to Anne to convince her that it was unavoidable.

'It is just not possible. When we're scraping about for every penny we can lay our hands on, it just isn't common sense.'

She did not say – though Agnes had no doubt that she meant – that if Brack's business was to be rescued by Worksop the Brackenburys would have to accept Worksop's terms in full.

'What's more, she ought to be at home with you. She's old enough to help out.'

'And perfectly willing,' Agnes assured her.

'I know that well enough. Anyway, she needs to be there. No more maids. You wouldn't have one now, would you?' Agnes did not reply quickly enough to satisfy her sister. 'At least, no more maids paid for by us. We'd feel happier with Enid there to look after you – to keep an eye on you all the time. That's the important thing, not saving the money.'

It was not an ultimatum – for that would at least have allowed Agnes to refuse the offer and take its consequences. It was a statement of the inevitable. Fate, circumstances and Worksop allowed no other possibility. The message would not have been more clear and categoric had Anne simply said, 'We won't pay the fees.'

Agnes expected to leave for Shirebrook – which she was careful to call home – next day. But Ernest suggested that she waited until the end of the week. 'Why not let that husband of yours take you? He'll come over here in his motor car on Friday. He can take you and Enid back with him. It won't do any harm for him to worry about what's happening for a day or two.'

'How do you know that he'll come here on Friday?'

'He will when he gets my letter. You mark my words. I'll tell him to be here at five. Our business will occupy him for about half an hour. I don't want him hanging about. If you can be packed and ready . . .'

Brack knocked on the back door of Brook House at exactly five minutes to five. Anne let him in. A dog that Brack had not seen before panted by her side.

'Say hello to Chum,' Lottie told him in her most reproachful voice. 'He's trying to be friendly. He's just settling in. Poor old Prince passed away in his sleep.' Reproach turned to recrimination. 'I don't understand how you can just walk in without speaking to him.'

'I didn't notice.' Brack dangled his hand in Chum's direction and the dog began to lick it with salivating frenzy.

'Is Ernest here? He said—'

'He's in the garden,' she told him, 'moving slugs.'

'Moving slugs!'

'They're on the lettuce,' Lottie explained. 'He's moving them to the dock behind the rubbish heap. They don't like it very much. But it saves the lettuce and it keeps them alive.'

For a second, the explanation diverted Brack's attention from the serious business which lay ahead.

'Why do you want to keep them alive? It's best just to wash 'em off and tread on them.'

Lottie was scandalised. 'It's not their fault they live on lettuce.

421

That's how God made them. We don't believe in killing living creatures. They have their purpose like we have ours.'

Ernest's arrival – his sleeves still turned back to protect his cuffs against the ravages of vegetable and weed – ended further speculation about the slug's place in society.

'You must forgive me.' He held his dirty hands in front of him to prove that the delay was unavoidable. It took him several minutes to scrub them clean under the cold water of the kitchen tap. It was because he felt nervous that Brack began to defend himself before he was attacked.

'You better understand straight away that I've not come here to be preached at.'

'I never thought you had. You're here to listen to a business proposition.'

Ernest Skinner set out his terms. He had taken legal advice. His original idea was for Brack to declare himself bankrupt – for bankrupt in every real sense of the word he certainly was. But if that were done with the agreed intention of selling his business to a relative it might be regarded as fraud.

'Selling the business! I thought from that bloody letter you were going to save it.'

'So I am. Just listen and try to take it in.'

'Just tell me what you want to say and I'll be off.'

'The idea of going bankrupt and me buying the business cheap just won't work. So I'll have to pay your debts.'

Brack's spirits visibly improved.

'I'm very grateful.'

'I doubt if you will be after you've heard what's on offer. I put it wrong. I should have said buy your debts. I'll buy them with the rest of the business.'

'Who said I was selling?'

'We're not here to bargain. You've got nothing to bargain with.'

Brack stood up. He meant to do no more than relieve his tension, but Ernest thought that he was threatening to walk out.

'It's take it or leave it. It's my last offer and probably your last chance. I'll buy your business – coal, goodwill, what's left of the wedding car, that motor car in the road outside, everything. I'll pay off your debts. And that's a lot. I don't know exactly how much but it's a lot.'

'Not as much as she makes out.' He jerked his head in the direction of the kitchen. 'Aggie's always been against anything on tick. You can't start a business without credit. She'd rather go without than have easy terms. She's daft about it. Don't take her word about how much we owe.'

'I want it all written down by Monday. Hire purchase on the lorry and the cars. Petrol not paid for, money owed for coal . . .'

'You can't expect me to write down where the coal comes from. It's colliers' free coal. They'd get the sack if anybody found out that they'd sold it to me.'

'They should have thought of that before they sold it. I want it all written down.'

'It'll be a tidy sum.'

'I'll buy it all with the business. Then you work for me.'

'Bloody hell. I was beginning to think you'd say that. Then I decided that you didn't have the cheek. How much? How much are you going to buy it all for?'

'A pound. A pound to make it legal.'

'Christ almighty.'

'I'll thank you not to use that sort of language in this house. My sister is next door.'

Despite his anger, Brack noticed that it was Anne alone who was to be protected from his blasphemy.

Agnes had faced enough trouble for one day, so she waited until they got home to Shirebrook to break the news to Enid.

'But you've got another fortnight. Your aunt Anne's paid till the end of the month so you don't have to leave before the start of the Christmas holidays. You'll be all right until a week on Friday.'

'If I'm leaving, I'm not going back now. They're nasty enough to me as it is. I can hear Winnie Horsey laughing and saying that it wasn't the place for a miner's daughter in the first place and Bridie Smith saying that it served me right for being teacher's pet and reading all the time.'

'I thought they were your friends.'

'They are. They are my friends. And I'm never going to see any of them again. If I'm going to be a skivvy, I'll start skivvying straight away. I'll wear a mob cap and an apron, if you like. I might as well.'

'Don't be so silly, love. There's no point in wasting a fortnight's fees. Besides you like it so much.' Agnes realised, before the sentence was finished, that she had not chosen a line of argument which was likely to reconcile Enid to her father.

'Well, I'm not going back. If I've finished, I've finished. Finished for good.'

'You'll have to go to Worksop and get your clothes.'

'Let him go. He's caused all this. He's ruined my life. I don't like any of those clothes anyway. They're mostly customers' cast-offs. If he wants them, let him go in his motor car and get them. I hate him.'

'Enid! It's your father you're talking about.'

'I know it is. And he's spoilt everything. I'll never forgive him. Never.'

'Whatever he's done, he loves you in his way. Couldn't you tell that last week in Chesterfield?'

'What did he do last week?' Enid knocked Jeffrey Farnol's *The Money Moon* off the chair arm and on to the floor. 'He flashed his money about in front of his friends. He bought me those three old Shakespeare books with their silly pictures and funny printing. I couldn't take those to school. They're out of a museum. He doesn't understand what I want and he's stopped me getting educated and I shan't forgive him, ever. And I'm not going to Worksop tomorrow.'

Enid spent Monday morning performing household duties. She cleaned out the ashes before anyone else was awake and by the time her mother – startled by the sound of brush and pan on grate and hearth – joined her downstairs, she had laid the fire. She insisted on black-leading the oven before she had her breakfast and, whilst her father was still chewing methodically on his breakfast, she announced that she was going to start the weekly washing. Brack was hugely amused.

'You wouldn't know how. You couldn't light the fire under the boiler.'

'If Betty could do it, I can do it. Or perhaps you went out into the washhouse and lit it for her.'

Agnes waited for Brack's violent reaction but he was too startled even to speak. Enid rattled the cups together and began clearing away the breakfast pots. She poured a kettle of boiling water into the washing-up basin and then turned on the kitchen tap with such force that the sudden jet crashed into the dirty crockery and bounced over the side of the sink. Brack watched his daughter leap back and look down at the greasy water that had soaked her dress.

'I told you. You can't be trusted to wash t'pots. Too posh to put an apron on. Best leave that to y'mam and sit down and read a book. I reckon that's all you're good for.'

He did not consciously lapse into a north Derbyshire vernacular when he wanted to annoy his wife and daughter – although enthusiasm for their irritation always had that effect. It was an instinctive impulse, a reflex that resulted from his complete commitment to their annoyance. At such moments, his entire being – his whole existence – was dedicated to offending them. He had no need to clear his throat, but he turned and spat into the fire with a convincing and

424

triumphantly revolting imitation of a miner with incurable chest disease.

Determined as Brack was to cause his wife and daughter maximum offence, Enid was even more dedicated to proving that her father had underestimated her talent for housekeeping. After using only half a box of matches and recoiling from only three minor gas explosions, she managed to light the boiler. She rotated the dolly peg in the tub with such manic energy that there was a real danger of the wet clothes being torn to ribbons, and she turned the mangle handle with almost as much frenzy. The clothes line was full and flapping by eleven o'clock.

'What now?' she asked her mother, not so much a question as a challenge.

'You'll have to help me start your dad's dinner in a minute. Sit down and read for a bit. We'll have a cup of tea.'

'I've given up reading. All that's finished. I'll clean the bedrooms out.'

'Oh dear, Enid. You are being silly. Make the best of it. You'd have left school next summer anyway. I can't stand all this unpleasantness. I'm just not well enough. Sit down and finish your book.'

Enid, apparently shamed into silence, began to search for her place in *The Money Moon*. As soon as she found it, her mother suggested that she went and read in the quiet of the front room. She moved without complaint and sat shivering on the cold, leatherette sofa, wishing she could return to the warm kitchen without having to endure her mother's constant interruptions. Before she had finished the first page, Agnes hobbled into the doorway. 'Nip along to Ellis's for me, love. I've no baking powder left.' She felt in the pocket in the front of her apron and pulled out her purse. It was fastened with both a clasp and a buckle and Agnes fumbled so badly in her attempt to open them that the purse fell to the floor with a thud. 'Pick it up for me, love.'

Enid obeyed with bad grace and then ignored her mother's outstretched hand. Whilst her mother watched, she opened the purse and extracted a shilling. Then, in a gesture of flagrant condescension, she dropped the purse back into the front of Agnes's apron and, before her mother could move, she was through the kitchen door and running down the road with her coat hung across her shoulders like a cloak.

She arrived at Ellis's just as Owen Ford was leaving. 'No school today? It isn't Christmas holidays yet, is it – even in that posh school you go to?'

The feeling of outrage, which had partly disappeared during the sharp sprint in the cold December air, immediately returned. But

Enid did not turn on him as she would have turned on her mother. She did not intend to make a spectacle of herself with a relative stranger. 'I've come home to help m'mam. She's got worse and I'm needed at home.'

Owen longed to ask about the burned-out car and the devastated lorry. But he was a man of obtrusive conscience and he knew that it would be wrong to speak to her about the terrible conclusion to their trip to Chesterfield. All he could think of was a stale question. 'Have you read your books?'

Enid forgot herself. 'I have. But I don't like them much. I read *The Amateur Gentleman* as soon as I got it home. Then I got *The Scarlet Pimpernel* through the post. That was all right. But *The Money Moon* is just silly. I'm reading it because I've not got anything else, but it's very boring. It's all romance.'

'Where are you going to get books now?' They stood together in the doorway.

'Mam's going to see if I can join the Institute library. And we'll go to Worksop some Thursdays. That's my auntie's half-day. We used to go to the library on Thursdays, Mam and me. She says we'll still go when we're over there for the day.'

'But no romances, eh?'

'Now I'm at home I can read what I like. Aunt Anne – well, Aunt Lottie really but she didn't say anything – wouldn't let me read the best things. They stopped me reading *Tess of the d'Urbervilles*. That's a romance, but it's real. It's not all silly invention about living happy ever afterwards.'

'Don't you believe in living happily ever after?'

'No. Not in real life I don't.'

'If you really want to finish it, I'll lend you mine. If you want . . .' He was worried by how serious she seemed.

'Yes, please. Can I come and get it this afternoon? After dinner?'

The mention of dinner reminded Enid of her mission to buy baking powder. She pushed past Owen Ford into the shop. He shouted after her, 'I'm back after tea. I'll bring it with me. If you want it, come round here tonight.'

It was Enid's first visit to the back room and Owen Ford expected her to be uneasy in the strange presence of the living corpse which lay in the long wicker cradle but she walked straight across to the window where Arthur Ellis lay, looked down at him and speaking in her best Ashleigh House voice repeated the greeting which Ashleigh House had taught her.

'Good afternoon. How are you?'

'If you really want to know, bloody awful. That's how I am.' Arthur stared at the ceiling. 'How did you expect me to be?'

Enid's composure was completely destroyed. Owen Ford hurried across to help her. Taking her hand he led her back across the room and sat her on a hard chair near the table. 'Poor old Arthur's had a bad day. He's had a lot of pain this morning,' he whispered. 'That's why I came round again.'

'I can't hear what you're saying. Speak up. Is it Brack's daughter you're talking to?'

'Yes, it's Enid Brackenbury. I was saying that we were going to read a bit more. That's right, isn't it, Arthur?'

'Well, what's she got to say for herself?'

Although she had begun the visit bravely, Enid's confidence had gone. She was frightened by the sound of the eerie voice echoing from inside the long low cot. She sat, knees and ankles together as Ashleigh House had taught her, too nervous to reply.

Owen answered for her. 'She's come round to get a book, Arthur – a book I'm lending her. Did you see her when she came across to the window?'

'Not really.'

'She's about fourteen, very tall and, I'll tell you, a good-looker. She's got blue eyes . . .'

Enid's spirits improved. She had never heard herself described before. It was an enjoyable experience. Her back, which had been pushed hard against the chair, bent as she began to relax.

'What sort of hair does she have?'

'Mouse. Pure mouse.'

The novelty of hearing herself discussed by two men had begun to lose some of its charm.

'Can you read?' The voice from the sepulchre was clearly directed towards her.

'Of course I can. I could read when I was three.'

'But can you read out loud? Can you read straight from the book.'

'Try,' said Owen Ford. He handed her a volume so thick and heavy that she could hardly hold it. A bookmark guided her to a page almost in the middle.

'Start there,' Owen said. 'Start at the top of the right-hand page.'

Enid drew her breath and balanced the book on the table at an angle which both allowed a clear line of sight and enabled her to hold up her chin in what she believed to be a becoming manner. 'And now for what the sermon says about secular individualism. Here are the Beatitudes with which the sermon begins, printed by Ruskin side by side with their modern perversions.' She paused. 'Do I read down or across?'

'If you can't read, just say so.' Arthur Ellis had not the slightest interest in John Ruskin's critique of materialism but he had got used to the tedium of his day being relieved by the comforting hum of an uninterrupted voice. 'If you can't read it, give it to Mr Ford.'

'Give her a chance, Arthur. She's just asking what to do. She's done very well.' He turned to the prodigy. 'Do you know what beatitudes are?'

'Beautiful thoughts.' She answered with an immediate certainty that almost convinced Owen Ford that her answer was correct.

'Read across, one after the other,' he said.

'"Blessed are the poor in spirit: for theirs is the Kingdom of Heaven. Blessed are the rich in flesh: for theirs is the Kingdom of Earth." I don't understand. It doesn't make sense. They're different.'

'They're supposed to be different,' Owen Ford told her. 'They're what Christians say life's like compared with what really happens. It's what you were saying before. Happy ever after. Happy in heaven compared with what really happens.'

'I still don't understand.'

'Neither do I,' said Arthur Ellis. 'He doesn't read all this stuff for my benefit. He reads it to amuse himself. If he did it for me, he'd read detective stories. That's what I'd really like.'

'I'm getting a Sherlock Holmes book. Mr Ford's brother is going to send me one from Chesterfield. I'll read it to you if you like.'

'When'll it get here?' Arthur Ellis could not hide his excitement.

'The weekend, I think.'

'Do you want more of Ruskin on religion until your blood and thunder comes or would you prefer complete silence?'

The sarcasm was lost on Arthur Ellis.

'Is your dad coming round after work? He usually comes on Thursdays with the *Sporting Life*.'

Enid did not answer. She wanted to say that what her father did was of no concern to her and that, as she had not spoken to him, she could hardly be expected to know his plans for the evening. But, since she had not decided how to explain her return home, she was not quite ready to make her feelings public. Enid was determined that the neighbours should know what a success she had been at school – that her teachers had told her that leaving was a scandalous waste of talent and Mr Parry himself had written to her aunt saying that it had been a pleasure to have her in Ashleigh House. She knew that the official reason for the sudden end to her education – agreed between Aunt Anne and her mam and repeated to her over and over again as a guarantee of family respectability – was the need to look after her crippled mother. But she found perverse delight in the thought that her brilliant future had been destroyed by the lust of her wicked father. It was not the promise never to reveal the truth about that awful night which restrained her: she had simply not made up her mind about whether fact or fiction would do most to improve her reputation. So she stayed silent.

Nothing better being on offer, Arthur Ellis agreed that they should return to Fabian Tract Number 132, *Socialism and Christianity* by the Reverend Percy Dearmer, MA, Vicar of St Mary-the-Virgin, Primrose Hill, and Secretary of the Christian Social Union. Owen read for an hour, sustained only by the encouragement of Enid sitting at the table and doing her best to look as if she understood. When Arthur, who had been half asleep from the beginning, began to snore, the bound volume was silently closed and all hope of moving on to Edward Carpenter's *The Landlord and the Village* abandoned. Enid and Owen crept silently out together and filed down the narrow passage into the road.

'You shouldn't just read rubbish, you know. Not a clever lass like you.'

Owen Ford spoke from over her shoulder. Out in the sunlight of the street he stared at her, face to face, and made his point again.

'Sherlock Holmes is all right but you ought to read something more serious.'

'I didn't understand what you read in there. I tried, but I didn't understand.'

It was not an easy admission for Enid to make, but she wanted to understand and she did not know how else to ask for help.

'It's easy enough when you get used to it. Didn't you pick up anything?'

'I recognised Ruskin. You talked about Ruskin on our way home from Chesterfield. But I don't remember what you said.'

'Ruskin's a man. A writer amongst other things. There's a college called after him at Oxford University – a college for working men. That's where Percy went.'

'I don't know about Oxford University either.'

Owen Ford explained. Standing on the dirt pavement in Austin Street, Shirebrook, he told her about Oxford. His account owed much to *Charlie's Aunt* and *Zuleika Dobson*, for the two ancient universities were indistinguishable in his mind. As a true disciple of Ruskin he described the ancient buildings with loving care. He passed quickly over the foundation of the colleges – lest ideas about the charity of kings and the benevolence of bishops be planted in an impressionable young mind. He was weak on the curriculum and strong on the social life, of which he passionately disapproved. He barely mentioned sport.

'And your brother went there?'

'He did. Percy went there all right. And I went to see him. Twice.'

'How did he get there, with all the lords and millionaires and . . . and . . . ?'

'Working hard.' Hard work was, in Owen's system of values, a virtue second only to commitment. 'The Association sent him. Nearly all the students at Ruskin come from the labour movement.'

'What's the labour movement?'

'It's the party, the ILP and unions. You ought to join the party one day. One day soon.'

'How old do I have to be?' Enid was visibly thinking.

CHAPTER THIRTY-FOUR

The Resurrection Men

For close on two years, Enid read to Arthur Ellis on almost every afternoon and then, in the early evening, Owen Ford read to them both. Enid entertained the cripple with whatever books Percy Ford sent from Chesterfield as his contribution to Arthur's amusement, but Owen chose his texts with meticulous care. He read for education, not pleasure, for although a miner by trade he was a teacher by instinct. Like all the best teachers, he was anxious to learn.

Arthur endured the selections from socialist thinkers and the *Manchester Guardian* leaders as the price to be paid for entertainment, and the bookseller and his brother knew it. But they continued to leaven the lump of crime and detection with the higher forms of literature to educate Enid. They always felt profoundly guilty when she was diverted from the route to the classics which they had planned. Once Arthur discovered Edgar Wallace, his demands were so insistent that for several weeks she read nothing else. Owen tried to compensate for the deterioration in tone by drawing the young woman into the political discussions which followed the thrillers. The political discussion almost always concerned strikes.

'It's simply stupid,' said Father Froes. 'If the roof falls in, there won't be any work for a year.'

'Let the colliery managers and owners take their jackets off and man the pumps.' It was Arthur Ellis quoting, from the depth of his cot, a speech that Owen had read to him so often that he had learned it by heart.

'That's even more stupid.' Froes was red-faced with irritation. 'The Manverses and the Devonshires won't starve. It'll be your members and their wives who go hungry.'

'It's no good, Father. They won't do it,' said Owen. 'We had a difficult enough job persuading them to keep the engine room working.'

'I don't believe they're that stupid. They wouldn't cut off drinking water to their own houses. There'd be no water and no electricity.'

431

'Brack was at the meeting yesterday.' Arthur spoke with malicious glee. 'Tell him about it, Owen. Brack urged them to fight to the death. Their death, of course. Not his. He's become a big socialist now. If you meet him on the street, you better look out, Father. He'll denounce you as a class traitor. He's learned all the jargon.'

'I'll say to him what I said to you. If they cut off their own water supply, they'd be stupid . . . That's all.'

'Stupid and desperate,' Owen Ford corrected him. 'They've been desperate ever since the railwaymen went back.'

'God bless Jimmy Thomas. Say a prayer for him, Father. He's saved you. Made it a land fit for the coal owners to live in.' Arthur's laugh turned into a choking cough.

Owen went on to talk with obvious understanding about the Sankey Commission, the Federation's seventy per cent proposal and the end of the War Wage. All that Enid could really understand was that the miners were about to lose again and the railwaymen were to blame.

Ignorance of detail did not prevent her from giving her passionate support to the miners' cause, which she thought of as a political event. The socialism of the Derbyshire coalfield was all the politics that she knew. Conservatives – like coal owners – were objects of unremitting scorn and hatred. After two years of total immersion in Owen Ford's basic principles, his convictions had seeped into her system and she was no more capable of questioning the fundamental truth of his philosophy than she was of doubting Uncle Ern's innate wisdom or rebelling against Aunt Anne's authority.

Brack still called at the Ellises from time to time to collect Arthur's bets but his hostility towards Arthur, although suppressed, never faded. His daughter, who sat on a stool in the corner of the room listening to Owen's diatribes, never spoke to her father for she was unable to hide the dislike which she felt towards him. She fidgeted in such obvious impatience for him to take the stake money and leave that Arthur could sense her antagonism. When Jack McGovern came with him, her wish was always granted, for he left as soon as his business was done. Then Enid's composure was quickly restored. When he came alone, he always engaged Owen in argument. His enthusiasm for controversy was matched neither by knowledge nor by humility. Assertion followed assertion and expressions of indisputable fact – self-evident to him if to no one else – were heaped upon each other. When Brack (with betting slips) faced Father Froes (with communion wine), the priest's convictions were matched against the haulier's certainties and they bombarded each other with volley after volley of badly directed prejudice.

'It just doesn't work, any of it,' the priest said. 'Why do you think that millions of women and children are starving to death in Russia?'

Owen had the facts of Soviet food production at his fingertips, but before he could quote them Brack entered the fray with his personal view of history.

'Because of Winston Churchill, that's why. He's behind it. First Archangel. Then the blockade. Rich capitalists starving them to death on purpose. I'd have thought you knew that, Owen.'

'They're not starving to death. They're eating more in Russia now than they ever ate under the tsars,' said Owen weakly. Nobody took any notice.

Brack launched another assault. 'Call it Christianity! The Pope hasn't said a word. Millions starving to death and not a word out of him.'

'You can hardly expect him to support Bolsheviks. They crucified priests in Russia. Not just Russian Orthodox. That would have been bad enough. But they killed Catholic priests as well. No Catholic, let alone the Holy Father, is likely to defend your Mr Lenin, I can tell you that.'

'What about Ireland, then? All the people they've shot there? What about the man they shot the other day, Michael Collins? They were all Catholics who did the shooting. All of them are. Sinn Fein, they're Catholics. Why does the Pope bless them and forgive their sins?'

'Unlike some of my colleagues – my Irish colleagues – I've never supported Home Rule. But that's nothing to do with it. Nobody in Sinn Fein questions the miracles, or advocates free love or burns down churches.'

'What about John Wheatley? He's a Marxist and a Catholic. He said so.' Owen sounded triumphant.

'He couldn't have said any such thing. Socialism and Christianity just don't go together.'

'He said it. He's a Clydesider, a Red Clydesider he's called. And he's a big Catholic in Glasgow.'

'I know where the Clyde is, Brack.' Father Froes stood on his dignity. 'This Wheatley man may call himself a Catholic but I doubt if I'd regard him as one.'

'That's not even good theology.' Owen Ford was near to despair. 'If you don't even understand what you believe in yourself, how can you take part in a sensible discussion?'

Father Froes was not to be deflected. 'They don't believe in private property, Owen. And property is the foundation of the family and therefore the bedrock of the Church.'

'I thought that was St Peter.' Owen Ford rarely allowed himself a

433

joke and each of his rare degenerations into humorous self-indulgence was always followed by stern observations on the human condition. 'I knew property would come up sooner or later. Property's behind it all. I knew it would be.'

'Property is theft.' Arthur Ellis, forgotten in his low bed, offered his opinion without the passion which had characterised the rest of the conversation.

'What the hell does that mean?' Brack asked.

'Don't ask me. Just lie here and listen to him. Ask Owen. He's been saying it ever since he first came here. I've never understood what it means. I just said it in case you were interested.'

There was a scraping at the door and after it had slowly opened Jack McGovern slunk in. He leaned against the wall and waited in silence. As soon as the cobbler arrived, Brack wished the whole company good night and, without appearing to notice his daughter, left. Father Froes left with him, not (as Owen Ford assumed) to take part in some game of chance but to deliver a lecture on a father's duty to his children.

'You really shouldn't let her spend so much time at that place. It isn't good for her. She hears more rubbish than a young girl should listen to in a lifetime.'

'No good saying what I should or shouldn't do. She takes no notice of me. Anyway, it keeps her out of trouble and out of my way. And you'd be surprised what she learns. She doesn't half come out with some ideas, I can tell you.'

'I don't doubt it. That's what worries me. They'll make her a Bolshevik. You mark my words. Her soul's in danger.'

'Her soul's nothing to do with you.'

Brack slapped the priest on the back with a vigour which might easily have been mistaken for high spirits. But Father Froes knew that it was both a warning and a punishment. Brack did not want to be bothered with problems about his daughter's conduct and character.

In the Ellises' back room, Arthur had also grown impatient. 'I've had enough of politics for one day. Enid love, are you still there?'

'I'm here, Arthur. Over in the corner.'

'Let's finish *Fellowship of the Frog*.'

'I want to ask Mr Ford something first. Mr Ford, what books ought I to read to find out about Russia?'

'I'll get Percy to send you some. We'll read them together.'

'Come on,' said Arthur. 'Let's have a bit more Edgar Wallace.'

The *Fellowship of the Frog* was never finished. Enid read twenty more pages before she went home to supper and with Owen Ford sulking on the couch she read fifty more during the next afternoon and evening. But that night Arthur Ellis died in his sleep. Sally Ellis behaved as a proper Catholic wife should and sent for the priest before she called the doctor.

'He was a good man,' Father Froes told her. 'A good man and a good Catholic. He never lost his faith, right to the end. Despite all he went through, he never questioned God's will. Now he is with the saints. A blameless life. The reward of a blameless life.'

The widow responded to the mood of the moment. 'I think it was faith that saw him through, Father. Lying there all these years. And he was only a young man, even at the end.'

'Is your mother coming over?'

'She will, when she knows. I'll ask Mr Ford to go to Ollerton and tell her. I don't want to leave Arthur on his own. I'll lay him out before she comes. I'll . . . not that he needs much. He's been like a corpse . . .' Sally could not finish the sentence.

'Don't distress yourself. You did all any wife could. I wouldn't ask Ford to go for your mother if I were you. He'll only say something to upset her. Can't Brack go in one of his motors? Or Enid? She's old enough. I'll make all the arrangements. Leave all the arrangements to me. I'll see Brack and ask him to go to Ollerton.'

As he bustled out, he almost collided with an angry Owen Ford. Owen's first words to the widow were not of comfort but complaint. 'I only just found out. Why didn't you tell me? A woman told me in the street. She'd seen you going into the presbytery and she noticed that the curtains were drawn.'

He reached out and held her hand and thought, for a moment, of taking her in his arms. But he feared that she would know that he wanted to offer more than comfort. She gripped his fingers so tightly that the knuckles ground together.

'Everything's done, Owen. Father Froes is doing everything. Mam will be over soon. He said that Arthur was a good man.'

'Froes wouldn't know a good man when he saw one.'

'Please, Owen. It's neither the time nor the place. He was a great comfort to me. He said that Arthur's faith had seen him through.'

'You saw him through. You and your cooking and your surgical spirits. That's what kept him alive. Not faith and communion wine.'

'I know you mean well. I know you're thinking of me . . .'

'I'm thinking of Arthur. It's respect for him. He didn't believe it, you know. Not a word.'

'Don't say that, Owen. It's a terrible thing to say.'

'It's the truth. He said as much to me. If you go through all the rigmarole in church it will be an insult to him. He wouldn't want it.'

Sally Ellis let go of Owen Ford's hand. 'I do not want to see you in this house ever again.'

'I shan't come.' Sally was surprised that his anti-Catholic passion was so strong that he was moved to tears. 'And don't expect to see me at that pantomime in church.'

It was a big funeral – a funeral of which, as Father Froes said in his sermon, anyone would be proud. John Hicken represented the Miners' Federation and all of its Shirebrook members who were on the morning shift sat in rows behind him. Some of them had come straight from the pit. Although they had scrubbed the coaldust from their faces and hands, they eased themselves into the pews like men who were afraid that they would soil all that they touched. Sally had hung Arthur's safety lamp on the statue of St Joseph, and the colliery manager – on the instruction of the owners – had filled the church with flowers brought all the way from Nottingham. Brack – born, like John Hicken, a Methodist – sat uncomfortably amongst the shop-keepers and neighbours. Lacking the union leaders' experience of strange rituals, he was glad that Jack McGovern was at his side to prompt him at appropriate moments. He filed self-consciously out of church and would have passed the widow with barely a nod, but she held out a hand and stopped him.

'Thank Mrs Brackenbury for the note. It was kind of her to send it. Tell her I understand why she couldn't come and that I'm very grateful.'

'Enid wrote it.' Brack could think of nothing else to say. 'She couldn't. It's her hands, you know. All twisted now. She'd decide what to say, but Enid wrote it down.'

'I thought I'd see Enid here.'

'She's looking after her mother. Agnes wanted her to come but she insisted on staying. I'm sure she'll pay her respects later.'

Most of the graves in St Joseph's churchyard were new and neglected. Only a few of them were marked by headstones. The rest were no more than mounds of earth. The date of burial could be roughly calculated by the degree to which the land had been reclaimed by grass and dandelion. The ground was littered with the remains of wreaths, some of them still attached to cards with messages that read 'Gone but not forgotten' and 'Always in our hearts'. A few graves were decorated with slime-lined jam jars, still half filled with the remnants of decomposing flowers. St Joseph's churchyard had a special excuse for being neglected: half of its graves were the last resting place of Irishmen who had come to Shirebrook to sink pits and dig coal. They had lived and died in the village, single and alone.

On a night when thick cloud covered the moon and the air was damp with mist, St Joseph's churchyard would have looked like no more than a bumpy field had it not been for the single stone cross which – one of its arms decorated by a beer bottle – was just visible in the half-light that shone from the bedroom of the presbytery. But the potholes, where the graves had sunk with the collapse of coffins, and the mounds of clay, which moth and dust had not yet under- mined, made it hazardous terrain to cross in the dark. Three figures – the first carrying a miner's lamp – made careful progress towards the most distant, and most recently used, corner of the burial ground. They were laughing.

Percy Ford had no reason to know that a churchyard at night held no terrors for Enid so, fearing that she would be as frightened as any other young woman, he had tried to lighten the atmosphere with the only sort of joke which he knew. 'If anybody sees us, they'll think that we're Resurrection Men.'

'What's Resurrection Men?' Enid hissed back.

'Body snatchers.' As soon as he had said it he thought that, instead of calming her fears, he had increased her apprehension. But for some incomprehensible reason, the name reduced Enid to uncontrollable hysteria. Both Owen and Percy found her laughter irresistibly infectious.

It was Enid who struggled to behave with appropriate solemnity. 'We ought not to be laughing. It's a churchyard. We ought to be behaving ourselves.'

'Arthur would understand.' Percy Ford had never met him.

'Would he buggery.' Owen Ford laughed no longer, but Enid and his brother had started again.

Enid stumbled over a tuft of twitch grass.

'Are you all right?' Owen Ford held her arm. The shock had sobered them all. 'Hang on to me. We're almost there.'

In the far corner of the churchyard, they stood by the side of Arthur's grave. The clay was still damp and they felt their feet sink into the soft ground. Percy held the lamp whilst Owen fumbled in the inside pocket of his greatcoat. He pulled out two carefully folded sheets of paper. Each one was covered in his own handwriting.

'Hold the lamp down a bit. I've written it out big. But I can still hardly make it out.'

'I can remember it, more or less. My bit that is.' Percy Ford was proud of his education.

'Better get it right.'

The lamp was held down and the paper was moved into the arc of its limited light. Owen leaned forward to focus on his paper.

' "Neither the religious stolidity of the British, nor the post-facto conversion of the Continental bourgeois, will stem the proletarian tide . . ." '

He read on and on, turning over the first sheet and reading from both sides of the paper. Then he handed the second sheet of paper to his brother and, in turn, took the lamp from him.

Percy began to read in his almost cultivated voice. ' " . . . Communists disdain to conceal their views and aims. They openly declare that their ends can be attained only by the forcible overthrow of all existing social conditions. Let the ruling classes tremble at a Communist revolution. The proletarians have nothing to lose but their chains. They have a world to win." '

Owen Ford picked up the first handful of wet soil and dropped it back on the grave. Percy picked up and dropped the second. Then, palms still moist with earth, the brothers solemnly shook hands.

'Can you remember the words, Enid?'

'Of course I can.'

They sang together and they sang so loudly that Father Froes, on the point of putting out his light, heard them and stealthily opened his bedroom window. The tune seemed vaguely familiar and he could only catch a few words. 'With heads uncovered . . . we all . . . till we fall'. They were enough to convince him that, whatever was going on in his churchyard, it was not a poor imitation of witchcraft. He decided that they were drunks and would do no harm.

The Resurrection Men went back to the road round the dark side of the church and, feeling self-conscious for the first time, they began to walk towards Langwith Road in silence.

'Well!' It was Owen who spoke first. 'At least we gave him a decent send-off. Something he'd appreciate.' He hoped that he did not sound too defensive.

'Will it be all right at home?' Percy asked.

'Dad never gets home before midnight and Mam was fast asleep by ten as usual. I'll either creep up to bed or read for a bit. That's what I'm usually doing when Dad comes in.'

'The gas is on.' Percy was beginning to lose his nerve.

'I left it on.' Enid's confidence reassured him. 'Dad expects it on when he gets back. If Mam woke up and it was off she'd come down.'

'It's very dangerous, leaving the gas on.' Owen was a careful man.

They were outside the yard and the heaps of coal were just visible through the mist. Owen and Percy Ford stood in the shadow of the wedding car that still belonged to Uncle Ern as Enid tiptoed towards the front door. She turned the handle slowly and with a meticulous determination to make no sound. There was a faint creak as the hinges swung and, startled, she paused before she stepped forward. As soon as she crossed the threshold, she ran into the living room in case the noise had woken her mother. Uncle Ern was standing by the fireplace.

'You're for it, young lady. Wherever you've been, you're in for it.'

Enid was too frightened to move, or to speak.

'It's your grandad. He won't last the night. Your mam's putting some things in a bag. The taxi should have been here ten minutes ago. If we don't leave soon, she won't see him before he goes.'

CHAPTER THIRTY-FIVE

New Friends for Old

As was so often the case, Uncle Ern at his most certain was Uncle Ern at his worst informed. William Skinner lasted the night, and on the following morning sat up in bed and demanded bread and butter. Next day, he insisted on coming downstairs. He sat by the fire in his favourite chair and smiled contentedly whilst Enid read to him from *In Chancery*. He fell asleep before the full horror of the divorce was revealed. Enid innocently asked her aunt if she had ever known a divorced woman.

'Of course not,' Anne replied, without having to consider her answer.

'Not one? Not ever?' To Enid, seventeen, it seemed that Anne had lived so long that she must have seen everything and known people of every sort.

'Divorced women go away and hide themselves. Nobody speaks to them.'

'There's one in this book. Everybody speaks to her, everybody likes her.'

'Then you shouldn't be reading it. Can't you read something nice – something about goodness – if you have to read at all.'

Enid was suitably crushed. Anne was remorseless. 'And don't go talking to your mother about all this dirty rubbish. It will only upset her.'

Galsworthy having thus been elevated to the heady status of the impure and improper, Enid took her book into the kitchen and, sitting at the table, read until she was moved off to make room for supper.

Young Dr Anderson – the new partner in his father's practice – advised that the old man be allowed a breath of fresh air. It was a popular proposition only with the patient himself, but Anne carefully balanced respect for professional opinion against distrust of youth and decided that ten minutes would do her father no harm. His topcoat was buttoned over a jacket and two pullovers and then augmented by a rug draped over his shoulders. Suitably weighed down, he was allowed out into the mild spring air. Anne, who had taken up temporary residence at Grove Cottage, supported him on the left and Enid, who had been temporarily forgiven for her late-night excursion, supported him on the right.

Agnes had warned her daughter that they would return to the subject of Enid's thoughtless irresponsibility as soon as they returned to Shirebrook but it was always clear that the threat would not be carried out. To Enid's surprise, her mother had believed her story about a sudden impulse to visit Arthur's grave, an invention which was convincingly reinforced with details of wreaths and the overgrown state of the churchyard. Morbid sentimentality warranted a less severe penalty than blasphemous disregard for convention. Both crimes were clearly less serious than other offences which Agnes had, at first, suspected but never mentioned. She did, however, enquire if any young men had joined in the expedition, and was obviously relieved to find that they had not.

'She'll forget it in a day or two,' Lottie had said and, as usual, Lottie was right.

Within a week, Agnes decided that her father was well enough for her to return home. Her departure was delayed by William's demand to be allowed to visit the herb garden and his need for Enid to support him on that expedition. Anne was reluctant for him to venture so far, but in the end she agreed for no better reason than the fear that the agitation of argument would be more damaging than the exertion of a gentle walk.

The herb garden looked like a herb garden no longer. The previous autumn's seeds still hung from withered stalks and stems. Fennel, cat mint and calendulas had spread into each other's beds and were half obscured by twitch grass and dandelion. Rue and rosemary had grown into scrawny bushes and the terracotta pots had broken and lay in pieces like neglected antiquities. Only the cast-iron frame of the seat had survived wind and weather. Across the corner which it had once proudly guarded, a wheelbarrow had been turned on its side. One of its wheels had been removed for repair.

'Are you all right, Dad?'

Anne had no reason to fear that her father felt exhausted. It was the sort of anxious question that she always asked.

'I'm fine. But I'd be better if this garden hadn't gone to rack and ruin.'

He bent down and grasped the brown, dry husk of a dead poppy flower. He disintegrated it between his fingers.

'You'll get cold, Dad. Just standing there. We better be on our way back.'

441

'I'm going to speak to young Mr Hodding about all this. His father must be turning in his grave. He loved this garden.'

William was almost in tears. When he sat down on the side of the broken wheelbarrow, Anne left him for a moment to compose himself. Enid picked sprigs of lilac and made them into a bouquet.

'What *are* you doing?' Anne seemed outraged.

'Smell it.'

'I know what it is. And it isn't yours. That's stealing. Put it back at once.'

'What's the point of putting it back now?'

'Don't you argue with me. Put it back. It doesn't belong to you. Put it back now. We've got to get your grandad back home.'

'He's fallen asleep again.'

William Skinner's head had fallen on to his chest and the hand which had held the dead poppy had opened and spilled the seeds on his knee. Anne did not need to pick her way over the broken flagstones. She knew that her father was dead.

It took Ernest Skinner several days fully to understand what had happened. His father's death was reported to him within the hour by young Mr Hodding, who telephoned the woodyard at Retford. But whilst he knew that William was dead – knew it to be a fact to be recorded in the *Worksop Guardian* and registered at the town hall – the real meaning was not clear to him until a week after the funeral. He understood only when he locked the Grove Cottage door for the last time.

He had chosen not to travel to Overend Road with the pantechnicon and as he began his long walk past Worksop Manor, Beard's Mill and St Anne's Church, it seemed impossible that Darfoulds had become part of his past. He had expected to feel an immense sense of loss, for he had loved his father and lived in gratitude for the love he had received in return. But he was not prepared for the fear that his father's death had, somehow, marked the end of the best part of his life. He felt that he was mourning the passing of forty years. When William died, Ernest's youth died with him.

. Old Mr Hodding, Gerrard Knock and his red-headed wife who had fallen through the ice, Arnold Hirst's lessons with Indian clubs, Vincent Sweeting and Lucy – he thought of each one in turn. They had all become part of a past which was now so far beyond recall that he was no longer sure how much of what he remembered had existed only in his imagination. His marriage and Lucy's death now seemed beyond belief – even though he possessed a mahogany cigar box and a house in Overend Road to prove that it had all really happened.

As he opened his front door, he saw, in the half light of early evening, two pictures from Grove Cottage. He had chosen to keep them, not because of their artistic merit or because of sentimental attachment, but because his father had told him that they were valuable. In the half-light, they looked even more bizarre than usual – two portraits of prize cows which breeding, or painter, had made grotesque. As a boy he had always wondered why the heads were so small and the udders so big. Now as the pictures stood on the hall floor, waiting to be hung on the empty expanse of grey wall, he was tempted to put his foot through the canvas. But that was not Ernest Skinner's way.

He lit a single gas jet in the living room and then moved his plywood model of the Eiffel Tower from one end of the mantelshelf to the other and put in its place the two-pint cask which the coopers of Wisbech had given to his grandfather – the perfectly made miniature barrel that Jacob Skinner had taken into the fields at harvest time and had given to his son when William left for Lincoln and the great adventure of building an arboretum. There were other items of his inheritance to put in place. The console table, which William had bought to convince Elizabeth that a gardener's wife could live in comfort, was put in the front room and, like every other piece of decent furniture, covered with a sheet. His father's retirement gifts – silver chalice from employer and matching cream jug from fellow servants – were locked away in the sideboard. The oak clock from the Grove Cottage kitchen – its picture of a busy beehive now chipped and faded – was already in place in the alcove by the fireplace.

The table was half covered with years of fretwork. Most of the pieces were gifts he had made for his mother and brought for comfort to Overend Road when Lucy died. The rocking chair, the letter rack, the windmill and the pipe-holder, once the prize exhibits in the collection, had all been broken with the years. He moved them tenderly to one side to make room for a folded cloth which he spread across one corner of the tabletop. That night he would not walk to Brook House for his supper.

He was concentrating so hard on mixing his mustard – the invariable accompaniment to the invariable pork pie – that he did not hear the motor car draw up outside his house. The heavy hand on the glass panel made him start. It took him several minutes to release the locks and bolts which were in place for the night but his visitor, hearing the sound of movement, waited. When Ernest Skinner opened the door, standing on his step was a small and immensely fat old man. In the half-light of dusk and nearby street lamp, he did not recognise Vincent Sweeting.

'I thought I'd got the right house. Should have done, all things being considered.'

'Good evening,' said Ernest, made extra polite by the Rolls-Royce at the end of the garden path. 'Can I help you in some way?'

'I've only just heard. My chauffeur told me when he picked me up at the station. I've been in Sheffield for a few days. I came round on chance. Just to express condolences. I couldn't see a light but I thought you'd be in.'

'I was in the back.' Ernest thought it was important to apologise for the lack of illumination before he expressed gratitude for the kindness.

'You don't recognise me, do you?'

Ernest tried and failed. He went through the owners of companies with whom the woodyard did business. Most of them he would have recognised at once. None, to the best of his knowledge, possessed such a motor car.

'It's Vincent Sweeting. God, I knew I'd changed but I didn't think it was that bad.'

'You'd better come in. Come into the front room for a minute.'

Vincent Sweeting kicked against the frame of one of the bovine portraits and blundered after his host. Ernest decided that, despite the cold and dark, it could not be the living room. A visitor who arrived in a Rolls-Royce could not be entertained across a half-laid table which boasted only half a pork pie, a mug of tea and an opened packet of digestive biscuits. As they turned out of the hall, the guest felt instinctively for the electric light switch.

'Haven't you got the electricity?' he asked, sinking into one of the sheet-covered armchairs. The silence confirmed its absence. The deprivation made Sweeting feel particularly apologetic.

'I've meant to come round, time after time. But somehow I've never done it.'

Ernest nodded into the gloom.

'I hear you've done very well at Hirst's. Chief clerk now.'

'They've taken on a second man. He does most of the estimating. I stay in the office these days. Accounts, invoices and wages. That sort of thing.'

'It sounds very interesting. I just wanted to say how sorry I was about your father. I remembered you were very close. He came round to Sparken Hill—'

'I remember.'

'Could we have the gas on for a minute? It's difficult to talk in the dark.'

'There isn't any gas in here. I've never had it connected.'

'When I built this house five years since, the mains were in.' He

444

looked up at the walls. They were decorated with ornate brass gas brackets. 'All you had to do—'

'I never did. Not in here. It is in the back.'

'Well, let's go in the back. I'm not particular but I do like to see who I'm talking to.' He fumbled his way out of the front room and into the dim light of the single gas mantle.

'I was just having my supper.'

'I'll have a cup of tea with you. But first I've got to use your toilet. Still down the yard, is it?'

When Ernest Skinner followed him out of the back door, Vincent Sweeting said that he could find his own way. Then to his alarm he noticed the bucket. 'Out of order, is it? Broke?' He almost decided to wait.

'That's for the tea. I'm going to fill it at the pump.'

'Are you telling me that there's no running water in this house?'

'There's a tap in the kitchen but the water comes out of a tank. I like fresh water for drinking. It's healthier.'

'Bloody hell.' Vincent Sweeting was not sure of which eccentricity his son-in-law was guilty. But he knew that Ernest, whom he had always thought strange, had grown stranger with the years.

Good cups and saucers – china bought for him by Anne when he had moved into Overend Road – were pulled out of the kitchen cupboard and quickly washed under the tap. The kettle was put on the hob and swung over the fire whilst the teapot was warmed on the boiler by the side of the grate. Vincent Sweeting settled himself in an armchair and began a fascinated enquiry into Ernest's habits.

'Don't you boil your kettle on a gas ring?'

'I haven't got a gas ring.'

'Do you do all your cooking in here?' He flapped his hand towards the black-leaded oven.

'I don't cook much.'

'But you don't have a gas cooker?'

'I don't trust them. You can taste the gas in the food.'

'Nor a gas boiler?'

'I've never bothered.'

'You keep the house neat, I'll say that. Does a woman come in?'

'I do it all. There's not much. I go to my sister's most nights.'

Vincent Sweeting could not work out why a man who polished his grate so bright and hung such clean lace curtains at his window had never, in a quarter of a century, bothered to put paper on his walls. They were still the same naked, mud-grey plaster that they had been on the day when he had paid off the builders and handed the keys to

445

his widower son-in-law. He reached across the table and contemplatively cut himself a slice of pork pie.

'How do you spend your time, Ernest?'

'With my sisters mostly. I used to go down and see Dad a lot.'

'Are they married?'

'Aggie is. But she's not the one I see most of. Anne lives in Newcastle Avenue with . . . There's an adopted sister there as well. They have a dressmaking business.'

He could not bring himself to relate his answers to the old times. Nothing would have been easier and more natural than to say 'Aggie – the married one – came to dinner in Sparken Hill' or 'Anne, and her partner Lottie, made Lucy a driving coat. That's when I first saw her, when she went to get measured.' But somehow he could not build bridges with his past. Vincent Sweeting could not bring himself to mention the name of his dead daughter.

'Married sister got kids?'

'One daughter. She's not very well. Aggie that is. She's got rheumatoid arthritis. The doctors say it's nothing to do with Dad's trouble but it doesn't make sense to me. Two things go together.'

It was several moments before Vincent Sweeting replied. He was eating the remnants of the pork pie.

'It's not for me to say but life hasn't dealt you much of a hand, one way and another. If you took my advice, you'd find a nice little widow and let her look after you. Plenty about, thanks to the war. Plenty that would jump at a house like this and a husband with a good steady job.'

'I know you mean well, Mr Sweeting . . .'

'I'm not suggesting it, because I know you won't do it. But start taking an interest in something. Something besides your maiden sister and Hirst's timber yard. Take an interest in your niece. A nephew would be easier . . .'

'She's a young woman, Mr Sweeting. Almost grown up. There isn't much she could learn from me.'

'Perhaps not. But there might be something you could learn from her.'

To Ernest's relief, Vincent Sweeting announced that it was disgraceful to leave his chauffeur sitting outside for so long and, after slowly finishing his third cup of tea, he felt his way down the dark hall and into the starlit night of Overend Road.

Enid Brackenbury was eager to learn from everybody who would teach her. She had requested, and had been refused, permission to take a job in a Shirebrook drapery. Life would have been easier if she had worked from eight to six behind a counter but her commercial ambitions had not been frustrated to save her hard work. She was required to concentrate on hard work at home – looking after her mother and Brack and performing all the tasks which might have been the duty of a housemaid. Brack believed that she would be reconciled to the drudgery as long as he demonstrated his continued fondness for her.

Her father was working hard and doing well and he hoped that the new prosperity would soon enable him to pay off and buy out Ernest Skinner. As he struggled to reclaim his own independence, he schemed to make Enid increasingly dependent on him. His plan was to buy back her affection but he was sure that even if his investment did not produce that dividend, he could win at least the show of respect by lavishing gifts on his ungrateful daughter. He was wrong.

Another new tennis racquet was purchased complete with a complicated press which kept the frame rigid and strings taut between matches. Enid informed him that it would be too much trouble to tighten the wing nuts after every game and suggested that the press be chopped up for firewood. Subscriptions were taken out to every tennis club in the district – Clowne, Cresswell, Cuckney and Ollerton – and a brand-new bicycle was bought to take the new member to and from tournaments. Enid said that she preferred to play in Shirebrook and push her mother to the courts in the newly acquired wheelchair. Agnes was instructed to order tennis dresses from mail-order companies but Enid said that she would be more than satisfied with the Suzanne Lenglen imitation that Auntie Lottie had made for her seventeenth birthday. Only one of Brack's presents pleased his daughter – and that he gave to her by mistake.

Brack had spent a Sunday afternoon ratting with Jack McGovern. It was in many ways an unrewarding pastime. It was impossible to have a good bet on ratting. A real gambler might put a shilling on how many rats the dog would kill or how long it would take to despatch its most determined victim but ratting had none of the excitement of rabbit coursing. The only real pleasure was watching the dogs at their ruthless work, burrowing into the ditches and drains until they found a nest and then methodically despatching the whole family one by one and tossing the broken-backed corpses into the air. Jack was employed, at a penny a rat, to clear barns and hen houses all over the area. Brack went with him for pure enjoyment. The cobbler never did anything just for pleasure.

McGovern's best dog was Peg, a pure-bred wire-haired terrier for whom he claimed the title 'champion ratter of Nottinghamshire'. She had grown old in her trade and, since she had been in pup for half of her adult life, loose skin hung from her distended belly. But she was still fierce and, according to her master, particularly vicious when about to whelp. It was not only the five-shilling fee that caused Cobbler Jack to match her with a collier's dog as soon as one litter was weaned. On the day that he agreed to clean out the old middens behind Scott Street, Peg was – in McGovern's words – 'within days of dropping them'. He expected the whole rat colony to be gone within a few seconds.

The event began in the usual way with stones prised up and lumber pushed aside so that the dog could get the scent and burrow her way into the nests. Before the path had been properly cleared, Peg began to pull on the rope that held her collar and give out a continuous growl which sounded like the engine of a motorbike straining to be in full throttle. When at last her lead was slipped, she gave a terrible scream and charged in the direction of a pile of rotting sacks. There was a howl and a crash and Peg dropped into the deep cesspit below.

Jack McGovern peered cautiously over the edge of the hole that the sacks had covered. 'She's still alive. I can see her back legs twitching.'

'She won't be for long,' said Brack. 'Fall like that. Best just leave her there and get one of the farmers to come and shoot her.'

'Bugger that. She's in pup. She might not rat again, but the pups are paid for.'

'Well, I'm not going down there and you can't either.'

'If you help me, I can.'

'The whole bloody thing might fall in.'

The argument was ended by two young miners who were taking a short cut home after their Sunday pints.

'What are you two buggers up to?' The larger of the two young men spoke in a soft Dublin accent.

'It's my dog,' McGovern told him, 'fallen down this hole, poor thing, and we can't get her out.'

The young Irishman seemed to take the description as a challenge. He took off his jacket and handed it to Brack. 'Poor bloody thing,' he said. 'Doing no harm to anybody and falls down this bloody great hole. You can't leave the poor little bugger down there.'

'I'll go. You've got your best suit on.' The Dubliner's friend spoke with the slow deliberation of a man who thought very carefully before he offered an opinion and then held to it with absolute certainty.

For a moment it looked as if the two young men would fight each other for the privilege of jumping down into the disused cesspit but common sense prevailed. The smaller man would be lowered down by his larger companion. After much flexing of muscles, the descent was completed with a splash as smart best shoes landed in the ordure which still covered the cesspit floor and curses as it splattered the legs of the blue-serge Sunday suit.

'For God's sake, take this bloody dog and let me get out of this bloody stink.'

Peg was held at full stretch above her rescuer's head but she was still out of reach from above the hole. She whimpered and tried to move her back legs.

'She's bleeding on me now. Take her or I'll drop her, I'm telling you.'

'Can't you kneel down and get her?' McGovern spoke reproachfully to the miner who had remained on the surface. 'You got all that muck on you, lowering your mate down. There's no sense in two of us ruining our suits.'

To Brack's surprise, the young man agreed and Peg was lifted out and laid on a dry piece of sacking.

'Is she dead?' The young man who had performed the act of mercy pulled himself out of the cesspit hoping that the sacrifice of his suit had not been in vain.

'Is she buggery,' said Brack, staring in disbelief at the dog. 'She's whelping.'

The first three pups were born dead, but the fourth kicked and spluttered into life. It was the runt of the litter, too small by normal standards to survive even an untroubled birth, but the birth in the disused midden behind Scott Street in Shirebrook ended with the death of the mother. Peg gave a deep sigh which might have been mistaken for contentment. Then she lay, head back, legs stiff and mouth open.

'What do you want to do about the pup?' asked Brack. The runt, although still blind, was struggling to stand. 'He's a game little 'un.'

'Not game enough,' said its rightful owner. 'He'll be dead in half an hour.'

The smaller of the young miners, overcome by best bitter and the miracle of creation, was silently vomiting. The other turned angrily on McGovern. 'We got ourselves covered in shit getting that fucking dog out of the hole and you don't care a bugger.'

McGovern assumed his most caring manner. 'You don't understand, young man. That puppy's done for. It's a kindness to let it die. I'd drown it here and now but it'll be dead before we fill a bucket of water.'

'Half a dollar,' said Brack. 'Half a dollar. I can rear it.'

'I wouldn't take your money.'

'Then it's mine, is it? If I can rear it it's mine?'

'It's pure bred that is.' Jack McGovern was beginning to fear that, somehow, he was being cheated.

'Then half a dollar, I can rear it.'

'If you want to chuck your money away, I can't stop you.'

Brack was already wrapping the puppy in a piece of the sacking. He carried the damp bundle home inside his jacket.

Agnes was ready to complain as soon as he took the parcel from inside his coat and laid it on the draining board next to the sink. 'Is that meat you've got there? Is it a bird you've caught?' Blood was soaking through the rough hemp and the smell of the cesspit was unmistakable even before Brack opened the package. 'In heaven's name, what is it?'

The question was reasonable enough. For the pup, umbilical cord still dangling from its belly, bore no resemblance to a dog. The small parts of its body which were visible beneath the coating of slime were pink hairless skin. Huge sightless eyes were sunk deep in a head that looked as though it belonged not to a terrier but to a giant eel.

'It's a dog, you great tripe-hound. What do you think it is? It's a thoroughbred dog that was born half an hour since.'

'Is it still alive?'

The thought that he might have carried a dead dog home under his coat was so absurd that he could not bring himself to reply.

'Where's Enid?'

'She's out.'

'Always is when she's needed. Can you heat a drop of milk in a pan?'

'Poor thing. It would be a mercy to let it die.'

'For God's sake, just do it.'

He opened the cupboard under the sink and took out a handful of the old rags which were kept to use as dusters and floor cloths. He chose two of the softest and wrapped them round the puppy like swaddling bands before laying it in the corner of the hearth in the living room. It was almost an hour before it learned to suck warm milk off his little finger and it only just began before his patience was finally exhausted.

'It would be kindest to put it out of its misery,' said Agnes.

'Bugger off,' Brack told her. He had poured warm water from the kettle on to one of the rags and was gently sponging the dog clean.

'Is it a pig?' Enid asked when she got home.

If her mother had asked such a question Brack would have dismissed it as wilful stupidity. Since it was asked by his daughter, he pretended to be charmed by the naïvety. 'It's a wire-haired terrier. A thoroughbred. It's less than half a day old. I've nursed it like a baby.

450

It would have been dead otherwise. I can't get it to drink the milk.'

'At Ashleigh House they fed kittens through those rubber things inside fountain pens, that or valve rubbers.'

Brack was already halfway out of the doors shouting, 'I'll pump the tyres up, after,' over his shoulder.

Next day, the puppy was on its feet. Enid kissed her father for the first time in more than five years. 'I've always wanted a dog of my own. Now I've got one. Wait till Auntie Anne sees him.'

'What are we to call it?' Agnes asked when she was finally convinced that compassion did not require the pup being put down and realised that it had to be prepared for formal introduction to her sister.

'Teddy,' Enid queried, with the Prince of Wales in mind.

'Some right bloody socialist you've turned out to be,' her father told her. 'I'd have thought you'd say Ramsay or Lenin – one of Owen Ford's heroes.'

'Not Lenin.' Enid was deadly serious. 'Mr Ford would want me to call him . . .' She could not remember A. J. Cook's first name. To the idolaters of Austin Street, the miner's leader was 'A. J.' Dogs had to be given names, not initials.

'Call him Spot.' Agnes peered into the orange box which, lined with an old blanket, had become the terrier's temporary home. 'He's got that black patch over his eye.'

The suggestion not even being worth contemptuous dismissal, Brack announced what the dog's name would be. 'He wouldn't be here if it weren't for a couple of drunken Irishmen who fished his mother out of that stinking cesspit. I wouldn't have done it and neither would Jack McGovern. We ought to call him after them.'

'Paddy,' offered Agnes.

Paddy had been Brack's original choice of name. When his wife suggested it, he changed his mind.

'Mick,' he said. 'We'll call him Mick, not Paddy.'

CHAPTER THIRTY-SIX

A Parent's Duty

The Mick who had saved the dog's life lived in Hucknall in a boarding house owned and run by Edna Ferguson. All the lodgers were Sligo men. Mrs Ferguson and her husband had come to England from Calooney more than twenty years before and the priests in that town still recommended her boarding house to young parishioners who set out on the great adventure that started on the boat to Holyhead and ended in the coalfields of Nottingham and Derbyshire or on the London Midland and Scottish Railway. The Fergusons had not made a fortune out of the Church's patronage for Edna felt that she had to live up to the reputation she had gained back home for providing Calooney men with superior lodgings at reasonable prices. Her food was significantly better than that which was served in similar establishments. Bed linen was changed every fortnight. No more than three men shared one room. Sewing and darning – like good advice – was available without extra charge.

Edna Ferguson, who had produced only daughters, thought of her lodgers as her adopted sons. She wrote to their natural parents in Ireland with reassuring accounts of their health and conduct, taught them to clean their teeth, encouraged them to drink in moderation and to respect all women as images of the Mother of Jesus. The house at Hucknall was intensely Catholic. Sacred Hearts beat over every fireplace and pictures of popes decorated every bedroom wall. It was also oppressively practical. Edna Ferguson could remember when her lodgers' insurance premiums were due, the last time they attended confession and the dates of their birthdays. She was the perfect Irish landlady in all respects except one. Edna Ferguson had favourites.

Her maternal passion for Jack O'Hara was born at the first moment that she saw him. Jack was the other sort of Irishman – not the red-faced, thick-necked, brilliantined Paddy of popular imagination but, in appearance at least, a Celtic poet with high cheekbones, pale complexion and a look of wistful vulnerability. When, after the first of the pithead baths had been built and he came home as clean as if

452

he had been to work in the council offices, she knew that he was the young man of her dreams. She had never before even contemplated one of her daughters courting a lodger – the idea was far too like incest and only calculated to upset the calm efficiency of the boarding house. Jack O'Hara proclaimed by the way in which he held his knife and fork that he was the only man for her Sheila.

There was no need to put the idea into Sheila's head. It was clear from the way she gave Jack extra mashed potatoes and made his bed with especial care that she was infatuated with him. In looks they could hardly have been more different. He was tall and elegant whilst she was short and homely but she shared the passion which ruled Jack O'Hara's existence. Sheila Ferguson wanted to better herself.

Jack's concern for improvement was a gentle ambition. He felt neither ruthless determination to fight his way out of the pits nor a burning desire to make a fortune. He thought of personal improvement entirely in terms of manners, appearance and social acceptability. He longed for plus-fours, two-tone brogues and membership of the Carlton-in-Lindrick golf club, but realising that those ambitions were beyond him he excited the contempt of his colleagues and the admiration of their wives by being the only collier to wear white flannels whilst playing tennis on the Miners' Welfare court. Money that other miners wasted on beer and betting was saved and used to buy a tailor-made suit in Nottingham. Edna Ferguson's judgement of his character was confirmed when, in defiance of convention, he began to wear underpants. When he bought a box of toilet paper and hung it on the nail which had previously only held squares of old newspaper, she knew that she had a gem in her top attic – a jewel far too precious to lose.

It was because of his neat respectability that she found it so difficult to believe that he had come home with his best suit covered in evil-smelling slime. It was almost three o'clock and she was serving dinner when he hurried past the dining-room door and up the stairs towards the bedroom. When she saw him out of the corner of her eye, her first reaction was relief for it was not like Jack to be late and she had feared some sort of accident. But, when he did not immediately reappear, relief turned into apprehension. Her husband was sent to investigate.

Finbar Ferguson left his roast beef and cabbage in silent resentment. Dinner was always late on Sundays to allow his wife's lodgers to have a well-earned drink after mass. He had waited long enough. By the time he got back, his gravy would be cold and congealed. It was, he told himself, wholly unreasonable to send him on such an expedition. It was not the first time that a young miner had come home on Sunday too ill to eat his dinner. Admittedly, this Jack O'Hara was not the sort to drink himself sick. Indeed, if he had a fault in that direction it was that he drank too little. But it was easy enough to imagine him becoming the victim of his own courtesy and the resolution of some normal colliers to get him drunk for the first time in his life.

When Finbar came back downstairs and explained that Jack had ended his morning in a disused cesspit, Edna told him not to talk stupid. He knew that he should resent being insulted in front of the lodgers and that it was his duty to assert his manhood. He framed the rebuke in his mind and said, 'Well, see for yourself. Or smell for yourself. He stinks like a blocked drain.'

The young men tried not to laugh by concentrating their attention on second helpings. They were amused to find that Finbar had fallen for so obvious a deception and looked forward with immense pleasure to Mrs Ferguson discovering, from the vomit on his lapels, that the paragon was less than perfect.

'How could he have fallen down a cesspit?'

'I didn't say he'd fallen in. He jumped in. Him and Eddie Eames, who lodges in Ashfield.'

The young men no longer attempted to hide their amusement.

'Ask him,' said Finbar.

Jack had appeared in the doorway. He was in his stockinged feet and had obviously dressed in a hurry. The waistcoat of his second-best suit was still unfastened. He tried, unsuccessfully, to button it with his right hand whilst his left smoothed down his hair. He gave the winning smile which was intended to disarm anybody who came within its range. Before he could apologise, one of the young miners asked him, 'Is it right you've been in a cesspit, Jack?' It was not a sympathetic question.

'I surely have. Can't you smell the stink of it on me still?'

He had been asked a simple question and he gave a simple answer. He was a simple man. The idea that he was being mocked never entered his head.

A second young miner feigned innocence. 'Why did you jump into the cesspit, Jack?'

'To get the dog out. The dog that fell in. Eddie and me got it out.'

After that answer Edna Ferguson took over. Her faith in Jack O'Hara had been justified. He had ruined his best suit and sacrificed a hot dinner in order to save some poor dying animal. She should have expected no less. 'You're a good man, Jack O'Hara,' she said. 'Sit yourself down whilst I warm up the Yorkshire puddings. Sit yourself down and tell us all about it.'

454

Jack tried to tell them, but every time he began his story Edna Ferguson interrupted him in order to improve upon it. She deepened the cesspit and made the dog rabid. It was the third time that she described its owner as a poor old man which reminded Jack that he was telling the story, not her. He began to correct her errors.

'He wasn't that old. Bit more than forty.'

'Then why didn't he go down into the cesspit and get his dog? Was he a cripple?' Mrs Ferguson was scandalised. 'Why did he let you and Eddie do it?'

'He had a hair-lip.'

Jack described the deformity as if it were, in itself, justification for leaving the dog to die.

'The man . . . the man with the hare-lip. Was he swarthy like a dago? Did he have greasy hair?' Edna asked.

'That's him. Do you know him?'

'He's called McGovern. He's called "Cobbler Jack",' said Finbar. He realised at once that he should not have spoken and slumped back into the half-sleep which always followed his Sunday dinner.

'I think it must have been him,' said Jack. 'He talked about going back to his shop.'

'McGovern is not the sort of man that your mother would expect you to make a friend of.' Mrs Ferguson always relied on the authority of unknown mothers to confirm her more controversial assertions. Mrs O'Hara's death, on the day following Jack's birth, in no way prevented her from being called as a witness for the prosecution.

'The other man looked respectable enough. Tall man, very straight. He had a moustache. He took the pup away. The dog died but we saved the little pup. The man said he was going to keep it.'

'Brack,' said Finbar, who had been a keen cyclist in his time.

'Brackenbury.' His wife repeated the name with obvious pleasure. Because of a dispute in her own parish she did many of her good works for St Joseph's in Shirebrook. She thought of Brack as a prosperous businessman.

'If Brackenbury's got the dog, he can pay for a new suit.'

'I couldn't ask him that, Mrs F.'

'I could. When I meet your dear mother one day, I won't be able to look her in the face if I've not got it at least cleaned.'

'I can't see Brack paying a penny,' said Finbar.

'Wait till he gets my letter.'

The young miners, who had almost finished their treacle tart, were not sure if they felt happier for their landlady's motherly concern or afraid that she would act with similarly public fortitude on their behalf.

'If he doesn't pay, I'll get the priest to write to him.'

Having threatened the greatest intimidation she could think of, Mrs Ferguson began the final episode of her Sunday afternoon ritual – eating remnants of meat and vegetables that had been left by her healthy lodgers and greedy husband.

It was Brack's idea that Enid should go to the Saturday-night dances organised by the Catholic Women's League in the old army hut that Father Froes called his parish hall. Previously, all suggestions of help for Agnes – visits by the Society of St Vincent de Paul and gifts of the partly faded flowers which the Society of Mary had removed from the altar after weddings – had been brusquely refused. Brack had not changed his attitude towards the Church, which he distrusted, or towards Catholics, whom he generally despised. He was simply anxious to ingratiate himself with the Hucknall boarding-house keeper who had written him a threatening letter. He felt no obligation to pay for the dry-cleaning of the young man's suit. But he had agreed because of the business card which Mrs Ferguson had put in between the folded sheet of lined writing paper. It described her house in Hucknall as an hotel and, not knowing that the description was fraudulent, he had hoped that a reconciliation with the proprietor might produce custom for his car-hire business. When he sent a three-shilling postal order, made out to Pullar's of Perth, he had expected no more than a note of acknowledgement in return but pinned on to his receipt was a ticket for the Women's League Whit Monday dance. Mrs Ferguson clearly expected him to buy it as a sign of goodwill. He decided to send Enid as bait for business. Enid refused to co-operate.

'You'd enjoy yourself, instead of sitting here reading every night.'

'I enjoy reading.'

'You do need to get out, love,' her mother told her. 'Perhaps I could go with you and sit in my chair at the back.'

Enid had anticipated the suggestion. Indeed, it was her principal reason for dismissing the idea out of hand. She would not consider going out in the evening without Agnes and she could not imagine enjoying herself whilst worrying about the hunched figure sitting in her wheelchair near the doorway.

'Your dad and I used to go to dances at Whitwell, and the Miners' Welfare at Rhodesia. We went every week for years and we didn't half enjoy ourselves. I think you ought to go.'

'I can get another ticket for your mam.' Father seemed desperate for his daughter to dance.

Enid's immediate suspicion was that, in her mother's favourite phrase, he was 'up to something'. Determination to frustrate whatever plans Brack had made for Saturday night hardened her resolve.

'Doing the veleta with middle-aged Irish miners? No thank you very much. I'd rather read a book any time.'

'They're not middle-aged. I took a wedding car to Hucknall this morning. There's a house full of single young men there.'

'All Irish and all miners.' Enid was not asking a question. 'No, thank you.'

'I thought you were supposed to be a bloody socialist. What's wrong with miners?'

'Nothing, except I don't want to spend Saturday night dancing with them.'

'All right,' said Brack. 'I'll tear the ticket up.'

'Don't do that, love. That's a silly thing to say.'

Until that moment, Brack had not even considered destroying the ticket. He had hoped to bully and bribe Enid into using it. And, if that hope were not realised, he had every intention of returning it to the Hucknall landlady who had sold it to him and reclaiming his half-crown. But, his wife having forbidden it, honour required him to reduce the pink pasteboard to confetti.

'Oh, Brack. Why did you do that? I would have persuaded her to go.'

'Bugger that.'

Brack threw the tiny scraps of pasteboard vaguely in Enid's direction. Most of them landed on the table. Some stuck to the butter. Others floated in the milk. Enid, assuming an expression of exaggerated disgust, began to remove them one by one.

'It's no good playing Lady Muck with me. I'm not impressed.'

Agnes began to cry. 'I don't know why you both want to upset me. You're terrible. You both like trouble. You revel in it. You're both as bad as each other.'

'I don't want any trouble . . .' Enid was looking at her father. There was no way of telling from her expression what she would say next. Agnes hoped for reconciliation.

Brack anticipated surrender and decided to press his advantage home. 'You should have thought of that before.'

'I don't want any trouble. If you want to bring one of your women round here on Saturday night, just say so. We'll go to Worksop. You only have to tell us the truth. But don't try to send me to an awful hop at—'

It was the first time that Brack had hit Enid. He struck her twice, once across the side of the head with the flat of his hand and once – after she had flinched and half turned away – with his fist. The fist landed on the forearm she had raised to protect her face and glanced off on to the coil of hair which she wore pinned up over her ear. The dull pain in her bruised arm was matched by the sharp sting of hairpins pushed into the soft skin in the nape of her neck. Mick growled and bared his teeth. Agnes tried to push herself out of her wheelchair. Enid swung a great looping punch in her father's direction. Brack caught his daughter's wrist before the blow landed and twisted her arm viciously behind her back. It was the end of all resistance.

'You'll break my arm! Stop it! Please stop it! You're breaking my arm!'

Agnes poked him with her stick and screamed something almost incomprehensible about sending for the police. Brack – ignoring his wife's threats, his daughter's entreaties and Mick's attempts to tear the bottoms off his trouser legs – marched Enid through the hall and towards the front door. He leaned past her, turned the handle and pushed her out into the muddy yard. It was all that she could do to keep her balance. A youth, filling sacks with coal, looked up and grinned.

'Stay there till I tell you. If you come round the back, you'll get another thumping.' He turned to the grinning youth. 'And you get on with your work or you'll get a thumping an' all. This is none of your business. This is family matters.'

It was half an hour before Brack left the house. When Enid came back inside, cold and shivering, her mother did not even pause to express sympathy or concern. 'We'll have to go back to Worksop.'

'But they don't want us, Mam.'

'How can you say such a thing, when they've been so kind?'

'Mam, they've had us on and off for years and they've had enough. They want to live in peace, just the two of them. Ginny upstairs isn't so bad. But in the living room they want just the two of them.'

'Don't be so silly. You talk about them as if they were man and wife.'

'Just believe me. Can't you see? Can't you believe the evidence of your own eyes? They like us calling round, even staying a day or two. But if you turned up tomorrow and asked if we could stay for good, they wouldn't want us, Mam. I can't believe you don't know that already.'

'You can't stay here.'

'For a bit I can. We both can. We both have to.'

'For how long?'

'Until we can escape for good. Until then, we'll have to make the best of it. But we'll get away. You mark my words.'

'That's easy to say. But it won't happen, ever. I could stand it when it was only me. You don't know how many times he's hit me and I've hidden the bruises. I stuck it for you. But if he's going to start hitting you . . .'

'I'm telling you, Mam. We'll get away.'

'How are we going to do that?'

'To begin with I'm going to that dance at St Joseph's.'

Brack was magnanimous in victory but he was magnanimous at great length. He dismissed the idea of Enid paying at the church-hall door as beneath the dignity of any daughter of his and went on to describe in detail the inconvenience of making a special journey to Hucknall to buy a replacement ticket. It would, he explained, be perfectly reasonable to report the original as lost or destroyed and ask for a free replacement. But parental pride required him to lose the half-crown without complaint or explanation. He proposed to buy three tickets so that he could escort his wife and daughter and make sure that they both enjoyed themselves. It was at that stage that Agnes expected Enid to announce that she had changed her mind a second time and had decided, after all, to stay at home on Saturday. But she smiled sweetly and asked her mother's advice about what to wear.

Enid wore a pale-blue dress with a sailor collar and a short box-pleat skirt. It was the age of energetic dances, none of which had been taught on Wednesday afternoons at Ashleigh House. But, to her parents' surprise, Enid attempted the Charleston as soon as a young man invited her on to the floor and gyrated with such enthusiasm that both her parents were shocked by the way in which her hem rose several inches above her knees.

When Father Froes came in at the interval to draw the raffle and thank the organisers for their efforts, he paused by the door and said to Brack, 'Your daughter *does* seem to be enjoying herself.'

Brack knew that the priest was being offensive, but he was not sure how to reply.

'She's having a lovely time,' Agnes said in obvious gratitude for the priest's kind words. 'Brack and I used to go to dances when we were young. The Miners' Welfare at Rhodesia mostly. We danced every dance.'

'Not like that, I trust.' Father Froes moved on towards the saxophonist who led the three-piece band. 'In great form tonight, Mac. In great form. I saw the old lady in the bathchair tapping her feet.'

'Her daughter's a stunner, Father.'

'And her father's got a temper like the devil himself. So you be careful.'

The drummer demanded silence with a crash of his cymbals and

459

the formalities of the interval began. The first number out of the bowler hat was claimed by a gnarled collier who, to nobody's surprise, chose the three bottles of stout. A girl with a limp and a stain down the front of her shabby dress drew second prize. She chose the cheap bottle of scent. When Father Froes called out 'Fifty-seven', Enid had to examine and re-examine her ticket several times before she was really sure that the box of chocolates was hers.

'If nobody's fifty-seven . . .' Father Froes was about to feel inside the hat again.

'Wait a sec!' Enid blushed and rushed forward, looking at her feet and the floor.

As she made her nervous way to collect third prize, young miners whistled and the saxophonist played the first few bars of 'Ain't She Sweet?' A drum-roll greeted the priest's presentation of the chocolates and Enid skipped back to her mother in the wheelchair, glowing with pleasure. 'They're chocolate almonds.' She began to tear the Cellophane paper from the box.

'Leave them until we get home.' Brack was trying to release the brake on the wheelchair.

'Isn't Mam very well?'

'She's upset. Upset by your behaviour.'

'What have I done?' It seemed only right to ask her father rather than address her mother direct. Brack was massively in command. He had decided that it was time to leave and all questions concerning why that must be were for him to answer.

'You know very well what you've done.'

'No, I don't.'

'You've made a show of yourself and you're making a worse one now. Home, young lady, this minute.' Brack turned the wheelchair with such violence that Agnes, unable to grasp the wooden arms, curled up in her seat out of fear that she would be thrown out and on to the floor.

Enid prepared to leave in resentful silence but whilst Brack was still struggling to point his wife towards the door Father Froes called down from the stage, 'I hope there's a chocolate for me.' He hurried from one end of the hut to the other. Enid handed him the box, but he ignored her and turned to Brack. 'Three-thirty at Worcester. Can you tell Cobbler Jack I'd like five shillings each way on . . .'

The priest's confidential manner both attracted the dancers' attention and forced them into demonstrating that they were not trying to overhear what he was saying. After the initial furtive glances, only one young man looked directly at the conspiratorial group. It was the smaller of the two Irish colliers who had rescued Peg and her litter

460

from the disused cesspit. The priest was about to place a bet on the next race on the card when the young man approached him. No respect, thought Father Froes.

'Excuse me, Father.'

'What is it, my son?' The form of words was pastoral, but the tone was impatient.

Brack was on his way to the door, but the young man put a hand on his arm and asked him, 'Did that pup die?'

'It's all right,' said Brack. 'She's got it. It's her dog now.' He jerked his head in his daughter's direction.

The young man nodded to Enid. It was a perfectly courteous greeting. But it began and ended casually and Enid was used to young men treating her more seriously. They were supposed to look at her, turn quickly away and then look again. After that, they would blush and stammer, talk too quickly or attempt to impress her with their wit and worldly wisdom. But they were not under any circumstances to nod casually and prepare to carry on a conversation with somebody else.

'Is it a dog or a bitch? I've never been able to remember, if ever I knew.' The young man smiled.

It was, Enid decided, not the smile of a man but a boy. The young Irish man was a natural, unspoilt by the ravages of either learning or experience. He was not at all the sort of person whose company she sought or valued. She also believed him to be the most handsome man that she had ever seen.

Jack O'Hara took Mrs Ferguson's warning seriously. It was because he respected both her judgement and her wishes that until the night of the dance he had made no attempt to see if the pup had survived. And it was her stern injunction, ringing in his ears, that had made him treat Enid with such perfunctory bad grace. He had recognised Brack, standing at the back of the St Joseph's dance, as the man who had gambled on the life of the puppy and could tell him about its fate. But he had also recognised him as the companion and friend of the man whose company he had been told to avoid – on pain of offending his dead mother. In consequence, he asked about the dog and quickly passed on. But, before he hurried away, he had noticed the young woman who stood, nervously resentful, by the side of Jack McGovern's companion. She was beautiful. But, more important to him than beauty alone, she was beautiful in the superior way that particularly appealed to Jack's instincts for self-improvement. To be seen with such a woman – smart, Mrs Ferguson would have called her – could only improve his social status. But she was the daughter of McGovern's friend and McGovern was, on the word of Mrs Ferguson

461

herself, an undesirable. Jack told himself that there were plenty more pebbles on the beach, fish in the sea, strings to his bow and, if all went well after the interval, irons in the fire.

The dancing resumed with a ladies' invitation waltz. Jack knew there was no escape from Sheila Ferguson and capitulated gracefully, with barely a second glance towards the several young and highly attractive potential partners who had been intimidated into retreat by Sheila's proprietorial advance. He completed two circuits of the floor before the leader of the band announced that the dance had turned into a 'ladies' excuse me'. A polite queue formed behind Sheila Ferguson's back. The first girl to tap her on the shoulder was Kathy Mann, whose mother cleaned at the billiard hall.

'Was that Enid Brackenbury you were talking to?' Kathy asked him.

'I was talking to a man.' Jack felt strangely defensive. 'I don't know his name. I saved his dog. It fell down . . .' The story of the cesspit rescue had been told so often and greeted with so many combinations of ridicule and disbelief that he decided not to describe the incident. 'It's her father I know. 'Cause of his dog.'

'Her father's a communist.'

'How do you make that out?' Jack wanted it to be true. He had never met anyone who was notorious and he longed to have saved the life of a dog which belonged to a scoundrel.

'My mam told me. He went to a meeting in Derby and shouted Jimmy Thomas down – shouted that the railwaymen had betrayed the miners. And he's not even a miner himself.'

The case against Brack having been made and his guilt established beyond all reasonable doubt, Kathy Mann gave way to the young lady who hovered behind her and she returned to her chair by the wall, deeply satisfied by the combination of awe and incredulity which registered on Jack O'Hara's handsome features.

'Was that Brack's daughter you were talking to?'

Jack O'Hara looked down at the tiny, worried face of Mary Farrell and gave an immensely comforting answer. 'I was talking to Brack himself. At least I think I was. I don't know the gentleman personally. But I'm told that Brack – that's to say Mr Brackenbury – is his name.'

'He's not a Catholic, you know.' Mary's accusation was so vehement that she lost her step and trod on Jack's foot. In normal circumstances, the shame of such an error would have destroyed her entire evening but she had embarked upon a crusade against the ungodly and she had no time for such vanities. 'So his daughter's not a Catholic either. Because he isn't and her mother isn't and I know that she's not had instruction. I know it for certain.'

Jack O'Hara's expression registered nothing except bewilderment. Mary Farrell decided that an explanation was necessary. She did not want to give the impression that she was motivated by spite or, even worse, jealousy.

'People say they're Catholics, because the man hangs about Father Froes. But they're not. I know it for a fact. He and Father Froes are personal friends. That's all.'

The idea that priests had personal friends was not within the comprehension of the normal Irish collier. Priests occasionally called in at the Welfare for a pint, where they were treated with a strict formality which ensured that guests and hosts were equally uncomfortable. They sometimes went to race meetings. Indeed it was said back home that the ferries to Liverpool were black with clerical suits on the Friday before the Grand National. On rare occasions, priests' relatives were to be seen making furtive exits from presbytery front doors or sitting at the back of mass whilst their sons and nephews distributed the sacrament. But priests did not have friends in the way which ordinary men had friends – equals with whom to enjoy a joke and share a confidence. Jack expertly guided Mary round an almost stationary couple of elderly ladies who could not remember which partner was supposed to lead and which to follow.

'Brack's a friend of the priest?' He did not disguise his scepticism.

'Yes. Of Father Froes, here at St Joseph's.'

'I don't think that Father Keogh has any friends. I've never seen him with any.'

'I don't know what happens in Mansfield.' Mary Farrell spoke of Jack's parish as if it were part of a still unexplored land. 'But Father Froes and Brack are friends. So don't forget. She's not . . . none of that family is. They're not Catholics.'

It was Mrs Ferguson's turn. She had walked to the front of the queue of young ladies who hoped for the privilege of a single circuit of the floor with the handsome Jack O'Hara. Mrs Ferguson had withdrawn her social services from her own parish – St Philip Neri in Mansfield – because of a dispute over whist drives and had put her talents at the disposal of St Joseph's. Her status as dance impresario combined with respect for her age and her temper to ensure that no objection was raised when she elbowed the other prospective partners aside. She clasped Jack's hand in a grip of iron and, holding him at arm's length as if she feared that the cesspit slime still stuck to his lapels, looked at him as if he had committed some awful crime.

'My word, we are in demand tonight.'

Jack grinned. He was pleased that his landlady had noticed.

'I wouldn't smirk if I was you, considering . . .'

'Considering what?' Jack was still off guard.

'Considering what people are saying about you.'

Delighted that they were saying anything at all caused the smirk to widen into a grin. Mrs Ferguson decided that the *coup de grâce* was called for.

'They're saying that you'll let our Sheila down.'

The last notes of the waltz – played by the saxophone which finished the number several seconds later than the rest of the band – died away and the master of ceremonies and maestro crashed the cymbals in preparation for announcing the next dance. Jack was saved. The wronged mother looked menacingly at the musician who had betrayed her. To her regret, bands being in short supply, she would have to employ him again the following week.

'Now, ladies and gentlemen . . .' Pleasure oozed out of his voice. 'Just clear the floor for a moment whilst my excellent assistants here . . . Thank you, Paul. Thank you, Pat . . . spread a little more french chalk . . . . Just clear the floor for a moment, if you please. Then it's the Gay Gordons by special request of the McDonald family who came all the way down from Ayrshire . . . Just clear the floor for a couple of seconds . . .'

Jack O'Hara was so disturbed by what his landlady had told him that he completely forgot the stern injunction which ended the chapter on ballroom dancing in his book of etiquette. He allowed Mrs Ferguson to return to her seat unaccompanied.

Fortunately, Father Froes was on hand to comfort her. 'Is that the young man your Sheila's going to marry?'

'He is, Father.'

'Don't worry about him eyeing Enid Brackenbury.'

'I wasn't, Father. He's a good boy.'

'And she's a terrible snob. He's safe enough unless he takes out a subscription to the lending library and spends his nights with his nose in a book – which I think we'll both agree to be unlikely.'

When the Nottingham County Council opened a branch library in Worksop, it prudently decided to keep the general public as far away from the books as possible. Instead of exposing its shelves to potential readers, it exhibited a full list of all its stock on a massive notice board. Novels and biographies, travellers' tales, craftsmen's manuals, political texts, religious tracts and guides to better gardening were, therefore, protected from the ravages of those who might, irresponsibly, choose to browse rather than to borrow. Coloured discs hung alongside each of the titles. Green signified that the book was available only after application to other branch libraries and would take a week to obtain. Blue was a warning that the book was already on loan and reserved by a substantial waiting list of would-be borrowers. A red disc meant that the book was on the premises and ready for immediate issue. Few red discs hung on the board.

Enid Brackenbury arrived in front of the library notice board at exactly half-past two on every Thursday afternoon. The time never varied for the circumstances which brought her to that place at that time never changed. Thursday was half-day at Harthill and Skinner and the front door of Brook House was closed behind the departing seamstresses at one o'clock sharp. Enid, who had arrived earlier in the morning with her mother, waited to hear the sound of the big bottom bolt sliding into place and then gently lowered eight new-laid eggs into the pan of water which was boiling on the hob. During the next four and a half minutes she cut eight slices of bread and buttered them according to the various tastes for which she catered – thick for her mother, sparse for Lottie and, for Anne, not so thick as to make her feel over indulged but not so sparse as to make her feel neglected.

At ten minutes past one Lottie always said, 'This really is a treat.' By a quarter to two the lunch was finished and the washing up done. Agnes settled down for the afternoon and Enid was on her way to the library, where she always stared at the notice board with mounting frustration until, despairing of finding a book which she really wanted, a sudden and reckless selection was made from the few titles which were immediately available.

'Have you chosen anything?'

It was the unmistakable voice of Owen Ford.

'They've never got anything I want. In the end I'll get some rubbish that isn't worth reading.'

The conversation was casual enough, two old friends who had not met for a long time exchanging pleasantries on the subject that had once brought them together. Enid could not quite speak to Owen as if he were an equal. She was no longer the girl who sat at his feet in awe and wonder but even though their ages – separating them by less than twenty years – seemed to have converged, she still thought that he was too old, as well as too wise, to be treated with anything except nervous respect. She was not even sure that, with him at her elbow, she dare withdraw the novel by Ian Hay against which a red disc had suddenly appeared. She had read and enjoyed *Knight on Wheels* and had recognised it as exactly the sort of romantic nonsense against which Owen had always warned her. He looked up at the board. In ten seconds he had dismissed all the titles as unworthy of attention.

'There's never owt here. It's much better in Chesterfield, though

Percy wouldn't put it that way. Sales have suffered since the library opened. Percy sells magazines now to make ends meet.'

'How is Percy?'

'He's in great form today. I've just come from the stall. He went to Oxford last Saturday. Ruskin reunion. Set him up for six months. That's what I came to see you about.'

Enid had not even considered the possibility that their meeting was anything other than chance. She had thought it strange that he should waste his time in the inadequate public library but the idea that he had travelled to Worksop for the explicit purpose of seeing her was too impertinent an assumption for her to make. The library assistant, who was hooking a new batch of coloured discs against the list of books, stared reproachfully at Owen over the horn rim of her spectacles.

'We can't talk here,' said Owen. 'We're supposed to be quiet here. Come and have a cup of tea.'

'M'mam will expect me back. She'll be worried if I'm not back by half three.'

Owen took her hand and pulled. She followed him as much out of embarrassment as enthusiasm. As they left the library, he gave her his first lecture of the day.

'It's about time you grew up. Most women of your age are thinking about children of their own. Tell your mother that you couldn't decide on which book. Tell her that the big bad wolf caught you in the forest. Best of all, tell her that you had a cup of tea with me. But for Christ's sake don't go on about being out late as if you're fifteen and it's past midnight.'

'You don't understand.'

'I understand only too well.' They were outside the library and on their way to the Abbey Tea Rooms. 'I understand that I told you about the suffragettes and you thought they were wonderful. Well, they didn't chain themselves to railings and throw themselves under racehorses for you to stay at home in Shirebrook pushing your mam's bathchair.'

'What else can I do?'

It was a whole series of doubts – real and rhetorical – encompassed within a single question. Enid had no doubt where her duty lay and she was uncertain about both the alternative opportunities and her ability to seize whatever sudden chance came her way.

'That's what I've come to see you about.' Owen sat down at a rickety wicker table. He had not bothered to take off his coat and, although a waitress hovered at his shoulder, he ignored her and went on talking. 'The real thing is whether or not you want to escape. Sometimes I think that your mother is just an excuse. You can blame it all on her. She held you back. You don't have to feel guilty.'

'Guilty about what? What have I to feel guilty about?'

'Guilty about wasting your talents.'

The waitress coughed and waved the menu in Owen's direction.

'A pot of tea,' Enid told her. 'A pot of tea for two.'

'Nothing to eat?' The waitress sounded cheated.

'Nothing to eat.' It was Owen's one concession to his surroundings. Then his assault on Enid was renewed. 'It's the easy way, saying "I could have done it, if only I'd been given the chance." It'll be a great consolation in your old age, telling your grandchildren – that's if you have any – "I could have done something with my life, but I had to look after m'mam." It's the easy way. But it isn't the right way. That's what I've come to say.'

'Owen,' Enid was calmly pouring the tea, 'I don't have the faintest idea what you're talking about.'

'You've got very social of late. That's what I'm talking about. Dances, including dances at the Catholic church. Tennis every afternoon except Sunday. Bicycle rides with all sorts of young men.'

'Very rarely,' said Enid, thinking that she wished it were not so. 'I slave all day in the house, looking after Mam. I go out once in a blue moon. I don't understand what you're on about. I sit in with Mam most days. Don't you expect me to have a game of tennis if I get the chance? Anyway, Mam likes it. I wouldn't do it if she didn't.'

'I want you to do something worth doing. Do you still read?'

'Of course I do. What do you think I was doing at the library?'

'When I say reading, I don't mean reading anything. In the old days we used to read serious stuff and talk about it.'

'That was when Arthur Ellis was still alive. I thought we did it to entertain him.'

'I did it sometimes because I thought I was helping you – especially after you left school.'

'I didn't realise.'

'Be fair. I offered. I said come round any Wednesday when I was on mornings, or any Saturday afternoon. Now you've got to decide.'

'Decide what? Tell me quick. I've got to be on my way back home. M'mam will be worried sick if I'm not there soon.'

'Decide on Ruskin. You've got a real chance. In a year or two that is.'

'Owen, I've got ten minutes before I have to go. Tell me. Tell me so I can understand.'

'It's Percy. He was at Ruskin last Sunday. They're on the look-out for women. They said that to get more women in they were prepared to lower the standards. Percy thought of you straight away. It wouldn't be this year. But next October perhaps . . . You'd have to work . . .'

'Owen, I couldn't.'

'Of course you could. It isn't a written exam. Just an interview. I'd prepare you for it. We both would, Percy and me.'

'I don't mean that. It's no good, I couldn't.'

'Are you still a party member?'

'I've not paid my subscription for months.'

'Your dad comes to ward meetings regular. We'll get you back into good standing. Brack will pay your arrears. It will all be as right as clockwork, you'll see.'

'Have you talked to my dad?'

'I don't need to. I can tell you now. He'd be as pleased as punch. Can't you hear him boasting – "My daughter at Oxford." I tell you, there's nothing to stop you.'

'There's my mam.'

'Don't be such a bloody fool. Miss this chance and the best you can hope for is a husband and kids.'

'That's what most young women want.'

'Young women at the tennis club.'

'Don't sneer about it, Owen. It's escape for me.'

'I'm showing you the way to escape for ever.'

'Well, I can't take it.'

'There isn't a young man . . . ?'

'Nobody special. To be honest, nobody at all.' They both laughed.

'When you change your mind, come round. Come to Austin Street or to the pit. Leave a message in the checkweighman's hut. It's there for the union business. Ruskin, that's official business. You'd be entitled to come and see me about that.'

'My word, you are getting on. Recognition? Is that what you call it?'

He did not realise that she was mocking him.

'We've been recognised long enough. But not respected. They'll have to learn a real lesson before they respect us. But it's not far off. When it happens, you'll be playing tennis.'

It was because he was so upset that he left the room without paying. Fortunately, Enid had a florin in her purse.

'I've taken your name in vain.'

Owen Ford tried to avoid speaking in clichés, but at moments of unusual tension he sometimes relaxed his high verbal standards. When he was particularly nervous, banality followed hard on the heels of banality. He winked at Brack, inclined his head and lifted his elbow as if to give him a playful dig in the ribs.

'Thought I'd have a word in your ear before a little bird told you.'

Owen peered through the dusk of Jack McGovern's back room. He had hoped never to visit Cobbler Jack's but braving the gloom that surrounded the scratched and bottle-littered table was his only way of seeing Brack that night. He tried to ignore the florid lady with whom his quarry was in desultory conversation and repeated his explanation.

'Thought I'd have a word to the wise.'

'What you been up to, then?'

There was no reason, of which Owen knew, for Brack's antagonism. During the early months of Arthur Ellis's infirmity, the two men had spent part of almost every afternoon together and it was only reasonable to suppose that, when Brack began to take a real interest in politics, they would build a serious friendship around their mutual interest. But Brack had unaccountably turned against him.

'Just done my good deed for the day.' Owen took a deep breath and made a determined attempt to talk sense. 'I've been talking to your Enid.'

'Oh, aye.'

It was no more than an indication that Brack was ready for the explanation to continue but to Owen it sounded like a challenge. Because he was frightened, he accepted.

'Nothing wrong in that, is there?'

'Nobody says there is.'

'My brother Percy's just got back from Oxford.'

'Is this what you talked to our Enid about?'

'Well, it is, surprisingly enough. Percy went back to Ruskin College and they've got special places for women. We could get Enid in, if you'd let her go.'

He knew that he was scandalously overstating the prospect but he could not admit that he was causing so much fuss about a vague hope.

'Did she say that I'd stop her?'

'She said she'd have to stay at home and look after her mother.'

'And what do you think I should do about that?'

'Persuade her. Stop her from throwing her life away.'

'It's nowt to do wi' me. She takes no notice of me. If she did, things would be very different.' Brack smiled. He felt no malice towards Owen Ford and wounded him purely for pleasure. 'If she did what I told her she wouldn't spend every night with a different young man. None of them with a sensible thought in their heads.'

Owen turned gratifyingly pink. Brack decided to stab him again.

'I'd speak to her about it tonight. But I doubt if I'll see her. She won't be back when I go to bed. She'll be gadding about somewhere all hours.'

CHAPTER THIRTY-SEVEN

Struggle

Until a bare week before the appointed date, it seemed that the Twenty-Fifth Annual Meeting of the Hucknall-in-Torkhard Byron Society would not take place. Canon Barber, rector of St Mary Magdalene and president of the society, had been unable to obtain a speaker. He was on his way to post the notices which cancelled the meeting when he was approached in his own churchyard by a man whom he recognised at once as a ruffian. Relying on the stranger's pugilistic appearance, Canon Barber assumed that the fellow was in search of the memorial to Benjamin Caunt, champion prize fighter and son of the parish. To the rector's surprise, the stranger, speaking in the accent of an insurance clerk, asked him if it was possible to see Byron's tomb.

Canon Barber answered curtly that it was not.

'Are you sure he's buried here? Some say he's not. Some say he's in Greece.'

'I have no doubt that he lies beneath the nave.'

'All of him?'

'Certainly all of him.'

'Contemporary accounts say that they took out his heart and entrails in Missolonghi.'

'You seem to be something of a Byron scholar.' Canon Barber did not mean to sound complimentary.

'When I was at Oxford I wrote an essay on "The Prisoner of Chillon" – "The Prisoner of Chillon and the Instinct for Liberty".'

'You read English?'

'I read politics . . . and economics and philosophy and geography and trade union studies . . . And history.'

'In my day there were no such courses,' said Canon Barber.

The rector, deciding that appearances do sometimes deceive, led the way in through the ancient porch and marched towards the chancel steps. He pointed at an iron ring attached to one of the flagstones. 'It's down there. Steps lead down to the vault.'

'Can we go down?'

'No, we cannot.'

'Is that because you're not sure it's there?'

'Look.' Canon Barber pointed to a slab of green marble. It was engraved with the poet's name and dates of birth and death. The inscription ended: 'Presented by the King of Greece'. The rector snorted triumphantly. 'You see, the King of Greece thinks he's here, even if you don't.'

The visitor seemed convinced and studied, with proper reverence, the other Byron memorials. 'I've always admired him. Always. Ever since I studied him.'

Canon Barber made his request at once. Agreement was immediate.

Notices were printed and distributed on the following day. They advertised – to the speaker's slight concern and great pleasure – an address on 'Byron and Revolution' by Percy Ford Esq. BA.

The turnout for the Annual Meeting was twice as great as the rector had anticipated. The front row was filled with miners, all of whom were in their best suits and, to the Canon's consternation, wore in their buttonholes enamel red stars or badges which bore the head of Lenin. The president had barely begun his introductory remarks when the door of the Carnegie Library was pushed noisily open.

'I can't be back until after nine.' Brack, who was pushing Agnes's wheelchair, made no concessions to the meeting.

'You said *by nine*.' Agnes was too anguished to worry about who heard.

'I told you. The train doesn't get into Derby till half-past eight.'

'Shush, Dad,' Enid told him. Mick, who was fastened to the footrest of the wheelchair, growled.

Agnes turned on her daughter. 'You shouldn't have made him bring us.'

Enid replied, in a stage whisper, 'He was coming here anyway, Mam.'

Brack was almost out of the door. 'I'll go straight to Fergusons'. They'll want to get home after that journey. You'll have to push her across there.'

Enid busied herself tightening the screws which held the folding wheelchair rigid.

'It is, therefore, with the greatest pleasure . . .' Canon Barber had almost regained his composure, '. . . the greatest possible pleasure that I introduce our speaker for the evening, Mr Percy Ford.'

There was a ripple of applause and Percy, in a manner more

471

appropriate to a public meeting, announced, 'I dream'd that Greece might still be free . . .' as if it were a text and he was giving a sermon.

Agnes was asleep in ten minutes, but Enid, sitting next to her mother on the chair which Owen Ford had brought to her, was enthralled. Mick stood guard for the first half of the lecture and then turned several tight circles before stretching out across Enid's feet. After half an hour Percy reached for his *dénouement*.

'That is the message of "The Prisoner of Chillon". Only the morally feeble accept servitude. The strong struggle for liberty however long they are in chains. After a thousand years of serfdom, the Russian people rose up against the tyrant – as willing to die for freedom as the Greeks had been in eighteen twenty-two. Had Byron lived one hundred years later, he would have stood shoulder to shoulder with the men who stormed the Winter Palace.'

Percy raised a clenched fist and the men with the red stars and Lenin badges returned his salute. The rector, who had stood up in a moment of unthinking enthusiasm, sat down again. The lady who was pouring out the tea knocked over her milk jug.

'Your Percy's very clever, isn't he?' Enid felt obliged to say something and she hoped that a compliment to the lecturer would at least endear her to his brother. 'He does know a lot.'

'All talk,' said Owen, 'and the time for talking's gone.'

Agnes radiated distress. 'There isn't going to be another strike is there, Mr Ford? I pray it won't happen. It does nobody any good. I can remember nineteen-twelve.'

'We won't take less, Mrs Brackenbury, I'll tell you that. The lads would kill anyone who suggested it. It's nothing to do with all this fist-clenching rubbish. Percy will be all right whatever happens. I'll get you some tea.'

Enid took one of the cups and held it in the direction of her mother's lips. Agnes craned her neck towards it and Enid, who was not concentrating, poured half its contents down her mother's dress. She took the digestive biscuit from the empty saucer in Owen's hand and carefully fed it to the dog.

'Where are you going now?' Owen asked. It was clearly time to change the subject.

'Mr and Mrs Ferguson are coming back from Ireland tonight. Brack's picking them up at Derby station.'

Owen pushed the wheelchair, Agnes winced at every bump in the road and Enid talked from start to finish of the journey. She talked about Mick with genuine authority and about Byron with real interest. But most of all she talked about the Russian Revolution without the slightest idea of what she was talking about. She was still confusing

Bolsheviks and Mensheviks when they arrived at the Fergusons' front door.

Only Jack O'Hara was at home. He would have been playing billiards at the Welfare had he not been in bed all day with a bad cold. Mrs Ferguson did not believe in her young men going out in the evening when they had not been to work and the force of her personality maintained proper discipline even when she was somewhere between St Pancras station and home.

Owen took charge. 'Miss Brackenbury and her mother are meeting Mr Brackenbury here.'

'Is this the dog?' Jack O'Hara was on his knees.

'I beg your pardon?' To Agnes, he seemed to be at prayer by the side of the wheelchair.

'Is this the pup me and Eddie Eames got out of the cesspit?'

Even without his interest in Mick, Enid would have remembered him from the St Joseph's dance. His eyes were red and watering and the end of his nose was swollen and raw from constant sneezing. But he was still the most handsome man she had ever seen and he was still more interested in the dog than he was in her.

'I've met the young man, Mam. So have you, but you won't remember . . .'

'Do you have a dog?' Agnes had a talent for the inappropriate question. She did not wait for an answer. 'There's no need for you to wait, Mr Ford. We're very grateful for your help as it is.'

'I wouldn't dream of leaving you here. Percy's happy enough. He's starting a revolution in the nearest public house to the library.'

They waited till nearly eleven o'clock, sitting uneasily in the living room and making sudden darts at disjointed conversation and watching Jack O'Hara blow his nose. Then there was the sound of a motor car drawing up outside and they knew, for motor cars were rare in Hucknall, that the Fergusons had returned.

'Jack, you ought to be in bed, you'll get your death.' Mrs Ferguson seemed not to have noticed the strangers in her room.

Owen tried to make the introduction. 'I'm sorry—' But he was cut off by Agnes.

'Brack, we thought that something must have happened to you. We thought that you must have had an accident. Where have you been?'

Brack was in a bad temper. He had hoped to be home in Shirebrook by ten o'clock and in Cobbler Jack's by half past.

'Come on,' he said, 'let's get her out and this contraption folded up. You'd better get your mother into the car.'

'Just let me say thank you to Mrs Ferguson,' said Agnes.

'It'll be thanks enough getting out of her house.'

Mrs Ferguson had gone to heat milk to go with Jack's aspirin, muttering, 'Sheila should have done this.' Her husband told Agnes that there was no hurry. Brack was already pushing the wheelchair towards the door.

'I thought something must have happened to you.'

'The train was late, you silly bitch!' He tipped the wheelchair up on its back wheels to bump it over the threshold. Agnes gritted her teeth.

Enid was outraged. 'For Lor's sake be careful. Are you trying to hurt her or what?' She did not wait for the answer but grabbed at the wheelchair's handle. Her father pushed her away. She grabbed again. The wheelchair spun round in the doorway and crashed against the wall.

'You bloody fool,' Brack said. 'You're just showing off in front of this young man here.'

He half pushed, half struck, at her shoulder. Enid staggered back theatrically and did a fair imitation of hitting her head against the doorjamb.

'You stop that.' Jack O'Hara had returned to the hall with the half-drunk glass of hot milk in his hand.

It was the timidity of the reproof that made Brack pause and turn. There was something inherently absurd in the young man's behaviour. He was threatening Brack whilst holding a glass of milk in his hand. Brack did not want to offend the Fergusons, for he hoped that they would become regular customers. He moderated his reply. 'I beg your pardon?' It was intended to intimidate the lodger without enraging his landlady.

Jack took the question at its face value. 'I said stop that. It's not a gentlemanly way to behave.'

It was at that moment, or a second later, when Jack began to sneeze uncontrollably, that Enid decided that he was the man to save her from Brack, for ever.

Fortunately Jack O'Hara had come to exactly the same conclusion. His irritating habit of appearing not to notice Enid had been no more than protection against the danger of revealing his true feeling. Enid looked and spoke and dressed like the girls in magazines which he read for social inspiration. She went with the plus-fours and the golf-club membership, the Catenians and a clean shirt every day. She was so far above him that at first he thought it was foolish to aspire even to talk to her on equal terms. Then he saw her tyrannised by her father and he knew that, although unworthy, he had been sent by Saints Catherine, Theresa and Agatha to rescue her.

For the next two weeks there was no dance in the old army hut that St Joseph's called a parish hall but neither Jack nor Enid doubted that they would meet when the three-piece band struck up again. They would not immediately dance together – respectability required a ritual – but by the end of the evening they would be the most handsome couple on the floor.

Their confidence was justified. The next dance was all they had hoped it would be. For the first half of the evening they hovered in each other's vicinity showing no more sign of recognition than a curt nod and half-smile. Then, when the night was almost over, Jack walked over to the corner where she sat and, giving the little bow he had learned from the book of etiquette, asked if he could have the pleasure of the next quickstep. He danced well, she badly. But, despite the need to concentrate on her steps, Enid talked without pause. For most of the time she boasted – boasted about the books she had read, the sophisticated life she lived in Worksop and her distinguished family. Jack managed to do little more than ask her about the dog. Then she boasted about tennis.

'I play tennis,' Jack said.

'Which club?'

'I play at the Welfare.'

'It's better at a proper club. Tournaments every Saturday. I won the ladies' singles seven times last year and the mixed doubles.'

'How do you join?'

'You've got to play in white. White flannels. It's compulsory.' Enid had a vision of Jack in cheap plimsolls, a flannel shirt, from which the starched collar had been detached, and braces.

'I've got white flannels.' He showed no resentment at her assumption. 'I've had them ever since I came to England.'

Jack spoke as though his whole life had been a preparation for that moment.

'You'll have to be proposed and seconded . . . But I dare say I could find you someone . . . That's if you really want to join . . . If I asked, somebody would do it . . . They'd do it for me . . . You'll have to pay the full subscription, even though the season's started.'

'That doesn't matter.' Jack longed to know how much it would cost, but feared that it would not be gentlemanly to ask.

It was an eventful May. On the first day of the month, the miners – who had, as Owen predicted, refused a wage-cut – were locked out of the pits. Two days later the General Strike began. It seemed to Enid that management and men had conspired to ruin her life. Whatever his feelings towards her, a miner, locked in bitter combat with

475

the Staveley Coal and Iron Company, was not in a position to carry her off like young Lochinvar.

Throughout the month, they stalked each other like two wary gladiators, trident against net. Jack played no tennis – he could no longer afford the court fee – but he did go to the dances in the old army hut with a ticket supplied by his still hopeful landlady. He travelled to and from Shirebrook with the other Hucknall lodgers and, like them, treated Sheila Ferguson with detached courtesy. Occasionally, Enid and Jack danced together. She talked, he listened. Twice he walked home with her – not walked her home, but walked in the same direction. Once, when it was raining, he insisted that she put his jacket over her shoulders. He was clearly tempted to linger by the fence that separated Brackenbury's yard from the road – but that was only to get a close look at the motor cars which the increasingly successful haulier offered for hire or sale. One day, when he knocked on the front door of 11 Langwith Road, Enid thought that there must be some sort of mistake. Owen Ford, who stood a pace behind him, inevitably spoke first. 'I believe you know this young man.'

'Yes, I do. I met him at St Joseph's dance.'

'I might have guessed. It was his idea we came, not mine. I wouldn't have troubled you, knowing that you're not really interested any more. He said to come.'

'It's not really you we've come to see.' Jack blushed at making so base an admission. 'It's your father. But we thought you might put in a word, being a sympathiser and all.'

'A sympathiser for what?' Enid asked.

'For socialism.' Jack declared his allegiance as if he had been born under the red flag. It was Owen's turn to blush.

'And how long have you been a socialist?' Enid asked.

Owen answered for Jack. 'After that meeting at Hucknall. He says he heard about it from your mam. But I can't remember her saying much. Anyway he saw the rector and then wrote to our Percy. Percy guessed he was a Catholic and would not have anything to do with him. He passed him on to me. He's as keen as mustard now.'

Jack beamed. 'I'm helping with Thursday's meeting.'

'Oh, the strike.' Enid pretended to be more bored than she felt.

'It's not just another strike,' said Owen. 'It's what I've told you would happen. It's our chance to stand up for ourselves – or it could have been. Not just the miners. All the labour movement. If we give in now we're finished.'

'And I'm helping with the meeting.' Jack could not disguise his pride. 'I thought that you being sympathetic might put in a word with your dad. We need a car to get the speakers from Chesterfield and then on to Staveley. We thought your dad might let us have one cheap.'

'I'd have asked him myself . . . but this one here insisted we did it through you . . .' Owen was apologetic again.

'That's all right. What are you standing outside for? Come and say hello to m'mam.'

Owen listened to Agnes talk about the strike, the weather, the world heavyweight boxing championship, the temperance movement and the pains in her legs. Jack asked if he could have a closer look at the cars and – leaving Owen to act as audience to her mother – Enid led him into the yard.

'I didn't know you were interested in the union, less still politics,' she said.

'I'm not,' he said. 'Honest to God, I'm putting my soul in jeopardy working with these syndicalists.' Suddenly, he sounded like a real Irishman. 'Doesn't Father Keogh preach against them every Sunday from St Philip Neri's pulpit?'

'Then what are you up to?'

'I heard that you and your dad were great politicians. Indeed, you said so yourself. For sure, I thought it was another way of seeing you.'

Jack O'Hara left the tennis club within weeks of gaining full membership, for despite possessing a pair of flannels and a flashing forehand the other members made it clear that he was not welcome. He was a striking miner and tennis-club members were, almost to the last pair of mixed doubles, against the General Strike. Jack had believed that the miners' cause was just from the day in June when John Spicer had read out the offer made to the 'Workmen of the Staveley Coal and Iron Company Collieries' and described the terms of surrender on which the company was prepared to reopen its pits. He had not fully understood what the company proposed but Mr Spicer spat the proposal out with such contempt that Jack had realised at once that it was not worth accepting.

'For a seven and a half hour day a minimum percentage of forty per cent on the present basic rates. . . . The wages of no adult worker shall fall below seven shillings and threepence per shift. . . .' That proposal was greeted with a howl of rage. Mr Spicer's entire speech was interrupted by only two outbreaks of cheering. The first followed an attack on 'Judas Spencer', the Nottinghamshire Miners' Trustee who had described the strike as 'the biggest fiasco in the history of the trade union movement'. The second greeted his proposal that the company's terms should be rejected with contempt. His proposal to

477

fight on was carried unanimously, but his promise that the miners would fight on alone was received in bitter silence.´

It was a dismal summer in Shirebrook and a desperate autumn. Not a single miner returned to work, despite the temptation placed in their way by deputies who haunted the public houses, offering to buy drinks for any man who accepted the new terms. Children went hungry and rent was unpaid. The miners' conduct was described as 'generally exemplary' – by the Chesterfield magistrates when they convicted Henry Webb, a full-time organiser for the Communist Party, and Percy Ford, a bookseller. Both were guilty of conduct likely to cause a breach of the peace. Most traders sympathised with the colliers' cause and supported them with continual credit. At 11 Langwith Road, Ernest Brackenbury – who had only just paid his debts and bought out his brother-in-law – faced ruin by strike for the third time in his career. Weddings were postponed so the white Humber was rarely out of the yard. There was no 'concessionary coal' heaped outside miners' cottages to be illegally bought and sold cheap to the semi-detached houses on the edges of the pit villages. Removals were almost all the result of evictions and bailiffs do not hire removal vans. Small shopkeepers, on the verge of bankruptcy, saved money on haulage by expecting boys with barrows to push heavy loads for long distances and the boys pushed the barrows gladly because there was no other work. But Brack stood loyally by the miners. The Independent Labour Party – in which, thanks to his strong opinions on every subject, he cut a dash – and the Co-op, which still did its best to put business his way, had no doubt that the colliery owners were to blame. Even when the strike began to crumble in other parts of the coalfield, Brack remained resolute. At the end of September, he found the few pounds which Enid had saved out of the summer housekeeping as a protection against the hard winter. He gave it to the strike fund.

Enid herself, suddenly surrounded by the drama of conflict and confrontation, fell hopelessly in love with the theatre of politics. Jack was temporarily forgotten and her father briefly rehabilitated. He had become a political figure in the area, pronouncing with equal authority on ideology and organisation. She began to admire what she believed to be his grasp of economic theory. He was, she decided, a genuinely clever man. To Enid, that partly made up for his multitudinous other sins and she glowed in the respect with which he was treated by other local politicians. The idea of his standing for the county council in the following May seemed no more than the obvious next step in his irresistible political advance. She was not at all surprised when he announced, over breakfast, that he was to drive Mr A. J. Cook, General Secretary of the Miners' Federation, when he

478

visited the Derbyshire coalfield. He was infuriated to discover that there was to be no meeting in Shirebrook.

'That's what you get for loyalty. We're solid here,' he insisted, as if he were a collier living on strike pay. 'Because those bloody scabs have gone back at Warsop, we've got to go there to stiffen the rest up.' His identification with the miners was total.

The first day of A. J. Cook's visit began badly for Brack. The loyal miners who were his neighbours decided to march to Warsop behind the jazz band which normally played at St Joseph's parish dances. It was an unreasonably joyous occasion with the young colliers singing the popular songs of the day and sometimes breaking into a little jig. Shopkeepers came to their doors and applauded. Wives and children followed behind, with the little boys whose bicycles had still escaped the pawn shop ringing their bells and standing up on their pedals in the hope of seeing the great figures at the head of the column. The great figures included A. J. Cook, who had declined the offer of the white Humber and chosen to march with his men. Being allowed to march in the third rank was little consolation to Brack. When the procession crossed the railway line and the marchers expressed their opinion of the railway union by spitting down on to the track, his anger was not confined to Jimmy Thomas, who had led the still not forgotten desertion of 1912. He was cursing the fate which had, once again, relegated him to the second order of men.

A. J. Cook was welcomed to the Warsop meeting with a great cry which to the accomplished ear was recognisable as the slogan which inspired the striking miners, 'Not a penny off the pay. Not a minute on the day.' They expected him to reply in kind. Instead, he told them the simple truth. If Nottingham and Derby cracked, the battle was lost. The Federation would return to work in shame and the miners would live in poverty for ever. He believed that the tide could be turned, that colliers – the bravest and most sensible men in Britain – could be persuaded to carry on the fight. The first tactic was to stop the tide of returning strikers before it became a flood. He believed it could be done. He paused, and smiled. 'At least, that's what I usually feel. Despite what they say in the *Daily Mail*, I'm human. I have my moods. Sometimes I feel downhearted.'

There was a cry from the far corner of the crowd. 'Enough to make you downhearted, some of these bastards.'

The meeting dissolved in affectionate laughter and Cook bade his members a grateful farewell. Brack was at the side of the platform to applaud him down the steps. But before he had a chance to offer his congratulation on the oratorical triumph an official of the Derbyshire Association caught him by the elbow. 'After Clipstone you're to go

479

back to Shirebrook and get the car. They'll take you in the van. Take the car to Mansfield. After the Nottingham meetings, A. J. wants to go straight back to Chesterfield.'

Brack resented the order but welcomed the opportunity. He decided not to stay at Clipstone, but to make his own way home by bus. As he changed his collar, he barely had time to tell Enid of the important part he was playing in the class struggle before he had to make his way to Mansfield. The stewards outside the town hall looked suspiciously at his three-piece suit and the pointed toes of his highly polished shoes.

'I'm with A. J. Cook.'

They seemed unconvinced. Brack swallowed his pride.

'I'm his driver.'

Grudgingly they let him in.

It was not a happy meeting. Mansfield was a railway town and the miners who were still out on strike felt bitter towards the railwaymen and colliers who had capitulated. Those who had gone back to work hated the irreconcilables with the special hatred that comes from guilt. Cook's claim that ten thousand blacklegs had been shamed into renewed solidarity was greeted with sceptical whistles even by his own supporters. When the meeting was over, he slumped into the back seat of the Humber without a word. Frank Hall, the new General Secretary to the Derbyshire Miners' Association, climbed in beside him.

'Soon as you like,' he said to Brack.

It was not until they got to Shirebrook that Hall realised that they were not on the road to Chesterfield.

'Don't you even know the bloody way? No wonder we can't run a strike if we can't find a driver who knows how to get from Mansfield to Chesterfield.'

'I'm taking you home first for a drink and a bite to eat.'

'No, you're bloody not,' said Hall, leaning over from the back seat.

'Let him, Frank. Longer we keep away from Psaltergate the better. They won't have any good news for us.'

'You'll enjoy the half an hour's rest. It's a nice comfortable place and I've told my daughter to get things ready.'

'That's very good of her,' said Cook.

'She's very keen. Pleased to do it. Very political. There was talk of her going to Ruskin, but she's got a sick mother to look after.'

'We can't stay very long, Arthur. You've got to telephone Wales.'

'I've got a telephone.' Brack congratulated himself on the wisdom of paying his bill rather than allowing it to be disconnected as his finances dictated.

480

The dining-room table was set. The kettle, already filled, stood on the unlit gas ring in the kitchen. There was a bottle of whisky and four glasses on the sideboard. Brack took out the cork.

'Not for me,' said A. J. Cook. 'But I'd like a piece of ham and a pickled onion. I can't remember when I last ate. Can you, Frank?'

'How do you think it's going, Mr Cook?' Brack asked.

'Let him sit quiet. He's had a hard day.'

'Manners, Frank. Our host's entitled to ask his question. Let's put it this way. If you were a gambling man, which I'm sure you're not, I wouldn't back the Federation. Not even for a place, if you know what that means. Nottinghamshire has done for us.'

'It's that bastard Spencer. He's made our home stink.' Frank Hall spoke with the passion of a man betrayed. 'I'd kill the bloody Judas if I could.'

'Will you go on fighting?' Brack asked.

'Whilst there's a chance I will. But it's no good starving women and children . . .'

'For nowt.'

'That's right, Frank, for nowt.'

'Why do you think so many men followed Spencer and went back?' Brack asked, anxious to emphasise his willingness to fight to the bitter end.

'They thought they were scrapping for a few coppers. But they were fighting the class war. The colliery owners know it. They fought like I'd have fought if I'd been on their side. They decided to smash us. Our lads didn't understand.'

Out in the hall Enid was sitting on the stairs. She leaned forward so as to catch every word of the conversation and be ready to dart away when she heard chairs pushed back from the table. Her father had told her, as he had told Agnes, that it was no place for a woman and obediently she had gone up to her bedroom as soon as the car crunched across the yard. But the temptation to hear history being made was too strong to resist and she had tiptoed silently back into the hall.

When Cook decided it was time to go, he stood up without a word and, in a single pace, crossed the room and opened the door. Enid did not even have time to stand up.

'You should have come in.' He spoke over his shoulder as he walked out into the night. 'Your father says you're a great politician.'

'I told you to come and have a cup of tea with us, you soft ha'porth,' said Brack. 'You know how these young girls are, Mr Cook. Won't be told anything. I wanted her in with us.'

'I made the tea,' Enid said.

*

481

There were three shillings left over from the money Brack had given her to buy the special supper and Enid had no intention of returning what she regarded as her profit on the deal. When Brack was safely out of the house she took it upstairs to be added to the other silver that she hoarded, as a squirrel stores nuts to feed it through the winter. She reached up to the top of her wardrobe, where she kept the old purse that was her hiding place. Her savings were gone.

When Brack got back from Chesterfield, Enid was still sitting on the stairs as if she had not moved since he left, but she was holding the old purse in which she had kept her secret savings. It was empty.

Brack greeted her in great humour.

'You still up? Make us a cup of tea, love. What about that, then? Arthur Cook in our dining room.' Then he saw the purse. 'What the bloody hell is that?'

'It's my purse, my old purse, as you know very well. It's the purse you stole the money from.' She threw it on the floor. 'What did you spend it on, horses or women?'

Sitting on the stairs, with her arms wrapped around her knees, she was easily able to duck under her father's swinging fist. So he kicked her. The hard sole of his shoe struck her across the shin and caused such sharp pain that she rolled over on to the hall floor. He kicked her twice more, once in the small of the back and once on the thigh. She lay still, looking at the highly polished, patent-leather shoes and waiting to be kicked again but refusing to cry and wake her mother. There was, she decided, no alternative. Whatever his prospects, Jack O'Hara would have to get her out of this house before the year ended.

CHAPTER THIRTY-EIGHT

Talking

Arranging her escape proved more difficult than Enid had anticipated. She had no doubt that Jack was infatuated with her. It was, after all, no more than the natural reaction of a healthy young man and she had noticed that, when he thought she was not looking at him, he gazed at her with the 'cow's eyes' which young women of the time regarded as the true sign of love. But circumstances – and Jack's retiring nature – conspired against their making formal progress towards engagement and marriage.

On Guy Fawkes' night she persuaded her mother to allow her to wander along to the bonfire which had been built by young Catholics on the waste ground behind St Joseph's Church. She was not surprised to find that Jack had come across from Hucknall or that he immediately elbowed his way towards her. The first rocket of the night burst gold and silver in the sky. Without speaking Enid buried her head in Jack's shoulder in a fair imitation of fear. He had patted her head only twice before a large shadow appeared from around the blazing fire.

'I've got the roast potatoes. They'll be cold if you don't eat them now.' It was Sheila Ferguson. Enid spent the rest of the night listening to an earnest clerk from the station booking office explain why good Catholics like him did not enjoy the celebration of a papist hero's murder.

Enid spent a depressed Christmas Eve and distraught Christmas Day cooking for her father and mother. On Boxing Day, she was to visit Brook House and end her seasonal celebrations with an afternoon spent talking in the fitting room, which had been decorated for Christmas by replacing the bulrushes in the Chinese vase with holly. At the last minute, Brack, who had offered to drive them to Worksop, remembered that he had a job to do and was no longer available. Enid knew that there was no point in arguing and began to prepare her mother for the railway journey. They waited for over an hour at the station, for they had forgotten that the Boxing Day timetable offered only a skeleton service. They were cold and miserable when the train arrived. After ten minutes at the back of the unheated goods van in which the wheelchair was tethered they were frozen and dejected. At Cresswell, Jack O'Hara was standing on the platform.

He did not see the Brackenburys at the end of the train even though Enid leaned out of the window and waved to him with the passionate determination of a guard on a runaway express. But it was all change at Shireoaks and as only three passengers had made the Christmas journey a meeting was unavoidable.

'A merry Christmas,' said the eternally proper young man, '. . . if it's not too late.'

'Where are you off to?' Enid had less patience with the convention.

'Rhodesia. Union's giving a kid's party at the Welfare.'

'I used to go there,' said Agnes. 'I used to go dancing there with your father.' She looked anxiously down the line in the hope of sighting the Sheffield-to-Retford train.

'Thought I might as well give a hand. I'd nothing else to do.'

The train appeared and Enid began to push the wheelchair along the platform. Mick smelled another dog on a porter's barrow. He splayed out his feet and refused to move.

'Let me look after your ma.'

Jack and the guard got Agnes aboard without mishap. The whistle was blown, the green flag waved and the lantern swung.

'Get off, Jack.' Enid was near to being agitated. 'It'll take you to Worksop.'

'I thought I might as well go to Worksop.'

'Well, it's very nice. Very nice to see you,' said Enid. 'And nice to have you help us off at the other end.'

Jack helped. Then he pushed the wheelchair to the barrier. The ticket collector had decorated his cabin for Christmas. Jack took a small piece of mistletoe from behind the hook on which the Sheffield schedules were kept and, holding it over Enid's head, kissed her lightly on the cheek. Then, without a word, he turned on his heel and disappeared into the dusk and steam on the other side of the bridge that crossed the track.

'What's the matter with Mick?' Agnes asked. 'He's fussing and growling as if we've been set on.'

A young woman, barely older than Enid and almost as striking in appearance, sat on a high stool just inside the sitting-room door. She was Hilda King, senior seamstress at Skinner and Harthill and Christmas guest at Brook House. By the afternoon of Boxing Day she had begun bitterly to regret accepting Lottie's invitation.

Lottie had intended only to be kind. The girl's parents were spending Christmas with her brother in Scotland and Hilda, having recently recovered from a mild attack of shingles, felt too debilitated to face the long journey. Lottie could remember what it was like to spend Christmas alone so Miss King – as she was always called in Newcastle Avenue – had been persuaded to leave her lodgings in Bridge Street and move, temporarily, into the attic above the bedroom in which Ginny lay, purple and several times larger than life.

Hilda King longed for Christmas to be over. After the holiday, she would be able to return to her sewing machine and the comparative ease of her normal working day and recover from the hard work of her holiday. But Anne had been unable to think of her as a guest rather than an employee. She had certainly made apologies for her constant demands – 'Your legs are younger than mine . . . I don't want to take my hands out of the stuffing . . . It won't be like Christmas if I'm not downstairs when Agnes gets to the front door.' But demands had been made nevertheless. Miss King had been up and down stairs half a dozen times each hour: carrying Ginny's tray, taking the latest delivery of Christmas cards for her examination and making sure that windows were locked, gas turned off, door closed and all the other safety precautions, by which Anne was obsessed, properly taken. She spent at least ten minutes of every hour searching for Chum, who was never allowed to sleep peacefully in the privacy of the space between the horsehair sofa and the wall. Anne liked the dog to be visible and when he was within sight she expected him to keep up a constant conversation with his owner. 'Look . . . he knows every word I say . . . Can you see him smiling at me . . . He's talking. That's him talking. Saying he wants a little walk.' There was no rest for the dog and no rest for the visitor. In the moments between protecting Chum from the dangers of the brook, walking him down to Beard's Dam and responding to his desire to be scratched, patted and rubbed, Hilda made tea, laid tables, washed pots and dusted furniture. Each instruction was preceded by the request that she 'just . . .' and normally ended with the request that she then 'nip up to make sure Ginny's all right'.

'Is Ern not here?' It was Agnes's first question.

'He's gone back to Steetly. The graves were terrible when he went up last week. He couldn't leave them like that. Get your coat off and we'll have a cup of tea. Hilda—'

Anne did not need to finish the sentence. Hilda was already on her way to the kitchen.

'Is Chum there?'

'He's asleep, Miss Skinner.'

485

He was asleep when Anne called but at the sound of her voice he rose slowly to his feet, scratched his genitals with his hind leg and yawned so extravagantly that it sounded like a cry of anguish. Anne had a favour to ask Enid. She made the request in a confidential whisper.

'Hilda's been cooped up in the house all Christmas. It can't be good for a young girl. Just sitting about the house. Persuade her to go for a little walk. Take Chum and Mick.'

Mick snarled and snapped all the way to Stubbin's Meadows. It was the beginning of his life-long aversion to a dog he clearly believed possessed none of the aggressive instincts of a decent rat-catcher. Hilda made no attempt to protect her amiable charge.

'Have you had a nice Christmas?' she asked.

It was a genuine question but Enid suspected offensive irony. It was necessary to defend family honour.

'Lovely. Best ever. Ate till I nearly burst. Mam made our own mincemeat. She never uses bought.'

'Is it the same as we had?'

'I'm sure it is. Granma's recipe.'

'It was like treacle. All the currants and raisins minced up and mixed with sugar.'

'I've never known anyone who didn't like it.'

'It's probably just me. I've not liked anything this Christmas. It was a kind idea, but it just didn't work. Don't go telling your aunt I said so. I've got to sit behind that sewing machine on Monday morning.'

'Of course I won't. I'm sorry. It must be awful not to enjoy Christmas.'

'Your uncle Ern's a strange one.'

Enid bristled. 'I don't think he's strange. He's a very handsome man, and very well read.'

'He's good-looking but he's interested in such funny things. He talked nearly all Christmas Day about french polishing.'

'That's because he works with wood. Head clerk at Hirst's wood-yard in Retford. It's a very responsible job.'

'Has he been married?'

'Years ago. She died.'

'Marriage doesn't seem to run in your family. Have you got any-body – anybody serious?'

'No,' said Enid firmly.

'Me neither. I had, but we broke it off. Wish we hadn't now. He's getting married on New Year's Day.'

Mick buried his teeth in Chum's left ear. Enid hoped that the confusion of howls and snarls would enable her to change the subject. She had no wish to hear of Hilda's emotional problems and was desperately afraid of being cross-examined about her own. She made the mistake of bending down to separate the dogs. There was nothing to stop Hilda relieving her feelings.

'I never talked to anybody. That was the problem. It wasn't my fault. I didn't really have anybody to talk to. Nobody of my own age, anyway. And you couldn't talk to my dad and mam about things like that. Next time, I'll know better.'

'Next time?' Curiosity overcame caution.

'Well, I'm going to get married one day, aren't you? And there won't be any secret courtships. Unless you talk to people, you don't believe in it yourself. It doesn't seem real. Next time I'm going to tell everybody straight away and the minute he proposes I shall snap his hand off.'

'What if he doesn't propose?' Enid asked.

'I shall propose to him. Women do it these days. Not only in leap year. Women smoke and drink and everything now. At least they do in London. You should hear what goes on at Welbeck. The maids tell us when they come in for fittings. You wouldn't believe some of the goings-on.'

'Well, I wouldn't propose to a man, ever. He'd have to ask me.'

'You won't have to wait long,' said Hilda.

There was an argument when they got back to Brook House about whether or not the mince pies should be heated in the oven. Agnes said it made the crust hard, but Lottie believed that it gave the mincemeat extra taste. Anne said that mince pies were always reheated at Grove Cottage, so the dispute was resolved, as disputes always were, in the interests of the past. Hilda bit, chewed and swallowed with obvious difficulty.

'Have another one, Miss King. I know you like them.'

'No thanks, Miss Harthill. I'm full.'

'An elegant sufficiency,' said Agnes in mock reproof. It was one of her favourite jokes.

'I'm sure you can squeeze one in. After all, it's Christmas.'

'Go on,' said Anne. 'There's plenty in that biscuit tin. Nip into the kitchen and put some more in the oven.'

Hilda ate a second mince pie and then, on Lottie's insistence, a third. Enid watched the slow mastication of each bite with a growing certainty that, when the next right man came along, Miss King – rather than seizing the moment – would wait for him to propose to her.

'Aren't you having another one?' Anne asked.

'No,' said Enid firmly. 'No, I am not.'

She had given herself a year – a year until the following Christmas. She would take the world in her hands and shape it to her will before Boxing Day 1927.

Although Enid did not believe Hilda King's claims to brazen independence, she was profoundly impressed by her advice about talking – an activity which she believed to be much superior to listening. Jack, she felt sure, was on the very edge of declaring his intentions. She proposed to take him over the precipice at St Joseph's New Year dance.

Jack's own preparation for that great event did not go well. Mrs Edna Ferguson had become reconciled with St Philip Neri and was – as a result of her *rapprochement* with the parish priest – prepared to do more at that church than attend mass and make confessions when she was sure that the young assistant priest was on duty. Her complaint against Father Keogh concerned his rage for rebuilding and the consequent emphasis he placed on fund-raising by dubious means. Mrs Ferguson believed that Catholic social events should primarily be concerned with pleasure, and refused, point blank, to cut down on refreshments and decorations to make a bigger profit for the rebuilding fund so she moved in on St Joseph's, organised dances in the old army hut and waited for Father Keogh to come to his senses. When her patience was eventually rewarded she received a handsome apology for past errors, a promise that no future expense would be spared and a desperate request to persuade the jazz band, which usually played at St Joseph's, to transfer its affection to St Philip Neri. Father Keogh's Irish fiddlers had gone home to Cork for the New Year holiday.

Mrs Ferguson agreed and accepted the priest's offer of a dozen free tickets. Father Keogh rightly took it for granted that, if she transferred her loyalties from Shirebrook to Mansfield, her daughters and lodgers would all be expected to shift their allegiance at the same time. Only Jack O'Hara rebelled.

'I shan't go to St Philip's. I shall go to Shirebrook.'

'But Sheila's got to come with me. If I'm taking over the refreshments, I'll need her in Mansfield.'

'Look, Mrs F., there's something that you don't understand. Sheila does. I thought that she'd explained.'

'Well, she hasn't.'

So Jack O'Hara explained there and then. He did not tell Mrs Ferguson of his intention to marry Enid Brackenbury – indeed, he left her with the firm impression that he proposed to remain single

488

and celibate all his life – but at least she lost her illusions about him marrying Sheila, and that, in itself, was an act of peculiar bravery. He found his first excursion into heroism so rewarding that on the following Saturday – when the gramophone broke down and the dance at St Joseph's was abandoned – he invited Enid for a walk and, having kissed her twice, told her that he loved her.

The love affair did not progress at the speed which Enid anticipated. Jack kissed her, moderately passionately, each Saturday, danced with her often enough to encourage coy jokes amongst the other dancers, took her to the cinema in Langold or Clowne whenever the picture houses were showing something suitable and occasionally invited himself to tea at 11 Langwith Road. But he never spoke of their future together. She decided to clear her mind by taking Hilda King's advice and talking about him. She began with her mother.

'Can Jack come over to tea on Sunday, Mam?'

'Not Sunday, love. You've forgotten. That's the day I go to Sheffield to see the specialist. If he doesn't do something about this pain, I don't know how I'll manage.'

'Sunday, Mam. Not Monday. We go to Sheffield on Monday.'

'Have you arranged for a car? You know your dad won't take us in the end. He says he will and then, ten minutes before it's time to go, he changes his mind.'

'It's all arranged, Mam. Father Froes is going to drive us. He's got to go to Sheffield on Monday and Dad's going to lend him the new Morris. He won't let Father Froes down, so we'll get a lift. But that's Monday, Mam. I want Jack to come round on Sunday.'

'Monday, yes, I know. It can't come too quickly for me. It's my neck now. Can you get me an aspirin, love?'

Enid decided that a frank discussion with Anne and Lottie might prove more helpful. On the following Thursday, when lunch was finished at Brook House, she announced that there would be no visit to the library that afternoon – a decision of such significance that it seemed certain to alert her aunts to her disturbed state of mind. Within minutes of the table being cleared and the dishes washed and dried, Agnes fell asleep in her wheelchair. Enid decided to insinuate the subject into conversation. Lottie provided the opportunity.

'We've not made you anything for months. Have a look at the spring fashion books.'

'I want a new tennis dress. I'm going to play a lot this year.'

'You seemed to play a lot last year.' Anne suspected that tennis was enjoyable.

'We like you to play tennis,' Lottie insisted. 'It's so nice for your mother. She loves sitting there watching.'

'On fine days,' Anne added. She had often warned them both about the risks of pneumonia.

The time had come for a subtle change of direction.

'I expect I shall be playing a lot of mixed doubles next summer.'

'Is that wise, love?' Lottie seemed worried.

'Why not?'

'Because it might not be fair.' Anne was surprised by the question.

'Not fair in what way?'

'To the young men. I said to Lottie before Christmas when your mother told us about all these dances you go to. I said to Lottie, it isn't fair to the young men.'

'They might get ideas. That's why they go to dances in the first place. As Anne said when we talked about it, even with Aggie sitting there they might not realise about you.'

'Realise what, for heaven's sake? I've not got anything that's catching.'

'Realise that you couldn't leave her . . . if he ever . . . or you ever . . . if ever anything happened. Well, you're not free, are you? Girls who go to dances are not usually . . . usually, they're free.'

Lottie, realising the pain her partner was causing, offered a few words of comfort. 'Not that you're interested in that sort of thing. You're far too sensible. We know that.'

Enid decided that her only hope was to ask the advice of the wisest man she knew. Owen Ford would treat her like an adult.

'I can't see you settling down with a Catholic.'

'He isn't much of one. It's what he was born to, that's all.'

'And you'll convert him, will you? Convert him to socialism?'

'He votes Labour now. And he's very active in the union. You know that.'

'I'll tell you what to do. Tell him you're going to Ruskin and you'll be away for a year. That ought to force him into something, though I'm not sure what.'

She could not believe that Owen was laughing at her.

'I couldn't do that. I couldn't tell him a lie. Anyway, he wouldn't believe me. He knows I wouldn't leave Mam. He's got to help me to look after her.'

'I think you better let things take their own time. Have you heard about Percy? He's going to Moscow, for a month. Russians are paying for everything, lucky sod.'

It was the first time that Enid had heard Owen swear. It was, she decided, a sign of the emotion he felt at the thought of his brother's absence.

Enid, although annoyed by the absence of acceptable advice, was consoled by the joy of possessing an item of exciting news. When she got home, her father was in the yard examining a dent in the mudguard of his new Morris. She could not wait to ask him the sort of question that always irritated him.

'Do you know what Owen Ford just told me?'

'I'm hardly likely to, am I?'

'Percy Ford's going to Russia.'

'And I hear you've got something planned yourself.'

'What do you mean?'

'I hear you're thinking of settling down.'

'What?'

'Don't be clever with me. Father Froes told me.'

'Told you what?'

'That red-faced Paddy told the priest at Mansfield that he's going to marry you.'

'I don't believe you. He wouldn't do that.' Enid was too startled to resent the description.

'Well, he did. Had to, didn't he? You've got to turn Catholic. The Mansfield priest asked Father Froes if he'd do it.'

CHAPTER THIRTY-NINE
Instructions

If Brack had understood the Irish, he would not have been surprised to learn that the parish priest knew more about Jack O'Hara's intentions than had been confided to the intended herself. Jack O'Hara was twenty-seven and – his attitude to life being essentially rural Irish – he believed himself to be far too young for marriage. There were no wild oats to sow. He was born to settle down, but there were conventions to be observed as he approached that happy state. The idea of being married whilst still in his twenties was, like the thought of signing the pledge or being cremated, beyond his powers of comprehension.

True to the Irish tradition, he also believed in making an early decision about which young lady was to be kept waiting whilst youth and hope slowly died. Because he thought of himself as a gentleman, he decided that Enid's long wait would be graced with a ring and the title of engagement.

The thought that she might not want to marry him had briefly disturbed his methodical plan when he saw her, evidently happy in her own company, as she walked her little terrier out of Shirebrook towards Scarcliffe. Then, when he touched her on the shoulder, she started, turned and blushed and he remembered what a catch he was and that half the girls in the district, Catholics and Protestants alike, longed to join him on church walks or meet him inside the picture house. And he had never been so conspicuously gallant with them as he invariably was with Enid – walking her home even when he was really going in a different direction, taking off the jacket of his second-best suit for her to sit on when they visited Clumber Park and fetching and carrying for her wherever they were together. Enid's progressive reputation was the cause of his second sudden panic. She was not a Catholic. Then he remembered that her error in being born into a heretic family could, with the grace of God and the co-operation of the parish priest, easily be rectified. He consulted Father Keogh at St Philip Neri in

492

Mansfield, who passed him on to Father Froes in Shirebrook, where Enid lived but did not intend to worship.

The telephone call from Mansfield to Shirebrook was made within ten minutes of Jack O'Hara leaving the presbytery, and Father Froes sat down in front of his fire to consider not so much the implications of the message as how even a fool like Father Keogh could have made such a mistake. It was, he believed, inconceivable that Enid Brackenbury would ever consider marrying an Irishman and he did not intend to behave like an idiot by suggesting that she had. He had a low opinion of the Irish, whom – with the exception of Edmund Burke and the Duke of Wellington – he believed to be boneheads. Enid he heartily disliked because of her pretension. He could not imagine disdain and stupidity coming together in holy matrimony.

The more he thought of Enid becoming Mrs O'Reilly or O'Brien the more improbable the idea seemed. That, he decided, absolved him from any obligation to keep the story confidential. He would dispose of the matter by telling Brack about the silly tale which was being told about his daughter. He convinced himself that it was his duty to scotch the rumour. Later that day, he drove his new Morris down to 11 Langwith Road feeling a malicious pleasure at the thought of the embarrassment which he was to inflict on Brack.

Brack was in the yard supervising the bagging of coal. When he saw the priest draw up he walked across to the petrol pump which was his latest bad investment. Without being asked, he began to fill the priest's tank, pumping away with vigour for vigour's sake. After a couple of pulls on the handle, petrol sprayed over his trousers and shoes. Brack swore.

'Sorry.' Father Froes was grinning. 'I got filled up earlier. I didn't realise.'

'If you're amused somebody must be in real trouble.' Brack doubted if his shoes would ever recover.

'How's your daughter?' It was not a question Brack expected.

'Fine. Health's fine. Still all airs and graces, as you know well. Still all books and half-baked theories. But her health's all right.'

'Is she courting?'

'Why, have you got your eye on her?'

'I've never thought much of your sense of humour. Father Keogh at Mansfield says she wants to take instruction. Says she wants to be baptised.'

'That's bloody rubbish. Must be. She hates Catholics. Always has done since she used to go and read to that cripple in Shirebrook. All

493

of them there went on and on about the religion and the damage it does . . .'

'Well, according to Father Keogh, she wants to marry a Catholic. He says that she wants to take instruction and come into the Church.' Father Froes waited for an explosion of anger or amusement.

'I'm not surprised by anything the silly bitch does. She's playing games. She's playing games with herself. She probably believed it when she said it, when she said she'd marry him. But I'll bet my bottom dollar that she doesn't mean it now.'

'What about the instruction?'

'That's for you to decide. I wouldn't waste my time. I'd tell her to bugger off. It's not worth talking about. Have you come up here just to tell me this daft story? And I thought you'd come with a good tip.'

'I'll give you one. Speak to that daughter of yours.'

'I'll talk to her mother first. I'll get more sense out of her.'

'Turn the engine over, will you, Brack?' Father Froes offered him the starting handle.

'Sorry, I've got to clean the petrol off my shoes.'

Father Froes took Brack's advice. His refusal to give Enid immediate instruction was not couched in the language her father had recommended. He simply asked her to wait for a little while and think very carefully about her intentions. When Enid told Jack that the instruction was not to begin at once, Jack told Father Keogh and Father Keogh explained to the Bishop. It was, Bishop Dunn told his secretary, at least possible that Father Froes's refusal to give instruction to this young woman in Shirebrook was attributable to nothing worse than a sudden attack of excessive piety. Bishop Dunn was notorious throughout his diocese for his ability to see virtue where others recognised sin. In some men, it would have been an endearing quality. But Bishop Dunn, immense and perpetually smiling, seemed to be challenging the world to dent his moral complacency. And the rest of the world found the challenge difficult to resist.

'But, my lord, he burst in here spoiling for a fight. I'd never heard about this woman until he more or less accused Father Keogh of "peaching on him", whatever that may be.'

'That's the problem with being educated at a Protestant public school. We escaped that and we ought to be sympathetic towards those who were not similarly blessed. He seems to think that Father Keogh told tales about him.'

'My lord, do you think that Father Froes should have some sort of medical help?'

'He needs help, Thomas, but not of the medical variety. He needed help years ago and nobody provided any.'

'You're very charitable, my lord. But he's not had a bad life out there in Shirebrook. And it's a life of his own making.'

'What chance did he have out there in that Godforsaken . . . that desolate little village? My predecessor, God rest his soul, was a saintly and gallant man, but what did he know about places like Shirebrook? Stuck a pin in a map, I wouldn't be surprised.'

At such moments, the secretary had no idea how he should behave. If he agreed with the Bishop's strictures he was likely to be denounced as a whited sepulchre when his lordship made one of his sudden shifts of moral direction. If, on the other hand, he immediately defended those whom the Bishop had denounced, he was guilty of the sin of presumption. Since he never ever considered saying what he really thought he was almost driven to make an apology for earlier errors. Bishop Dunn himself solved the dilemma.

'The poor man now wants to retire.'

'Indeed, my lord. That was the purpose of his visit.'

'Wish I could let him. But he'll have to soldier on for another year. He'll have to stay until the new man is ready and he won't be for another year. I've chosen him already.'

The Bishop's secretary did not reply. But he hoped that the priest who was sent to Shirebrook would possess an iron constitution, an inner security and a private income. He feared that he would be one of the young men from the diocese whom the Bishop was in the habit of picking out in boyhood and preparing for the priesthood like caged linnets which are blinded in infancy so that, being denied light, they sing to defy the dark.

'We'll not get in now.'

Jack O'Hara stood on the edge of the pavement and looked petulantly over Enid's shoulder at the line of hopeful cinema-goers which stretched, two abreast, from the foyer of the Regent Picture House down Sherwood Street, curled round the bank on the corner and disappeared into Walton Terrace.

'Why didn't you get into the queue? You'd have been inside by now.' Enid did not readily accept blame.

'I was afraid to miss you. Anyway, it was halfway down the road an hour ago when I went past.'

'Then we wouldn't have got in, anyway. We should have come earlier.'

'I didn't know how late you'd be. For all I knew, your mother had been taken bad again and you wouldn't come at all.'

'You should have come with me. You should have got the same train.'

'I told you, I couldn't. If I told you once, I told you twenty times. I had to be here at four o'clock.'

A commissionaire, wearing more gold braid than an Admiral of the Fleet and a peaked cap several sizes too big for him, began to shout, 'Can you keep close to the wall, please. Don't block the pavement, please. We'll be moving in a moment.'

'We won't get in,' said Enid. 'We might as well go home.'

'It's worth a try.'

'We've wasted ten minutes arguing. The queue will be twice as long now.'

A busker began to sing, further whetting already lively appetites.

> 'There's a rainbow round my shoulder
> And it fits me like a glove . . .'

Enid smiled, hummed and turned to Jack. 'I would like to see it. Let's see.'

They ran to the back of the queue and were at first immensely comforted by the arrival of other couples who, despite having less chance than they, still hoped for a seat in the second house. Jack noticed that the other couples faced the ordeal of waiting with cheerful fortitude.

'What's the time?' he asked.

It was almost seven o'clock. They had still an hour to wait. Enid moved restlessly from foot to foot. The strap which held her left shoe in place cut into her instep and the toes of her left foot were crushed in the tight leather of a new shoe. Yet she was restless not because she was uncomfortable but because she was bored. And she still had an hour to wait before the performance began.

'Do you know how much the train fare cost . . . ?'

Enid did not expect Jack to know the answer. The enquiry was a conversational device she had picked up from her mother. It was intended as a bridging passage between a comment and the unrelated assertion which followed it. The rhetorical question was also meant to emphasise the importance of what followed and, by eliciting a grunt or nod, confirm that the listener was still attentive.

'It cost me almost four shillings to come to the pictures! Two and five for the railway and—'

'You haven't got in yet. And if you do, I'll buy your ticket. Don't cry before you're hurt.'

'If you don't want to pay for me I can pay for myself.' Enid was already fumbling in her bag but, although it contained the return half of a third-class return between Nottingham and Shirebrook Junction, it did not hold one and sixpence.

'Now, did I say that? In the name of mercy, what's got into you this evening?'

The busker had worked his way back to the rear end of the queue.

'I'm sitting on top of the world
Just rolling along.
Just rolling along.'

He attempted a tap dance, but the flapping sole of his shoe made him stumble. The more jovial members of his audience applauded and he took advantage of his brief popularity to remove his greasy cap and hold it out in what he believed to be an appealing gesture. Jack threw him a threepenny bit.

'What did you do that for?' Enid sounded outraged.

'It's only threepence.'

'When I think what I have to do to save threepence. I walk a mile to save a penny on the groceries. And you just throw your money away.'

Jack decided that changing the subject was better than arguing. 'It said in the paper that thirty-three ladies' handkerchiefs were found in the picture house after the first show.'

Enid sniffed. But Jack had yet to tell the whole extraordinary story. 'All of them were wringing wet with tears.' Not even the second sniff could dampen his enthusiasm. 'A woman from Arnold cried for three days without stopping . . . and a man from Bulwell wrote to Jolson offering to send his kids to America for adoption to make up for the one he lost.'

'It sounds stupid to me.'

'It's the magic of motion pictures.' Jack intended no irony. He spoke with awe and wonder. Enid giggled but his enthusiasm could not be crushed. 'And talkies in particular. The miracle of sound.'

'It'll be a miracle if we get in.'

Jack, dispirited at last, fell silent and Enid began to describe the plot, characters and particular fascination of *The Moon and Sixpence*. She set out the story in meticulous detail, correcting herself if she detected the slightest error in her narrative, returning to descriptions she feared were inadequate and emphasising, by repetition, points of particular interest. There was still half of the book to go when the commissionaire reappeared, Mons Star rattling against Victory Medal.

'Move along now, please. Move along. Have your money ready, please. Correct change if possible. Stalls to the right when you get inside. Circle to the left.'

They shuffled to the foot of the cinema steps and were actually within the pool of light which spilled out of its swing doors when the commissionaire held out an officious hand.

'Bugger all.' Jack had not meant to say it but it slipped out.

It seemed to Enid that every man and woman on the steps in front of them turned round and stared. She was suddenly filled with anger. 'If we hadn't stood there arguing, we would have been inside by now.'

She spoke in what she believed was a voice so quiet that only Jack could hear. He replied, in his usual Irish boom, 'If you'd have got here on time we'd have been inside ten minutes since.'

No sooner had he said it than he realised that retaliation was a mistake. Enid always won every argument for she would say anything, no matter how disparate and damaging, to confound her enemies. So he conciliated.

'Let's not argue about it, love. We'll go and have a cup of tea somewhere.' He did not think that his offer of a truce would be accepted but waited for the blow to fall, wincing in anticipation of both her assault and the sensation it would cause around them.

The commissionaire reappeared. 'We can take another fourteen.' He counted methodically. Jack was number ten, Enid eleven.

She did not cry, even when Al Jolson sang 'Sonny Boy'. Nor did she marvel at the magic of talking pictures. She scratched, shuffled her feet, wriggled in her seat and leaned down so often to make sure that the shoes she had kicked off were still within reach that even the concentration of the old lady behind her was broken. When the old lady's husband tapped her on the shoulder, she sank down into her seat and hoped that Jack would notice she was not watching the screen. Halfway through 'Mammy', Jack began to tap his feet and, emboldened as well as excited by the rhythm, he reached out surreptitiously for Enid's hand. When his fingers touched hers, she first clenched her fist and then ostentatiously folded her arms.

They stood to rigid attention for 'God Save the Queen'. Men in the audience who had forgetfully replaced their hats removed them again, hoping that their treason had not been noticed. As they pushed their way out, Jack looked on the floor for abandoned, tear-soaked hand-kerchiefs.

'Well, we've done it. We've seen a talkie.'

'I don't think much to it.'

'I thought Al Jolson was great. Did you know that he's married to Ruby Keller? There was a picture of them in the paper. Jolson had a trilby on with a big wide brim. I'm going to try and get one.'

They walked on towards the station. Enid was silent. It was, Jack knew, always a bad sign. He cursed his luck that this night, of all nights, should be ending so badly. It was, however, too late to change his plans.

'Have you got time for a cup of tea at the station?'

She walked into the buffet without speaking and sat down in the deserted far corner of the dingy room. As Jack walked over to the counter and waited to be served he felt for the little package in his jacket pocket. It contained the ring he had bought that afternoon. By the time he had carried the tea back to Enid, he had still not decided whether to take it out with a flourish or press it secretly into her hand under cover of the stained tablecloth. He had not taken the greaseproof paper from under his cupcake before she asked him the question.

'What about this priest?'

'What about what priest?'

'Don't treat me as if I'm stupid. You know what I mean.'

'I swear to God I don't.'

'The priest you told I was going to turn Catholic. The priest who's going to teach me how to kneel down and cross myself and bow in front of the altar.'

'Who told you about that?'

'My father.'

'Who's your father? Do you mean Father Froes?'

'I mean my father, stupid. I mean my dad. He knows. Father Froes told him that I was going to marry you. Nobody told me. But you told some priest in Mansfield and he told Father Froes. So what have you to say for yourself?'

'I don't know what all the fuss is about. I had to ask him, with you not being a Catholic. Father Froes shouldn't have told your dad, I'll give you that. But I had to make sure it was all right before I asked you.'

'And it's agreed, is it? You've got permission, have you?'

'Yes, it's easy enough done. You take instruction – that's where Father Froes comes in. You're one of his parishioners – or will be after you've been baptised. There's nothing to stop us.'

'So that's all right, then?'

Jack was immensely relieved. He prepared to bring the ring into play. After all, his day had been a complete success. He had bought what looked like a diamond ring, he had seen Al Jolson in *The Jazz Singer* and he was about to become officially engaged to be married.

'Yes. You've nothing to worry about.'

499

'I haven't, but you have.'

'What do you mean?'

'I mean that you haven't proposed and that when you do I won't accept.'

'What, in the Name of God, has got into you?' He looked round furtively, fearing that his raised voice would carry to the other passengers on the far side of the buffet. 'I've always taken for granted—'

'Perhaps you have, but I haven't.'

At last the worm turned. 'If you feel like that, why did you come to the pictures? You were happy enough to come to the pictures.'

'You are so stupid. I wasn't happy listening to all that tripe and stopping you pawing me in public. I was just happier than I would have been at home, worrying about m'mam, worrying about money and worrying about where m'dad was. I wish I hadn't come now. I shouldn't have left her in the first place. She'll have been on her own for four hours or more.'

'I never pawed you . . . I wouldn't.'

'And another thing. I came so that I could have it out with you. I wanted to get it straight.'

'To punish me, more likely.'

'You deserved it.'

They boarded the train in silence. It was, as Enid had predicted, crowded and she chose to squeeze between giggling girls rather than sit close to him. They rumbled on through the mining towns – Eastwood, Seiston, Kirkby-in-Ashfield. As they pulled into Mansfield, she willed him to get out and leave her to travel on alone to Shirebrook Junction. He did not move.

He handed her down from carriage to platform with his usual careful courtesy and they walked out of the station side by side. He offered her his arm and she decided that it would be more wounding to ignore him than to refuse so he trudged on with his hands in his pockets. He could feel the ring-box bouncing against his knuckles.

When Brack told his wife that Enid was planning to turn Catholic and run away to Ireland, he intended to do no more than enjoy the brief pleasure of her momentary panic. He expected her to shriek with anguish, beg him to tell her that it was not true and then say that he must hate her very much to torture her with such obvious relish. If his plan had worked, as he had intended, the evening's entertainment would have been over in ten minutes and he would have been warm in bed chuckling with pleasure at the memory of his escapade.

At first Agnes did not seem to understand his message. She was sitting hunched and half asleep in her wheelchair waiting for Enid to return home and help her to bed when Brack woke her up with a start which rattled her spine and sent flashes of pain through her elbows, wrists and knees.

'Is she there? Tell her to come in straight away. I should have been upstairs two hours since.'

'She's still out. Out with that man I was telling you about.'

'Which man?'

'I've told you. That red-faced Paddy old enough to be her father.'

'No, you haven't. I thought she was at the pictures with Jack O'Hara.' Agnes did not recognise Brack's caricature.

'That's him. She's going to marry him. The priest told me. She's going to turn Catholic and then they're off to Ireland.'

Agnes screamed. At first, it was very much the scream that Brack expected but it went on and on. Then, when it seemed that Agnes was trying to hold it back, she began to choke. She coughed, spluttered, retched and attempted to swallow. Her face turned purple and the veins in her neck began to swell. Brack, believing that she was going to suffocate, slapped her on the back.

The second scream was shorter and louder than the first. It also ended more spectacularly. Agnes slipped to the front of the wheelchair seat and then slumped to the kitchen floor. She lay before the fire. Her left leg twitched with a macabre regularity and her face, which had drained from purple to grey, was no longer ribbed by bulging veins. Brack decided that she was not dead but dying. He bent down and tried to pick her up without having any idea of what he would have done with the twisted body which had so suddenly lost all its sharp rigidity and lay, on the pegged rug, like a half-full sack of potatoes. Before he could take firm hold, the kitchen door opened and Enid walked in. Afterwards, he often wondered if it was the sound of her footsteps or the sudden draught of cold night air which revived his wife. Whatever the cause, the result was instantaneous and extraordinary. She struggled to sit up, failed, struggled again, and then cried out, 'Don't hit me again. Please, don't hit me again. I beg you, don't.'

Enid leaped at her father. She beat him on the chest with both fists, and used all her weight to push him away from her mother. Brack staggered back, astonished at her fury.

'Keep away,' said Enid. 'Just keep away.' She reached theatrically for the poker. 'Don't you come near her, that's all.' Brack did no more than steady himself on his feet. 'Just you dare. Just you try to hit her again, that's all.'

'Don't be so bloody silly. I never touched her.'

Life stirred on the pegged rug.

'He did. He knocked me out of the chair.'

'If you've any bloody sense you'll get her up. If you leave her there whilst you argue with me, she'll roast to death if nothing else.'

Agnes, made suddenly aware that she was within a few inches of the blazing fire, rolled away from the hearth.

'Don't move, Mam. We'll get you up.' Enid turned to her father. 'If you try anything . . .'

Brack, even at that moment of crisis, could not prevent himself from speculating about what his daughter feared that he might try. None of the possibilities he considered proved convincing. But when he grasped Agnes under the arms and she screamed again at his touch, Enid looked at him as if to warn him that she would not give him a second chance.

'You come and get hold here. I'll take her feet.'

Agnes screamed again when he touched her feet, but by that time Enid had pulled her halfway up. They lifted her back into the wheel-chair. Agnes moaned and her head, usually so stiff on her neck, lolled down on to her chest.

'Wouldn't it be better to lay her down?'

'That just shows how much you know.' Enid told him. 'That just proves how interested you have ever been. She doesn't even lie down at night. I prop her up in bed every night and you don't even know. And you're supposed to be her husband.' Enid was rubbing her mother's neck.

'Are you really marrying an Irishman? Are you really going to Ireland and leaving me with him?'

There had been a second miraculous recovery. But the remission was brief. Enid, without answering the question, rubbed on. Agnes's eyes closed and Brack, believing that he saw her tongue begin to poke out of her lolling mouth, was afraid for the second time that she was dead.

'It were just a joke. I didn't think she'd believe it. I just said it . . . said it to hear what she'd . . . say.'

'Say you're not.' Agnes still looked like a corpse, but she spoke with a conviction born of desperation. It was an order. But it was an order which Enid did not obey.

'Get her a drop of brandy.'

Brack hurried away in search of a glass.

'A cup will do,' Enid told him. 'I hear you all drink out of cups in Cobbler Jack's.'

'For Christ's sake, don't be so smart.'

Agnes groaned. The profanity had penetrated her stupor.

502

'Shouldn't we get a doctor?' Brack asked. 'She looks pretty bad to me.'

'I've seen her like this dozens of times. Not because she was knocked on to the floor. Though I doubt if it's the first time . . .'

Agnes's head was held back and the glass, pressed to her lips, was gently spilling a tiny rivulet of brandy across her cheek and down her jaw.

'She's not getting any.'

'It's the fumes that revive her. Like smelling salts. You get out. I don't want you to be the first thing she sees when she comes round.'

Agnes watched him make his anxious way across the room. She only opened one eye. But it followed him step by step to the door and stared unblinking at his back until the latch fell into place. Then she sighed and seemed, for a moment, to fall asleep.

'Are you really going to go to Ircland?'

''Course not, Mam.'

'Then why did he say it?'

'You know him. He said it to hurt you. He likes causing us both pain.'

'Can I have another sip of brandy? Don't go to the kitchen. What's left in the glass will do.' She drank the last drop and ran her tongue over her dry lips. 'You really mean it. You'll really not go to Ireland . . . ?'

'Not to Ireland or anywhere, Mam. He made it up.'

'He wouldn't have just made it up, love. There must be something in it.' Agnes was half asleep.

Enid pulled the wooden footstool from the side of the fire and put it so close against the side of the wheelchair that when she sat down the tartan rug which she had spread across Agnes's legs covered her own knees and kept her warm as the fire slowly died. She sat, without moving, for more than two hours, and waited for her mother to wake. Agnes, as always, talked in her sleep and Enid – who spent the start of most nights sitting by her side – tried, as always, to follow the ramblings about the old times which increasingly obsessed her. It was two o'clock before Agnes woke and Enid, try though she did to put the idea to the back of her mind, could not help thinking that her mother would doze her way through half of the following day whilst she cooked her father's breakfast and cleaned the house, made the dinner and performed all the other tasks which were her daily routine.

'It's turned cold. The fire's gone out. Are we still in the kitchen? You should have got me upstairs before now.'

Enid accepted the rebuke without argument and began the hauling and pushing necessary to get her mother up to the bedroom.

503

'I shan't be able to do this much longer. Whatever your dad says, I'll have to put up a bed downstairs.'

'One more heave, Mam, and we'll be on the landing.'

'Did I dream it or did your dad talk about you going off to Ireland?'

'That's what he said. It isn't true.'

''Course not. Did I fall out of the chair?'

'You were on the floor when I got home. Dad was trying to get you up.' Enid was so tired that she was not sure herself of what had happened.

'There was something I wanted to tell you. Something very important. But I've forgotten what it was.'

'Tell me tomorrow, Mam. You'll remember in the morning. Come on. Just put your arm up a bit whilst I get your dress off.'

'I've remembered. It's the butcher in the Cut.'

'Yes, Mam.'

'The dog. The dog you got for him, a sort of lurcher. Great scraggy thing.'

'Yes, Mam. I remember. If you don't keep still I'll never undo these little buttons.'

'He starves it. It's locked up all day in the little yard behind the shop. You can hear it crying. And he hits it. The poor thing's terrified.'

'Yes, Mam.'

'Did your dad really say that you were going to marry a red-faced old man?'

'Yes, Mam. But he isn't old or red-faced. That's Dad being nasty.'

'Just trying to upset me. I remember now. He said you were going to get married and you said you weren't.'

'No, Mam. I never said that.'

Ernest Skinner sat in the window of his undecorated drawing room and peered over and round the piles of furniture which stood in the places they had occupied since they had been brought from Grove Cottage. Anne – half hidden behind a glass-fronted cupboard, which should have been stood against a wall – sat in her father's old rocking chair and braced her feet against the floorboards to make sure that it did not rock. Agnes lay along a horsehair sofa. Lottie perched on the edge of a blanket chest which had been on its way to the front bedroom for over ten years. Enid, in her best dress, had pulled back the dirty dust sheet that covered a shabby armchair and, having almost been choked by the cloud of dust she released, had chosen to lean against the wooden form of the exposed arm, after polishing it vigorously with her handkerchief. She hoped that she had retained her natural poise

– despite being the first item on the agenda of the family meeting.

Ernest had initially enjoyed the prospect of presiding. He was the undoubted head of the family yet he had not been asked to exercise any sort of authority over it since his father had died intestate and he had been asked to adjudicate at the division of the furniture. He hoped that Anne did not feel resentful that he had taken his share of the better items and then left them shut up in his unused front room. The way in which she stared at the mahogany console table – the proudest of his parents' possessions – had raised the first doubt in his mind about the wisdom of assuming his responsibilities. He leaned forward, making the bentwood legs creak beneath him, and said, 'Now, Enid, what are we to do about all this?'

'It's simple enough. I'm getting married. I'm not sure when. Now I'm engaged to be married.' The little *savoir faire* which had survived the concentrated attention of the other women vanished and she began to cry. 'It's normal enough. It's what girls do. I don't know why . . .' She was about to say 'it's anyone else's business'. Then she remembered that everything that she and her mother had ever done had always been Anne's and Ernest's business.

'Most other girls don't have crippled mothers.' Anne nodded at the end of her sentence to confirm that she had said the last word on the subject.

'And fathers who—'

'Wait a minute, Lottie.' Ernest asserted his command. 'We'll talk about that when all this has been decided.'

'It has been decided.' Enid, though still weeping, was defiant. 'And I'll tell you this. It's the best thing for Mam as well as for me.'

Enid could not believe that they could be so stupid. She could not tell them that marriage to Jack O'Hara was to be escape – for her and for her mother. Surely they must understand? They could not believe that Jack was the love of her life. Jack was respectable and gentle and they would live gentle and respectable lives together. But did any of them really believe that she would have settled for gentle respectability had it not been for her father and the bruises on her back? If they had told her that she ought to do better than marry an Irish collier she would have understood because she would have agreed. And if they had said that it was wrong even to consider becoming a Catholic she would have known that they were right. But they did not want her to wait and make a better choice – a match worth her looks and her intelligence – they did not want her to get married at all. They did not love her or they would not expect her to shrivel into lonely middle age. They were stupid, for marriage to Jack

O'Hara was escape from Brack for her mother as well and, although she could not say it, they ought to understand.

'You know that I'll take Mam with me.'

'You say that now but . . .' Anne could not bring herself to describe what would really happen. 'And I'm sure you mean it.'

'So does Jack.' Enid turned to her mother. 'He wants to look after you.'

'He hardly knows her.' Anne did not mean to imply that a better acquaintance would cause Jack to change his mind.

'Men say these things at first.' Lottie was sorry to see Enid suffering. 'And he probably means them today. But in six months' time . . .'

'What if there was a baby on the way?' Agnes was genuinely concerned about Enid being able to lift and push whilst she was pregnant, but Anne looked at the carpet as if they had been shamed by a lewd joke.

'Mam, whatever happens, we'll look after you. Better than you're being looked after now.'

Ernest looked his niece in the eye for the first time. 'Will you do it, Enid, if your mother asks you not to? If we all advise you against and your mother asks, begs, you not to leave her?'

'I'm not leaving her, Uncle. I tell you she'll come.'

'Very well. That's clear enough. You're going to do it, sooner or later.'

He took out the notebook in which he had made a thousand calculations of the price of living timber. Once upon a time it had gone in his Gladstone bag with the sovereign balance, the bradawl and the folding ruler with the brass hinge. These days, he carried it in his jacket pocket. The indelible pencil was as sharp as ever.

'Five hundred pounds. That accounts for five hundred pounds.'

'Whatever for?' asked Anne.

'She'll need something to get started. From all I hear, this Mr O'Hara won't have any money. We'll talk about your contribution in a minute. Now, let's move on to the next subject. This young woman. Is she really . . . er . . . you know?'

'Not now she isn't.' Enid was much recovered.

'Was she ever?'

Anne did not wait for her sister to confirm that the girl had been pregnant. She swept out of the room expecting Lottie to follow rather than stay and have her ears defiled by such conversation. Lottie sat tight, fascinated by Ernest's cross-examination.

'And she asked for two hundred?'

'Two hundred and fifty.' Agnes was surprised that he had forgotten.

506

'She'll settle for a hundred, you mark my words. Who's going to offer it to her?'

'I'll do it,' said Enid. 'Nobody else will. I'll have to.'

Ernest made another entry in his notebook. 'Now about the business . . .'

'The business is doing well enough.'

'Not as well as it would do, Mam, if he worked at it properly.'

'Then why doesn't he buy the girl off himself? He did that last time,' Ernest asked.

'He thinks he can blackmail Mam and me. Why should he raise the money somewhere else if he thinks that we'll get the money from you?'

'Well, that's it, then. When do you think the wedding will be?'

'Not for a long time yet.' Enid felt a sudden panic. 'We haven't thought about where to live or anything.'

'Have you told your father? Does he know it's definite?'

'I've not had a chance. We haven't talked about much except that girl since she knocked on the front door last week.'

'You better tell him. He is your father – whatever he's done.'

Enid told her father that night after she had put her mother to bed. She decided that the news about buying the girl's silence could wait. Brack would be indifferent to Ernest's generosity for he would not mind if all Shirebrook knew that he had made a young woman, less than half his age, pregnant. But her decision to get married would, in a strange way, worry him. The cause of his concern was too complex for her to understand but she looked forward to watching his look of disturbed surprise.

'Is it because of me – because of me and that girl?'

''Course not. I decided weeks ago.'

'Well, if it is you're more stupid than I thought. And I'd be sorry to think of you throwing yourself away on account of me.'

'It's nothing to do with it.'

'I can't see it myself. You're a clever young woman and a good-looking one. Last year you were wanting to go to Ruskin College. This, you're going to marry a red-faced Paddy collier.'

'Not this year, Dad. Next. Or perhaps the year after. And don't be daft. You know he's not like that.'

She was pleased by the flattery and, had the conversation ended there, father and daughter would have ended the evening feeling something like affection for each other. But it was not in Brack's nature to kiss Enid goodnight and go contentedly to bed.

'I suppose you need the two years for the lessons.'

'What are you talking about?'

507

'Don't start playing daft all over again. You know what lessons. The lessons to teach you how to be a Catholic.'

'They're not lessons.'

'Froes says they are. Takes them very seriously. That's why he made you wait till you were certain. He doesn't think you really believe in wine turning into blood and biscuits into—' Enid was halfway to the kitchen door. Brack shouted after her. 'I'll tell you this. You'll have a hard time learning. Froes is going next year. The curate from Mansfield's going to get the job. Specialises in heathens . . .'

'It's no good, I'm not going to bite.'

'Smart young man. Bishop's blue-eyed boy. Very severe. He'll make you learn every bloody word.'

Brack had lost more than a pound at Cobbler Jack's but he felt that, by the end, it had been a very enjoyable evening. Enid had thought she could out-talk him. But, with all her airs and graces, he had still had the last word.

CHAPTER FORTY
Bubbles

At first, Brack was openly hostile. Then Jack O'Hara bought a bicycle and, more important, bought it after taking Brack's advice. Enid could not remember telling him about the cycle shop or talking about her father's occasional and improbable boast that he had once been a professional racing cyclist. But Enid had talked to him so much and told him about so many things that she was not really surprised when Jack prefaced his questions on a model and make with expressions of gratitude. He gave thanks not to Brack himself but to the assortment of saints who had arranged their meeting.

Brack continued to abuse Jack behind his back, affecting astonishment that his daughter should look twice at a Paddy collier and telling his wife that she was about to be abandoned to his personal and exclusive care. But the hope of more flattery, and perhaps even continued respect, made him treat Jack with either formal courtesy or the aggressive jocularity he believed to be a sign of sophisticated male friendship.

Freed from the tyranny of the railway timetable, Jack spent almost all his spare time with the Brackenburys. He sat, silent and composed, in a corner of the living room, only speaking when he was spoken to but always ready to perform tasks Enid asked of him. When he was offered food, he ate it. If he was handed a newspaper, he read it. When he was told that it was time to go, he left. Both Agnes and Enid found his calm presence immensely reassuring. Jack remained an outsider – observing the family rather than preparing to join it. But whilst he was there Brack always behaved himself.

'I want you to find out something for me, unless it's too much trouble.'

'Yes, Mr Brackenbury.'

'You mean it is too much trouble, you idle bugger?'

'No, Mr Brackenbury. I meant I'd do it.'

'Then get up off your backside, you lazy bugger, and come and look at this.'

Slowly and carefully Jack put his cup and saucer on the floor by his chair and made his methodical way across the living room to look over Brack's shoulder at the paper he was reading.

'It's our local rag.' Jack sounded apologetic. 'I left it last night.'

'Do you know about this?'

It was an enquiry, but it sounded like an accusation. Jack was not sure of his offence, but he feared that he was guilty of something. The tension was heightened by Brack's impatience. As Jack struggled with the print – silently forming the words with his lips – his accuser leaped ahead and read the advertisement out loud.

'Grand Whist Drive. St Philip Neri, Mansfield. First prize guaranteed value, ten pounds . . .'

'It's the curate. The one who's coming here as parish priest.' Jack felt that somehow he was being held responsible. 'I only know about it because of Mrs Ferguson.'

'What's she got to do with it?'

'She's against it.' Anxious to avoid even guilt by association Jack struggled to remember the reasons for his landlady's indignant opposition. 'She says the wrong people will come – not just to the congregation but the sharks who go after the big money prize. She says that the parishioners won't come because they've put up the entrance fee to two bob. But Father Keogh says they'll try it for once.'

'What's the prize?'

'It was given by one of the curate's rich friends.'

'But you don't know what it is?'

'Mrs F. says she'll sell it. Not that she'll win. She's not a card player. But I don't know what it is.'

It was a reproduction of *Bubbles* by John Everett Millais, as big as the original painting and framed in solid ebony. Brack carried it home with amused pride and dropped it on to the living-room floor whilst he triumphantly removed the bill from his inside pocket.

'It's lovely,' said Enid. 'It's Little Lord Fauntleroy.'

'It's bloody awful,' Brack told her. 'But I reckon I can get seven or eight quid for it. Not bad for a night's work.'

'You're not going to sell it.' Agnes had already picked a spot on the wall opposite the window.

'I am. You don't think I spent all night with those old biddies just to hang it up over the fireplace do you?'

'It's too big to go over the fireplace.' In the corner Jack O'Hara had come back to life. 'Did Mrs F. go?'

'She doesn't like me, your landlady. She was the nastiest of the lot.'

'Nastiest? Why were they nasty?' Agnes was still ready to defend her husband.

Brack paused before he answered. The explanation was complicated and he knew that he would be bored long before it was completed.

Enid leaped at him. 'What have you been up to?'

'I've been up to nowt. Quite the opposite. I just made them stick to the rules and they didn't like it.'

'If you were such a goody-goody what was all the trouble about?'

'An old bird revoked. She must have been ninety if she was a day – hardly able to hold the cards. I'd won first prize already. It was the last hand and I'd won every one up till then. Anyway, she throws away on diamonds and I take the trick. Then she announces, calm as you like, that she's got a diamond all the time. She puts a three down, and then starts trying to pick up the cards on the table. When I tell her to stop she drops a jack and a four of clubs on the floor. So I called the MC over – that young chap, the curate who organised it all – and told him she'd revoked. You could have cut the atmosphere with a knife.'

It was time for Jack to be on his way home and he was worried about the reception he would receive. His landlady would undoubtedly find him guilty by association with Brack.

'And Mrs F. was the nastiest of the lot, was she?'

'No. The old priest was the real trouble. Never said a word to me. Just gave me the picture, no presentation ceremony or anything like that. But I heard him telling the curate off.' Brack gave what he believed to be an imitation of an Irish accent. ' "Did I not warn you, Father? Undesoirables I said. And undesoirables is what we've gone and got!" He meant me. He knew I could hear.'

'And all you'd done was insist on the rules being kept?' Enid found difficulty in believing in her father's innocence.

'Then the young priest apologised. He knew I could hear, an' all. Real la-di-da.' Brack attempted another imitation. ' "If I'd have known that sort of thing would happen, I'd never have done it – however much we make. I should have taken your advice!" And all about bloody nothing. All about a daft old woman who revoked.'

'What's he like, this new curate?' Enid asked.

Jack, always a thought behind, told her what she already knew. 'He's the one that's going to come here. He'll give you your instruction.'

'He's just like Froes said.' Brack was pleased to move on from the boring account of the previous night's injustice to a topic which seemed likely to embarrass his daughter. 'He has those glasses that clip on to your nose. I doubt if he's had a pint in his life, or a bet. And we know that he hasn't . . .' When Agnes failed in her duty to

511

register shock at the anticipated vulgarity, Brack changed tack. 'And they say he's very religious. I'm not surprised you keep putting off going to see him.'

'There's no hurry,' said Enid quietly. 'Do you want a cup of tea before you go, Jack?'

Her father was not so easily deflected from his purpose. He turned to Jack. 'Wouldn't you like her to get on with it? I don't know why you don't put your foot down. Anyway, how long are you going to wait before you make an honest woman of her? When I was a young man—'

'We won't get a colliery house for the best part of a year.' Enid was suddenly serious.

'Well, that doesn't stop you becoming a Roman. I bet you that's what Jack would like.'

'It's no good, Dad. You can try all you want, but there'll be no row tonight. Jack and I know what we're doing. And you can't cause trouble between us. So don't waste your breath trying.'

Brack put his arm round Enid and squeezed her so hard that she could feel the skin bruising on her shoulder under his fingers.

'What a lass! You see why I don't want to lose her, Jack. Puts her old father in his place. Not afraid of anything or anybody.' He gave an extra squeeze and Enid imagined that she heard the crack of a splintering rib or shoulder-blade. 'She'll be a handful, Jack. But she'll be worth it.'

Agnes glowered to see husband and daughter in such harmony. Jack paused in the act of putting on his bicycle clips and concentrated all his energy on swelling with pride at the thought of marrying such a paragon. Enid waited for the bombardment to continue with a salvo which even her mother and her fiancé could not fail to recognise.

'There is one thing though, Jack. I wouldn't like to think that she was having you on . . .'

'Having me on in what way, Mr Brackenbury?'

'Having you on about joining, about becoming a Roman. If you ask me, she thinks she can marry you without signing on.'

'And why should she be wanting to do that, Mr Brackenbury?'

The hideous imitation of an Irish accent was again attempted. 'She'd be wanting to do that because she doesn't believe in a word of it. No more do I, for that matter. But you'll not be wanting to marry me.'

'Why do you have to spoil everything?' Agnes asked.

Jack, bicycle clips in place, wished Enid goodnight. As always, Enid offered her cheek in the manner of an ancient aunt saying goodbye to a barely known nephew. But Jack, carried away by a moment of sudden passion, kissed her both left and right as if he were the President of France and she was a legionnaire who had won the Croix de Guerre.

The furniture shops at Worksop, Chesterfield and Mansfield would not believe that a lifesize reproduction of Millais' *Bubbles* – even in a solid ebony frame – was worth ten pounds. And even in Nottingham and Derby the best offer that Brack received was two pounds ten.

'And that's really for the frame.'

'I've spent nearly that on petrol, carting it about.' Brack remembered the name over the shop window – Ignatius McCarthy – and decided to take refuge in the Church's authority.

'The priest in Mansfield said it was worth ten pounds. I've got a receipt here.' He handed the smart young man a piece of paper which had grown creased and crumpled with continual examination.

'I don't doubt that someone paid ten pounds for it. But that doesn't mean it's worth any more than two pounds ten. Your benefactor was cheated. I can only pay the proper price.'

Brack saw a glimmer of hope. He had clearly convinced the young man that the Church was to be the beneficiary of the picture's sale. He would make one last – Catholic – appeal to his better nature.

'We thought some church might buy it, him being a religious painter.' He concentrated hard on the little speech Enid had written and made him rehearse.

'The *Light of the World*?' asked the young man.

'Well.' Brack had only been prepared for one painting. 'I was thinking of *The Angelus*!'

'I'm afraid that's a different painter. Doesn't even spell his name in the same way.'

Whilst Brack was deciding exactly what he would say to Enid when he got home, the smart young man changed mood. 'Look here. I thought you were a crook but it's plain enough now that you don't understand a thing about pictures. Let me tell you what I think. You won't like it but at least it'll stop you making a fool of yourself anywhere else. I'm sorry for the way that you've been tricked. I'll do you a favour. I'll offer you three pounds.'

It did not seem like a favour to Brack and the explanation which followed was an insult. 'I think this picture started life as an advertisement or perhaps a prize. Pears Soap. Have you ever heard of Pears Soap?'

Brack confessed that he had not. He had heard of carbolic, but not of Pears.

513

'Perhaps the frame was put on for the presentation. Or perhaps the recipient framed it himself. It's a very nice frame.'

'And the painting?'

'I don't think that it can rightly be described as a painting at all. It's a print and not a very good one at that. I can't really tell through the glass, but I have my suspicions it might have been given away at Christmas. If I could see the back, I could possibly tell you. It may have a Pears trademark on it. I think that I could slide it out by just slitting the brown paper on the back.'

'No, you don't.' Brack clasped *Bubbles* to him for safety.

'Get another opinion, by all means. But I very much doubt if you'll hear anything different.'

'What I want to hear is what that curate in Mansfield has to say for himself.' The car cranked into life with the first turn of the handle. He was in Mansfield in twenty minutes.

The curate at St Philip Neri did not like trouble so, when he opened the presbytery door and saw Brack standing on his threshold with *Bubbles* in his hand, he said a quick prayer and invited his unwelcome guest inside. The presbytery door did not open on to the road but raised voices carry and the priest did not want to risk the sound of unpleasantness reaching a parishioner who might be passing by.

In the whist drive, Brack had barely looked at the curate and, as he followed him through the kitchen and into the sitting room, staring at the back of the worn cassock, he was surprised to see how big a man he was. He was big and broad enough to be a policeman – Brack's invariable criterion of acceptable shape and size. When the priest turned round it seemed that his whole character changed. Suddenly he looked far too ascetic to walk the beat. The damaging illusion was, Brack decided, created by his haircut and his glasses. The hair was too short, parted too near the middle and held into perfect place by too much brilliantine and the spectacles were pince-nez. Clipped to the nose of an elderly schoolmaster, they might have seemed at home and in place but perched below the broad forehead of a well-set-up man of less than thirty, they looked ridiculous. The thin gold safety chain which looped across the side of his face and disappeared behind his ear added to the absurdity. The curate wore spectacles which were designed to fall off. Brack had no doubt that he would bend him to his will.

'You said the painting was worth ten pounds.' There seemed nothing to be gained from beating about the bush.

'And so it is. You've got the receipt.'

'Nobody'll give me ten pounds for it.'

'Well, ten pounds is what my aunt—'

'Your aunt? Your bloody aunt? What's your aunt got to do with it?'

'She bought the picture. The receipt's in her name.'

'It's a bloody conspiracy. That's what it is. A family conspiracy. The best thing that you can do, young man, is buy it back.'

'I didn't sell it.'

'It's no good bandying words with me. I was deceived. I read that advert. First prize worth ten pounds.'

'Believe me, there is nothing that I regret more than arranging that whist drive.'

'You'll regret it more if I don't get my ten pounds.' Brack thought that he noticed clear signs of nervousness. 'You'll regret it more if I write to the Bishop.'

'I can't believe that you'd be so unreasonable.'

'Unreasonable, after you've cheated me out of ten pounds?'

'You talk as if I've put it in my own pocket.'

'For all I know, you have.'

'I've not had ten pounds in my pocket in my life.' He felt through the opening on the side of his soutane and took a handful of coppers.

'I'm not saying ten pounds.'

The curate reached into his pocket again and pulled out a silver-plated cigarette case. At first Brack thought that he was to be invited to join in a friendly smoke as a sign of reconciliation. 'It's no good you trying to get round me.'

There was only one cigarette under the band of gold-coloured elastic which was supposed to hold ten. But there were, alongside it, two folded pound notes. The priest offered one to Brack.

'An offer of goodwill.'

'Two. You've got two there. I'll settle for both.'

'It's all the savings I've got in the world.'

The priest's voice and his gold pince-nez made Brack sceptical.

'Both or I'll write to the Bishop.'

The priest put the cigarette case back in his pocket.

'It's up to you. I don't want any trouble. It's worth a pound you don't deserve. It isn't worth everything I've got. Take it now and get out or get out without it.'

To the curate's relief, Brack did not call his bluff. He had hardly been gone two minutes when Father Keogh returned from his visit.

'Anybody called?'

The curate shook his head. It was not, he told himself, a real lie. The nameless man was a person of no consequence.

*

515

'I've decided to keep it.' Brack carried the picture in front of him in the manner of St Michael driving the devil out of paradise in the cheap mural on the wall of St Joseph's nave.

'I am glad,' Agnes told him. 'What made you change your mind?'

'I knew you liked it. It's your birthday present.'

'Her birthday's three months away.' Enid looked up from ironing.

'It's nice to be early. Let's have it on the wall opposite the window.'

'Don't be so daft. You'll never see it there for the light. When the sun comes in, it'll shine off that glass like a mirror.' That was exactly the place where Brack had intended it should be but he felt that he had already been too agreeable for one day. 'It'll have to go behind the door.'

'The door will bang it.' Enid sounded pleased at the prospect.

'You'll have to be careful, won't you? Instead of running about ram-stam. It's your mother's birthday present. You'll have to treat it with respect.'

What came to be called 'the painting' – as if there was only one in the world and the Brackenburys owned it – hung safely in Brack's chosen place for six months. Occasionally the door was pushed open with such force that the knob struck against the wall and deepened the depression that it had made with the years. But the two frames – door and picture – never met, so the glass stayed intact and the little boy with golden curls and velvet suit blew his bubbles in safety. Then one day Jack, ever eager to help, rushed to help Enid as she gently manoeuvred her mother's wheelchair through the door. It was never clear if Jack or the chair itself hit the painting. But whatever added the extra weight dragged the hook out of the wall. Everybody was astonished that – having slid so slowly to the ground – the glass smashed, the frame came apart at the corners and the picture fell out and lay, face downwards, on the carpet. Agnes screamed and Jack stared, transfixed, at the destruction.

Crudely stuck to the back of the picture was a cartoon which seemed to have been cut out of a humorous magazine. It showed a filthy tramp, bundle by his side, writing a letter. Jack struggled to understand the humour of the caption. 'Since using your soap a year ago, I have used none other.' Then Brack, who had heard the crash in the yard, came in to recriminate.

'Oh, Brack, I'm so sorry,' said Agnes, as if she had smashed the picture herself. 'And it was your birthday present.'

Brack picked up the picture without a word and began to read the legend printed on the back.

A nice little boy with a nice cake of soap,
Worthy of washing the hands of the Pope
    The Jackdaw of Rheims
    by the Reverend R. H. Barham 1788–1845

So it was, after all, a religious picture as he had expected all along.
He then read the second message.

    A Christmas present from Pears
    Not to be given to retailers who
    order less than one gross of de-luxe
    toilet soap.

CHAPTER FORTY-ONE

The First Christmas

Callers who came on business knocked on the Langwith Road front door. Friends went round to the side (which was called the back), tapped gently on the fluted glass and then walked in. Agnes sat in her wheelchair by the kitchen fire. When, out of ignorance or perversity, someone defied the proper procedure and forced her to shout through the door, she did not try to conceal her annoyance. Staring at the remnants of her birthday-present picture, she felt particularly irritated by the noise of a visitor who knocked but did not come in. When the latch was not lifted at once, she shouted an immediate ultimatum.

'Come in, if you're coming.'

The clear implication was that the stranger was expected to come in or go away but the message, if received, was not understood. A second knock, barely louder than the first, drove her to frenzy.

'Can't you hear? Come in, whoever you are. I can't get to the door.'

The door opened so slowly that, at first, Agnes did not realise that it was opening at all. Then a face, young and pink but creased with anxiety, peered into the room. It was the gold spectacles which she noticed first. Then she saw the short, neat hair. The clerical collar, which she did not recognise until the whole man had eased himself into the room, came as no surprise. The face unmistakably belonged to a priest. After an agonising silence, the visitor spoke.

'I called to see Mr Brackenbury.'

'Can you close the door? There's a terrible draught.'

'I'm sorry.' The door was closed with a crash which shook the whole kitchen. 'I'm sorry.'

Agnes was not clear if the young man was apologising a second time for causing the draught, a first for slamming the door, or in general for his intrusion and existence. She was not to blame for the confusion. Apology was, to her visitor, a way of life. He often said that he was sorry, in complete sincerity, without knowing exactly what it was that he was sorry about.

'Is it coal? Have you called about coal?'

'Father Froes recommended that I come here.' He waved an old bill to prove the authenticity of his claim. 'I thought Mr Brackenbury would be here. I'm sorry. I'll come back.'

Agnes hated being alone. 'Why not wait? He'll be back in a minute. The kettle's almost boiled. If you poured it on the tea . . .'

It was clearly the priest's duty to help the cripple. He bent to lift the kettle from the hob, burned his fingers on the hot handle and apologised. Agnes looked up at him from within the folds of the rug which was draped across her shoulders. It seemed to the priest that her head rose out of her shoulders without the intervention of a neck. The cripple bewildered him. He had heard from Father Froes that the coal merchant had a strange and difficult daughter. But he had been told nothing about an elderly invalid.

'You'll have a cup of tea yourself, won't you, Father?'

The priest was reassured. She addressed him properly. Propriety comforted him. The crippled lady was not wholly ignorant of the True Church and its practices, but he still had no wish to remain and make stilted conversation. He did not enjoy small talk.

'I really should be on my way.' Even as he said it, he knew that he would not go. 'I'm the new parish priest. I'm Father Froes's successor.'

'We knew that you were coming—'

'Of course, your husband and Father Froes . . . I'm sorry. I interrupted. Please go on.'

'Father Froes bought his coal here and his petrol.' She was clearly eager to dispel any idea that the two men were friends. 'It was Jack who told us . . . Jack O'Hara from Hucknall . . . He's going to marry our Enid. She'll be back in a second. She's just gone to have a look in the butcher's yard. She's late today. Usually she goes before this.'

It seemed a strange assignation, but he already knew that Enid was a strange young woman. Father Froes had done little to prepare his successor for the problems which faced him but, as well as advising a swift purchase of cheap coal, the retiring priest had warned him about the coal merchant's daughter and her periodic desire to join the Catholic Church. He wondered if it would be impolite to enquire the reason for Enid's unusual, and apparently regular, visits to the back of the butcher's shop. Before he had made up his mind, there was a crash against the bottom of the door and then what sounded like a scream of fury. Disconcerted though the priest was by the events outside the kitchen, he was even more unnerved by Mrs Brackenbury's behaviour. Making what was clearly a superhuman effort, she

519

lifted her feet from the wheelchair's footrest and held them, despite the obvious pain, in the air.

The door opened and a small white dog rushed into the room with the unthinking velocity of a meteor – a leather lead, still attached to its collar, was dragged behind it like the tail of a shooting star. The dog ran in a straight line towards the opposite wall and then, at the last minute, splayed out its legs and stopped within inches of knocking out its brains on the skirting board. It turned and began to race madly round the room, bumping into every chair and table leg, the high corners of the black-leaded fender and the wheels of Mrs Bracken-bury's chair. Because her feet were off the ground, the invalid was shaken but not bruised.

'This is Mick.' Agnes introduced the terrier as if it were a favourite nephew. 'He belongs to Enid. Never goes out without her.'

Instinctively, the priest flapped his hand in the dog's direction. The terrier leaped at him. It twisted in the air as he pulled away. The teeth snapped a fraction of an inch away from his fingers.

'He's very friendly. He can tell when people like him.'

The priest put both hands behind his back.

'Don't worry. If he'd meant to get you, he'd have caught you right enough. His mother was champion rat-catcher of Nottinghamshire. Show that you like him and he'll be friends.'

Foolishly, the priest obeyed. Mick's second attempt at severing his wrist was more successful than his first. He caught the cuff of the black clerical coat between his teeth and began to shake the sleeve as if it were a long worsted rat.

'Drop it, Mick. Drop it at once. He can understand every word that you say, Father. Tell him to drop it. If he knows that you mean it, he'll let go.'

The priest did as he was told but his message did not get through. The dog was still pulling at his sleeve when the latch rattled again and Enid walked in. This, he remembered, was the young woman who, according to Father Froes, was toying with the idea of taking instruction in preparation for a Catholic marriage. He had no idea if his predecessor had been right to say that she did not intend to marry the young Irishman. But it was clear enough why the young Irishman wanted to marry her. Father Hattersley knew nothing of women and had no wish to learn but he recognised that, to ordinary men who were susceptible to romantic emotions, she would be irresistibly attractive. She was dressed in what he took to be the fashion of the moment, itself an extraordinary sight in Shirebrook. Under the felt cloche hat, huge blue eyes took in the whole room, without apparently focusing on him.

'It's still there, Mam. I think it's been there all night.'

'This is the new priest from St Joseph's,' her mother told her. 'He's come about coal.'

The young woman, wholly preoccupied by her morning's adventure, ignored the visitor and continued a story she had obviously begun before she left home.

'I don't know why he took it in the first place. He didn't want it. He doesn't love it. I can't see him even looking after it.'

'He doesn't like dogs.' Agnes turned to the priest. 'You either love dogs or you don't. And he doesn't. We'll have to find it a good home.'

'I'm not sure that he'll part with it.' Enid stamped her foot on the dog lead that was snaking across the carpet in front of her. The terrier came to a choking halt. It began to cough instead of howl. 'That day I told him not to hit it, he said that it was none of my business.'

The mention of business emboldened the priest to force himself into the conversation. Holding out his hand, he advanced on Enid. 'Miss Brackenbury, can I introduce myself? I'm the new parish priest. My name's Hattersley.'

'I know,' said Enid. 'My father is a great friend of Father Froes.'

'It was Father Froes who recommended that I come here for coal. I thought that Mr Brackenbury would be in. I'm sorry . . .' He was apologising for forcing his custom upon them. 'I'll come back.'

'Stay.' Enid meant it to be a command. This was the man who, one day, would give her instruction. She meant to establish her dominance straight away. 'He'll be back in a minute. Stay and drink your tea.'

'Do you like dogs, Father?' Agnes had dogs – particularly neglected and maltreated dogs – at the front of her mind. She did not mean to be easily diverted from the subject.

'Yes, I do.' He was sure that he had given an honest answer. Mongrels had roamed through his boyhood in the back streets of Nottingham, and he was sure that he had liked them. He thought that he remembered the head gardener at Ratcliffe College owning a dog of some sort, though perhaps it was just a stray that wandered in from the Fosse Way. The memory of it, like all the memories of Ratcliffe, made him sadly happy. Roman dogs had been a different matter. Any dog that wandered in the Via di Monserrato was likely to be rabid. But he felt sure that, if there had been a proper dog at the English College, he would have liked it.

'I knew you did.' Agnes was scratching along the terrier's spine with the end of her walking stick, whilst the animal – working in exact rhythm – beat one of its back legs on the floor. 'Mick knows too. They can tell who likes them.'

The priest did not reply. He sat nervously on the edge of a hard chair holding his cup and saucer and staring at Enid. Bending down to unfasten Mick's collar she saw him out of the corner of her eye and blushed. She was sure that he was sizing her up in preparation for instruction.

'I can take the order, if I can find my dad's pad.'

'I hoped to take some with me now.'

'You're going to carry a sack of coal down to St Joseph's?' Enid enjoyed laughing at him.

'Well, perhaps not a whole sack . . . But there's none left in the cellar . . . And that presbytery gets so cold.'

Agnes misheard him. 'Scott's emulsion. That's the thing for a cold. Enid, get that bottle off the pantry shelf. The poor chap can have a spoonful straight away. Has it gone to your chest? I thought you sounded chesty when you came in.'

'He says that the presbytery's freezing, Mam. He's got no coal. Father Froes took every bit with him.' She turned to the cold priest. 'When Dad gets back he'll get someone to fill a box for you, to last you out until the proper delivery tomorrow.'

Enid had no intention of losing the order. The priest must be kept talking until her father returned. The problem of explaining why they could not make a full delivery before the next Monday could be dealt with later.

'Did you say that you liked dogs?'

'I did. Yes. Very much so. Very much indeed.'

'There's a lovely collie tied up all day at the back of the butchers. He's filthy now. Hasn't had a bath for weeks – or been fed properly. You can count his ribs. Some people aren't fit to own dogs. And he hits him. If you put out your hand to stroke him, he cowers back . . .' She was no longer making conversation but, carried away by the horror of what she described, was denouncing the wickedness of a world in which only she and her mother really loved dogs. 'One day he could hardly put his back foot to the ground. He must have kicked him.'

It seemed to the priest that Enid described the dog's degradation with something approaching pleasure – pleasure not at its suffering but at her own righteous concern for its welfare. She had disturbed the priest from the first moment that she came into the Langwith Road kitchen. Suddenly he believed that he knew what it was that made him feel so uneasy. Thanks to his priest's instinct, he had realised that, under the smart clothes and supercilious manner, Enid Brackenbury both recognised the world's wickedness and determined to triumph over it. Of course she would be welcomed into the arms of Mother Church.

522

'Would you like a dog, Father?' His reverie was disturbed by Agnes's question. 'Would you give him a good home?'

'I couldn't possibly . . . I'm sorry but I couldn't.'

'He would keep you company,' Enid promised him. 'You'd not be on your own in that big, dark house.'

'Who'd look after it when I was out? I don't have a housekeeper.'

'All he wants is love,' Enid answered with what Father Hattersley regarded as saintly certainty. 'He would rather be locked up by somebody who loves him than taken for a walk by somebody who doesn't care.'

'Anyway' – Enid could tell by the deflating preface that her mother was going to spoil everything just as she was about to get the dog a good home – 'anyway, anything is better than being tied up all day and night in that filthy yard.'

'I'd like to . . .'

'You'd like to!'

Both women spoke in perfect unison. He was about to add that, despite his personal preference, duty prevented him owning a dog when the back door opened again.

'Hullo, Father.' Brack tried not to seem at all surprised. 'Fancy finding you here. Seems a long time since you swindled me over that picture. It's in pieces in the other room. Take it if you want it. I won't charge you anything.'

'I've come for coal.' Confronted with the monster of the ten-pound whist drive, it was all that the priest could think of to say. It sounded less like an explanation than an excuse.

'Then coal you shall have.'

Brack held out his hand. Father Hattersley took it automatically and allowed his arm to be pumped up and down.

'Don't touch your face.' Enid told him. 'It's one of his regular tricks.'

He looked down at his palm. It was black with coaldust.

Until he moved into St Joseph's presbytery, Father Hattersley had never been on his own for more than a few working minutes at a time. He had often been lonely. But he was usually lonely in company. Despite all the talk of prayer and meditation, priests live gregarious lives. Father Hattersley was an essentially solitary man who relied on those surrounding him to help him through his solitude.

As a boy in Nottingham – the third son in a family of seven children – he had shared a bed with his younger brother, competed with his elder sisters for second helpings, lived according to the rigid rules which his mother had laid down and rejoiced in his father's company.

523

Herbert Hattersley laboured long hours at the Raleigh Cycle Works and spent most of each evening at the Grove Hotel. But when he was at home he sang, reminisced about the old days in Yorkshire, boasted about his sporting achievements, proclaimed his patriotism and generally filled the house with his genially irresponsible presence.

It was an ideal, if unconventional, preparation for Ratcliffe College. Boys from working-class families were supposed to cry themselves to sleep for the first month, but Father Hattersley had felt at home from the moment he arrived. It was at Ratcliffe that he had first been called Rex – a nickname that he believed vindicated Bishop Dunn's decision to send him to the school and confirmed his natural affinity to the world of ivy-covered cloisters, boat houses, High Mass, Latin grammar and, above all, an easily accessible library.

There was no room at Ratcliffe for foible or idiosyncrasy, and that suited Rex very well. He was happy to be shaped in the precise mould of a Catholic public school. Everything in his life was certain. He was made free from every sort of doubt and from the unpleasant duty of making decisions for himself.

In Rome there had been a moment when his faith faltered. All novitiates questioned their vocation at some time during the seven long years of unremitting study. But Rex had questioned everything. Yet even then – when he feared that his doubts about God's love would soon turn into disbelief – he still felt a profound affection for the institution in whose purpose he no longer believed. He felt comfortable in the discipline of an ordered life and secure in the affection of friends who, like him, knew that the duties they performed today were the same obligations as those they would discharge in ten years' time. When he regained his faith and decided that there was a God whose will he must obey, he embraced the Church with the passion of a lost child reunited with its mother.

When Bishop Dunn sent him to Shirebrook, he fought hard against the sin of pride but he lost the battle. However he wrestled with his conscience, pride seemed the only appropriate reaction to his appointment as parish priest at the age of twenty-six. He decided, after considerable thought, that regret – regret that his mother was not alive to witness his triumph – was an acceptable emotion for he could accept that she had witnessed it from heaven and still feel sad that she was not by his side. Father Hattersley took his moral obligations extremely seriously. It was, therefore, with something approaching hysteria that he woke up on his third day in St Joseph's presbytery filled with the worst of all the mortal sins – despair.

It had taken him barely forty-eight hours to discover that, despite his title and appointment, there was no real parish of which he could become priest. He had said his first Sunday mass to a congregation of sixteen souls, nine of whom had taken communion. There was no choir and, the organist being ill, he had been forced to lead the singing and prompt the responses like a Methodist minister at a revivalist rally. The single altar boy had been late, so Rex had rung bells, swung censers and performed all the other tasks which, in a well-ordered church, he would not have even organised for himself. He saw no prospect of improvement. There were simply not enough Catholics within his parish boundaries to justify St Joseph's independent existence and, despite his seven-year preparation as a missionary to England, he was doubtful if he could make sufficient converts to fill the first four rows of pews.

On the third morning, he forced himself out of bed thinking that he would be lucky not to celebrate mass alone. His night, like the two nights before, had been disturbed in the most unexpected way. In place of the usual nightmare of expulsion from the Church, he had dreamed of dogs – some terriers, some collies but all led on golden chains by Enid Brackenbury. Late each night he had woken from his dream determined to rescue the dog from its tormentor. And in the early hours of each morning he had fallen asleep again certain that the idea was absurd. On the third morning, reflecting that the dog was still occupying too much of his thoughts, he counted six parishioners spread about the church and felt grateful for their fidelity. When the mass was over, he slowly removed his surplice in the vestry and tried not to feel resentful that there was no housekeeper back in the presbytery frying him eggs and bacon. He imagined himself feeding the unwanted rind to the dog.

By a great effort of will, he succeeded in not lighting a cigarette as soon as he passed under the porch, but for reassurance he felt in his pocket for the paper packet of ten Woodbines. As he turned the corner of the path to the presbytery, Enid Brackenbury was standing at his front door holding, on a dirty piece of rope, an immaculate long-haired collie which Diana herself would have been proud to have in her elegant pack. Inevitably, she spoke first.

'We got it yesterday afternoon, so that I could give it a bath. Mick's been terrible. He won't let anything near me. But he's jealous as well – jealous of everybody. Everyone except Mam, that is. He loves her. Not as much as he loves me. But he loves her. Isn't he a picture? We told you he would be.'

The vestments which Father Hattersley carried over his arm flapped in the cold early-morning wind. The priest opened his door and led his two visitors into the presbytery. He carefully smoothed down his hair and hung his surplice in its appointed place before he spoke.

'It certainly is a very handsome dog. What do you call it?'

'The butcher calls it Pal. But what sort of a name is that for a dog? Call it what you like.'

'What I like?'

'It's only a pup. It'll take to a new name in a week.'

It was only then that he realised what the young woman intended. He reacted not with the hostility which he had anticipated but with pure joy.

'You mean it's for me?'

He sank to his knees on the hard carpet and began, as his first proprietary gesture, to untie the rope from round the dog's neck. The collie rose magnificently to the occasion. First he licked the priest's face and then, when the rope was removed, pawed at his liberator in an irresistible demand for more attention.

It was Agnes who had suggested that the lonely priest and neglected dog be brought together but Enid had worked at a scheme by which the union could be arranged. She planned to arrive at the presbytery with the washed and brushed collie as if her visit – and the gift – were expected. When Father Hattersley protested that she had mistaken his intentions she would affect distress at the humiliation of returning it to the brutal butcher. If the priest did not capitulate at once, she would employ the technique that was so successful in promoting business in the pet shops which she and her mother so hated. She would suggest that he took it on trial, and the dog would do the rest. She had been so proud of her stratagem that she resented the ease with which the dog had made its conquest.

'I'm glad that you like it. We had to pay the butcher five shillings.'

The priest reached for his cigarette case. 'I'll pay you, of course.'

'No, you won't. It's a present from Mam and me.'

Her moral ascendancy had been established. When the dog began panting in a way she would normally have described as laughing, she took command.

'Is the kitchen at the back?' As she walked out of the living room, she announced, in tones of deep reproach, 'This dog needs a drink.'

Enid returned with a pudding basin so full of water that it slopped on to the carpet with every pace that she took. She put it down in the corner of the room with such force that half of its remaining contents spilled out on to the oil cloth. Pal – who was not in the slightest degree thirsty – ignored the bowl and licked the rivulet that ran to the skirting board.

'You'll have to learn about dogs if you're going to look after him

526

properly. You'll have to spend time on him. Taking a dog is a big responsibility. He'll have to be your hobby now.'

'Hobbies aren't much in my line.'

'Don't you do anything for pleasure?'

'My job is a pleasure.'

'But apart from that?'

'I sometimes watch football. I go to cricket matches. I read . . .'

'We read all the time, Mam and me. Two or three books a week. I can't stand people who don't read. Though there's plenty round here. I'm reading *The Rainbow.*'

'Isn't that by Lawrence?'

'Yes,' said Enid proudly. 'A man I know has a brother who's a bookseller. He sent it to me. It's an early Christmas present. What . . .'

It would, Father Hattersley feared, be impolite to rebuke his guest and benefactor even for reading an author whose work was specifically prohibited to Catholics. He made a mental note. When her instruction began, he would deal expressly with the corrupting influence of literature.

'What are you reading?' Enid took it for granted that everybody was always reading something.

He was reading *The Incredulity of Father Brown* but he felt that to admit it would be to make himself sound ridiculous. On the sideboard was the book sent to him from Ratcliffe to mark his appointment to a parish of his own. It was unread, because it was unreadable. He waved in the direction of *Christian Architecture in England* by Augustus Welby Pugin. Enid stared blankly at the handsome presentation volume. Her silence – which he had already recognised as unusual – unnerved him.

'I'm very interested in churches.' When she still made no comment he felt that he had to apologise for his peculiar tastes. 'I started when I was in Rome. I lived in Rome for seven years.'

Enid was, for once, impressed. But she recovered quickly. 'We're going to an old church next week. My grandad's buried at Steetly. He was a wonderful old man. Very intelligent and very well read – very well read, that is, for a man of his sort. You and I wouldn't think he was well read but he was. We'll be taking the Christmas wreaths as soon as they're ready.'

The collie had stretched out in front of the fire in the rigid position of a dead stag in a Landseer hunting picture. Father Hattersley leaned down and first stroked one of the front legs that were pushed out towards the fender and then scratched the belly, which was warm from the heat of Brack's burning coals. Enid noticed, to her surprise, that the priest behaved as if he had been brought up with dogs.

'I must go to see it one day. What do you say it was called?' He struggled to sound detached. But he felt all the signs of incipient anxiety – the dry throat, the constriction across his chest, the itching shoulder-blades. He wanted Enid Brackenbury to go home. For reasons he did not understand, her presence in the living room made him deeply uneasy. He hoped that if he did not encourage conversation she would leave.

'Why not come next week? Father Froes used to drive us. He used to drive us to Sheffield.'

'I'm afraid that I don't have a motor car.'

'Dad'll lend you one. There's always one standing doing nothing in the yard. He'll lend you one if you take us. Can you drive?'

He had never sat behind a driving wheel. Father Hattersley could not understand his own reaction, but despite himself he hoped that, by the time his services were needed, he would be able, honestly, to answer that he could.

'When do you want to go?'

'Next week or perhaps the week after if we haven't finished the wreaths. Do you know how much shop wreaths cost? It's a scandal.'

'I'll take you with pleasure.' It was, he knew, an absurd offer to make. But he had no choice. Something in his heart or head compelled him to make it.

'You'll have to lock the dog up. Mick would kill him if they were in the car together. He'd be so jealous. We can't leave him at home. He loves going to Steetly. It's a real treat for him.'

The priest stopped rubbing the dog's ear. Wanting more attention, it sat up and began gently to chew his fingers.

'Look,' said Enid. 'He knows that we're talking about him. Have you decided what to call him yet? Pal won't do. Pal's a silly name for a beautiful dog.'

'Peter,' said Father Hattersley. 'Peter. It's a good name for a Catholic dog. I shall call him Peter and on this rock I shall build . . . I don't know what. But I'll build something.'

The dog stood up and wagged its tail, much to the pleasure of the priest, who was beginning to wonder if he had been guilty of mild blasphemy.

'I told you.' Enid was triumphant. 'He understands every word you say.'

After less than a week in Shirebrook, Father Hattersley knew no one except his handful of parishioners and, amongst them, only the butcher possessed a vehicle. Rex approached him with almost incoher-

528

ent diffidence. The butcher was a kindly man and gladly agreed to teach the priest the rudiments of driving.

'Thinking of buying yourself a car like Father Froes?' They were out together on the morning delivery round, with the priest behind the wheel and the butcher leaning nervously towards him.

'That's not very likely. I'm going to borrow one from Mr Brackenbury next week.'

'I guessed that they were friends of yours when they brought you the dog.'

Rex had been careful to keep Peter out of the conversation. He liked the butcher and was grateful to him. It seemed best not to raise a subject which might require him to complain about how his dog had been treated.

'I'll miss him but it was all for the best. Being on my own these days I couldn't leave him at home. All I could do was tie him up all day at the back of the shop.'

'So I understand.' The learner driver was making his third attempt to find top gear.

'He didn't half used to enjoy his walk after I'd locked up. But Miss Brackenbury was right. It wasn't really fair to him.'

'Miss Brackenbury is very fond of dogs.'

The gears crashed. It was the butcher's concern for his van which made him speak more frankly than he had intended.

'Mind you, it was her idea that I should have it in the first place. I suppose she was being kind, my wife having just died. But she knew that it would be tied up all day. Still, it was better than he'd been used to. Miss Brackenbury saved him from the Johnsons in Albuera Street. Used to beat it with a stick. Mr Johnson married a Frenchwoman during the war. They don't know how to treat dogs over there. Do you know that they eat horses in France, Father?'

Rex pulled on the handbrake with undisguised relief. 'I doubt if I'll be ready by next Tuesday.'

'You will, Father. I don't doubt it for a minute . . . You are borrowing one of Mr Brackenbury's cars, aren't you? Not thinking of taking this?'

'I've taken your dog. I won't take your van.'

'Believe it or not,' the butcher said, 'she offered to pay me for it. Cheek!'

Enid enormously enjoyed the trip to Steetly. The priest drove slowly, which, although not in keeping with the dashing character of which she was so proud, protected her mother from the pain which Agnes was forced to endure when Brack raced recklessly through the potholes and Father Froes plunged without thinking over the humps and hollows of the narrow road. Mick's behaviour gave her special pleasure. The dog snarled menacingly at the priest throughout the journey and, when Father Hattersley attempted to help her on with her coat, leaped at him with a splendid ferocity. Most important of all, she dominated the conversation.

At first, Father Hattersley had wanted to examine the chapel. But, after the briefest inspection of the exterior, interrupted several times by Enid's insistence on pointing out every mark made by Cromwell's cannon balls, he gave up the struggle and submitted himself to Agnes's questions and Enid's constantly changing narrative.

His answers to the old lady's enquiries were all suitably sentimental. The pain of his mother's death had never quite passed. He had worshipped his eldest brother Bert, killed with the Sherwood Foresters at the Battle of the Somme. The thought of being reunited with his younger brother at Christmas – Syd from Ratcliffe College who would one day follow him to Rome – filled him with joy. The bronchitis from which he had suffered as a boy had turned into nothing more debilitating than an allergy to pollen and a tendency to headcolds. He cooked for himself only rarely, living mostly on bread and cheese, fish and chips, tinned salmon and Nelson squares. Agnes wallowed in the pathos of his replies.

Enid rejoiced at their brevity and entertained him with a series of lectures on Thomas Hardy, Jean Borotra, hardy annuals, the iniquity of fox hunting, John Galsworthy and the paragons of virtue who made up her maternal family.

'Does your family come from Nottingham?' Enid asked.

'My father came from Sheffield.'

'Good Lord. So does mine.'

'So I suspect you hear a lot about it, a cross between the Garden of Eden and the new Jerusalem.'

'You bet.' Enid was working hard to master fashionable jargon.

'Bramall Lane.'

'The Wicker. The River Don.'

'The Moor.'

'Paradise Square, where John Wesley preached. Have you ever seen Paradise Square?'

'I've never been to Sheffield.' Rex felt guilty again.

'I go to see a specialist in Sheffield,' Agnes told him. 'Father Froes used to drive me there.'

Enid turned away to lay the holly wreath on her grandfather's grave. She looked to the grey sky above the poplars that separated the churchyard from the fields.

'"The rude forefathers of the hamlet sleep." Actually he wasn't really a forefather of Darfoulds – that's the village down the road. He came here from Wisbech, where he'd been workhouse master, a very responsible job. He came down in the world. But he didn't mind because he loved plants and flowers. He was head gardener.'

'"Let not ambition mock his useful toil."' Father Hattersley meant to do no more than play her game but he felt that she resented him matching her quotation for quotation.

'We're very political. All of us are Labour Party members. Dad is very active. We don't understand how a Christian could be anything else.'

It was clearly a challenge. Enid assumed that, like all priests and clergymen, he was Conservative. She hoped he would admit it and enable her to mount an assault upon him with the support of various Biblical quotations. She had not decided whether to accuse the Church of complicity with capitalism – 'the poor ye have always with you' – or denounce him for denying the obvious socialism of the Bible – 'it is easier for a rich man to pass through the eye of a needle' – when he offered what was supposed to be an anodyne response.

'I've never been very interested myself.'

'How can you say such a thing! How can an intelligent man say he's not interested in politics? It's at the heart of everything. Politics decides what we eat, what we can say . . .'

The priest nodded feebly, hoping that his agreement would look like an admission and an apology. It did not satisfy his inquisitor.

'Don't you understand that?'

'I suppose I do, yes.'

'Then why don't you do something about it?'

'Were you not even interested when you were a student?' Agnes asked. 'Students usually are. Weren't you even interested whilst you were in Rome?'

He was not sure whether he regretted or welcomed Mrs Brackenbury's intervention. As he decided how best to reply, Enid began to list the names of Italian patriots which were known to her.

'Cavour, Garibaldi, Browning wrote about Italy.'

'I saw Mussolini, once.' He spoke in desperation.

'A Fascist,' said Enid, clearly implying that she would not be surprised to learn that they had been close friends.

The journey back began in silence. Then after two bumpy miles, Agnes passed judgement on the day.

'It's been lovely, lovely just listening to you young people talk. Can I call you Rex, Father? I know you're a priest, but I'm old enough to be your mother and I'm not a Catholic, anyway.' When Rex did not answer at once, Agnes moved on. 'Have you enjoyed it, Rex?'

'Very much. Very much, thank you.' Rex would have enjoyed it far more if Peter had been with them. After barely a week he had grown so attached to the dog that he felt guilty to think of it locked up in the presbytery.

'I've loved it too,' said Enid. 'I don't see very many intelligent people these days. There aren't many well-read people in Shirebrook. I had to leave school early, you know, to look after Mam. I stayed a year longer than most girls do, but the teachers said I should have stayed until I was sixteen. And that was at Ashleigh House, a private school in Worksop. You must come to our house so that we can have a sensible talk, Rex.'

'Yes, you must.' Agnes did not aspire to being a participant. 'I'll love listening to the pair of you.'

Rex decided, there and then, that he must avoid the Brackenbury literary soirées at all costs. They would, he had no doubt, be exactly the sort of occasion which he detested. He hated tension and loathed controversy and he could imagine the bogus passion which Enid would generate as she disputed the origin of a quotation or the underlying meaning of a verse of poetry which she did not understand. Yet it was not because he would find the evenings so unpleasant that he determined never to accept Agnes's invitation. He could never go because he wanted to go so much – wanted to go to be with Enid.

CHAPTER FORTY-TWO

And Glory Shone Around

It was Jack O'Hara's idea that they should all go to Midnight Mass. Agnes was doubtful and Brack – who spoke eloquently of drunken miners vomiting in the churchyard – said that he wanted to be out of the house by three o'clock on Christmas Day, so he expected his dinner to be on the table by one whatever time Enid and her mother got to bed.

'I'm going,' said Enid. 'We can't go all the way to Mansfield. But as long as you mean here in Shirebrook, I think it's a lovely way to start Christmas.'

For the first time in her life Enid was not looking forward to Christmas. She had promised herself – twelve months before, walking with Hilda King on Boxing Day – that she would start a new life before the year was out. Yet nothing had changed. She was talking about marrying Jack but she was delaying every attempt to move towards Church and marriage. Brack still loomed over her life.

'Don't think she's weakening.' Her father had noticed that Jack was beaming with pleasure. 'She'll not join, whether she goes to church or not on Christmas Eve.'

'I'll come.' Agnes sounded almost enthusiastic. 'If you can get my chair inside. I don't want to be lifted about.'

'I'll see the priest.' Jack sounded as if, because of his special Catholic status, he could arrange suitably wide aisles.

Father Hattersley greeted Jack with suspicion. He had spent the week since his visit to Steetly avoiding the Brackenburys. It had not been easy. Meat for the dog had been sent to the presbytery in blood-stained parcels. Written invitations to tea had been pushed through his letter-box. Books had been left on his front step – sometimes before the jug by which they stood had been filled with the day's milk. One morning he had met Enid in the grocer's and she began at once to make arrangements for the excursion to Sheffield which he had promised, but never meant, to make. She was so obviously offended when he said that he could promise nothing definite

533

before Epiphany that he thought she would punish him by spreading the rumour that he ill-treated the dog. Peter, by his side, was the picture of canine contentment. But Rex knew that those who looked for sin could find it anywhere. Enid and her mother, expecting cruelty, would easily convince themselves that giving him the dog had been a terrible mistake.

'Of course. If Mrs Brackenbury wants to come, we'll make sure that she can. I don't think the church will be very full. How wide do you reckon her chair is?'

Jack held out his hands to signify the span of the wheels.

'We can get that down the centre aisle. Bring her early and put the chair just in front of St Joseph's statue. She'll see everything from there.'

Jack and the Brackenburys arrived at the church shortly before half-past eleven. Jack wore his best Nottingham-made suit and a starched white collar which was so high that he could barely turn his neck. Enid, on his arm, was barely visible under a wide-brimmed felt hat. She had insisted on wearing the coat which, since Worksop had made it as her Christmas present, should have remained in the wardrobe until the next day. It had a wide fur collar which she had convinced herself, without any evidence to support her conviction, was imitation. Agnes, despite fearing the pain that the pressure on her neck would cause, agreed to cover her head.

The church was half full — mostly the parishioners who, as Enid tartly observed, had not been on their knees since the previous Christmas. By midnight there was a respectable congregation. Agnes looked round for evidence of recent drinking but noticed nothing to complain about except the poverty of the people around her. They sat in sober piety waiting to be told that Christ had come into the world to redeem their sins.

Enid occupied the thirty minutes before the service began by letting her mind flutter around the details of her surroundings — the faded murals of Biblical scenes which she could not identify, the ugly statue with a lily in its hand which stood like a sentinel on guard over her mother, the muscular youth with thick horn-rimmed spectacles and thicker eyebrows who bustled about on the altar steps in preparation for the priest's arrival. Then Rex came into church.

For a moment, Enid did not recognise him. She had often thought of him with affection since they had visited Steetly together but she had thought of him as the diffident young man with the pale-blue eyes, scholarly manner and no aptitude for driving. She would have described him as modest, shy and self-effacing and so little concerned with the vanity of this world that he wore a shabby black suit with frayed cuffs and a patch on one elbow. And she liked him for those modest virtues. Suddenly he was a high priest, robed in the glory of a feast day's white vestments and performing, with unerring confidence, the rites of a religion which, by its own canons, set him apart from other men.

She made no attempt to follow the order of service. Even in her own church she would have paid only perfunctory attention to the prayer book. But that Christmas Eve in St Joseph's she simply stared at the priest as she slowly began to understand what being a priest meant. In the churchyard at Steetly, he had been mortal – different from anyone else that she knew, but at least a member of the same species. In church, celebrating mass, he was no longer flesh and blood. She tried, and failed, to imagine him feeding the dog, shaving, mopping egg yolk from his breakfast plate with the last piece of bread. It seemed impossible that she had called him Rex when they said goodbye. Then she made the ultimate admission. If she met him again in the grocer's shop, she would not know what to say.

It was at that moment of supreme and wholly uncharacteristic loss of confidence that her mother began to demand her attention by tapping at her ankles with the walking stick which was kept in the wheelchair for exactly such tasks.

'Enid,' she hissed, dissatisfied with the speed of her daughter's reaction. 'Enid, look.'

The line of communicants who were shuffling their way towards the altar steps stared at her in outrage. But Agnes tapped and hissed again. Jack edged away in the hope that nobody would realise who had wheeled her into church.

'Enid, look. Look at his shoes.'

Agnes pointed at the soles of Father Hattersley's feet, which were clearly visible below the golden brocade on the hem of his white cassock as he knelt with his back to the congregation. Both soles were worn through. On the left, the hole was so large that the sock inside had almost worn away. Pink skin shone through the thin wool. On the right, the hole was smaller, but the uppers were no longer attached to the welt and the heel was missing altogether.

It was all that Agnes could talk of on the way home. 'Poor man, his feet must get soaked if there's a drop of rain.'

Nobody argued.

'And if he gets a stone in his shoe, it'll be agony.'

Everybody agreed.

'As soon as the shops open after Christmas, we'll buy him a new pair. He was so kind to us last week. Will you find out what size he takes, Jack? It's a disgrace that anyone in his position has to live like that.'

535

Enid was not listening. She had decided that, although the promise of last Christmas had been broken, she would make the same promise again this year. One year. In twelve months life would be different. By next Christmas she would have escaped. It would not be the escape she had planned on Boxing Day during her walk with Hilda King. It would be a complete liberation. And she would be free by next Christmas. Jack was earnestly explaining the reason for Father Hattersley's poverty.

'There's no money, Mrs Brackenbury. It's the parish. There's not enough Catholics. I doubt if there are five hundred altogether.'

'Five hundred and one now,' said Enid. 'I'm going to get instruction and be baptised.'

At first, even Brack believed that Enid was going to marry Jack O'Hara. And Agnes looked forward to what she saw as a way of leaving her husband which neither jeopardised her respectability nor imperilled the romantic illusions about her marriage which had survived almost thirty years of neglect and brutality.

'We'll manage very nicely.' Agnes took advantage of Enid's trip to the library to reassure Lottie and Anne. 'Enid's very careful and he's earning a good wage.'

'A good wage for a miner,' said Anne, as if a miner's pound was worth less than the twenty shillings spent by a professional man.

'Isn't it about time we met him?' Lottie asked. 'Enid hardly talks about him at all. All we know is what you've told us.'

'We'll bring him next Sunday,' Agnes promised. 'But don't ask Ern till late on. He's a quiet lad and he'll be frightened to death by all the family sitting in that fitting room like judge and jury.'

'Ernest can come round at teatime.'

Anne was more understanding than Agnes had believed possible. Unfortunately, despite the rare moment of sensitivity, she decided that family fidelity required her to invite her brother to Sunday lunch.

When Jack O'Hara arrived at half-past three, Ernest Skinner was waiting for him. He advanced, hand outstretched, to do his duty by his niece. 'I think you and me should have a little talk in here.'

Ernest guided the visitor towards the fitting room with what he believed to be a show of courtesy. It involved the young man leading the way. Unprepared for the tailor's dummy which stood, fully clothed, in the half-light by the door, Jack collided with what he at first believed to be a silent and statuesque employee of Skinner and Harthill. Ernest laughed in a way which was intended but failed to provide confidence.

536

'Switch on the light. They've got electricity in the fitting room.'

Jack was used to colliers' cottages which were lit only by gas. But he could not believe that Uncle Ern – the celebrated fretworker, chief clerk at Hirst's woodyard, a devotee of fencing and an expert with Indian clubs – was so impressed by the light switch on the wall. He was not sure if he was being patronised or insulted.

'Careful when you sit down,' said Ernest. 'There are pins everywhere. Did Enid tell you about the cottage pie that Miss Skinner sent to Shirebrook?' He did not wait for a reply. 'It was years ago. The young madam had just arrived and her mother had just started with the pains in her neck. I was sent with cottage pie in my Gladstone bag. Gravy, of course, was in a bottle. As long as I held it level, nothing spilled. Fortunately I've got a steady hand. I've never drunk, that's why. I got it there without a drop splashing the lining.'

Believing that Ernest was waiting to be congratulated on his achievement, Jack was searching for suitable words of praise when the raconteur remembered the end of his story.

'Aggie heated it up and Brack started to tuck in. Then he started chewing. Gristle, Aggie thought. Soon, he's pulling something out of his mouth. Six inches of bias binding. Fortunately no pins.'

After as close an inspection as he thought polite, Jack sat down on the chaise-longue.

'We brought up your Enid,' Ernest told him. 'And we wouldn't like anything to happen to her.'

'Anything like what?'

'Anything bad. We want her to be happy. She's had enough trouble in her life. So has her mother. They both need a bit of looking after.'

'I'll look after them,' said Jack. 'I'll look after them both. I want to look after them. You ask Enid.'

'The important thing,' Ernest was speaking very slowly, 'is to be steady. At first Enid won't want that. She's not a great one for steadiness at the moment. But she's young. You don't look flighty to me.' Jack was about to confirm that no one had ever called him flighty when Ernest added his codicil. 'Though that's not a miner's Sunday suit you're wearing. That looks tailor-made to me. Don't let her make you flighty.'

'She's very careful, Mr Skinner. Very careful with money, just like her mother.'

'They've both had to be. But that's not quite what I meant. Don't let her make you flighty with ideas. She gets above herself. That's no good. Take it from me.'

'I won't, Mr Skinner. I just want a bit better life. Ordinary, but a

537

bit better. Dance on Saturday evenings. Game of tennis now and then. I want people to think that I'm a gentleman. But nothing special. And I'm a hard worker.'

'I'm sure you are. Do you drink?'

'Half a pint now and then.'

'I'm sorry to hear that. You say half a pint now and then. But it grows on you. When I think of the trouble that I've seen caused by drink . . . Do you smoke?'

'No, Mr Skinner. Never have.' Jack looked as smug as it was possible to be whilst sitting on the edge of the chaise-longue.

'That's a pity.' Ernest took out his tobacco pouch and felt in his pocket for his pipe. 'I was going to give you one of my pipe-racks. One of the very best that I made when I really had an eye for fretwork. Lovely thing it is. Still, if you don't smoke . . .'

'Why do you want to be a Catholic?' The collie stood by the side of the chair. He rubbed its ear as he spoke.

'I don't honestly know. I'm surprised myself. But I do.'

'No doubts?'

'No doubts at all.'

'Is it because you want to marry Jack?'

'It was Jack who put the idea into my head. But he'd marry me, Catholic or not.'

'Has he told you what it would be like if you weren't a Catholic when you married him – what sort of wedding you'd have?'

'We've never discussed it.'

'Good. I wouldn't want you to join the Church so that you could have a white wedding.'

Enid grinned.

'It's been known. The ceremony for mixed marriages isn't very . . . very . . . very . . . romantic. I suppose that's the word. No music. No flowers. It would all happen at the back of the church.'

'The ceremony wouldn't matter to me.'

'It would matter to Jack. He won't feel that he's married if he hasn't had a Nuptial Mass. It'll matter to him all right. And it will have to start mattering to you, if you're going to be a Catholic. The ceremony is important. It's a symbol of one Church, doing the same thing everywhere and for ever. Obeying the same rules. You'll have to learn that if you're to become a Catholic.'

'If you want to catch me out, you'll find it easy enough. If I knew all the answers, I wouldn't be here wasting your time.'

'I'm sorry. I wasn't trying to catch you out. I just wanted to make sure that you were here for the right reasons. It's easy to—'

'Of course I'm here for the right reasons. What wrong reasons could there be?'

'Jack could have persuaded you. Or he could have bullied you. Believe me, it's been known. It's wrong but it happens often enough. Young man says, "I'll only marry you if you become Catholic" or "My mother would never forgive me if I didn't have a proper wedding." I don't want that. We haven't had forced baptism for four hundred years.'

'In the Congo. They did it in the Congo, just before the war.'

'Who told you that nonsense?'

'I read it somewhere.'

'That doesn't make it true. I used to have a saying: "I've read it in a book." That meant that it was a fact. No argument possible. Now I wish that I had a pound for everything that I've ever seen in print that turned out to be a lie.'

The mention of money made him look down at his shoes. They were a size too small and, although he never laced them tight, they still crushed his toes. He had tried to work out why they were less painful when he stood up than when he sat down and had concluded that, when the weight was on his feet, the hard new leather was somehow spread out. It was an unconvincing theory. There were only two things about his shoes of which he was certain: they hurt and his feelings for them were disturbingly close to idolatry. After much troubled thought, he had decided that they were so precious to him because they symbolised the generosity which is essential to a Christian life.

'Were you brought up a Nonconformist?'

'Church of England. My mother was Church of England.'

'And baptised?'

'Christened? Yes, I was christened at Steetly, where we went the other day.'

Enid blushed and looked down. She had forgotten that he was no longer the self-effacing young man who drove so carefully and seemed afraid of her mother, her dog and – most of all – her company. When she looked up, he was blushing too.

'If you've been baptised into the Church of England, you don't have to be baptised again. We admit you into the Church. An informal little gathering. Sponsors, not godparents. I shan't have to splash you with water. Have you got a certificate from the Church?' He immediately regretted asking a question which seemed to imply that he doubted her word. 'It doesn't matter if you haven't. The thing now is to have our talks.'

'When do we start?'

'This week if you want to.'

'Whenever you like.'

It was not the answer which Rex expected. He was immensely ambivalent about Enid's wish to become a Catholic and he suspected that his reluctance to instruct was influenced by his feeling that she was about to make a wholly unsuitable marriage. He had convinced himself that his reservations about the match were properly pastoral – the fear that wife was so superior to husband that they could not be happy together. But he had reconciled himself to a tragedy which, even within his limited experience, was not unknown. Enid would marry Jack in his church and he would probably perform the Nuptial Mass. He assumed that it was her wish that the wedding take place as soon as possible.

'It takes a long time. We probably have to have twenty meetings. There's a lot of ground to cover.'

Enid looked pleased. It was clear to the priest that she still did not understand.

'Say one a week. We'll miss a week or two because of Lent and Easter. You won't get married before June.'

'That's all right. There's no hurry. Jack used to say that no man should get married until he was thirty-five. We've not written off for the colliery house yet. We probably won't even do it in June.'

'Do you want to begin now?'

'Yes, please.'

They began with the importance of faith. He would, he promised her, move on to the Seven Proofs of the Existence of God. She might, at that point, be interested to read Hilaire Belloc's *Reply to Mr H. G. Wells's History of the World*.

'I've read things by both of them before.' It was true. But she was never quite able to remember the exact titles of her reading. 'I've read "Mr Kipps" and "The History of Polly". And poems by Hilaire Belloc. "The day we went to Birmingham, by way of Beachy Head . . ." And I've read a Fabian pamphlet by H. G. Wells. It was called—'

'We'll deal with Mr Wells in a week or two. In the meantime I want to impress this upon you. Faith is the main thing. There have been many miracles. More than we know. They happen every day. Miracles are proof – proof of God's love and proof that the saints in heaven intercede for us. But do not ask continually to put your hand into the wound. Our Saviour did not come down off the cross. He did not provide evidence that would stand up in an English court of law. He required us to have faith. Do you understand?'

'Yes, Father. And whilst I remember. Mam hoped you'd come round for tea on Saturday.'

'I'd be delighted.' All thought of faith and morals had been driven out of his head. His only regret was that he would have to leave Peter at home. Dog and priest had become inseparable.

It was at tea on Saturday that he agreed to drive Mrs Brackenbury to Sheffield and to come back via Worksop. Rex initially declared himself too busy to visit Worksop Abbey, but was quickly shamed into it by Enid who *could not really believe* that an educated man had lived so near for so long but did not even know that Cardinal Wolsey had stayed there during his last journey to London.

'"I charge thee, Cromwell, throw away ambition. For through that sin the angels fell." That's not Oliver Cromwell, of course. It's the other one. The one in Henry VIII's time.'

'It's Shakespeare,' Agnes explained. She had heard Enid quote the lines a hundred times before. 'Do you like Shakespeare, Rex?'

'I don't really know much about him. I haven't read a word since I was at school.'

Enid expressed *absolute astonishment* that anyone who claimed to be educated could admit such ignorance. Jack O'Hara, who was not used to priests being patronised, explained her behaviour in a way he hoped would placate the priest without offending her.

'She puts great store by education, Father. Especially by reading. It's a great pity that she didn't stay on at school. But it wasn't to be. She could have gone a long way, given the chance.'

'There was a man,' said Agnes, 'who wanted her to go to Oxford. You never see him now, do you, love? At least you could talk to him about interesting things.'

'You see, I've had no education worth speaking of.' Jack announced the absence as a fact to be recognised more than a failing to be regretted or rectified.

'Why don't you take her in hand, Rex?'

'Mother!'

'No, I'm serious. When she comes to you for your talk about religion, why don't you give an extra half-hour on . . . on . . . on the things you know about. Enid says you're an expert on churches. That's a lovely subject.'

'I used to visit churches in Rome in my spare time. That's all, Mrs Brackenbury.'

'Well, there you are, then.'

Rex capitulated.

'We'll start off with Worksop Abbey and see how we go on. See if you can get Thomas More's *History of England*.'

Jack coughed in preparation for making a speech.

'We really are grateful, Father. It'll make me feel better. I often

541

feel guilty about keeping her here without anybody who's well read. I know your time is precious but it would be wonderful if you could teach her things. If there's anything that I can do at the church . . . Pay you back, so to speak.'

'Let's start with Worksop Abbey and see how we go on. We may all be tired of each other's company when we get back.'

They were not tired of each other when they got back from Worksop, so they arranged to visit Nottingham the following week. In Nottingham, Rex was tutor and guide. He pointed out – but did not suggest visiting – The Trip to Jerusalem, which he described as the oldest public house in England. He was more vague about Mortimer's Hole. The first time that they drove past the entrance, he called it a dungeon. During the second circuit of the castle rock – searching for the path to the top which they had missed by looking at the cavern door – he described it as a secret passage. On the third, it was both. On the fourth he ignored it altogether.

Agnes sat in the car on the castle esplanade looking out over the city whilst Rex took Enid into the Sherwood Foresters' Museum to see pictures of the battle in which his brother Bert had been killed. The war, which had hardly touched her, seemed like ancient history and the sepia photographs of soldiers meant no more to her than the porcelain vases in the next gallery. But Rex was moved by every map and diagram. By the time they got to the last glass case – ten faded portraits of pinched, working-class medal winners – he was in tears. Enid took his hand. She had never touched him before and she assumed that he did not pull away because, in his sadness, he had hardly felt her fingers pressing into his palm.

On the way home, they passed Newstead Abbey and agreed that they must visit Lord Byron's house as soon as possible. After Newstead, it was Keddleston and after Keddleston, Southwark Minster. One Saturday they drove all the way to Lincoln to see the arboretum that Agnes's father had built. On the cathedral green an Irishman, thinking that he recognised a fellow spirit, asked Rex if he had seen the prison from which Eamon de Valera had escaped. He sent his best wishes to the priest's sister who had by then returned to the motor car. Rex radiated hatred through his pincenez.

In March, just after they had planned to visit the Major Oak, Agnes decided that the travelling days were over.

'It's just too painful getting in and out of the car. But you two have to go. Edwinstowe's lovely at this time of year.'

'I'm not going to leave you on your own, Mam, while we're off enjoying ourselves.'

'We wouldn't dream of it, Mrs Brackenbury.'

They went to Edwinstowe and walked in Sherwood Forest. It was a late spring and the buds had not broken on the horse-chestnut trees. Instead of the thousand different shades of green which Agnes had promised, the world was grey and brown and the leaves which covered the paths were wet from early-morning rain. The Major Oak was certainly a disappointment and probably a fraud – no more than the hollow stump of a dead tree. Rex calculated that it would hold half a dozen merry men at most, few of whom would remain merry for long inside the rotting trunk. Enid could think only of the names. She repeated them to herself as she waited, in vain, for Rex to follow her inside.

'Will Scarlet, Alan Adair—'

'I'm frozen through. Let's have tea in the Hop Pole at Ollerton.' Rex felt the change in his pocket and confirmed that he could afford a pot for two with scones and jam.

Rex ate and drank with one hand held to his throat as if he were examining his neck for swollen glands. He believed that if he half-obscured his clerical collar, couples at other tables would not recognise him as a priest – despite his black suit and, because it had not had so much wear, his blacker stock. He had developed a new ambition in life. His aim was to be ordinary, and it was impossible for him to be ordinary unless he was inconspicuous. He did not fear the special infamy of being a priest out at tea with a beautiful young woman, but the general notoriety of being a priest at all. He had not even thought of leaving the Church since the crisis of faith in Rome. But had there been an order of monks, committed to invisibility as the Trappists were pledged to silence, he would have wished to join. He had become part of the Church Reticent.

He had meant to leave the car in the yard and walk home to the presbytery without going into the house. But Jack O'Hara called from the back door. 'Can you come in for a minute, Father? Mrs Brackenbury wants a word. She's got a favour to ask.'

Each of Mrs Brackenbury's favours was more difficult to perform than the last and they were all requested in a manner which suggested she was not asking favours but awarding privileges.

'I'll tell you what it is, Rex. I got Jack and Enid tickets for the Sheffield Lyceum next Friday. Shakespeare. *Antony and Cleopatra*.'

'I don't know anything about it.' Resolution failed. 'I suppose I could get a copy and talk to them about it.'

'That's not what I want. Jack's working. He's got the chance of an extra shift. And with them saving up . . . She can't go on her own and I couldn't sit in those theatre seats. Seems strange now. I used to go a lot when I was a girl . . .' Agnes's plea faded away into silent reminiscences of imagined delights.

543

'I'd be very grateful, Father,' Jack said. He went on to demonstrate a delicate sense of propriety. 'It's all right, Father – being Shakespeare. It's not a music hall or a smoking concert.'

So they went to the Lyceum in Sheffield and saw Owen Nares in *Rose Marie*.

'I didn't know. I swear I didn't.'

Rex had never thought that she did. He was silent not because he thought that he had been trapped into a musical comedy but because he had remembered what they should have been doing that night.

'Wasn't it awful?' She hoped that he had not noticed her foot tapping during 'The Indian Love Call'.

'I rather enjoyed it. More than I would have enjoyed Shakespeare.' He fell silent once more and did not speak again until they were in Langwith Road. Enid, half asleep and mortally afraid that she sensed catastrophe, managed to resist every temptation to speak. Outside the gate, Rex turned towards her.

'How are we to deny ourselves?'

'What?'

'How are we to deny ourselves? It's a catechism.' She had never heard him sound so aggressive. 'Come on, it's a catechism and you're supposed to be learning the catechisms. *How are we to deny ourselves?'*

'Heavens above, there are hundreds of them.'

'And I'm supposed to teach you every one. *We are supposed to deny ourselves by giving up our own inclinations and by going against our own humours and passions.'*

'I've told you. There's no hurry. We've heard nothing about the colliery house.'

'Why are we bound to deny ourselves?'

'Don't be silly. It's been such a lovely evening. Don't spoil it.'

'We are bound to deny ourselves because our natural inclinations are prone to evil from our very childhood; and if not corrected by self-denial, they will certainly carry us to hell.'

'Next week. We'll have a proper lesson next week.'

'No, we won't. We're going to stop pretending. We might as well have been on the stage as in the audience tonight. It's all acting and it's over.'

Enid was frightened. The gentlest man she had ever met was trying to frighten her with his tone, his manner and his harsh message and he was succeeding. It was not a very convincing imitation of brutality. But the fact that he attempted it was enough to send her out of the car without saying either thank-you or goodnight. He called after her up the yard. 'If you really want instruction, send Jack to see me. Don't come yourself. Send Jack.'

CHAPTER FORTY-THREE
Above Reproach

As Enid ran into the house with Rex's stern ultimatum following her across the yard, she felt only a brief depression. Before she reached the back door she had calculated that by learning twenty answers a day, she could memorise the whole catechism in barely a fortnight. When she arrived at the presbytery, an expert on The Seven Great Means of Grace and The Christian's Rule of Life, Rex would have no choice but to ask her in to discuss Virtues and Contrary Vices. She believed devoutly in the power of conversation. Once they were talking again, the brief interruption in their friendship would be over.

Her mother were asleep by the time she got home. Instead of waking Agnes and preparing her for bed, Enid reached down the little book from behind the clock on the mantelshelf, sat on the stool by the side of the hearth and began to read the section entitled The Apostle's Creed. There were earlier sections of the catechism which she still needed to learn but the Apostle's Creed filled almost a full page and she already knew the Anglican version. Within five minutes she could convince herself that she had disposed of a major part of her task. Unfortunately, her father arrived home before the five minutes had passed. The first casual and disorganised assaults on selected parts of the catechism ended immediately. It was much the same with every feeble search for grace. Invariably her meditations were disturbed by The World, The Flesh or Her Mother.

By the end of May she had completed only half of her task and her learning rate was slowing down. The more slowly she went, the less urgent the work seemed. And the longer the time which had passed since the visit to Sheffield, the less important it seemed for Rex to become again her guide, philosopher and friend. By the beginning of July, the catechisms were abandoned in favour of tennis. It was the month of the weekly tournaments, scratch competitions at which she excelled. Winning, and the admiration which it generated, was, like time, a great healer.

The one disadvantage of the scratch tournament was the rule which

545

required the partners in mixed-double matches to be drawn by lot. Had she been able to play each Saturday with Jack, victory would have been a weekly certainty. In one match, she was paired with an elderly man who could barely serve. The next she was forced to play with a visitor whose limp was such a liability that not even Jack, opposing her in the fourth round, was unable to throw the game away and send her victorious into the semi-finals. On the Saturday of the big Bank Holiday event she was drawn with a schoolboy whose appearance seemed vaguely familiar. She almost tied Mick's lead to the wheelchair and pushed her mother back to Langwith Road, but Jack said that it would be impolite and identified her partner as the youth who had helped the priest officiate at Midnight Mass.

The schoolboy was called Syd – a name so unprepossessing that Enid made no further enquiries about his temporary membership of the tennis club. He wore immaculate white flannels and cheap shoes which, although they allowed him to play on grass courts, had clearly been designed for the beach at Skegness. The confusion of his appearance was compounded by his horn-rimmed spectacles and an ugly swelling over his left eye which he attributed to a boxing injury. To Enid's astonishment he was a superb tennis player. Largely because of him, they won the first three rounds in straight sets. When their third triumph was accomplished, he told Enid that when they played in the semi-final on Bank Holiday Monday his brother would come to watch. His brother was Father Hattersley, parish priest of St Joseph's Roman Catholic Church in Shirebrook.

Enid and Syd won the tournament even though each of them, for different reasons, was distracted by the group of spectators which stood anxiously beyond the wire netting. Most anxious of all was Father Hattersley, who suffered torments every time that Enid drove out of court or Syd volleyed into the net.

Rex was a silent partisan who demonstrated his involvement only by nervously running his fingers along Peter's collar. Agnes, next to him, was almost invisible under layers of rugs. From beneath the folds of thick wool she gasped disappointment, cried encouragement and muttered dissent at every dubious line call. Jack scurried to and fro between Agnes and the pavilion, carrying glasses of lemonade and cups of tea. Enid missed at least six shots by catching sight of them out of the corner of her eye and remembering the time when they all made weekly trips together – all, that was, except the dark handsome young man in sports jacket and open-necked shirt who stood – part of, but aloof from, the tableau – smiling as if he knew something that the others did not know. He was part of the cause of Syd's concern.

Syd was performing in front of both his brothers. But, despite the strain of fulfilling their expectation, he and his partner won.

They walked home together, through Shirebrook Market Place along Station Road and past the Waggon Works. Jack pushed the wheelchair and Agnes held the silver mixed-doubles trophy on her lap. The sunburned handsome young man smiled with the silent certainty of someone who had much to say but feared that it would be wasted on his immediate company. When they got to 11 Langwith Road, it was taken for granted that the trophy would decorate the Brackenbury mantelshelf. Enid and Rex both waited for Agnes to suggest a summer outing. When she failed them, they looked hopelessly at each other.

Then everybody spoke together. The dark young man, who conceded a willingness to be called George, said that he still had a month before he must return to Valladolid. Syd complained that he must be back at Ratcliffe on the first Tuesday in September. Rex consoled him with the thought that they were to spend next day at Beeston on the river. Enid announced that she had nothing to do for the rest of the summer and Syd, in a sudden fit of misplaced gallantry, tried to convince her that life was hard for them all.

'We might not be able to go to Beeston. It all depends if we can borrow a bike for George.'

'You can have Enid's. If you don't mind riding a lady's.' Jack O'Hara was incorrigibly generous. 'Enid's not ridden a bicycle for years.'

'I'm riding one tomorrow.'

Jack did not believe her but he did not argue. Enid's dislike of the priest came as no surprise. Father Hattersley had, he knew, been dissatisfied by the way she prepared, or failed to prepare, for admission to the Church. If she wanted to exact the terrible retribution of denying him the use of her bicycle, there was no advantage to be gained by arguing with her.

'Why don't you borrow one of Brack's cars?' Agnes had not followed the unconvincing account of Enid's renewed enthusiasm for cycling, but she wanted to help the young people enjoy their leisure. 'There's two or three standing doing nothing all day. If Enid asked him, he'd lend you one.'

'Can you drive?' Syd asked his brother. When Rex admitted that he had learned during the winter, even the silently superior George looked at him with something approaching admiration.

They all went to Beeston – George, Syd and Jack crushed into the back seat of an Austin Seven, and Enid, with Mick on her knee, in the front passenger seat. Peter was left at home, locked up in the presbytery with nothing to look forward to except the midday visit of the cleaning lady and a brief moment of freedom in the garden. Rex believed that they could have made room for him in the car but Enid said that he was too excitable in company and could not be trusted to behave himself.

'Highly strung,' Enid explained.

'Spoilt,' George suggested.

'As long as he doesn't spoil our rowing.' Ratcliffe, being on the Soar, was a rowing school and Syd looked forward to demonstrating his prowess in a hired boat.

But it was decided that Mick, Peter and the Trent were incompatible and Mick, taking precedence over all other dogs and most people, was the chosen passenger. At Beeston, instead of sitting in the prow like Montmorency, he stayed on the bank with Jack. George sat silent and intimidating, looking into space from the balcony of the boat house. Syd and Rex rowed and Enid urged them on from her seat beside the tiller. Rex was again transformed. He pulled on the oars with a muscular enthusiasm that neither his diffident manner nor his priestly vocation had encouraged her to expect.

'Can we come again tomorrow?' Syd asked when they were tied up against the duck-boards and Rex was examining his hands.

'We're supposed to be going to Newark tomorrow,' George told him. 'That's if we can get a bike for Syd.'

'Why for me?' Syd asked. 'It could be for you. We're just a bike short. It could be yours or mine.'

'Not tomorrow,' Rex told him. 'Not for me anyway.' He opened his palms as if Syd were Doubting Thomas. The blisters on his hands had burst and the loose skin had sloughed off. 'I've not rowed since Palazzola. I've got soft since Lake Albano.'

It was the sound of the warm Italian words which excited Enid. They were words that Robert Browning might have used. Perhaps Keats had visited Lake Albano or Shelley had stayed at palace . . . she could not pronounce the word even in her mind.

'We could have the car again tomorrow if you wanted it.'

'I can't come,' Jack told her. 'I'm working. But I hope you'll all go.'

For the rest of August, Enid and the three brothers toured Nottinghamshire and Derbyshire together. Syd, who believed himself to be an artist, made charcoal drawings of market crosses and church spires whilst George, who had collected coupons from *John Bull* magazines and become the proud owner of a Box Brownie, took pictures which he pretended he would develop and print himself when he got back to Spain. Rex and Enid walked and talked and looked – at the castles and churches, into shop windows, out over valleys and up towards the summit of hills but, most of all, looked at each other. They were conspirators who plotted against themselves, as they pretended – even when they were alone and they planned the next day together or remembered the last – that their relationship was wholly innocent. They tried to make it so. Or, at least, they worked hard to create an atmosphere of innocence. Enid declared that George and Syd were her friends no less than Rex. Rex was scrupulous in making sure that throughout that summer they did everything together as a family of four – three brothers and a sister. Sometimes they were joined by the man who would one day become the sister's husband but he was not yet part of the family. He was welcome amongst them, but their jokes were not his jokes, their enthusiasms were not his enthusiasms and increasingly, as the summer wore on, their memories were not his memories.

Enid chose to deceive herself because she was carelessly happy and thought only of enjoying the next day. Rex thought continually of September. For he knew that, when the autumn came, their friendship would have to end or be so changed that, by the end of the year, he might barely believe that he had spent the summer in Arcady. But he also knew that it need not end until September. Whilst his brothers were with him, living the lie which they believed to be the truth, he could preserve the myth of their platonic friendship. Once someone suspected – and confronted him with their suspicions – he would face more than the risk of suspected scandal. He would be expected to deny the rumour that he loved Enid Brackenbury. That he felt unable to do.

It was Brack who, although unqualified for the task, cast the first stone. Fortunately, he aimed only at Agnes.

'You might as well know, people are beginning to talk.'

'Talking about what?' Agnes feared that he was about to confess to an indiscretion which was already known to everybody in Shirebrook except her.

'Talking about your daughter, that's what. She's never away from that priest. I don't know why Jack stands it. He must know what people are saying.'

'What are they saying?'

'They're saying that she and that priest are up to something. Stands to reason. It's obvious to anybody normal.'

'I thought you liked him. You argue with him enough when he's here. I thought you liked Enid seeing him.'

'I like him better than I like that bloody Paddy she says she's going to marry. But that's all part of it. Nobody believes that she's going to marry him. It's all part of the game, isn't it?'

Agnes gave the gasp of horror for which her husband had hoped and followed it with a cry of anguish which exceeded his greatest expectation. When she had composed herself enough to speak, she made clear – much to her husband's disappointment – that she believed the allegations to be baseless.

'You ought to be ashamed of yourself. No decent man would think such a thing of his own daughter.'

'What do you think they're up to, then?'

'I think he's a good man and she's an innocent young girl who enjoys talking to somebody educated.'

'But you don't think they're tupping in the presbytery?'

'If she was, I'd know. I'm her mother.'

It was, Agnes knew, the wrong answer. For it implied the possibility of an improper relationship. She made an attempt to retrieve the lost ground.

'All I want is for her to be happy. Anybody with eyes in their head can tell how much they enjoy each other's company.' The second attempt to defend her daughter's reputation being even less successful than the first, she tried again with even worse results. 'Anyway, his brothers are leaving on Saturday. It'll have to end then, whatever's going on.'

On the morning that the brothers left Shirebrook, Enid walked into the presbytery at half-past eight and, with the unthinking impertinence that only George found irritating, began to clear up the kitchen in preparation for cooking a belated breakfast. The taxi was not due until ten so there was still time for Enid to argue that the Austin Seven was available for the journey to Nottingham and that it was silly to waste money on a hired car. Rex was surprisingly firm and Enid typically persisted.

'I can't understand you. The car's just standing there in the yard.'

The brothers were upstairs in the bedroom which they shared – George carefully folding his clothes and packing them precisely into his suitcase, Syd rolling up his belongings and dropping them into the cabin trunk in which every Ratcliffe boy was required to keep his personal possessions. Nevertheless, Rex closed the kitchen door.

'Just stop for a moment and listen. Concentrate for once and take it in. I mean it.'

Enid put the frying pan down on the gas ring. She had seen Rex solemn and angry. But this was her first experience of Rex severe.

550

'You won't get any breakfast if I don't start it now.' She picked up the frying pan again.

'For heaven's sake. Just listen for once.'

'It'll burn if I leave it there without anything in it. I know now why you don't want to borrow Dad's car. You don't want me to come with you to Nottingham. George and Syd would like me to. You ask them.'

'George and Syd won't be coming back from the station.'

'Do you mean that you don't want to be by yourself with me? Are you ashamed to be seen with me?'

'You know that isn't true. I'm very proud to be seen with you. That's all part of the problem.'

'What problem?'

Rex was not sure if he was confronted by invincible innocence or intentional evasion.

'The problem that I have to end this morning. The minute Syd and George get on their train, the summer is over.'

'The holiday's over.'

'Living like this is over. Days out are over.'

'I don't see why. You don't want them to end. Neither do I. I know you've got to go back to work—'

'Do you understand the work I do?'

'Don't be stupid. Of course I do.'

'Do you remember how our friendship began?'

She remembered but she did not answer and Rex, although he knew that she remembered, forced himself into the painful discipline of setting out the truth.

'You came to me for instruction. You said you wanted to become a Catholic. I shall be, indeed, I already am, your parish priest. One day I shall marry you . . . One day I shall marry you and Jack. We're not supposed to spend our time together skimming stones across the lake in Clumber Park. I'm supposed to be explaining papal infallibility and why we know that the Virgin Mary ascended bodily into heaven.'

'But you can do that and we can still do nice things as well.'

'Enid, I'm a priest. I've taken vows. I've made promises to God. One of them was to avoid temptation . . .'

It was the first time that either of them had conceded the possibility of anything except friendship. The suggestion delighted Enid, but because she was caught up in the argument she took immediate advantage of Rex's unexpected honesty.

'What sort of temptation? I don't feel any temptation. And I'd no idea that you did.'

551

Rex knew that she was only playing games. He did not argue with her but moved on to his next objection.

'Temptation's only part of it. I've got a duty to my office. I've promised to do nothing that might bring it into disrepute. I mustn't do anything that lets evil-minded people pretend that I'm breaking my vows. It's not my reputation we're talking about. It's the reputation of the Church.'

'What about my reputation?'

'That's a silly question. What I'm saying will protect your reputation. If we go on like this, all Shirebrook will start talking about you.'

'That doesn't matter to me. I know what's right and what's wrong. I don't need anyone to teach me.'

'Well, I do. How far did you get with your catechism? *I must believe what God has revealed. . . . I know what God has revealed by the testimony, teaching and authority of the Church.*'

'I know the last answer. When I tried to learn them, I looked at the last page in that little book that you gave me. I learned that one because it sounded so stupid. *After my night prayers I should observe due modesty in going to bed.* I've never heard anything so daft. And after you've done that, gone to bed modestly, you're supposed to think about death. Not me, thank you very much.'

They had not noticed the door open and Syd, who caught only Enid's last few words, did not recognise the irony in her gratitude.

'You haven't given them to her, without us!'

'Of course I haven't.' Rex was irritated but he was also relieved. He was not sure if he was glad or sorry that the argument was over. He hated friction, but he knew that his brother had ended more than unpleasant bickering about the catechism. He would never talk to Enid like that again. When next they met, he would be a priest and she would be a potential parishioner.

'I'll go and get George.' Syd plucked at Enid's sleeve. 'Bring him into the living room.'

Rex walked out of the kitchen without a word, pushing his way through the hall door ahead of Enid. Syd was surprised by his display of uncharacteristic bad manners and Rex was embarrassed by Syd's apparent belief that he would do everything that Enid told him. He was going to make his own way into his own living room at the time of his own choosing.

There was a brown-paper parcel on top of the bookcase. As soon as George came downstairs, Syd reached up for it without waiting for Rex's permission. Ignoring his brother's outstretched hand, he offered it to Enid.

'It was Rex's idea. We searched and searched for a *Golden Treasury*. Then we found this set in a second-hand book shop . . .'

Enid opened the parcel very slowly. It was her nature to cut string and tear off wrapping paper but it was not the moment for haste. When the package was opened, the summer would be over. After she had untied the binding, she put the package on the living-room table. Then she revealed its contents, like a conjurer materialising a dove from under a silk handkerchief. She sighed with pleasure at the sight of four small kid-bound anthologies of poetry.

'Read inside. Read inside the brown one,' said Syd and, before Enid had time to obey his instructions, he picked up the *Golden Treasury*. He opened it at its gilt-edged rice-paper fly leaf and waited for Enid to read what they had written there. She read the message out loud.

'With love from the Three Musketeers. Syd, George, Rex.'

'We were all going to write messages in one of them,' Syd told her. 'We were all going to write a quotation from one of the poems. George found one straight away . . .'

George smiled and handed her the brown Tennyson. Inside he had written 'Enid made sweet cakes to give them cheer. Idylls of the King.'

'I couldn't find anything in Keats, anything suitable. And neither could Rex. He's written his name in Browning. But he couldn't find a quotation.'

'Well,' said Enid. 'That's not surprising. Mostly, Browning wrote love poems.'

CHAPTER FORTY-FOUR

Life after Death

Enid and Rex did not talk again for the next three months. They passed in the street and Enid smiled and looked away when Rex smiled and raised his hand as if to touch the brim of an imaginary hat. They stood, almost side by side, in the Co-op grocers, and when Rex, who had undoubtedly arrived first, allowed Enid to be served ahead of him, she thanked him in a single sentence which did not contain a word about her mother's health, the books she was reading or the remarkable number of total strangers who stopped her on the street to share confidences or compliment her upon her appearance. One day by coincidence, they both trespassed in Scarcliffe Park at the same time and, arriving at Owl Spring together, feared that their dogs – which had been released from their leads – would set upon each other. But Mick did no more than sniff at Peter and Peter ignored him, concentrating his energy on urinating against a tree.

'Is he behaving himself?' Enid asked.

'He's marvellous,' Rex told her, unsure of whether or not to add that the dog now slept at the foot of his bed.

'He could do with a good brushing.'

'I brushed him this morning.'

'You didn't do him properly underneath. It's easy to miss underneath if you don't know about dogs.'

Rex touched the peak of an imaginary cap and hurried on. Enid walked back to Langwith Road so slowly that there was no escape from her mother's anxious enquiries. Enid was barely inside the house before she was required to confirm that she was all right, nothing had happened and Mick was not dead or injured.

It was different from their first separation. Then the sense of loss had quickly passed. But that was before the joys of August. All that was best in her life had been compressed into that single month. It had become the sum total of her past, the full extent of her memory and the yardstick against which she measured each moment of incomparably trivial pleasure. She longed to see Rex and her longing was increased by Agnes, who constantly asked inconsequential and insensitive questions about why the priest never called round to see her and what Enid had done to offend him.

Time after time during every day she dreamed of ways of arranging a real meeting. She did not imagine that August could be recreated but she wanted to lay the glorious summer to rest with all the rites appropriate to the dearest departed. In particular, she wanted Rex to know how much she regretted her bitter words about the poetry anthologies. She could not bear the thought that he might really believe that she knew only Browning's love poems. She spent restless nights repeating the titles. 'Bishop Blougram's Apology'. 'The Grammarian's Funeral'. 'Fra Lippo Lippi'. 'Andrea del Sarto'. 'Sohrab and Rustum' – or was that Matthew Arnold? She was so obviously unhappy that her father swung wildly between urging Jack to cheer her up and suggesting that he gave her something to be really miserable about. Complaining about her long face became a nightly ritual.

When one night Brack came home, unusually, worse for drink, Agnes and Enid – with Jack silent and apprehensive in the corner – prepared themselves for a ferocious assault.

'I've got something to say that's best not said in front of strangers.'

'You'd better go, Jack.' It was going to be a bad evening. Enid did not want to make it any worse.

'I'm damned if I will. You've stood enough, you and your mam. It's about time somebody told him what's what.'

'Why didn't you tell me what's what years ago? You've been sponging here for years.'

'Go home, Jack.' Agnes sounded genuinely frightened. 'There's no reasoning with him when he's in a mood like this. I know you mean well. But it won't help.'

Moved as much by pride as love, Jack slowly advanced on Brack.

'I'll go if Mrs Brackenbury really wants me to. But I've got one thing to say to you before I do. If you ever lay a finger on Enid again – her or her mother – you'll have me to answer to!'

Jack's face was so close to Brack's that he could smell the beer on his breath. Brack belched, seismically and with premeditated malice. St George was inspired, not intimidated, by the dragon's fire.

'Just don't touch her, that's all.'

Brack stood absolutely still. Agnes had not expected him to be intimidated by Jack's threats, but she was surprised that he showed no sign of being offended or enraged. He spoke very slowly.

'You're a nice enough lad, Jack, but you've got a lot to learn about life. I could look after you with one hand tied behind my back – old as I am. But I won't because you're more to be pitied than anything else. Sit down and listen to what I'm going to say.'

'Sit down, Jack,' said Enid. 'Sit down. We don't want any more trouble.'

'I'm going to have to spend some time away from Shirebrook. Three nights a week, I reckon.'

'It's that woman at Mansfield, isn't it? Jack told me that everybody was talking about it. You disgust me. You're my own father and you make me feel sick.'

'Bring it all out if you want to. That's your business. All I'm saying is that I shan't be here weekends.'

'Why don't you come straight out with it?' Agnes was pressing so hard on the arms of her wheelchair that she was able to look her husband in the face. 'Why don't you act like a man and tell me that you're leaving? With all that Dutch courage inside you, it ought to be easy enough.'

Brack was still cold, composed and sardonic. 'You've been leaving me for two years or more. How many times have you told me that you'll be off as soon as he makes an honest woman of her?'

'She is an honest woman.' Agnes was not in a colloquial mood.

'That's as may be. But she's going to take you off as soon as she has a place to go to. You didn't think that I'd stay here and look after myself, did you?'

'I didn't think you'd shame us all—'

Enid did not have the chance to finish the sentence. Her father walked towards her and Jack sprang between them. Brack looked at his daughter over Jack's shoulder.

'I'm sick and tired of hearing how ashamed of me bloody Lady Muck is. It's time you were put in your proper place. You might be entitled to tell me how to behave if you hadn't been running after that Roman Catholic priest. Talking about bringing shame on this family. Sleeping with a priest—'

Jack swung his fist approximately in the direction of Brack's head. It was not a real blow and Brack parried it almost casually. He caught Jack by the wrist.

'Don't you dare hit him.' Enid tried to sound fierce, but sounded only afraid.

'I wouldn't touch the poor sod.' Brack did not so much let go of Jack O'Hara's wrist as discard it. 'Now you know. Don't say that what's been going on between her and the priest comes as a surprise.'

He left the living room without looking back. Agnes wept. Though she did not know it, it was relief more than sorrow that made her cry.

Enid tried to console her. 'We'll be all right for a bit. I'll get a little job if he's awkward about money.'

'Don't you think it's time?' Jack had enjoyed his masterful moment and intended to live up to his new reputation for decisive courage. 'Don't you think it's time you and me got married?'

'I haven't done the instruction.' Enid knew what he meant.

'You don't have to. There are mixed marriages every day.'

'Rex . . . Father Hattersley told me that they're not approved of. You don't have a proper ceremony.'

'Is that what you want?' Jack asked. 'Big wedding with Brack to give you away?'

'You wouldn't like it, Jack, me not being a Catholic yet.'

'You can become a Catholic afterwards. It happens every day.'

'Where would we live?'

Enid feared that she had asked one question too many. But if the new Jack O'Hara – bold and assertive – noticed her reluctance, he chose to ignore it.

'I'll find somewhere. We can't be far away from getting a colliery house. I'll find out tomorrow. We've got a month to look. The banns will take nearly that. Then it's nearly Christmas.'

'Thank you, Jack.' Agnes was no longer crying, but because she could not raise her hand, her lined face was wet with tears. 'I want to get out now. I've stuck him as long as I could for the memory of what he was. But I want to go now as quickly as I can. Will you go and arrange it all tomorrow, Enid?'

'That's my job,' Jack told her. Agnes's gratitude was not yet exhausted and, since Enid was unusually quiet, she did not have to edge her way into the conversation during one of her daughter's brief silences. 'And you were very brave, standing up to Brack like that. He's a very violent man.'

'I had to, Mrs Brackenbury. I couldn't let him get away with saying those terrible things. I couldn't let him say those things about a priest.'

It was three days before Father Hattersley sent for Enid. She knew that the call would come. Jack had warned her that she would be expected to live a Catholic life whether she joined the Church or not and she was reconciled to making the promise that canon law required. She expected to be summoned to the presbytery within minutes of Jack's return from delivering the solemn message. As she waited for the call, Enid became increasingly nervous. Agnes attributed her daughter's undisguised anxiety to the apprehensions which afflict every bride.

The invitation came by picture postcard – a sepia and white relic of Rome which showed the Swiss Guard on duty in the Vatican. Enid was invited to choose any morning that week. She elected to go as soon as she had changed into her best dress.

Agnes, who had been born and bred in the Church of England, was not at all surprised by her daughter's obsessive preparation for her audience. She would no more have gone to church at Steetly in her old coat than she would have sent for the doctor without cleaning out the grate and black-leading the fireplace. True to her traditions, she insisted on sending the priest a gift – six new-laid eggs which had been collected from the hen house that morning. They proclaimed their special status by the feathers which were stuck to their shells by patches of fowl-droppings.

'From my mother.' Enid stood in the doorway.

Rex took the brown-paper bag and looked inside it cautiously.

'They're eggs. New laid. Better go somewhere cool.'

'Everywhere's cool in this house. I'll take them into the kitchen.'

He was about to say how well she looked and how pleased he was to see her when Peter bounded into the hall. Enid asked the dog if he had yet been taken for a walk, where his lead was, if he could smell rabbits and who was a good boy.

'That's done it,' said Rex. 'There'll be no peace now.'

'He wants to go out.'

'Well, don't let him, not until you make sure—'

It was too late. Peter bounded past her and out through the still open front door. She had not closed the gate.

The driver of the six-wheel coal lorry neither saw the dog nor knew that he had hit it. There was no screeching of brakes or screams of agony. But both Rex and Enid knew what had happened. Rex was the first out into the road.

Peter lay in the gutter, a bloody heap of fur, bone and entrails from which his head, still intact, looked up without sign of pain or fear. Rex fell on his knees in the road.

'He's dead, Rex.' It was obvious enough, but at moments of crisis words unguarded by thought spilled out of Enid.

Rex had the dog's blood on his hands and, as he rubbed his eyes, it smeared across his cheek. He began to cry. At that moment she loved him because he was so desolate and because he looked so grotesque. The hair was still brilliantined in place. But the face beneath it was crumpled with grief and, every time he tried to wipe away a tear, another dark-red mark blotched his face. At that moment, Enid had only one wish – to take him in her arms as if he were a child and tell him that somehow she would make it up to him. She knew how much he needed protection from the pains of the world and she wanted, more than anything else in life, to be the one who protected him. Because she knew that was not possible, she felt sick with despair, and she said the first thing that came into her head.

'When a dog dies, the best thing is to get another one straight away. That's what they did at Worksop. When Prince died they got Chum.'

'I don't want another dog. I never will.'

'You need somebody to love. Somebody or something. You really do.'

Rex looked up. He spoke with the slow certainty that Enid remembered from Midnight Mass.

'I love you. I loved you the first moment I saw you.'

'I love you too. You know that.'

She touched his blood-stained cheek and Rex stood up. He seemed wholly incapable of deciding what to do next and she loved him for his vulnerability. It was her duty to be strong, to decide.

'Let's bury Peter.'

Enid led the way back into the presbytery. They found old sacking and the sides of an ancient packing case in the cellar and, swallowing back her nausea, she supervised the collection of the fur and offal which had been a dog. Rex dug a shallow grave in the back garden. The whole job was done in twenty minutes.

'Wash your face,' Enid told him. 'I'll make some tea. Then we'll talk.'

'What is there to say? We both know—'

'Wash your face.'

He hated waiting. But he did not have long to wait. Enid began talking as she poured the tea.

'You know that we can't see each other any more. You know that this is the end, don't you?'

Rex had believed that Peter's death marked not an end but a beginning. He was almost speechless with astonishment.

'But . . . I thought you said . . . You said you loved me.'

'I did. And I do. I truly do. But now that I've said it we can't pretend any more. I'm going to marry Jack. Then we'll move away.'

'I don't know how you can say such a thing. We love each other. That's all that matters.'

'You're a Catholic priest. That matters.'

'I don't want to be.'

'That's what you say now.'

'I'm not sure that I ever did. I tried to give up when I was in Rome. But they persuaded me to stay.'

'I can remember you telling Syd that he'd have doubts before he was ordained. You said that everybody did.'

'I'll tell you something else. On the day that Syd and George went back, I saw the Bishop. I asked him to move me anywhere – curate again, cathedral, anything. He told me to come back here and resist temptation. He said that, if I ran away, I'd never be any good as a priest again.'

'And that's exactly what you did.'

'No, it's not. I came back by train and I spent all the journey praying for guidance, praying for a sign. That's what priests do. And when I got home, George had left half his clothes here. George, who's so neat and careful, had left a jacket and a pair of trousers. A shirt. Even a tie. I sat in this chair and thought it's the sign. God wants me to go on seeing her, but he wants to keep the Church clear of scandal. I can go out with her in secret in George's clothes. Then I thought it was all wrong.'

'How do you mean wrong?'

'Wrong to take you out like that. Wrong to do it in secret not because of what God might think about me, but because of what I feel about you. I wanted to marry you or nothing.'

'And you decided nothing?'

'First of all, I decided that all the stuff about signs and guidance was nonsense. George just forgot, left his things by mistake. Then I decided what to do – decided as a man, not a priest. I've only been half a priest – half at best – ever since.'

'But you decided not to see me. You didn't come up Langwith Road and tell me you loved me.'

'I didn't think you'd have me. I thought you'd want to do better for yourself.'

'You thought I'd do better for myself by marrying Jack! Don't make me laugh.'

'I never thought that you'd marry him. Not until he came round last Monday and asked me to put up the banns.'

'Well, I've got to now. I've got to get my mother away. Jack's the only hope.'

'Marry me.'

'That's a stupid thing to say. Cruel and stupid. You'll not marry me in a million years, because you can't. If you tried to leave, they wouldn't let you. Your family would be round—'

'My father's not even a Catholic.'

'Your brothers then. And all your old friends from Rome. They'd be round here one by one. You'd have to deny everything that ever happened to you.'

560

'If you marry me, the past won't matter. We'll start life again today.'

'You're not strong enough. Nobody is.'

Rex was frightened by the passion with which Enid argued, because he did not understand it. At first she barely understood it herself. Then she began to realise that she wanted not proof that they must part, but certainty that Rex really wanted them to be together. He had come so near convincing her that she felt safe to admit its possibility.

'You really want to do it? You really think you can?'

'I can if you help me. I can't do it on my own, because I'll lose my nerve. I'll think that you're going to change your mind and that I'm giving all this up for nothing . . .'

Looking round the ugly, badly furnished presbytery, it seemed to Enid that it would be no great sacrifice. He was a parish priest without a parish, and so poor that he could not even afford a decent pair of shoes. As far as she knew, he had no friends, except his brothers. And they were destined to follow him into the same solitary vocation. All he had to lose was a single idea. But it was the idea which had dominated his life.

'I can't help you. You'll have to do it on your own. If you can't do it on your own, you can't do it at all.'

'But it will all take time. How many people have we got to tell? We've got to break the news gently. It'll take a month for a letter to get to Spain. I can't do it if I'm not seeing you.'

'You mean that you'll send me home today, home to Jack O'Hara, who thinks that he'll be married in the New Year?'

'I've got to tell the Bishop.'

'You're still a priest, Rex. And I'm not going to persuade you to give it up.'

'I don't want you to persuade me. I want you to help me.'

'If you really mean to do it, you'll do it on your own.'

'Today?'

Facing the prospect of total defeat, Enid made a tactical retreat.

'Perhaps not today. But soon. I can't wait for ever. We've got to get out of Langwith Road.'

. 'Six weeks. And we'll go on seeing each other whilst we plan it bit by bit.'

'Six weeks and we don't see each other till you've decided.'

'I have decided.'

'Until you've done it, then. Until you've left the Church.'

'Not even Christmas?'

'Don't talk about it.'

Christmas was to be spent at Worksop. Agnes had written to her sister on the morning after the announcement of Brack's intended desertion and Anne had replied by return of post – not offering the anticipated immediate refuge but suggesting a four-day holiday in a month's time. Jack had thought it a wonderful idea and cheerfully agreed to celebrate Christ's Nativity alone in his lodgings. Brack had rejoiced at the thought that he could divide his time, without complaint, between Cobbler Jack's and the lady in Mansfield. But he had described Agnes's decision as leaving him to fend for himself.

It was the second Christmas Enid had chosen as the turning point in her life. As she sat on the edge of the sofa in St Joseph's presbytery, she felt mortally afraid – afraid of life going on just as it was and equally afraid of the cataclysm which would precede a change.

'So I won't see you until then?'

'You won't see me until you're ready.'

'Tell me what to do.'

'If you want me, come to Worksop on the day after Boxing Day. But don't come unless you've finished with the Church. Come to Brook House, number seventy-five Newcastle Avenue. And come in George's jacket, not as a priest. If you've not told everybody by then, including your precious bishop, I shall go home next day and marry Jack.' Enid shook her head.

'You can't marry him now, whatever happens.'

The suggestion that the future was still not certain and secure filled Enid with terror.

'It's up to you. As long as you really mean it, I shall marry you, not him.'

'I'll show you how much I mean it. We can't let Jack go on believing that you're getting married after Christmas. Tell him you're not ready. Say that I won't marry you in church or anywhere else. That ought to be enough proof for you. That's finished me as a priest. A priest who still believed and did that would expect to go straight to hell.'

'Don't risk your soul for me. You might need it. I'll tell him that I couldn't sign the papers.'

Enid longed for him to insist that he would sacrifice his soul without a second thought. But he did no more than beg her to help him survive through Advent.

'Will you send me a message just before, a message saying that you still want me to come?'

'I'll send you a Christmas card from Worksop as soon as we get there. It'll say that I'm still waiting. Will you write to me?'

'I'll write every day.'

'Just once. Just once to Worksop. Then I'll be ready.'

CHAPTER FORTY-FIVE

Comfort and Joy

For Agnes the journey to Worksop from Shirebrook was painful and expensive. Inexplicably Enid had refused to ask Rex to perform his usual errand of mercy and chauffeur them in Brack's Austin. So having been balanced precariously on the back seat of the local hire car – with Mick in the apex under her arthritic knees – she was driven over the potholed, pitted roads with a scandalous disregard for her condition. Every lurch of the car's rusty springs caused a stab of pain in one of her atrophied joints. But she enjoyed the journey.

When it ended, outside Brook House, Enid counted out four and sixpence into the driver's hand with such bad grace that even her mother, on the back seat, could detect her daughter's resentment. Despite the feeling that they had been cheated out of coppers which they could not afford, she felt happier than she had felt for months.

For a week she would be free from Brack. And she would be free from Jack O'Hara sitting silently in her kitchen, night after night, and behaving as if he really believed that one day Enid would marry him. Looking at her daughter – so tall, so thin, so beautiful and so haughty in bearing and in character – Agnes was not surprised that she had come back from the presbytery with another excuse for postponing the wedding. She was surprised that Jack O'Hara had believed all the nonsense about religious doubts. But Jack did believe it, and they were well rid of him for a week.

Enid pulled the suitcase and the string bag from in front of the seat on which her mother half sat and half lay. Mick, disturbed, yawned and banged his hard skull against Agnes's painful calves. At that moment Anne and Lottie appeared at the bay window of the fitting room. The split second's glimpse of the white faces and tightly drawn grey hair made Agnes forget the pain. She had fled to Worksop in so many times of crisis and Anne and Lottie had always been ready to share her suffering and to offer advice, comfort and ready cash. She could not believe that they did not enjoy her staying with them. The idea was just a product of Enid's sensitive imagination.

Visiting Worksop when she wanted nothing but the pleasure of her sister's company was her proof that she loved them for themselves, not just as a refuge. Agnes could not wait to begin the week of pleasure which she was to share with the two women who had helped her through so much pain. She craned forward from the back seat to look out of the car window so that she could see them hurry down the path to meet her. Then Lottie called out again, louder and even more urgently. 'Get hold of Mick! Chum's out!'

Anne appeared over Lottie's shoulder. 'Chum's out!' she cried. 'Get him, quick!'

Mick – far from being got – recognised the agitation in the women's voices and was excited by it. Suddenly he smelt, saw and heard his old adversary. Excitement turned into hysteria. He leaped from the car, ears pricked and hackles bristling. Screaming like a soul in torment he hurdled the low front-garden wall and closed on his quarry.

'Get hold of him, Enid!' Agnes cried, rubbing her swollen knee with her twisted fingers.

Enid fumbled with the latch on the garden gate. Lottie put out an ineffectual hand. Anne attempted to impede his progress with her foot. All failed. Mick caught Chum by a hind leg and bit hard. Chum howled.

'He'll kill him, Enid!' Agnes called in anguish from the car.

Then, as if by miraculous intervention, Mick turned away from his wounded foe and stood absolutely still, ears pricked again and hackles raised more fiercely than before. He seemed to be staring into the shallow waters of the brook.

'He's seen a rat,' announced Enid, as much in pride as in relief.

'Don't let him get it!' shouted Agnes. 'He'll kill it!'

Chum limped into the house and Lottie, with rare courage, caught Mick by the collar and held on to him as he twisted and turned, snarling and snapping. It was not clear if he most wanted to escape or bite the hand which held him.

'You'll strangle him.' Enid looked frightened for the first time. 'It's only natural.'

Anne, who had followed Chum from the field of honour, reappeared in the doorway.

'It's all right, I've put him upstairs.'

Mick was flung inside the kitchen and the door slammed behind him. Then Agnes was lifted into the wheelchair and pushed down the path that ran alongside the little stream. Enid returned to the car for the suitcase and the string bag. The driver thought of asking for an extra sixpence to cover the time that it had taken to unload his strange cargo. But as Enid, weighed down with luggage, approached the side door, he heard the wire-haired terrier screaming its pleasure at the sound of her footsteps. He started his engine, pointed his car in the direction of Shirebrook and accelerated towards sanity.

The kitchen into which Agnes Brackenbury collapsed was in chaos. One chair was heaped with flat cardboard boxes, another with pattern books and a third with a pile of tissue paper which was held in place against the draughts by a flat-iron. Cards of buttons, papers of pins, books of needles and half-rolled spools of ribbon covered the top of the sideboard. Bobbins of coloured cotton stood on the mantelshelf like ornaments. Two bales of worsted which had been swept from the sofa in order to accommodate the invalid lay on the floor surrounded by samples of lace and velvet. The table in the centre of the room was piled high with enough holly to decorate every picture and fill every vase in Brook House ten times over.

'Ern only brought it yesterday. Said he had to search all over. There's been a lot of frost. It's been a bad year for berries.'

'We've got the old wreaths back,' Lottie added. 'Ern brought them after he'd been to church in Steetly last Sunday night.'

'Have you stripped them?' Agnes asked.

Neither woman admitted their failure. Enid, correctly interpreting the silence, tried to reassure them.

'We'll do them between us, tomorrrow.'

'You'll have to take them tomorrow,' Anne told her. 'There aren't any buses on Christmas Day any more.'

Enid was indomitable.

'Then we'll do them tonight. We'll start on them as soon as we've had a cup of tea.'

'We can't.' Anne, Agnes felt, was not suitably apologetic. 'We've been worked to death. We'll be finishing orders until the small hours of tomorrow morning. Miss King's staying to help. I've got a coat and a skirt and Lottie's got three dresses.'

Overhead, the sound of a sewing machine's treadle sounded like a call to arms.

'Then I'll have to do them myself,' said Enid, still trying to sound cheerful. 'I'll start straight away.'

. As they waited for the kettle to boil on the black-leaded hobs of the kitchen grate, the four women exchanged the casual pleasantries with which a more normal family might have begun its reunion. Agnes insisted that she felt 'better than for years' and that the journey had 'not been half as bad' as she had expected. Lottie said that Miss King had recovered miraculously from the needle which she had driven through her finger on the previous day and Anne added what a blessing it had been that Ern had just called round with the holly and was able to pull it out with the pliers from his old toolbox.

'When's Ern coming?' asked Agnes.

'Tomorrow. He's going to go to Steetly with Enid,' Anne replied.

'He wouldn't miss that for the world,' added Lottie.

There was a clear tone of reproach in Anne's voice as she continued her brother's plans. Ern never let his sisters down. Agnes should have known that and should have felt no need to ask for reassurance.

'He'll be here in time to catch the bus outside Beard's Mill at ten past six.'

'Ten past six?' For the first time, there was a hint of rebellion in Enid's voice.

'It's the only way he can get to Retford before nine. As it is he'll be an hour later than usual.'

'Then we'd better get started,' Enid suggested, trying to sound less disgruntled than she felt. 'The call of nature takes me down to the yard. Is the washhouse open? I'll bring the old wreaths back with me.'

'Enid!' Aunt Anne had, at least in public, never acknowledged the existence of bodily functions.

'She's in a strange mood,' Agnes explained as her daughter disappeared.

'Even so, there's no need to say things like that.' Lottie had echoed Anne's sentiments for forty years.

Agnes ignored the reproof.

'She had such a lovely summer – playing tennis and reading books and all sorts of interesting things. But now she seems very unsettled.'

'I blame that O'Ryan or whatever he's called,' said Anne, 'trying to make a Catholic of her.'

'He won't. There's no fear of that. No more risk of that than that she'll marry him.'

'Last we heard,' Lottie said, 'it was January. I was worried about the wedding dress with so much work on.'

'Well, it isn't January now. She thought up another excuse.'

'I don't have any patience with her,' Anne said. 'She ought to just send him packing.'

'Will you help me down the yard?' asked Agnes, using the proper euphemism.

Enid and Agnes met at the door. It was only because of Enid's agility that a nasty accident was averted. Mother was balanced precariously between a sister and a walking stick and daughter was running whilst carrying in each hand an ancient wreath. Brown and broken holly leaves were still attached to the dry moss and rusty wire.

As she came to a sudden halt, dead berries fell from their wizened stalks and dropped with a patter on to the red flagstoned floor.

When her mother and aunt had disappeared she turned to Lottie.

'Can I light the gas? They're full of bits of old wire. I'll cut myself to pieces if I can't see what I'm doing.'

'Of course,' said Lottie. 'Help me on to a chair.'

She made the dangerous ascent and struck a match. As she reached up to hold the flame against the mantle, Mick tried to bite her ankle.

It was still dark when Uncle Ern knocked on the front door. Enid handed over one of the wreaths she was holding and stepped out into Newcastle Avenue without a word. They walked to the bus stop in silence, each one carrying a wreath with a stiff formality which owed less to the solemnity of the occasion than to their desire to keep the damp moss off their best coats.

The bus was late and, as they waited, Uncle Ern asked his first question. 'How's your mother?'

'Ever so much better. She's happier than I've seen her for absolutely ages. She got a terrible lot of banging about in the car yesterday but she slept very well last night. What she needs now is more rest and quiet . . . She had an awfully nice summer, but she rattled about a lot. She's very tired.'

Uncle Ern thought, but did not say, that Agnes's chances of rest and quiet had disappeared at the time when her daughter learned to speak.

'This week will set her up wonderfully. She was so well in the summer. She had a lovely summer . . .'

Enid, much to her uncle's relief, allowed the sentence to die away. Before she had the time to collect her thoughts, the bus appeared in the dark distance, a pattern of golden specks of light piercing the gloom.

They sat silently together until they reached Steetly. Half a dozen young quarrymen, late for the early-morning shift, rolled and smoked their cigarettes, read their newspapers and examined the sandwiches with which their wives or mothers had filled their snap tins. The quarrymen were still snuffling their way out of sleep and in the warm of the bus Enid began to doze. But Uncle Ern sat upright and alert. His flat cap was square on his head. His muffler was tied with geometric precision under his chin and his double-breasted topcoat was buttoned and buckled into rigid place. His moustache – bushy yet neat – completed the picture of respectable insignificance. Enid, crushed next to him on the double seat, fought against sleep for she feared that her head might fall on to his shoulder. Despite her determination to remain awake and alert she had to be nudged into movement when the bus arrived at Steetly farm.

The quarrymen, reluctant to lose more than an hour's pay, were first off the bus. Uncle Ern followed and, with elaborate courtesy, helped his niece to descend from the platform. In the Steetly farm yard, the cocks – whose ancestors had fought at nearby Shireoaks – were screeching their welcome to the dawn. Uncle Ern unlatched and pulled open the gate in the briar hedge which surrounded the churchyard. Then he plunged his carefully polished brown boots into the long damp grass in the ditch below the briars in order to hold the gate open for Enid. Before he followed her on to consecrated ground, he removed his cap.

They stood side by side, in a corner of the churchyard which was shaded by the branches of a hawthorn tree. William Skinner would have chosen to be buried with his wife but at Steetly the soil was too shallow and the rock beneath it too hard for double graves so their son had two mounds to cultivate, two crosses to scrub and two lengths of cast-iron chain to keep taut and black along the boundaries of the two Skinner plots. Uncle Ern laid his wreath on his father's grave and turned away as if he were afraid that to remain would expose his emotions. Enid Brackenbury bent down and half dropped her heavy holly memorial on to the closely cropped grass. She turned to see if her uncle had noticed the sacrilege and saw, to her relief, that he was already standing reverently in the porch of the locked chapel. He bowed his head in an act of genuine reverence. Realising that his niece had noticed his act of piety, Uncle Ern hurried off down the path and struck a more secular posture at the bus stop. He took a pipe and a tobacco pouch from his inside pocket.

'You won't mind?' he asked, turning to Enid.

''Course not. I like the smell.'

'Not everyone does.'

It was well after eight o'clock when the bus arrived and Uncle Ern was struggling to avoid revealing his anxiety about missing the Retford train. It was concern for the time which made him sound peremptory – even by his own high standards – when he told Enid to climb to the top deck and sit on the right-hand side of the gangway. Instead of sitting by her side, he occupied the seat in front of her. He was still unconvinced – or so his niece assumed – that she enjoyed the smell of his pipe.

For the first few minutes of the journey, Enid, who knew that respect required her to think of the past, thought only of the future. She had come to Worksop for Christmas, as if Christmas was all that mattered in her life. Yet before New Year's Day life would have changed – wonderfully, dramatically, irrevocably and, without doubt, dangerously. At least she hoped it would have changed. The more she thought about the details, the less sure she felt that the dream would come true. She struggled to convince herself that her worries were absurd, that a letter would be waiting for her with the Christmas cards when she got back to Newcastle Avenue and that it would describe every detail of the wonderful life which was about to begin. When she had convinced herself that she was really about to be rescued, she began to worry about the consequences of escape. She had always taken it for granted that her mother would make the dash to freedom with her. But what if, when the time came, her mother did not want to escape? Suddenly she wondered if she had made a terrible mistake. Not in deciding to leave but in the manner of her leaving. Perhaps she should have broken the news before she came to Worksop. Enid could imagine how her aunts would react. 'But your mother's an invalid. You can't ask her to take such a risk.' They had said it a dozen times before. Perhaps she should have told her mother and got her on the side of hope and joy before Anne and Lottie were given the chance to argue for disappointment and despair. 'I know', they would say, 'that Ern would advise exactly the same.' Perhaps she ought to speak to him now, now that she had him on her own, and convince him that what she was doing was right. He had been married. He ought to understand. But what if, having convinced him that she must leave, the letter did not come?

Enid's confused thoughts were suddenly interrupted by her uncle, who turned round in the seat in front of her and spoke with an urgency which had no thought for the tobacco fumes and smoke with which his niece was suddenly engulfed.

'See that. Do you recognise it?'

He tapped the window.

'Of course I do. It's Grove Cottage.'

'Do you recall your grandmother?'

'Hardly at all.'

Enid knew that it was the wrong answer. But she feared that if she lied she would be cross-examined about Elizabeth Skinner's life and times and forced to reveal her deception.

'How old were you when your grandfather passed away?'

Grove Cottage was a mile behind them. But, as the bus sped on, Uncle Ern could think of nothing except his family and the years they had spent together in the service of Squire Hodding. He did not wait for his niece's reply.

'Did you know him when he was still head gardener or had he given up by the time that you remember?'

'I think that I can remember him when he was still gardener. My mam told me about you going out at night to do the digging for him because he was too ill to work.'

'Head gardener,' said Uncle Ern, 'he had two men under him. I didn't come out to do the digging. Just to tidy things up a bit. The two men did the digging.'

'Well, anyway, I remember. I remember him and I remember his stories.'

'What stories?' Uncle Ern's façade of rock-solid serenity seemed, for a moment, to be in danger of cracking.

'Stories about the docks at Wisbech. Stories about building an arboretum at Lincoln and about Christmas at Harness Grove when Squire Hodding had a great party for all the workers and Mr Knock the coachman dressed up as Father Christmas . . .'

The bus began to slow down in preparation for its stop outside the flour mill in Newcastle Avenue. But Enid, nervous as well as naturally garrulous, was in full flood again. Even as she made her uncertain way between the seats and began to descend the swaying stairs, she still talked of the tales her grandfather had told her.

'He told me everything about you – about fencing and boxing and skating to work along the canal in the year of the big freeze. He told me that you once knocked down a man for being rude to my grandmother and that when my dad called round . . .'

She had forgotten that Uncle Ern was not getting off at her stop but travelling on to the Worksop railway station and his train to Retford. As the bus moved away she looked up and saw that square, precise, disappointed face looking down at her from the window. Uncle Ern was smoothing his moustache with the back of his hand. He was looking down at his niece but he was thinking of different people and of different days. Ernest was thinking about the past and Enid was thinking about the future.